Efemona

THE AFRICAN WOMAN WITH BALLS

O.O. KANDISON

ISBN: 978-1-63950-133-5 (sc)
ISBN: 978-1-63950-134-2 (e)
Library of Congress Number: 2004099827

Writers Apex

Gateway Towards Success

8063 MADISON AVE #1252
Indianapolis, IN 46227
+13176596889
www.writersapex.com

DEDICATION

- To my three beautiful children: Verita, Ehimare, and Oziengbe, who missed and love their daddy dearly. I love you all.
- And to my good friend: Fela Anikulapo Kuti. Let it be known you'll never be forgotten for the truth in your music against the Generals and Zombies who drained Nigerian's economy.
- To my father Mr. S. Ojiehebho.
- To Christiana and Albert, who raised me when things were tough for my dad and mom.
- To Marthina Ogba. You'll always be my sister.
- To Sunny. How can I tell you, you're a true brother? Keep up the good work and keep the faith in Almighty!
- To Muriel Skelly, my attorney, who as a matter of fact first glanced through these manuscripts and who helped to get my children back to the United States.
- To Jersey Ward. Thanks for all the complimentary rooms at Reno Hilton, where most of these manuscripts were written, reversed and edited.
- To Gordy Case. Without you, this work would not be possible. I thank you for all the payroll draw/advances which enabled me to purchase a computer for this work.
- To Jamie Sorenson for your kindness and understanding knowing that I was skipping work on a regular basis just to complete this work and never fired me.

AUTHOR'S NOTE

This is entirely a work that I imagined. There are, however, places known as Ogoni, Ewu, Irrua, Bornu, Onitsha, Ukpenu and so on. They are all located in Nigeria. Never-the-less, their locations, or the way they are used and or the people and the names used in no way are intended to resemble the towns, cities, villages, or characters of this story.

This is a story of Efemona, who rose from the bitter streets of Ukpenu, South of Benin City in Nigeria to come to America on her husband's ticket where she has since been influenced by Western tradition to become Nigeria's greatest black woman from a poor family to bring down the Government of the dictator of her country: Bad Dudu Abacha. Efemona, an orator and smarter than most African women in Reno, NV, she formed the most powerful organization: African Women Against Marriage Movement (AWAM), which made her an instant celebrity. Here is the supreme triumph of Nigeria's new novelist and critic that told of: corruption, brutality, and nepotism in his own way.

ACKNOWLEDGEMENT

I have been fortunate indeed to have had the support of many individuals in writing this book. Without their help and suggestions, it would have been impossible, and therefore I would like to thank them: Dr. Chris Acholonu, Prof. Wole Soyinka for his UNR visit and kind advice and also Prof. Marvick of the Foreign Languages Dept. at the University of Nevada, Reno for the French translation in this book. I also want to thank Peggy Tamborino for her tireless and professional rework on the manuscripts for this book.

* * *

Ogbebor K. Ogbesia was born and raised in Nigeria. Upon graduation from high school he moved to Reno, Nevada where he attended the University of Nevada, Reno. He has lived and resided in the state of Nevada more than 43-years. He is the author of *The Court Circus Mess/ Underclass and Injustice and A CITY OF BLOODSUCKERS.*

PREFACE

This work began three years ago as an entirely different work. It was to have been about a brutal dictator. By its very nature, it was to have been a pure political novel, the result of extensive research. However, Efemona's life, certainly, wouldn't have been a part of it at all. As it turned out after the puzzles and hardships in her Country, Efemona became a part of it. The story of Efemona that now somehow transcended the facts that my beliefs about her as a smart woman may not have been told. As years passed, I learned that the dictator in my country, at the very vortex of an ever-spreading Oval Office probe was in fact a coward, as Efemona would show.

To write a book about a dictator in another African country is one thing. And to write a book about Bad Dudu, the man everyone came to fear in their country is another. Therefore, this fictional book would not be about a faceless name in tabloids, about one unknown out of the over one hundred and fifty million people in Nigeria. It would be about Bad Dudu, and his son Mohammed and their cronies who destroyed their own people and wreak havoc on their country's economy which Efemona couldn't stand.

I might never have thought of writing this book if I'd not married Efemona, the woman whom my father had arranged for me to marry, who later became smarter than I, her teacher, her husband.

As a freelance writer and photojournalist, I managed what I was paid, while Efemona as a registered nurse spent hers alone. As a matter-of-fact, my pay as a freelance writer and photojournalist was a bit challenging. And although I had a bachelor's degree in journalism from the University of Nevada, Reno, I had done nothing on the degree on any manuscripts.

As a new writer, on the market and with a master's in Political Science, I now challenge Efemona and Bad Dudu.

It is my pleasure to share with you who Efemona and Bad Dudu really are.

—Ogbebor K. Ogbesia

*   *   *

Efemona! What do you have in-between your thighs, female genitals or balls?

—General Bad Dudu

WHAT THEY SAY

A CRITIC ART FORM OF FICTION . . . Truly will bring all military rulers of the Third World countries to their heels.

—*Prof. Chris Achulonu*

* * *

CRITICALLY WRITTEN. EFEMONA TRULY GOT THE BALLS . . . to bring down the government of the dictator of her country with her voodoo spell.

—*Dr. Sam Okorie.*

* * *

FOR SURE, THIS WORK WILL SURELY ENLIGHTEN THIRD WORLD LEADERS.

ABSOLUTELY POWERFUL! Kandison knows what held back the most populous country in Africa-NIGERIA.

—*Jordan A. Randolph,*
(Bartender: Stardust Las Vegas, Nv.)

* * *

POLITICS AND FICTION AT ITS BEST.

—*David Ortiz*
(Bill Heard Auto Salesman)

A HECK OF A THRILLER AND GRIEVANCE
AGAINST CORRUPT GOVERNMENT . . . typical
Kandison with a narrative that will hold one spellbound
as they keep the page turning until it roars towards the
final showdown.

—Prof. Howard Michell,
Social Psychologist, University of Nevada, Reno

* * *

I COULDN'T PUT IT DOWN. Incorporates
qualities of critics for which Kandison is known: fast-
paced, believably annoying characters, current events
background, so authentic that it was Efemona and
Kandison who invented it.

—Troy Urie

PART I

THE BUSINESS OF ZOMBIES ARE FOREVER
ZOMBIES

—OGBEBOR

And tortures him now more, the more he sees
Of pleasure not for him ordained: then soon
Fierce hate he recollects, and all his thoughts
Of mischief, gratulating, thus excites:
"Thoughts, whither have ye led me? With what sweet
Compulsion thus transported to forget
What hither brought us? Hate, not love, no hope
Of paradise for Hell, hope here to taste
Of pleasure, but all pleasure to destroy,
Save what is in destroying, other joy
To me is lost . . . ."

Paradise Lost: Book IX
(Lines 469-79)

Chapter

1

....

Though he was greatly feared by her countrymen and women with three hats on, only Efemona saw him as a joke. She'd barely lived in the United States for a couple of years when she realized that somebody had to wake up and challenge him. And it happened by chance, and by divine intervention that Efemona became the voice of her people. In history as we know, a man lives not only his personal life as an individual, but also, consciously or unconsciously, the life of his epoch and his contemporaries. That was then. To Efemona, times have changed. Civilization has wrought the Universe, through the Americans.

Efemona is not the sort of celebrity you would like to meet by chance, or in any other way, for that matter. She's uniquely a Nigerian by birth, and a naturalized citizen of the United States. A woman like Efemona would be on the run if she was still in Ukpenu, a small town south of Benin, in Nigeria; a nurse by profession actually. But also, she came on my ticket to the United States and had lived and seen how the system functioned, her new redefined self and civility came into the open.

I remember when I was 12 years old, the first time I saw the man with two hats on. He was touring his nation then. All primary schools and grammar schools boys and girls would line up by the side of the road to view, cheer the man who ruled his nation. We would be there on the street rain or shine, with market men and women who also wanted to have a clue on how the man looked.

The day he finally came to my state, he'd stood upon an American made long automobile, what the Americans call a limousine, top opened, and wearing two hats, as the driver drove slowly along the asphalt. Market men and women had booed him, but we, the primary school children, with our nation's flags on our palm to wave him by. As he too was waving to us, my mother was busy telling me a story about the man, that the man with two hats on was from Lagos, then Nigerian capital. He was the president of the most populous country-our country. And that Lagos, prior to the man putting on two hats, who assumed the leader of Nigeria, had ceased power from a man who was wearing only one hat. And Lagos at the time was beautiful, had all the amenities of a First World. And that when the man wearing two hats had ceased power, people started to realize that they were hungry, their mouths felt filthy. Also, the people started to realize that as they walked through the streets, they had no where to urinate, they were broke, and more often, cursed the day, the army was formed.

As the man with three hats came along, things had gotten out of hand. More than often, the streets of Lagos were quiet, too, most of its bright lights were out. Here and there women selling their carnals were apparent. Here and there, men with brutal manners of brutality were everywhere looking for places to rob to satisfy their palates and their wives and children. She'd also reminded me of how our two dominant strands of Muslim culture and Christians-coexisted in harmony with no apparent contradictions when Mr. Life Goes On had ruled.

What do I know then?! It goes to show how naïve and dumb I was at the time to know why all the market men and women booed at the man wearing two hats as our president and as his entire entourage drove slowly by. After all the cars nosed gently by and were out of eyesight, I'd then vowed to my mother on our way home in the rain, that I must wear two hats like the president, but she insisted that it was not a good idea and no matter how I cried for her to buy me two hats to put on, on the Holy Week before Easter, the week the Reverend Father Iramen had decided he would wash the feet of a dozen men, children, and women of his congregation their feet, she declined my request. The ceremony, of course, was supposed to symbolize the humility of the great toward the small. And it was the day the Jehovah's Witness preachers predicted that Armageddon would struck the Earth and everyone would perish. So they had advised that everyone who had farms should reap what they'd sown and eat the proceeds, spend every Naira and Kobo and give to the house of Jehovah what they could not eat and spend. The Catholic faith of the Iramen House had contended that such a thing would never happen which was why the Jehovah Witness hated the Iramen House of the Catholic faith believers at Ukpenu which Iramen, Efemona's father helped get across to his believers. He'd stuck to business, preaching to his congregation, letting his believers know that Armageddon will never happen, but that instead they should celebrate with him on the remembrance of the birth of Christ the Savior, who will come again to help the people of Nigeria to redeem their country they had believed in when Mr. Life Goes On had ruled. So, on this controversial day, even though I was only 12 years old, I'd needed my feet washed and had wanted to wear my two hats to the church to celebrate, too, in my own beautiful way.

At the time, we were still living at Zuma Avenue on the first floor full of rats and roaches of the oldest building ever built at Irrua at the time, by Dr. Okojie, a small town southwest of Benin City.

My poor mother. May God sanctify her grave *now*. Noting her deaf ears to my cry on the glorious Holy Week celebration, the day I could've worn my two hats to look different among my peers while imitating the president, to all present, I jumped off the fifth floor of the building onto the concrete at the time and landed squarely, but bruised. I never knew how the glorious Holy Week had ended and who had gotten their feet, heads, and arms washed. When I woke up five days later in the hospital and was finally discharged, I came home with my mother and witnessed my father and his age groupies, men who loved each other and life, sitting in the balcony on a harmattan, hazy, but sunny day, mosquitoes and dragonflies buzzing around the corners of their cheap palmwine sweetened lips. Matter-of-factly, they were not noisy drunks, but men who loved, cared for themselves and their country and lashing out at the man with two hats on who ruled the nation-, "A nation of literate men and women with Ph.Ds made illiterate by the man with two hats." That was how he'd put it to his age groups at the time.

It was a dream hazy harmattan season as I'd mentioned before, one that I will always look back at with pleasure as my father had discussed with his buddies. After all, "in wine there's truth" has always been true to this time. The truth was, to wear two hats in Nigeria, one has to be a General, a Lieutenant, or a Major in the Army, trained at Sandhurst Army Canon University in Britain and therefore must know how to fire different weapons of destruction without missing target. He was saying to his peer groups, "The Generals in the Army are usually from the North. They have the upper hand because they are given the power by the Britishman after their training in England to repress the Southerners. And if they are strong-headed trying to stage a coup to oust a Northerner from power, they should arrest them, pluck their eyes out and cut their tongue off and eat their nose and cheek and brains." He chuckled.

"Hum huh, but you know something? In this country, the 'us' and 'them' has become a cancer, a virus. I see our children these days getting more interested in the old ways of when Life Goes On was in power. I see it with my uncles, nieces, and nephews and even my own kids," his friend Oyagbau concurred.

"Apart from the power given the Northerners after graduation from Sandhurst, they are told to move all the armored vehicles and cannons and motars to Kaduna, somewhere in the North, so that any time they want they can fool the people of this country. And you know something, they always succeed in coups and counter coups," voiced out another man.

I was captivated in the gist so I hanged around, though I was to go catapulting with my age groups. Usually my father was harsh when I was not reading or doing my homework. But on this day, he did not shout on top of his voice at me to get down to business of reading and doing my homework. He continued his sermon to his peer groups, "Just as stock brokers are blamed when something goes wrong in the market, the military juntas has and always has blamed the civilians and or the military man on top who rule: an excuse to assume power. They also use the same tactics to hand over power to the next man in command, when they stage a bloodless coup."

That day, my father and his age groupies were having the best time of their life, the day which marks the traditional time when the sky suddenly darkened and the Earth shook and Christ was said to have died on the cross for our sins. Actually the opposite because The National Power Authority had cut off the electricity so that the coup would succeed. And it did.

At one point it seemed almost too interesting to me to see that they all got up from their seats and hugged each other, jubilating and making mockery of the people that hanged Christ on the cross, when the news came on Voice of America (VOA) that the time of the man with two hats on, had expired while on top of *Thai woman toto*, fucking with big bucks. However, the news concluded that Bad Dudu has ascended the throne, stating that himself would wear three hats, claiming the man with two hats on was too corrupt, and him with three hats on was the messiah to save the country. Interesting, I thought. I still remember that day in history.

They sat again after the famous news from VOA and Isiaka, another of my father's drinking acquaintances, declared, "With the sudden death of the man wearing two hats, whose time had expired while eating the forbidden apple of some imported Thai damsels, the once restive ethnics which had been influenced by University students across the country, whom the masses had also supported to result to the streets on numerous occasions on a non-violent demonstration mainly to protest a General who was not duely elected by the people, killing, jailing, robbing the nation in cold-blood of billions of dollars and siphoning the loot to foreign banks, would now finally cease."

Here, I realized that what he meant was that Nigeria needed a Savior to rescue them from Generals wearing one hat, two hats, and three hats. One who would try as much as possible to resuscitate a cancer economy seemingly resistant to change with men wearing bogus hats in the most populous country-Nigeria.

Another of my father's acquaintance group noted, "Inflation has been high, poverty rampant and had reached its summit. You think anyone in this country would mourn him amidst what he did to men and women of this country? Teachers were not paid their salaries due them, and workers also were complaining of low monthly wages. Amidst all these, the Generals have billions stashed in Britain and Switzerland banks. We all know that they crooked all the billions out of our country making the people of this country to suffer."

My dad summed up, "The Southerners in this country are toiling everywhere in chains."

All these memories still linger on my mind coupled, that six months later, the man wearing his three hats dropped one off stating that a General with common sense shouldn't wear three hats to address his nation. That he'd worn three hats so people would greatly fear him, and that he'd realized that two hats on was just as good as three on. And I must admit that these atrocities of the Generals wearing one, two and three hats fully came to light late in the last century and although they have been condemned by great journalists, to tell the stories of these men with remarkable accuracy, they were tortured and hanged. Also the chaos, debt they talked about was to grow still more, with the European countries welcoming the crooks into their banks, to build their towns and cities, with these crooks loots after they die.

Here Efemona would be introduced and be remembered as the only woman who got the balls.

Chapter

2

....

The executive seat of the building on which he sat is a resemblance of Sandhurst Army Canon Depot in Britain.

He's also a several times supporter of successful coups in his country, a one-man media control machine as a dictator and a self-proclaimed hero who takes no nonsense from critics who try to challenge his authoritarian regime. This man and his army junta regime in West Africa is known by his people he ruled. He is illiterate and surrounded himself with Lebanese men and women crooks and cooks. Where he hails from in his country beyond the city of life of the hot seat he occupies and of death is an empty place. The city is now the country's commercial capital. But leave the city's commercial capital and driving up North, Ukpenu, Bornu, and Ogoni areas, to mention but a few, far away from his village, you'll certainly run into a lot of wide open voids occupied with lots of cattle and goats and rodents.

In short, cattle and goats and rodents out-numbered thatched-huts and corrugated homes. The expanse of land at Borunu, Bornu off Sundan on Ogoni road, his birthplace, barely known by most Nigerians except by this renounced man-General Bad Dudu's own people, scarcely appears on the map of his country. The only sign of local life are thousands of cows that marooned on the vast expanse of land that face starvation with his people. Overnight however, General Bad Dudu, the man described, had transformed only his brother's compound and his cattle ranch pastures. Whereas, the inhabitants of this expanse of land suffer, Bad Dudu, didn't care about anybody else except his pocketbook and those of his brothers and in-laws from Lebanon. Few of his villagers had trudged through the vast land to wander to Lagos, the commercial capital to engage in black market selling the dollar and pound sterling currencies.

The entire people in the country he has absolute power gave him the name General Bad Dudu. Those in his village call him the Cattleman General with no mercy.

What baffles most people in his country is that the Cattleman General knows little about 'government of the people by the people'. But he has sexual experiences and preferences with only Lebanese, Indian and Thai women. To the typical farmers and market women of his country, it seemed to them that General Bad Dudu made love to them and gave them millions of U.S. dollars and British pounds.

General Bad Dudu, the man described, had assumed the presidency of the most populous nation in West Africa, ending the regime of the man wearing two hats. It was Dudu Junta: a cadre of high ranking military officials who had seized power that ended the life of the man with two hats on, with barricades of bullets to his skull-Mafia style assassination, whatever one may call it for that matter, when he was on top of *toto:* the female carnal. Due to Bad Dudu's philosophy that the strongest man always wins, his control of the National Radio by his junta regime out gunned the loyal forces of the man wearing two hats when he was having fun with the females.

In Dudu's speech, before he occupied the executive hot seat where he then gave orders, he'd accused the man wearing two hats of lacking physical development and trying to undermine the well being of the populace. Dudu also charged the man wearing two hats for being too soft on persecution of men who challenge authorities as well as arbitrary stoppage of money flowing into the palm of certain people who don't deserve it, which was not part of the rules laid down in secret meetings at the Buckingham Palace in England that the Northerners alone have the right to rule and siphon the nations money to Britain and Swiss banks.

Bad Dudu and his junta group then were very critical of ousting the man wearing two hats accusing the beneficiaries of over ambitions to rule and relegate some technical share of the pie of the nations wealth to the common people who don't deserve to eat, but to starve to death.

The thing is, lacking the premise of a true democracy of government of the people by the people, for which Bad Dudu has no knowledge, that common people come first in the house of representatives, he quarreled with the administration's transition to Civil Rule Handover arguing it was designed to favor a section of the country who are vast and prone to *'419' activities-the dubious acts of smart people from certain parts of the country to acquire millions from the white man overseas.* But Bad Dudu was against this. He, as figurehead of his people prefers to carry billions with briefcases out of his country to foreign countries.

But to the typical farmer, market men and women of his nation, the reason for the coup Bad Dudu gave to his nation meant a heinous reversal of the aggressive steps forward of the man wearing two hats. The poor common people knew that some of the radical changes the man wearing two hats wanted to make had been tested over and over before and the populace being governed found them highly undesirable. They also knew that the man wearing two hats was buckling on the idea of how he would wipe out the virus of corruption and to purge those officials of his regime who engaged in such acts draining the country's resources and treasury. The man wearing two hats had had a mission. To him, Nigeria, despite a rich nation that exports crude oil to other countries in the world, is for the most part a barely functioning nation. He knew there were the usual shortages of electricity failures, no running water, fuel shortages, patchy waste removal, unchecked pollution, crumbling and worn infrastructures were legion and legendary. A change was needed he'd reasoned.

But, it does not take a genius to know that the man wearing two hats was heading towards the right direction for his people. And that Bad Dudu wearing three hats the day he announced to the nation, he was wearing three hats on the hot seat had opposite motive. The people being ruled however, knew that it was all the same trickish way they all fool the people they rule. They are all one and the same.

Who would challenge the man wearing three hats on his head in this populous country, Nigeria, was the question.

* * *

It baffles businessmen and women who visited this most populous nation of West Africa-Nigeria, that when they visit for business trips they are perplexed to see government abandoned projects, panhandlers on every street they turned, and garbage heaps everywhere. They are prone to wonder why Bad Dudu hasn't completed his tasks as he'd promised his people after he seized power with a hole in the head. Adam Khan knew why.

Adam Khan was a Lebanese well-known businessman who regularly visited Nigeria every six months after successful coups had taken place. The last time he was there after the man with two hats on was ousted by Bad Dudu, he was surprised to see a nation in chaos. He'd visited during the rainy season. To Adam Khan, a former foreman of the Shell Oil Drilling Inc., a flamboyant man with a seamed face and a body that was heavy with a protruding Gulder beer belly, it was ironic to him that among the several oddities surrounding the abandoned highway constructions—of bridges, roads, schools and hospitals, since Bad Dudu seized power, none of these several abandoned projects had been completed. This time, ten years of his absence had turned Adam Khan into a complete stranger, that as he dashed into an unfinished building in Lagos as he landed at Muritala Mohammed Airport, the unfinished building which was turned into a Booka-restaurant anxiety flipped his stomach.

Actually, this was a restaurant I also knew very well in those days when I was growing up. A rowdy place where women discuss business of buying homes and land before poisoning their husbands who were rich. At least it was the myth when I was growing up. That time, I'd listened to Princess Akinzua a not too pretty woman, but who knows how to insinuate her daughters in America to swindle millions of dollars from their husbands who were married to African Americans who are based in New York, Philadelphia, and New Jersey. That's another story.

Anyway, to Adam Khan tharch homes, roads similar to dirt track still remained to be where they were when the last coup was staged and executed. The Booka he'd dashed into for shelter was operated by a lone woman, Bad Dudu had taken her husband's life for investigating him of corruption while occupying the executive hot seat. The question that immediately occupied Adam Khan's mind was how could a nation like Nigeria rich in crude oil bed reserves not be able to complete all its government abandoned projects and create new jobs for high school graduates? Well!, he thought, Nigeria is ruled by zombies. I am here again to make my fast millions from the zombies! Contracts or no contracts, I'm sure to leave the country with at least $5 million dollars. Adam Khan was right. It was the idea of biding for the contracts to build new schools, hospitals, and bridges and explore new oil wells that lured him to Nigeria for the tenth time.

Adam Khan who has been a crook all his life, looked around the Booka and saw the hungry, preening men and women ordering *fufu* and *eba* and rice without meat in their soups and threw a mocking question at widow Abayomi, the owner of the Booka. Though the women were hungry, they still had their sense of humor and all had a common passion to wear bright, colorful and cheap dresses which amount to their madness. They never stop talking about good quality materials and where the money might come from someday for them to keep buying *okirika wake up—Salvation Army clothes*. In reality, they had wished Almighty could bring back Life Goes On when he was in power and everyone will have enough again to buy their wants and needs.

Adam Khan asked a young woman, widowed Abayomi had served eba with no meat in her soup. "You don't like to eat cow meat, goat meat, fish, chicken? How come . . . ?"

The young woman was mute. In reality Adam Khan just wanted to ridicule her. She became more involved in her food, swallowing with pride but with pain and not looking at him. But Adam Khan looked at widow Abayomi again and said, "I asked a simple question and your customer ignored me. Do you know it's a shame to eat food in Lebanon without meat?"

"Come on, the people of Lebanon don't have that much money to satisfy their palates!"

"With Nigerian zombies ruling we Lebanese can satisfy our hunger these days."

I guess that might be the reason why you're in my country then. Abayomi said. His reply chatted out, "We Lebanese crooks, businessmen heard that Bad Dudu was looking for able, fit men and women who could carry as much as thirty-seven briefcases loaded with cash out of his country coupled with the fact he could award more contracts in the next few weeks. That is what brought me to your country. But tell me the truth, did Bad Dudu actually promise that under his new command everyone in your country will have enough to eat? Or Bad Dudu was just another jerk to con your nation of billions of dollars within the next few months of his regime?"

Widow Abayomi and her customers became nervous. Abayomi doesn't trust anyone any more who might snitch up on her to get the bullet in her temples overnight as they did to her husband.

Finally, she summed up her courage and sighed deeply. Rather than replying to him, she tossed a copy of an old Daily Times newspaper to him she'd kept for a long time.

And Adam Khan glanced through the front page of the newspaper and he read: "We are a nation of modest means and we have to acknowledge my junta regime do not have the money to complete government abandoned projects which other regimes of junta military rulers in this country have abandoned for years. What my own junta regime planned ahead to do is to award new contracts to contractors to build new schools, new hospitals, new bridges and new roads." It was Bad Dudu speaking to the press. Adam Khan knew why Bad Dudu would rather award new contracts to foreign contractors rather than Nigerian contractors to complete the old abandoned projects. The fact is this: He would swindle more billions out of the country through Lebanese, Stragfbarg, Dumez, and other foreign crooks contractors within a few months of his regime.

Adam Khan finished reading the story and he carefully folded it and handed it back to her. He knew widow Abayomi was afraid to let out the truth to him. He too, knew he was a party to Bad Dudu, carrying briefcases loaded with foreign currencies in millions and billions out of the country for him, and he receives up to $2 million in kickbacks for the job. That was how Adam Khan was making his fast money for the bid of contracts of building new schools, new hospitals, maternities, and new roads.

In reality Adam Khan grieved for the young preening men and women eating eba and fufu without meat in their soups. Recollecting how much money he had carried out of Nigeria in briefcases, he sighed deeply and looked at widow Abayomi after reading the newspaper. He let out his opinion and thoughts. He said to Abayomi, "Nigerian military junta led by General Bad Dudu, who devalued your nation's currency, which was once stronger than the dollar itself, is a country at war with itself. Your country is one of the very few countries in Africa that would've had as an original, a rare and classic work of art deco architecture and good infrastructures. To the preening men and women, and market men and market women, farmers and palmwine tappers-suffering the illness of your major Generals who rule your country, Nigeria was supposed to have one of the nicest examples of good living standards compared to other African countries. Your country is supposed to have good roads, good grammar schools, and good universities, nicest hospitals and maternities in villages ever built and above all, teachers paid monthly and regularly."

Adam Khan paused and asked for a glass of water. After drinking it he cracked up and continued, "You know, your country is one of many countries in the world God had blessed with plenty of minerals found under the ground. It was also one of the first countries in Africa that was influenced by the British and Roman's arts and crafts movements, etc. and many other important twentieth century art and architecture designs with different styles. Could you tell me why these such necessities are now neglected for a rich country like Nigeria, your country?"

Embattled widow Abayomi was to blame the growing junta coup and counter coups and corruption scandal in her country on a pervasive manner and attitude of more Generals in line ready to take over by more bullets to the head instead of calling for election for literate men to rule her country. Mute and unwilling to answer his question, but in which she would've replied, the coups and counter coups all for the purpose of draining our economy and in which rogue military juntas including Bad Dudu allegedly beat, shot, and jailed people and sometimes celebrated their misdeeds in Britain, would not be told by her. The thing is, a dozen women she knew, who now are widowed because Bad Dudu silenced their husbands for the truth, still hasn't changed the way the economy should be revived. Then she thought for a long time of the hunger and of starvation of children and of men and women of her country. Tears rolled down her cheeks. Afraid the man before her asking her these heinous questions might snitch up on her and then she might be arrested by secret plain clothes juntas of Bad Dudu and silenced by bullet, finally looked sternly at Adam Khan taking cover in her Booka. She summed up the courage, "After the rain why don't you take a tour of this city and the country when you have the time." He nodded. He didn't want to pressure her to talk. After the downpour, Adam Khan bid her farewell, then stepped out of the Booka of the unfinished building into an untidy asphalt road and walked along Iyamu Crescent Street of more abandoned and boarded-up houses huddled together in narrow, non-asphalt road. Animal carcasses used for voodoo now soaked in wet flood rain, stinking, lined the side of the streets. In reality the rain had made sodden messes of the carcasses and garbage all piled high on both sides of the street. The garbage inshort would probably remain there for another decade as long as Bad Dudu was in power, he thought. Adam Khan knew the city very well when Life Goes on was the President or Head of State of this nation. During his regime, everyone in Abayomi's country had enough to eat, he pondered in his heart as he strolled. I can now understand why widow Abayomi wanted me to take a tour of the city and draw a conclusion for myself. He shook his head in disgust- actually the opposite.

* * *

Adam Khan had strolled more than three miles into Alausa Avenue and then headed to Akinzua Street in Benin, the city where Efemona attended elementary school. It has just chimed 4:30 P.M. when Adam Khan spotted the Ministry of 99% Poverty Restaurant owned and operated by Princess Akinzua and Judas Iscariot where Adam Khan and Dogoyaro had arranged to meet. This restaurant owned and operated by Princess Akinzua and Judas Iscariot is where Bad Dudu and some of his crook Lebanese businessmen meet regularly to discuss and to reach agreement for the purchase of various hotels, such as the Eko Hotel which Dudu had purchased for $100 million dollars including the demolition of several houses owned by poor people; the houses which did not meet the standard of houses in the areas. Adam Khan looked here and there and shook his head. The reason for that was, this street itself had become the people's talk of the city emblem of urban decay and poverty except for where the Eko Hotel stood.

But the Ministry of 99% Poverty Restaurant owned and operated by Princess Akinzua and Judas Iscariot was a restaurant in history Adam Khan remembered too well before he dashed in. He'd known that Princess Akinzua and Judas Iscariot were both crooks in their own way, using the restaurant to cover up from all the deals they receive from the junta crooks of Bad Dudu.

As they settle, Major Dogoyaro sat opposite Adam Khan then took off his raincoat, hat and rain boots. They sat down after the ease of men hand shakes and ordered pounded yam with equesi soup with plenty of stockfish and beef meat which an ordinary farmer and market women and family men can not afford in this country, anymore. After so many years of doing business in the country with the junta members, Adam Khan was used to the food himself. They ate to their satisfaction. After all, if you have money, you can afford to buy anything you want. So, after they'd finished eating, Major Dogoyaro ordered more star bottles of beer and *pepper soup* while poor women and men customers swallowing their *eba* with pride with no meat looked and envied them. With another glass of wine and shots of Cognac, Dogoyaro became more talkative than normal. Adam Khan noticed he felt a twinge of embarrassment when he realized that the entire restaurant customers were listening to him describing how they repress citizens for truth and draining the Nation's treasury through Lebanese crook businessmen like Adam himself.

Matter-of-factly, Adam Khan had wanted him to continue so he could extract some valuable information about the proper channel he could get hold of top other members of their junta regimes then suddenly he told himself to shut up and smile. Princess Akinzua understood the meaning of the laugh, too, and smiled.

Princess Akinzua, whose real name is Madam Kalamazoo, five and six, heavy set with dimples, was busy clearing the table. She seemed a little put off at the moment, touching her braided hair regularly. For the first time, Adam remembered that Madam Kalamazoo was not what he'd heard about her: slim and beautiful. She was ugly as to Sumo wrestler than first class women of Aba and Ghanaian gold scale women to lay. But Madam Kalamazoo was good for arranging press conferences with crooks from Lebanon to meet high military officials at her restaurant. Who in this country, called Nigeria would suspect Kalamazoo to be a member of the underground making millions? Her ugliness was the reason she was inducted into the *OZO* society moneymakers. They had reasoned that with young, beautiful female acquaintances, with wine, they are prone to reveal their secrets of making money through dubious means. Madam Kalamazoo was therefore, the best for the job.

In contrast, Judas Iscariot was not too ugly. His status fit the profile of a broomstick, but he is also good in talking and conning the government of lots of money in the Dudu's regime. Though his head was like that of a coconut, it can retain millions of information without putting the facts on paper when meetings were held at their restaurant with high ranking military junta officials. He can retain how contracts would be awarded and how much was to be siphoned out of the country without the knowledge of the people being ruled with iron hands of the junta military council regime.

To crown Judas Iscariot and how slim and ugly he was as a broom stick I'd saved him from the point of being hacked to death by his wife Elaingotcha. The story: I was at his home one day to discuss with him that the military junta regime of his country was draining Nigeria's treasury and what I planned to do to stop it was imminent, when his wife, Elaingotcha, had a cane to whip him and a chef's knife to slice his throat after whipping him. Before it happened, I was on my knees begging and calming her. She listened to me, being a family friend for over ten years.

When she'd calmed down I'd asked her, "So what seemed to be the problem with you and my friend Judas? I have never known you to lose your temper in this manner before me."

She had tears in her eyes. Then she said, "I'm just sick and tired of my sickle cell anemia motherfucking husband talking bad about you behind your back."

I almost cracked up, but restrained what would've been a raucous laughter. She knew I'd be interested to hear more. So she made a face to deceive her husband then said, "I've kept the sucker quiet for a long time now insulting you and me before high ranking military officials of Dudu's regime when they come to our house. A stingy, ugly fool who thinks you, Ekiaqueta is his rival. For one, Judas my husband shouldn't even compete with you because you had wrote and had passed mathematics examination in the university. Whereas, my husband and Bad Dudu paid other students to write it for them. What annoys me the most is that he has been scandalizing your name before the junta men of your government. He'd labeled you before them that you are a drug pusher and jailbird in order to tarnish your image and get more acquainted with the Generals and Major Generals so that he would continue to get more favors from their wives and mistresses who'd run away from their Generals and Major Generals' homes for fear of being killed and tortured by their husbands. Time and again, Judas, my husband knows that if he says Efemona, whom you planned to marry is a whore, a bitch that would be true. To tell me that you are a drug peddler when he knows that you don't even smoke cigarettes is madness. I'm sick and tired of his lies against you.

She looked at me and said, "Don't you think your pen is more powerful in the fiction form on paper manuscripts than the sum total of everything my ugly, dumb motherfucking husband says he has matrialistically?"

"Yeah, you're right." I'd said.

"Then let me kill the motherfucker before you once and for all. I've told my husband time and again that I don't like gossip and yet he kept undermining my ability and how I felt about it." Though I concealed my irritation and looked at Judas Iscariot, my friend, I'd sympathized and so I was in the middle trying to separate a fight with a chef's knife. I held Elaingotcha and said, "You know, your husband is suffering from Kwiarsioko. He'll die by himself rather than by you taking the law into your own hands." She sobbed and dropped the huge chef's knife on the floor.

Iscariot cracked up. I wondered why. Elaingotcha frowned at him. Finally she said, *"Judas Iscariot, the ugly stinking fool, motherfucker knows if he gives me shit I go give 'am shit. If no be you, Ekiaqueta, I go quench 'am today."*

"Please don't kill him before me. You can do that when I leave," I'd said. Come to think about it, I wondered how Elaingotcha knew how to speak broken English. I looked at her ugly face with plenty of acne and her long lips with style. Man! My man Judas has no good taste. Anyway, I'd said to Elaingotcha, "Please don't insult my friend before me."

With style too, I looked at Judas Iscariot, a distinguished- looking thin man with a deep-cupped chin and two deep laugh lines on his face. A face that I could've turned down if I were a youngwoman. Still my man Iscariot is very pompous with his looks when in the company of the Generals and Major Generals of his country junta rulers. Hum! My man Iscariot! Between his two distinguished laugh line marks, stood his big nose, almost bigger than his head. And to worsen his situation, his gray hairs gave another crooked dimension of drama to what otherwise would've discouraged Elaingotcha my ex-neighbor's sixteen-year-old daughter from marrying him. But because he has a black Corvette which she didn't even drive or know how the inside looks it had naturally took her breath away coupled with the riches from the Generals and Major Generals dubious activities he'd acquired. Secondly, thanks to 'just for men' which had worked its miracles on his hair to disguise him as a young man. To be real to the point, I know he does wonderful concealing of his age when in the company of his junta Generals and Major Generals who rule his country, whom he'd ties of dubious activities. He is most notorious when in the company of the ex-wives of the Generals. Though he admitted he's thirty-years-old, his face is like the back of an oak tree. He is very stingy. To say the least he might socialize to buy drinks for the women of ex-wives of the Generals. However, the next time he comes across the women in bars he demands his money back. The reason for that is because he doesn't want the people of his country in poverty to know he has ties with the General's siphoning his nation's money to Swiss banks. Also, Judas Iscariot likes to get close to people at parties who have money as himself to know how they made it before he carries propaganda against those who have problems with their ex-wives who were strictly his adversary at a time. The few people who are his bosom friend apart from the Generals who rule his nations he calls, "First Class," meaning that they are artful dodgers who were able to steal thousands from the Eko Hotel and Federal Palace Hotel and Casinos and never got caught like himself when he'd worked at Eko Hotel and Casino as a keyman before he was discovered by the junta Generals and Major Generals he was a man who could be made rich overnight.

But one thing I'd hated about Judas Iscariot the most was that though he's filthy rich, he goes to church and sits in the back pew throughout the service without participating in the sermon, like a beggar on the street who came into the church seeking temporary relief from harmattan cold weather in the mornings.

From the information I'd received from sources about Judas, I'd trailed him to his church where I'd watched him neither recite the hymns nor receive holy communion and when the man collecting offerings comes nearer him, he kneels down with his face down pretending to be praying, therefore avoiding dropping a dollar in their basket.

Hum! My man Judas! He calls himself a gigolo and the father of all exotic vehicles who married the youngest woman among his peers. The thing is, he'd married Elaingotcha when she was sixteen because he believes she was still a dunce. To intimidate Elaingotcha, he'd advised that she address him as 'Sir', always which Elaingotcha honored because of the Corvette he'd just purchased with kickbacks from the Generals who own casinos. And at his wedding at the 'Good Hope Wisdom Church', there was a holdup and the guests became restless that they began to entertain doubts if the wedding was ever going to happen or be postponed. The hold-up of course had been that Elaingotcha then had realized that she'd been flattered by the eargality of passion Iscariot aroused in her life-forty years older than her in actuality instead of thirty.

Being a good friend of Judas, I'd led the way to investigate why the hold-up for Elain tying the knot. I found out that the parents of Elaingotcha, Mr. and Mrs. Gbassa had insisted that Judas sign a prenuptial agreement, which was a last minute idea because their daughter was too young to make her own decision and that if Judas were to pass out while he was screwing their daughter who has more strength to engage him in hours fucking the son-of-a-bitch, without the prenuptial documentation, Judas' next of kin would inherit his wealth he has accumulated through dubious means. Therefore, Elaingotcha would be left with nothing. While I then confronted Elaingotcha for clarification for the delay, she was mad to hear that her parents were behind the stalemate for Iscariot to slide the ring onto her finger. Elaingotcha had then quickly confronted her parents. She'd told her parents that, even if Judas doesn't sign the agreement she knew best on how to deal with him when the time comes. She knew best how to handle him for all the insults and humiliation she'd entertained from the stingy, ugly motherfucker all those years before proposing to marry him. Elaingotcha then confidently told her mother how she would kill the son-of-a-bitch for insulting her all those years, calling her a dunce and making her kneel down for hours when, by joke, she was replacing his artificial dentures upside down in his mouth. She knew that the motherfucker was getting close to his grave and if he doesn't pass out when he was screwing her, she knew when to hurt him. Where she would hurt him was when he was climbing National Electricity Power Authority (NEPA) poles installing cables. And that the best way she'd planned to kill Judas, she'd told her mother was; she would trail the son-of-a-bitch and watch him climb the pole with a ladder and then she would take away the ladder, which would force him to jump to his death. Then the detective who would handle the case would be forced to believe that he committed suicide. Then she would inherit his wealth and ship them to Morovia and also she would claim his retirement plan and his life insurance policy in excess of $5 million dollars the military junta regime has in his name.

Elaingotcha also had recalled to me how Judas Iscariot had met her and her friends then invited her friends only to the party without her, but told her to come after the party to provide a late amusement for him after the dinner and party were over. Knowing what late amusement and come see me after the dinner party meant later, she vowed to kill the motherfucker after marrying him.

Anyway, Elaingotcha finally looked at my face as I felt for her deeply what she'd been through. Her mother who'd been mad carefully listened to her daughter explain to me her plot on how she'd planned to kill Judas. She was relieved and then gave her a go ahead to marry him at the last minute in the church. Defiantly, Elaingotcha looked at me and said, "Because of the way Judas had conned me to marry him and had even told me I will have access to the keys to the Corvette which I have not driven since I knew him all these years-and you were a witness at one time when he ridiculed me that I was a dunce, how do you think I can eliminate that from my mind?"

But then I'd calmed her down. She'd always respected me. I gave her a tissue to wipe her face. She could not contain herself.

Looking at me with tears flooding out from the socket of her eyes she said plainly, "Ekiaqueta! You are Judias savior today. You warn your friend not to bring up or gossip with your name before me."

"I'll do just that," I'd promised her.

The one thing I'd gathered from Elaingotcha relating to me her experience, I immediately know why the military junta high ranking officials choose Judas Iscariot as their partner for making dubious money through ghost contracts and paper manipulation and before siphoning the money out of his country with his accomplice Princess Akinzua.

* * *

Dogoyaro and Adam Khan were now finally drinking their star beer when Dogoyaro called on Princess Akinzua. Princess Akinzua turned around, Adam Khan noticed for the first time Princess Akinzua, whom he'd heard so much about in Obiageli Newspapers, was not at all the way he'd imagined she would be: as beauty is to Vanessa Williams as Princess Akinzua has pimples all over her face, and as Princess Akinzua is slim and watches her weight as she was fatter than a Sumo wrestler, and her children bought her all the houses at Benin Government Reserved Areas (GRA), as Princess Akinzua's daughters are happily married and their husbands decide how their money should be spent. As tall and average built, but with the appearance of a Sumo wrestler and therefore engage in fasting. It was hard for Adam Khan to imagine that Princess Akinzua could've fallen in love with all the high profile military junta of Bad Dudu's regime who deserve the best and not an ugly bitch as herself who is poor and wretched. Adam Khan heard from the horses mouth that Princess Akinzua had in fact, instigated her daughters to file for divorce and carry their loots of multi-million dollars the court in America will award them to Nigeria to buy homes, which was a smart move because Princess Akinzua herself believes in Nigerian Banks than in overseas banks. In reality, the money Princess Akinzua was making from the junta's regime was invested in Nigeria.

Anyway, Dogoyaro finally motioned Princess Akinzua to their table. He liked to flirt with beauties and uglies. He said to her, "By the way, how much do we owe you for the food and drinks?" Princess Akinzua was rather continually touching her braided hair. Dogoyaro and Adam Khan could tell she'd just perhaps braided her hair by the way she was poking and reacting to the base of the root stem of the braid to ease the pain underneath because they were too tight.

Dogoyaro asked, "Did you just braid your hair?" At the same time he praised the style and complimented the lady who braided it. Then he stood up and looked at the hairstyle again, "Who made it for you?"

He touched it and felt it for her. Princess Akinzua reacted in a throaty contratto purr. "Oh! It hurt. The girl down the street made it yesterday in a hurry for me. Her name is Rose Ose," she answered and added, "She's good, but this one is too tight for me."

"I can see that," he said and sat again with Adam Khan. "Well, why don't you grease the base with baby oil to ease the pain," Dogoyaro suggested and she stood up.

They flirted together a few more seconds and Princess Akinzua asked, "By the way, who is this gentleman with you?" She knew him but just couldn't remember who he was or just wanted to fool the people in her restaurant.

"Well, meet Adam Khan, our man good in doing business with us." She shook his hand. "Adam Khan is here looking for new contracts with the junta regime. He flew in from Lebanon early—and he's strolling the streets to survey the areas of this country that need new developments, and most important, to find out where our oil reserve beds are to be developed and drilled for our man Bad Dudu."

Princess Akinzua knew what he was talking about. He added immediately, "And how much do we owe you?"

Adam Khan noticed she'd a calculator. She punched the calculator a few times and came up with her total. "Only ten thousand Naira, General."

Adam Khan couldn't believe that the food they'd ate was that expensive. In his heart, he was thinking how many people can afford that kind of money to feed themselves in a decaying Nigerian economy. Then he raised his head up, "Really?" he asked, joining the conversation.

"Ah! We are biting the dust hard here in this country these days. Those who rule don't care anymore in this country. The money is worth nothing. Our money use to be worth more than the dollar. Now it has no inherent good value. I think of it now as worse than the Mexican Pesos. Bad Dudu and his men are fighting for-their-own-pockets."

Adam Khan listened as Princess Akinzua aired her bitterness. She added, "You must include me on the contract calendar when you get it from the main men on top. I'm tired of suffering the illness of our leaders," she voiced out with bitterness to confuse the rest of the customers eating in her Booka, and Adam Khan understood.

But the preening men and women around in the Booka all nodded as if instincts told them to, at the same time. "*Money Pala-va* these days is worse than it used to be," one of the men eating eba responded, unaware that Princess Akinzua was part of the problem in her country.

"I try my best to feed pay me. I give them five the hungry and the poor even if they can't months to pay me."

Adam Khan looked at her. Then he said, "Good of you Princess Akinzua. Allah, which Bad Dudu believes in will reimburse you for your good deeds for the poor you're feeding in this country."

But then, Adam Khan, Dogoyaro, and Princess Akinzua all listened with secret amazement to the rest of the preening men and women complaining about the thunder and lightning and the rainy weather and hardship in the country because of greed by General Bad Dudu and his junta regime in cahoots.

"The motherfucking damned thunder and lightning burned down my house yesterday. My children, my wife and I will be homeless. It took me damned fifty years to complete roofing my building," a family man who said he has ten children and twenty grandchildren complained. "It would be hard for me to build another one in fifty years if Bad Dudu is still in power as a dictator." "My son was shot dead yesterday by a group of uniformed armed soldiers who came up to my house and dragged him outside and tortured him before my eyes. After torturing him they shot him and killed him point blank," Madam Katu, a Christian, the mother of Giwa, the famous renounced journalist voiced out as she swallowed her last mounded eba.

"The junta regime of Bad Dudu believes in Lebanese crooks helping them to siphon our oil money to foreign banks," another market woman eating *amala* and *ogbono soup* without meat voiced out.

Then another preening trader held Adam Khan and the rest of the customers in the Booka spellbound as he swallowed his *pounded yam*. He too had gisted: It was on a Saturday morning. The day had just dawned bright and clear from harmattan haze. I'd woke up early and walked a few distance around my unfinished building which my father later had converted to a palmwine parlor. When I came in, I got dressed then had a cup of coffee, while I tried to decide what good road to take and bike up to Ukpenu, south of Benin to see my mother who'd been killed by a lunatic with a Magnum. My God! There were potholes on major roads I biked to go to Ukpenu. At times I get down from the bike to walk and pushed my bike through. The worst of all, the taps for water along the roads were dry. And at Ukpenu, the people I talked to told me that the poverty level where Bad Dudu hails from in the remote areas of the North called Bornu-bordering Ukpenu was even worse than the poverty level at Lagos where he rules-to ditch out orders who he wants jailed for life. An egg of a chicken at Bornu and

Ukpenu now cost N120, a tin of peak milk, N150, and the smallest yam tuber, from N200-N500.

At Ogoni, where the oil reserves are, where I thought men and women were enjoying the wealth of our nation alone, graduates there don't even have jobs. The only good government paying jobs is for Arabic teachers. The one thing that stunned me the most was that there are more armed men on the street of Ukpenu and Ogoni. By night, market men and market women and farmers stumble along using torchlights if they can afford one to avoid deep potholes. That means our National Electric Power Authority is a failure. General Bad Sudu's grandchild, Amedu, and Efemona grandmother both drowned in one of the deep potholes. From what I learned, the potholes were deeper than Lake Tahoe and Lake Victoria. Desperate to see for myself when I heard these stories from my natives, instead of grieving the death of my mother who was killed, I biked to Ogoni areas. My friends! Ogoni was actually a place one cannot imagine biking through. It was too baffling to see too many

shops filled with coffins. The shopkeepers who operated the shops I noticed were sitting alone in the gloom. I could tell that they, too, were trying perhaps to re-create a normal life despite that the signs of poverty were imprinted on their foreheads as in any other part of the country. The people at Ogoni and Ukpenu where Bad Dudu hails from rode bicycles and at most Honda and Vespa motorcycles to go to work and, to their cattle and chicken raring farms. Bad Dudu's father rides a fifty-year-old bicycle. After work he uses it to carry those who can afford to pay his fares to their shops and farms. That's how he survives to take care of himself and his family and great, great grandchildren. I have never before seen a billionaire so stupid as Bad Dudu believing in foreign banks than his country and his own people."

Major Dogoyaro, Princess Akinzua, Judas Iscariot, and Adam Khan wished he would just stop the gisting and eat his damned *eba* with *ogbono* soup with no meat in the soup. Finally Major Dogoyaro interrupted him, "What is your name my friend? And what part of the city do you live?" he'd asked for a reason.

"My name is Ukikankon-Dituan," he answered and swallowed his mounded eba on his palm.

"Your name must've meaning?," Dogoyaro asked.

"You bet. It means that if a man is poor beyond poor, he should strive not to get up at all to have a penny."

Ukikankon-Dituan knows better not to give his real name for the fear of Major Dogoyaro to consult his equals to eliminate him or send men to his home to torture him before they kill him.

Everyone in the Booka laughed. Ukikankon-Dituan continued to eat and gist.

"It was during the rainy season that I biked to Ogoni too. The rain being too heavy to resist, I decided to dash into a small Booka to take shelter. I'd only a few Naira and Kobo in my name. There were not too many people eating and patronizing the Booka, but there was little potential for lively conversation. Because I could not speak a word of the Ogonis, the Booka owner reasoned and never bothered me to order more food. He was very hospitable and somehow I managed to communicate with him a few words in the roofless building. I waited until his customers were gone before I appealed to him to spend the night. He honored my request. When his customers were gone, we both sat together in the mud brick—protected rear of the building he'd started to build when Life Goes On was in power, only to be abandoned when General Bad Dudu seized power and no money to complete it. He was a teacher, too, who'd not been paid for several months. Prior to my biking to Ogoni areas, I'd biked to Maiduguri, Sokoto, Kaduna, and Kano on my mission to know how the people live and die. To my surprise, the people still live in tharched huts. I wondered why Bad Dudu and his in cahoots that rule us would have millions and billions stashed up in foreign banks, killing and maiming innocent people who voiced out their concern about our economy—and his own people still live in tharched huts. I tell ya! Traveling to those places was fun: You know, for me it was adventure, sight seeing, meeting people and questioning them how they feel about General Bad Dudu and his junta regime. Fortunately, the more people I questioned on my stopovers about Bad Dudu, the more they resent him and his regime.

Anyway, arriving at the home town of Bad Dudu, flies and mosquitoes wrestled with me when the rain fell for several days, flooding the roads with no gutters and adequate drainage, reminding me so much of Lagos when it rained. The gutters were full. Broken bottles were everywhere. Ramshackle homes littered with piles of trash heaps and beer cans were symbols of the site that had organized parties of loud noise, and drunken fights, most in front of the Shell Oil Drilling Corporation, the seat of con artists, where Bad Dudu currently visited to say the least, was an eye- sorely foul. To tell everyone here the truth, there was no major difference between what I saw where Bad Dudu hails from and in Lagos-the present commercial capital where he ditches out orders to ruin our nation. Instead of churches, small mosques dominated his doomed birthplace. Even Bad Dudu once traveled home and prayed in one of the mosques. From what happened to him, he vowed never to visit his people, but punish them. The fact behind that was, his $2 million dollar man made shoes and his British made car worth millions of pounds the Lebanese crooks imported for him from Britain were stolen at the mosque when he was praying and had to go home on foot without shoes and his Rolls Royce. Though it was an exclusive Muslim village where he hails from and felt welcome and safe, they resent their own man-Bad Dudu, because they felt he has not done anything tangible for his own people in Bornu where he was supposed to develop. They had to sell his shoes and his car they'd stolen from him to build themselves a new and magnificent mosque. On my way back to Lagos, my bicycle tires had worn out. I had to abandon it and walk on foot. It took me several months to get to Lagos. The reason for that was, passengers transits and commercial vehicles can't make it to Lagos anymore because they are too old. To my surprise, the villages and towns I'd passed all ended up at different sleepy villages with huts. However, cattle, goats that frolicked in puddles in the main roads increasing their usual sound of gaggle as they fall into the potholes paved my way to direct me during the night.

Though I'd no torchlight with me, the moon shun on the roads. I was able to see that homes in Bornu off Ogoni by the side of the refineries where our oil is pumped exceed vast acres of land in square feet. And for a typical Bornu village style where the inhabitants don't even know if their country uses Naira and Kobo as legal tender, in picturesque simplicity, built their homes with adobe and grass."

Adam Khan's sympathy for the Ogoni and Bornu and Ukpenu people as Ukikankon-Dituan gisted as he swallowed could be seen imprinted on his eyelids-that sympathy that can't fit nicely on the head of a pin, with room left for saints to gavotte and sing the blues. Here too, Adam Khan remembers Ogoni, where he'd lived and built homes in the land of the oil prospectors seized from the poor landowners when General Bad Dudu seized power to rule with absolute power. He knew that men who prospect on oil drilling in these areas make at least $5 million dollars a year and business oil men from across the globe worry not for the Ogoni people who own the land if the government does not intervene. The nouveau riche as he might call them, build nice houses for themselves, the Ogonians envy and therefore had to finally speak up. He too knew that the Ogonis can't afford the homes they themselves built for sale out there, because the median price of homes in the area for the oil executives is close to $1 million dollars. Maybe it is and maybe it isn't. All he knew is that he would go there and have his own cut and chunk out of it. He does know that if the government intervenes to give the Ogoni people their share of the pie, they will ask for more incentives. But to the tragedy, the nouveau riche (oil executives from across the globe) spend several days in the swamps pumping out thousands and millions of barrels of crude oil from the ground at Ogoni without compensation and degrading their environment.

Which reminds me, that in America for instance, they consider environmental protection to be a fundamental responsibility wherever they operate in the world. Operating in an environmentally sound manner is as important as providing a safe workplace for their people. For their companies to conduct its operations in a responsible manner, each of them must make environmental protection part of their every day routine. They know drilling crude oil, which is necessary for modern society, affects the environment. Through their reasoning and sound planning, continuous monitoring, responsible reclamation, careful operating practices and attentive management, all can be accomplished right from day one. The Americans know that operating and drilling crude oil can be like raising a child. Each poses particular challenges and opportunities. They know that no two oil-drilling sites are the same. Innovative design is required to address each site's unique environmental setting and geologic character. They are committed to meeting those challenges and opportunities. Thanks to their leaders in Washington.

Anyway, Adam Khan sighed deeply, looking at Major Dogoyaro. Major Dogoyaro had wanted to interrupt Ukikankon- Dituan. But he gisted on. "As I was thirsty, I arrived at a little town south of Benin City known as Ukpenu, Efemona's birthplace, who they said is now a famous woman in Reno, Nevada. Here, a barefoot 12 year-old boy with no clothes on ran up to me, the stranger with city life clothes on, in amazement, of course. I inquired from him, "Where can I buy a bottle of beer?" He pointed me in the right direction and my smile immediately found an echo in the distance. I tell you all the truth, all activities seemed to end when I walked into this little town. All I can still remember seeing on the store shelves were roast suya and guguru and ground nuts. The store owner could not speak English, but somehow we managed to communicate a little. I bought suya and a bottle of beer. Then, when I tendered him a twenty Naira note, he shook his head. I figured he had never seen the color of money before. They still traded by barter. I watched him. He pointed to my shoes, and my shirt and my wristwatch. Instantly, I knew what he meant. So I took off my shoes and pulled over my shirt and gave them to him. He too, gave me what I wanted. I was damned hungry my friends! Finally I got back to Lagos where life was supposed to be fair to everyone. Hum? Not quite. My feet were all worn out. They became swollen as those of elephants. But, as I look back through my journey back to Lagos, my sufferings and adventure, the people I met to give me an insight about the sufferings of the people in the villages-all made me to get well to tell my story to the world. But my friends! Do you all know what baffles me the most about our leaders who rule this country?"

Everyone in the Booka looked at him and shook their heads. He shook his head, too, in a way to say, my people! Then he continued, "When our junta military rulers return from Britain and other European cities as they visit, our journalists asked them what they liked about those cites, and the funny thing is that they are quick to reply along the lines of, "We dined at a cozy sidewalk café in a beautiful plaza on a warm afternoon by a cool fountain where people were strolling, good enough to look at-not preening men and women-relaxing without flies and mosquitoes wrestling with them, and the cities are wonderfully built. Their soldiers don't parade the streets with guns and motars and raping young women on their streets. Still when they return and are settled in their offices where they quickly affix signatures to swindle millions out of their country they tend to forget and ignore the problems of their countries.

High rise buildings and good roads in England, United States big cities can be seen in Nigerian villages if not greed by the juntas, who are naïve, stupid and dumb fools who cannot write their names except through Lebanese crooks who help them to manipulate the papers. These crooks Lebanese men care more about the junta regime and their egos and political careers than building a city for the people who actually live here in Nigeria because of the kickbacks they receive from the not-so-bright men in power who rule our country. You see my friends! I find it unbelievable that the Nigerian Union of Traders, Teachers, market men and women and the Ph.Ds of this country have dealt nothing but underhanded cry calling for divine intervention to our political spectrum in this country. Few men and women, including magistrates called for a meeting to meet with General Bad Dudu, but have since been imprisoned and tortured to shut up my people. We all know the reason for the killings and torture. It is because the Oval Office is mute."

He swallowed his last mound of *eba* and drank a glass of pond water. He was ready to greet the day out of the Booka, if dysentery does not take his life before the junta does. He got up and said good-bye to all in the Booka.

Major Dogoyaro was flinging his keys and moved to the door. "Well, it's been a very enjoyable and interesting evening at your restaurant listening to bullshit. I am proud of you Princess Akinzua."

"Truly," Adam Khan agreed.

The preening women listening to Ukikankon-Dituan all did their chorus as women and headed out of the Booka to their poverty ridden homes.

"I'll see you again sometime. I've to go now. The food was excellent," Major Dogoyaro complimented.

Adam Khan shook his hand again and walked out of the Booka, then continued on his mission: strolling.

Chapter
3

....

My introduction in absentia to Efemona by my father, Mr. Ojie, was imprinted on her heart. After a careful thought of her country and the economic chaos and her sugar daddies dying by the numbers by bullets, by accidents and by natural causes, Efemona thought about herself, that one day she wrote a letter to me (Ekiaqueta) in the U.S. to consider her for marriage. Efemona had written:

"My Dear Ekiaqueta,

I know it is strange to hear from me. The last time I saw you was when you came to my village with your father to see my parents. You might have forgotten, but I haven't. You played soccer with naked children and you played so wonderfully as I clapped for you dribbling everyone in the field. My father calls me Efemona. My mother too, calls me *Udonomonrele*. I know after twenty years in America you might have forgotten what it means. Just in case you might've forgotten, it means a woman having balls bigger than those of a real man. I know you'll smile to that. Anyway, I've good- looking bottoms and average boobs you'll admire when I join you. And I hope that after you read this letter you'll have forgotten all other women you are flirting with in America. From this moment on, tell them you are now married. I have brown eyes. I know you will like me. The several credits I have received over the years from my former sugar daddies make me feel good about myself. I am now a nurse by profession and my father is now the Principal of Edo College in Benin City. I am the fourth child of my parents. I have two brothers and two sisters. I also have half brothers and sisters. I have just graduated from the academy of professional nursing in my state. I cannot say I was among the very brightest in my class, but I was among those who passed. The nursing school I attended allocates its graduates to different hospitals and maternities across the Nation. I've just been allocated to Ewu-Ishan Maternity Home. I've since worked there for the past eight months. I am glad to meet with your father once again still holding on with the poverty he has entertained all these years. He visited my parents to propose me for you in absentia. I hope you come home soon to get me. He told me to communicate with you immediately and to break the news to you. By the way, how is the U.S. of A? I know you guys are enjoying over there. We are stuck here in the country. Bad Dudu makes new laws every day in this country. Every day that passes by that we still have a life, we thank our Savior. You will not believe that I am allocated to the worst village you can imagine. They have no water, no electricity and no transportation. Transportation these days is for the affluent. Those we regard as affluent are the local government officials riding bicycles and at the most, Honda motorcycles to work. My last sugar daddy rides a twenty-year old Honda 175 motor cycle. After work he uses it to make money taking people to their farms. People pay a fare of twenty Naira per drop. That's how he survives to take care of me and his family of twelve children. Everyone here is really feeling the heat of recession. I wonder where this country is heading five years from now. Right now, most graduates in this country have become *armed robbers and '419' crooks-that dubious activities of the smart graduates without jobs to con the whiteman of millions of dollars and pounds through fraudulent acts . . .*

Though I am happy to have a job, it is better not to have a job at all, because for the past six months, I've not been paid. For the teachers of this country, they have not been paid for more than nine months. To worsen everything in this country, the ruling oligarchy had devalued our Naira, which was stronger than the dollar. This country was better in the '70's when everyone had enough and Udoji award was awarded to every worker. Today, there are more armed men on the streets. By night people stumble in the streets using torches to avoid deep potholes on our roads. My grandmother drowned in *one* as she walked home from the village market without her usual lamp she carried along with her every night when coming home. Two weeks ago, I traveled to Aba to visit my sister and her husband. The coastline there has been badly ruined. However, people sit on the beaches ignoring the heap of garbage the government itself had created. Day in and day out, the women of this country are harassed and mocked at with bad vibes from the soldiers with weapons on our streets and it's getting worse. To tell you how I love you in absentia, I enclosed my picture for your eyes only. And remember, my father would gladly welcome you into our home as his new son-in-law from America. Just bear in mind that the dowry would not be much for your buxom Efemona to be.

My mother, as you may or may not be aware, is from a Royal family-a Countess.

Yesterday, armed intelligence agents stormed the offices of a prominent Nigerian newspaper, assaulting several employees and looking to arrest the editor-in-chief. And what was his crime? Virtually writing about the sufferings of the men and women of this country. Nine officers had armed themselves with submachine guns and pistols looking for what they call "subversive and incriminating documents" during which a five hour raid at the Abuja offices of THIS DAY which they searched. And what was the crime of the editor-in-chief? Obuigbena had received several threatening phone calls in recent times which had warned him to stop publishing stories implicating Aliyu Mohammed Gusau, in massive graft under Bad Dudu's junta regime, of stealing billions of dollars from our treasury, bankrupting our oil reserve money and causing the economic infrastructure to collapse. The fact is that THIS DAY had published stories alleging that Aliyu Mohammed Gusau knew about and may have been involved in several corrupt deals, including a multibillion dollar scandal involving a Russian-built steel plant. This is just a common practice of our ruling junta's authoritarian regime to shut up our journalists writing the truth about our zombies in the high offices of our country. I hope these things are not happening in America? Sweetie Pie! I hope to hear from you soon. Cheers. Efemona."

* * *

Nothing could be more appealing to me when I received Efemona's missives on a Good Friday, the day which too by coincident had marked the traditional time when the sky darkened and the earth shook and Christ was said to have died on the cross for our sins. I was still a small boy when I went with my father to visit Efemona's parents and his relatives at Ukpenu where Efemona was then. Here, Efemona's father was the Rev. father of the church on the glorious day for the ten o'clock mass for the observance of Good Friday. It was the day the sky suddenly turned dark with thunder and clouds in heaven and everyone thought Christ was actually coming back to earth from Heaven. I could not sit still in the church so I ran out of the church to play soccer with my age groups and wondered what the hell was going on, when my father came and grabbed my hand and led me back into the church. On this day in history, Iramen House of God was filled with well-dressed men and women with traditional wear except with very few people who dressed up in Western style, and Efemona's big brother held the wine for his father and his father looking resplendent in his Holy Week Crimson robes, stuck to business reminding all his believers about the death of Jesus Christ.

Anyway, I traveled to my homeland after the famous darkness when the earth shook to get Efemona to the United States. On a fine evening, when I got to Nigeria I found myself among real enthusiasts willing to see me and Efemona get united. What surprised me the most was the natives and my age groups had set up a ring where a wrestling match was to take place between two antagonists. Wooden chairs, the folding type, had been lined up in a square around the ring at my father's compound. A well to do from America had come to get Efemona to the States was the talk of the town. I will never forget that day.

Few minutes later when I landed, with my entourage from America, the drumbeat began. *Pounded yam, fufu and egusi soup was served.*

I sat with my father and relatives of Efemona in the cool of the evening and talked. As I watched the events progress, my father Mr. Ojie, talked and explained to me because he'd the most to talk about in whispers to my ears. "Efemona would be a good wife for you, my son."

I was amazed to see so much of a crowd, like a swarm of bees, all hungry to see me while the wrestling match was in progress between Iyansu and Asuku, the two well known antagonists over a period of two decades. In fact, most of the length of the onlookers had been filled with plenty of elderly men and women. To be real to the point, not one of these crowds could take out their handkerchief from their pockets to clean their face without causing serious bodily harm to his neighbor.

Few minutes later, Iyansu and Asuku came into the ring with faces designed like zebras. They'd no time to waste. Little by little, they started to grab each other with power and struggle but with defiance in technique, to win early in the rounds.

I must tell you that I was thrilled in a beautiful way to see what I hadn't seen in twenty years. But the wrestling match only lasted about ten minutes when Iyansu landed Asuku on his back until the gong was rung by an 86 years elderly referee in the ring, who then pronounced Iyansu the winner. Everyone with Naira and Kobo threw it into the ring for the winner while Asuku hurtled shamefully out of the ring. Before Asuku hurtled out of the ring, he'd tears in his eyes for the shame of being defeated, but regarding tradition which by the elders, Asuku must sacrifice seven cows and seven goats. Where the money would come from to satisfy the elders was his pain. He'd no job and to crown it all, he'd lost his manhood in his village until he could meet his elders demand of the seven cows and seven goats fine. The match, according to my father, was to remind me that culture must not be forgotten, and therefore it elicited memories of when Life Goes On was in power everyone had enough and marriage was deserved by *anyone* above the age of twenty, at least.

Though Asuku was pardoned by the elders of his village to sacrifice the seven cows and seven goats, the elders cursed Bad Dudu depriving them of the rituals which is to say, they would have had enough to eat if Asuku could afford to buy the seven cows and seven goats to receive their blessings to redeem his manhood.

Having witnessed the wrestle of the evening, between Iyansu and Asuku, the crowd poured into the shining moon and the stars. I shook my head knowing that history had replicated itself, because based in history, Irrua people are tough to wrestle to the ground, though Bad Dudu had successfully repressed them with his authoritarian regime, thereby damaging their culture. So I whispered to Efemona and explained, "tradition and animosity is merciless. Vengeance is sweet.

One day, the people of this country will know who the people destroying our economy are. Bad Dudu and his in cahoots characters will regret."

Efemona pondered in her heart as we both watched elders and spectators disappear slowly without any energy left for them to walk home, regretfully sorry for the young man that had been defeated because he was so skinny and had not eaten before the wrestle.

*　*　*

Sunday morning had just dawned bright and clear. Efemona was thrilled to be with me in the privacy of her room. For the first time, I'd the urge to look at her perfectly. I looked at her insistence, as we sat alone. For sure, I could analyze Efemona's mind to read: "Thank God I found me a man."

After all, a husband as far as Efemona was concerned would bring respectability to her and her parents and to her brothers and sisters. She would now marry a man who'd been away from Nigeria for several years who was famous and pretty rich.

To Efemona, I was good looking or handsome, and soft spoken, which surprised her the most. As we relaxed, I said to her, "How is life in this village anyway?"

She looked at me and smiled. Then she said, "I've waited all along for a savior like you. Every day in this village, I'm faced with ugly situations. Life in general is exciting, but I'm tired of the low life now."

She kissed me as a sign she was sociable. Then she said, "I understand that there are no mosquitoes and tse-tse flies in America? Is that true?"

I nodded. "You will see for yourself in America."

She took my hand in hers and walked me around the yard, which was like a hostel. I walked majestically with her. Within a few seconds, a mosquito buzzed around my face and then entered into my nose. I stifled the impulse to sneeze as my eyes became red, but soon faded out.

"My God, I could've sneezed to death," I said as Efemona looked at my face.

"You can see what I go through every day in this place," she said and cracked up. "You see, in this village, everything is so far away if you don't have mobility. Here, you can't hail down a taxi as you can in Benin, Lagos, Enugu, Aba, Kaduna or Kano. Beside, there are not even taxis, anymore."

I listened with interest. Efemona opened her cupboard and brought out a bottle of London Gin. She served me and served herself. Efemona waited for the drink to get the grip on me before she said, "In this village, life is hard and it's becoming unbearable. Mosquitoes and flies rampage rooms. People are forced to buy mosquito coils and nets and in fact, they don't seem to work much. It was recently that I discovered they are made at Aba, by the Ibos of Eastern Nigeria. They're the people who produce imitations of any imported items that come into this country from abroad. We hardly have electricity twice a week and also there are no modern amenities as in Nigeria as in America. I mean homes with water systems and bath tubs are hardly seen. In this village we bathe in the open. Our pit latrines are abomination. My patients suffer a lot at night. I try to do all I can to help, but I am now exhausted," she sobbed.

I sat with her a moment with anger, ignoring her sobbing. Finally I gave her tissues to clean up her face. When she was done I patted her on her back. And I said, "Listen to me Efemona! The Ibos of this country are the people we should all be proud of."

She interrupted me. "Why?" She asked.

"Well," I said, firstly "In the entire African countries I see no race in Africa that could stand and measure up with the Ibos in scientific thinking. Secondly, in our country, the zombies who rule us believe in that famous saying, *You chop, I chop!*" But the Ibos don't believe in that. They believe in commerce and technology. They try. Thirdly, as a Nation, a populous Nation as ours, by now we should be able to measure up with North and South Korea, Singapore, Taiwan, Hong Kong and India. Yugoslavia had just launched a car on the world market known as the Yugo and it now runs in all countries of the world. Our country should count on the Ibos. We should praise them for trying at all." Efemona became swoon.

"Don't you think the Federal Government of Nigeria should allocate to the Ibos during fiscal year budgetary a substantial amount of grant to carry on their research on high tech studies on how to manufacture bicycles, toothpicks, perfect the mosquito coils and nets, silver spoons, and needles? And don't you think they have the brains?"

Efemona became dumbfounded. Her eyes widened and were blinking more than usual. "The Northerners are stealing our money by night and day. Isn't it about time they realized that the Ibos can perhaps manufacture for Nigeria something better than the Yugo and Honda motorcycles to transport farmers and market women to their destinations?"

I looked at Efemona and watched her peel a banana and put it in her mouth, reminding me of American women, the way they suck on dicks on XX channels. When she finished eating it, she said, "You know! I think you're right."

I knew as much that I was right.

Efemona insisted, "I've never actually sat down to think it over. From now on, I'll surely count on the Ibo man."

As soon as she finished, two gentlemen I recognized as Hidiamen and Ehimire knocked. It was as if they had entered on cue. Efemona ushered them in. Both gestured towards me where I sat, then extended their hands. I took it and insisted they sit. They hesitated. Finally, Ehimire sat.

From Hidiamen's actions and expression on his face, I could tell he had words to unload. Furious with Efemona, he said, "There is never a time I visit you and you don't talk negative vibes about the Ibos. What again has the Iboman done to you?"

I watched Hidiamen release his vexation. Within a few minutes of their presence, Hidiamen had said a thousand words and never intended to stop. Ehimire said, "Hidiamen can you please sit down?"

Finally he sat. I introduced myself. "Nice to meet both of you." "Nice to meet you too."

We all became silent for another few minutes. I raised my head and saw Efemona looking at me with admiration. Then I looked at Hidiamen, a bright, pleasant and articulate young man, and bold. From all indication he's one that is never too afraid to air his grievances—against dictators and oppressors. Not too many a man looked like him because he's handsome and lightish brown in color, medium height with no fat in him, fashionable in his own way. Very oratorical, thoughtful, alert, and seems to be untouched by his day's excitement. From my point of view, you can equate Hidiamen as someone from the city. Hidiamen, who is not quite forty, could be a teacher, however he was a true politician, trained as a barrister from London, England. Still disappointed with Efemona's reference to the Iboman as a people who flood Nigerian markets with imitation gadgets he said, "I challenge you Efemona. Flip a coin. Head or tail you lose. I'll tell you that my Americana here with you will agree with me that the Iboman are the smartest human beings in Nigeria, if not Africa. I heard your remark about the Ibos making imitations of all gadgets that you believe now flooded the markets in this country."

Efemona held and squeezed my arm hoping that Hidiamen would just stop. He continued anyway. "The amazing thing is that when you have poor farmers giving the black power salute of a poor man beyond poor in this country, it is a sign they hope will deliver them someday from the corrupt oligarchy rule of the zombies in uniform. Nigerians ruling junta's regime has given a new meaning to the working poor, new hope since the first coup happened in this country to hope for hopelessness until death do them part. This was the time the Iboman woke up to think, then develop their brains in making shoes and manufacturing other little gadgets they think the nation needs the most: like candles, toothpicks for the zombies when they're finished eating stockfish, which *only* the very rich oligarchies can now afford. They tried everything to survive. The same way I believe, the super powers started."

"That's right," Ehimire agreed.

"Interesting," I said. Efemona nodded in agreement. We slipped back into a companionable silence, then I turned my attention back to Hidiamen. "Please to lecture Efemona for me to know what's going on in this country," I said.

I smiled again, then kept my mouth shut. Efemona looked at me as if to say: "You're from America, the God's own country where the tallest Tower of Babel are now built and African Continent was then cursed to wrought in hopeless confusion to speak different languages and to be wicked to each other. Why don't you challenge the young barrister from England?

Hidiamen added, "You see my friends, I have learned over the years to know that no man is so dumb enough, blind enough, not to know right from wrong. Nor does he miss his mouth when he was hungry and swallowing *fufu with equesi soup* with pain and hardship."

We all laughed again. Hidiamen did not stop there. He continued, "The ruling class in camouflage uniforms pretends that the nation has no problems, but indeed the problems can never be solved until we all realize that we are all one Nigeria."

Ehimire, who'd been sitting idle was tempted to interrupt Efemona. "You don't sound all that Southern anymore. I used to count on you Efemona, but now I've trouble understanding where you're aligned. Isn't it about time you count on the Pope before the Jew? Or on the Ibos before any other ethnic group?"

"That's not the point." Hidiamen said. "My point is why did Efemona not recognize the Iboman whom we all should rely on in Nigeria or in Africa? The Ibos are a race who could manufacture anything the country needs. They can dismantle an armored car vehicle and then reassemble it in order to make it even perform better in shooting average than what the super powers had intended it to perform."

Again, Ehimire was tempted to interrupt, but he was reluctant to spoil the mood of exhilaration that seemed to have gripped Hidiamen. And Efemona at the moment looked dumb and gave a non-committal grunt. Finally, Efemona said, "I know I'm a woman, naïve. I wasn't thinking right the first time, but now that I'm enlightened, I'll carry with me the praise for Ibos anywhere I go."

I nodded but said nothing. But Ehimire said, "What do you mean by naïve? You weren't born and raised in this country yesterday! Isn't that true?"

Efemona leaned down and put her innocent face next to my stubby cheek and said, "I'm sorry."

Hidiamen said, "You got to be. Tell you what you can do to make a deal with everyone here. I recommend that you buy made in Nigerian goods stamped Ibos, but England."

"That's right," Ehimire said, almost jumping to his feet.

"And advertise at Ukpenu, Irrua, Bornu and Ewu that Ibos made toothpicks are better than imported toothpicks from England."

"True enough," Ehimire said.

"Colonial Master's Navy blue made in England for police and their rifles are not better than those made in Nnewi by Ojukwu's scientists." Absolutely I yielded.

"Zombie oligarchy siphoning the Nations money to overseas will say bullshit," Ehimire voiced out and then slapped the bed frame pole with his palms. Again, there became silence in the room except the music coming out from the boom box. It was Gregory Isaac playing, "Night Nurse."

Finally Hidiamen broke the silence after the music, "I need a drink."

"Oh! I am so sorry I didn't ask you both what you would like!" "That's okay. We didn't give you the option. We were on your ass the moment we walked in," Hidiamen said.

Anyway, she got up and brought out her ice chest from under her bed and opened it. Then she brought out four bottles of Star beer and served everyone. Finally, she said to Hidiamen, "You should've been a politician rather than a lawyer. I bet you know pretty much the history of this Nation."

"Not exactly. But I know a little. Would you want to hear more? I'm mad as hell with Bad Dudu's government and his son and his in cahoots."

"Why?" Efemona asked.

Hidiamen said, "This country has money. It is being managed by dunces and zombies. Listen to this! I'd the opportunity to attend a grand party with Bad Dudu last year with dignitaries as Bimbo Robert, Stagger Lee, Alex Kondi, Babagida, Dim Pascal the economist and stock broker, Elton John, Madonna and John Major to mention but a few, at the Abuja new capital building. Man! The place is almost heaven. Southern oil money at work. I even recognized Umaro Diko, Dan Juma and Dan Tata. I was surprised to find them partying hard, too, considering their positions in the Nations highest offices. But like their pals, Abubaker, Idris, Babagida, Buhari, Shagari to name but a few,

Babagida and Bad Dudu are one of the greatest flies that buzz around *yanshes and toto.* I mean pussies. I mean Oriental women, Lebanese women and Thai women who came to Nigeria to make money selling their carnals to the oligarchies whom Americans have refused entry into their country, denying their visas to go screw real white women abroad."

"Oh yeah!" Ehimire echoed softly while Efemona was lost for the meaning of pussy.

"They say all can drink tea too and smoke Cuban cigars and eat gworo cola nuts," Efemona said, though, to be in the conversation.

"I saw for myself how they lavish our money and spray them foreign women they dance with, with dollar currencies pasted on their foreheads while their maids collect the money with a tray on their hands. I'm mad as hell."

Here I will say that I actually witnessed all these happenings when I was growing up. I witnessed it first hand when they dance Owanbe music with those foreign women whose figures of women from Thailand, Lebanon and England asses were bigger than three Onitsha women asses combined. The ones I think are rejected by their men where they hail from because they were damn too fat and ugly.

Hidiamen stopped and sipped on his booze. Efemona's eyes rolled a bit in my direction. I said, "I really can't believe that a country with all kinds of natural resources will request to borrow money from the World Bank (IMF).

Efemona tilted her head and rested it on my shoulder while rubbing her right hand on my belly, more captivated. She looked at Hidiamen and he looked at her back. Finally Hidiamen cleared his throat and said, "Efemona, if you want to know more about our country I'll be glad to let it out from the depth of my being. I know Ekiaqueta here, the Americana will agree with all I've to say."

"I'll be glad to listen, Hidiamen," Efemona said and looked at my face. In some husbandly way soon to be, I was happy that Efemona was listening and her orderly in the maternity has not come to fetch her with a bad news of so and so is having a baby in the ward and she's bleeding, or the baby is out, but the mother is dead-and so on and so forth.

Hidiamen thought that was nice of Efemona to appreciate hearing more about the history of her birth rite which she didn't know and had not been told by an enlightened teacher. Efemona asked, "You mean that our country's money is being lavished on unnecessary things this country doesn't really need?"

"You're thinking fast ahead of me, Efemona," Hidiamen said. Then he added, "But you're certainly not aware that in the seventies our country was the USA of Africa . . ."

Efemona jumped up in shock.

The mere mention of USA set Efemona's adrenaline pumping.

Then she repeated, "The USA of Africa? You must be kidding me. How did that come about?"

"Yes! Our country was the USA of Africa. Everyone enjoyed our oil wealth so vast Nigerians seemed able to buy all the security it could ever want after the civil war, when the Northerners in the name of Nigerian soldiers to unify Nigeria as one, nearly exterminated an entire race, the Biafran (Ibos). After the war, the Ibos toiled hard enough to restructure their infrastructure, developed and manufactured lots of gadgets for the nation. Most of the gadgets were rejected by our people who liked made in England than Ibo made. The Federal Government did not encourage and give an incentive to them to do more with all the money our nation had and still had. So what happened? They ended up in the Atlantic Ocean. The heart of the matter I mean, was that, the Federal Government didn't motivate them. True enough was that they had no money to carry on. But today, the Ibos are still existing and trying harder. I mean they are still surviving. Nigeria crude oil sale or no oil sale."

I shrugged in reaction of crude oil sale or no crude oil. Efemona noticed my reaction but said nothing. Finally, I interrupted Hidiamen and said, "They got the pipe line past my father's backyard to Kaduna and Kano with England's technology and Barclay's Bank financing."

"Hell yeah. They got it past the Doddan Barrack without consulting with the people they rule and not even with the Ogoni people where the oil is being tapped," Ehimire said.

Of course, that's power and money and corruption. And if there's one thing we know, the Northerners oligarchy have money. I mean they are filthy rich."

I shrugged again. "Politics is intelligence, you know, to fool all the people because the people can't do shit in this country. We're all a Nation. They can extend the pipeline to England through the seas if they choose to. The Englishman is there to receive the proceeds and back them up."

Hidiamen concurred. "We're being ruled by a notoriously power hungry uniform men club, gargantuan, corrupt ruling relay race men of not so bright with no education and ideology. My friends, don't get me wrong. I'm prepared to die for my country if it's the conclusive truth that would heal my Nation. You see, a decade of uncontrolled spending, Bad Dudu and his men claimed before they took power has since wreaked havoc with our Nation's finances. If an economist from Aba, Onitsha, Ondo, Oyo, Benin or … had warned of the chaos and the devaluation of our currency which was stronger than the dollar to befall our country in this century, who would've listened?"

He paused. Efemona and Ehimire looked close to tears. Ehimire said, "That's right Hidiamen. I think there's a need here to explain to Efemona that a dog in the South needs a mat or something to sleep on. Tell her more. Go on! Go on, please!"

I watched Ehimire. His gregarious, direct, seemingly unflappable in-group associate, but privately very human, said before Hidiamen finished sipping on his drink. "Today my country has devalued our currency that was the dollar of Africa, stronger than the dollar itself, and the yen, too. It was the only money in the world that measured up to the British pounds and sterling, and what happened?" Ehimire asked, but answered his own question. "The motherfucking zombies know that Nigeria's once colossal cash reserve has shrunk by at least one-third, based upon the figures of 1978 to 1979. Moreover, domestic debt has inflated to trillions as per capita income for this country over one hundred and twenty million inhabitants. Per Capita income was from fifteen hundred dollars in 1979 to fewer than fifty dollars now in Bad Dudu's authoritarian regime. Unemployment among those who have recently left school hover around ninety-five percent, that they deemed armed robbery is the key to their fate if they should survive." "Ah, no wonder they killed my mother and savaged my brother, Sunny with bullets to his chest," I said to remind everyone that Iwamon was my mother who died like a chicken because the hospitals in our country *are not well* equipped though the doctors are as well qualified as American doctors or the Japs doctors. "Yes! They don't joke. If you are there at the wrong time you pay your price. The price is indelible because they want to prove a point to the junta regime of blocking the roads and collecting one Naira from poor motorists on our roads."

"Why don't they look for Bad Dudu and his brothers steeling our money, rather than my mother, a poor woman?"

Hidiamen looked pained and looked at my face. Then he said, "Where was I before Ehimire interrupted?"

Ehimire refreshed his memory and he immediately remembered and gave him the clue. Hidiamen began, "My contention is this: Tens of billions of Naira were squandered on contracts-I mean ghost contracts that were neglected by the Dudu's regime, institutionalized bribery and lavish life of their relatives and wives from Lebanon and their buddies they award contracts who stashed all the wealth in Britain for them and themselves. For instance, the popularly known Adam Khan, the ugly homosexual was fucking Bad Dudu good. He fucked him because he knew he was a zombie. Anytime Bad Dudu netted a deal worth over $5 million dollars, he handed it over to Adam who goes to England and Switzerland to deposit the money for him. On his way he would split the money into half. Matter-of-factly, all Nigerians now regard these oligarchy families as thieves and artful dodgers.

Who would challenge them is the question. We have no weapons. They have the weapons in the North."

He looked at Efemona and said, "Efemona do you know how this country has come to accept what she is today?"

"No! How?" She asked with interest.

"Okay. I'll tell you. Ekiaqueta, your husband soon to be as you said, should know this as well. That, this country and its diverse ethnic inhabitants were brought under control by the British Colonial masters.

British and American drillers and French drillers began to extract oil in the early 1960's. As the country grew in population, so was their affluence. It then remained a sort of relay race oligarchy of the mostly Northerners. Since that time immoral, members of the ruling class family has since dominated our government with their General ranks- and Majors and Brigadiers in the army then ruining our economy. Following the oil boom in 1979, oil prices quadrupled. New roads, airports, seaport, industrial centers and Universities were built at an astonishing rate. Then the new Generals who shot and killed our civilians ruling us at the time turned around and jailed most of the governors and premiers for a reason."

"What was the reason, Hidiamen?" Efemona asked with a smile, willing to learn.

One thing I like about Hidiamen is that when you ask him a question, he doesn't fumble. He answers straight away. He said looking at Efemona, "The reason was that they had used the money for developing the country, which was building new schools, new hospitals, and new roads. Some Governors were humiliated, beaten arrested for building Universities in their states. Did you know that most of these Governors like Ali, even Obasanjo . . . who were mostly from the west and Benin or from the south to put it in a lame man's tongue, some died in our jails because of division in the system during that era and some of them caught tuberculosis?"

I almost jumped to my feet to clap for Hidiamen because in my Reno office in the United States, I heard through VOA the story of The Movement for the Survival of the Ogoni People (MOSOP) confirming that 20 Ogoni men who had been held without trial since Bad Dudu seized power were released from Port Harcourt Prison, Rivers State but had all contracted tuberculosis, paralysis, blindness, and heart diseases. Coupled with the problems of breathing, hearing and loss of vision. My joy of course was not the mere mention of good men jailed contacting tuberculosis, but for Efemona to know that the Southerners are being repressed in their own country. And also that as recently as August tenth, 1998 a 73 year-old man-Mr. Michael Nkpagayee- died from injuries sustained when he was severely beaten during raids by the Rivers State

Internal Security Task Force on the Sogho community. His decomposed body was later released after money was extorted from his family-all activities that were carried out by Bad Dudu and his people. For the benefit of Efemona I explained interrupting Hidiamen—"Ogoni is a land of half a million people in the Niger Delta region of Nigeria. Since 1958, oil companies such as Shell have exploited Ogoni's oil wealth, degrading their environment, while the Ogoni people have suffered economic depravation, the environmental devastation of their land and the discrimination policies of successive junta regimes for which The Movement for the Survival of the Ogoni People demands economic justice, human rights-including the right to choose the use of their land and its resources is what Ken Saro-Wiwa was killed for by Bad Dudu."

I could see Efemona's reaction and could tell that she became loaded with malice against Bad Dudu and his junta regime of the repression and torture and of death to those who challenge his regime. Efemona asked, "Do you think the zombies are naïve, don't love their own country or they are being manipulated by the British people?"

"Very good question, Efemona," I praised my wife to be. "It was mostly that some had believed that they would rather stash millions in foreign banks than to use our oil money to feed the poor hungry men and women of this country. Because they rule this country as juntas, their reasoning was therefore to have carte blanche to purchase the most advanced weapons in case of an uprising from the people they rule, many of the weapons which the country mediocre army are unable to use and still lying waste at Kaduna. Indeed we did not really need them. What the country needed then were industries and food stuff for its own people."

Hidiamen's voice floated across the room, mellow and funeral while Efemona tilted her head towards me and whispered, "So our leader(s) are actually ignorant?"

"You judge for yourself, Efemona." Ehimire said. As I looked at her, there was a time genius-a flicker of a smile crossed over her face. Then she said, "There will be a time when I'll get involved in the affairs of my country like all of you. I will not be scared of anybody to air my feelings. I will probably be the nurse to bring the South and the North to Christianity, so that we could've a true democracy."

I said nothing; neither did Hidiamen and Ehimire. But Hidiamen got infuriated and bit his bottom lip. "You be quiet, Efemona. You are just a woman. Do you know how many men have died for the truth in this country? To think in terms of a woman bringing the South and Northern states to Christianity? I advise you to think of something better to do and become when you join your husband in America. If you plan to be a good nurse to bring the South and North together, study what to solve the problem of their river blindness in the Bornu areas. Better yet, study to be a journalist to expose the millions and billions of oil money they stacked in foreign banks, and doing so be prepared to receive a hole in the head or a letter bomb through the mail. Therefore, what happened to Dele Giwa, a fearless journalist this country had produced would befall upon you. Hope you know that Nigeria doesn't have freedom of speech and freedom of assembly, though we claim we have a democracy. Good luck, Efemona."

There was now a deep silence in the room. And the sun had sunk below the blinds of Efemona's window. Somehow we had to pay close attention to sun dawning in this village or we miss the subtleties of what is before us on the table for discussion. In a flash though, I remembered Hidiamen's remarks about the stockpile of arms in Kaduna lying waste. Then I said to break the silence between everyone, "I can't believe a nation like ours would build up arms and not use them to fight against apartheid in South Africa when the tension there was high. You know, our country didn't actually need the stockpile of arms anyway. Besides, this country was not at all at war with any neighboring countries. Only Libya and Cameroon tried us, we did not respond. They could've walked over us in the battles. By the way how strong is our army in Nigeria anyway?"

Ehimire was on his feet and suddenly caught in. "First," he said, "The thing about our military junta government of Bad Dudu is that they use the weapon powers to shut us up. It was of recent I found out for myself that the army junta is the ultimate in the Third World countries for repressing and terrorizing its own people instead of protecting and guarding them. It is the weapon that our military rulers both in this country and in Africa in general uses to extricate itself for blaming the civilian regimes for corruption and mismanagement of their country's economy. Behind that premise too, are so many problems, contradiction and military obstacles that we the people should feel extremely sad about, that the war we've had in Nigeria had been fought with ourselves. I had to quit the army because I'm strongly committed against the evil it perpetuated among my Southern people. We have the Hausas, who believe the army is the only tool to hold Nigeria one. Second, we have the Benins and the Yorubas who are yes sir people behind the Hausas. Third, we have the Ibos, a committed spiritual people destined with God given talents to manufacture everything our country currently purchases from England and other developed nations of the world, but are not recognized in their struggle. Fourth, we have a lot of other ethnic groups who are not even recognized in the Nigerian Army. They are just there to stand in the rain or shine to help support any coup. My brothers! A soldier is a soldier, when it boils down to toppling his government, especially in our country. What they do is secretly organize themselves to carry out the coup. And you know, to my understanding, very little of the weapons the juntas purchased from Britain, Russia, Japan and India were used against demonstrating University students along with their families who were fed up with the tyranny of Bad Dudu's regime. The students, to me, had a mission. All they wanted to do was thwart Bad Dudu's regime. For that reason he slaughtered and killed a lot of students and their families. The day all this happened in Lagos, the commercial headquarters, I was gravely ill on admission in a private hospital in the midst of a deathwatch, when everyone heard the firing of motars and canons. In an hour the carnage was all over. Everyone dispersed to their respective homes which was what Bad Dudu meant to show that he was the real Caesar or Pompey to intimidate everyone. The students and their parents, women with their children and elders who were rambled by Bad Dudu's bullets and left to die on the streets of more than 18 states, all moaned softly as they lay in red pools of their own blood. You know something folks, I probably might be dead today if I were not in the hospital sick. But my heart goes out to those students and everyone who died for a true democracy of this country."

Hidiamen was tempted to interrupt, but Ehimire anticipated him. He added, "Some of the rifles and pistols also ended up on our streets in the hands of armed robbers who used them to slaughter civilians and rob them of their precious life savings."

Hidiamen, anyway, ballooned his cheeks as he looked on and listened. Looking at Ehimire and Efemona who was still swoon, I caught in. "It was the guns that they used on my mother and my brother."

"No doubt about that." Hidiamen said and yelled at Ehimire, "Ehimire? Ehimire, let's be realistic here, even the Americans use their prisoners to test their experiments."

"Not with weapons on demonstrating citizens. If they do it is about new drugs for the cure of diseases like AIDS," Hidiamen said as Ehimire whined on the bed. With his lips bouncing up and down he said, "Well, it is not so here. This country would be backward fifty years to come. The junta regime of Bad Dudu still makes bizarre decisions without regard to the people they rule. Don't you remember the history of the oil pipeline from the South to the North? The cost of laying the pipes was more than fifty times the aim of the project? Do any of you know why? The reason for that was: Buoyed by the rising oil price in the world market, Bad Dudu asked his junta supporters to reverse the benchmark for the fiscal appropriation bill to $20 per barrel from the former N18. What he did then was to offer subsidies to farmers-not just farmers, but in reality to their relatives. This was a small technical share of the oil bounty to the farmers. The era which marked the famous saying *"You chop I chop God no go vex, or you give us some of the wealth and then, She'd do whatever you want to do."* It was the time Bad Dudu tricked the nation to lay the pipeline to the North. Today the students in this country cannot even write their names because when the farmers were given a small technical share of the pie, they lured their children to the farms neglecting education. What the teachers did then was go to the North and purchased cows and goats and pigs and marched them to their classrooms to teach them animals instead of human beings."

Actually, I remembered that myself when herons, hens, pigs and cows then in the replacement of humans in the classrooms cannot think logically, add one and two together, but became dumber and dumber. I think it was somehow funny, that the pigs and cows and hens and herons don't actually sit on their seats in class, but rather sat on top of their desk and chairs with them spooky funny look of hunger on their faces because they too are hungry enough not to listen. There at Ukpenu, Ogoni or Bornu all the oil beds flows into a curving red serpent that turns out to be crookedest villages and towns in the nation with no pipe borne water, hospitals or beautiful schools. And the roads on which these animals trekked who are now in the likeness of humans to their classrooms wraps around degrading, swampy and flood covered potholes. But still, with these negatives which Bad Dudu and his in cahoots are aware, they don't give a damn. Still, the dollar, pounds and the German mark comprised in a pictorial long stride, moves on to foreign banks. And of course, these huge stacks of our oil money now buried in the world all over, from where they are, shine on our decaying infrastructure and on the hungry men and women of our country. I leave it at that my friends.

"Oh! That might be the reason the teachers in the country are not paid monthly but every nine months," I said.

"You bet," Efemona and Hidiamen concurred.

"Here we are lamenting about the country woes. Bad Dudu, Babagida and all their junta members who rule this country are in Britain now having the best time of their lives, while their wives and mistresses are vacationing in the Cayman Islands or having babies in America to become American citizens," Ehimire said and bowed his head, thinking several thoughts.

I thought about that for a second. Efemona let a meaningful second pass before she said, "You're right. Bad Dudu's wife recently vacationed in Britain with thirty-two boxes of luggage all loaded with $5 billion dollars and pound sterlings; while during the past few weeks, some men have been cannibalizing on their fellow human beings. Among the notable feeding on grilled hands, feet and wrists on his makeshift stove was Clifford Orji who was later arrested after it was found that he was killing and then eating, people underneath one of Lagos's busiest highways. I do not blame Mr. Orji eating and selling their private body parts to prominent men in the city, because the startling juxtaposition of a high-minded democratic process with the basest of human behavior might not be as incongruous as it appears at first. And over the decades since the British handed us our independence, our Nigerian military dictators had brutalized the populace, mostly Southerners, by a succession of dictatorial military rulers-by nepotism, fostering of corruption and ruthless repression of political dissent. I believe Mr. Clifford Orji was not only hungry, but also bent on vengeance.

Who knows if it was Bad Dudu's people's flesh he was feeding on? Maybe or maybe not. The morbid populace interest in the macabre events under the highway is a reflection of the abiding wretchedness of ordinary people's lives like your mother and your brother who were shot and robbed. It could have been the opposite. You know what I'm talking about?" Efemona explained and called on my name for me to look at her sincerely in her face.

Noting that most of our wealth has ended up in private bank accounts all over the globe, and the populace are hopeful that they have voted to get some of the outside wealth back when Abiola won the election and most of our problems soon stem from the fact that the National Treasury was robbed blind in broad day light and that independence in 1960 of course, Nigeria's regions received one hundred percent of the wealth they generated, and since the zombies took office, it whittled down to one-point-five- percent, I said to compliment everyone and particularly to Efemona remembering Clifford Orji as a prime good example of what the zombies in our country had driven some people to become. I said, "Never, never, never again shall our wealth be alienated from its people or our people from the land where the wealth is rooted."

Hidiamen and Ehimire did not hear me. Only Efemona did and she nodded. Finally Ehimire stood abruptly, cleared his throat and said, "Loans are guaranteed to all the citizens of Libya, Saudi Arabia and Kuwait. Electricity and water flow in abundance, but my country. What makes me sick the most is that my country is also a member of OPEC. We probably export more crude oil than the Arab countries combined."

Efemona shook her head in disgust. Then she said, "My God! How do you know all this?," Ehimire said.

"I'm not a dummy. I read everything in the papers and magazines. I also listen to Voice of America (VOA) and BBC first thing in the morning. These two world known broadcasting stations in the world said a few days ago that, "Only the very few zombies of the Bad Dudu's regime siphoning their nations wealth overseas enjoys the life of spectacular opulence. You think they are wrong? Hell no! They are right, my friends."

I said, "It's so in other parts of the world. Even in America," just to end this conversation.

Ehimire looked at me and shook his head. Then he said, "Ekiaqueta! I don't think so. Everyone in America enjoys the life of good living. If there was corruption in America it was probably of high class: like screwing in the oval office and polluting the atmosphere and lying about it. But an American will never carry thirty-two cases of luggage loaded with millions of dollars out of his country. They invest their money in America. That's why you see the Tower of Babel in Chicago, New York, Seattle, Washington D.C., Reno, Nevada, Las Vegas just to mention some big cities for the record. But in our country, corruption is open. We take the money in the open signifying who cares or gives a fuck. We all saw what happened when Ed Bradley of 60 Minutes landed at our International Airport-the customs boldly taking bribes from him and his entourage. Didn't we? That's just but how corrupt Bad Dudu's regime was. The budget in this country runs into the billions yearly. The wealth is distributed at the discretion of Bad Dudu though no one elected him as President. He now even calls himself the President. Based on information through the interpol of corruption organization repelling Third World countries from carrying out billions from their countries, Bad Dudu owns a half of Britain's Banks. His members of the ruling class receive generous salaries of doing little or no work. Every year, they too, award contracts to their families and relatives who also skim millions from ghost official projects."

He paused and drank the remains of his beer in the bottle. Efemona's mouth was wide open. When he finished, he added, "Compared to the

Americans, all corrupt elites are caught while they are in office. Every criminal on the street gets caught. For major crimes, convictions run ninety-five percent. Therefore, any criminal or corrupt Congressmen and women know from the outset that they are going to be caught. Here in my country, the conviction rate is below ten percent. And those ten percent are mostly from my state. Ekiaqueta! I cannot tell you how mad as hell I am now. A junta criminal in Ukpenu, Ogoni, Bornu knows he probably isn't going to get caught and if he did get caught, he ditched out currencies from the crime he had committed to bribe Bad Dudu's men who can arrest, convict or kill without debate about it. And in America, every study of police effectiveness shows that the American detective solves their cases. But in my country, they never get crime solved."

As he talked and talked, I asked him to sit down. His gaze flitted over everyone in the room. When he finally sat, Efemona said, "I'm surprised."

"Surprised my ass. Don't you know that even Mr. Abiola reportedly received millions in illegitimate commission for his large Telecommunication deal from his bosom friend until Muritala Mohammed himself was assassinated. In truth, that's why he's still in prison. Not because he swept the election with grand slide, but because Bad Dudu believes he's a Yoruba and by no means should have access to a million dollars in British Banks, or a billion pounds in Swiss Banks. By the way, didn't you read my articles in the Obiagele Newspaper in which I stated that in America men and women run for Congress if they are lawyers, doctors, professors and actors who can stand for hours on the podium to address their equal World leaders in a summit. In contrast, I also stated it is only in this country of ours and elsewhere in Africa who are Sandhurst trained to carry Uzi's and AK47 rifles in their Khaki camouflage and Agbada to intimidate market men and market women and their children on our roads and on the streets. You saw what happened. Didn't you? I was jailed for ten years. My hair shaved from my head? Didn't you?"

He was getting humiliated by booze. So I watched Ehimire sit, got up again and threw a fist to his chest and then added, "I'm mad as hell. As Hidiamen."

"You have every reason to be mad as hell. Everyone here, including me, in this country now feel the corruption and the pain of my people being jailed by Bad Dudu for revealing the truth about his regime," Hidiamen said.

"That's right. We don't need Allah and Christ to come down to tell us that you're right, Ehimire," Efemona concurred. Hidiamen added, "Yesterday one expatriate over the VOA sighted that at his Abuja Station, there was shortages of parts needed to fix broken bicycles, vehicles, caterpillars and motorcycles used for errands by civil servants in the ministries. He also lamented that his salary was never raised over the cause of his laborious sweat for the junta regime of Bad Dudu. The reason for that was that he was not a Lebanese. But guess what? The expatriate also said the ruling juntas had just about enough to build mansions at Allen Avenue at Ikeja, buy homes in Britain, in their relation's name before they deposit huge sums in foreign countries." Efemona had tears in her eyes.

I patted her on her shoulder and she too knew that I was impressed with these two gentlemen with us. I complimented both for helping me to enlighten Efemona. Both laughed heartily.

Ehimire looked at me as if to say I envy you, because men from America do have flesh on their cheeks and bones. But Hidiamen added, "Despite all the wealth of our nation, we have the dumbest cruel and unusual punishment for our journalists. It's only in my country on earth that lacks freedom of speech. Write any stuff juntas don't like, they call it criticism and then they nail the journalists on the cross like Jesus. And most annoying is that we do have political parties and elections in this country, but are they real? No. Because the willingness of my people to be distracted, albeit temporarily, from their weighty affairs of state perhaps also indicate a degree of skepticism about the elections in this country. The transition of doubt and the process has generally been accompanied by a marked sense of weariness and cynicism among my people. Even in elections, we'd all political promises before and do not see any difference, the voting over the past years when the junta would promise to hand over power and they never do. The reason for that is because the ruling juntas usually wait until the elections are over then pump in money to the crooks who ran to shut them up and go about their business. Absolutely, it is money that dictates which party, stood in the elections in Nigeria. Man! I pray that one day my country leaders lift freedom of speech so that Efemona would not be hanged if she decided to become a journalist instead of a nurse when she comes back to this country." Ehimire concurred with Hidiamen. "As far as I know, political prisoners in this country are detained indefinitely and are even denied legal representation, subjected to human rights abuses and humiliated with prolonged physical abuse. Some are even hanged and the public is never told the truth as to how they died. So what does that suggest?" Hidiamen answered his own question. "It suggests to me that if a fool doesn't go to the local market to buy the rotten meat, the meat would remain with the butchers. That means no one would buy their rotten meat."

I shrugged. Hidiamen and Ehimire shrugged too. "I know I wouldn't buy rotten meat from a butcher," I said.

"Me too," Efemona said.

"Me too," Ehimire concurred.

I looked at my wristwatch and it was getting too dark. Hidiamen and Ehimire both rose to go. They each had finished a fourth bottle of larger Star beer. They put out their hand and I took it. Efemona and I walked them to their cars. "Goodbye my friends."

As they drove off, Efemona and I watched silently as they drove into the dusk of the shining moon.

Thus, Efemona had learned a lot. And I knew she would perhaps ponder those thoughts forever in her heart for life. And I believe the stage is set for Efemona in the near future if not now.

Chapter

4

My first night together with Efemona, I noticed that her pussy was all wide and used: Like a doorknob, every man got a turn on it in her country. The reason for that was probably because she was screwing around with too many sugar daddies in order to be able to take care of herself. And for that reason I'd asked her why. This was her reply: "Honey, it was the only way unmarried women in this country can make money to take good care of themselves."

Well, I did not crucify her. I forgave her and told her not to do it with anybody else except me. Even with the regular nursing job she had, working in a village maternity in her country, the mean salary was not enough for her to buy her favorite lipsticks and the things she loved, that were imported from America.

Before communicating with me, who later married her and shipped her to Reno, Nevada, in the United States, Ukpenu was Efemona's favorite place. The truth is, she understood why. She grew up there, that any other place beside Ukpenu and Ewu, a little town after Ukpenu where she was later stationed as a nurse was alien or another planet. The dirty alleys thick with dust and trash heaps, black market that flourished like the poverty, the canny urchins, the arrogant preening sugar daddies, the weary women, and the beautiful girls who looked old by twenty-five was what she was accustomed. Efemona loved it all, the haggling, the hustling, the howling, the high drama and low life, the most beautiful town Ukpenu and Ewu, she knew of.

The seasons of Ukpenu for instance, is what strikes Efemona the most. Merely a small ethnic group on the Southern part of Benin City,

61

it was headquarters of the greatest armed robbers on the planet earth. Efemona and myself who would later ship her to America, knows that Ukpenu itself, let one admit, was ugly until Governor Ogbemudia civilized its people. It has red soil and garbage heaps all around the city's surrounding, with lots of criminals for a reason. The air quality is foul and one does not need time to discover what it is that makes it different from so many other towns and cities in our country.

For instance, how to conjure up a picture, of a town without industries, without infrastructures, good water, or where one had never seen men and women curse their neighbor with *'Shango'— god of thunder,* or where one never hears the beat of drums of the Royals in the Palace and the town crier-a thoroughly negative place, was where Efemona's whole life was based.

The seasons of this negative place Efemona was acquainted are rainfall and dry seasons. All that tells you of rain is coming down is the cloud without notice. And you know that the dry season has arrived when the sun bakes the houses bone-dry, sprinkles mud brick walls and tharch roofs with reddish dust, and one has no option but to survive the bitter hot season in suffering and inhaling of dust which made the majority of the people in the town to have a bad cough. Without stipulation, Efemona and I would say the easiest way of making a place like Ukpenu, where she grew up, acquaintance is to ascertain, how the people in it live, cooperate, observe morality and their culture, mingle with one another, or how they love and die young, because of hunger and poverty.

The heart and the truth of the matter is this: that at Ukpenu, everybody is bored. Though Ukpenu produces half of her country's Ph.Ds in different fields, they have no jobs in a country rich in natural resources. If the Ph.Ds voice out their mind in the media, they are arrested and perhaps executed through firing squad. Even those who are lucky to have teaching jobs or hold government jobs are bored when they have nothing to do. Therefore, the inhabitants became farmers by force of circumstance and thieves by night.

Efemona, before I shipped her to the United States, had worked hard in a town maternity home where she helped pregnant women to deliver their babies. Sometimes, Efemona worked around the clock because she got paid for the number of babies she helped to deliver. Efemona working around the clock had a motive: the purpose of getting rich quick. In short, if I'd not married and shipped Efemona with me to the United States, Efemona would've found a way using an AK47 to waylay her own people in the quest to become a rich woman.

To say the least, Ukpenu seems to be a town without imitations, which is to say, it is completely alienated from other parts of her big cities like Aba, Warri, or Lagos, the present commercial capital where Bad Dudu occupies the hot seat of the nation's executive seat.

Like in any other part of her country though, Ukpenu is the hardest hit in poverty. Men, children and women die young because of hunger and because they have no money to buy their needs and medicines. Though being sick is never acceptable to the man who is married with lots of children, the women still stand by their husbands in sickness or in good health, rich enough or poor beyond poor.

At Ukpenu or elsewhere in her country, the violent rainfall or the violent temperature makes one look older than his or her years, being him a graduate or a Ph.D. holder. To Efemona and to my observation, it's somewhat haphazard to reveal what her town is like. But what Efemona and I are trying to convey is the banality of her remote place with lots of graduates with no jobs, the town's appearance and life and days with trouble of death and wailing every hour of the day. To please the gods of death, Efemona's town's people slaughter dogs, goats, hens and place them by the roadside which further contributed to the sanitation problem the nation had.

Efemona and I know that Ukpenu is like no other place in Nigeria. It is a place where civilization is doomed. The road to the town swing in from Ogoni, another place in the Nation where the masses have suffered shootings, rapes, arbitrary arrests, mass looting, extortion and imprisonment in degrading conditions at the hands of a military that is armed by and paid for by the Shell Oil Company, which deposits millions of dollars monthly into Swiss Banks for Bad Dudu.

Along the road leading to Ukpenu, one could see over the palm trees vegetation. Further along are steep slopes, terraced valley garden farms, where rubber plantation and palm trees out number the houses one sees by the roadside. When the sun had not yet peeped over the steep slopes, colors played in the sky over the houses, and banana trees and over the ponds become more reddish of dust. Houses too, stand staggered above one another where one hears birds and owls waking and chirping intoxicated. You could see cows, goats, hens and roosters rambling across the road. Also, gangs of naked children play soccer on dirt ground available to them. Soccer playing on any open space is a ritual to any male youth growing up at Ukpenu.

At the nearest local airport to Ukpenu, a few distances away from Benin and Ogoni village, as soon after you enter the city, one will certainly encounter military patrols: mobile police, yellow fevers, regular police, soldiers with their usual rifles sitting idly and bored, watching and waiting to deter crimes of their own invention and creation. Efemona ain't no fool not to know in fictional style what I'm talking about.

One certainly knows that he is at Efemona's town of Ukpenu, when the flies hover on your face or eat with you, rats fight and struggle the dinner food with you on your dinner table. Also, your vehicle dances Owanbe as you drive along the street or run 5 MPH not as a result of too many pedestrians, but mostly as a result of potholes. You're at Ukpenu when the smell and remains of animal carcasses used for voodoo placed at the roadside by Efemona's grandmother before herself drowned, to please the gods are strong enough that you place two fingers into your nostrils. You're at Ukpenu when the sanitary arrangements are both primitive and inadequate and the air around you is foul from pit latrines. Efemona would leave it at that fictionally.

When it rains at Ukpenu, there is always a deluge. And with the deluge the streets with no adequate gutter as in any other part of her country, remains a sea of mud. The males visiting their female friends and mistresses usually fold up their trousers up to their knees and walked into the deluge to their destinations. If one was not careful, one was doomed to drown in the deep potholes of Efemona's streets at Ukpenu. I rest my case, folks!

* * *

The slogan of the people in Efemona's country is: *'If you can't beat them, you join them.'* Victoria, Efemona's friend and co-graduate of the Maria Gorritti Academy of Nursing in Benin City believes in the slogan. Victoria knows the drill and believes that if one joins the member elite club of Bad Dudu's ruling junta regime, one can help reshape the corrupt system or make quick money from bribes and kickbacks.

Bawuh, Dudu's Aide, believes in Victoria as much as Victoria trusts in him. Bawuh had met Victoria at a party where Victoria seduced him and screwed him the same night they met at Eko Hotel where the party was held for a funeral of Bawuh's friend who was also a member of the ruling junta regime who died of an overdose of eating too much *stockfish*.

At the party, which the ruling junta party had termed 'Spray Money at Obitos for Love Ones', Bawuh was the guest of honor.

He too, was Bad Dudu's Aide. After Bawuh had finished spraying money on the dancers on the floor, Victoria carefully found her way to sit by him. Victoria was able to seduce him and they made love after the funeral.

Bawuh at first was not interested in her conversation until he became wasted on Cognac and Remimarthins. Then intrigued by the impassioned sex appeal of a beautiful woman before him, he succumbed.

In the beginning, after they screwed, Victoria did not like the idea of Bawuh spraying that much money in a funeral, to the women who danced with the rich and famous of the ruling junta's regime at the obituary. She'd preferred that Bawuh go to her village and spray the money where men and women did not know the color of money the nation currently used as a legal tender. That waside, she also had preferred that Bawuh spray the money in her village market to the poor who has not enough to eat until they die.

The one thing though Victoria did not know was that Bawuh, forty-five who flatters, was a rich and successful member in General Bad Dudu's junta regime. Six feet and two, with tribal marks on both of his cheeks, brown eyes, and an earnest, but arrogant power of money he was, Victoria thought was one of a kind of rich idiots with no education.

As though reading Victoria's mind, Bawuh had leaned across from the guest of honor's table and said, "Money is meant to be spent. Eat today, forget tomorrow. The oil money is only for us." "At least that is you and your ruling junta buddies, Bawuh!

The people of this country are hungry, too," Victoria propelled from the depth of her soul.

Victoria knew that General Bad Dudu is the ringleader of his regime who does what he likes best without the input of his Aides sometimes. Bad Dudu himself had dodged import duties while on the hot seat of Doddan Army Barracks on tires, cars and computers at the Appapa Wharf. Bad Dudu as authoritarian of his people gave his close associates and Lebanese crooks the license to import, give orders to seize goods on the high seas of private businessmen who does not regard him as the president of the country. For that, Bad Dudu gave orders to his crooks to claim their goods in the high seas leaving them penniless and before they are arrested.

Victoria knew that Bad Dudu was violating the law of the land. But who was she to blow the whistle? If she does, it could have a devastating effect on her economic implication of her people, now that she'd hooked Bawuh with her pussy and seduction. Bad Dudu might ask Bawuh to wipe out her family from the earth. He could also ban all her brothers and sisters, all the high-ranking officials of her state from leaving the country until they are all arrested and their hairs shaved from their head and private parts before they are tortured and killed.

Victoria before she graduated from Maria Gorritti Academy of Nursing was a truant from school as Efemona was. Meeting sugar daddies who were smugglers made her a wealthy woman coupled with her nursing trade as a Nursing Sister. And with wealth came her power to mingle with powerful junta members of Bad Dudu's regime to attend parties she was not invited. She was to build her own private Maternity Hospital where she could take care of pregnant women from all over her country. The news of her promotion as a Senior Nursing Sister came to her in her remote village of Aro-Chukwu as a surprise. She took advantage of the promotion. The brain behind her promotion was Bawuh. What a good feeling knowing a high-ranking military junta official of Bad Dudu's regime?, she thought and celebrated with her peers to the news of her promotion to Senior Nursing Sister of her country.

Chapter

5

T he day I first met Efemona was on a Friday in September at Ewu Maternity Home, an eighteenth century built maternity home by the British Colonial masters that had catered to the pregnant women over thirty something years. Based on the description of Efemona by my father, Mr. Ojie, who had introduced Efemona to me and arranged the marriage in absentia coupled with the buxom Efemona photograph she'd personally sent to me through the mail, I boarded a taxi and headed straight away to the Maternity Home to see her for the first time.

She had regarded me, the man, the adventurer from the United States from a distance. And I too, regarded Efemona as she approached, dressed in a white gown work uniform. At first I thought she was one of those local market women who goes to market on the seventh day of the week to teach other local women in the market how to take care of themselves, but then as she drew nearer, I recognized her face from a photograph she'd sent me.

Efemona Irabor Iramen was the sort of nurse you would like to meet by chance, or in any other way, for that matter. She is a uniquely Nigerian nurse, a trained one. A nurse like Efemona would be a hot cake in some parts of African countries, but in Nigeria where the zombies rule and care for themselves alone and nobody else. The zombie wives, for the record, go to England and elsewhere in Europe to deliver their babies. She, Efemona, is an ugly woman nurse, a nurse that no known zombie junta member wants to meet and deal with because they believe she's evil, wild mannered and too flippant. Efemona is what Bad Dudu junta elites mean when they tell you, "Oh! Shut up, she's coming our way." And then they would disperse until she was out of sight.

So, as this flippant known nurse woman approached, I could not for the life of my appearance, guess how she recognized me immediately, only that I was dressed sharply and do have some flesh on my bones. Then she ran to me and embraced me. Nevertheless, I hugged her and kissed her in return. Perplexed, I said, "Yes, I believe you must be Efemona."

"Yes, I believe you must be Ekiaqueta."

You know in Nigeria as in any other part of Africa, African names do have a meaning. Looking at me a second time, and hugging me tighter, Efemona said, "I admire your name too much. I believe it means *'What Can I Say'*."

"Yes that's my name. I'll be your husband from now on. My father has done his job. It's my duty to take you to America where you will have all the freedom in the world to eat three square meals a day." She laughed and embraced me again and again, the fact that, I could've refused to hug and embrace her at all, the way she looked to my liking. But the fact that my father had arranged the marriage for me in absentia, I'd overlooked her appearance and statue.

On the other hand I made some grunt mockery of What? What am I looking at silently or I think your face is too ugly for my liking for a wife. However, my face remained impassive, but on the other hand I may have twitched that I said, "Oh! So my father, Mr. Ojie couldn't see a beautiful woman in Nigeria other than Efemona standing before me?" I'd murmured within my being.

But anyway, Efemona smiled. Thus Efemona and I chatted a minute or two and noted each other's weak points.

In parting, I embraced her again with definite plans to see that she join me in America within a short time frame. But in reality, it was the most mundane of circumstances. And as my taxi drove off from the Maternity Home, I realized I have encountered an uncustomary mismatch into the future, noting that I did not like what I saw, Efemona being too vibrant. As the first son of my parents, culture must be preserved and so I honored my father's words, "Efemona is the right mate for you."

*   *   *

I left the Maternity Home and headed back to America after staying with my parents for about a week in Nigeria. From time to time, Efemona was corresponding with me through the mail and on the telephone. On several occasions she'd written to inform me of having terrifying dreams-the dreams in which she'd noted: she'd slept one night and went into the subconscious state. And that she would go to America and join her husband. And second, a long time acquaintance was visiting her in Reno, Nevada in the United States. Perhaps it would be informative to understand that nature of having dreams in Nigeria, especially being a nurse and stationed in the remotest place to live. Having a dream at Ukpenu, Ewu, Ogoni, Bornu or elsewhere in Nigeria or in general, Africa where the army rule their people is terrifying. Reno, for instance, is quite simply the best city in America to live, making Nigerian cities the oil producing country of the world, seems eye sore. For instance, I myself had once had a dream in Reno, Nevada whereby a man and his wife, both white and elderly couples had cornered me to board a taxi I was driving, to drive them to Circle Drive or what the man called 'Young Circle', where they would teach me how to work on top of water (river) where the very nouveau riche who practices millionarism occultism-the occult society that ruin the poor of Reno residence who came to Reno, Nevada from Nigeria to make their life better. Till this date it still baffles me what the dream meant. It was in broad daylight at the Reno International Airport, when two couples I believed working for the underworld Mafia, or the CIA remember me too well. As I later found out through my forefathers in their graves through voodooism stronger than those of the occult group in Circle Drive, it was a society that makes poor people who stood to challenge the powers that be in Reno or England of oppression to either talk to themselves on the sidewalk of Downtown Reno, sorting through garbage heaps or if that failed, are eliminated from the earth's surface.

In my case, 'Man pass Man' is how a true Nigerian cooked for seven days and seven nights would put it. I'm a true Nigerian and I believe in Baal worship and voodooism that surpassed that of Circle Drive or Young Circle in Reno, Nevada.

On the other hand, Efemona's dream was the one that inspired, which means that she would come to America to ruin her husband or go home to Nigeria to destroy the government of Bad Dudu. How that would happen for Efemona to become the first president of this most populous nation in Africa, the dream did not explain. But the dream had flashed a name of a woman in her heart-Miss Philomena Drake, who would meet her first at Port of Entry to instruct her about American ways and life and possibly tell her future.

Anyway, from the horse's mouth, Efemona has always been a smart little kid when she was growing up despite the poverty that wrought her village and her people. At the age of 13, she was already screwing around with sugar daddies. Anywhere there was a party she was not invited, like Nathan's party where I learnt that she was seen wearing a colorful green skirt and top, she was the first to know, hear about the party, and the first to get there on the day of the party.

Efemona being a truant from High School in Benin City where she learnt how to talk and be flippant with her teachers, Efemona, I learnt, followed the footsteps of her mother and sister named Anegbo who first met a rich sugar daddy at the age of 12. And because Ojimelu, her sugar daddy was rich who visited Nigeria regularly from England, where he resided and had worked and trained himself at Oxford University, Anegbo then poisoned him.

It is perhaps instructive too, to note that Ojimelu was paid with British pounds and schillings, the money that had became the object of worship in Nigeria after the dollar.

Because Ojimelu was rich, Anegbo decided to con him to her garden. Being vicious, Anegbo knew that Ojimelu, her sugar daddy had thousands of British pounds and schillings, enough to purchase three bungalows at Government Reserved Areas in Benin City and Ukpenu. She then plucked a mysterious fruit from her garden and handed it to him.

Hum! A man in love, what did he know? The goddamn poor Ojimelu! When he ate the fruit, he instantly had a swollen stomach. After a few days, he was defecating in his pants, which lasted for seven days and seven nights, until he died. With her intention of getting rich quick, Anegbo then immediately inherited his wealth and told Ojimelu's parents to fuck off and she became the Queen of the night to henchmen in the area, making big bucks from marijuana sale and selling her carnal to rich junta members who can afford her for her beauty. Though the masses in her village were plagued with poverty, Anegbo and her parents knew not whether there was hardship in Nigeria.

Before Anegbo poisoned Ojimelu because of his wealth, she'd lived just like the typical market woman, who carried *Ugborele- that famous spice that stinks when fermented and prepared then added to soups turns the flavor superb.* Ugborele was what Anegbo used to carry on her tray to her local market on her head to be sold for a few pennies.

Anegbo's one room apartment, I tell ya, would always be my metaphor for Heaven, Purgatory, and Hell. When she poisoned Ojimelu, she soon earned herself a new name. She became the *'Oyinbo'* of the town which means that she was fair in complexion and the preening, haggard men of Ukpenu and in general, Nigeria liked her for her complexion and then dated her. On the other hand, Efemona soon became hooked on London Gin because Anegbo introduced her to it.

Anegbo, for your information, also looked a cross between Los Angeles famous Heidi Fleiss personality and the famous women in X-rated movie channels. The *'Oyinbo'* Anegbo soon became the richest woman at Ukpenu and in Benin City. Soon after, all the working men there became her sugar daddies. On Fridays for the record, Anegbo has an escort standing by as early as nine A.M. to transport her loot and profits from all her sugar daddies to the bank. The place Anegbo lived was filled with contradictions. I mean, it was inhabited by the normal collection of people because she, too, had recruited other women to work for her selling their carnals, Aisioke and women's bubba and wrappers and head ties which were expensive African attires.

Some may ask how my Efemona made it to America to become internationally acclaimed and famous a woman tougher than Anegbo who poisoned her sugar daddy so she could inherit his wealth and despite the fact that as rumors had it, had defied her culture and morality at Ukpenu and was cursed?

First of all, it all happened when I visited Ukpenu to bring Efemona to the States. In the quiet of her bedroom, we'd quizzed ourselves when she'd made me drunk to tell her my life history in America. It happened that I was so drunk that I laid beside her on the same bed where we had talked in whispers, the most intimate conversation of adults. Efemona then had loved every bit of my gist. I'd told her of places in the United States we'll visit, like places of tourist attractions: the Lake Tahoe nude beach, the Disney Worlds and the seasons of changes and why's. She too, had told me of the harmattan cold seasons and the monsoon seasons, which she'd believed were probably similar to the winter cold months in America. I'd explained to her the differences. The harmattan I'd said, "brought hot winds and dry climate while the winter was extremely cold and brought snow to the mountains and rooftops of houses. Sometimes, some cities in America experience minus 30 degrees." My Efemona was surprised. She opened her mouth and stared at me. Finally she said, "I'll prefer to see for myself soon."

When our conversation finally graduated from geography, I then switched to boys and girls stories of the past. It was here I'd confessed to the sins of my lifetime: How I met a young woman in Reno, Nevada named LJH through whom I lost my virginity being a graduation night for her in the backseat of her car and finally in her bedroom. I'd said to Efemona, "I'd never before seen a naked woman with pubic hairs before LJH, not even in pictures because my father was a strict Catholic. I dare not come into his domain with pictures of women. Even Playboy and Hustler and other magazines of nude females were censored by the Federal Government. And I knew those same ruling oligarchy who banned and censored these magazines watches them with the Lebanese women and their mistresses all over the world in the privacy of their home. As a result of that I'd no strangest idea what a naked woman's body looked like, talkless of penetrating a vagina." As I talked and recalled my first fumbled attempt to consummate the act, Efemona had laughed and then gripped me.

I knew Efemona was enjoying the gist so I chatted on. I also told my Efemona that LJH was an experienced woman in the act and hence I didn't miss the real gate because she'd guided me throughout the act. How LJH and I became perfectly matched lovers and how she showed me a lot of styles during the act before I gained knowledge and stamina and became a pro myself.

She'd interrupted me. "What styles did LJH teach you, honey?" "A lot, honey pie!" I'd said.

I knew Efemona was damned too interested to know so I explained, "LJH would love it when I would want to *come* and she would tell me not yet. She would rather make sure she *come* first by turning in different positions and enjoying it and I following in the act like a ninny. That it was LJH who taught me what oral sex was by showing and performing it with me-the blow job or what she called the flute note. That she'd also showed me the 6996 positions and all the erogenous stimulus zones of the female body where I could touch her and she was wet without being fucked. With passion, Efemona gripped me and interrupted me and said, "So you then became LJH Casanova of lust in her sack?"

"Absolutely," I'd responded. Then she turned around and kissed me. She pressed her mouth harder against my throat while my hands clutched at her back. As she was getting a reaction, I asked, "Do you want to hear more?"

I knew she wanted to hear more. Her actions told me that. So I'd then added, "Me and LJH enjoyed sex on the grass in parks and the beaches of Lake Tahoe. At first LJH did not like it, but later she admitted it was the best sex she'd ever had doing it on the beaches with me, nationwide."

Coupled with that gisting, something also had told me to tell Efemona about the famous Mustang Ranch Brothel. After all, I'd said everything. Why wouldn't I tell her how I'd paid for sex twice after I caught LJH cheating on my bed? Then I'd said, "You know, I'd also paid for sex in the Ranch, the most famous Brothel in the world, the one so much talked about."

Remembering her pussy was all wide and used by sugar daddies in Benin and Ukpenu, she asked with happiness, "I know you must like swimming in their sacks."

"Not exactly," I'd said.

"Why not?" I'd said nothing. But I'd thought about my answer for a long time if I should tell her and she too will do the same when she joins me in the States. Finally I'd told myself to trust my Efemona. After all, we are Africans. Once we tie the knot, she would keep my interest up. She would honor our culture and traditions until death do both of us part. And even if I should die before her she would honor me and give me the respect for several months before servicing other men.

Finally, I then said, "I caught LJH making love to my friend on my bed which I'd shared with her for over five years and even so I'd felt guilty paying a prostitute for revenge and I had wanted my money back after screwing the fucking bitch in the Ranch. The worst of all, the bitch LJH had serviced my friend with my own booze in our refrigerator before they got into the act.

Efemona laughed then said, "Honey, I forgive you with all my heart. I promise to be a perfect African woman when I join you soon in America."

With her assurance, I even went as far as to tell my Efemona how I must've been in the best shape of my life after LJH had done that to me. How I'd ran in and out of beautiful African American women's homes of single women. Instead of me making the move at them, the women made the move at me for my good looks and the way I talk. White and Blacks, no exception. I didn't really know what it was exactly, the times, my attitude, the place I was staying or maybe it had something to do with my being young and lanky in stature. The place was near my University campus: 621 Spiros Bungalow, North Sierra Street. I had lots of friends then, male and females. I'd lived with other African students, six of us from Nigeria. Spiros Bungalow had two floors of socialization, of bizarre scenes, bristling IQ's, where women of all races were welcomed home. Here we partied all the time. Each room was occupied by a party loving animal. A place which then was finally renamed as "Party Bungalow Palace", where most of our friends from all over the world usually stopped by to ask whoever was home, "What's on the agenda today or tomorrow?" But you know, the words were flashed around the city, the Africans from Nigeria are having a party at the 'Party Bungalow Palace'. We'd wandered in and out of each other's rooms, feasting, drinking and screwing for days, missing classes. In the city's neighborhood or at the Job Corps, you hear the boast of those who'd attended the Nigerians' party once before at the Spiros Bungalow saying, "I survived the hangover at the Bungalow." Even when I was in class, my room or those of my roommates were always unlocked for females to walk into and relax. And when we'd no parties, with as much drama, comedy, love or whatever made human beings sensitive to relate to one another, love had so much to do with the atmosphere of the Bungalow. We all lived as brothers and the women we dated were treated as sisters. Friends were welcome with open minds. No attitude nor attention-spasm-tantrum was ever displayed. We all were real to the point of borrowing each other's money. And from time to time, exchanging beautiful women with nice asses and boobs."

Again, Efemona interrupted me. "And you'll promise me now that you'll be the best husband in the whole world over-night?" She'd said while her hand had curled around my neck. "Supposing I want to make love to you right now? This time of day?" She said knowing that fucking in the afternoon is strictly against our culture. I thought about my answer for a few minutes. Then I'd remembered at Ukpenu or in other African villages, we do have morals. Married couples don't make love in broad daylight. They have other things to think and worry about-the issue of money and hunger, of course.

But anyway, I'd said, "It makes no difference to me because in America we do it anywhere and anytime of the day. Back then, nobody knew what AIDS was. I dig those times doing it in the afternoons. And because the Americans have no culture. Or to put it in a lame man's tongue, the culture of the Americans is only about fucking-night and day. Those times, a friend would say, "I dig that woman. Timson, Achuko, Okorie, Eze, Gilbert, Kandy, Clement, Odira, John Muthana, Mibiti, or Nathan has. Can I get some from her? I mean, would you mind? It was no big deal. We were all open to one another to that point. That was then, my dear. Even, I'd once asked Achuko if I could get some from his beautiful girlfriend and he'd said to me in these words, "Ask her. If she doesn't care, why should I care? It's not my buttocks nor my *yansh,* so go for it." It was that easy to get some. I dig those times, my dear."

"What do you say to the women when you have the permission from your friend to have some?" Efemona had interrupted me again. "You mean what should I say to her or how should I tell her?"

"That's what I mean, dear."

"Well, I just ask her if I could dick her sometime in the morning, afternoon or evening. The choice was left to the woman. When she comes, I take the drinks to the basement floor. It was that simple. The women! So many women. You see honey, I can close my eyes now and recount so many faces I dicked who were friends to my buddies. It's the American way, sweetheart. Nobody gives a fuck. And we fucked them anyway because they don't give a fuck. In retrospect, we'd personalities of all types then, breasts of different sizes and shapes, some resembling yours now before me, the left one belonging to Odira or Achuko or Okorie. Their buttocks, too. I would squeeze the right one and the left belonging to another. We didn't discriminate. I dig those times."

My Efemona was silent for a long period. Finally, she then had ran her fingers through my ass and my bare back. From the corners of her eyes, I could see her in trance, maybe thinking two things. Revenge when she set her foot on American soil or seduce me quickly as she seduced her former sugar daddies to make love to her while she cleaned their wallets. Not quite. Anyway, I was compelled and sure that little remained of her face, which had turned sour. She stared at me with silent mutiny. Finally she'd said, "I see."

Thus, Efemona got civilized before she wound up in America to join me. And I must be frank that my dad did not know of course that my Efemona he had chosen and arranged for me to marry had messed or farted at Ukpenu local market. I bet that if my dad had known in detail he would've moved forward to look for another woman for a wife for me. The fact was, the culture at Ukpenu village was highly respected and observed that when Efemona went to her local market early at the age of 13 and messed, in the midst of merchants buying and selling, she denied that she'd done it. The gas that permeated from her ass was too strong that the merchants gathered and cursed who'd done it. Though

Efemona did come forward to admit that her sister's baby she had tied on her back had done it, the merchants did not believe her. Before she got home she had a high fever and was near the point of death. Efemona then quickly sent an emissary through the town's crier to inform the Oba, the Chiefs and Elders she'd something to tell them. When she came before them at the Oba's Palace, she then knelt down before them with tears in her eyes. She must've knelt down for sixty seconds unable to say something when the Oba finally asked her, "What is it you want to tell us, my dear daughter at your age?"

Efemona looked at the Oba, the Chiefs, Kings and the Elders and sobbed. "I'd lied against my sister's son whom I'd on my back when I messed in the local market and the merchants buying and selling gathered and cursed who did it. I believe the smell polluted their noses, which they couldn't resist. I believe I might die if I don't tell the truth."

His Highness did not seem happy with her for lying against her sister's baby, but he did grasp the meaning instantly. The Oba then had asked her again. "What did you do that made you to be sick when you got home from the local market?"

Everyone in the Palace looked at Efemona to hear the truth. Rather than answer the Oba's direct question, Efemona's face was down looking at the floor of the Palace. Finally she'd raised her head up and sobbed again. "Your Highness," Efemona said, "I'd gassed in the midst of thousands of merchants buying and selling their goods and polluted the food in the local market. The gas from my ass was too strong for everyone to bear. I could understand why they cursed whoever had done it. I'd lied that it was my sister's baby on my back that did it."

His Highness was pissed. He looked at Efemona, and their eyes met for the third time. Then he looked at everyone in the Palace and asked his second in command, "When is the next market day coming up?"

They all had looked at Efemona. "Tomorrow, your Highness." Efemona answered before anyone in the palace, before His Highness.

The Oba then had said, "The crime of lying against newborn babies is absurd. I fine you seven goats and seven hens. And tomorrow, go back to the market at peak period with a whistle and a gong and announce curtly that the mess of last week in the local market was not from the son of your sister's baby's ass but from your own ass."

And so it went, degenerating very quickly into Palace histrionics. All had loved it. Except His Highness himself, who asked everyone to shut up. "Enough!," then he looked at Efemona. "Efemona! My Palace appreciates your moral integrity and is impressed with you to come forward to reveal the truth. Go in peace and inform all my market people."

Efemona left for the market and stood in the middle of the market as early as eight A.M. to tell the truth. On her arrival at the local market she then blew the whistle and then the gong again and again to draw the market people's attention. That done, she announced curtly, "My fellow market traders, the mess in this market last week that polluted every merchant's nose and the food they were selling was from my ass and not from the ass of my sister's baby. I want everyone here today to forgive me. I beg everyone here today to carry the news to their neighbors who are not in the market today."

"You are forgiven. Don't do it again," the market people booed.

Before Efemona got home she became well and sound.

*   *   *

Thus, the mess in the local market was enough for me to have turned down our introduction and marriage, if I'd known. But the other story of how Efemona became internationally acclaimed goes like this: It happened that a palmwine tapper who was my father and later became a laborer clearing the bushes surrounding the local maternity Efemona was stationed working for free for the local government had met her there. It's even ironic that the government of Bad Dudu did not even recognize this palmwine tapper and laborer to compensate him for his effort as a good citizen for his country, a country that employs immigrants mostly Labanese to pay them for their labor, could not even recognize the palm tapper and laborer to pay him a nickel, a dime, or one kobo.

Anyway, at Ewu, Efemona was the Florence Nightingale who cared for the pregnant women to deliver their babies. Here the palmwine tapper or laborer discussed the possibility of marrying his son who was in America. Efemona agreed without hesitation to marry me (Ekiaqueta) in absentia.

After a distinguished career as a Nursing Sister at Ewu Maternity for which the government of Bad Dudu's junta regime did not recognize her work, I visited her and took her away to America from the culture of poverty.

On her arrival to the United States through Los Angeles Airport, the city that makes the world go round, her first impression of the huge airport and the beautiful city told her that Ukpenu and elsewhere in her country, where town planning was an alien concept, must be challenged someday.

Her eyes soon rambled from one point to the other. Then she surveyed the beautiful city from afar. She was amazed. All the high-rise skyscrapers were all arranged in grid system and well patterned to modern American civilization architecture. Even the sidewalks were of polished granite and the circular driveways were veneered in ceramic tile. She couldn't believe what she saw. But it was real. The difference between this city and Nigerian cities was evidenced at a glance. First the Tower of Babels were almost touching the heavens or hell, standing still. One day, Efemona then thought, would hear God's voice and where *HE* was hiding. She thought, the Tower of Babels here are standing still and she wondered if at one time or another God ever cast *HIS* spell and put confusion on the American country when they were building them as *HE* did in Africa. God must be wicked to the African race, and their Continent but good only to God's own country: America. But my country, Nigeria, is rich in everything. Does it all meant that only the leaders in my country who ruled us are cursed not to think righteously to invest in their country to build modern Babels everywhere? And when God cursed the African race, did he refer only to zombies ruling *us* in Nigeria? All these questions were then beginning to register in the back of her mind.

Looking further, the airport in itself was beautiful and it was a spectacular piece of architecture and design. Surrounding the airport was a glorious park of lawn, man made lakes, waterfalls and statues of the Mayors and civic honorary men and women. Nothing like that in her country. She shook her head in disgust. *"Wan day be Wan day,"* she murmured to herself. Shaking her head she thought again of the white man, of how clever they are perhaps. The world where life does not echo in hopeless of confusion of different languages as in Africa, especially in her country. Thinking and trying to forget about her country's predicaments, she opened her purse and took out a dollar bill, walked up to a vending machine, which was still alien in her country. She slotted in the dollar and it was rejected. She didn't know why. So she looked at the dollar bill again. It was the first time she then had noticed the inscription, "In God we trust." She placed the dollar back into her purse and continued to observe as more thought flashed behind her back.

* * *

Looking around helplessly, Efemona could almost hear the sound of money being printed on her forehead. In reality, she was flabbergasted by the way of life of the men, women and children who walked the streets of L.A. as she stood perplexed. There were no vendors, no hordes of strangers and mean looking spirited soldiers with Uzis, no *Agbellos* or motor parks tugs as in Benin, Lagos, Ewu, Enugu, Ekpoma and Ukpenu. There were no small boys and small girls carrying fruits on their head running back and forth selling their bananas and suyas. Efemona thought, in my country, there are nature in humanity the body bears because people cannot afford to buy bar soaps any more to take their bath. Lots of people had passed me by, I have never sensed body in humanity.

She'd been standing for quite some time, still perplexed, when a white woman, blond, noticed her from a distance wearing colorful African attires and walked towards her. She was one of those radicals at U.C. Berkley who liked Bob Marley's Kaya album and African attires. She admired Efemona's colorful native attires that she couldn't help to give her compliments and introduce herself.

"I'm Philomena Drake, a student at U.C. Berkley in Oakland, CA. I like the way you are dressed," she complimented again.

They chitchatted for a while. "By the way, did you say you came all the way from Nigeria to join your husband down here?"

Efemona nodded. Miss Drake was about to go when Efemona gave her a compliment too, "You are dressed gorgeously."

With satisfaction, she accepted the compliment and was about to watch herself disappear among the crowd at the airport when she decided to give Efemona more attention.

"Oh! Thanks! Yours is even better-and eye catchy. I see you do have a deep accent. So what part of Nigeria are you from?"

"Ukpenu, a little town in Nigeria, south of Benin City." "And what are you doing in L.A.? Oh! Never mind. You told me already, E.J.D! Isn't it? Huh?"

Efemona didn't know what she meant. Before she could ask, Philomena answered her own question. "I mean Efemona-just-dropped-huh?"

Efemona became more fully aware of her surrounding *now*.

She nodded. Philomena chatted with her for a few more minutes and noticed that Efemona could be influenced and lectured before African Americans got to meet her. Then she looked at Efemona directly in her eyes, "Well, welcome to America, Efemona."

Efemona thought she would disappear. But not yet. Philomena continued, "It is easy to make it in America. There are lots of opportunities in this country if one wants to work. Our land is the land of freedom. *'Women struggle for their rights in this country not because we regard equality as inherently just, but because we believe that by sharing equality with men the power to shape and govern societies, we can then create a better world for all people,'* she'd quoted a powerful congresswoman in Washington.

Efemona became swoon. Philomena added, "Here in America women have choices, we can take a job or refuse one. We can be married or remain unmarried. We can be lesbians, too. Whatever makes us happy. We have the right to stay on Welfare and collect from the State. It is called the Welfare Supplemental Income. It enables us to take care of our children. The more children we have, the more money we collect from the government. In no time, you'll be qualified to get such money on a weekly or monthly basis. In America though, one has to be very careful because we've crazy people all over the place here in L.A. and elsewhere across the country."

Efemona caught the phrase of lesbian then asked, "What do you mean when you say women can be lesbians?"

Philomena smiled. "I should explain to you. You see Efemona, I shouldn't tell you this because you came from a different culture quite different from ours."

She paused. "Well, Efemona, it's a love affair between two women, mostly practiced by women who want to be independent, tired of their husbands coming home broke from the casinos. Here in America, the artificial roles are played out in different manners of a stud and her lover. The stud is the bull dyke in control of satisfying her lover with an artificial helper. The stud is the man because she assumes a man's role when she needs to be entertained and be satisfied. They also change their names. For instance, Alice becomes Alexan. And Efemona can become Ifeanyi. Ifeanyi, now the man, has the right to invite Patricia or Virginia to the house and give them an artificial dick helper to entertain her until she has an orgasm. They both can eat each other's up, too, until they wet themselves. The stud who assumes the role of the man then cuts her hair short and dresses like a man and walks like a man. She also teaches her partner how to lick pussy until she'd enough of it. Like Efemona, now Ifeanyi, would no longer cook, but her lover whom she controls, who does the cleaning in the house, does the dishes and laundry and also does the ironing for her as well. Strange, huh? Only in America, Efemona! As you become settled you'll learn more of my country."

"That's really strange."

"Yes it is! Anyway, I was saying in America, we have crazy people all over the place. An American can kill you over a nickel, a dime, or a quarter. It was just yesterday here in San Francisco that a man I'll call C.J. killed another man over a quarter. He'd approached Mr. DD, an Exxon gas station attendant to inform him that the soda pop vending machine which he'd dropped his coin failed to dispense his selection. He then demanded his quarter back, but the attendant had told him the vending machine was not his and that he would try to notify the company that owns it in which case he would get his quarter back in a check through the mail if his address and information about him was still current. Mr. C.J. was not completely satisfied with DD's explanation. He then went home and came back with a magnum and shot him point blank.

We will meet in heaven he told him and walked away." Philomena finished talking, then hugged Efemona, creating a mood that was more friendly *now* than just a mere passerby and admirer of her attires. She looked at Efemona again and said, "You look tired now after the long flight from Nigeria to this country. I can give you enough information to lead you a long way so you know how my country—," she giggled at Efemona.

Efemona didn't know how much time had passed, but she was aware of the fact that if her husband was late picking her up, Udomiaye, who lives twenty miles away from L.A. was to pick her up. She was aware that if they do come to pick her up they would page her. She was relaxed and silent for a few seconds. She was glad to run into the right person, the ultimate admiration of her attire by Miss Drake. So she said, "I like your company. Please tell me something."

Philomena looked down at her wrappers, then touched her head tie. "What are they made of?"

"They are all brocade," She anticipated her response. She began as the words poured from her, crowding one another in their rush to flow out. "You might as well hear this gruesome tragedy then, Efemona."

She cleared her throat again. "This happened in Lake Tahoe a few days ago. A young man named Ike, sixteen years old who put a gun to the head of his bosom friend, BT Express and pulled the trigger at least seven times. Ike and his friend had been arguing over who should control some money less than one hundred dollars they'd stolen from a woman at the mall. Armed with a .22 caliber semi-automatic pistol, Ike drove his friend and another of his friends Judoka to a field a few miles away from where they live and shot him several times in his head. To make sure that BT Express would not wake up and get even, he went back to his car and reloaded the gun. He came back and shot him several more times on his two eyes to make damn sure he would never see again if he was to wake up. Killing in America is universal, Efemona. They kill women, too. Women kill, too. A man or a woman can walk into a crowd and try their new weapons on innocent people. That's when you hear so and so was there at the wrong place at the wrong time. These are just but some of the crimes of this great country. I only told you those tragedies not because I want you to go back to Africa, but because it would guard you throughout your duration of stay here in America. I want you to be very careful as to who you mingle with, Efemona. You won't hate me for this, would ya?!"

For sure, Efemona had had enough, but not quite. She looked at Philomena's almost perfect political mask, a pleasant half-smile, candid eyes that rarely blinked, a long jaw of resolution, a mouth that was full with more stories. She'd a vaguely student professional look, and possessed a laugh so hearty and infectious that Efemona could not guess if they were rehearsed. Efemona finally smiled and said, "No," being enraptured.

Philomena could tell that Efemona wanted her to continue. "I'll stop if you want me to, but I just want to make damn sure you get the message."

A man was selling newspapers on a corner close to where they stood. Drake signaled to him and said, "What's up?" while Efemona looked on.

She passed him a dollar, without looking at him as the man handed her the papers. "Oh!" She said, "I will look at it later Efemona. And I was saying . . ."

They stood in silence and the city of L.A. stood in the distance. A bright sunlit day now with a soft breeze blowing into the walkway. Efemona said finally, "My husband is not here yet. His uncle was supposed to pick me up at a certain time. I'm enjoying your gist and your company. Please continue."

Philomena, who'd longed to continue anyway, cleared her throat again. "In this country, a woman can sue their husbands, employers, their daycare managers, landlords and their bosses where they work for sexual harassment and even the president elect of the United States. Women, as a matter-of-fact, can participate in general elections and run for offices. We can screw any man we like or choose, even if they are married or they are our husband's best friends. What is most exciting about it is that we can do threesomes, foursomes, and more. We can also service our husband's friends with his own booze in the refrigerator before we screw them on the floor of our livingroom they house us.

It is the freedom our forefathers granted Americans when they drafted our constitution. I bet that no other Constitution in the world surpasses ours, Efemona. Once you get yourself acquainted, you'll begin to see things the same way everyone in America sees it. Another exciting good reason about my country-already your country, is that you're already protected under the law when you arrived. And even if your husband caught you red handed screwing his best friend on his couch he dare not lay his fucking hands on you or he will spend the rest of his life in prison. You can sue him for laying his fucking hands on you and knock him out of business. There's no status of limitations on when to sue the bastards who abuse women. I divorced my husband three months ago and the jury awarded me $3.5 million dollars. Pretty good deal, huh? Only in America, Efemona. The American legal system works. In our legal system, it is easy for judges to convict and we women always win. What kind of job does your husband have, anyway?"

"He's a businessman. At least that's what he told me and my parents," Efemona replied with a beautiful smile.

"There you go. I can see you in the near future as a millionaire. Here in America too, the law permits us to cut off the penis of our husbands or loved ones if they mistreat us, cheat on us and abuse us. We can also kill our parents and plead insanity in our courts. Ninety-nine percent of the time, the woman wins if we can prove and have a justifiable reason why we committed the crime. Only in America, Efemona."

"Wow-o! Oh, yeah," Efemona exclaimed.

"That's right. And a year after the jury awarded me the $3.5 million, I took another couple of millions from a fast food, food chain. Only in America, Efemona. I love my country and I know you will too. Hey! Write down my phone number if you should have any problem to the city that you are heading."

She dictates, "Nine-one-six, three-five-eight, five-five-five-five. Call me. Sorry to take so much of your time. I have to go now."

Efemona thanked her again for all the lectures and gists. But she said, "Before you go, please tell me how you were able to take a coupla millions from a fast food, food chain?"

"Oh! I should explain to you. Well! I slipped on a peanut as I walked into the restaurant, my dear. So I sued and I won. My final advice to you, Efemona is that this is a great country. You can acquire a lot of knowledge in this country and go home and help your people. My country-America is a land of great opportunities and freedom for all. If you are smart enough to read, and watch soap operas all day and all night, you will know and learn where you come from and where you're going from this moment on. I've got a prediction for you, that you're gonna be great and one hell of a woman who would challenge the president of your country. And when you become famous remember me, Efemona. Good luck to you, Efemona." And she deserted her.

Chapter

6

B y now you will have known that my name is Ekiaqueta, but also known as 'What Can I Say' and that I'd gone to Nigeria to marry Efemona, whom my dad had arranged for me to marry. I cannot say I was poor, but I was living a middle class life in Reno, Nevada as a good citizen. My life before I left my country to come to America to make my life better was hell. Born in a small town a few miles away from Benin City where I was raised in abject poverty and where there were no industries, everyone learned to adjust and eat cheaply what they cultivate from their farms. My father, Mr. Ojie, to meet ends devoted his time off after working with Efemona at a local maternity hospital as a laborer and as a palmwine tapper, devoted his time to his private shoe factory. My dad, Mr. Ojie, taught himself to make shoes, which earned him local fame more than just a laborer and palmwine tapper. He was the first man in our entire community to design a sandal popular with the working farmers which utilized the rubber from discarded automobile tires as soles and then sold it to farmers in the area.

If all the leaders and their in cahoots who had ruled Nigeria were like my father, Mr. Ojie, moral and honest, Nigeria would have enough for everyone to eat. What I mean to convey here is that with the sales from his shoes made locally from his factory, he was able to feed his five wives and twenty-seven children.

My father, Mr. Ojie was also the first man in the entire community local division to advocate the need for the ruling junta oligarchy regimes in Nigeria and in Africa to stop siphoning their nation's money to foreign banks. The heart of the matter was far-fetched, which was that, though Nigeria had wealth and the money was not distributed evenly the way it should've been throughout the nation, he successfully rallied his drinking acquaintances to collect taxes which they later used to purchase a generator to provide electricity, fix the potholes and sanitation problem in his community. He was also the first man to see the need for electricity and therefore rallied round among his people to collect money from them to purchase a huge generator from America to serve his own people as the National Electric Power Authority was a failure. I, being the first born of my mother and the twenty-first son among my brothers and sisters, the chances of putting me into school was slim. As I was growing up, I was combing the streets and the compound of Zuma Memorial Hospital where I grew up with my buddies: Daniel, Margie, Rose, Sunny, Maetu, Hidiamen and Ehimire. At the time these buddies of mine were all placed in schools I was still combing out the garbage heaps on the streets and my compound. I might as well admit here that I graduated from garbageology before my uncle finally placed me into elementary school.

What I'm trying to convey here is that my father had no money to place me into school in a country where billions of money in crude oil sale revenue is generated, but siphoned out to foreign banks by those who rule Nigeria. And I would be dumb and stupid if I don't thumb-up for a Swiss judge, George Zecchin, who finally indicted the son of Bad Dudu, the famous Nigerian dictator in connection with a billion-dollar money-laundering scheme. It was George Zecchin who finally accused Bad Dudu's son, Mohammed Abacha Dudu, now in prison awaiting trial on murder charge of killing and torturing to death the wife of Abiola, his father's rival who spoke out on behalf of her husband who'd won the general election, but denied the executive hot seat of his country. Moral minds like George Zecchin who saw the need to indict Mohammed of money-laundering, fraud, mismanaging public funds and belonging to a criminal organization should be commended for his role that frozen $670 million linked to Mohammed alone. That aside he also urged all Swiss banks to freeze another $600 million and more money in Britain that Mohammed had crooked out of Nigerian Treasury.

The one thing to note in these revelations is that these millions are tied to only one man in Bad Dudu's regime and how about other high-ranking officials of his regime? I believe Bad Dudu and his son Mohammed operated accounts in Germany and France and as many as 100 banks could be involved as a dumping ground for Nigerian money across the globe. If Mr. Zecchin could see the need to help the Nigerian Government to recover some of these millions, what then stopped the Oval Office from taking steps against corruption in Nigeria?

Anyway, Nigeria's junta regime of Bad Dudu killed several students and hung as many civilian literate men and women who spoke out against his authoritarian regime. The long and dwindling economy in Nigeria was known as the haven for luxuries and most probably was unknown to most Americans except to Bill Clinton and his congress and probably still is, unless people happen to catch sporadic reports on the international segments of the CNN news while preparing their dinner or drinking their booze. Washington Oval Office knew all along the egregious acts of persecution and brutality of civilians by the Dudu's junta regime, which has debilitated Efemona's country, even when they don't make the lead headlines in America, were common. The truth is, only news reports and magazine articles provide an actual glimpse and situation of what it is like to live in Nigeria under Bad Dudu. To witness the atrocities in person is another thing. Across the country, there are no more food stuffs in local markets, agriculture is no longer encouraged and mechanized as when good moral minds like governor Ogbemudia were in power, who had made available incentives to farmers and market men and women. I believe for instance, that Americans are aware of the genocide that occurred in Kosovo. In the same manner the Oval Office should've realized that while an estimated 10,000 people were killed in Kosovo's war, the Nigerian heinous military atrocities of Bad Dudu is equally weighty. What can the Oval Office do to revitalize a dwindling economy and stop Bad Dudu from killing and silencing innocent civilians who saw the need for free elections and true democracy? I think an obvious solution could've been a U.S. ban on importation of crude oil. In fact, millions of dollars sold from crude oil is drilled and sold by Bad Dudu, Babagida and their in cahoots in government. Money from crude oil sale is siphoned out of the country and the rest they use to screw prostitutes from abroad. Oh! Excuse me! Am I going too far? Some may say that a sanction on my country would jeopardize its financial stability. What good is it for only Bad Dudu and his in cahoots to embezzle the billions out of Nigeria, leaving the masses they rule in poverty? Writing this book, I will tell you why this is necessary. Any American President, not just Bill Clinton must consider the changes the people in Nigeria are going through. As I mentioned earlier, as a child when I was growing up, it was difficult for my parents to put me into school as a result of hardship. But here I am now! I, who had witnessed the beginnings of resentment for the Bad Dudu regime government and intuitively knew that it was time to leave the doomed country, leave my brothers and sisters behind, because I foresaw the atrocities: thousands of men and women suffering and innocent men and women jailed for life. Therefore, I took great advantage of the opportunities the American people gave me; a college education and a chance to become a writer. However, I still have my people suffering from the hands of a dictator—Bad Dudu. As I write this chapter for this fictional story, I pray constantly for the day Bad Dudu will fall or call for election for my people.

But Anyway, I will confess that based on my recollection before the Americans gave me the chance to become internationally acclaimed, now writing fiction, my uncle, who was barely able to support himself and his wives, put me into school and prior to that I had been shipped around the family tree. Because of the humiliation and suffering, I had once run away from my uncle to live with my niece, Néné, who was also unable to feed herself and her children. When she was finally able to place me in primary five where I'd stopped, I was made a butt of jokes by my classmates who'd enough to eat before coming to school. As a struggling woman, Néné for instance, was noted for her versatile snack preparation around town. Before six in the morning, she'd prepared and fried *akara-balls* made out of black-eyed peas for early risers who go to their farms before the cockcrow. Each akara-ball was prized one kobo, the equivalent of one cent. My duty as a houseboy and a servant was to help Néné to sell the akara-balls to the villagers. I must perform this ritual each morning before going to school. Sometimes, the competition would be so much in town that I could hardly get anyone to buy from me, because consumers would take a look at it and tell me it's too small for the price. To satisfy Néné, I would carry the tray of akara-balls on my head going from door to door shouting at the top of my voice-as an appeal or as a town crier to get people's attention that I was around with akara- balls for them to buy. As a result, I would go late to school.

For that reason my teachers soon became aware of my regular tardiness and warned me on several occasions. One morning, as I walked into the class, my teacher, Miss Getrude, whom I now perceive to have a fake chest, asked everyone in my class to come forward and give me a stroke of the cane on my naked butt. That aside, after the whipping from my classmates, she would asked me to come forward, which I did to avoid more whipping. Facing my classmates, she would asked me to kneel down where I would remained for long hours. As she would finally asked me to go to my seat, and as I would walked to take my seat, I'd to look back for fear of being called back to be whipped.

But one day, Miss Gertrude was glancing through the famous Nigerian Edo Times and she saw a nice bold headline about a child being moved around a family tree in order to survive. And in a way, I thought it might have been me. But I did not feel a twinge of embarrassment. After all, I have been whipped several times and humiliated, and it wasn't going to be the last time.

My teacher, Miss Getrude, seeing the article then bounded on her seat then said some faint words to me as I looked back at her with silent animosity, "Ekiaqueta, I'm very sorry for asking your classmates to give you a stroke of the cane every morning even when I had not been paid for more than nine months as your teacher."

"Don't feel bad. I think I deserve to be . . ." I said with a brief frown and vexation. "Bad Dudu and his in cahoots draining our economy and treasury are the cause of my being late to your class, if you'll pardon my expression," I'd said as I walked to assume my seat in class as usual.

"My sympathies, Ekiaqueta. Would you forgive me?"

As I looked back again, I saw that she was wiping tears from her eyes.

"Forget it," she walked toward me and held me close to her body as if I was her little child. The affection and bondage of a child coming late to school for helping his niece to sell akara-balls to survive could be seen in my teacher's facial expression.

Getrude said, "The Edo Times newspaper I was reading mentioned that Bad Dudu and Babagida and their in cahoots are the brain behind why children are absconding classes, because rather than being in school receiving lectures from their teachers, they have to help their guardians at home selling akara-balls to survive the hardship in the country."

My mouth slipped open as I lowered myself into my chair in the class. But then Miss Getrude stood over my shoulder and placed the paper on my desk as she consoled me to forgive her. It was then my eyes caught the material riches of the junta regimes in Britain, Switzerland, France, Germany and Hawaii. My mind told me that Bad Dudu and his in cahoots were all suddenly in the presence of serious wealth. Like Getrude and everyone else in the country, Getrude knew that Bad Dudu and Babagida had cut every citizen of her country off wealth for their only good.

"I know why you are late to class," she said to me finally. "Why?" Everyone in class glared at her.

"Because you must perform the ritual of helping your guardian every morning to sell akara-balls." She said and finally strutted away to take her seat, while I lamented if I will ever graduate from her class for going to school late selling akara-balls for my niece in the mornings.

* * *

My teachers resenting the ills of the generals who rule Nigeria, some of my fellow classmates soon followed my footsteps of helping their parents and guardians in their farms to toil the land for survival. As a young man who was moved around the family tree circle, there was something truly forbidden of a child: challenging one's guardian. I was truly destined to be literate in life. But because of my tardiness at school and the ridicule from those whose parents were able to clothe them and buy them books, I dropped out of school to devote my attention to full time akara-ball seller for my niece. And still, the days I am unable to perform the usual rituals of helping to sell the akara-balls for her or because I was physically unsound, I was an enemy for days. Here I confess that I never did get to know my natural mother real well who wandered under the hot gamma rays of the sun, toiling hard to earn a living working for people who had money so as to conquer her own abject poverty rooted in her country. I still remember the day of her death: the sun, too, refused to shine because it, too, was perhaps mourning the death of my mother. I know my mother's spirit *now*, is calling on those Generals who did away with Nigeria's wealth and money in her grave before she died through armed robbers who claimed her son in America was rich, sending her dollars to take care of herself. Having no dollars on her the day she was waylaid going to the local market, she was hacked to death with a machete and an ax.

By now, you may have perceived the life I endured, which means that whoever had enough money and food in any given year took me in. After all, in Africa, it takes a whole village to raise a child. When I finally went back to school and finished my elementary school, I was again shipped to join my father's distant relative, a Principal of a Grammar School.

Mr. Odion, may his soul rest in peace. He was a remarkable man of a tall, huge, strong make, and of bold, stern aspect. Always the leader who presides over town meetings and other congregations. He was the one who finally convinced my dad that he would place me in college, what we call a Grammar School in the Third World. Mr. Odion was harsh on me pretty much, bullied and punished me continually. Sometimes two or three times a day. I feared him so much that my bones shrank whenever he arrived from school.

There were moments when I was highly frightened by the terror he inspired daily in my upbringing. Though teachers were highly looked upon as role models during Bad Dudu's days, they too were poor beyond poor. I never ate and be satisfied. I had to run errands for everyone in my compound to stay alive making quick bucks. Sometimes I laugh *now* seeing on television here in America, kids coming forward to testify against their parents for spanking them, which is somewhat an abomination for a child in Nigeria up to this date.

For the record, I hereby challenge American kids to travel to Nigeria or elsewhere in Africa and see how discipline, abuse and caning in schools and homes by our parents and teachers can be. Which reminds me for the sluggish progress of the children growing up and sleeping late and rough doing their homework. I would gladly say I was not an exception sleeping rough because, Mr. Odion wakes me up each weekday morning at six to perform housemaid duties. More often than not, my age groups in America I can *now* see are still under their blankets sleeping because they have everything under their roofs. What else can I say, only to add that they wake up to find new refrgerators and brand new carpets and new computers in their bedrooms. What then would make an American kid not to shine in schools? To my observation since I have been in America, the kids in America certainly have it all. So much of the American kids and discipline in schools in Nigeria and Africa as a whole.

Anyway, going to this then capital of Nigeria, Lagos, was like going to America. The day I left the village to meet my uncle, Aigbedion, was perhaps my happiest day after I graduated from a Grammar School. Aigbedion, too, was a man of no nonsense, a bully, short and quick at slapping his brothers and sisters and even his wife. It was in Lagos I witnessed Mr. Aigbedion almost killed his wife because she was not quick enough to open the door when he'd returned from work. On my arrival to live with him to get me a job in this capital, I soon became his slave in his household.

True enough, Aigbedion was the Human Resource Manager of one of the biggest Iron and Steel Industries in Lagos. When I'd stayed with him for about a year of wasted time cleaning his car in the morning before he goes to work, my instincts told me to think twice. So I got fed up that one afternoon I walked into his office and knocked on his executive office door. I remembered my uncle shouted at the top of his voice saying, "Come on in", thinking maybe an applicant desperately in need of employment was with an envelope containing money to bribe him to gain employment under him. I guess he was greatly disappointed to see me instead. I recalled him asking, "Why are you here?," referring to me.

"I can't stay at home anymore doing nothing except cleaning your car in the morning for which I am not paid. It's either you place me somewhere in Lagos or you give me transportation money to go back to the village to become a skilled thief," I insisted.

My uncle, Aigbedion looked at me and shook his head. Finally he said on the defensive, as if a razor blade had been introduced into his skin by those who hate his guts where he works and earns respect. Then, he walked to his open window and looked at the busy streets of Lagos with millions of people roaming about with no jobs and looked at Dodan Army Depot, which was just down the street. Stories were legions of people who came from the southern part of Nigeria other than from the North who trudged long miles and distances to walk to Lagos were denied employment in offices where military men reign supreme who are Hausas. My uncle himself was denied employment several times until he learned and figured out how to write Arabic and speak Hausa language.

To cut the story short, Aigbedion was a man whom I heard so much about, helped other people not related to him to get them placed up in different employment fields in the capital. But to that remarkable compliments from horse's mouth, my thought was, if my uncle was so influential, why don't he place me with a company that would pay me a good salary? As I write this book, the answer came to my being: the 'Us' and 'Them' syndrome is in built in a typical Nigerian, that is, to say, Nigeria is a diverse country prone to tribalism. Thus, my uncle was lucky to have a job and if he were to give me a job where he was working with the not so bright people, and I, smarter and brighter they might conspire against him and he could lose his job.

And a country rich with natural resources, all the countries in the world want, my country could then have boasted of the best schools, hospitals, and most important, create good jobs for its people. According to statistics, after Bad Dudu ceased power, malaria was unable to be cured by Nigerian doctors because they have no medicines to dispense. Then an outbreak of cholera for the record was said to have killed thousands of people in Bornu because of lack of good water for them to drink. Why would one expect to live his life in a country like that? To me therefore, it is good to follow the footsteps of long ago ancestors and philosophers like St. Francis of Assisi loving his ancestors of five or six centuries ago who mingle not a little emotion and gratitude with love. So if one may hope everything of a child who loves their leaders and guardians who taught them to be responsible and beware, through harsh discipline and encouragement, then they were for the age that loves history and who then had directed me on the right track to write this book. Realizing to be a genius and to succeed in life, I had to put in more effort and struggle on my own, which gave me the idea of coming to America and leaving the zombies behind to destroy the giant country of Africa: Nigeria and its economy.

*　*　*

For the record, I should tell you that Nigeria is non-aligned with the world, though it did have good diplomatic relations with the West when Life Goes On had ruled. It was the era of the Nigerian oil boom. Lest you might not know, the West is Nigeria's major trading partner, buying 40 percent of the country's oil export, the backbone of its National economy.

Two days after I'd made up my mind to go back to the village to become a farmer or become a skilled armed robber, American Embassy in my Capital started to appeal to young scholars to travel to America. Their ads soon filled the airwaves with such slogans as, "Visit the land of perfect freedom."

As I tried to ponder the ads on my mind, Ken Abusche, a friend of mine, stopped by and told me he would soon be going to America. Surprised, I exclaimed, "America?" Then I looked at Ken Abusche, my good friend, and saw the sincerity in his eyes. Though I'd impregnated his sister, leaving her with no money to take care of herself, and finally decided to abort the child for lack of resources to feed the baby when he/she was born, he forgave me and told me we could move ahead and forget the past. However, his father condemned her from the pulpit and a month later, because of the humiliation, she committed suicide. Remembering this incidence, I knelt down and begged Ken Abusche for forgiveness.

On the day Ken visited me to give me the news of going to America, I was fighting hard to fight off the malaria that had gripped me. He noticed then that my fevers had risen and fallen, the chills had hit me like ice in my belly, then faded away. The nausea as I stood with him came unexpectedly in waves. For that reason he'd pitied me and patted my arms and promised me he was not going to leave me behind in Nigeria to die like a chicken. Then he put his hand on my shoulder and looked at me in the eye. With sincerity he said, "Ekiaqueta, you and I have to get out of the poverty in this country. They say Nigeria is the richest country in Africa, but here we are suffering, sick and with no money to buy malaria tablets, High School graduates with no jobs! For years now, we have been roaming the streets in search of employment, employment that is not forthcoming in our favor. All the Ministry jobs in this country are in the hands of Northerners. This is a land of no opportunity for us. No one lives like the way we do in this country as in America."

Listening to Ken, I knew he must've read all kinds of literature about America. For one, Ken is not the type of a person who just talks without meaning or because he just wants to talk. A six-footer who has aspirations in life, finally said with tears in his eyes, "This country we are born into is meant for Generals with camouflage khaki uniforms from the North, my friend. We must've to leave this country. Americans welcome anyone to their country who have high ambitions."

He looked at me again in my condition, sweating, "Think about it, my friend. Are we going to remain in this situation in this country and be tempted to become armed robbers?"

"We can engage in '419' activities," I replied.

"Not a good idea, my friend. We might be caught and our hands might be amputated from our bodies. Look what's going on in this country. Close to a thousand people have died in clashes between Christians and Muslims that began in the Northern city of Kaduna over proposals to introduce the Sharia—that crude law of the Muslims which practices the Hamurabi's Law of taking your limbs and amputating your hands from your body. The violence has since spread to Bornu State. At least 15 people had been slaughtered. Four churches and two mosques had been razed to the ground by fanatics. And last week, the Northern State of Zamfara, the first to introduce a hard line aversion of Sharia, modeled on Saudi Arabia's code, breached an agreement with the Central Government to suspend Islamic Law, then amputated a convicted thief 's right hand. My friend, I don't want to become an armed robber or sleep with a married woman who wants to be laid and my dick would be cut off because of Sharia Law code of the Northerners," Ken explained.

"Are you saying we have no more Federalism type of government any more in this country?" I asked.

"That's basically what I am trying to convey to you, my friend. The State Sharia courts have been committed also to flogging men and women for drinking alcohol and committing adultery. Are you going to stay in this country to witness the medieval acts and human right violations and atrocities?"

Looking at Ken, I said, "It might be a good idea for us/the Southerners to cut the Northerners off for them to practice their own laws."

"That would not solve the problem. The Federalism that bound us together as one Nigeria is now destroyed. This is why you and I will leave for America and leave the Northern oligarchy alone, and the people that made away with our country's oil money to foreign banks making us to think of dubious ways to make a living."

Finally I saw his point. No man in this country is so dumb not to know that. In the Southern part of the country, where the women these days imitate the Western cultural style of fake boobs in their chest, to which my sisters are prime candidates, they might travel to Zamfara and be stoned to death, like Stephen the mytre in history.

So I said to Ken, "All said, man! I wouldn't want my sisters to be stoned to death by Sharia Law. I'll think about the good news of going to America with you."

As Ken left me that evening, my mind was whirring, and transformed that if Ken left me behind in Lagos to go to America, I might become a notorious robber. Sleeping did not come easily for me. But when I finally slept, I felt about as bad as I'd ever felt in my life remembering my parents, of how poor they were. That evening the American Embassy ads again woke me up early, reminding me of Ken's visit the previous day. The premise and phrase of 'Abraham Lincoln' was registered at the back of my mind that poverty for my family was not forever and that, though Bad Dudu and his junta regime had dwindled the economy of Nigeria to a great degree unimaginable, and that among other things, men facing adversity for good or evil as a predicament to conquer, the abject suffering was soon going to be over.

Thus, resenting Bad Dudu and his men in power who rule the giant Nation in Africa and are draining the oil money as fast as they could, making graduates to turn armed robbers on Nigerian roads, I vowed to venture to the American Embassy to obtain a visa together with my buddy, Ken. It was during this struggle in our lives, my life with Ken to travel abroad that I believed in the saying that "For men to love each other truly, they must've shed tears together."

I loved Ken just as much as he loved me. Therefore, our interest to travel to America grew even more that when we come upon anyone with the same ambition, who has not only the interest, but knows some history of the American ways of life, we join in their conversations.

Anyway, we obtained our visas and Ken traveled to America before me. The reason for that, was, his parents were able to rally round to buy him a flight ticket to leave the country.

My parents, on the other hand, were poor beyond poor. They were unable to purchase my travel ticket. Who on Earth does not know that the first duty of the historian is to forget his own time and country, then become the sympathetic and interested contemporary of what he relates? Or that it is difficult to give oneself the heart of a Greek or a Roman because it gives us a heart of the thirteenth century?

I do. So truly enough as I slept, I remembered that my dad had a rubber and palm produce plantations. But, stupidly enough, rather than tapping the rubber myself to sell and be able to raise the money to purchase my travel ticket, I decided to get a job at Ogbemudia Rubber

Processing Plant at Ekewan Road; off Ugbowo Cemetary, where the Royals of Benin cast spells on people they hated their guts.

* * *

At Ogbemudia Rubber Processing Plant, what strikes me first when I'd walked through the plant to seek employment was the foul odor-a thoroughly negative place, so to speak I tell ya!

As the man who would be my boss took me on a tour of the processing plant, I saw men and women hauling wet, hot foam rubber off of conveyor belts on their backs. A job I thought machines should be doing. But truly, Nigeria can afford one hundred machines to do the job with the millions generated from it's natural resources, if not for corruption rooted in Nigerian Generals' veins. Anyway, because most people don't like to do this job, no matter how much they were paid, I was hired right on the spot. Here, I was placed into an entry-level activity. My job then involved that I circle around in wet foam rubber discards, shoveling the cast bits into drying ovens. And it was here I saw Osajie, one of my uncles whom I never knew where he worked. He too, was surprised to see me. I could read his mind that he didn't want me to work in this plant. Though he hugged me, I could read in his expressionless face, a man with a Doctorate Degree working in a place like that. Osajie was a strong man, silent type, too, and like a lot of men around this plant, he didn't waste words. He too, was a man who never liked to ask questions, so I volunteered, "So what are you doing here working with a Ph.D. in this kind of place, a place Bad Dudu should be and you in his executive hot seat?"

He nodded his head, looked at me and said, "Men like us don't argue with men with weapons. *Wan day be wan day. Bad Dudu go get e own with a bullet to e head.*"

Sounds too good to be true. I nodded.

We must have stood for about five minutes when my new boss said to my uncle, "Okay now! Let me take him around to see what we do here. Seeing the way you look now, Ekiaqueta might change his mind about working for me here."

Not at all. I need a job badly, and most importantly, destined to go to America where every man has it all I pondered in my heart, saying nothing in response.

I followed my new boss, but this time with some sense of urgency. Five minutes before, when I saw my uncle, stinking like a dog that fell into a pit latrine, I could have given myself very good odds of getting away without wearing the plant's overalls. Still, my odds were fifty-fifty, and it was a gamble I was willing to take, because in retrospect, when Osajie comes home he uses three buckets of *well* water to bathe. His hands, when he shakes with you, were like torns/rocks. And looking at his face, it appears he was having an odd discoloration. His hands to say the least, were almost white like those of a white man's skin. I will not be surprised if Osajie had told me he shit strange shit from his ass. Truly, why would another man ask another human being to do that work is beyond me.

Anyway, on my first day on the job I was asked to take on the 'Hole'. What a gruesome place?!

I watched the conveyor belt, which was set up to discard tallow dripping through the slits into a basement hollow hole tank. My duty was to keep cleaning up the 'Hole'. Due to the smell, I could've walked out, but I was desperate and happy to get paid to have money to purchase my flight ticket. Nobody, I must admit, knew of my plans. As I would shoveled off the scrap of tallow hot rubber foam from the 'Hole' from the floor, some would drip on my neck. Before I knew it, I had blisters all over my neck. And each time I go to work knowing that I was working in the 'Hole', I would say a silent prayer to God that my face don't look like my uncle's before I travel. God heard my prayers. After a month of doing this gruesome job, and I'd made enough to purchase my ticket, I walked out of the job.

* * *

I finally bought my ticket to travel to America. On the day of my travel, I took the taxi to Lagos International Airport, a port that was similar to Las Vegas strip, where you see people from all over the world during a popular boxing match between two antagonists when boxing fans flood the streets after the fight. Lagos International Airport was like that. Men from all over the country who came to Lagos in search of jobs paraded this port to hustle to support their parents rooted in poverty. Lagos itself was a Capital of pirates. I leave it at that for another story.

But I will remind you though that these hustlers, whether in khaki camouflage uniforms or on civilian clothes, could tell who was travelling out of Nigeria and who wasn't. In Lagos Airport, it was the customary rule of the men and women to believe that bribery was morally acceptable for one to get through the day without trouble. For instance, everyone bribes the police, the soldiers, the yellow fevers who control the jammed traffic and even those who help to bear the burden of carrying your luggage.

My concern here is what are the Americans doing to halt the suffering and corruption of the most populous country in Africa? Hear me out. As a young man who'd just graduated from a Grammar School desperate to leave his country, what do I know? I do know that Ed Bradley and Morely Shafer, both of 60 Minutes, had done their best to expose the nature of bribery and corruption in Lagos Port. More graces to their elbow. Here, I confess that they should do more to expose those in power. I mean the Generals themselves who siphon my Nation's money to Swiss and other thousands of banks across the globe.

As a young man, and as far as I was concerned, after I graduated from Grammar School, I'd believed bribery was good and perfectly legal, as it was the customary legacy left behind by the Colonial masters: the Britishman for my country.

Here is the truth, that when I got to the Airport, I was approached by custom men who scrutinized my luggage and documents, who pretended to be doing their jobs. In real life, they were hustlers. They demanded I open my luggage, which I did.

"And why?" I asked.

The three custom officers who then had surrounded me all frowned. One of them said, "We are having high class smuggling these days in this Airport and it's starting to get worse. Quiet men like you, who are not carefully searched, are those who go to America with cocaine, crank and hard drugs, to give our country a bad name."

His accusation quickly dumbfounded me. Here I thought anyway that my country already had a bad name because of Bad Dudu and his ruling oligarchy, including these three custom officers who'd surrounded me. But then I stifled my impulse to maintain my anger.

"I beg your pardon?" I'd managed to say. "Open the box," another had yelled at me.

I can tell you I was boiling that finally I'd said, "The nature of crimes and criminals has skyrocketed since Bad Dudu and his junta regime assumed power by motars and canons, and I bet the customs and Bad Dudu's men at this Airport will never change their ways of collecting bribes from the poor men and poor women of this country."

They ain't no fools not to know that I knew what's up. So they let me loose. But as I got closer to the departure gate, I was yet again engulfed by other plainclothes security men, so that I could only see the jet within a short distance from where we stood, but couldn't cross the geese with their flippant tone of voices. One of them, wearing a shapeless suit and a turtleneck, came up to me and tapped me on the shoulder. *"Ah! Oga, we have some problems."* "What kind of problem are we talking about, now?" I'd asked calmly.

"The visa, the passport, health card, please."

"Okay. My plane is taking off in a few seconds," I informed him. "Deaf ears."

My common sense told me that I should grease their palms, otherwise I would be delayed. But at second thought, I thought about my hard-earned money from the rubber processing plant barely enough for my pocket money. How to squeeze out a few of the dollars for bribery was the question.

So I stood there like a zombie, dumbfounded, which was a stupid move. But finally, I gave the nosy man my documents for travel. He looked at it and passed it on to the next man beside him. My passport, thus, was exchanging hands with men I don't even know who they were, only that I'd then figured they were after my money. As you can put it nicely: bribing them.

Anyway, my passport with the visa had exchanged hands with the fifth man when one of them opposite me motioned to me and with his right eye blinked. I wasn't that dumb enough not to know what he meant. After a few seconds, the man reminisced a little about the people I was going to join in America.

He'd said, "By the time you come back to Nigeria, you'll surely be a Yankee."

I ignored his comment, but fished out a fifty dollar bill which I'd bought from the black market from Bad Dudu's own men whose only job at the gate of the Doddan Army Barracks was selling currencies of all denominations to tavelers who are fortune seekers. The plainclothes man grabbed the money with impunity and said to the others, "Let him go. He's just another of those High School graduates going to America to wash dishes for the white man, where they would eventually teach him how to eat hamburgers rather than cracking the bones in this country."

What a mockery, I thought. "I wish I could import hamburgers for the entire population who'd nowhere to turn," I said jokingly too to him.

Then he handed me my passport. "Run and catch your flight," Idolo said to me.

I looked at him with silent hatred. I never thought the man would be a complete idiot, but neither did I think I'd hear words such as, "Have a *save* journey." For he'd forgotten the pronunciation of, 'Safe journey', after he'd pocketed my fifty dollar bill.

Chapter

7

....

Saturday morning dawned bright and clear from harmattan haze. Adam Khan woke up early from the fifteenth floor of the Dupe and Ruined Nation Hotel and walked a few distances around the hotel. He came in and got dressed, then had a cup of coffee, while he tried to decide what good road to take to Edo, Benin, Irrua, Zuma Memorial Hospital to see his bosom friend.

Talking about Irrua where his mind directed him to travel first, I too had spent most of my life in Irrua where I learnt how to deal with abject poverty, that if one was not rich, one was doomed to be poor beyond poor. It was the city where I'd read the most weirdest shit I could find in the garbage walking and combing the compound of Zuma Memorial Hospital at Irrua where I grew up with Peter, Daniel, Hidiamen, Himire and some orphans like Betty, Marie and others I can't recall their names. To be real to the point, it pains the fuck out of me sometimes in a beautiful way to think that I learned, figured out, studied a bunch of garbage from papers thrown away by the nurses who'd came from far away from different parts of the country to study at Zuma Memorial Hospital where Doctor Okojie was their lord of course.

And say, for instance, you put Irrua on the map of Nigeria! I would say put Irrua to its knees! Probably yes, but I imagine Adam Khan could get the Nation's attention of how bad this road leading to this little town was. The Nigerian Government ruled by zombies with camouflage khaki uniforms should be able to lure American business, if only because it has vast expanse of land, uncrowded, clean and inexpensive that rich businessmen and Bad Dudu and Babagida both Generals who looted

Nigerian treasury can afford to come in and build industries. Nigerians know that and they won't for the heck of it argue with me on it. I grew up there and got back often to visit the people I left behind in poverty. The rich Generals beside Bad Dudu and Babagida who stole our money could have been able to lure business into this countryside during Bad Dudu's regime or any other regime of the oligarchies. Lots of vast lands being it from Bornu, Kaduna, Mbieri, Irrua, Ogoni and so on, have all been a huge economic neglect-but the average houses here are huts and corrugated zinc homes unfinished. The roads are an abomination and the history and natural beauty of these areas are under daily neglect and assault by Shell BP and the sprawl reaches from Bornu, Irrua, Warri, Ewu and Ogoni of the Nation where mostly the environment has been assaulted day in and day out by crude oil prospectors Bad Dudu knew about.

Those under Bad Dudu consider it progress. My point, though, is that if you're among those who believe the Nation's money should be invested in Nigeria, these expanses of land in Nigeria could be used for industries to employ graduates who have turned armed robbers on Nigerian roads.

Anyway, Adam Khan continued to stroll. Ten years of his absence since he had last visited these places for contracts had turned him into a complete stranger. Brick homes, tharch homes, roads similar to dirt track still remained to be where he'd left the towns, the cities ten years ago. There had not been new development, no progress, government projects abandoned as a result of financial chaos, the ruling junta regime of Bad Dudu claimed they had no money to complete. Beside these bad roads and abandoned government projects, are coffin shops operated by those who are poor beyond poor, hoping to hear the wailing of death, of natural, accident, or mayhem or by a hole in the head from armed robbers.

Adam Khan summed up the courage to meet one of the shopkeepers who operated the coffin shops. He said, "You seem to have too many coffins in your shop. Why is that?"

The old man, with veins and marks making a statement on his forehead, looked at Adam Khan and noticed that he was dressed very neatly from the rest of the people in his country and beside he was like an Arab man. He said to Adam, "My son, there are now more deaths not only in this town, but in the entire country, than one can imagine in any country in Africa that doesn't have oil, but farming. Four days ago, Anini and his men raided a bank down the street and shot ten people who died on the spot. Benin, Irrua and the Nation at large has revisited Mighty Joe and Oyenusi, the two great notorious armed robbers Nigeria had produced. I tell you, my son, hunger claims the majority of us, too. You can see my condition. My days are numbered. Can't you see my gaunt face and bony skin?"

Adam Khan sympathized greatly with him and then tossed him a twenty-dollar bill before he bade him goodbye noting that the entire street of coffin makers would've engulf him if they'd seen him tossed the bill. Quickly, he headed to the hospital of his destination.

In the still of the day, not many vendors this early morning, as crush of humanity had filled the air. The passage through which Adam Khan walked was lined with the darkest of dark people on the earth's surface the sun had baked to charcoal. In short, Adam Khan could read inscriptions on their foreheads: like, please, I'm dying of hunger, please help me out with a kobo, a dime, a nickel. Adam had watched and noted with keen interest that everyone before him learned to dress cheaply because of inflation. He also noted that the patients before him lining up in the brick hospital had all waited for favors from the gaunt-faced clerks themselves. And that even the clerks, too, learned to avoided eye contact of their friends, but only to worshipped their files in their hands as they rushed by everyone. In Benin, Irrua and elsewhere in the Nation, even before Adam left ten years ago to resurface again when Bad Dudu had seized power, the lines of sick patients never seemed to move. That was the case this beautiful morning at the University Teaching Hospital, Benin (UBTH). Only that the lines became much more longer when Dudu ceased power.

Adam Khan had seen children who wailed and sucked. Women who sagged. Men who swallowed saliva and pain, and curses but to wonder why the ruling juntas were wicked to the nation's men and women and corrupt without explanation, and yet there would be no more answers in the next eight more hours, only to stare aimlessly at their crying children, the walls and the red soil on which they stood. And the drizzle this morning was not very sympathetic to the men and women and their children, to say the least.

Finally, Adam Khan sought refuge at the nearest kiosk owned by someone he knew during Life Goes On when he was first awarded the biggest contract to build the prison that now houses millions of graduates who had turned '419' crooks and armed robbers on the streets of Nigeria. Unfortunately, his friend had gone out, so there was not many questions jamming answers why he was in the country.

As the drizzle had ceased, Adam bade goodbye to the preening young woman in the kiosk. And before bading her goodbye he said, "Inform Jerry that Adam Khan is in the country." "I'll surely do that," the young woman had said.

As Adam walked along he observed that more children twisted and tugged and struggled against weary mothers and their fathers' arms, breaking away for precious moments of freedom before they are dragged back into their arms. Even so, the multitude had began to grow as 9 A.M. had snapped. Then more gaunt, thin, sunken, bald, painted frustration of faces in gaunt dark beyond dark men of humanity, stood patiently, heartbreakingly, compliant.

Occassionally sharp words in tribal tongues muffled above the loud noises of the clerks who refute ties as alien to those who'd not the least an option of how long before they would see a doctor than to wait and get treatment for whatever their illness was. When the stone-faced clerks' eyes jammed their counterparts, they smile occasionally if they understood their counterparts tribal tongue, but sharp rebuke when the tribal language was different from his/ hers to understand, cursing as a result. Adam watched as one stone- face clerk asked a man with ancient tribal designated face to shut- up for no apparent reason and then told him, *"Go si dawn."*

The man with the tribal marks and the clerk exchanged a few insulting words with themselves. With much vibrating mouth of more insults to the clerk he called on the police on duty to take him away. Adam watched as the policeman took his arm then walked him to the end of the que where he might not be attended to by a doctor for the day. Looking at the scenario, Adam shook his head.

Adam Khan walked on. The smell of antiseptic, seclopin, streptomycin, and more, the septic smell from boiling syringes combined with bodies in humanity had assaulted his senses. Jesus Christ! Something never changed all these years of my absence, he wondered and murmured to himself.

But Adam Khan had, after being gone for ten years and living an expensive life in Lebanon and sometimes in America with the loot of millions of dollars he had made from the zombies in power. He could afford to take his bath and stay in the most expensive hotels, when the people in Benin, Irrua, Bornu, Sokoto, Owerri, Ondo, Oyo, cannot afford to buy bar soaps to take their baths.

Anyway, Adam Khan walked through the crowd. And as he got to the elevator, a man in police uniform, still navy blue, as usual, and wearing an ugly hat, a legacy of the Colonial Masters Administration, stepped out of nowhere to block his way. He was thin with wrinkles of high drama and problems written all over his face. His shoes had all worn out too. Adam Khan could see, or imagined that the navy-blue pant had counted over 20 years. The navy blue had turned navy yellow where the iron had inscribed its own remarks: I'm British made. When Adam first arrived ten years ago, he'd applied to get the contract to sew new uniforms for the Nigerian Police Force. For some reason he was late filing his application with Bad Dudu's right hand man at the time and so he lost the contract.

The policeman looked at Adam Khan and shook his head. Finally he said to him, *"Where you dey go Oga?"*

"I'm here to see my friend, Dr. Peter Aburime to negotiate a contract with him to purchase new gadgets for this hospital."

"Well! Dr. Aburime did not tell me he's expecting anyone." "Must Dr. Aburime inform you that someone was coming to see him before you allow them in?"

The policeman, with his rifle, did not answer. So Adam said, "I am Mr. Adam Khan from Lebanon. I know my way around here in this country. I came from the United States a few days ago where I now live hearing the news of Bad Dudu taking over your Government and to see my friend Ekiaqueta's mother, who was shot by armed robbers. And most importantly to survey your city, this city, to know where the roads are worse to repair so I can put in my application for the contract to fix it. Also I have a letter from Ekiaqueta to be delivered to Dr. Peter Aburime for Efemona, the woman Ekiaqueta wants to marry. In short, Ekiaqueta, my friend, has married this woman in absentia. Dr. Aburime knows the girl well."

As the policeman heard Adam mention the United States, he engaged him in a friendly conversation. "Did you say you came into this country when Life Goes On was in power? Well, Benin City is no longer what it used to be. Hum! It is you people from abroad we here in Nigeria are now looking up to these days. Everybody is struggling to eat one meal a day, that is, if they have the money to buy what they want to eat."

The policeman did not even feel sorry for Ekiaqueta, whose mother was hacked to death by armed robbers, or maybe he didn't hear Adam Khan's explanation. So Adam repeated, "Oh! That must be the reason armed robbers outnumber the struggling men and market women of this city-your city-to murder innocent people in cold blood."

"Oga, I no do-am. Who do-am God go punish am well, well."

The policeman looked at Adam as he racked his brains out to engage him with more questions than answers to see if he could draw his attention to see his pain and suffering. Without being told, Adam knew he needed sympathy more than Ekiaqueta who was about to lose his dear mother. After all, let those alive eat bread and those who are dead to bury their own heads was what the policeman was thinking. He, the policeman, desperately needed reward of the dollar from a man from the United States, because the dollar was now the object of worship as God.

Adam evaded all his requests. Finally, he asked Adam, *"Oga, you get ID card?"*

"Ah! Common, you and I know Nigerians don't have ID in this country. Since when have your government given ID's to the people to carry in their wallets?" Adam joked.

Adam did not want to prolong the conversation any longer. Then he brought out his billfold. The policeman could see the dollar bills. Adam then brought out his Nevada Driver's License. The policeman took it, looked at it for a few seconds and then he said, "The immigration officers in this country didn't give you an ID before you entered this country? *This ID no be Nigeria ID. You get Nigeria own?*"

Adam fished out another ID. This time UBTH's, which he'd used to obtain the contract to build the University of Benin Teaching Hospital when Life Goes On was in power. The policeman looked at Adam and the ID again. "It doesn't look like your face." He looked at Adam again, "When did you take this picture?

It's been a long time this Teaching Hospital was built. We no longer use black and white ID here. *Color ID cards are what we use here now, Oga.*"

Adam concealed his anger and said, "Sir! Asemota studios took the picture ID ten years ago when I built this University Teaching Hospital."

The policeman had changed completely and did not want to listen to Adam any more what he'd to say. As a matter of fact, Adam had the urge to ignore the policeman and walk his way in to go to his destination. But then Adam realized that he could be shot while the policeman identified him as an armed robber. So he changed his mind. But if Adam had decided to take a chance to walk to his destination, the policeman had no walkie-talkie as it was still an alien concept instrument despite the billions the country had made selling its crude oil to the United States and Britain. However, the policeman did have a British rifle, which of course, was lying beside his chair he'd sat on and even forgotten he'd one when he engaged Adam in conversation. Anyone could've walked away with the rifle. Finally, Adam said, "It seems to me that things had tightened up a bit, since I left this country ten years ago."

Fell on his deaf ears. His face became more gaunt. Finally, the policeman said, "Ah! Bad Dudu and his junta regime are the only people enjoying the nation's wealth. *This ID wey you show me dawn baje my brother. I mean e—no good again.*"

Adam Khan knew technically the policeman was right. It was clear to Adam as he, too, understood how the system functions even though he'd been away from the country for ten years. Again the policeman frowned and pocketed the black and white ID card. Two wrongs don't make a right. So Adam said, "My friend, what seems to be the matter now, pocketing my ID card which is still alien to your leaders in this country?"

Now you know of course that Adam Khan understood the Queen's English more than Nigerians. The policeman said, *"You need another wan, my friend. I'll tell you wetin you go do if you give me something."*

Somehow the policeman noticed Adam was not listening to him anymore, so he repeated in English, "You need another one. I'll tell you what you can do if you give me something, sir."

The policeman had entered another phase of the conversation. The 'something' he doesn't want to hint on directly was of course money. Adam said, "Okay. I'll give you something if you tell me what I can do to get another ID now and when I see my friend Dr. Peter Aburime as soon as possible," Adam answered knowing others of his type would be asking him to produce an ID when he visited places he hasn't been for ten years of his absence.

Adam Khan condescended a little. "Awrite. What something are we talking about?"

Adam knew what the policeman was after. It was all about a bribe. In truth, it was cheaper to give him the money rather than have his ID taken before he could cross his path to go and see his friend. Then Adam gave him an option. "Don't you think it would be better to give you the money than to pay someone else to have my picture ID taken?"

He kept mute, but looking at everyone in the line to make sure he doesn't have to shout. Adam changed the subject and said, "If I decide to have my picture taken, how long would I wait before I get it?"

"It depends, *Oga*. You have been in this country several times before. You know what to do. With a man like you standing out in the crowd-flesh on your bones-who cares how many people are ahead of you? This is a country where corruption and bribery is rooted in our blood."

Adam thought of that for a few seconds. He knew the policeman was right. The policeman looked away. Anyway, Adam said, "I have a lot of appointments to keep today, but I must first of all see Dr. Aburime. If you let me in, on my way out, I'll take care of the ID *shit*, my friend."

"We don't eat shit in this country. We might be hungry . . .," the policeman rebuked him.

Then he inhaled on his British 555 cigarette, then saw the line that was growing longer and longer each minute he interrogates Adam and Adam engages him in the never ending conversation. But after several minutes of the conversation that was yielding no promising fruit from Adam Khan, he saw a child playing with his rifle he'd abandoned for several minutes. "Excuse me, Sir," the policeman said.

He left Adam and walked towards the mother of the child. Doing that Adam didn't want to offend him and walk to Dr. Aburime's office. He waited for him. He watched the policeman send the mother and her son way behind the last person in line. As he came back, Adam expected him to smile and change his mind to let him in. He engaged Adam with more conversation, but breathing heavily after he scolded the woman and her son, smoking and expelling more smoke from his nostrils.

"I'm really surprised," Adam said, "Since when did this ID stuff come into use in this country?" Has the government of Bad Dudu finally seen the need for ID's or what?" Then Adam frowned. "Look Mr. I am really pressed for time. I'm here on a special assignment to expose corrupt men and women working in this hospital accepting bribes from sick patients before they are treated."

The policeman laughed a mocking laugh.

Adam, realizing that bribery is a way of life in Nigeria and the policeman was unmoved, he said, "How about if you give me a visitor's ID card and I'll give you something, my friend?"

"Now you're talking, my friend! Sounds good to me."

The future, the policeman saw fit was looking tentative. He looked at Adam and smiled, "Who did you say you came to see?" "My friend, Dr. Aburime," Adam said, mentioning not all other appointments he may have had to keep.

"Okay, print your name here" he instructed Adam then opened up the visitor's register for him to sign in. The register, to Adam in itself looked older than the hospital. As the policeman had opened it, the fan blew off two sheets. Who cares? He didn't go after them, but rather watched Adam Khan with his gaunt red-eyed instincts and sighed deeply. Adam knew he wanted to ask him where's the money. But Adam said, "Follow me and show me Dr. Aburime's office."

He walked with Adam and for the first time he noticed what Adam was wearing. A pair of Levi jeans and a T-shirt which bears the inscription, "What part of no don't you understand?" on the front and on the back was "screw all Bad Dudu's junta regime government men and women who don't believe in Swiss banks."

As they walked and strolled, Adam asked, "Lots of crimes these days, huh? In Benin or . . . ?"

"Yes. Anini and his forty thieves are terrorizing this city and some parts of this country. They are killing people indiscriminately. Anini could walk into this hospital unnoticed and rob it without being caught."

They both walked together on a long hallway where Adam must've counted several numbers of more doors left and right until the policeman pointed to the office of Dr. Peter Aburime. *Now* he'd remembered he'd a rifle lying down by his security post so he said, *"Oga, I dey hungry well, well. I never eat anything since yesterday."* Adam realized that was probably the reason his face was so gaunt to look at. He had sympathy and finally he reached into his breast pocket and fished out a fifty-dollar bill and handed it to him. He thanked Adam and blessed his family, then cursed who ever hacked my mother to death Adam had told him.

As they parted, two female orderlies were pushing towards him in his front a gurney with a young man who'd just been run over by a Lexus and the man had suffered severe head and neck injuries. The orderlies, young, probably around twenties with braided hairstyles, were good looking, too. At least Adam was proud of them. Both had manners. They were neat and polite. They'd Ukpenu style of respect for their elders. They looked at Adam and greeted him with Benin language, *"Do—o—mon, Sir."*

Adam nodded his head and replied, *"Koyor."*

They pushed the gurney past him and Adam Khan watched as they settled the youngman at the passage where he would remain throughout his agony.

As Adam thought of the way this young man will eventually die, an elderly man, whom Adam presumed was literate, walked by and shook his head. He couldn't help but voice out, "In Libya, Kuwait, Saudi Arabia, it is no problem. Those countries also export oil and have used their sales to equip private hospitals and government hospitals. Even, they used their money to irrigate their deserts to make the soil humid and fertile for growing food crops for their people. This young man could've lived if he'd been transported to Libya, Kuwait, or Saudi Arabia."

Adam Khan wanted to engage him in a conversation, but the elderly man had walked away faster than Adam could now walk. Adam became surprised that the two young doctors who'd came to inspect the youngman in the passage ridiculed the dangling neck, flipped it left and right and then debated with themselves. The youngman was bleeding terribly *now*. Can't they do something to stop his bleeding? Adam thought. Their actions became more repulsive to Adam. One of the doctors said to his buddy, *"Oh boy, you think sey dis one go make 'am?"*

"Ah! This one dan go to yonder. Make we just leave am jare."

His buddy, Moses nodded. "There's nothing we can do for him, I suppose"Moses said.

Mike shook his head. "Nothing. It won't be long. He's dead already. His pulse is already out. You feel it. Remember, our operating room has not been equipped since the Britishman handed us independence in 1960? Today is the twenty-fifth. I still haven't heard anything about the gadgets I ordered from England. It's been five years now. We need an MRI scanning machine for this type of injury. Look at his head and jawbone! They are broken. What else can I say? Look at a fine youngman, was a healthy- looking man. Probably never had a day's illness in his life. He might be hungry since he came back from Brazil to this country a few months ago. Now he's here to die a painful and slow death. Look at this! I'm sorry for him but . . . ! This accident smelled a sudden death to him. It is the country we live in man!" he said, looking at Adam.

"Just can't disguise his face, beautiful face with brown eyes. A man who I saw at the disco last night at the City Belles, enjoying himself with women as his friends were dancing. He even declared twelve bottles of Star beer on my table. *Now* he's dying a painful and slow death in his country because of lack of equipment to save his life in a country that is very rich in mineral ore talkless of crude oil too."

Mike flipped his head left and right. Again and again. Adam noticed the jerry curls oily sheen hair had just been retouched in a nearby salon, beard and mustache well trimmed, broad nose, masculine jaw, very white set of teeth just showing through his wide parted lips, with slim, masculine shoulders and long hands.

Mike looked at Moses. "Moses," he said, "You know what I just discovered about this youngman? He's an athlete. You can tell from his stout long legs and perhaps he was a draft for the Brazilian soccer team." He raised his left hand and then his right legs, then dropped them causally.

Moses shuddered and brought his head up again close to his face, flipped it to the right and then to the left and he said, "Take note, Mike, that he has an attractive face, humorous, determined to live but-no medicine to dispense even if we perform the operation."

The youngman, he thought, was probably from Irrua. Before Mike could write down any more history, as Moses flipped his head again to the left, the eyelid dropped. "I told you he won't make it," Moses said.

Adam watched in horror and awe, when the doctors in Nigeria will even learn to try to save lives even without gadgets to help treat ailing patients to live. As the doctor walked away, Adam followed and tapped one of them on his shoulder. He introduced himself. He asked Moses some provoking questions, which Moses could answer without much thinking. Moses looked at Adam with a baffled face, "The money this country has is being siphoned to Britain and the Cayman Islands by the zombies with khaki uniforms who hail from the Northern most part of this country." Adam wanted to say something, but Moses pressed on. "The super powers should come quickly to take everyone to heaven with nuclear bombs, but leave one newborn male and female, one from every tribe of this country, and take them to America, not Britain, and train them to be clean citizens when they grow up to become adults." *He meant that would end corruption in his country.*

Mike concurred with Moses and said to Adam, "The rich men of this country go to overseas for regular checkups when they are sick because they have all the ill-gotten wealth stacked up in foreign banks, especially in Britain, Switzerland and the Cayman Islands. They look down on us as if we are not trained doctors.

Who cares if a poor man dies in this country? All the hospitals are empty of modern equipment."

Adam saw their point. They walked side by side until they parted. Another few more strides to Dr. Aburime's office was the outpatient which was now filled with hundreds of people. Adam saw in amazement, sneezes and bad coughing, tiny people waiting to get treatment for TB's.

Adam Khan got through, past the matron's office where he saw in Hausa language: be as healthy as Babagida, Adamu, Abacha and Abubakar Adul Salami. Slightly above these huge posters of these leaders, were the state vaccination regulations of chicken pox for children, just say no to drugs and be like Mutombo. Adam wondered why not Aikeem Olajuwon. Instincts told him Aikeem was not helping his people, that is, he was not bringing all the millions he's paid playing basketball to survive in America to Nigeria. They'd wished he brought the millions to his country to build ultra modern hospitals, modern mosques as Mutombo did in his country, Uganda.

Across from the matron's office Adam noted were dilapidated wooden cupboards filled with files. The files on top of the cupboards were more than the files inside. Adam noticed nurses and orderlies alike exchanged words and searched the wooden cupboards and drawers for patients' files. Patients and their children hurry past others to the pharmacy to collect their prescriptions after seeing a doctor. Adam noticed that prescriptions were never available in the pharmacy except at private hands or private clinics, and private chemists. What a country, Adam murmured to himself.

Adam finally got to Dr. Aburime's office-which was a door left to the matron's office. His office was well above average, well decorated with Western posters of medicine and anatomy of the body. His room was huge, about fifteen by twenty, filled also with Western books of literature, history, magazines, physics, chemistry, biology, philosophy and politics. His chair was ultra modern in style, similar to those of CEOs in America.

Adam noticed a difference right away as he walked in between a 'being to' and a Nigerian educated doctor. Everything about 'being to's' is that they stand out among others in their homelands. Dr. Aburime sat on his seat talking to one of his friends who'd been food poisoned by his wife and then ran away with his three children to join their family who had moved to Portharcourt where they couldn't trace her whereabouts by the erring husband's family if he survived. Peter had on black slacks made of wool and a white shirt with black stripe lines. When Adam walked in Peter didn't notice at first. But when he looked up, saw Adam, he put down his writing materials, smiled and stood up, shouted, "Adam Khan" in amazement.

"I knew someone walked in but never thought it was you. I thought it was one of my nurses."

"First of all, I'm sorry to inform you that one of my good friends, Ekiaqueta, also known as What Can I Say, lost his mother to the armed robbers of this country. The poor, helpless woman suffered a great deal in her life for nothing. Even the sun refused to shine on the day of her funeral. It, too, seemed to mourn her, knowing that she spent all her life under its hot rays, working the land to survive."

Adam thanked Dr. Aburime graciously for all he did for her during her burial. Then Adam added, "I thought it was important I see you to hand over a letter Ekiaqueta has for his wife, Efemona. Learnt he has married her in absentia because his father arranged it."

Peter nodded. Then he said, "I knew you were coming, but I wasn't told when. My wife just briefed me that you called to say you have business to transact with the Generals of this country. By the way, when did you arrive?"

"Three days ago."

Adam looked at his puffy cheeks. Aburime had gained an enormous amount of weight. Time had not told much on him despite he was close to fifty. "What kind of business are you in *now* that makes you unable to communicate or call me?"

Adam apologized. "You know how things are in America. The bills never get paid. So I was devoted to working nine to five, man, when I'd lost all the money I'd made from the Generals of this country gambling in Las Vegas and Reno, Nevada."

Dr. Aburime cracked up and looked at Adam. "You are right. I know how it is. By the way, what can I get you to drink? So! You have come to make more from the zombies?

"What do you think?"

Finally, Peter motioned Adam to sit down.

"It seems to me you're doing just great, man! Look at all the gold you have on! I'm sure you have some stuck in your damned ass!" Adam teased Peter.

Peter cracked up and motioned him again to the beautiful chair facing him made out of an iroko tree. By the side of the chair was a small end table with a Western lamp. And dangling proportional above it was a basket full of magazines with books, which hadn't been dusted for quite some time. Adam said, "Red dust hangs tough in these magazines, my friend."

Peter yelled out on top of his voice-to alert the attention of a nurse passing by. Justina was the first to walk in, in response.

"Please take down that basket containing magazines and clean them for me," Peter said.

And as Justina took down the basket to clean the magazines and books to glance through, Adam took one of the books. Unfortunately, the hard cover had been ripped off. As Adam flipped through the pages, he noticed it was George Orwell's Animal Farm which then quickly had refreshed his memories of his High School days.

"Hum! George Orwell again," Adam echoed. In a few minutes, Justina came back with the basket with the rest of the magazines and books. Peter said, "Put them aside for now. I'll put them where they belong later." Then he flicked Adam a glance, but spoke to Justina, who asked, "Am I being helpful today, Dr. Pitt?" Justina's voice took on the assuring, slightly patronizing tone of an overworked nurse trying to chat with Peter's name. Then she said, "I believe Piiiitt is taking me out to dinner tonight," she stretched Peter's name in several syllabi.

"See me later, Justina. I have a visitor right now from America." Justina smiled and walked away. Then Adam looked at her butt and salivated as Justine was walking out.

Peter and Adam chatted about Orwell's Animal Farm then agreed he was one of the greatest writers of all time.

Dr. Peter Aburime finally sat on his executive chair facing Adam Khan and laughed aloud each time Adam shot him a question or complimented him. "You look terrific, man."

Another big crack up, as if he thought he was being cajoled by Adam. Or won't you be quiet or give me a break? But anyway he accepted the compliment and said, "You too, Adam. Have you been making money through the wire services from the zombie rulers of this country?"

"Last year I made $5 billion dollars just by carrying briefcases for Bad Dudu's wife travelling to Lebanon every two or three days." Standing again and rearranging his table, Adam told him what he encountered with on his way to see him with the policeman. In reality it was not a new thing to him. *"I know. Since e-si sey you look different e-wan some thing for e-pocket. You chop I chop is the answer to everything we do here in this country. At least that's the philosophy of Bad Dudu's regime."*

"You're right. I gave him a fifty dollar bill," Adam said.

Dr. Peter looked at Adam Khan and smiled. "You made his day. He'll probably not show up for the next three months to work. This country is now a jungle. Only the strong survive these days. But ironically, no strong men again to challenge Bad Dudu. They have all been wiped out by Dudu."

Adam already knew that of course. He didn't need the Creator to come down to tell him to believe. He looked up. "Oh! I almost forgot. Did you receive the message I sent you that Sunny was shot a few days ago and he's now in a private hospital? Did you inform his brother?"

"Sunny who?"

"The son of Ojie. Ekiaqueta's immediate junior."

"What? You're kidding me. Did the armed robbers of this country have a vendetta against Ekiaqueta's family? Take me there now if you are not too busy."

Dr. Aburime took his keys. As they both walked towards the door, Adam looked back and read once again a sign on Aburime's table that read, "A clean desk is a sign of a sick mind."

They walked together in silence and finally Peter said, "Sunny was robbed two days ago. The armed bandits had shot him in the chest and took his 504 peugeot, leaving him to die in his own blood." They exited the gate, walked through the parking lot and Peter found his car. "Glad the damned theives around here had not broken into my car," he told Adam.

"He opened the door for Adam and Adam took his seat. He drove fast and in a few minutes they arrived at Isirame Memorial Hospital on 8 Idebiri Lane.

The hospital could only be approached by passing through a steel gate and then undergoing the scrutiny of security men in police uniforms with rifles lying beside where they sat.

They passed the first security man with ease, who had small flesh on his bones, but was drunk. The hospital itself was named after Peter's uncle which ran through the North end of Idibiri Lane beside Benin roundabout.

Magarette, who had stood waiting for Peter's arrival to help carry his attaché case to his office, looked up from her shoulder and saw Adam Khan.

Peter Aburime said to her, "Where is Maetu?" Then he groped for his stethoscope behind the back seat in the car. Then Peter said, "Have you notified or sent messages to Irrua to Sunny's family?" Magarette nodded.

"Yes Maetu, and her mother and father are on their way. I reached Adam Khan, a good friend of Ekiaqueta, myself. He flew in a couple of days ago, not for this present situation, but to deliver a letter for me for Efemona."

"And did you get him?"

He looked at Adam as if to say, introduce yourself, man. Then he looked at Magarette, rewarding her with a beautiful smile. "This is Adam Khan standing before you."

She hugged Adam and tears dropped from her eyes.

As they all walked along, a long time good friend spotted Adam with Aburime and shouted, "Adam Khan!"

Dr. Aburime and Magarette excused themselves and walked into the ward with ease to give Sunny attention with other doctors already attending to him.

"When did you arrive?" Daniel asked Adam.

"Three days ago, after I was notified this country has a new leader and my friend's mother was robbed and in critical condition. Here I am. My friend's brother's faith lies in the hands of armed robbers of this country in critical condition again. He's been shot in the chest," Adam told him.

"C'mon, I'll go with you," Daniel said.

As they walked together, a policeman again from nowhere jumped in front of them. *"Yes sir, where una dey go?,"* the policeman said.

"I'm here to see my bosom friend's dying brother on admission, shot two days ago by the armed robbers of your country," he mocked. In reality, Adam is a party to why armed robbers have emerged in great capacity in the country.

"You can go in. When you come out Oga, you give me something," the policeman said.

"No problem," Adam said.

Daniel's jaw dropped in surprise. Jesus Christ! He caught his eyes in the policeman's face, showed him a disapproving grimace and said, "Somebody's friend is dying in the hospital bed and you are asking for something? What a city we live in these days."

Adam Khan echoed silently in his heart. My friend's family is getting used to living in the hospital bed. They have all their families driven out of their homes and shot at.

Daniel, still mad at the mere words of the policeman, looked at Adam and said, "This city is getting worse every day."

The policeman with his rifle said, "Somebody dies, somebody is born."

Adam wasn't angry because he was desperate to see my brother alive. As they walked in, members of my family were already there in the hospital. They all watched silently as more physicians rushed to join Aburime in the operating room when Sunny's condition had worsened from stable to critical.

Adam Khan silently prayed in Lebanese language for Allah to forgive him for being a party wrecking the Nation's treasury in cahoots with the junta's regime. At the same time he prayed to let Sunny live. He caught one of the doctor's arms as he emerged to break through the crowd where Adam and Daniel stood with other patients thinking their own faith. "Can I at least see Sunny to know how serious his condition has been to inform his brother in America?" he asked and brought out his cell phone from his breast pocket.

"Are you a relative?," the doctor had asked sympathetically. "A good friend of the family over the years," Adam replied. The doctor drew Adam aside. "It's not a pretty sight, my friend.

I have been busy with other doctors since yesterday to bring him back to life."

The doctor felt sorry for Adam being a friend of his friend in the operating room, then reminiscent a little about Sunny, his mother who also was hacked to death from the armed robbers on her way to the local market. "Well, I suppose if you're his relative or friend," he said, "It's against our ethics and regulations here, but since you flew in from America as a result, come with me" the doctor said.

Adam Khan gingerly followed him into the operating room. There he saw a team of more doctors doing everything they could to save Sunny's life. Two doctors for the record were allowing the first pint of blood to be transfused. A tube was affixed into his nose. Aburime worked at massaging his heart to bring his pulse back to normal. Seeing Sunny in such a horrible situation, Adam resisted the tears in his eyes, but felt sick to his stomach, as he thought of the millions he'd come to make again in the country. As he looked back into the faces of those children who were in line with their parents sobbing too, he choked back tears.

Daniel and Adam remained silent. More nurses walked in and saw Daniel standing with Adam and found themselves at an impasse, but said, "Good afternoon, Dan. Who is the visitor with you?"

"Adam Khan. He's a very good friend of mine. I've known him since he was 18 years old, a character."

What that meant Justina didn't know and didn't want to know. But Jesus! There was the usual struggle of men and women in line who were gravely ill beyond ill to see their loved ones too who had been shot and no doctors to attend to them. There were also the usual preening men and women who'd blocked the entrance to which Adam and Daniel had to get in to see Sunny. Children and babies had clung to their parents sobbing for something precious. Adam Khan's best guess was that they were starving and no milk in the human chest to feed them.

My God, my Lord! The place was now crammed with police and soldiers, family members and Benin TV crews. As they pushed their way through the crowd, to see one of their own also shot by mistake by their own, another soldier in camouflage uniform with an Uzi stopped Adam Khan, Daniel and Dr. Sympathy. The soldier didn't know Dr. Sympathy was the brain behind Adam Khan and Daniel to see Sunny in his present situation. The soldier, an Igodomigo who only knows how to shoot without missing and totally alien that Adam Khan was well known to his Generals ruling the country, refused to let them in. Looking at the starving children with their mothers, Adam screamed his frustration.

"Get this hungry soldier out of my face before I make him kiss the ground."

He'd forgotten he was not in Lebanon or in America. Daniel said to calm him, "In this country, men don't argue with men with Uzis."

Hum! The soldier glared. His hands twitched aggressively to cock his Uzi.

Daniel looked at Adam's face and noticed he was ready to go off. Then he said, "Calm down, Adam."

Daniel took the soldier aside and had a conversation with him. But the soldier was still mad as hell, "Tell your friend, this is Nigeria. We are given the power to shoot anyone who challenges the authority of Bad Dudu. I can shoot him *now* if he doesn't mind his tongue and he'll die like a chicken with Sunny, whom he came to see."

Here, Adam could see jealousy written on his forehead that he, Adam does have flesh on his bones. With silent hatred, Adam looked at the bony soldier with his Uzi, sweat dripping from his armpits. No man born of a woman needs to be told why the arrogance is on his face. If the truth be righteously told, Adam knew his grievance, which might be that he'd not eaten today and yesterday even though he too was a solider. He was one of those who probably cannot spell his name, but given an Uzi by Bad Dudu to repress men and women of his country guarding gates and hospitals—the yes sir type.

Finally, he let them in after a twenty-dollar tip. Jesus Christ! Adam found himself asking Daniel, "How did Sunny get shot?" I was just in Nigeria four months ago. Numerous negative thoughts flashed through his mind. He asked Dr. Sympathy, "Have they caught the culprits who did it? And would Sunny make it?"

Sadly, Dr. Sympathy shook his head as he walked him in. Meanwhile, two other doctors Adam couldn't recall their names were flipping his head left and right.

"They don't seem to know yet," Dr. Sympathy said. "It doesn't look good, though my friend."

Adam Khan and Daniel became irritated with the other doctors' behaviors. Adam said to Dr. Sympathy, "Tell your other doctors not to ridicule my friend (Sunny) in his present state. They should either operate on him or stop flipping his head left and right."

As they were still standing, Néné and her daughter, Maetu rushed in. "Forget it," Dr. Sympathy said in a sad, toneless voice. "He died."

Adam Khan shook his head and thought: what kind of training are the doctors of Nigeria taught, anyway, in their teaching hospitals? As he thought deeply more and more of a rich country he'd helped drain their treasury, two other nurses wheeled in another patient with a cardboard paper printed Iwamon on her chest. She'd been robbed on her way to the local market too. The name Iwamon is well known in the country. She was the mother of Ogbebor living in Reno, Nevada. She was bleeding profusely with her mouth open. Apparently, still had life on her breath. The two nurses who'd jerry curls were taking off Iwamon's clothes which had been plastered to her body by her own blood. Quickly, one of the nurses called in Dr. ZK. He, Dr. ZK, felt her pulse and said to Dr. Andrew, "It seems weak and thready! Look! A splotch of blood has stained the front of her blouse and wrapper." Dr. ZK turned to the other nurse talking to Dr. Andrew who is supposedly an expert in taking out bullets from kidneys.

"So, what's the story here, Miss Ihioma?"

"Another of those sad news in our country-of bullet in the head, chest, lower back Doctor."

"Let's see if her lung is affected." The unheard doctor turned to his partner, "What do you think?"

And his partner turned her over, flipped her head left and right, as they'd done with Sunny.

"Lets send her into the X-ray room for observation of a stat chest X-ray."

"She's still breathing, it's a sign of hope that she might make it," Dr. ZK said.

Miss Chika said, "Dr.! You remember I told you a few months ago the X-ray machine was broken ten years ago and still hasn't been replaced. The order is waiting approval from Bad Dudu."

"Oh! That's right. I forgot. Run to my office and call Colonel Khadafi of Libya to deploy his U2 plane to take the X-ray via satellite or rush us his one of several X-ray machines. It's our only alternative right now."

As he spoke, he raised the jugular vein and began to observe it. He looked over at Dr. Andrew. "This is the spot the bullet penetrated. The pericardium's probably bullet ruptured."

Dr. ZK sighed deeply. "From my observation, it looks like the sac that protected the heart has now probably been filled with blood, thereby disturbing the heart from pumping the way it normally should have been."

Dr. Andrew coughed. "OK. Lets not speculate until Khadafi sends us the X-ray results. I know he would honor what I requested. He is humanitarian and very generous. Then Dr. Andrew turned to Miss Ihioma and said, "Please take her blood pressure."

Ihioma raised her left hand and took her pressure. "Oh, my God!" she cried out. "It's dropping fast on me doctor."

Dr. ZK and Dr. Andrew looked on. "Go, go. Chika, get the monitor for measuring patients' electrocardiogram," Dr. ZK shouted. "That, too, is broken. Bad Dudu finally placed an order in Britain just yesterday," she said, wiping tears from her eyes. Chika knew who Iwamon was. A well-known woman like Mother Theresa in her country.

With frustration, Dr. ZK said, "OK. Call Togo's president to rush us one. Tell him we're losing a philanthropist who toiled and worked hard all her life caring for orphans of this country. Tell him that Nigeria can't afford to lose her, because she's the only woman who cared for the poor of this country, as Mother Theresa, and we want her to live."

Without too much emphasis, Adam Khan knew why Iwamon was dying a slow and painful death. The hospitals around here are ill equipped. Embezzlement of funds meant for government run hospitals is rampant. He, Adam Khan as he stood watching, was a party to the embezzlement in this country. He dare not say something. All he could do was watch and listen to the secret amusement of doctors and nurses cursing the day Bad Dudu and his in cahoots were born, carrying the Nation's wealth to foreign countries to bury millions and billions in different countries around the world.

While Dr. ZK was still on the subject of losing a fine woman, another doctor rushed in with a faxed copy of her chest X-ray, taken via satellite with a note accompanying it from Khadafi's personal doctor saying, "Pericardial tamponade", which means the heart had a hole in it and the lung had collapsed. "If I were you doctors," the note stated, "I would get a tube in her first to expand the lung. That done successfully, you get an anesthesiologist to put her to sleep (though the armed robbers have put her to sleep faster than modern science) and then open her up immediately and intubate her. Then stitch the heart."

Dr. ZK looked at the note. With happiness he read aloud, thinking the right course to help Madam Iwamon to live was at his hand, but not knowing the doctors in his country were being ridiculed. As he read aloud, the nurses felt a chill into their spines as they, too, cracked up. The doctors with no shame anyway, waited for an endotrachaeal tube which they'd sent for from St. Anthony's Catholic Hospital at Nnewi. The endotrachaeal tube had taken Ojukwu and his scientists forty-five minutes to manufacture before they rushed it in. After another hour or so, Togo's president delivered one among their several electrocardiogram monitor machines with strings attached. "Please return it with good faith."

Adam Khan was thinking the opposite. This damn Nation with smart Easterners as Ibos manufacturing anything gadgets could hamper his bid for the contract to supply hospital equipment for Bad Dudu to swindle millions out of the country. But he dare not say. All he could do was swallow his saliva cursed and mocked the Ibos of Nigeria in his heart.

Finally, nurse Albert Salawe handed Dr. ZK an endotrachaeal tube and carefully began to push the tube into the unconscious Iwamon's windpipe. A bag was placed at the end of the tube and Dr. Andrew began to squeeze it in a steady manner ventilating the lungs. The monitor began to slow, but the curve on the monitor refused to move.

"What?" Dr. ZK yelled out. Another death has taken place in a rich oil country with no modern equipment in their hospitals and maternities. And though Adam Khan watched Iwamon die like a chicken, he left the scene quietly and strolled alone upstairs to see the children's ward, where Dr. Peter Aburime's wife had delivered a baby boy. To him he felt that it was important to see life as well as death, to try and balance his profound sense of loss of a woman with the feeling of rebirth. The children he thought would eventually suffer the illness of their Generals in office and those who are yet to rule. He was at their mercy to carry their briefcases any time they needed him was his last thought.

Chapter

8

....

I picked up Efemona at the Los Angeles International Airport almost three years ago to join me in Reno, Nevada, the so called 'The Biggest Little City In The World'. I became busy as soon as possible, taking some days off from my day job so as to plant the seed of life into her womb.

You know, as a young man whose dick was functioning right, I began to enter her day in and day out that within a month of her arrival to the States to join me, I'd planted the seed of a life inside her womb as I had anticipated. On a Sunday morning, as early as eight A.M., I'd woke up and made some tea for both of us as a normal ritual I made Efemona to entertain since she'd joined me. Maybe I was wrong this early morning to wake her up because it was strange for me to determine what was so weighty on my wife's mind while still in bed. You know,*(we)* men know when a woman has something to unload. This particular morning, I could almost see that little devilish, evil intention on her left eye and the angel on her right, both chattering in her ears. And believe me that if I knew that waking up my Efemona this early morning to have a cup of tea with me on the dinner table would cause me pain and anguish, I would've change the course of events. Her conversation she brought up was mostly about important social issues: like your mates are all buying houses and moving into fashionable million dollar homes. I want my mother to visit the United States and you've not shown a sign to welcome her into our domain. You probably hate my mother. You don't communicate with her, you don't send her money, you are not taking good care of your first daughter, something other men would be proud of having does not appeal to you. You zombie and so on and so forth . . . .

It's too early for these vibes, I suppose. So I looked up from Efemona's shoulder and immediately she realized it and then she frowned. The face I could see had turned as red as a billiard ball. I'd just noticed Efemona's attitude towards me on our way to a grocery store one evening. On our way back from the store, I'd the impression that there was something very heavy on her mind. In fact, if I thought about it as the way she was behaving that early previous and then this early, morning, Efemona's behavior I would say, over the past few weeks or so had alternated between periods of romance and bouts of rotten vibes from her flippant mouth and withdrawal.

Lets face the reality about pregnant women for a minute. Men with experience of their wives they have lived with for a long time, as my buddy Achuko once informed me, are prone to bouts of sulkiness and withdrawal, especially with women who throw up in the morning within their first or second week into their pregnancy. On the other hand, I wasn't quite outright sure if her pregnancy was the reason I was being entertained and insulted every now and then. Anyway, I became used to her mood, her rotten vibes and her sullenness and her general moodiness towards me and my immediate relatives in Nigeria, whom she had frequently attacked of being witches and wizards praying not for her good, but for her downfall.

This morning, to say the least, she'd insulted me and my immediate families that I couldn't resist to attack back. If I had not attacked, I probably would have punched her in the nose, which might've cost me thousands of dollars to reconstruct her ugly nose soonest. Finally it occurred to me that two wrongs don't make a right, so I patted her. Then she looked at me and said, "So what do you do on your days off from work?" the question that dumbfounded me.

Efemona did not stop there. She looked at me and said, "You know honey pie, I can now challenge God to a fight." What she meant by that, I must be frank with you, I don't know, nor did I ask. Finally though, for her rudeness I asked, "What seems to be the matter to have the guts to challenge God to a fight as you said."

"Because you never care to take me out since I arrived in Reno on your days off." And she threw an invitation card at me. "The Okories are having a birthday party for their daughter today if you care to attend. I know you'll rather go to work than to take me and your daughter out even for a day."

"Well," I said, "I don't have a yacht for us to sail around the world that's why I choose to work everday."

"I thought you told my parents in Nigeria you were a millionaire? Please, I didn't come to America to sleep all day and all night, honey." I watched her ready to get up. I held her down. Then I appealed.

To tell the truth for that matter, I'll tell you that Efemona, since she joined me, surprises me with little flashes of a sociable woman who'd perhaps mingled with sugar daddies with little money in Nigeria. But if I were a more manipulative man, as Efemona was, which now had occurred to me I would promote her sociability as a means of keeping her informed about the society she'd come to live and be merry with me. But I was a shy man, quiet, but her attitude this Sunday morning told me I should change my ways for our marriage to work. So I said, "I would like to cook for Efemona today. Would you rather I take you out or cook meatballs and cucumber for you?"

"No."

"Why not?"

"Because it is not only food I came to America to eat." Jesus, whatelse have you come to America for, I thought.

"You don't like Reno, the city that makes the world go round in the West? Reno is a Yankee state," I pointed out. "The good times roll in this city."

"You haven't showed it to me since I've joined you."

"How about us driving to Lake Tahoe then where the nouveau riche paved their asphalt road with gold and silver?"

"You can go to Lake Tahoe alone by yourself."

"Good answer." Flippant, bitchy, but good I thought. Nevertheless, it was time to promote her sociability I then realized. I watched Efemona stood up. "Better yet, Ekiaqueta, why don't you ask yourself what you've done for me lately? Now I am carrying your second baby. Probably, you are a damned gambler in the casinos of this town."

"Efemona, why don't you just shut up and tell me what's on your mind and see if I cannot handle it. You are indirectly insulting my intelligence. C'mon woman, sip on your tea! Goddamit."

"If that's the case, why don't I just tell you more stuff to get you to understand I've had enough of tea?"

"Please don't. Just tell me what you want me to do for you this early morning and I'll do it."

Efemona finally saw the need to know that I was damned serious to dance to her whims and caprices. So she said, "I want to go hiking. And I want you to go with me to Mt. Rose."

"Thank you! Why don't you say so all this time than to bitch about my folks and insulting your husband?," I said.

Efemona and I looked at each other, but neither of us, I presumed, knew how to hike. I finished my cup of tea and I stood. "I feel better now. Let me know when you are ready."

"Good, sweetheart. I think you just needed a mental enema for the expedition with me to Mt. Rose."

We both smiled and kissed. Actually, I did feel better, probably because Efemona would teach me how to hike. Efemona caught my eye and she winked the right one at me, which made me even feel better. I don't think I know how to hike. Thus, our problems were just getting started with a woman who thinks she got the balls.

* * *

For Africans from Nigeria to go hiking was strange to me. Twenty years I've lived and resided in the city of Reno, Nevada, I'd never ventured even the lowest aspect of a foothill. After we ate the Sunday morning oatmeal, Efemona arranged for a nanny to come to our house to baby-sit our first daughter. I knew she didn't want to be bothered. On our way to Mount Rose, Efemona sat behind the wheel of our new 4x4 Toyota pickup truck. Surprised to see Efemona behind the wheel, I said, "Oh! Honey, I was gonna teach you on my next day off how to drive."

My Efemona smiled. "It's too late. My friend, Miss Porcupine, had taught me how to drive." Actually, for her friend teaching her to drive, it relieved the burden from my hectic work load, both at my job where I do the meaner job at a factory and the verbal abuse at home from my Efemona if I don't do the dishes or respond to her immediate question of why I was home late.

I must be frank with you to say that I wondered how my Efemona had adjusted very fast. As she drove, I said to her, "Be happy I'll always be beside you to enjoy yourself. Whatever makes you happy I'll do for you."

To make my Efemona happier I instructed her to turn right at the Boomtown roller coaster World Park Disney. Here, I paid for Efemona to ride the roller coaster which was higher than the splash mountain of Los Angeles Disney World. Here, the deafening music of Michael Jackson she adored so much blared over the coaster ride and faded into the background, then higher and higher Efemona rode with such electric manipulated strings unto the high peak roller coaster. I could tell immediately that Efemona liked enjoyment and it pained the fuck out of me to deny her such enjoyment even when I could afford it.

Anyway, what made every human to holler when they're on it, only made Efemona to smile and wave to me down below. She loved what she saw, as the strings of flashing colored lights from the rides flickered like fireflies above and below. Efemona's occasional laugh was clearer and more raucous than her co-rider in the same din. But on the overall, all the men and women below, some with their mouth full of pop corn, hands clutching loved ones, looked like an army of ants as Efemona rode higher and higher smiling and waving.

I watched my Efemona as she bent her knees and leaned her body against the horizontal bars of the cylindrical cage supporting her and her co-rider. Then she looked down the entire city of Reno stretched between several mountains but well planned below her. "Hum Nigeria?," I guess she'd murmured in her heart. She could see the dazzling flashing lights of the huge casino skyscrapers as beautiful in the distance and below her, flushed, dazed, sorrowful faces of broke gamblers heading back to California.

I could tell what my Efemona was thinking: the whiteman surely knows how to enjoy. Why wouldn't I enjoy in a country full of enjoyment of all kinds.

After the ride, I noticed Efemona's mood had changed from sulliness and nuttiness of a few days she'd entertained with me to rather chattering of past and present events to happen in 'The Biggest Little City in the World' we resided.

"I loved the ride," she finally admitted. "I know you did," I responded.

She hopped into the truck and sat behind the wheel as usual. As she drove, so many thoughts flashed behind my mind: like, I know my Efemona had made lots of friends in this city, based on the way she now speaks like the typical Yankee cowgirl. Truly, you'll agree with me that women have that tendency to grasp linguistics more than men. I mean, my Efemona could speak and add some typical American Yankee vibes to her intonation. And compared with the way I still talk, I know I will probably go back to Nigeria with my strong accent I came to the United States with. With Efemona, she could intone perfectly the word, "Please," with many syllables to suit the moment when she was with her bitchy friends arguing. Without being told, I also knew that my Efemona does nothing else in particular other than to watch enough soap operas and probably planned to set up a Television Station of her own at Ukpenu some day. Or that, our house was made a den of visitors, both wanted and unwanted when I was away from home who were teaching her how to get around. Or most probably gossip all day with some bitches I know whom I'd warned her about who studied this little city slang of the Yankees in Nevada for decades and don't intend to speak in their broken or Pidgen English and are not interested in going back to Nigeria some day. Like Patricia and Virginia, her famous notorious bitches I'd warned her about, they can speak what I guess you would call the Western typical Yankee gossip slang without a break. But on the overall, I did figured the good visitor which I haven't met had taught my wife to drive. So I said, "Honey, I know you *now* know how to drive. But remember in this city everyone needs a driver's license to drive because this city has been declared Nationally by the Casino

Lobbyist Association as a city where judges and police are biased to ruin da niggas."

"I passed my driving test a few days ago. Our neighbor, Miss Patricia Porcupine, took me to the DMV after months of coaching me to drive. Isn't that nice of her?"

She'd driven ten miles when she exited on route 66 and stopped at the Boomtown Ranch off on I-80 West. I was surprised. So I asked, "Honey, why are we stopping here? I thought we were on our way to Mount Rose to ski, go hunting or hiking?" I joked.

In a flash her answer chatted out. "To rent a horse."

"But honey, I don't know how to ride a horse. Now! What's the deal gonna be with the horse?" I asked.

"Well, I do honey. I'll teach you how easy it is to ride a horse. You'll know the deal after we rent the horse."

I watched my Efemona do her thing. Then she rented a space for our car and then approached one of the cowboys of the Ranch. There, she made me paid and rent an Arabian horse of probably five years-old breed. Efemona inspected the horse thoroughly. With her own words that the Arabian horse was physically sound to ride to the woods before we hike our way to Mt. Rose, I pulled out five hundred dollars and paid the rancher before she mounted on top of it. But I was afraid to mount on it beside her. Seeing me afraid, the cowboy breeder and trainer explained to me, "This five-year- old Arabian horse's nickname is 'Enjoy'. And Enjoy has a good temperament, unlike most of the horses here I've trained and bred. This Arabian horse can be ridden hard and slow depending on how your wife wants it," he explained and smiled a mocking smile. I guess he knew what most civilized women can do with Arabian horses which I didn't know at that moment. But with the mere mention of *enjoy*, by the Yankee cowboy, I remembered what Mr. Achuko, a good friend of mine had told me about my wife. I believed Mr. Achuko not to be a liar. Here I will quickly reflect that once a bitch which pussy is all wide and used by sugar daddies, excuse my expression here, will always remember the good old days and remain a bitch. The thing is, you may not know that Efemona and I had separated within a year of her arrival to join me. But, I can't really tell you or recall what'd sprung the incidence of our separation. But I can tell you that a woman who wants to get laid by other men will find a way to do so.

Anyway, with the money I was paid by the judges of this little city who live double lives of the casino gurus and I screwing them and their wives and mistresses, I was able to send Efemona money to take care of my child. And with the money, she invited Mr. Atlanta to Reno to continually service her during that separation. Achuko, bitter enough seeing Efemona holding hands with Mr. Atlanta, also known as Aghator Oyeghe, at the entrance to the Harrah's Roof Garden Restaurant, had then walked up to them.

After some pleasantries, Achuko said in a jovial manner, "Man! You mean to tell me there are no single women in Atlanta, Georgia to come all the way to Reno to fuck my friend's wife in Reno, Nevada to humiliate him, just within a few days of their separation?" Aghator Oyeghe looked at Mr. Achuko and smiled. Finally he said, "Single women or no single women, if a woman gives you her car and bought the gas, too, would you refuse?"

"You mean to tell me that Efemona bought your flight ticket to Reno, Nevada just to service her?" Achuko asked then gnawed his teeth. "Hum that expensive pussy man."

"What are you talking about? You don't want me to *enjoy*?" Efemona had asked Achuko with sarcasm.

"That's not the point, my friend. She wants to humiliate Ekiaqueta because he has a small dick, according to Efemona."

"Oh, well have fun then," and Achuko had no more words, but walked away.

Achuko relating to me the encounter with Aghator Oyeghe, I immediately remembered who Oyeghe was. The incredible Aghator Oyeghe had grown up with Efemona at Ukpenu. My memory told me that Efemona and I had seen Oyeghe at the adult

BX movie channel when the going was good without separation at that time. We were sitting in the living room then when my Efemona flipped on the XXX channel on the TV and saw Oyeghe screwing a beautiful blonde woman. I still remember it clearly. The picture of Aghator Oyeghe was previewed at the upper right hand corner of the TV with his full posture posing nude and his synosis of physique description carefully described. He was at least five eleven and eyes of a frog with a voodoo urn charm on his neck which El-Iyari-the voodoo doctor at Benin made for him before he left Nigeria to the States. The description also revealed that he was the most sexy man alive with the longest and biggest expensive dick for separated African women who are now in America *today*. Even before my wife and I had seen Aghator Oyeghe on the adult channel on TV, Efemona had repetitiously displaced before me a Playboy magazine showing and describing Oyeghe in an article about his dick that it was as big as a water melon. As soon after Efemona saw his profile as a celebrity now residing in Atlanta, it naturally took her breath away. Now you know why Efemona started to insult me day in and day out until we separated without incidence for a while.

Actually, you may want to know that Aghator Oyeghe and I used to compete while in the same Grammar School in those days. But I was smarter than him in my class. While I maintained straight A's, he maintained a C minus average. Truly, he used to compete with me, too, on virtually anything I do in life. The only thing he defeated me on, was competition with women, who should be able to lay as many divorced and separated women first before such women were labeled notorious by the entire community. I respected and dumped my hat for Oyeghe when he boasted before me that he'd laid as many as ten women in one night.

You might also want to know that Aghator Oyeghe was a youngman who was suspended from my school for failing in English and mathematics. With peer pressure in Efemona's coed Grammar School where he later ended up, he continually smoke the famous *Ubiaroko Grass*: marijuana, the most enhancing and talked about grass in the world. I'll tell you that if one's gene was not strong enough to handle it, one was doomed to dust. And indeed Aghator became doomed.

I still remember very well to this day, when my father used to sit me down for hours telling stories and preaching about *Ubiaroko grass: marijuana*. One time he'd said to me, holding a ratan whip in his right hand, "That thing that alters youngmen's attitude to make them throw away their clothes to become madmen on the streets, don't ever try it.

You see the son of so and so, that's what they'd smoked. They call it *Itabeleme,* some call it *goof, Igbo, we- we*, afitito and so on and so forth."

Actually, talking about the best *goof or weed* in the world, it is the famous *Ubiaroko grass* which my friend, the famous African musician, Fela Anikulapo Kuti once advertised through his music in his 'Shrine' where he played his Afro Beat music. Matter of factly, I did gisted Aghator Oyeghe that I'd smoked Marijuana and the effect it had on me. But I'd lied. Somehow, Aghator Oyeghe was competing with me at the time, but couldn't handle it just as certain people cannot handle booze. This was a handsome young man in his prime twenties, suddenly was roaming the streets of Uromi, Ukpenu and Benin City on foot naked and his huge ding dong then was swinging along with his body movement on the streets.

As he roamed the streets, notorious women who ran away from their husbands and sugar daddies after they stole their money and known to be outcast to the community men soon discovered Oyeghe for their sexual pleasures and enjoyment. These runaway women separated and divorced on their way home from the local market who had never had orgasm for several months because their clitoris are mutilated, and because the community men look down on them for their notoriety would trick Aghator Oyeghe giving him a penny to go with them to their homes to do yard labor. On getting to their home, the story was different. They would force Oyeghe to perform all kinds of sexual activities until they had had orgasms. Aghator Oyeghe soon became their celebrity simpleton for them, because it was a myth to these notorious, famous women where Efemona then had grew up that when a woman sleeps with a mad man it would bring them good luck to find other rich men to marry so they can trick them and steal their money and become more *notorious* to be known in their villages, towns and cities.

Anyway, Efemona seeing Aghator Oyeghe before her again after so many years she'd admired his dick swaying beautifully in nude as he roamed the streets in those days, in her village local market it naturally took her breath away. Immediately after Oyeghe ejaculated and the blond had an orgasm before her and I as we both watched, Efemona picked up the phone before me and dialed his 800 number at his Atlanta, Georgia home. "This is Efemona," she'd said.

"Oh, hi baby."

"Still remember me?"

"Of course. Our teacher used to give you a ruler those days to whip me at the back of my knuckles when we argued in the class and you'd always won."

I watched my Efemona choking with laughter. She was happy it was the famous Oyeghe she'd known. They chatted for a few minutes and Efemona said, "My husband and I saw you making hot love with the blond the other day. I thought it would be nice to inform you that I am now in Reno, Nevada."

She described Reno, Nevada to Oyeghe, a city she explained to Oyeghe, he could make thousands and millions of dollars screwing separated African women and divorced American women and other women who'd came to America and lost their self cultural identity.

Though I didn't know what Aghator Oyeghe had said on the other end of the phone, I figured he'd said, "Well baby, this is America, a land of no free launch. It's good to let you know up front that *notorious* women no longer take advantage of my ding dong and give me a penny to use me for their sexual gratification. I do it now for a thousand bucks."

The reason I know that to be true was that Efemona cracked up and said, "I know a woman soon to be separated from her husband in Reno, Nevada."

My impression of Oyeghe was the reply, "Well, send me a ticket right away. I'll be there in Reno, Nevada to make love to all the divorced and the separated women in Reno, for a thousand dollars a night."

"My AWAM supporters can afford the price, baby," Efemona said and hung up the phone.

After she hung up the phone, Efemona looked at my face and smiled. Now you know where an African woman, *soon to be notorious,* was heading.

* * *

Anyway, as the cowboy lectured me about the Arabian horse's cool temperament, my fear of falling off the horse soon melted away. Efemona said to me, "Hop on it behind me you chicken."

I looked at the huge jackass and the trainer thinking of how he would spend the five hundred dollars I'd paid him to rent the horse for my wife to enjoy and be happy. Finally, I hopped on the horse without hesitation. I mounted beside my wife and she kicked Enjoy and Enjoy began to trot her way.

We continued across the foot trail unto Mt. Rose, a trail path I figured several horses had trotted on a million times.

Thus Efemona trotted Enjoy into the quiet of the sunny afternoon in the woods, a luminous broad day light, the harsh and deserted mountain that she loved to hike with me after the horse ride. It was here that an owl, with its round yellow eyes stared at us, from a pine tree. Looking at it closely, I was scared, but it was beautiful and full of mystery.

Efemona trotted the horse gently as our hearing became keen. Then the owl took fright, flew up silently among the trees and disappeared. After criticizing the owl before me, Efemona trotted Enjoy again, then looked around and saw the first tender flowers of the yellow gorse showing amongst its thorns. "How beautiful," Efemona made me aware as she trotted Enjoy by. I nodded my head.

Finally, she diverted the horse into a steep slope. It was now about six-thirty P.M. The breeze felt good on our body and the scent of thyme was still in the air around us. At this moment in time, only the sounds of Enjoy's hooves on the dry fallen leaves around the pines and birds chippering their notes from the pines could be heard. Here, I must admit that it was a perfect sunny late afternoon in the first week of summer.

Efemona continued to trot the horse here and there in the woods as we rode across several other trails, then down on the base of Mt. Rose. About half a mile away to the North, far away we could see the top of Mount Rose as the sun shone brightly on it. Efemona stopped and then reigned Enjoy around, then said to me, "I want you to hop down and start getting naked. Be cooperative and sociable."

"Why?"

"Nature called around here, honey."

The first, and probably the only, thought that you envisioned here is that when you heard the phrase Efemona had used, was maybe answering the call of nature, which to a lame man means eliminating some waste product from our bodies. Obviously Nature, that is human nature, reminds us of the need to eliminate the bad products that our bodies have completed processing and utilizing. Our failure to regularly eliminate waste products from our bodies can make us sick. I was dumb for a few seconds. And I know some of you would have probably thought that Efemona had meant I should start defecating to fertilize the soil around us. It was strictly not what my Efemona had meant.

After much debate and my hesitation to get naked instantly as she commanded me she looked at me with a crooked smile.

"Because I want you to. You should know that I came to America to enjoy and learn new stuff. Just get down and do what I asked. And if you don't hop down and do what I asked, I will blow my whistle for hunters around to come over and experiment with me what I dreamt about."

"Oh, please. I should be the one to be in control here," I said. "How can you be in control when you don't know how to ride the horse and speak Yankee slang all these years you've been in America?"

She hopped down from the horse and helped me down. I watched her tether Enjoy to a pine tree and then stood facing me. "I'll help you take off your clothes if you don't take orders from an African woman with balls," Efemona said.

She commanded again, "I said take off your clothes."

I shook my head. "I am the man who is supposed to give orders in a foreign land or in an enviroment like this."

"No you ain't! I am," she said and smiled.

I stood motionless for a minute, then she pulled off my T- shirt, exposing my bare chest and threw it down beside Enjoy and looked at my shy face and my unwillingness to comply. "I thought you said you've done it in parks and the beaches of Lake Tahoe?"

I nodded. "Well, this ain't different. I want to show you *'nine-nine'*, that I'm more sociable than the rest of the women you have laid."

"Do I really have to do this, sweetie?" "Absolutely."

She unzipped my fly, then pulled off my Fila running shoes and Fila socks. Finally, I saw she meant it, so I helped myself out of my Levi's 501 jeans and she smiled. She stood beside Enjoy and looked down at me standing naked before her in the hot, sunny summer weather.

"Not so dumb now and shy, are you, Ekiaqueta?" "No ma'am."

To be honest with you, I guess this was Efemona's idea of remembering her sugar daddies and to keep our marital sex enjoyable and keeping me to remain in line to be more sociable when we engage in an act like this. Though to be frank, I'm not complaining about acting out Efemona's sexual preference on Mount Rose. I'll say the truth that matter-of-factly, these dramas are scripted and directed by Efemona, who in fact wanted me to be more sociable casting for her as a Hollywood actor at the aspect of Mt. Rose. "In a few minutes I'll teach you what you'll remember and I guess you have never before done with any other women you know."

"Really?"

"That's right. After doing it here in this environment, as time goes on, and as you become more sociable as a realman, I will decide where next we'll do it again in the city. Alright, Ekiaqueta?"

"Sounds good to me," I said.

Actually, this was the first sociable play acting of the summer season Efemona had initiated, which caught me by surprise after the Disney World episode. But as I looked behind the history of the world, with Adam and Eve, in the Garden of Eden, the realization of who said it is not possible of a woman commanding a man to get naked and consummate the act with her flashed my thoughts: the fact that I think God created Adam and Eve naked in the Garden of Eden for a reason: to be able to move freely in their Garden, shit and pee anywhere they choose, to fertilize the soil around them to produce nourishing fruits for them and the animals HE created for them. Above all, to make love anywhere they choose in the Garden without shame. Don't you think it's against God's will that man has recreated the environment to compete with HIM? And we all must render why on HIS judgment day? But you know, I think we should go back to history and honor Adam and Eve in the Garden. You think about it! Ain't we disrespecting our Creator who made us without clothes? I think we should go back to nudity so man and woman can choose who, for instance, has a bigger ding dong and which woman has the most beautiful round ass for men to choose from and lay any time they choose to do it, or women choosing among the ding dongs they want when they see a man they like without judging with the fingers. And I think it is fair enough to ask ourselves if there is actually anything obvious or something about a man standing naked before his wife in the wilderness, such as on Mt. Rose, that had appeals to my Efemona. Or that the flouting of modern conventions regarding where love should be made should be dictated by men alone? If your answer is no because man has made the law, putting people in jails, charging them for indecent exposure-weren't Adam and Eve doing it in the open? Anyway, I figured Efemona knew this and wanted to be the first African woman from Nigeria to experiment it with me on the horse.

Occasionally though, women like my wife who command their husbands to tell them when they need it are rare.

Finally, I said, "What do you intend out of this command?" "None of your business. Just do as I command. I just want you to entertain me the way I please, the way I want it done-please me in the American way, baby!"

Efemona looked at me standing erect and motionless thereafter and perplexed as her new Diana Ross-like hair blew in strands across her face. Then she immediately climbed on the horse again. Efemona on the other hand knew I'd no acting background, only that I'd been trained as a journalist. Some instincts told me though, she'd probably performed these acts with her preening looking sugar daddies in Nigeria at Ukpenu and Ewu with those who had little money to get the day worthwhile with her drinking her regular London Gin while they ride their motorcycles instead of the horse.

Anyway, for all accounts, I was naked, defenseless, but about to experiment love making on top of an Arabian horse with a woman with balls.

In fact, my heart was pounding, thinking that a hunter might mistake us for a deer playing on top of a horse stolen by two niggers. "Please, ma'am do what you will with me, but do it quickly before the police and judges who turned hunters in Reno, Nevada on Mt. Rose mistake us for a chimpanzee riding on their stolen horse."

Efemona cracked up and I must admit that since she'd joined me, is good at impromptu games, and she does it well. Sometimes she makes me a saint and her the barbarian cave woman of the sixteenth or seventeenth century.

She hopped on the horse and reached out and cupped my chin in her hand. "I know you are embarrassed?"

"What do you think! And why wouldn't I be?"

I should mention that Efemona since she joined me often takes the dominant role, and I'm the one who plays the part of a naked slave about to be auctioned or a prisoner of war who is stripped and about to be whipped to perform on the horse whichever way she wanted.

"Hop on the horse behind me." And I did.

"Put your right foot in the stirrup." I put my bare foot in the stirrup and she pulled me up behind her while I wrapped my arms around her breasts. Then she raised up her green leather skirt. That done, she yanked off her top and flung it on top of my T-shirt. Finally, she whipped Enjoy and the leather whip caught me in my right eye, though I stifled the impulse to say, "Ouch," when Enjoy began to walk. She realized the whip had done damage to me, but didn't know what part of my body.

Anyway, she raised her ass up enough for me to penetrate and enter her from behind. "Put it in," she commanded me.

I said, "I do this only to make you happy, my dear. And besides, I want to be more sociable so as to spend the rest of my life with you."

"I doubt that," she said. Then I hesitated. Noting that she was not feeling a thing inside her, she commanded again, *"Put it in well, well now, honey."*

"Okay, raise your ass up a little for me." She did and I penetrated into the right hole.

She kicked Enjoy and Enjoy began to trot Efemona's way. I held Efemona tighter as I squeezed her breast since I couldn't cram one of them into my mouth. Finally, Efemona was moaning. Poor Enjoy! What did he know?

As I was completely caught up in the heat of the moment, and Enjoy trotted along Efemona's wishes and direction, our bodies and the odor of ejaculation rising between us, Efemona increased the trotting of the horse.

Lord, have mercy! Efemona was breathing hard now on my rigid penis, and moaning out words of pleasure, me panting even harder and pumping as the horse walked, the wetness oozing between us. Poor Enjoy! For five hundred bucks I guess the cowboy trainer and breeder of Enjoy will have a job to do when we return it to the ranch.

Efemona climaxed first and Enjoy could hear it that he, too, reacted and jerked forward, making us almost tumble over the horse. A few seconds later, as the horse slowed its speed, I flooded her womanhood. And as we were catching our breath, Enjoy bent down his head and began to graze, as if nothing had happened. Efemona and I hopped down and clung to each other, trying to relax and catch more breath.

And looking at me in the face, Efemona said, "Wasn't that a good ride. And wouldn't you want to do it again with me sometime?"

"Absolutely. It was definitely a good ride." And I will tell you this was the first time I knew that my Efemona was wired up in the psyche.

As we finished catching our breath, we helped ourselves to our clothes and dressed up. Efemona said, "One more thing we have to do before we head home is to hike up the peak of Mount Rose." For a minute I thought she was joking. I watched her tether enjoy and said, "C'mon. Let's go."

She held my hand for a few minutes. When she finally let me go I trailed behind her like a zombie. By no means, however, I was not a slow walker, but Efemona walked even faster with her cowgirl boots dragging me after her and chattering like a squirrel all the while. While I responded to her chattering sometimes with a whisper, "Yes," and, "No," or at the most, "Yes," she made me look like I was the one who just landed in America.

The one thing that really made me inferior was that Efemona kept saying before me, "How beautiful," and kept on repeating like white people do and flipping her swirely hair backwards. So, anyway I watched my Efemona flying like a bird while I wondered how the hell we could come down and get the hell out of the peak of Mount Rose. Finally, I reached the top where Efemona had been resting and waiting for me.

In spite of Efemona's high-heeled cowgirl Gucci boots, she darted down the peak with her boots, like an arrow. I became ashamed of myself while I struggled to get down. She stood at the base smiling and cheering me and offering to come to my aid to drag me down. How could I be so chicken-hearted? With great difficulty, I crawled at intervals and finally managed to make it to the base of the hill. Efemona yelled out at me boldly, "Bravo! My darling the chicken has made it down."

As I experienced these social activities that my wife had introduced me to, I began to entertain the happiness that my wife would help me financially to measure up with my social acquaintances from the same country who'd all purchased houses here and there in Reno and all driving Lexus and Mercedes cars. I was mistaken. My Efemona had a different agenda. I'll tell you that this horse engagement which Efemona initiated, will perhaps not be the last of an African woman trying to teach a husband by example the real meaning of an African woman in America that American society has civilized and about to germinate balls, nuts, testicles or whatever you may call it.

* * *

The one thing I realized when a man is hurt screwing a woman is that when a woman hurts a man by accident when fucking, her man doesn't feel the pain until they are done. Efemona noticed for the first time that one of my eyes was swollen and reddish and finally asked, "Did I do that to you when I had whipped Enjoy to trot my way and the whip got you?"

"That's what love can do, honey!" I said.

It was nearly seven P.M. when we returned the horse to the ranch then hopped into our truck and we headed home. And as we got home,

I thanked the nanny again for looking after our daughter and paid her fare home. In a few minutes I fell asleep on the couch in the living room. But then, it was hard for me to believe what we had done on a horseback ride. Five or ten minutes into my nap, I felt a pinching on my nostril, then on my eyelid.

After a while, I heard a voice, "Open your eyes, Daddy. Open your eyes." I managed to open my eyes. It was my daughter, Verita, who'd just turned six, trying to pull my eyelids up with her small, tiny fingers.

"Verita! Why don't you go and play?" I managed to say.

She was gone. In a few minutes I heard her talking with her friends.

Then in a faint, I heard some chattering in the living room close to the couch that I laid. "Daddy? Open your eyes. Open your eyes, Daddy."

"Daddy is very tired, kid. Is your mama back yet?" I managed to ask Verita.

She answered me not and paid no attention to my question. "Daddy, open your eyes. Daddy? Daddy, open your eyes!"

I knew that Verita would surely continue saying the same thing over and over, until I opened my eyes and played with her. So I sat up and rubbed my eyes. "Daddy was napping, Verita. Can't you understand Daddy is still very tired? Go and meet your mother," I said and laid down again.

"Mama went shopping for Adeze."

My daughter was right. She remembered that I'd told her that when I returned from Mt. Rose with her mother, we'll go and party with the Okories.

"Mama said you should dress me up for the birthday party for Adeze."

Quickly, I rushed into the bathroom to give her a bath to avoid bad vibes from her mother when she returned and Verita still hasn't been dressed up. Anyway, Verita entered the bath tub. As I sprinkled some water onto her body, she asked me, "Daddy, don't you love mama? Mama said she don't love you because you are poor and can't afford to take good care of her and me and the baby she's now carrying in her stomach."

One thing I know is this: children can hardly make up stories. I mean they don't lie. So I asked her, "When did your mama say that?" "I heard mama talking on the phone with someone she addressed as Anegbo and sometimes her sister and saying she planned to buy a new house in Nigeria after divorcing you and suing you in the court of law of the United States."

I said nothing. Then she asked, "What does mama mean when she said she would sue you and divorce you and show you 'nine, nine'?"

My daughter is always very aggressive in questioning. To prepare her to be a good writer in the near future, I explained to her. "It's all about witching someone you don't care about anymore, which will personally inflict pain or humiliation or both on the victim-like on your father by your mother."

"Really? Why would mama want to hurt or witch you and humiliate you in the courts of the United States, Daddy?"

"You can ask your mother," I said. But deep inside my being I know she would not have the nerve to ask or she would get a hard knock on her head as the way Efemona was brought up in her country-Nigeria by her father-not mother.

"Daddy," Verita said, "I want to be with you always. She stared at me, waiting to hear me continue to say something, but I kept mute. Then she said, "Does mama have an Uncle in New Jersey?"

"I don't know. Why?"

"I heard mama one night say she would leave you and take me along to see him. She also said that Uncle in New Jersey is richer than you. Uncle has a Vette and a truck," she said and nodded solemnly, the way she always did when she was telling me what she thought I should know. Finally, I said, "Is that right?"

She did not listen to my question. But she asked, "Are we going to the party when mama comes?"

I finished bathing her. As I toweled her soft, tender body, I answered, "Yes, sweetheart."

* * *

I'd just finished dressing Verita up when Efemona walked in with gifts wrapped for Adeze. She, too, had already dressed up where she'd done her shopping or gone to without my knowledge I supposed. And for the record she was dressed with tight, short jeans upon a halter. I figured they were either Gucci or Givenchy. The high-heel shoes no doubt matched the resemblance of Givenchy made. I looked at her a second time. She'd surreptitiously pumped up her breasts on her stubby chest over her halter which then made me to salivate. How in the world could I have not admired my wife with this kind of wear that attracts the libidos?

My God, my Lord! I said, "Glad you made it back for us to take Verita out to see Adeze and her brothers and sisters. And more so to show off what you have on to your friends." She looked at me with distaste when I touched her nipples, sort of a mockery compliment, she'd presumed.

My daughter was getting impatient to go to the party. So I held my daughter's hand and we all headed to the truck and hopped in. I sat behind the wheel. You may want to know that the Okories live down the Clear Acre Foothills off the city. So at the rotary I turned left and drove about two miles to get to their house on Tora and Canan Street. I'd followed Sam Okorie's directions well that I couldn't have missed the house. There house was a two story building which they had just purchased over the foothills off the city with half-a-million dollars, I guess.

I knocked on the door. Sam came out wearing tight Levi jeans and a Levi jacket over a white T-shirt. He let us in with gratitude of self-consciousness. My daughter embraced Adeze, whom she hadn't seen in a couple of months and immediately settled in with their toys.

Efemona and I found ourselves gazing through floor-to-ceiling glasses of the faraway downtown high rises of the evil empire of the casinos. As I stood in the middle of the living room admiring the Okories' new home and the incongruous images of the high rise building with their neon lights, it struck me that I'd not taken Efemona lately to see some of the celebrity shows at the Flamingo Hilton or even taking Verita to the Circus Circus to watch the circus acts.

Finally, Efemona said to UK, "Your place is beautiful."

Doing so, they admired each others' outfits and also commented on how slim and in general how beautiful and young they both had become after having children of their own.

Sam Okorie nodded and looked at me. Then he said, "The advantages accorded both of our women in America over their age groups in our country where the prices of food stuff had risen exponentially."

I nodded in reaction to his comment. "Absolutely," I said.

"It is hard to see flesh on the faces of women of our country," UK voiced out.

I should point out here, that UK had just visited and returned from Nigeria and she was talking from her observation of the women she saw-I mean her age groups whose days were perhaps numbered from malnutrition.

Sam looked at Efemona and his wife. "Every morning both of you should get on your knees and thank us for bringing y'all to this country—America."

Both women said nothing. I know Efemona was thinking of something to say, but I changed the subject. I said to Sam, "We missed our way on our way to this place," I'd lied.

"We thought as much." He paused for a second, then asked, "What can we offer you both? Don't worry about the children. Verita is having fun with her friends."

"How about dry gin?" "London Gin okay?"

"Yes. My wife would settle for London Gin if you have it." "Certainly." I smiled to myself as Efemona and I walked behind Sam through the sitting room, noting our surroundings as we talked. The decorations in their living room caught our eyes. They were excellent. Their furnishings had combined the very modern with carefully placed antiques-a sofa and a long couch, a rocking chair, and an oak roll top desk neatly placed around some great books and a computer with CD Roms-which Efemona guessed were purchased from street peddlers of the ghettos for a cheap price.

Though Efemona knew nothing about the Okories background, she remembered that I'd introduced them to her, and then she started visiting them alone on her days off. She knew they were Ibos. From the Okories' stories building and their furniture, Efemona guessed that, like Ekiaqueta, her husband, (sitting with her) Sam must know the neighborhood gangs breaking the laws, breaking into malls and looting from cooking pots to furniture to jewelry and there was simply no way that Sam and his wife could have bought such a good home and furnish it nicely based on their salary as a casino dealer and a car salesman.

By the way, I could see the envy on Efemona's face, which is one thing wrong with the Nigerians in the City of Reno. You might want to know why. The reason for that is we don't give credit to those who deserve merit and emulate them for their success. Instead, we envy those who climb up the ladder step by step and pray that the IRS or the cops get them into their computer blotter systems to ruin them or reduce them to become nonenetities. As I knew what was heavy and weighty on my wife's mind, I said, "Pray with me for God to bless the efforts of those whom merits are due."

Sam stopped at the refrigerator and opened it. Efemona and I scanned the kitchen area. It was spacious with a wine and liquor cabinet, a cooking space ideal for married couples with children. Sam served me my request. To Efemona he served London Gin. "Thanks," we echoed together.

We all sipped on our drinks, including UK, with her plain diet coke on the rocks. Walking with us back to the sitting room, Sam said, "Would you guys care to go upstairs? It's a pleasant evening and we might even be stuck inside making love to our lovely women all night."

Efemona grabbed my balls. She said, "I'll castrate my husband now, if that's what we are going in there for." Though it was a joke, she probably meant it. Sam and his wife laughed, but I didn't think it was funny.

We walked with them upstairs. It was also beautifully decorated with the same furniture setting as in the living room. The bedrooms were decorated as the Lincoln room of the Oval Office, with flowers in all four corners of the room. Here we could see the beautiful city of Reno with its arch glittering the sign, 'The Biggest Little City in the

World.' It was as if the couples had arranged the semblance of a perfect world, a cocoon for a kind of retreat.

I was not vicious that my family friends were doing better than I was. The reason for that was, without Efemona, I thought I might have been able to compete. After all, UK is helping Sam with his bills, therefore making him a perfect realman to compete in the real world of material stuff.

In contrast, Efemona had been working but never one day try to help pay off our bills. She'd knew more about American law than anyone else among the African community in the Little City of Reno. What she does with her money was of course unknown to me.

Finally, we were ushered to the dinner table. We all sat and picked at our food, talked and smiled with each other. Everyone was busy eating the fufu with okra soup when Sam broke the silence. "I can't wait to tell you, Efemona, that Ekiaqueta is doing his best to take good care of you. Your dressing pattern these days has changed. You'll make a big difference now in Nigerian elections if you run for office to set an example to the African women here in Reno how to dress. Thank your husband and the American TV influence."

Listening to Sam, Efemona wanted to remind him that she and I were visitors at their house and were part of the ridicule if Sam should have the nerve to pick on her alone.

Efemona reacted, she accepted the compliments and cleared her throat after swallowing a big mound of *fufu* on her palm. Then she looked at Sam and UK. Finally she said, "Thank you for your observations and compliments."

Sometimes men know that women in the company of their family friends are sometimes dramatic. I watched UK's frivolous and dramatic manner as she tried to prove a point. She was squirming on her chair. She caught Efemona off guard and sided with her husband. She said, "That's right. Efemona has puffy cheeks these days than when she first came to join Ekiaqueta here in Reno, Nevada. At a time, I thought Ekiaqueta had married a woman having Kwarsiokor. How did Ekiaqueta manage to know you, Efemona? I understand you are now the talk of the town here in Reno as soon as you formed your movement?" Sam interrupted UK.

UK was lost. "What movement are you talking about, baby?" "Oh! Efemona has a movement known as the African Women Against Marriage Movement (AWAM) she had secretly formed here recently in Reno."

"I haven't heard about it."

Efemona concentrated on her food. For a time I was lost too, with AWAM formation. I let it die in my heart.

I could tell Efemona didn't like the revelation. But she endured partly because she was a guest. After a few seconds, Efemona faced UK. She said slowly, "When we were coming over here, my husband didn't even give me a compliment. Because I like you and Sam as our good family friends, I wouldn't like to disrupt Adeze's birthday party with her friends."

Efemona's eyes met mine coolly, not quite defying me, but just testing how I will react. I said nothing.

Efemona said, "I wish. I want my husband to listen, too. He, my husband is too native and zombie. He's not a realman as I thought he was. He's too tired to talk adult conversations. He's too tired to take me out. And I don't even want to talk about that of sex! I had to finally take him to Mount Rose and initiated it on top of a horse with him before we came here. Right now it looks like I am the man. He knows it. The little money my husband makes, he sends to his folks, and the remaining he takes to the casino to double it, hoping to make a fortune and then he comes home broke."

She looked at my face, then to Sam. "Mr. Broke! Show me some dollars. Ask my husband sitting beside you how much money he has in his pocket *now*? This is not a joking matter, Sam. Because of his behavior, us together without money is sparks and fire. We both had an inner light and inner energy that moved us forward for a while. My husband saved and bought cars from the Government Auctions and sold them for a huge profit. Today he has nothing. He has sent every dime of the capital and the profits to his father and his relatives in Nigeria. And here I am suffering. Ekiaqueta comes home now and eat if he has the strength. After eating he lies on the couch like a log. Thereafter, a high pitched snoring would tear through our entire building, shattering the night. Our neighbors across from us are frozen in their room as they try to determine from which building the snoring was coming out of. You ask your friend, Sam. He's sitting down here with you as if I'm telling tales against him. I dare him to say something. I hate him now. The Bible says, 'He who is not for you is against you.' It is how I know the Bible is right. So you see, Sam, I'm against my husband *now*, very much. I could careless what you people would think about me in the meantime with my African Women Against Marriage Movement I have registered with the National Organization of Women (NOW) here in Reno. UK and I know that women age fast. I'm aging fast. If I don't act fast, Ekiaqueta will ruin my life."

I thought, what life has my wife got when I met her in that village picking firewood? I'd wanted to say something when Efemona interrupted me. She said, "My husband's father and his immediate senior sister who are witches in Nigeria will not plan my life for my family. I don't understand why they wouldn't let me and my husband live our lives peacefully. My husband has just installed a telephone for his father in the village and myself and our children are here and he's treating me like shit, and as a second class citizen, as if I'm a fool dug out from a pit latrine. Right now I'm no longer a fool or a pit dawn woman. I have taken my bath and put on my make-up. I am awake and ready with my knocking boots."

At a loss for words, Efemona finally paused. UK noticed she'd finished her London Gin. "Have another?" she looked at Efemona. She nodded. She filled up Efemona's glass. UK shrugged, "I'll not side with you on that, honey. This is not our country. I'm also a woman like you, Efemona. Our parents in Nigeria are number one we should think extremely about because they are aging fast. The reason for that is because they have no money to maintain themselves out there. Secondly, they have no means of getting here where everyone has an opportunity to get a job. We have jobs here and we get paid for the work that we do here. Our parents are there suffering and besides, Ekiaqueta bought your ticket to come to America. He has the right to send anything to his father, brothers and sisters and relatives if he chooses to do so and if he has the money."

Efemona didn't like that and didn't want to hear the truth. For an African woman having the thoughts of showing her husband 'nine-nine', she said, "I'll refund my husband his air fare ticket money he paid for me to join him in this country."

Frankly speaking, I may or may not have lowered my voice when I'd retorted to ask Efemona why she was disrespecting me before my family friends, but the stereo automatically came on, and so, everyone listening to me had to listen to Efemona singing with Frank Sinatra, "My Way". What a great song! And I thought Sam Okorie just wanted to ridicule Efemona by playing the song with a remote control.

I gave him my thumbs-up to indicate that I knew what he meant, though I was not in the best of moods as you may have thought. So, despite the fact that I was impressed so far with Sam and his wife, I said finally to my Efemona, "How about all the documents I sent to you to obtain the visas. And how are you going to pay my father who introduced you to me, smart ass?"

UK caught me short. She said, "You said Ekiaqueta is a gambler," she continued in a friendly manner of consolation. "My husband was also a gambler, but I made him stop it. You can do it, too. Getting into a confrontation over little things like that would be a grievious breach of our tradition. Think about it, Efemona. You need to see those people that I grew up with. I was surprised, sad when I saw how some of them had become haggard looking. I could see where dried tears hung tough around their eyes and cheeks. I even touched and hugged my best friend, Lucy, whom I attended the same Catholic School with. She was fat when I left the country seven years ago. I could feel her bone-like, thin, frail hands and her ribs. Her once fat cheeks had shrunk and her jawbone had jutted out. I am aware you know why that is, Efemona? It's because she has no money to buy her necessities. The only women with flesh on their bones before I left the country are those dealing with drugs with the juntas. Like Miss Oyakilome, Madam Mariam, Bad Dudu's wife, and one other notorious one that brought down the

Babagida's junta's regime." She tried to remember her name, but she couldn't. "I'll tell you in a minute when I remember her name, honey."

Meanwhile, Efemona had ignored UK's sermon. Finally, she winced at her and said, "Fill up my glass with gin, madam story teller."

UK stood and walked to the center table where the gin bottle was still waiting to be consumed. And UK had wanted to say no baby, it appears to me the gin is bringing out the demon in your head. But she didn't. As UK walked away to serve Efemona her drink, Efemona murmured, "Ekiaqueta's folks can all go to hell. I have only one life to live. My husband even had the guts to tell me the other day that he would use the money on his 401K plan to build a house for his father in their village. What kind of nonsense is that?"

I guess she wanted me to hear her, but I was busier than ever swallowing my fufu. After the dinner, the couple walked us to our car. Efemona sat behind the wheel and waved good-bye. My daughter stayed behind with her friends. Everyone had fun except my wife who gnawed, grinned and whined on the steering wheel as she sat. After cursing, she had the guts to ask me, "Where to?"

"1632 Wedekind Road, Apartment E," I said.

She zoomed off. On the freeway, I had the nerve to ask my wife about the AWAM movement Sam had knowledge about, but me. "You'll know after I show you 'nine-nine' in this city. She slammed on the brakes. I was wondering what she was going to do. "Get the hell out of this car or I'll call the police for verbal abuse."

I was scared. So I hopped out of the car. Efemona drove home alone leaving me in the middle of nowhere on the freeway, which about summed it up that Efemona was getting possessed about the possibility of planting balls in-between her legs.

Chapter

9

Quite frankly, I arrived home shortly after mid-night on foot. You and I know that in America, you don't trust anyone to give you a ride on the freeway. Though, three beautiful, single women had volunteered and stopped to give me a ride home, I declined their offer, but thanked them graciously for their generosity. As I got home, I tried to reconstruct the event that led to my walking home. For me to ask Efemona why she did what she did was weighty on my mind. How to confront a woman who was ready to germinate balls between her thighs was the question. Anyway, I took off my sunglasses for her to see how swollen my right eye had become. Efemona saw the eye and pretended not to see. Then I walked to the refrigerator to help myself to a beer because I knew she would not entertain me in the first place. I mean Efemona became cold and rustic, called me names I can never forget: like zombie and pig immediately I'd walked into the house.

Here, I felt my skin had been sliced off my body like a lamb in the slaughter. We fought, physically, all over. We insulted each other and fought in the kitchen. I tell ya! Efemona became a strong woman. It took me as many left hooks and right crosses as I could uncork to keep her honest in the African way. What a strong woman she'd become!

Here I'll tell you that African women usually kept their mouths shut when their husbands were talking. Things had changed with Efemona and I drastically. Despite my carefully planted hooks and jabs, there were times when Efemona's hooks saw tactics that penetrated my defense and I'd wind up with a face full of cuts from her nails and jabs.

I tell ya! It was war of nerves with Efemona and she knew it.

America had Americanized her. Can I stay awake another night arguing with Efemona, who has known more about American law than I? By the way, what the hell have we been arguing about for the last three nights . . . not my swollen black eye I received from her when she whipped Enjoy to trot her way to moan pleasure of release. It was about mostly mean things and how I should become a realman: like uhhh, Ekiaqueta, zombie, what're you doing standing over my shoulder? Why do you buy R&B music and not cowboy music of Kenny Rogers or cowgirl music of Dolly Parton? What a new woman Efemona had become! Nerves. "Efemona!

What the hell are you doing?! Why don't you shut the fuck up?!" "Get the hell out of me. I want to die. I don't want to be a part of your life any more. I want to go to New York to join Okoro. Send a message to your father and sisters that I want to leave my life as the Romans."

"Quick! 911 operator please send me an ambulance to 1632 Wedekind, number E. My wife passed out in the bath tub. Had too much London Gin as a downer, possibly cognac and marijuana as an upper to be flippant and nonchalant."

Numerous suicide attempts! Maybe five attempts! By the time the last one occurred, I was hoping she would just do it! In any case, it was a different feeling to come home on my lunch hour and find my wife in the kitchen table sitting butt naked drunk and passed out and forgot to get the kids from their baby-sitter. Even the bills for our baby-sitter became another problem. Does Efemona give a fuck? Absolutely not!

The quarrelling and howling each day at our residence became a concern to our neighbors. It was to be one of the lessons that would land me in trouble: verbally abusing my African wife. We were still arguing over who should do the dishes in the house when Dapor Ogundemu Akintude walked in one evening.

I should point out here, that Akintude was Efemona's boss at Rossy Medical Center located in Medieval Street in Reno, Nevada. I guess they were secretly doing their thing and Efemona had telephoned him to come over and deal with me on a man to man thing. The one thing you may not know is that men fucking their friends' wives visit in order to humiliate the man before the woman.

But anyway Dapo walked majestically in without knocking on the door in a place that I pay my monthly rent and take care of my children, then looked at me funny. And he had the nerves to ask, "How are you doing baby? Is he doing the dishes today?" What a humiliation and insult?! I thought.

How could an African man also married with children come to my home to disrespect me? I dared him to recount his words. He was reluctant. Efemona knew better not to invite her dick reliever to my domain.

Anyway, it wasn't until we were watching the Oscar awards on the TV of the evening that it dawned on me that I'd shared a lovely dinner, enjoyed the warmth of a stranger in my home and experienced no bad vibes. The only negative thing about the whole thing was that I was in my house with a visitor who loved my wife more than his own wife he kept indoors and hated my guts because they've been screwing behind my back. So to speak I thought.

Nevertheless, I noticed Efemona in deep thought. I knew what she was thinking. I can tell you that she was searching her mind time and again whether it was her who'd changed or me whom she now had upperhand in controlling because the American System of Law says so. Obviously, it was me who is unsocial, very native who doesn't want to change his ways of his forefathers, and therefore, Efemona doesn't mean a damn thing. My father and my relatives mean more than herself and her children. I, Ekiaqueta would have to choose between his father, sisters and relatives or there would be no more peace. She looked at Dapor and said, *"E-soyakwékona!* What a fuck!" She jumped to her feet. They talked for a few seconds. I must tell you I was scared in my own house merely looking at Dapor, a man having frog-like eyes and stout looking, with biceps bigger than mine. You never know what a man fucking your wife will do if you turn your back, so I made sure I was facing him throughout. The thing is, I might turn my head and he would use his machoness to grab my head and deep it inside the pot of boiling water on the stove and after that, make up a story with Efemona to tell the cops of Reno.

For that I sat down a moment like a drone contemplating about the build-up of animosity for the news of Dapor screwing my wife. As I summed up the courage I said, "Akintude! Dapor! Ogundemu! Get the fuck out of my house!"

"Dapor stays and you leave," Efemona voiced out.

I said to Efemona, "Tell Dapor I do not want to see him at my house anymore from this moment on."

"You damned stupid fool with no dick enough to satisfy your woman…" Dapor said, which annoyed me that I could not resist to use any object at my disposal.

So I started the commotion. I slapped the fuck out of his face. I watched him stagger and held his face with his two hands between two chairs of our dining table. When he regained his vision he yelled out, "Dammit! You should be happy I'm helping you to fuck your wife."

"You might be happy, but am not," I said.

Actually Dapo had penetrated my defense that left me with a broken nose and a gash on my right eyebrow, the same eye that had already seen it all when Efemona engaged me on the horse ride fucking me her own way to socialize me.

Little did I know that Akintude knew more about my home than me. He ran to the drawer of my kitchen and fetched out a chef knife to cut my throat. Seeing him coming towards me like a wounded lion, with the huge knife, Efemona screamed, but it was too late. Not what she'd intended to happen perhaps-also the opposite. The knife was in the air for me and I leaped to avoid it when Dapo swung it to penetrate my ribs, but I fell on the kitchen floor. "Stop it, stop it," I yelled out. He tried to stab me, but I gripped his ankle and we struggled like wrestlers on the floor.

I might be slim, but I succeeded in knocking him out with my left fist which rendered him unconscious. But then, I thought we were even. He wouldn't buy that. He became more furious and aggressive. Then he yelled out, "I'm gonna teach you a lesson, pardner."

"I'm not your pardner, sucker. Efemona is your pardner, buddy," I managed to say.

I'd blood dripping from my right eye and it had completely closed. I could hardly see. I yelled as Akintude and Efemona had now attacked me in an attempt to attract my neighbors for help, but Akintude seemed glued on top of me like a male duck mating with its opposite.

No sign of neighbors.

I finally managed to wrestle him off my back, clubbing him down with my right fist, a man twice my size. Then he jabbed a strong fist at my left eye, a blow I ducked from nothing but instincts, and I tried catching him by his right arm and then flinging him against the kitchen wall. I thought I'd flung him on the stove, but he was tough to resist and he connected with another of his deadly fists to my head that left me unconscious once more. In short I had a head hemorrhage and I was about losing the fight in my own house, which made me even more angry, but not much I could do because Efemona had teamed up with Dapor to reduce me and make sure I don't win the fight.

She came behind my back and knocked me ancient and modern with a hard fist in my lower back. But as I ducked another of Dapor's fists and twisted around with a deadly blow that would have ended the fight, it caught Efemona on her face-the blow that made her crawl away moaning. I watched her suddenly rise to her feet and come after me with her high heeled Gucci shoe and her watery eyes said much that I'd done some damage to her. With the heeled shoes in her hand, momentarily determined to club me with it, I shouted, "No," but she'd already got me hard on my balls. I fell.

Dapor raised his foot over my head to stomp me for the fight to be over. I hissed fiercely with pain, still reacting to the nail-heeled shoe, then turned toward Dapor, dodged his foot, turned to Efemona and kicked her, targeting no part of her body anatomy in particular, but hitting her at her knee cap and she fell on her butt. She yelled out, "No man does that to a woman in America!"

"Damn right. But I did," I yelled back.

More angry and furious, Dapor said, "Dammit!" and he connected another left hook to my skull and I fell again. Once more, the fighting fury had turned to blood and tears. Efemona's wailing voice roughened and was still determined that I must pay a price for laying my hands on her boss who gives her the beef behind my back more than I give her, perhaps.

Suddenly, our children woke. I could hear their siren voices. "Daddy! Daddy!" Verita, Ehimare, and Ozie all came out from their rooms and saw their daddy in a pool of blood. But Efemona wanted me dead and yelled at them, "Shut up and go to bed."

I laid my hand on Efemona's umbrella and rammed the tip of it into Dapor's face. But he deflected it with his elbow. Not quick enough, it penetrated into one of his nostrils.

"That serves you right," I managed to say. Man, it was an ugly scene.

With my one eye to see now, I could see that blood had soaked Dapo's clothes, like mine. I was about to descend upon him like a wounded rattle snake, when Efemona grabbed me from behind. As I twisted with strength, and about to land a powerful punch to Dapor's face, she staggered backwards, but was stunned by the force of my blow and she fell on her face again. "You deserve it, bitch," I yelled at her.

Efemona got up, furious as ever, and cursed the day my mother gave birth to me.

Akintude managed to get up and he said with his eyes closed, "Goddammit!" He roared like a wild beast, but I could see that his vision was blurred by the damage the umbrella had done to his nostril. He'd lost quite a bit of blood, but could still see. "Sonava bitch!" he yelled at me imitiating a cowboy intonation and reached again for the chef's knife under the dining room table. He swung with it and before I could defend myself, he rammed the knife in my right eye-the eye that had seen it all, with the deadly whips of the horse from Efemona and deadly blows from Dapor. I fell and was unable to get up, finally.

Efemona called out, "Yeah-hoo! Go for the gold, Akintude. Kill him. Kill the sucker who doesn't want me to *enjoy* in America." The thing is, I wasn't gonna let the sonovabitches hack me to death. As I lingered in pain, I could hear Dapor and Efemona laughing at me and calling me names. But who gives a fuck as long as I still have life with me? But I was mercilessly dazed. Finally, I heard the sirens fast approaching our apartment building and thereafter I was relieved. Probably I thought: my neighbors had heard the commotion and called the cops.

As Efemona and Dapor soon clutched each other like husband and wife I tried to haul myself off of the kitchen floor, when I heard tires hiss to a stop in front of my apartment. Within a few seconds, there came flourishes of knocks on the door and some figures I could faintly see, then emerged like a silhouette through the bright beam of security lights. The figure was that of a policeman.

"Thank God," I murmured within me.

"Is he okay?" the officers I could hardly see asked.

Truly speaking, I must admit I was hyperventilating, making up for life's revival of lost breath. I managed to say, "I'm fine officer." However, the officer didn't think I was fine. It was a stunned moment of disbelief and horror when suddenly I fell on the officer's foot. The officer squatted down and felt around my eyes and chest, searching for my pulse beside my mouth to render CPR. As I woke and gathered strength and momentum, the officer helped me to my feet, propping me against the dining room table. He examined my condition and said with a low voice, "I think you might need an ambulance."

"No! No! I'll take care of myself," I managed to say. He did not buy that. Somebody must be shipped to Parr 911 Jail Boulevard. With that I began to sweat, trying to recover and trembling. The officer finally plies me for my story after he saw my eyes and my condition. Some statement I believe he must enter on the paper for his day's trouble.

"It's a long story," I managed to say.

"Just tell me (us) a little of it," he insisted.

Meanwhile, Dapor and Efemona had separated from cuddling themselves and Efemona was wiping tears off her eyes and cheeks when the officer walked up to her. He asked her, "Ma'am, are you alright?"

As he was talking to her, I fell again on my knees. And Efemona looked in my direction and then into the officer's eyes. "He's pretending," Efemona said with impunity vibes.

"I think Ekiaqueta might make it to the nearest hospital," the officer said.

Efemona sniffed in her tears while the officer consoled her. "I better call in some ambulance."

One ambulance arrived within a few minutes. The personnel team looked at my right eye. "What happened?"

"They pounced on me," I managed to say.

The officer standing and watching the ambulance personnel waited to hear my response with his notepad to the ready, ready to take some confession.

"Who pounced on you?" his question chatted out.

"Efemona and Dapor, her new dick reliever when I'm at work." "With a reason that is more than that," Efemona voiced out. Two more officers listening laughed. "American versus African, I suppose," the officer said, of course thinking Efemona was American because she was speaking the Yankee more than the Yankilians.

The officer looked down at me and saw the blood stumps that were on my right eye, nose, mouth and my rib cage. He screamed even louder.

As I became fully aware of my surroundings, I gave my full version of the story. After my confession, the officer instructed the ambulance personnel team to transport Efemona and Dapor to St. Mary's Hospital first. I could visualize Efemona laid on the stretcher, shoved into the ambulance as the dazzlingly lit ambulance split the night while taking charge with professional heartiness and treating Efemona like a baby inside. But truly she'd no bruises. She was treated and then released before the officers. I figured Efemona knew the bill they would send to her in the mail would probably be more than treating me, her brutally dazed and wounded husband. So she hopped down from the ambulance, so that the personels would give me immediate attention.

I was helped into the ambulance which departed immediately and then dropped off at the Washoe Medical Center in the emergency room where some nurses had directed Lt. Larson and Sgt. Truce to join me later to take my full confession. Here I need not be told they were doing it for the interest of law. Looking back to how Efemona got involved with Dapo, I would say bravo to her for deceiving me of all people which gave her the edge of a good humor and laughter seeing the news on the local channel at four P.M. which I knew did not bother her, the fact that she wants me dead.

But then, I am glad that American doctors never let down their patients and their profession.

*   *   *

It was now six A.M. on a Sunday morning when I heard Charles Looman, an amiable gentleman working for the state by day as a Rev. Father and a doctor and a warden by night came to see me. I guess he was on his ritual of doing his morning rounds and praying to the sick to get well. At my bedside he stopped and looked at my eyes. Then he delivered a nicely pointed sermon on morality with African women screwing around with their husbands' best friends, when they came to America, but specifically not mentioning that Efemona had broken the Ten Commandments and should repent her sins so that I would be healed. Efemona, standing beside my bed, figured that Looman had read a transcript of the previous day's incident and therefore, got the right to say any rotten sermon as an American. Dr. Looman didn't mention names, of course, but Efemona smart as she could be was pretty sure Looman was referring to her. Efemona was happy though, that Looman didn't mention Dapor's name for the community now growing with quite a number of Africans from Nigeria to hear and know about Dapor's adultery with her and almost killing the man who brought her to America in his own house. More often than not, Looman hardly preached to his patients on their sick bed. But in my condition he figured he had to because Washoe Medical Hospital was not a Catholic hospital where they have Reverend Fathers praying for those on a death watch.

Looman looked around my bedside and saw a number of nurses with Sgt. Truce and Lt. Larson he knew and Efemona with my children with teary faces. Sgt. Truce, Lt. Larson and all the nurses looked at me in my condition and shook their heads. Finally, Looman made some oblique reference to my predicament by reminding everyone standing beside my bed that though in America women were the weaker vessel, more sinned against than sinners themselves, Efemona, an African with Dapor coming to America had changed the course of events. I can imagine what entailed- which means that America is Americanizing the African women whom their husbands paid their way to join them in America.

After the ridicule, Looman asked me, "How are you feeling, my friend?"

I thought it was an unnecessary question for a sick man in my condition at that crucial moment.

So I said, "The prodigal son which Efemona think that I am is tired and in serious pain."

Looman smiled mischievously. "What a pity. I came here to treat you to get well, my friend."

He turned me around on my bed and used his two hands to press on my stomach. "It hurts," I said.

"It is why I'm here to take a look and treat you before we decide on your faith for verbal abuse of Efemona and of a good samaritan."

I figured that's what the police had put on my charges. Anyway, Looman glanced at his watch and said, "I'll be back."

As I waited for him, my pain increased. I wished he hadn't woke me up. This was the first time I realized that time was slow when one was in a miserable condition. A few minutes later Looman showed up with a tube in his hand. Then he said to Lt. Larson and Sgt. Truce still at my bedside waiting for the outcome of my faith. "I'm afraid there's really nothing we can do for Ekiaqueta. His left eye is badly hurt and might be ruptured. We might have to remove it and replace it with a cow eye. You guys can save the eye and lose a customer who would make plenty of money for the State, the judges, the lawyers and the public defenders or you guys can let me take off the eye and replace it with a cow eye and have a one-eyed man destined to live and still live with Efemona to raise their children when he is released and at least Efemona would still be happy having a husband to look up to. We are talking both ways here, folks."

Looman looked at both officers again in their deputy uniforms. Then he continued, "This young woman," he looked and smiled at Efemona, "Would have a man and the state judges and public defenders make more money. Think about it deputies."

Hearing that I then sat up on my bed, feeling my world was about to fall apart. Everything was happening so fast as in a movie to someone else, but me that I had listen in awe as if hallucinating. Looman added, "If the eye is not removed now, Ekiaqueta will die within a week."

I must be frank to say I commend Dr. Looman and his nurses who tried all they possibly could to save my eye first before he contemplated to replace it with a cow eye or just seal it with rubber cement, in which case I might live up to a year while my left eye ended up like the main character of the famous movie: Scarface. And I could hear Efemona reacting, "Oh man! You got to be kidding."

And above all she was thinking that: if Looman replaces it with a cow eye, my Ekiaqueta might still be able to see. I'd rather have them both taken out and replaced with a goat and a cow eye so that he couldn't read his bank statements anymore and she could then siphon the little money I have in my account to her family in Nigeria to sustain life. And she looked at me. She knew I have no mind of my own to think at this crucial time. So she said, "I swear with the Oba's Palace in Benin that I'm gonna take everything you ever owned before I met you and after I leave you. The children and I wouldn't miss you very much. No, I retract that. The children might miss you, but not me. I also swear with Princess Akinzua and my mother that I'll acquire everything you've got."

Finally, my Efemona made up her mind. She said to Looman, "I object to that Dr. Looman."

"Give me a reason, Efemona," and he laughed.

"Because, What Can I Say right eye would still do the work of two and my children and I would be greatly scared of his face when he's released."

"So what are we to do, Efemona?"

Efemona suggested, "I prefer the eye be replaced with a matured eye of a big goat and of a big cow so that I could see him every day with the goat and cow eye walking on the side of the street like a real big goat or big cow. In that case, I can feel young again and be able to *enjoy* myself and also, be able to use my new sex appeal anyway I choose to shun men. Also, I could choose from Forbes top 100 most attractive men in

America if my husband should die on the operating table. And wherever they take me out to, and I see my husband walking along the street to Winnemucca where I lined up men with a bigger dick to satisfy me any time of the day, and him gazing on the sidewalk, I could spit on him while I chew my Extra Mint gum as I drive by him."

The truth about that ofcourse is that it is not a mistaken notion that the nature of a woman who wants to be independent will tell her life story to every Dick and Harry. But it is not so with a man. You and I know by now that women are objects of worship in America. For that Dr. Looman excused Lt. Larson and Sgt. Truce for a few minutes. They contemplated what to do, noting that Efemona has Americanized. When they came back, Looman said to Efemona, "We all agreed with you, because we must satisfy your request, that an African woman like Efemona now in America has the right accorded all Americans in this country. We have decided that a goat eye or cow eye be used for this kind of operation and your husband would be the first man we would use to perform the experiment."

With that encouragement to Efemona, I was wheeled to the Operation Room. And as I laid on the operation table in the operating room, I could hear the music humming while they performed the operation on my left eye. I was not myself as I think of my children. So many thoughts flashed behind my memory: like life as an orphan can be dementing and worse for children ages: eleven, ten and eight who are sometimes mistreated, molested, sodomized by their caretakers and step parents. As I recollected about the fight once again in my place with Dapor, which led to my predicament for Efemona to have a negative attitude against me, so many other thoughts flooded my being. That I shouldn't have fought with Dapor. I should've given Efemona the liberty to *enjoy* herself in America to avoid the fracas. Now my children would pay the price for all this mess. The abominable things parents got themselves carelessly into. And what I would give for one more advice to my children before I die on the operating table. I knew at their ages, they are not yet aware of the finality of what death is.

I swallowed my pain.

Efemona was watching the television in the waiting room with our children, smoking her last cigarette of the minute, ignoring the news of the operation when the nurses wheeled me back to the ward. Then Efemona stared at me on the gurney as they wheeled me by then suddenly jumped to her feet.

"Walking beside Looman she asked, "How was the operation?" "The operation was successful," Looman answered over her shoulder.

"Successful?" she asked then sighed. And I knew why she'd sighed after cajoling the American doctors for their expertise in the field of medicine. She'd wished they flew me to Nigeria where I would remain on the gurney before I die without an operation in the operating rooms with no scalpels and tools to perform such a rare type of an operation of an eye taken out and replaced with a goat or a cow eye.

Looman had wanted to ask her to give me a kiss, if only on the cheek, because he'd figured I'd definitely gone to the other side before waking up after the operation.

"When was your last kiss with Ekiaqueta, Efemona?" he wanted to ask Efemona. "Do you love Ekiaqueta? How much? Or you still believe in what you told Achuko, 'you don't want me to enjoy'?" But he kept his question to himself, and instead he narrated about the new development of the goat and cow eye operation soon to be approved for Africans from Nigeria by the Food and Drug Administration.

As he was still talking, my cow eye fell out of its socket. Looman exclaimed, "Oh! What's going on here? Maybe his body immunity had rejected it because the cow eye we used was too mature and old."

Looman became greatly disappointed. He looked at Efemona while Dr. Larson, Sgt. Truce and the rest of the nurses looked on. "Ekiaqueta must be shipped back into the operating room if he must live. All of you do have a choice. You can take another chance and decide not to have the surgery done on him again. In that case, Ekiaqueta might end up in the cemetary. Or all of you can let me do what is best for him and replace the eye with a young calf's eye. Then he would have a ninety-five percent chance to live and the city of Reno would be glad to be making more money on his head for performing the operation, while we charge the Federal Government thousands and thousands of dollars. What do y'all think?"

Efemona looked at me on the bed, then to Lt. Larson and Sgt. Truce. I know she preferred me dead. But the city would make the money. She was thinking fast.

Lt. Larson and Looman looked at themselves while all waited for Efemona to say something. Finally, Looman looked at her in her eyes directley. And Efemona smiled.

"So it's all up to me now to decide for my husband?"

"Pretty much so. Yes!" Larson said. And Looman and his nurses nodded and looked on as they smiled a mocking smile at Efemona. Doctor Andradae, who was Looman's assistant was pissed. He couldn't hold back any longer, so he asked, "What's going on?

Make the decision and let's wheel him out of here."

Andradae fully remembered Efemona, who had now changed into a taffeta black velvet backless gown, with her titties pumped up. The backless velvety taffeta probably cost more than Ekiaqueta earned in a month, Andradae thought. He looked at Efemona's face, then her head. He could see a black head-tie on her head. He thought she'd probably worn it to mourn her What Can I Say. For that he decide he'll do his best to ruin Ekiaqueta at the slightest chance he has when Looman was out of the operating room because What Can I Say had once exchanged words with him at Parr 911 Jail Boulevard that would've cost him his job.

Finally, Lt. Larson said to Dr. Andradae, "Just a disagreement."

"Disagreement my butt. I would want the cow eye replaced immediately with that of a young calf eye and the city of Reno make more money, ruin him, kill him on the operating table," she said.

Andradae was not still satisfied. "What do you think?"

"If my husband should die on the operating table, will the city of Reno make any profit?"

"Just about the same as if he survives," Lt. Larson said and Sgt. Truce nodded.

"Oh! Well go ahead then and replace the eye with a young calf's eye."

All smiled amicably. Then they gave a thumbs up for Efemona, gave themselves a high five and Lt. Larson said, "Thanks, Efemona. The city of Reno loves you. All the African men verbally abusing their wives under our care are almost being released on death watch on our hospital beds and in jails except What Can I Say, who is still in our custody at Washoe Medical Center. From this operation the city could bill the Federal Government one-point-five million dollars. In that case, me and my counterparts could arrange where to meet to share the proceeds among ourselves. I could go to Hollywood and buy me another home or boat."

Efemona smiled. Then she said, "That's what capitalism is all about."

All of them gave Efemona a bear hug, one by one, the very truncated hug of a typical Yankee American. They said one after the other, "Reno loves you. We love you, too. We shall let you know when Ekiaqueta is released. We do advise you to call the cops any time you go for a dinner with him. Create a scene on the highway. Invite Dapor to entertain you with a dick helper or a corn on the cob. We'll arrange for Reno cops to get him here. Is that alright with you?"

Efemona nodded and watched as they wheeled me away to the operating room. And Lt. Larson said to her, "I'll recommend that Efemona's name be nominated for a name of a street in this Little City of Reno."

"That would be wonderful," Efemona affirmed and gave Lt. Larson a fatherly kiss on his mouth. Finally she walked in front of the gurney on which I laid, while looking helplessly at the ceiling with so many thoughts again about my faith and our children.

I could visualize her moon eyes shining with a diabolical gleam looking at me. As I laid thinking my faith, I heard some faint fragment of words from my Efemona, "You ain't had much of nothing anyway, except the 401K retirement benefit, so to speak. But God bless you with Verita, Ehimare and Ozie through me. I'm gonna raise them with other men in place of you. Bye and I hope you don't make it." And she left me in limbo with the doctors and the state.

Looman, Larson, Andradae, and Truce all coughed. I could visualize them standing beside the gurney on which I laid like alter boys in the operating room, I looking drained, pale and miserable, they glowing with good health and watching Efemona and other nurses with shining long legs, how they would screw them when my operation was over and salivating and so on and so forth.

Anyway, tears ran down my cheeks as I begged Lt. Larson for a Bible to pray for Efemona.

He laughed and looked at me, thinking: look at this fool relying on the Bible at this critical moment in his life. Then he said, "You believe in the Bible?"

"Pretty much in times like this," I replied. He did not stop there. He added, "I just want to know why you want to pray for Efemona?"

"I figure she knows not what she's doing to a man who brought her to America from the culture of poverty Bad Dudu and his junta regime had inflicted on our people and our country. She should've appreciated me and forgiven me for whatever I have done to her," I replied.

After about ten or so minutes, everyone beside me forgot or made believe they forgot that I was still alive. In fact, Lt. Larson went out of his way to be nice to me, explaining to me about my operation, making a few dumb jokes about a woman from Africa coming to America to sell her husband to the authorities. Finally he brought me the Bible and he watched me pray the sinner's prayer along with everyone beside me except Efemona, who looked away. I learnt to forgive and I believed that through men was salvation possible through HIM. So I forgave Efemona.

However, I'd a very difficult time accepting the loss of my freedom and I could resort to vengeance if I was released at that hour.

But at heart, I knew it wasn't worth the pain to bother Efemona since she only has one life to live. With permission from Looman who'd warned me not to strain my only eye to see until my right eye was completely healed, I opened the Bible at random and I saw the phrase, "Do not worry." So I continued to read it aloud, Matt. 6:34, which in further detail stated, "Therefore, do not worry about its own things, sufficient for the days is its own trouble."

I must be frank to say that this verse of the Bible made me to believe that HE wanted me to see the passage to tell me not to worry about my problems and leave the work up to HIM, because, WE-humanity as a whole-thought the human race and hatred or reality, whatever you may call it, came into existence and we can think it's the other way around by seeing all colors and creed as equal, which we all are if only Efemona realized that one day. But for a woman whom I believe wanted to be independent, knew nothing I would say to her would change her mind to stay with me at a time I lost an eye to her dick reliever. I would've loved to see her give me a last kiss, but there was no need for that, because she'd made up her mind.

On the other hand, my last operation on the operating table had been a hundred percent successful. As Lt. Larson and Sgt. Truce were gone, I wrote the full report of the incidence with Dapor. Nevertheless, I was cited for disturbing the peace and causing Dapor pain for helping to satisfy my wife-dick wise. Tossing on my bed, I tried to block out the visions, turn off the TV, erase the memories, but they refused to be eradicated. Efemona's attitude had hurt.

But the one thing good about this little city of Reno is that if the sheriffs and wardens are guarding you on your sick bedside and you are not well before your court date, the judge can arrange for video arraignment. If you plead no contest, which in fact means you are guilty with a reason, and you explain why you committed the crime, the judge might fine you. In my case, I pleaded no contest on the video arraignment so I was fined two thousand and five hundred dollars without having to stand before Hickman in his court to be ridiculed for not having a dick to satisfy my wife and assaulting Dapor for giving her the beef.

I was finally released after a month with one good eye and an eye of a young calf. My children ages eleven, ten and eight did not denounce me. For the love they'd all had for a good father, they all wanted the same eye which I had got from the famous experimental operation of a goat or a cow eye. But I guess they didn't know the negative aspect of it. Why my children needed an operation done on them, my Efemona took me aside and whispered to me, "Please, I want you to sleep twenty-four hours of the day so I don't have to see that eye. When you return from work, your food will be inside the microwave oven. And make sure the children are all asleep before you come in. If by chance my children are out of the house, go straight into the master bedroom and lock yourself in. I am only protecting our children from having to see your cow eye every day."

I accepted all of Efemona's demands because in America I found out that it is the sovereign right of a woman to dictate for their husbands and Efemona had known this. And if their husbands take it as humiliation and not honoring their request, especially women who like to fuck around, it was regarded by their women as rude to their men. They could make out trouble out of it, then call the cops who will ask the men to leave the house for twenty- four hours until the women were satisfied.

Anyway, I obeyed Efemona so that I could only see her only when she came into the master bedroom for her make-up, but without seeing my own children. It was here on my twenty hours indoors I then watched Efemona's critical appraisal of her image in the mirror, which determined that she looked as good as she could be. The funny part of the whole thing was that it was only when she demanded that I laid her was when my dick could only get hard. And when she needed it, she took every step to hold on until mid-night when she turned off all the lights in the house before she then tipy-toed in. It was at this critical time that I found her actually attractive. But I admit that all the rich men of Reno with business all saw Efemona as very pretty or Efemona saw them, too, as handsome. And by no means when these men had intermittently had flirted with her all night and day, all were delighted to discover how easy she was to lay because she just wanted to humiliate her husband with a cow eye. Some of these men of Reno whom Efemona soon found handsome with lots of money as they portrayed to her as my instincts told me at best were all drunks.

Achuko, a good friend of mine who once visited me at the hospital once described to me that one of the notable men whom Efemona had acquainted was very pretty, and had constantly flirted with her, was delighted to discover how easy it was to lay her. That Mr. Atlanta with Efemona at the Harrah's Roof Garden Restaurant was drunk and terribly weary, and was filled with an excitement which was close to panic, in fact, he'd burned his way to the outer edge of drunkenness and weariness, into a diamond-hard sobriety. And that with the voice of Mr. Atlanta, the dead of Reno cemeteries all had sprang out of their graves, serving him and Efemona more wine and London Gin. And that Mr. Atlanta had asked the spirits to please help Efemona to boost her moral to carry along her African Women Against Marriage Movement (AWAM).

Listening to my friend Mr. Achuko did not change the course of events. However, the one thing that I know was that a beggar has no choice. Being too ugly with my one cow eye, I let her alone to do whatever she liked. And at a time I'd lots of pimples on my face because I hadn't fucked for several months. But Efemona drank, enjoyed, probably was shooting dope, whored, but I still had love for her and my children. It was life at the most precarious. Lots of things had happened. She'd conned and trick me always. Had put in a resurface with flippant wino tongue when she walks in to scold me and nut me out in my twenty hours indoors. Lots of tension existed but seldom fucked me when the pimples on my face were too much for her to see and resist. Life for me became sensationally chancy, but there was always tomorrow for her to change, so I thought or so I'd deluded myself into believing. And thus, Efemona was having more balls every day without challenge. Only in America.

Chapter

11

The Biggest Little City In The World had now become a revelation
to Efemona. Ukpenu and Benin City, Lagos mainland at Ajegule
to mention but a few names, had been the largest villages, towns or
cities Efemona had ever been, seen, but they were like hamlets compared
to the giant Neon Lighted Babylon, Reno-City. These villages, towns
or cities or whatever you may call them were loud, dirty and noisy with
armed robbers, Efemona *now* realized. She *now* realized that armed
robbers were not good for societies as in her country.

In contrast, Reno was now the haven where she can naturalize and
relinquish her citizenship, she thought.

It was a few days after dinner with the Patricias, a Saturday evening,
and Efemona, reacting to some remembered behavior of wine and
spirit consumption, decided to take a long walk through the cool of
the evening.

She put on tight Levi jeans and a sport white Nike T-shirt, got into
her Chevy Camaro Z28 and headed over to Patricia.

I should point out that Patricia, to be fair, is a number one bitch
capable of asking her girlfriends to get naked on the street and make
love to donkeys and horses and they obey her or else Efemona is not of
equal to deal with her that is, she's in an occupation whose temptations
would give Jesus Christ an anxiety attacks. Such was the case now,
because with Efemona over at her place and Efemona's red leather
purse dropped on her table, they could get drunk together and whore
all night together. You do the math and picture the kind of a human
being Patricia is.

176

Anyway, Efemona had not seen nor heard any sign of her new male friends during the past few days, and she was horny for a dick. At home Efemona had stayed within earshot of the phone.

Then she'd checked our mailbox a few times the whole day, and she watched the cars that sped by our apartment. In short, she'd reverted to a lovesick new remodel female, and the feeling was not entirely a good feeling.

It was at this moment in time that Efemona had a mail call forwarding and a caller ID cell phone. And within this period of our misunderstanding and transition, Efemona, too, had carefully changed and diverted her mail to her brother's in New Jersey, where in turn her brother, Mr. aka Downfall read to her the contents of her mail to her on the telephone if there were urgent messages from her father, mother, brothers and her sisters, but mostly from the notorious one, Anegbo.

Instincts had told me that Efemona wasn't getting any mail as she used to. For a man with a cow eye, what does he know? But, when she came back from her enjoyment, I summed up the courage and I said, "You finally made it home!"

"Sure." And she took my bottle of Coors beer from my hand, which was about to make me horny, too.

"What did you all do over at Patricia's?"

"You damn well know we were not just there sitting idle. We'd to put on slow music, turn out the lights, get naked, get high on weed and cognac and fucked different men of our choice."

I did not react to that because her balls were getting bigger and bigger everyday and I figured she might start something. Also, I know too that Efemona must've carefully persuaded her parents through telephone conversations, that the choice she'd faced with me in the same roof was stark. In that case, she must fight or die and relinquish her culture and tradition to achieve her purpose in America.

Anyway, to be jocular, I said, "Honey, you seemed not to get as much mail in this apartment as you used to. Why?"

"I diverted my mail anyway. I figured you were getting too smart and might discover my plans of AWAM movement and about all the speeches and rallies I have planned to march on in Reno and D.C."

And why would her parents, my so-called father and mother in-laws, cease to communicate with me? I baffled in my heart. The answer was not quite far away from me, which was that all parents in Nigeria whose sons and daughters are in America want them to send them money to sustain life. Therefore, no matter what Efemona does to achieve her objective as long as she could afford to send them money and file for her brothers and sisters to come to America to take the place of me, her husband, is none of their business. If she can do what her husband couldn't do, so be it. You get it?

So it was a long term plan on how to execute it. A thing that she'd then asked herself in the still of lonely nights and days when she was alone in the living room and me, in the master bedroom because of my cow eye, thinking how she would ruin a man of my caliber and then go about her business as a new African woman to be Americanized and remodeled. What it boils down to was: she would teach me a lesson I'll never forget. Showing me 'nine-nine' was the only answer. She knew Ekiaqueta knows nothing. My husband is a complete fool, she'd thought.

She was wrong. This is what I know: that one evening I was early to return home from work. That my Efemona had eaten and satisfied the children with stories at bed time. And that as I raised my head up to say hello, she knew why I was home. So she frowned. After several minutes of silence coupled with she was horny, she unlocked her heart and spoke to me to deceive me. On the other hand, I also had found out where she'd hidden five bottles of London Gin from which she was serving herself shots to get horny to command me to lay her at any time whether the mood for me was ripe or not. That is, any time she wants me to screw her was only when I can have it. You get that, too?

Anyway, that evening, I wanted to surprise Efemona being the week of our fifth anniversary when her father had pronounced us husband and wife. For that simple reason, I'd thought that we might talk and try to iron out our differences which she'd locked in her heart to be rude to me. For the most part I also had wanted to explain my unhappiness and maybe it might soften her heart, so that we both could recapture the closeness we'd once shared, rolling from one end of the bed to the other end while at the same time our children were happy.

"Well," I said, "How are you doing sweetheart?"

Efemona laughed a mocking laugh. Her eyes opened a second, veiled, and mean in a manner. So I lowered myself down upon her, slowly, allowing her hands to guide mine, before I tried to kiss her on the mouth. Instantly we locked together. Though, her hands fluttered downwards and settled on my lower back, I did not honor it. But I knew she needed it and she only wanted to rape me in broad daylight. Not surrendering to her wishes of her hornyness to have me, her battle and struggle began like a wounded hyena. It was unlike the night before when she'd commanded me and she'd used the same trickish manner whereby her hands moved along my back, up then down, something I'd least expected and which resulted that I brought her closer in, a beautiful indecision, which caused me brokenly, deep in my throat, to moan. That day she'd initiated it and opened up before me whereby I had no choice than to travel up on her savage, jungle, moist river which the rich and famous of Reno were *now* exploring every now and then. Noting that, I broke free. For that she was angry. And she said, "Haven't you heard of the movement I've formed in the City of Reno?" "What movement are you talking about?"

"The movement Sam Okorie reflected on before you at their dinner table."

Instantly, I knew what she meant, though I'd asked as if my Efemona was still the woman of yesterday who'd respected her culture and tradition and her husband.

Efemona looked up. And with a defiance this time, she screamed out, "African Women Against Marriage Movement, which is the lofty view that adultery is merely the application of democracy to love other men rich and famous beside you, Ekiaqueta."

Still I did not lose my temper. But I said instead, "As far as I'm concerned I've always had the impression that we both live happily together until death do us part, so that, that saying that 'long married couples begin to resemble each other,' would be evidence on our faces."

Efemona laughed another mocking laugh. As a new remodeled woman, I knew she wasn't going to be a part of that famous saying.

She would prefer to devote her full time and energy to her new plans and movement. She would then shun off men who are not up to the standard that she's looking for, then date the ones she feels are appealing-young and old who can satisfy her morning and night, so that where ever they take her, warm air would envelope them in a velvet perfumed room and more precisely, the perfume would emanate from her body most of the time, the usual Gucci fragrance. And then, while the young, rich men would command her and abuse her pussy, and she give them blow jobs and swallow, the old men would beg to eat her up, open for her a fresh bottle of champagne with a triumphant pop, and if no pop, they would try again until Efemona was satisfied-it popped the way she wanted it, then pour two bubbling glasses full, and then make a toast, before the usual London Gin straight up to make her more horny and flippant, even if Christ was before her to inform her, 'don't commit adultery and humiliate the cow-eyed man', your husband.

"Did you hear what I said?" Efemona asked. "I'm not deaf," I replied.

"Oh! I thought you were now deaf, too!"

I became mute by force of circumstance, thinking about some choices. I could stop gambling (the notion of gambling she'd made believed and concurted) to become rich and not be insulted day in and day out by Efemona. Finally, I pleaded in a manner of, we are in America. Don't let this society ruin your husband. And for Christ sake can't you forget the new look of my one eye general on my face and drop the subject of showing me 'nine-nine' once and for all? By the way, pass my dinner. I'm hungry. And after dinner can I sleep on my own bed tonight rather than on the floor?"

She laughed another mocking laugh, louder than a wailing dog's. Then Efemona said with boldness, "Look at me in the face! Dammit!"

And I looked at her damned new reconstructed nose on her face.

"No," she said. "Hum, me pass your dinner? You got to be kidding. I believe you know where the kitchen is. I need a divorce anyway. *Dinner kor—dinner ni!?*"

"What is that supposed to mean, Efemona?" "I mean dinner my ass!"

I couldn't make myself believe that Efemona, my wife, could respond to my being hungry or starving or my plight the way she'd responded. Even if she thought my pleading and being hungry was pure nonsense and bullshit. Thus, I slept-starved, not once, not twice, but on a daily basis.

*   *   *

The next morning I brooded over the events of last night. "What's wrong with Efemona for God's sake?" Of course I knew exactly what had gotten into her: she hated my guts for the incidence with Dapor that had become public that he was secretly screwing her behind my back. Anyway, I sort of accepted that, but was still convinced that she also did not love me as she used to, but other men, too. I love her, so she has to love me in return. What really bothered me was that she'd become feisty, went and actually took away my writing materials for this book. To crown it all, I know she'd always had a flippant mouth when she'd had enough London Gin, but she'd never ridiculed me so much for having a cow eye even though she'd approved it for me in the hospital when I couldn't think. She might have said 'one eye general', but not a cow eye. Now she was throwing insults at me over my head. "Maybe it's that time of the month. That cycle of her PMS monthly shit," I thought.

The thing is, I was still not getting it. I got the message when she yelled at me and said raucously, "Zombie" I said, I'll employ different men to cook my lunch and dinner while I shook them off their fruit of the loom and suck their dicks. And they too, will learn to screw and dick me the way I demand of them. Right now you're being placed on probation," Efemona said, with saccharine sarcasm. "From now on until I put you in jail, you'll be the perfect example of truth and justice in the American way. You'll learn how to keep your hands to yourself, don't worry about who is fucking your wife, and do me a favor, be a good husband and a doting father, a smiling, sterling pillar of virtue and integrity rather than a man abusing his wife who wants to *enjoy* in America. If my mother, Edmon, Clement, Anegbo, Emma, Fuck'em Good and Newman all say it's okay to forgive you, then you might earn back your place in my bed. Until the time they and I deem you worthy, don't even try to initiate sex with Efemona. Now do I make myself clear to you? If you feel you can bypass my words and the voodoo of my mother and grandmother guarding their children from time immortal of Oba's Palace, try me and you'll go to jail as many times as I want you to. You can be replaced with other men as many times as I deserve."

You know, I should tell you that I am a man who doesn't easily give up or get angry. Thus, my great love for Efemona, a woman I brought into this country, was at the verge of stardom when she fully realized that I'd become a real Zombie and a one-eyed general. But in real life, who gave her the room to shop all the malls of The Biggest Little City in the World before she was discovered by rich men or her discovering them. But then whoelse can erase the impressions with which she was born and raised? Efemona is the only African woman from Nigeria in The Biggest Little City whom the cops and judges of the City of Reno knows who can.

Finally I lost my temper. "What?" I bellowed.

She knew she'd aggravated my soul or to put it nicely, had disrespected me. She knew what she'd said was sacrilegious in the traditional African sense of married couples.

"Sucking other men?" I repeated.

I starred about her new anatomy that my money had helped reshaped. Breathing rapidly, which I could not control, I shook my head and swallowed convulsively.

She watched my containance standing tough. I could tell she was prepared to uncork as wicked blows, as I could uncork myself. Quickly I'd to restore moderately and dropped the mask of a lion indifference over my features.

"Good. Very nice, Efemona! I guess because I'm not a millionaire? Right?"

My Efemona did not give a shit, even when my only eye to see had dilated. So, finally I moved towards her, my right index finger pointed at her nose and I said, "Is it because I am not a millionaire that would make you suck different dicks in America to humiliate me?"

"That's right!"

"Aha! Pompey has come to Reno to humiliate and see Caesar's downfall," I murmured.

Remembering that her mother used to hail her as *Udonomoeirele-clitoris* with large balls, Efemona answered with vexation, "Pompey had better silence Caesar fast before Caesar got the chance to draw his spear."

It was the last straw to hurt the camel's back. I could feel the blood vessels on my head had bursted. I advanced on Efemona like 'Chaka the Zulu', the greatest African warrior, bent on vengeance for over accumulated insults of wild, unruly manners and of her knowing too much about American law than any other African woman in the city of Reno. Why me? I swallowed.

Though she, too, became adamant, she, too, tried to stick her finger into the only eye that I could see with, which left me with nothing but a slap on her cheek.

My Lord, my God! I trembled after the slap and I dare say my Efemona noticed it. It was an entirely novel experience, because I cried out immediately and begged to be forgiven. And I'd cried out not because the slap was painful to her, but because she could, if she'd been so minded, to pay me back later with the use of poison in my food or blind my only other eye to see.

The lesson for the exhibition between Efemona and I was not the spirit, but the brute in me. To her she never lied according to her upbringing. Her father never taught her to lie. With annoyance still, I said, "So! What about our three children?"

"Oh! Don't worry about that. I'll have them and collect child support every month through the Courts of this City. I've nothing with you," she affirmed sarcastically.

With that I frowned and looked at her face. And she looked at me back.

Finally, she said to me, "I am sorry for everything that has happened tonight. I know it's because of my not cooking for you that was a part of your vexation to escalate the lion indifference monster attitude in you."

"That's not the only reason. Screwing other men is another," I added.

"That must continue with me, though. I can't change that. I don't want to be sex starved in a country where men worship pussy and eat it as their food for breakfast, lunch and dinner."

"Over my dead body. Don't you think that would make my father angry as hell?"

"Probably! And who is your father anyway?" Efemona actually said.

"Do you think he'll get over it as an old man who'd arranged your marriage for me? You Efemona, whom I didn't even know well before I jumped into bed with you?"

"I sure do believe he would get over it. Do me a favor, Ekiaqueta. Tell your father that the next time he proposes any woman in absentia for any of his sons, he should do his homework first."

"You mean he didn't know you were a devil or you didn't show your true colors when he met you to propose you for me?"

Her hyena-like eye balls reverted, then she yelled out, "You know what Ekiaqueta? I'm no longer sorry if that is what you want to hear. I know you are good at writing. You can pick up the pen and write your father and your sister, Marthina, the witch. You have my permission to write my father, too. Next time you feel you are hungry like a tiger, you can go to the kitchen and cook for yourself. I am not your African slave or property anymore. Goddammit! Hey! Here is a pen for you . . ." She rummaged into her purse and flung one at me.

I watched her sultry mouth full of more words to unload, but gave no chance for it. Instead, I went into the kitchen to prepare a quick snack. May Efemona be damned. She'd emptied the refrigerator of all the groceries I'd bought three nights ago. I'd used close to six hundred dollars to buy the groceries. Seeing nothing in the refrigerator, I asked, "What happened to the groceries?"

"I gave them to the homeless of the City."

I did not buy that. I decided to comb out all the kitchen cupboards-nothing. I moved my search to the dishwasher where I found three bottles of London Gin. One was half empty. So I took all the bottles to her where she sat contentedly. She knew what I was about to say. Giving me no room to express my feelings about her drinking habits, she uttered, "Why are you showing them to me? Don't I have the right to keep anything in this house anymore?" "That is not the point. My purpose for showing it to you is because you've changed in habits and manners, to say the least.

Maybe it is because of your drinking habits that makes your clitoris to itch to get to have it with different men."

"None of your business."

"It's my business because I'm your husband and I brought you to this country to respect me and uphold our culture."

"This is America, honey. And don't you forget that before your father discovered me I made him aware that I'm the only *Udonomoeirele* in my family whom my mother and the Oba's Palace ordained to consume London Gin," she nodded and translated, I mean, 'clitoris with larger balls, bigger than your coconut head, if you have forgotten the meaning in our language, Ekiaqueta . . ." she stressed my name in several syllables.

She did not stop there. She continued, "I'm sure no one in my entire family can question my right to use London Gin, not even you."

"If I knew you were a goddamn wino, an alcoholic, I wouldn't have married you," I said.

That pissed my Efemona off. She threw one of the bottles on my head in an attempt to blind my only eye to see. "Get lost, Ekiaqueta."

I felt my head had exploded. So I walked towards her and landed another slap on her face. If only she would just learn to shut the hell up. I must admit that I felt the pain go up my arm.

And she was still standing, but rubber-legged as if she couldn't fall until I told her so. Then I put my hand in her face and pushed her down. Her head and attitude became wild as the beast. I grabbed her left wrist, and she struggled, hitting me with the other right hand. I broke her grip on it, and shook her hand off my arms. She finally realized that, *man pas man*, in some ugly ways like that. Finally, I said, "You can't make me do this. Sit down," I instructed.

"Deaf ears."

So I shoved her down on the chair. She was now crying out loud and her face deserved some pity. She tried to get up, but her feet were rubber-legged, but still uttering bad vibes.

I pointed to the chair. "You better sit down," I declared.

I knew what she wanted to do. I wouldn't give her the least opportunity to call the cops. I said instead, "I'll not even try to wreck my hand again. From this moment on, I'll use any object at my disposal."

Her mouth was working. Tears ran down her face. "I'll call the cops to tell them you have a gun to kill me."

"Quiet," I yelled at her.

She tried again to stand. I wouldn't let her. I pointed to the chair again. She warmed the seat as I dutifully had instructed.

After the differences, it was suddenly quiet in the room, so quiet I could even hear the sound of my own breathing. I thought I heard a soft voice. I was right. Efemona finally said, "The children are still over at the baby sitter's. Care to go get them?" she lied. All she wanted to do was have the chance to call the cops.

"The children can be with their nanny. I don't care," I said.

After another few minutes I heard another of her contralto chords of her faint pitch. So faint as a voice much more than a whisper that sounded as if it were being pressed out of her by my weight on her chest when the going of sex was good and I was in control.

I watched her stare at me. Then she dropped her face. The vibes again began to crawl with an acrid, velocity emanating from Efemona as she sat alone in the dining room chair with several thoughts. Was she thinking that I didn't mean to do what I'd done?

She saw that I felt bad and she said, "Don't! I caused it! But don't hit me again."

She looked at me and smiled. I returned the smile. If only I knew her motives! She took my arm and walked me into the room.

"Let's sleep and forget what has happened," she said.

I laid awake a long time, my heart filled with too many thoughts I'd no right to be thinking: like it's been a long time since I have been romantically involved in good sex, rather than a quickie. Nonsense. But it's true, lately for me. And this was I who saw not all women attractive. But I tell you the truth when I was on top of the world, if a woman was attractive and I'm in one of my frisky moods, I don't care if she's single, engaged, married, pregnant, divorced. I boldly tell them let's make love. Maybe that's because I was young and vocal with the women who like to flirt, too. Physically, I became very loyal, too, lately to Efemona. Anytime she needed it was when I could release. On the other hand, Efemona has also graduated in the school of flirteology, and one has to keep an eye on a woman of Efemona's type.

Anyway, she sat up on the bed and cupped my chin. But I was short of words to express my sad feelings of what I'd done to her. "I'm happy to lay beside you, honey," I found myself saying.

"Me too, honey pie," she said.

You must keep in mind that with my cow eye, I'd became ugly and I figured if Efemona should abandon me for good, no other woman would want me. I had forgotten if I'd told you, too, that Efemona and I had engaged in some interesting sexual practices she'd scripted or learned from other men abusing the pussy for her the way she wanted it. And when she comes into the room and wants me to do the same, at times doing it for hours for her, I get tired. Efemona, on the other hand, seemed more sure of what she wanted me to experiment with her tonight. For that thinking, she said finally, "Make love to me, Ekiaqueta."

That request in that manner meant that we were not going to play like cats, but are going to make love as primitive cave men because she was now melancholy. So my Efemona helped me kick off my shoes and kissing, we removed our clothes, helping each other undress until we were both naked. Doing the casting as we've never done before since we got married in a primitive arrangement, our eyes met, our hands touched, our lips smiled, her brow wrinkled. Holding her tighter, I said, "I'm very pleased to screw you the way you've never been fucked before."

"What style have I not experienced? I have seen it all, honey pie," she said and smiled and looked at me, and I could almost hear her mouth vibes making connections between her wide diabolical moon eye balls, ticking as the arms of a clock. And then she said, "I bought a resemblance Roman equipment of a dick helper slightly larger than yours to satisfy me the way I want it tonight. I'd bought and hidden it until the time was ripe for it when I am horny."

I thought: the angels in heaven were weeping for Efemona's sins all these years and could punish me for that. But on the other hand, if I refused, I would be denied fucks for several more months. And if I do it for her, I would be proud and sure of more fucks, proud of myself, too, despite the fact that what I was asked to do was not serving the angels of God, but serving the Western civilization for making equipment for women to satisfy themselves and humiliate their husbands whose dicks are small.

I let her cross her legs over on top of me, while I crammed one of her nipples into my mouth. Suddenly, she got up and reached under the bed and brought out a giant bottle of London Gin and two tumblers. She poured out the drink into the tumblers and handed me one. "You drink with me or we don't make love."

Here I clearly saw why some women change partners for variety. One is, if the man is unsociable and native. I toasted with her and we gulped it at the same time. Happy enough, I switched on the Roman dick helper and it was jerking and vibrating. "Lie down," I said.

She laid down on her back and straddled her legs. And I squatted inside her straddled legs with the vibrator and inserted it into her.

I watched her work her pelvis up and down and rocked back and forth, her eyes closed, her mouth open, moaning words of joy. Releasing her passions, she said, "Do you love me?"

"What do you think?"

I turned the vibrator off and inserted my dick into her. She straightened her legs and stretched her body out over mine. Then I rolled her over on top of me and watched her do the work. As she was losing strength, I rolled her over again. We embraced and continued to kiss as I entered her deeper and deeper while her hips rose and fell.

Efemona's body went tense, then relaxed, and she continued to move her hips until she was rigid again, then went limp again and finally her breathing began to sound labored, but continued on until she had yet another passion release. As I *came* too, her circle of climax was complete.

We laid panting as she lay with her head buried in my chest, her long Diana Ross-like hair draped over my shoulders. I heard her whisper between deep breaths, "Thank you, Ekiaqueta."

The truth is, it was very pleasant lying with Efemona for hours again, I on top of her, and her womanhood flooded several times that would ease the pimples on my face. How wonderful! And to crown it all, we rubbed our feet together.

I might've been sucking on Efemona's mammalian gland when I fell asleep on it, because when I opened my eyes, it was dark in the room and I was feeling a sharp pain in my dick. But not knowing why, I said, "It was good."

"It would be better if it was cut off."

She sat up, then got on her feet and said, "Stand up."

I tossed the coverlet over me aside on the bed and tried to sit up. I felt the sharp pain again on my dick. The scene I was looking at was that a heinous crime had been committed. A twine had been used to tie up the tip of my dick to the bed frame. She watched me struggle to untie it, then quickly rushed to the light and turned it off. Then she said, "It's a warning to you. Next time, I'll cut the damn thing off."

"C'mon. You don't want to be Lorena." "Lorena would be my hero." I dialed 911.

A few seconds later, there were flourishes of knocks on our door. I walked towards the door bare naked with the twine on my dick, unable to untie it as panic then had gripped me. As I peeped through the peephole, I saw a figure of a fire marshal and a policeman standing at our door. "I'm pressing charges against you for assaulting and trying to strangle my dick with a twine."

"I will press charges against you, too, for sodomy and rape," she said.

Standing stark naked, I shook my head. Who are the cops and judges of Reno gonna believe?

With that instinct, I refused to open the door. Thus, Efemona and I were even.

PART II

KNOW THE TRUTH AND THE TRUTH SHALL SET YOU FREE.

Y'SHUA (JESUS), THE GOSPEL OF ST. JOHN. 8-32.

THE GOOD NEWS BIBLE WHY IS THE WORLD CRYING WOE ABOUT '419' WHEN THE ENGLISHMAN INVENTED AND TAUGHT NIGERIANS EVERY CROOKED WAY THEY KNOW…NIGERIANS ONLY PERFECTED IT.

—OGBEBOR

EFEMONA AND VICTORIA INTERPRET CORRUPTION AND BAD DUDU ABACHA SPELLED IT LOUDER.

Chapter

12

....

If you've never been to London before, I will tell you that London was unseasonably warm in October, and the Englishmen and their tourists alike always took advantage of their bright sunshine. General Bad Dudu, as you may or may not be aware, was trained at Sandhurst Army Canon Depot University in London. The day General Bad Dudu arrived in London for his training, the noon traffic was heavy with tie-ups at Plastow Road, Cambridge Ave., and Oxford Street. The Queen and Prime Minister had arranged and instructed a white Daimler to drop off General Bad Dudu at the training depot. The Daimler had then turned off Oxford Street to New Bond Street, the Scotland Yard, and then threaded its way through the traffic, passing Roland Cartier, Geigers, and the Royal Bank Barclays of Liverpool. A few blocks farther on, it coasted to a stop in front of Sandhurst Army Canon Depot University. A discreet, polished sign at the side of the entrance read: FUTURE AFRICAN LEADERS WELCOME HOME. As they came to a stop, the leveried chauffeur stepped out of the limousine and hurried around to open the rear door for Bad Dudu. A young and tight-fitting British blond lady, wearing good make- up for the weather walking by, noticed a gaunt face in Agbada (the popularly known African wear) and thought, who knows how much money the nincompoop has come to dump in my country?!

The lady was not too far away from being right because she figured that American and European leaders all have common sense, and it was rarely common among African leaders. Which means that those who ruled and those waiting for the relay race baton to be handed over to them to rule all lack common sense. And she regarded General Bad Dudu among the several who lacked common sense.

General Bad Dudu is also not the sort of celebrity you would like to come across when he was growing up, or meet by chance, or in any other way, for that matter, because he is an evil General. He is a uniquely Nigerian Hausa, so to speak, though sources said he's from Sudan. He's mean and evil, a no nonsense gangster evil General in actuality after he was trained at Sandhurst. A man as wicked as Bad Dudu would be arrested, castigated, branded as a felon, branded as a human rights abuser in America, but in Nigeria where he occupied the executive seat of his Nation. After he'd bought the certificate of graduation from the Queen and Prime Minister he then came home to Nigeria and then ceased power.

Then as a dictator and as well as a citizen who didn't know anything about a true democracy, and didn't believe in paying taxes for the billions he siphoned out of his country, he became ruthless. He is what exiled men and women mean when they go to Washington to cry out to Bill Clinton and his former predecessors that another Hitler was alive who does not recognize the existence of minorities in his government, which makes up Nigeria. He is what Professor Wole Soyinka, first African Noble Laureate in Literature, Prof. Bolaji Akinyemi, Air Commodor Dan Suleiman (retd.), Dr. Peter Obadan, Chief John Odigre-Oyegrin, Senator Bola Tinubu, Senator Tokunbo Afikuyomi, Senator David Mark, and the Uromi-born Nationalist Mr. Enahoro mean, to regret that he and his compatriots in the liberation struggle stopped preaching liberation too soon, and it is our fault that we limited the scope of liberation to Nigeria and did not extend it to the Nationalists.

It took General Bad Dudu several years before he realized that in history, he who seeks learned advice, follows the golden rule as King David or King Solomon. So, sitting on his executive seat one morning, Dudu glanced through the famous Nigerian Arabic Times on his table, the first ritual he entertained each morning, then noted that statistics had shown that half the population of the people he governed with absolute power in Nigeria now have broken bones and jaws. Then and there, common sense told him that if half the population he governs are suffering from malnutrition and dying by the numbers from various diseases, he would have no one to govern who would fear him. He knew, too, that if all the political prisoners who have Ph.D.s in his country he broke their limbs and jaws before he imprisoned them, were not treated, all might die and Bill Clinton and United Nations would be after him.

It was time to care. He'd not thought about the 100 million less men and women from his country he ruled even though they live below poverty standard and ruined for him and his junta members to acquire billions of dollars in foreign banks of the world. He'd had the opportunity to do whatever pleased him: the transfer of money from one bank to another and from his country to foreign banks when he was still a lieutenant was a slow and laborious process. Not only did it require multiple forms to be filled out and dependant on his superiors signatures, it made him angry and thought one day enough was enough for his superiors to block his way from siphoning millions out of his country.

When he finally ceased power, it became a piece of cake to him in a beautiful way that with the high tech computer revolution, the situation had changed dramatically, and large amounts of money could be transferred within a number of minutes.

His day soon came. He was in charge. He became the all and all. He approved the numbers of barrels of crude oil sales to ships in the high seas and made records of transfers to foreign banks with Lebanese businessmen crooks. All transactions were in code, changed regularly to prevent unauthorized access. Each day, millions of electronic pounds, dollars, yen and other foreign monies his buddies want transferred out of his country passed through Bad Dudu's approval. It was fascinating work to be a Head of State wearing three hats, and also the life blood that fed the arteries of business with Lebanese cooks and crooks.

The Doddan Army Barracks where he sat on the executive seat had a big conference hall where he discussed business with his buddies and Lebanese crooks as to how much will leave the country on a particular day. Now it was the time to wake up. It was time to care for the sick and the lame. As he became sober enough that morning, two thoughts occurred to him: the replacement of a new Matron General for his country to take care of the sick and the lame was necessary. *And never in history have I heard of a white man dumping money in African banks to dupe his country. He shook his head. Things have got to change before I hand over power, he said to himself.*

* * *

In a clamor of deep thought of the problems that now confronted him almost daily, and from which he needed quick solutions, he picked up the phone on his desk and dialed his aide, Brigedier Talabi Bawuh.

"Bawuh?"

"Hello."

"Bad Dudu."

"Yes, General! What seems to be the matter this early morning to call me so early?"

"I couldn't sleep last night. I thought all night about the possibility of filling the post of Edna Obaze Adeniyi who passed away three months ago leaving the post of Matron General vacant all this time. Very soon I'll have no one to rule. People are all dying by the numbers. I want to save the lives of those in the hospitals around the country who are sick and cannot afford to buy medication in private chemists and private hospitals, all because of our dubious heinous activities in this country," he said and mocked to himself and to Bawuh.

"I'll see what I can do about that for you, General."

Bawuh started searching for a replacement. A few days later, after sleepless nights and hard work searching, he remembered Efemona and recommended her. He then submitted the names and left it on the General's desk at the Doddan Army Barracks, also the Nation's state building at Ikoyi. Bad Dudu couldn't have been happier walking into his office to find a file with thousands of names of nominees on his table. Quickly, he then decided to go through the nominees submitted to him for the vacant post of the Matron General by Bawuh.

Lest you might not know, the Doddan Army Barracks building which was designed in the early fifties was a resemblance of Sandhurst Training Depot of London of the period: pink, tan character building, dreary popular with its occupants, during the oil boom with civilian governments but which the Bad Dudu junta government later painted with camouflage warrior-like image of Caesar, the man popular in history.

To be aware of the facts, the Doddan Army Barracks was to move to its new capital at Abuja built in the middle of nowhere somewhere in the North, more than nine hundred kilometers away from Ikoyi, Lagos, the present commercial capital. This capital building, which cost the Nigerian Government billions to construct, couldn't have been in greater contrast to the Doddan Army Barracks Garrison. To international observers it was a product of the self- aggrandizing style of the fifties architecture of Britain, which was then tagged the Buckingham Palace of West Africa by the Queen when she first visited Nigeria, which gave it a vaguely ludicrous atmosphere. It was designed not to blend in with its environment of river blindness, but to stand out among other Nations for welcoming and receiving very important personalities and dignitaries from all over the world and therefore, the Criminal Investigation Department (CID) headquarters was the first to have its office within for protection against enemies and invaders of progress. Bad Dudu however, chose to remain at Ikoyi-Lagos until he met with a new Matron General to assume the post for which he'd lost not only a member of his administration who was loyal to him, but also a dear friend who held the post until she passed away.

Alahaja Edna Obaze Adeniyi had been dead for several months leaving the post vacant and yet nothing had been done. As a result of that, when Bad Dudu's government thought of what to do with the four Naira extra cash from the increase in the pump price of petrol from seven Naira to eleven Naira per litre, which was to fund hospitals for new gadgets, the dictator set up the Petroleum Trust Fund. In reality, the Trust Fund was for him and his junta members to make quick billions to transport to Britain and Swiss Banks. To ensure that the funds were not misapplied, a touted incorrigible Nigerian Alahaja Edna Obaze who was the Matron General of Hospitals, was appointed to head the PTF as executive chair lady. But in reality, this was to fool the people of Nigeria. However, she passed away leaving the country in chaos. To that end, the quick search for a replacement by Bawuh which took him only a few days to sort and recommend Efemona for the post, and Efemona he deemed necessary was capable to execute her post designed to improve the welfare of the people, of the armed forces and the sick and the lame and those of the police. Bad Dudu as dumb as he could be could spend another three months by himself trawling through the country and still not find anybody as good as the names of the nominess before him. And for him to pick out the right candidate was another problem.

Bawuh, his aide who'd been around and was slightly more intelligent, not in academics, but in quick thinking, strongly recommended Efemona because she'd been trained in Reno, Nevada in one of the best colleges. Above all, Efemona had lived in Ewu village and fought with mosquitoes where she helped the poor women who were pregnant to deliver their babies after nine months of their suffering in the farms under the sun. Bawuh had noted that throughout the years Efemona was in Nigeria, there was no other woman among the nominees who could measure up to Florence Nightingale in history. However, to Bawuh, Efemona was the Florence Nightingale of Ewu Maternity, where she'd worked. Efemona, he observed, knew how to circumcise the male and female new born babies. Above all, she had the knowledge of caesarian delivery. He need not waste his time to think over it again, just send a letter to Efemona in Reno with Bad Dudu's signature on it to demand her return to Nigeria through international cooperation would speed up the process. The letter might be lost in transit. To him that would cause a delay to fill the post. Bawuh, on the other hand, also heard in the news that the Ghanaian Government was searching for a well qualified Matron as well. So far Efemona in Reno, Nevada was the best qualified for the job. For a step above the Ghanaians he decided to move faster. General Bad Dudu would be delighted with Efemona's work, he thought. He kept his fingers crossed that Dudu would send for Efemona immediately in Reno, Nevada to fill the post.

* * *

It was six-forty P.M. when Bad Dudu finished going through the names of the nominees. He carefully followed the note that accompanied the file of Efemona's attached to the top of the folder by his Aide, praising Efemona's work before she left the country six years ago to join her husband. To Bad Dudu, he'd no choice but to honor and pick Efemona among the several nurses Bawuh had submitted their names. Efemona definitely qualified he thoughts. He rang Bawuh immediately the next morning as he sat listening to the sharp ringing of the phone, waiting for him to answer. The phone rang up to six or seven times before Bawuh picked it up.

"Bawuh, it's Bad Dudu."

His voice was mellow and cordial. "Good morning, Bawuh. And how are you this morning? And the family?"

"Everyone is doing fine, Mr. Dudu. Have you gone through the names I submitted to you?"

Dudu was short of words to express his gratitude. And finally he asked, "You're sure about Efemona?"

"I was sure before I recommended her. I believe she's the best qualified. Efemona is hot in the market in other countries *now*, unless of course, Alabon Close has dug up information that is bad about her."

"Not that I'm aware of. The CID cleared her. She had a good record before she left the country to join her husband. Hard working, party animal in the company of Victoria and Monica all love hard liquor and shared sugar daddies together, but not a problem. Efemona also fought the mosquitoes hard in the village. If nothing else, the mosquito bites she got in the village is enough to give her the job . . ." CID file also stated.

"I know that already. If nothing bad in particular is revealed about her by the CID, I suggest you move fast on it, Mr. Dudu.

She would be a great asset to the nation if she agrees to honor your post and invitation to come to the country to accept the job. You'll be delighted in her work" Bawuh said.

"I'll go along with your opinion on this, but how do we go about getting her into the country?"

There was a silence on the other end. Finally, he spoke. "Pardon me. I was choking," he said, "I know she has a good friend here in the country. Her name is Victoria. She's the person I know of to get her into the country with ease. No question about that. But you know it's been long since Efemona left the country. She probably believes in the American creed *now,* of *'no free lunch'*. So I suggest we arrange for her ticket and spending pocket money. That would boost her moral to come with Victoria."

"Very thoughtful of you," Dudu praised Bawuh and dropped the phone.

*　*　*

It should be noted that the rumor supermarkets and galleries in Lagos-Nigeria were all whirring in full force capacity since the passing away of Alahaja Edna Obaze and the immediate promotion of Victoria Osunde, also a good friend to Efemona before she left Nigeria to join her husband in America where she was to further her education. Bawuh, in favor of Efemona had accused the left- wings in their regime of steering the country dangerously toward only the Northerners having a good share of the pie. The nomination of Efemona from Bendel State, who was presently in the USA studying, was to halt this and return the country to the policy of one Nation with Muslims and Catholics having job opportunities for everyone and *you chop I chop God no go vess and everything will be alright.* At a time when a normally cynical populace seemed so unrestrained in its applause for Dudu's the regime's note-worthy performance since they took over the government, they thought there was reason to employ Efemona. Bawuh and his men behind Efemona were not so naïve. They knew Efemona, who was Catholic, was an asset. A great one.

On the eve of Efemona's arrival in the capital, a party was held at Bawuh's house in Lagos. It was both a security diversion and a strategic fortress against leaks that Efemona was at the verge of becoming the first Matron General who hailed from the Bendel State to visit Bad Dudu and Doddan Army Barracks to fill the post of Matron General.

Thus, the new or old, the money that was much envied by the women in this country, Nigeria was to be distributed. For that all the women who hailed from the south rejoiced and jubilated.

And they could see the rich and famous Hausas of Doddan Army Barracks and the beach houses they resided and their family fabulous gatherings on distant Ikoyi islands, and trust funds for uncles and nephews and perhaps even outright bungalows built in their names would now cease, at least when Efemona would arrive to redeem the poverty of the Southerners. The women thought. But only the weak women of the South in poverty thought in terms of that.

On the other hand, the strong with money who rule who planned the return of Efemona to the country became stronger with one thing in their minds, which was money-making. Money thawed them to a warmness they had never shown to the people of Nigeria they have stolen. It also thawed them to the point of becoming God themselves, which Nigerians know but are afraid to talk and criticized Bad Dudu's junta's regime for. It taught them openness to wickedness to install themselves in all high commissions in the country and made for a warm, cozy Hejira to Mecca. All these, the poor women of the South thought, when Efemona comes to assume the post, will all cease and be a thing of the past if she's smart enough to join the bandwagon to help her people.

Chapter

13

It was now August and the best-laid summer plans of a hard-working man like me went astray. I'd nothing to show for all the money which I made busting my ass except for the groceries and clothing I bought for our children. Efemona would not help me at all with the bills despite that she made more money than I did. I was then faced with a tough act to follow. Despite all the groceries in our deep freezer to last for a couple of months, Efemona wouldn't even cook and wouldn't even let me hold her. We became like a lion and a tiger in the den. Even to help pay for the long distance phone bills which she'd made to her brothers and sister which came close to $7,000 in a month was a problem. She would rather go on shopping sprees for new fashions, jewelry and shoes so that she could be seen and be noticed on the streets of Reno.

For the record, Efemona I should tell you, gets catalogues for shopping sprees from all over the universe where she'd made calls to. The fact is, I did not have the heart to stop her because of what her parents would think about me. After all, her parents gave Efemona to me thinking I could afford everything Efemona wanted and also to send them money to sustain life in Nigeria. It got to the point when I told myself I would remain poor for life. The bills at the dinner table with Efemona for discussion was uncalled for. What could I do? I swallowed my pride with style and let her carry on with her life and hope that someday she might change.

One afternoon, as it was our days off together, I sat her down to discuss our problems. I could tell that Efemona was reading my mind as a man with primitive instincts. Anyway, I sat on the couch opposite her. For the first time I'd the urge to ask Efemona to help me take care of some of the pressing bills, but I didn't want to strain our newly rekindled romance after she laid me with the incidence of strangulation of my dick with a twine for a bad humor. I did not bring that up, but instead I said, "Thanks for not arresting me with the cops the other night."

She smiled and rocked back and forth a few times on the rocking chair opposite me. Then I brought up a demand for payment letter from Gucci factory outlet mailed to Efemona totaling close to $10,000. I also brought out a red letter notice from the power company about to terminate our lights if payment was not received within seventy-two hours. That's not all. I held the telephone bill in my palm trying to figure out why the bill was a little over $7,000. Finally, I said, "I simply can't afford these huge bills anymore. You're spending more than I'm making." Efemona said nothing.

I looked at her and shook my head. I said, "If you help pay some of the bills it would not be piling up as it is now, my dear." "All right. IOU." Efemona said and walked towards the kitchen and murmured some fragment of words. "The devil sent me to you to burn you to your toes for deceiving my parents. You send money to your brothers and sisters for their education and you're concerned about my spending for attires here?! Shit! Ain't you a bitch?"

That baffled me and still I did not want to escalate our differences. Therefore, seeking respite from the agonizing images Efemona was putting me through, I donned my shorts and T-shirt and walked towards the balcony for a fresh breeze and to look at the beautiful sky. The afternoon was beautiful. The sky was bathed in bright sun light far away from the earth. I walked back into the house, unable to comprehend, napping couldn't come easily for me. All I could do was stare at my children who know not what the future holds. I picked up the phone and dialed Nevada Bell.

"Terminate our damn line." "For how long?" a voice asked.

"Indefinitely," I replied.

As I tried to nap again, I thought of different ways to commit a crime to be able to pay off the bills. After all, I didn't bring Efemona to America to starve her. In Nigeria, it was the responsibility of a man to take care of his wife (wives) and also provide the bread for his children. That's what Africans are taught and we live by it. As a result, I'd an idea which was to work twelve hours daily on the job seven days a week rather than committing crimes and fraudulent acts that would put me away for life from the judges and social workers of Reno, Efemona had alliance with.

As I worked twelve hours daily, Efemona increased her catalogue shopping spree for the latest fashions of Gucci, Calvin Kline, Yves Saint Laurent, Perry Ellis, Jacqueline Smith, and the Boss. Her secret organization AWAM was now well established world wide. And little did I know that it was the steady, faithful encouragement of her mother and her brothers Okoro, Newman and Clement who sparked the deed and whose passionate advocacies pushed her to form the AWAM movement, because I hadn't fulfilled the promise of robbing the banks to take care of Efemona, their daughter and families, money wise as a rich man from America. Everyone involved soon credited her fervor as the single most important factor to the success of her movement. Efemona became the President in America and Newman, her brother, then became the Vice President in Benin. I knew that Efemona had become a big guru, through the media and there was a time when she was getting mail from various women from all over the world. The mail that stunned me the most was from Anegbo, Efemona's junior sister, the same one who'd poisoned her sugar daddy, who was now desperate to marry and have children of her own. And not only was she interested to get married, she was desperately in need to leave Benin City for abroad with her man. It didn't matter what part of the world.

The heart of the matter was that Anegbo's female genitals were to be mutilated before the elders and before her mother and father decide to give her away to the man she finally planned to live her entire life with. Anegbo loved the man, but was against mutilation of female genitals. Efemona had read the letter and mistakenly had forgottten it on the dinner table. So I read the letter in secret. And what I read stunned me.

Anegbo had written: *"These days, advocates of female genital mutilation believers are mostly members of a dominant male hierarchy here in Benin. They zealously reverence the belief that uncircumcised women are unclean, impure and unfit to marry and bear children. They also believed that such women to whom I belong see beyond their noses and we seem to undermine respect and reverence in our tradition. They also fear that women would out screw them in bed and if we are not satisfied could be grounds for us horny day and night for different penises elsewhere. They charge the increasingly vocal opponents of the practice, many of us nurses residing in the capital, with trying to undermine the Benin or African culture and religion. These accusations obscure the appalling truth, a truth our mama, sisters, cousins and female friends understood too well, who have suffered agonizing pain, loss of blood, and Tetanus. Too many of these women to which I'll soon be a member if I'm not immediately sneaked out of Benin, have quietly bled to death or died of later complications. Most of these women, to my knowledge, face a lifetime of chronic vaginal and uterine infections, for they no longer possess protective labia, which bars the entry of germs.*

Efemona! I can only tell you so much that these women whom I know too well, all felt excruciating pain, agony and despair when their clitoris, labia majora and minora were all sliced off. Sometimes, they faint from the pain and die. And when these young women die, they equate them to be evil and witches. I want you to bear in mind that there are other side effects to this brutal mutilation and ritual you might want to take a serious look at. Such women who underwent this journey of pain will probably never achieve orgasm, but will endure painful intercourse and menstrual agony until menopause. To my understanding, it is the truth of female genital mutilation, a practice which I strongly believe is barbaric and medieval on its face, a practice that has claimed more than ten thousand young women in our village alone. Though I do understand that help may be possible through reconstructive surgery in the United States as nothing is impossible with the Americans, I resent having to go through the pain and the brutal ordeal in the first place. Hear me out, sister Efemona. I strongly support AWAM for which you and Newman stood your ground."

*   *   *

We still were on the dinner table with our children when Efemona broke the news to me about Newman. She said, "Honey pie, would you like to take a look at the news of our country?"

I must confess that I did not know what she was up to. All I know was that we'd just quarrelled and she'd malice. For her to unlock her heart and chat with me surprised me. For one, Efemona is quick to take offense, holding grudges, throwing out past mistakes up at anyone with whom she'd quarreled and nurturing grievances. Moreover, she never quickly forgives. Realizing that, I decided not to reply the fact that if I say something, it might offend her to continue to run her mouth until we both uncork our fists.

Anyway, I summed up the courage and looked at her for a moment. Then I nodded anyway. Then she handed me a copy 'of The Nigerian Observer' and pointed to the infamous news about her brother. And I read:

"The shooting of Newman, Vice President for AWAM movement, who is also Efemona's brother who now resides in the United States, stunned the entire nation of this country. The thirty-nine year old comedian, song writer and impersonator who'd risen from poverty to fame as the renowned son of the Principal of Edo College, an orator too, who could move the earth and the heavens, who spoke during Bad Dudu's takeover of his country quelling the unrest with his mellow oratorical speech was shot yesterday afternoon when he regaled an audience of all women at Oba market, when he was seeking Efemona's help to take them away from poverty to the United States.

"As the news flashed round the nation, it was though fifty million women had lost a good man, an intelligent man who cared for us," a young woman said of Newman.

The paper added, "The local news hounds were not immediately informed because it might cause unrest in the Nation as to who shot the handsome Oyinbo, the King of women's yanshes. And also because of the extraordinary attempts being made by Dr. Fredrick and his team of expert surgeons to revive Newman before the public was to be notified.

The police do not have suspects, but only his personal secretary Miss Ademola Okunbo, who was present at the time of the shooting, had made an official statement. With tears, Miss Ademola stated,

'Newman, a great man at his age, a fine musician and a source of inspiration to the women of poor beyond poor, the Vice President of

AWAM, supporting us in all endeavors to this date, narrowly escaped death."

When I'd finished reading the paper, I handed it back to Efemona and took my bottle of Heineken and went out to the balcony. So many thoughts. Efemona, who had had two shots of London Gin, crossing her legs on the center table came after me in the balcony. She asked, "Is everything all right?"

I nodded, but knowing not that I've so many thoughts in my heart. Finally, I said, "Your brother's shooting cannot be just because he supports the poor beyond poor of our country. Tell me something. What is the truth?"

"You know," Efemona said, "Newman was shot because the traders and farmers of Ewu, Benin and Ukpenu and elsewhere in the Nation were all fed up with his support for my AWAM movement, that he'd supported all young women to leave their husbands to start a new life of their own abroad. The farmers and traders then believed that I, Efemona, was the brain behind their support. Newman, for one, had lived his life exactly the way he pleased and matter-of-factly, doesn't give a damn about the farmers, palm wine tappers and traders. I also had secretly channeled to Newman thousands of dollars to fund women desperately in need of help who were in danger. As a result of that, the farmer, traders and palmwine tappers didn't like him. Newman was too vocal and they felt that he was using me to gain publicity for his actions, and because in reality he had just purchased the newest 560 SL Mercedes Coupe. With the money I'd secretly siphoned to him to help the women, so many of the young women then left their husbands and loved ones and ran to Italy and London and other countries to occupy the red light districts around the world which I formed, funded and publicized here in Reno, Nevada. Matter- of-factly, I've drafted a letter to Joe Conforte and to Dapor Ogundemu Akintude who are both my supporters to help me in all endeavors to be able to carry on my movements," and Efemona looked at my face to see my reaction.

"Each time you my husband was at work and I held an open rally in Reno, my brother Newman knows when to hold one in Benin with my photo placards mounted all over the city on all the electric poles.

After the rallies, thousands of women from Benin then vanish over night, since they themselves want to look as good as myself and have a chance, too, to be known while they start their new lives afresh because of the hardship in our country."

"Sweetie pie," she looked at me sipping on her London's Dry Gin shit and pressed on, "my cause helped finance jobs, living accommodations, money, if the need for the women to run away from their husbands was met with danger and as long as Newman had signed the approval in Benin. In Reno here, I'm the queen, the African goddess that all the African women *now* look up to."

I studied Efemona's facial expressions a moment. I was about to ask, what about what Ukpenu, Irrua and Benin culture preached to our women? As she looked at me to hear what I'd to say, I became dumb. I must admit that despite my cavalier attitude I was a bit concerned about the farmers, palmwine tappers and the traders who work hard to take care of their wives only to come home and their wives were gone abroad to occupy the red light districts of Italy and London all because of Efemona's movement (AWAM).

Finally, I asked Efemona coldly, "So whatever happened to Anegbo, your sister whose clitoris was to be mutilated?"

I thought Efemona would be pissed and react repulsively, the way she'd behaved when I discussed the bill problems with her on the dinner table. Instead, she laughed uproarously and said, "Aha! So you read my sister's letter secretly!" Didn't you Ekaqueta?"

I admitted. So she said, "On September the twenty-eight, at nine P.M., the day Anegbo's female genitals were to be mutilated, I sent an emissary to Princess Omonzua, the head princess of Benin, appointed by the Oba in charge of mutilating clitoris to spare Anegbo, noting that Anegbo had broken all the laws of the Ten Commandments of the Oba's rules for the people in Benin for lying, stealing, insinuating her sisters abroad to come home to Nigeria to buy homes without their husbands knowing, and also concealing information from elders and sleeping with different men without being married. Anegbo had followed some notorious women's footsteps, which had now backfired that laying different men was a taboo, an abomination to her culture, and now she would have to face the shame in the village's only market to spread her legs apart for the elders to see if her pussy is as wide as the Golden Gate of San Francisco."

I almost laughed. Efemona added, "The Princess, for the record, would've to place a dozen duck's egg inside her vagina for the elders to know if she'd perforated her hymen. As her senior sister and to bury the shame for Anegbo, who had then perforated her hymen at an early age, from the elders and the shame of humiliating our parents, I therefore sent an envelope containing $25,000 of your 401K profit sharing retirement to Princess Omonzua to conceal the truth when her legs were spread wide open in the middle of our local market."

I was about to say I know Princess Omonzua firsthand to reject Efemona's offer when Efemona dutifully interrupted me and said, "I am still bitter to this date, that Omonzua didn't honor my request. Instead, she faxed me a message to say: Efemona quoted, "Efemona! I know you are the champion of AWAM's movement, reactionary intrepid foe now Americanized in America. Ukpenu culture must be observed, preserved, respected and carried out. Your American dollars cannot destroy our culture," and I finally laughed.

Efemona had rested her gist before me when I asked, "So what did Princess Omonzua did with all the money you sent her?"

"You must be crazy to ask me that kind of question when you know that the dollar is now the God they worship in Nigeria."

She paused. Then she looked at me. "The motherfucker pocketed the money and I was humiliated in absentia. Anegbo was also humiliated before multitudes in our local village market."

I almost laughed again, but held it back, and thought anyway, no wonder our telephone bill was way too high. It was the content of Anegbo's letter that might've made Efemona to follow up on telephone conversations to prevent things like that before they happened. Which was true, and like most youngwomen growing up at Ukpenu or Benin, I resented the Oba's palace intrusions into their life pertaining the mutilations of their female genitals. So, I said, "Why did you not fax First Lady Hilary Clinton to get involved with your famous movement of AWAM with Newman on your side as a good speakers to halt the mutilation?"

Efemona then quickly reminded me of an event when she'd told me she'd a meeting to attend at her new job with her boss.

First, she apologized that she'd lied on that fateful day when she was dressed with a blue velvet gown with two shoulder straps with red high heeled shoes and her red purse stuck under her armpit. She'd said, "With my new Gucci velvet gown on, on that fateful day you remembered, I went to the Oval Office to appeal to Hilary Clinton about the future of women in Nigeria. I also regaled quite a number of the women before Hilary herself."

Needless for me to ask her the content of her famous speech Efemona chatted out, "I'd preached to them in the Oval Office, that this decade, marked the century of women. And I'll stand for any woman who will test their men and deviate from their crude manners against African women. This century, I said, will also make a historical milestone when women from Irrua, Ukpenu, Benin residing in Reno, Nevada will define where they have been and where they are heading. Within now and next year, I Efemona, intend to make Ekiaqueta, my husband, inferior within the law of the United States. The dollar, to me, was invented for the men to flash on our faces. If our husbands are so poor and reduced by the Internal Revenue Service (IRS), the cops of Reno, the judges, and therefore are unable to take care of us, we have the right to terminate the marriage. That's my theory, at least, that money was invented because corn, Cassava, melons, yam tubers, wheat and other forms of barter were neither secret nor handy enough to finance what we've go in between our thighs. By that, I mean and explained to the audience, before Hilary for them to know that prostitution is the world's oldest profession which the world's oldest kings of Benin Empire and Egypt and elsewhere in the world once used to pay the women. In those ancient times, they'd used a bag of salt, a bag of wheat, yam tubers, cassava, cowries and bags of garri. I made sure they understood me that women should refuse any form of barter in this century. What we need to see with our naked eyes is what money answers, that is, the basic need for women who were given away to men, like Ekiaqueta, my husband, should leave the marriage with alacrity. They should divorce, be independent, sue them, then wear the pants in their household. This century, women must need something to occupy their pockets. I mean the need to have bundles of currencies stashed into our purses and if it pleases us we have the right to ask the men who are interested to stick the bundles into our pussy. It is what God gave us. It is our bank. We must use it now to make money! money! money! Up, up my AWAM movement which I have formed."

She raised her glass to toast mine. I drew mine back. She murmured, "You goddamn fool, *Ohuan!*"

"I know I'm a fool. But by the way did Patricia and Virginia go with you during your visit to the Oval Office for the famous oratorical speech?," I asked not quite mad yet.

"Yes. Both stood in the front row and gave a standing ovation for me and immediately after them the entire audience stood, along with Hilary. I was thrilled. Never before been so happy in my life since I married you."

She listened to hear if I was angry. I didn't utter a word. But as my normal eye to see was itching badly, I rubbed my left hand across it to ease the itch. I noticed she did not look up to see my cow eye. Instead, she said, "I'm in the mood to screw you in the balcony. Do you have the strength? The kids are all napping."

The tricky manipulator Efemona knew the pimples on my face were becoming too much and I would be happy to fuck to clear them and I wouldn't refuse and she moved closer to me and added, "Close your eyes."

I did as she instructed. Then she kissed me and I became harder and harder in my pants. She felt it and lowered my pants for me.

Then she lowered hers, too. I imagined she held on to the wooden frames of the balcony before she said, "You can open your eyes now."

I did again as she instructed. Then she spread her legs. As I entered her from behind she started to talk. First: she said, "Honey, I beg you to take care of the children while I go to Nigeria to see Newman still in the hospital on a death watch. I'll be back within a few days. Will you do that for me? But make sure you don't blink the eye for the children to see."

There goes my trickish Efemona. No wonder she wanted me to make love to her after several months of denying me sex.

She knew I was enjoying the fuck and not quite ready to give her the juice. The heart of the matter was that I was holding it back. With a soft moan, I replied, "Yes, before you see Newman, I'll invite Sam Okorie and Ken Anukam, my bosom family friends to come over and dine with us for a tradition we have neglected for months because of our misunderstandings" I found myself saying after I *came*. Efemona, too, did not answer me, but continued to pull forward and backwards, enjoying it and trying to *come* herself. Common sense told me that if Efemona should *come* before me, her answer would be a different story.

Anyway, she managed to say, "Yes." Moaning soft words of joy, she asked me, "What will I cook for Sam and Ken?"

I listened to her in ecstasy moaning soft words of passion. I held my breath. When she finally *came* she said, *"I'll cook pounded yam with* ógbónó *soup."*

In reality, I knew I'd my last fuck of the century when she'd said, *"I'll cook pounded yam with* ógbónó *soup."* Which means that she's no longer a willing participant in one marriage as a proper African wife.

Anyway, I pretended I didn't know the meaning. But when I thought of my cow eye on my face, which has rendered me ugly for other women to date me if Efemona should leave me, I did not respond. Rather, I pumped harder and harder before she changed her mind to pull me off from ejaculating.

Moreover, remembering the famous tale of an African Princess my grand-father once told me about, who hail from Benin but raised at Ukpenu, who invited the Kings and Chiefs to her hut and cooked *pounded yam with* ógbónó *soup* then served them in the nude before taking them one by one into her private room and screwing them all to just to humiliate her husband, who was once a King himself, but dethroned, I declined the ógbónó *soup idea shit.* Or to use an analogy, an American Yankee asking a prostitute to have a banana split, which he knows the prostitute won't refuse.

Remembering the most humiliating part of the tale which was: that any time the Princess was done with each man in her private room, she came outside and rang the bell in the local market for the town crier to carry the news around town to humiliate her husband, who was once a King and then dethroned, then became peniless because his arch rivals then sold his lands and properties and golds to continue to screw her for her beauty the King had helped reshape with his money and fame, I said to Efemona, *"I would rather prefer that you cook pounded yam with egusi soup."*

She did not say a word. But we both had enjoyed the fuck. And after the fuck we dressed and went into the room and watched Night Line with Ted Kopple.

* * *

On a Sunday, the following week, which fell on a Thanksgiving day, Sam Okorie and Ken Anukam arrived to our house in the evening, as I'd suggested. As far as I knew, I had no immediate plans to see them again except maybe Efemona might invite them behind my back to cook ógbónó *soup* for them. The reason for that, as I explained before, was that Efemona and I had become a lion and a tiger in the den and by that I mean she became the social secretary in our house. She was in control. Though you may have realized I'd no more veto power because a tiger can sometimes withstand a lion, I did have full control on the invitation of these two gentlemen. Thus, at seven P.M. they arrived as I'd planned. Actually, I'd invited them to help me rebuke Efemona for her ways of trying to adopt the Western life style.

Talking about Sam and Anukam for a minute, Sam was a man who uses the intuition approach to help his friends accomplish a solution to their matrimonial discord. He was to me the folk hero of the Africans in Reno, Nevada. A distinguished gentleman, gifted with a spluttering oratorical way of speaking with good use of Ibo's proverbs, who has the look of a village headmaster. He loves it when any African with whom he cares invites him to mediate on a family dispute. His pugnacious face, piercing brown eyes made his face look brutal, in a way and intimidating. Efemona, of course, noted him as a man whose voice and manner were polite and conversational and then suspected that he absorbed only the facts he considered pertinent and sloughed off the rest of what was not important as inconsequential. As a man of six, ten in height-almost a giant, every one I know who is African in Reno, Nevada respected him and honors the same with other Africans, as it was our tradition. In contrast, Anukam was about his height. He was a man who greatly cherished his culture. Hard working man, though his wife had pulled him down any time he tried to climb higher on the ladder. Has eyes as aggressive as Sam's, but had dimples, which appeared and disappeared at will, relieving the belligerence of his face. He has a very dark complexion, as does Sam, but much darker, with his beefy forehead. His wife's attitude seemed odd at times. Odd, queer and peculiar I would say were the common words best known in humanity to describe women such as Anukam's wife.

However, a psychiatrist, looking at his wife and my Efemona would say, pathological, neurotic and maladjusted. That sums it up.

Anukam is sociable, laughter-loving, but a man who married a very unpleasant, ill-bred woman, as my wife had now become, both have similar nasty tongues.

Anyway, Anukam and Sam held out their hands. I shook them and each gave a powerful squeeze on my palm that caused me to wince after the shake, for my hands were not as strong and wide as theirs. Their fingers were as large, fat as hot dogs, which always had intimidated me anytime I shake with them. I almost declined to shake at all. And they knew why.

After our ease of men familiar with their counterparts, Anukam went into the children's room and chatted with them, while Sam sat and relaxed, his piercing brown eyes darting around the room in quick mental movements as if looking for hidden secrets. I noted his posture was contradicted by his busy eyes. Finally, Efemona got up and said, "Long time no see, strangers."

Sam and Anukam laughed and chatted with her. After a few minutes she ushered everyone to the dining table. I almost cracked up when I saw the goddamn steaming roast whole turkey lying on its back on the silver tray, legs parted. I made a joke out of the steamy turkey and my wife indicated her understanding of the joke with a nod.

We all sat at the dinner table. Sam and Anukam on my left. I could not see what type of soup was prepared for my guests. I can only tell you at that instant that I was busy enjoying my *egusi soup with pounded yam*. But I was perplexed when Anukam said, *"Dis ógbónó soup dey draw well, well. Where your wife buy-am?"*

Sam complimented her, too, for the good, tasty ógbónó soup. I said nothing. I did not want to embarrass my Efemona for serving me *equesi soup* and serving my guests ógbónó soup. Instead, I said, "UK, your wife, is also a good cook. I enjoyed the *equesi soup* she cooked on our last dinner together at your place, Sam." The dinner which had caused me a cow eye when I got home.

As Sam raised his eyes to thank me for the compliment for his wife, he noticed for the first time that I now have one different eye on my face. Then he asked, "What happened to one of your eyes?"

I hesitated. Finally, I said, "It's a long story, my friend."

When I finished relating the story, both men sympathized with me.

We all settled with our dinner. After the dinner Efemona served us a drink.

For Sam, it took only one bottle of Heineken to knock the edge off and loosen his tongue. And a second look at him, he made mockery of one of his friends, too, whose African wife had given a poached eye with a boomerang after the husband had yelled at her to stop insulting him. Listening to Sam tell the story, Efemona flung her head back and laughed uproariously, showing every tooth in her mouth, which were whiter than they used to be. Sam could not contain himself. He became angry and he said, "I remember when you first came to America five years ago, your dental structures and patterns were rough and yellow. It looks now that your teeth are whiter than mine, huh?" he joked.

To cut him short for what I invited him for, I said, "I invited both of you here to help me resolve the problems I am having with Efemona."

"What kind of problems?" Anukam asked.

I explained, "It is a memory of our marital discord, a memory of disorderliness and conduct of my wife I brought into this country to cherish me, my family and our culture until death do us part. In fact, I seek both of you to help me find a peaceful solution to our problem. I do not blame myself, nor blame Efemona, but at the end, both of you will find the root of the problem. I do not know where the trouble lies, but it could lay in the mismating of a palmwine tapper's son and a daughter of a principal who is way too social ahead of time for my hook-up. That is the truth, my friends. I respect my culture and honor my traditions, love to watch documentary movies and true stories, but hers are *now*

BX movies. I also like to save for a rainy day. But Efemona likes shopping sprees. I like taking the kids to the park. Efemona likes staging parties to show off her new Gucci leather stuff so as to compare and contrast who wears the most expensive stuff and criticize those who are not dressed to her standards, who humbles the pocketbook of their husbands. And you know what'd made me to marry Efemona? It is because I'd realized that we were both from polygamous homes, which is why I married her, which would be helpful to us while raising our children together until death do us part. And what is most annoying to me these days is that I pay all the bills, while Efemona keeps her checks to herself and sends the rest to her folks and relatives . . . She says I'm a gambler, I say she's an alcoholic. She claims that my sister is a witch and I said it's false and Efemona is fantasizing and wants to become independent so as to get all her brothers and sisters to the United States, rent her own apartment, lay different men, file the income tax and claim head of my household at the end of each year. In fact, Efemona had obtained her citizenship without my knowledge, which she claimed was a result of my senior sister's threat to kick her out from my life when we both go back to Nigeria. These are my concerns," I'd stated to my friends.

Efemona got up from her seat. "Excuse me," she said. I watched her walk up to the entertainment center and plug in a CD into the CD player. Her selection was a mix of R & B plus some contemporary hits. But, after 'Many Rivers to Cross' had sang, she reached over and turned the volume down. Then she came back and sat down and crossed her legs.

Sam said, "You might be surprised why we are here." He paused. "Ekiaqueta, or What Can I Say, your husband, invited us here this evening to iron out some little problems you may have with him. You heard everything he said. Do you dispute him?" Efemona looked up. "Both of you will never know the truth." "So what is the truth?" Anukam asked.

"I didn't hear my husband say he almost hacked me and Dapor Ogundemu to death. We have been having problems even before we visited you, Sam."

"Did you notify your respected relatives-I mean your in-laws that the merry joker Ekiaqueta tried to strangle you and verbally abuse you before you invited Ogundemu to eat ógbónó soup *with him?*"

"No comment." But she looked poker-faced at Anukam. Finally, she said, "They said it is not the nature of my husband and that I was having nightmares or illusions. That's how mean and native my husband's family are."

"Let's not get into the relatives stuff. What we care about here is the root of the problem, Efemona and Ekiaqueta have here in Reno, Nevada," Sam corrected Anukam.

Then he looked at Efemona with his aristocratic face. "We understand that you lavish huge sums of money on yourself alone and maintain a secret account and have since arranged with your relatives in Benin to purchase a home without Ekiaqueta's knowledge. He only knew that after he came upon an incriminating piece of evidence which was in your sister's own handwriting asking you to come home and buy a house. Is that correct?"

I watched Efemona's reaction with my good eye. She said nothing. Sam continued, "It's to our best knowledge that you've been working since you arrived in the city of Reno. How many years now, four, five?" he interrogated.

Anytime Sam would mention money, my cow eye would blink. I began to wonder why. Anyway, Sam added, "What do you do with all the money you are making? You don't have to give me an answer, but it is unfair that Ekiaqueta brought you into this country only to be Americanized overnight and blame it on his senior sister you claimed is a witch. I personally know Ekiaqueta's senior sister. She's a humble woman, respected and . . . you are not married to his sister, you are married to this man before you sitting here," he pointed at me.

Efemona tried to speak. Sam anticipated her. I know what Efemona was thinking and about to say, which was that: I ignore her when she was flippant and doing the dishes and I have done so for a long time, not caring about her feelings when I was mute, not replying to her abusive words. And that I never contemplate making any input into any argument she initiates or into any of her needs, such as new designer fashions she purchased from shopping catalogues nationwide, knew that anything she says would be met with ill-disguised contempt, making her inferior and I constantly reinforce the message of I'll know who brought whom to America . . . and a woman from Ukpenu to Ekiaqueta is supposed to entertain in the kitchen and shut her fucking mouth, that the mere fact of her opening a savings account and about having the idea of purchasing a home at the Government Reserved Areas (GRA) in Benin, which would make her as having a penis would now be foiled because of Sam and Anukam who are with us to mediate, she bowed her head, thinking.

Sam noticed her thinking seriously about my thoughts and said, "Now listen to me. Before ten o'clock tomorrow morning I ask you to go to your bank, wherever it is, and withdraw all the money in the fucking account. Dammit. Tender to Ekiaqueta even the nickels and dimes. Both of you could decide what to do with the money when the money is on the table. Work with What Can I Say. He brought you to this country. Dammit. Maybe you don't know we uphold our tradition that a man is the builder and the pillar of a good matrimonial home. Don't you remember where you come from anymore? Jesus have mercy! I still remember the mother fucking village with goddamn plenty of flies and mosquitoes you hail from, Efemona . . . Dammit."

He raised his voice. "Respect your husband and listen to him. Goddammit. And remember that no prophet is greater than his teacher, Efemona!"

He toned down, "We even understand that you said you'll pay Ekiaqueta the money he used to purchase your flight ticket to come to America. That's foul and rotten, woman."

Efemona could not contain herself. She considered Sam's rebuke as insults for a woman who has seen the light in America. Then she said,

"I thought in history it was question jam answer. It seems to me here it's no longer so. Rather, is question and answer your own question at the same time in my apartment."

Sam was not a man to bow down to such appeal. He mellowed down his voice a bit but as a typical village headmaster with a rattan cane on his palm walking the school compound, he looked sternly at Efemona.

"You know we try here in America to treat you women like goddesses. And you know damn well in our country it is not the woman whom our fathers train abroad, but their first son. Isn't that true? You don't have to answer me, goddammit. You belong to the kitchen in your village."

Efemona squirmed on her seat realizing that Sam was right. And as I listened to Sam talk, I realized that he'd an insight to who my wife really was than I did. So, for that I was concerned about my wife's future transgressions against me, such as gulping beer as a downer and gulping Remymartins, wine, champagne and marijuana as uppers to be more flippant to drive me away from the house any time she feels.

Sam added, "I must tell you in the presence of Anukam that you are damn wrong. Turning to Anukam, Sam asked, "Do you have anything to add to what I've said to Efemona?"

"Damn right, I do."

"Well tell her your mind and how good women from Nigeria raised in good homes by principals are supposed to behave when they are abroad."

"You said it all, Sam," Anukam said and looked at me. He saw that my cow eye was teary so he handed me his handkerchief.

As I began to clean my eyes, he said with caution, "I can visualize the pain you went through with the operation of your eye. Can you see with it?" He cajoled and my cow eye immediately moved in response.

I shook my head. Then he added, "Anyway, your wife also stated to us that you are a compulsive gambler. I'm not here to say that you are right or that Efemona is lying. Sam and I are here to get to the root of the problem. You probably gamble because you feel you have lots of bills to pay coupled with taking care of your extended families in Nigeria. It's not easy, but I tell you this, that men who are enslaved by gambling are willing to sell what they owned, even steal to support their habits. I have seen with my own naked eyes, married men who went into volatile terrain because they wanted to prove a point to their wives thinking they will win big in the casinos of these huge evil empire of the neon Babylon city of Reno. I have to tell you that it rarely ever happens. I have also seen married women who left their husbands and sold their carnals because their men fouled up their lives."

My only good eye to see was now carrying too much burden of looking left and right at interruptions from Sam and Efemona. But I could see Efemona nodding her head. She did not want to interrupt now. Instead she raised her finger up. Anukam said, "Just a minute. Wait till I finish."

But gone are the days when African woman like Efemona listen to men from Nigeria/Africa talk and she listen. Those women who does are ofcourse the idiot women who want their husbands to control them. Now that I live in America, and women are regarded first, Efemona thought, I can challenge and stop Anukam anytime.

I watched Anukam turn his face to me. Then he said, "You see, my friend, gambling therefore became their whole life and religion. If you do gamble, do it with common sense or might as well just quit."

Sam nodded. And Anukam said to Efemona, "Don't let your husband have that spirit in him to say what a mess he'd made in shipping you to America only to belittle him. I know that I am very often rather rational with my wife and sometimes don't take things as I should, but I really do not see your point in trying to grow a penis in the middle of the night."

I knew that pissed my Efemona off.

Anukam looked at Sam for comment. And Sam complimented him. He said, "I'm amused by your careful thought. I want Efemona to realize also that it is easy for men to make fools of ideas, which is true enough. But equally true enough is that notion that it is even easier for ideas to make fools of men and women. Both of them should work together for the benefit of their children."

It appeared to me that Anukam was reading Efemona's mind. And Efemona murmured some fragmental words which I could not hear because I'd blinked my good eye to see. Anukam reacted sharply in my favor. He looked at Sam and said, "It seems to me that if a young woman had made up her mind to the great wickedness of looking down on her husband and dictating to authorities for a cow eye for her husband, she would not appear distraught about it afterwards. To me, Efemona's actions from the way she's behaving now is a premeditated and calculated action against Ekiaqueta. And I do not think Efemona would take our words into consideration. I cannot imagine my wife from Aba or your wife from Onitsha coming to this country to team up with authorities to agitate for a cow eye for me or you when she know that there are millions of donated human organs of eye parts in eye banks throughout the fifty states of America."

"It depends on how you look at it. Let's admit we do not know the circumstances-and that's why we are here to resolve the matter." With that I was honored, not flattered, I suppose. My adrenaline rose and Anukam helped me out. "If there was a misunderstanding or a grave quarrel, it should have been kept within Ekiaqueta and Efemona in their domain. I'll say this, that is, this act of Efemona seemed to me to be surrounded by a foulness which stinks into my nostrils when I first heard the news of cops with Ekiaqueta in his own house with Dapor and later at the operating table at Washoe Medical Center, where Ekiaqueta was ill-treated with a cow eye. Efemona owes Ekiaqueta a great apology."

Efemona looked up and said nothing. Anukam waited a few seconds. The mere look on Efemona's poker face told him an apology was doomed. Then Anukam said, "I want you to realize that human beings are accustomed to making choices. Real choices come in different modes. You have the good and the evil. Hard and easy. The good ones are usually the hard ones. I'm suggesting that a smooth discussion of bills and important events should be discussed on the dinner table shortly before adult conversations to maintain confidence in your relationship that I foresee would be turned apart if you lived your life as the Romans do. The power and spending decision should rest with Ekiaqueta. It is the African way. We know our culture. We'll respect it anywhere. That's the hard part, Efemona."

He paused and looked at Efemona. Then he added, "I hope you are not offended, but remember we are not Americans."

I could see Efemona grinding her teeth. Right there and then, I knew what she was thinking because a man living with a woman in the same roof, fucking her, knows her better. What she was thinking I believe was: Ekiaqueta has had his moments. He'd stripped her of all dignity accorded all American women, including her. Philomena Drake came to her mind. I can't go shopping alone any longer! He challenges me in the presence of the sun and the rain. He even humiliated her and abused her in the presence of his friends. Finally she looked at Sam and as I turned to see her facial reactions, my cow eye was teary again. And Anukam gave me his handkerchief. I took extra precaution to wipe out the tears. She watched me finish and drew Sam's attention.

And my Efemona said, "You were there when Ekiaqueta grabbed me and almost blinded me with a right hook to my face in your house. You think about it! If the blow had met my nose, my jaw, I'd probably have ended up at Saint Mary's Hospital and . . ."

Sam gave her no time to finish. But he said, "You initiated it, Efemona, when you said, 'you'll show him *nine-nine*."

I didn't know Sam still remembered the incidence. And Efemona said, "Now the blame is on me, right?"

"That's right," Sam said.

Efemona murmured a few words, then resonated in a high-pitched voice. She said, looking at my cow eye still teary, "Ekiaqueta, you can narrate me to the Mayor of Reno, Nevada and the Senator of this state. You can narrate my whole life history to them. Now that I am in the United States, know what's up, I'll live my life the way I choose in this country. My money I made at my job is mine. Have a life or take a rope and hang yourself, Ekiaqueta."

I can tell you that the next few minutes witness Sam and Anukam a wife with flippant vibrations with her new Yankee slang tongue. A rebellion of a woman who feels she'd waited too long to have her freedom and there was nothing anyone says to change her new ways of the Western tradition.

Sam and Anukam rose to leave and Anukam looked at me and said, "We are sorry we can't resolve this matter you may have with your wife."

I rose, too, and I escorted my guests to their cars. Anukam stopped and lit a cigarette while Sam and I stood at the base of the stairs leading downwards. As he lit it, he glanced at me. When he finally joined us, we all stood together. Both looked at me with perfect composure. Anukam said, "It's important that I tell Ekiaqueta, my friend here, to get wise to himself. I see beyond certainty that Efemona will tear his home apart. In your own opinion, what do you think, Sam?"

Sam hesitated to answer him and looked at me.

I weighed the question in my being. "Well," I said, *"Ghandi once said, 'If a man gives you a drink of water and you give him a drink in return, that is nothing.' Real beauty, as I perceive it through Ghandi in his grave consists in doing good against evil."*

Both laughed at me. They have every reason to laugh, I thought. Maybe I must've quoted Ghandi, the man I love in history wrongly. But come to think about it, twice, I did know that reading Ghandi's text, it gave me an inspiration to carry on my life with my one eye to see.

"From the way I see things, my friend, Ghandi will not rise from his grave to tell you 'an eye for an eye' is what Efemona is up to. Wake up my friend!" Sam yelled at me.

"You know," I said, *"Fredrick Nitzsche knows best the meaning of evil. A master to Nitzsche is one who is superior to his slave. A master gives without expecting a return.* Looking at Efemona behind my being, I know she cannot hurt me more than she had already done, selling me to the authorities to gain fame, and carry on with her life to be able to dance *ojeke*, the famous dance of the Royals of Benin in the city of Reno," I said.

All said, I embraced both men before we parted. And as I walked helplessly into our condo, I recited my usual mantra, love lost is love gained. But NO. I did not settle for that premise. Efemona has three children with me. I must not compromise her wishes. I'll try my best to make our differences stick was my last thought before I dozed off on the couch.

Efemona traveled to Nigeria after two days of requesting that I do her a favor of watching the kids when she traveled.

Before she left, she'd warned that I should not blink my only eye to see when our children were looking at my face. She also instructed that I pray hard with her that Newman would be alive and well in the hospital bed.

With our children in the car and my goggles on, I drove Efemona to Reno International Airport to board her flight. Bear in mind that this was to be the first of an impromptu visit before her major visit to see Bad Dudu. She got to Nigeria and held to Benin, the time when the whole city celebrated the beginning of New Yam festival and Revelation of New Magic festival displayed in the Royal Palace yearly. Efemona got out of the taxi and started to walk towards the hospital, where her brother, Newman was. As she walked majestically with her suitcase carry on board in her hand, the next moment, she was swept up in the masquerade screaming and dancing of men and women in painted faces. She shook her head. It was culture *now* obscure to Efemona, because it was a black witch's display, a million witches, the old and the young magicians of Royal Palace at Benin were celebrating the death of her grandmother and possibly cast some voodoo charm on her to get more flippant with her husband when she returned to America. Efemona's suitcase was torn from her and disappeared, only to reappear in the Princess's right hand. As she looked at the Princess with her suitcase, she was grabbed by a fat man in a devil's mask and hailed. A deer-like man squeezed her breasts, a giant gaunt face zebra-like man grabbed her from behind and lifted her up yelling-*aye ye ye,* which she understood to mean Efemona would be somebody great in the near future. She struggled free to dash into Oba's Palace close to the hospital where Newman was being cared for, but it was impossible. They would not let her. She was hemmed in, trapped in the middle as they chant Prince and Princesses songs. And they knew who she was. Finally, she moved with the chanting witches and wizards, magicicans, tears of joy streaming down her face because she'd realized that the witches don't just come out to dance and display unless it was somebody who was out of the country who would be able to buy them goats and cows to make merriment and satisfy their palates, which they had not been able to satisfy since Bad Dudu had seized power. There was no escape until she dropped a few dollars on the ground for them. Finally, remembering her culture, she unzipped her purse and dropped a thousand dollars on the ground for them. As they picked up the dollars on the ground, they all disappeared one after the other, leaving my Efemona alone to walk majestically into the hospital ward of her destination.

* * *

A week later, Efemona arrived to America from the impromptu visit to see Newman. Our relationship got worse soon after. Late in the afternoon, two days after she arrived, she went to the famous Zion bar, also called the Trader's Dick, a few blocks from our condo. She'd walked the sidewalk, then saw the Zion bar was open, and walked in with the hopes of finding London Gordon Gin. Nothing but a London Gordon Gin, maybe two or three shots may make her mouth flippant when she come back to the house. And the truth is, I would be in the house waiting for her. It was Mother's Day and she could come back home after the London Gin gulps and bully me to make love to her, to make her happy on a Mother's Day remembrance. Right there, a wave of spell from the bottles of various gin in the name of demon of the witches fell hard upon Efemona, and she began to think. Soon after, realization seized her insane mind.

She'd seen the rows of bottles of hard liquor, all full and unopened, cognac, whiskeys, and gins and vodkas and names of other hard liquor she'd not heard of before, all lined up like pretty little cowboys in bright, colorful camouflage. Her mouth was instantly salivating for it. Her jaw dropped and her eyes opened wide. She grabbed the counter so she wouldn't waver, and her entire face contorted with happiness as she thought about me the, Ekiaqueta of a man with a cow eye getting more native and uglier every day, with not enough dollars, as she thought. So many thoughts flourished her mind when the bartender said something in a nonchalant attitude she'd not expected. Efemona glowered at him, bit her lip and remembered she has a man at home she has absolute control over in the American fashion. "Goddammit! Give me two shots of London Gin. Make it double," she said with no please. I have a man like you at home I have absolute control over," and she gulped it at a go.

He served her another at her request, but Efemona vowed not to stop until the bottle he was serving from was empty. As the bottle had only about one shot left, she paid him what she owed and walked with a purpose to the apartment, stepping around a group of other young women prostituting for men. So lucky are the young women, not married, she thought. No burdens, no children. Tomorrow is my turn, she murmured to herself.

She finally came back into the house, when the sidewalk cafés and bars were all closed until the next business day.

As she walked in, I noticed a change in her mood. The demon in the gin had just perhaps started to work its way into her veins. Then she sat on my lap. As I was getting ready and in the mood to screw her, she commanded me to enter her from behind while she held on to the arm chair. Within a few minute that I wanted to direct myself inside her with my right hand, there came several flourishes of knocks on our door. I quietly tip-toed and approached the front door. Noticing that the security lights were on and we were naked, I did not open the door after seeing the figure through the peeping hole. There I noticed a stranger, a pleasant-faced black female figure in her late thirties, with a vague, composed manner, with braided hair, slim with a nice ass. Looking at her titties from the peeping hole, I noticed, too, that they were bigger than a Hawaiian coconut fruit.

"Just a minute," I said after another knock. "Who is it?" Efemona asked me in a whisper.

"A figure I have never seen before, honey," I whispered back. We dressed up hurriedly. Efemona walked to the door, saw the figure and opened it. A figure before her stood as Efemona mumbled a greeting and was surprised at the figure before her. It was then six-twenty-five P.M. Still surprise, Efemona asked, "Yes, may I help you?"

The figure smiled. Efemona looked closely at her. Finally, she recognized her. With excitement, Efemona shouted, "Victoria?"

Efemona ushered her in and they embraced.

I was wondering who she was when Efemona introduced the stranger to me. I said, "Hi," and indicated with my right hand for her to sit. She sat.

Victoria looked at me and said, "I'm sorry I couldn't see you before you left the country with Efemona, my very good friend." I took my usual seat and sipped on my bottle of beer. Victoria turned to Efemona and said, "Fine home, good furniture you all have here, sister Efemona."

"Thanks to McMahon's discount furniture store that approved a credit line for me."

I noticed that Efemona did not say 'us', which reminds me of other African women married to African men in Reno, Nevada who try to heighten their husband's image despite they cannot afford to buy furniture of the type we had.

Efemona looked at Victoria numerous times. Finally, she said, "How did you end up in Reno to know where I live?"

"Don't you remember you are still on study leave of absence? By the way, the Federal Government of Nigeria still has your current and old address on file. You can run, but you can't hide from the powers that be in our country. Anyway, I'm running an errand for Bad Dudu, the General who has claimed he's the president of Nigeria despite no one voted him into the executive seat of Doddan Army Barrack."

Efemona became swoon. Her mouth opened and her jaw dropped. "About what? I'm surprised."

Victoria ignored the question. I was interested to hear what she had to say, too. Anyway, Victoria replied, "I have just been promoted three months ago by the President. I'm now in charge of monitoring all hospitals in the nation. I recommend to the administrator what our hospitals and maternites need such as new purchases of new beds, gurneys, oxygen tanks, disinfectants, needles, new drugs like Viagra for the military men, MRI scanning machines, respirator machines, incubators and . . . !! In fact, anything the Nation's Hospitals and maternities need. I'll try my best to monitor all these gadgets once they're purchased and in my care. My reason for that is because three or four years ago, the President, on his fiscal budget, allocated $100 million dollars for the purchase of new computers and hospital equipments. The items were purchased and delivered to the hospitals. You know what happened? Some of them ended up in private hands and the rest were seen in Ghana, Sierra Leone, Togo and the Cameroons for a profit of one thousand dollars in dubious pockets. Under my supervision, I promised the President that the items would be used in our hospitals and maternities across the Nation. I promised my sincere accountability. By the way, how have you been, girlfriend?"

"Congratulations. I'm very fine and doing good until I saw you standing in my door step. I'm nervous about your visit to see me here in Reno, Victoria. I must tell ya! Please tell me something! Is Newman, my brother, dead? I was just in the country to see him when I heard he was shot for supporting me and my African Women Against Marriage Movement (AWAM) about a week ago. Or are my parents still alive?"

"Your parents and Newman are well and alive."

"So what's up? What can I offer you?" Efemona interrupted.

Efemona walked up to the refrigerator and opened it. Then she opened all the kitchen cabinets and said, "We have Heineken, Guiness Stout, Goulder, Star, Korbel, London Gin and Coca-Cola and Sprite."

"Give me two shots of London Gin," Victoria said.

"Good old days," Efemona remembered. "You are still on it, ain't ya? I can't do without it, myself," Efemona said.

Efemona served Victoria and served herself, too, then sat down opposite to Victoria on the rocking chair and crossed her legs contentedly while rocking back and forth. Finally, she said, "Tell me Victoria, what's the purpose of your real trip? I don't believe the President would . . . ."

"It seems you're driving me away! I've all the time in the world to spend with you, unless, of course, you want me to leave. And supposing I tell you I'm simply on a vacation and was destined to see you? So relax! Are you heading someplace tonight?"

Efemona looked at Victoria in the eyes. She contemplated a few seconds, thinking it was too late now. But it occurred to her that maybe she should tell Efemona the truth. The problem was that Ekiaqueta has a way of analyzing things she might say and she didn't want him to know what she'd planned to do. Then she said, "Not exactly. But I'm just nervous, Victoria."

"Don't be nervous. Everything is perfectly fine sis-Efemona. I boarded the last flight form Lagos to Holland en route to San Francisco. And here I am with you at eighteen-fifty-five El Rancho Drive, condo three-three-O. I have all night with you unless you have an appointment to keep tonight. I suggest, too, that if you do have an appointment, you call to cancel."

Victoria looked at the telephone on the kitchen wall. She saw another on top of the end table by the entertainment center. She could not hold her breath. She said, "Everyone can afford telephones in America. But not in our country. I see you have one on the wall, one on the table. I guess you may have one in the bathroom and in your bedroom, too or even in your damn ass!," and she smiled.

"What do you think?" Efemona said and nodded, then added, "Yes, you are right. Anyone can afford a telephone in America.

Anyway, I will call and cancel my only appointment for tonight. I was gonna go out to have a few drinks with Virginia, my good friend across the street." Efemona said and then stared again at her guest.

"It's been a long time since we've seen each other. Your mom, father, brothers and sisters are fine, I hope?"

Victoria sipped on her London Gin, too, and glanced at Efemona. And the demon in the gin was bringing out their true colors. Clearing her throat, Victoria asked, "You are still on a study leave of absence, ain't you?"

"Yes, of course. I guess for a period of ten years. Why?" Efemona asked with amazement too.

Here I realized what Victoria was about to say: Meaning that in a third world country, like Nigeria, where files are missing or set ablaze to conceal stolen money from poor people on a daily basis and where computers are still alien to monitor bank activities and government officials, Efemona could go back after ten years of absence and collect a huge sum of arrears, which I think is bad for a developing country. Bear in mind, though, that this is not only happening in Nigeria. It is rooted in African countries and it's a way of bane of corruption whereby if Efemona goes back to Nigeria to stay, she could bribe high official of the establishment she'd worked for before she traveled and then get paid arrears for her study leave abroad. The thing is, how do we know that Efemona, or anyone else, was actually on a study leave and not prostituting on the sidewalks of American streets? The thing is, no one in Nigeira or elsewhere in Africa gives a fuck because the corruption is rooted in our blood, which is another reason why our forefathers sold their sons and daughters to the white man for nickels and dimes into slavery. I should also point out too that Bad Dudu and his in cahoots are no exception, if there was still slave trade today.

Anyway, though, I did not say a word. I sat patiently and listened to Victoria and Efemona's conversation as it progressed.

Efemona glanced up at Victoria briefly, her heavy-lidded eyes reveled. She then remembered that since she left Nigeria to join me, the Ekiaqueta of a man who is dimeless, Life Goes On had placed people he trusted in positions of power at different government hospitals and offices. Looking at Victoria moderately, she said, "This is but my fifth year on my study leave of absence." Victoria shrugged, then squirmed on the love seat, which she was seated across from Efemona. She, too, glanced at Efemona and said, "Now that I am already here with you, why don't we have a cigarette and just talk about what's been going on in our government?"

"I don't want to hear what is going on in Nigeria," Efemona cautioned.

Come to think about the embarrassing situation which Bad Dudu and his cronies had created in the history of Nigeria since Dudu assumed the Presidency for which no one voted him, Efemona realized that it should not only be treated as an emergency because one day Dudu would exterminate all the intellectuals of Nigeria which she was aware of, she also believe that one day he would send secret police to whisk her father away from his sleep and he would be missing as the rest of most learned men. She also belive that Dudu is well known in the Federation for his ruthlessness and his abuse of power through his military uniforms. Efemona knew for sure that the jails of Nigeria are full of intellectuals— men and women and even of University students and has no respect for anyone else in the country except his juntas. For that Efemona knew that Dudu was an embarrassment to the rest of the people of Nigeria who are of decent and of professional hard working men and women. Also Efemona knew that Dudu is a threat not only to the intellectuals of her country of which 1% are mostly from her family, but also to the attorneys who frequent the jails to see their bossom friends, the judges of Nigeria who dances to his whims and caprices because they're afraid they would be stripped of their robes and mostly to the thousand of other World Leaders who love their Nations and their people and for that Efemona strongly believe it was time that Dudu must go. With all these animosity on Efemona's mind she hunched her eyes up to protest against Victoria trying to tell her about what's going on in Nigeria.

Then she said, "Why do I have to hear it when Gambari, the former ambassador to the United Nations had pictures of our students who demonstrated against Bad Dudu's government in New York and all the students were executed as they traveled home on holidays?"

"Oh! Forgive me. I didn't know you are already aware of some of Bad Dudu's atrocities!" Victoria said.

Efemona watched Victoria calmly light the cigarette after Victoria apologized and then Efemona leaned back again on rocking chair, doubling her legs under her, without paying attention that she wasn't wearing an underwear. She sighed and looked in my direction. Finally, Victoria said, "It's nice to be with you again after all these years. Care to smoke with me as we used to back in the good old days together? I mean with all those Hausa men, sugar daddies we used to clean up their wallets?"

The mere mention of 'Hausa men' reminded Efemona of Idolo Imugu who comes regularly to the Nugget Hotel and Casino in downtown Sparks, Nevada, with whom she was having an affair. She smiled and looked at me. I looked at her in return. But you know, the respect for me at the time she first landed in America, cooking for me and doing the dishes alone has since been relegated despite my negative remarks about smoking, and so she said, "Sure, why not?"

Victoria lit Efemona one of the slim cigarettes. Then she cleared her throat, "Our Bad Dudu-I mean the man who claims to be the President of our country wants you back in Nigeria as soon as possible to assume the post of the Matron General. Miss Edna Obaze Adeniyi passed away. The best person for the job, which has since been vacant for several months, is you. Bad Dudu has chosen you, Efemona. He said that after going through your dossier he liked your devotion and dedication to your duties while you were with us five years ago. He's very interested in you because of your knowledge of C-sections on women who are unable to deliver their babies, and about your broad knowledge of cervical and breast cancer in women."

Efemona sighed deeply, but relaxed. After a while, she said, "There are qualified nurses and Chief Nursing Sisters in mostly the middle belt and all across our Nation to assume that post. Sis-Victoria, I beg you to go back and tell the goddamn Bad Dudu that there are more qualified people in that country to assume that post. Besides, my ten years study leave has not yet expired."

Victoria knew Efemona was damn right. But she was on a mission. She's now too embedded in the system of the ruling junta. She'll do anything to persuade Efemona. But Efemona had sent a chilly effect on her brain. Finally, she said, "Sis-Efemona! You'll do it for me. The money he'll pay you is good. From what I understand, your base salary would be fifty thousand Naira per anum. You could buy your own home at Ukpenu or GRA in Benin and also share Doddan Army

Barracks with Bad Dudu and his men in power. I know how you like to have orgasms," she joked.

At this time, the piercing begging of acceptance was felt deepest, that is, Victoria had thought Efemona would accept the post just because they were friends who dated and screwed the same sugar daddies in those good old times. That aside, Bad Dudu and Bawuh had also tried, by fax and e-mail, to appeal to Efemona. The thing is, our computer machine was plagued by a virus which resulted that I shot it down until the problem was solved.

Anyway, I looked at both women-as they battled to contain bounded emotions of long time no see as their eyes began teary. The discussion and appeal from Victoria was now far away from the usual animated sessions both women had had in the past. Right here at 1855 El Ranch Drive, number 330 condo, it was an insipid get acquainted once again of two bosom friends dropping words in easy, parley modulations.

After much thought, Victoria watched poker-faced as Efemona did the quick mental calculus. Efemona collapsed against the back of the rocking chair, tiny sobs escaped from her trembling lips. She opened her mouth to interrupt, but Victoria anticipated her. Here, Victoria and I knew why my Efemona had tears in her eyes. I did not say a word. My eyes were fixed deep on the video TV Late Night Show of David Letterman. With my one eye to see and my goggles still on, I saw that Efemona wiped the little tears and looked at her friend. Looking at me watching TV without input into their conversation, she said, "How much do you think fifty thousand Naira is worth? It's nothing, my friend. -N50,000 is just but chicken change for my position with International Games Technology (IGT), whom I work for here in Reno. Put it this way, -N50,000 is just but only maybe two hundred fucking dollars. Shit! I ain't going with you, man. Fuck Bad Dudu and his vacant post."

Victoria shook her head, noting that Efemona could in no way made that comment before the man who claimed he's the President without no one voting him into the executive seat he occupied. Victoria thought for a minute and asked, "Thought though you were still a nurse?"

"Of course. I'm still a nurse. In America one has the option and the right to work two or more jobs if one can handle it. My working for IGT is just a part time job," Efemona said.

Victoria was relieved. In her mind was the feeling that most Nigerians have no jobs and it's ironic that in America one can work three jobs if one is able and capable. Since Victoria was now a member of their teams-that team of *'if you can't beat them, join them'*, she resulted to beg further. "Sister Efemona," she called upon. "Please, you'll bare me out on this. Bad Dudu's junta members would think that I took the money meant for you for my personal gains. Please, you must go with me to Nigeria. Here is your ticket to make the journey with me. Bad Dudu wants to meet you at Doddan Army Barracks to welcome you back into his administration. Please don't fail me. Otherwise my job is jeopardized. Oh, I should tell you that you'll enjoy the new capital at Abuja with Bad Dudu."

Efemona listened as Victoria carefully described the new capital to her.

"ABUJA, our new state capital, what they call the 'Black House'," Victoria stated, "had been built to serve as a symbol for the massive intimidating power, Nigerian army juntas hoped to impress upon the African continent and as a fortress in case of riots; raids and revolutions from those who are fed up with the army iron hand rule on our civilians at home and from abroad. The place has a stark beauty and a pugnacious pride. The Black House, like the White House structure, from what I heard, cost the Nigerian government millions and millions of dollars more than Bad Dudu- our President had publicly admitted. Sources close to Bad Dudu said that the Black House was damn expensive to build because there was the problem of rock blasting of the foundation during the blasting and slicing of the huge stones. Though the giant 'Abuja stone' was too heavy for the British Hercules to tow to Britain or Switzerland to allow the building of the Black House, Bad Dudu and his junta members had to hire the best structural engineers of Lebanon and Britain with millions and millions of pounds and dollars."

As I listened to Victoria tell the story of Abuja, I began to wonder, too, that the place Victoria was describing must be almost Heaven.

I was right. Victoria continued, "The new Abuja capital is almost Heaven. The Black House contained over a thousand office suites housing many offices. I presume the President will give you an office there next to his office."

Efemona could not hold her thoughts. "How many offices are there for the staff nurses?"

"You'll know when we get to Nigeria. All I know is that the place I've described to you has sealed important offices just for transmitting information to Buckingham Palace on who will rule. And most of the important suites are protected by memos and urgent messages which are sent to Britain to the Prime Minister to make new policies will be revealed to you. You will be an insider rather than an outsider of the powerless of our Nation. The junta would always be on duty to guard you. To cut the story short, soldiers are always on duty. There is a sort of roundabout beyond the main gate. In the middle of the roundabout is the famous Nigerian flag. From the roundabout the guards command a view of the greatest circular drive and the street front. The roof line of the Black House has no vulgar bronze eagle yet compared to the Doddan Army Barracks because the President personally likes to rule from Lagos. But the green-white-green flag pole had been pegged on a stainless steel which stood firm in the middle of the roundabout flying till the day you will arrive to assume the post.

As the editor of the Obiagelli Newspaper wrote, the Black House at Abuja suggests that Nigerian politics are basically the allocation of West Africa power, if not Africa and had described the mood of Abuja building as 'one of a kind'. The Nigerian edifice similar to the White House had dignity and solidity. It's an avant-garde Black House, my dear. There are no windows facing the street on the first two floors, except for slits, which I think is for teachers with no pay having their offices shut, no windows and no lights because they cannot afford to buy candles and lanterns to carry along with them to their offices that would enable them to see and read their prepared lectures while they are inside."

"Have you personally visited the new Abuja capital?" Efemona interrupted.

"I've read about the place. I saw the architectural design and some of my friends had visited the place and told me about it. And based on the information from those who'd visited the place, they said that when the teachers' kerosene ran out of their lanterns when they were in their offices, they go home and sleep and their students therefore become dumber and dumber and are unable to add one and two together during monk examinations."

That almost turned Efemona off who remembered that Newman, her brother, was once a teacher and was not paid for about nine months before he decided to go to the Northern State of Zamfara to milk the cattle for the Sharia Cult farms.

So Efemona dealt her fist on the arm of the rocking chair.

Victoria knew why she did that. She, too, was a witness to the government not paying the teachers their wages for several months, because the Commissioner of Education, Mr. Bakari, had deposited the salary meant for all teachers in the Nation into his personal account to generate huge interest for him for five years. She looked at Efemona and said, "I know how you feel about that. Anyway, the whole place at Abuja was skillfully designed so that it could be closed off from Britain's Buckingham Palace by metal shutters with remote control. It is rumored that Tony Blair and ex-Prime Minister Margarette Thatcher have their own offices where they keep records of Major's and Bridgedier Generals who rule and are yet to rule and who would have the most money stashed away in British banks. Very soon Efemona you'll be among the Generals to rub shoulders with them."

"Hum! That sounds actually like almost Heaven," Efemona said.

Efemona finished her cigarette and asked for another stick before she got up to serve Victoria another shot of London Gin.

Victoria took the drink from Efemona. "Thank you sis-Efemona. You must think about my position. You must go with me because what you owe Bad Dudu, our President, is only the answer 'yes' or 'no' if you are not interested in the vacant post," Victoria said. "By the way, your husband just walked out on us without even telling us. That was rude of him."

For the first time, Victoria also noticed that Efemona had no marriage ring on her finger anymore when Efemona extended her left hand to Victoria for revelation of something. Then she smiled. With joyous feeling in the pit of her stomach, Efemona pointed at her ring finger to indicate to Victoria that she'd thrown the damn thing into the Truckee River so she could enjoy herself as the Americans do. Then she reached under the center table and brought out a folded newspaper of the Gazette Journal and extended it toward Victoria.

Victoria unfolded the front page of the gossip society section. There, in a picture no one in Reno could miss, were Efemona and an unknown gigolo, drunk as Jezabel dancing on the stage holding the gigolo she didn't even know. The gigolo's face was bent low over hers, which was low to her ears like a sunflower withering away when there was no sunlight. Efemona's smile to him was like, "Please take me home and screw me!" doing anything she could as if she was too drunk to move her legs. Under the picture the caption read: "Efemona was to meet some guy at the Reno Hilton Garage Bar, but didn't show up, so Efemona seduced Carlos, her daughter's godfather's son."

"What?!" Victoria was surprised and flung the paper to the kitchen and hugged Efemona.

After a few minutes, as they sat again, Efemona rocked back and forth on the rocking chair, then folded her hands behind her head, a sign of soon to be a successful woman. Finally, she said to Victoria, "The Reno Hilton Garage Bar is the place to be for African women in Reno who have it in their hearts to separate and live their lives as the Romans do. You know sis-Victoria, things are not alright with me and my husband as it used to be."

When I came in I watched Efemona take a long drag on her cigarette, then crush the butt out with a savage slash into the ashtray and looked at Victoria again straight in the face. "Right here in America, I planned to be the first African woman to teach one man a lesson he'll never forget."

Deep in my heart, I knew Efemona was about to cajole and humiliate me before Victoria. So I walked to the balcony to allow them to arrest their conversation.

As I came back in, again Victoria was nodding and still talking. Efemona leaned back, sipped on her glass of London Gin and stared at Victoria's eyes, then tapped on her thigh as if to say, Oh! Here he comes.

My husband feels he's the king for getting me into America with a ticket of only one thousand five hundred dollars flight ticket to travel and join him in America, which he knows I can *now* pay him back and leave my life alone as the Romans do," she joked.

I knew Efemona meant her words at the bottom of her heart. I grinded my teeth and shook my head in protest of that. She did not seem to see my containance, so I walked into the bedroom with extreme sadness. Two or three steps into our bedroom, I heard more fragments of words echoed by Victoria, "Well, this is your time and chance to elope Ekiaqueta and take the job in Nigeria the President has for you."

She paused to hear if I was listening, but I was humming *Asonogun* song suitable for *Ojeke* dancing at the Royal Palace in Benin. So she said, "I should tell you that your sugar daddy, Mr. Emeka Ngozika, I mean the man from Portharcourt, is one of the richest men now in the country. He's still single. He would be glad to have you if you are tired of your husband's bullshit here in Reno."

As I opened the door to come out, Victoria froze her words. I took my usual seat and sipped on my Heineken beer. I pretended I did not hear what was said while I was in the bedroom. Efemona looked at Victoria. I could see she was beaming with good will about Ngozika. Finally, Efemona said, "You mean Emeka is not married yet, after all these years?"

"He is right there doing better than ever. He quit his CEO job with Flour Mills a few years ago and took an executive post with Nigerian Petroleum Oil Company. You should see him now. His cheeks are now puffy looking. He has mansions and bungalows all over the Federation, including a whore house at Aba, where millionaires and tourists from all over the world come to hang out for pleasure. The discotheque at the joint is superb. Latest releases of well-known artists from America are played there all night. You name it. Rap, R&B, Jazz and more. When one is there you think you are in California's Beverly Hills in Hollywood. You can dance the night away with him at least for a night. He would be glad to see you again. I'm also positive that he could give you one of the several homes he has across the Nation. The Federal Government would compete with him to give you more money. In short, anything you ask for from Bad Dudu: housing allowance, servants, anything, Efemona! Think about it. All you have to do is tell the man with two hats on what you need. How about that, sis-Efemona?"

"I'll think about it. But first, after cleaning up the mess in the house tonight, I'll decide if it's worth going with you to Nigeria. I owe it a duty to tell you right now, Victoria, that you should apply your mind to who will be the next Matron General to tell the President when you go back home," Efemona bluffed.

"No! You must be kidding me. In our country, don't you know they, the ruling junta, operate on a hierarchy basis? Miss Edna Obaze Adeniyi is gone, you are the number two they remembered who is in America," she lied. All Victoria wanted to do was lure her to Nigeria.

"I don't know why I should even be debating this issue with you, Efemona. You have to start thinking of who would be your assistant when you meet with Bad Dudu, our President to assume the post."

After a long argument in which both of them did not concede to the other, Victoria was about to grow annoyed, but kept her cool. Finally, Victoria said to Efemona, "Girlfriend, please sleep on it if you can't give me a positive answer now."

Who would like to miss an opportunity like that to see Bad Dudu for the first time? I know I wouldn't. So Efemona looked up at her friend, "By the way, what time is the flight tomorrow, anyway? Oh! Never mind."

I watched Efemona look at her ticket Victoria had flung on her a few seconds earlier. I could tell she was showing a sign of interest to travel with Victoria to see the President.

"Five ten A.M.," Victoria said and looked up at her.

"Oh! Well, I think I might make the journey with you to please you. I'm not promising you I'll accept the post, but I want to do it just for you and also to see my dear Emeka, even if it's for one night, since Bad Dudu's regime has paid my way."

Victoria snapped to her feet and embraced her friend. Efemona said to Victoria, "How much did you say the President sent to me for pocket money?"

"Twenty-five hundred." Actually, Victoria had backed off a thousand.

Responding to Efemona, Victoria's mind carried her back to the good old days. In the same manner, Efemona's reward lay in the fact that she could go with Victoria to Nigeria to enjoy and celebrate the good old days. Then, slowly Efemona was eradicating Victoria's disturbing memories and replacing them with joyful ones. A few seconds later, Efemona took Victoria's hands and looked at me. I could see my Efemona with a beautiful smile beaming with beauty of what she would wear to see Bad Dudu. Looking at me with a diabolical glimmer of a smile, she said to Victoria, "Deal.

We'd better go to bed so we can get up early and be fresh for our trip to Nigeria tomorrow."

I finished my beer and walked to the kitchen to drop my empty bottle in the trash bin. As I walked, I turned and said to Efemona, "The time is getting late. Won't you make the bed in the guest room for your friend before we go to bed? Your friend would like a comfortable sleep before going back to Nigeria."

Instincts told me I was a fool to say a word. Anyway, she ignored my input and I understand why. My instinct told me that some women from Nigeria, like Efemona who's my wife, I mean who are from a particular tribe in Nigeria known as Ukpenu, who want to leave their husbands for other men richer than God, would do anything to humiliate their husbands when they step their foot on American soil to be Americanized, and become head of their household to reap the rewards of the welfare system and child support payments and alimony could be mean and ruthless. But the fact that I underwent a transformation, the horrifying surgery that netted me the cow eye which then made me ugly and wretched, Efemona made her decision right away without my input to travel with Victoria.

Anyway, I stayed silent for a minute. Both women looked at me. My cow eye that took several hours for doctors in Reno to affix into the socket of my left eye moved. Efemona and Victoria laughed a mocking laugh. Finally, Efemona said, "Girlfriend please, you don't have to look at his left eye. I gave the doctors of Reno the permission to perform the surgery with a cow eye. The thing was, my husband had a terrible beating from me on the side lover and then passed out. Having no mind of his own to make the decision for a regular eyeball, I made the decision for him for the doctors to replace his damaged eyeball with that of a mature cow. My mother had supported me, too."

Victoria gave Efemona a high-five and then changed the subject. She related how she had visited Sacramento, too, and their friend, Azeno, they grew up with at Ukpenu, had just been separated from her husband. Victoria had first made one round-trip a month to the city; during which she sat at the supper table with Azeno's newly richer than God millionaire man. While with Azeno, they had discussed how the Nigerian economy could be revived. And they ate in fine restaurants, went to concerts and movies, shopped and even attended an occasional social gathering organized by Bad Dudu and his buddies in Sacramento. Azeno, their friend, stayed in touch with her old friends, but was delighted with the new friendships of the millionaires richer than God. When the millionaire Azeno wanted to, she would ooze charm and engage in conversation on a wide range of discussions. Also, while Victoria was with her guests in Sacramento, Azeno handled business matters that demanded her input. Since Azeno got acquainted to the millionaires, she'd then been promoted to the CEO in Babagida's and Bad Dudu's oil refinery in Warri. Azeno also had worked as a volunteer *ojeke* dancer in one of the colleges in Sacramento.

Victoria finished. Efemona layed her hands around Victoria's waist. They walked into the guestroom that was decorated and made which I was not aware was made right before I requested Efemona to make the bed for her friend. The guestroom, for your information, overlooked the master bedroom.

"You know," Efemona said as they entered the guestroom, "The very moment you arrived at my doorstep, I became hot and wet." She helped take off Victoria's dress.

"Since we've been friends, you have always been hot and wet with various sugar daddies we used to hang out with." Efemona smiled and peeled her own dress over her head. She still hasn't worn an underwear and a bra since Victoria had disturbed our fuck. "You know, America has Americanized me," Efemona said and crammed one of Victoria's breasts into her mouth. "I go both ways *now*. I want to show you what I mean."

Victoria was perplexed. It was like a movie to her. Victoria did not know what to say. Shall Victoria say yes or please stop it?! She was mute and perplexed for one reason. That is, Efemona would go with her to Nigeria because she'd made a profit of a thousand dollars running an errand for Bad Dudu. If she refused Efemona's advances of lesbianism and Efemona turned down the invitation to see her President, she would have to cough out the money to give back to Bad Dudu who is too mean and ruthless.

Efemona pushed Victoria with her right hand with a slight push and Victoria landed on her back on the bed. Efemona spread her legs apart and shot out her tongue and then started to eat Victoria up. Victoria moaned softly. "You care to go with me now, as I have satisfied your lesbianism to see Bad Dudu and honor the post for which I was sent to get you into the country?"

"Just for you," Efemona said when she was done, then left her to sleep a comfortable, good sleep. Quickly she entered the master bedroom and packed a few clothes, including some spandex pants she'd recently purchased from Gucci factory outlet, which reports the good looks of her bottom.

I knew why she'd picked them. Despite my one eye to see, I'd admired her when she was dressed with them. Emeka and Bad Dudu no doubt would like it. With Efemona's newly reconstructed nose as those of Greenfall Evilfall, the most talked about District Master of Reno who loved to tell African women from Nigeria to divorce their husbands and sue them for child support and alimony, Efemona thought: I measure up with the gorgeous Indian women, Lebanese women, Thai women and by all means Bad Dudu would salivate when I was with him in his office, wearing my spandex mother of spandexes.

That thought settled, Efemona quickly dialed the limousine company of Reno-Sparks Cab Company to arrange for them to pick them up and drop them off at the Reno-Tahoe International Airport before five A.M. Victoria would surely appreciate it. And she knew

Victoria had never seen a stretched luxury car of that nature before. Victoria would sure jolly the ride, Efemona hoped.

*   *   *

At four-fifty A.M., the limousine picked Efemona and Victoria up. Victoria was surprised to see the chauffeur get out and open the door for them to be seated. He also closed the door behind them, which was more surprising to Victoria. Before the chauffeur had keyed into the limousine and moved, he'd asked the gorgeous women, "Coffee black, with sugar, or with dairy creamer? Scotch or Bailey's on the rocks? London Gin, or cognac or champagne?" At first Victoria was carried away and suddenly she glanced behind her and saw various hard liquor bottles all arranged in a cabinet beside her seat, all bottles staring at her like pretty soldiers with camouflage clothes on. Then she shrugged. Of course, they both love London Gin, if only for the grip taste, it also made them get flippant, and because Efemona pronounced first, "London Gin, please. Two shots each."

They toasted each other's glasses and drank. The chauffeur made it to the airport within a few minutes. They had no baggage to check in except a carry-on-board suitcase.

The flight, not Hejira as in prophet Mohammed from Mecca to Medina, it was from Reno en route to her country (Nigeria) on a special invitation with a mission and a purpose. The airplane finally departed. The sky was clear with no clouds to bump the huge craft as it was when Efemona first traveled out of her country six years ago and when she traveled again to see Newman on his admission in the Hospital when he was shot. This time, there was no sign of fear. The fear that gripped her on both incidents were completely gone.

*   *   *

When Efemona and Victoria finally landed at Mutala Mohammed Airport in Lagos, security was mounted in all corners of the airport. Both women were fully covered under Bad Dudu's junta regime because security, secrecy and privacy for Efemona in particular was the name of the game. Bawuh had made sure that the two famous women's return tickets first-class from Reno, NV-New York-Amsterdam-Heathrow-Lagos on a KLM flight, Efemona was flying into Lagos in false name. Having made the reservations he sent by faxcimile to the Liaison Office of the CIA security department shortly before the flight to inform Mr. Nichols who and why would actually be using the flight tickets.

At a stop over in Heathrow Airport, a coffin was loaded into the 747 Boeing without the knowledge of both women. It was a secret. The heart of the matter was, the President had put a reward of two million dollars dead or alive for anyone to capture Umaro Diko if his paid assassins were unable to do it within forty-eight hours.

I should tell you that Umaro Diko, who was also the right hand man of Bad Dudu, was the Agricultural Secretary when he cleaned up the treasury and cheated Bad Dudu on a deal that supposedly netted him five billion dollars, but Diko alone had ran with the loot to Britain and a street was soon named after him by the Queen, which made Bad Dudu angry as hell. The assassin who was working for Bad Dudu was an Israeli soldier of fortune, forty years old and had had several deaths to his name. Well-known politicians and students, market women and children and even those who had won elections who riot and tired of his tyrannical rule, Bad Dudu would name the names of the people, where they live to the assassin and they would be taken care of. He, the assassin, was also a well-known editor to which Bad Dudu censored whatever was to be published. He has three children and resided in Allen Avenue. A well-known writer and politician, but with Uzi and AK-47 connections. He carried out his first contract on the son of a famous musician, Bongos Ikwenu, whom Bad Dudu had taken his wife. Bad Dudu soon baptized the woman with two million dollars for her grief over her son's death to challenge Bongos that he was the 'Real' Caesar of Nigeria. Though Bongos was humiliated, he turned his other ear while he prayed for Washington to intervene for a country he loved so much.

* * *

The famous assassin for Bad Dudu had blew the pretty boy's brains out at point-blank range through the chest. The killing soon earned him great respect among the Caesars of various coup plotter emporors in Africa who rule with iron laws. However, other coup plotter emperors of Africa knew the culprit was the leader of his country who inspired and paid for the killing. His name was Baba-Ker. Silencing men and women on the sidewalk to him and Bad Dudu made no grave feelings on them. If he couldn't do it with bullets, he did it with a mail bomb. Even taking the life of children didn't excite him or trouble his remembrance. Just show him the oil money. It was a job along with his journalistic excellence as the editor-in-chief of The Heartbreak Newspaper for which I now work to write this fiction. To Baba-Ker, shipping in Umaro Diko from England in a coffin to sleep for seven hours en route to his country was the easiest job that netted Baba-Ker the quickest $5 million dollar reward. That's how Umaro Diko got into the picture for cheating his boss.

Anyway, so much of weird atrocities in Nigeria by Dudu. Finally though, the Boeing 747 finally began its approach to landing in Lagos through the Bar Beach overlooking Doddan Army Barracks and Victoria and Efemona were sitting at the right end of the wing, the best seat Bawuh had paid extra for them to view the entire city of Lagos through the beautiful Atlantic Ocean. However, Federal military regime in Nigeria prohibits any aircraft flying in from the Northwest because those who rule fear that if aircraft traffic was not carefully monitored by the airforce, some maniac might drop a bomb to exterminate them. But because of Efemona, Victoria and the coffin, the airforce did not divert the craft to Northeast, the normal route for landing of all aircraft landing at Muritala Mohammed Airport in Lagos.

Efemona on her seat looked out at the hazy city dropping acid rain in the distance, saw the heap of trash and pollutions and shook her head. One thing quickly flashed her memory: With all the billions the zombies of this country had siphoned out of this country, Nigeria could have been able to clean up the pollution of the city at large. She saw a newly transformed Nation and its people, all car-less who now relied on alternated forms of transportation to get them where they needed to go. On nice days like the one Efemona was looking at before her, people use their bicycles or run on foot to get them where they need to go. For the most part, most people rely on their feet more than decaying taxis that pollute the city's air quality most of the time with their smoking engines.

The one thing that baffles most people that live in Lagos these days, Efemona noted in her heart, was that Downtown Lagos was not the easiest place to call home as it used to. Efemona's father had even wrote her about his experience during the six months he visited his relatives in Lagos. He'd amalgameted his own *Tales of the City* to Efemona through the telephone she'd installed for him, and how he'd been approached by numerous eccentrics along Ekolai Meridian Hotel owned by Bad Dudu. How he'd been offered rides in the pouring rain by men as old as himself on bicycles with no tires on them. How he'd been greeted more than a thousand times by an outstretched heads through luxury cars owned and operated by the famous members of Bad Dudu's junta regime who yell out at him what he's doing in the millionaire's only neighborhood of the rich and famous draining the Nigerian economy. How he'd been yelled at by good Samaritans through flashing car windows, saying, "Old man, you shouldn't be walking alone in the rich and famous junta's neighborhood because they will rob you in broad daylight with a bullet in your brain and take your only penny in your pocket and deposit it in Britain for a higher interest rates. How he knew right then that Downtown Lagos, Obalende Suru- Lere, Bode Thomas and most Ikoyi Streets had become particularly dangerous, unlike when he'd lived there forty years ago when Life Goes On was in power. That was when he was able to travel out to overseas and live in various different continents as a student. But this time, he'd seen a city that lacks the warmth it had several years ago when men with morals and with sound education at Harvard and Yale ruled the nation and who knows the right button to push. He now hated Lagos at the bottom of his heart, for lack of electricity and water. He feels bad about the Nigerian Police blocking the major highways just to collect one Naira from the poor people they were meant to protect. He feels bad about all the dilapidated Grammar Schools with no chairs, chalk and blackboards for their students. How he'd seen it all as he walked the streets of Lagos, that there are no parks, no modern malls-you know, those big things he saw when he was in Britain, America, Germany, Australia and France and even in India, Mexico, Brazil to mention but a few countries. How it irritates his mind that Lagos, which used to draw tourists from all over the world, has no more reliable allies doing genuine business with Nigeria. How he watched as the Nation had fallen to its ebb through Babagida and Bad Dudu Abacha and their in cahoots who slowly destroyed the economy and looted Nigeria's treasury. How he'd noted and had asked Efemona if it wouldn't have been nice to have a vibrant and thriving Nation all other Nations of the Third World countries and the rest of the world would emulate for its riches and keep the money flowing to all its citizens? How he thinks the urban dwellers who do not even know the color of their Nigerian currencies would feel when they call Nigeria their country, a great Nation if they know the color of money to buy their needs, build nice homes and be able to feed their families. Optimistic father you might call him. Efemona shook her head remembering all of what her father had told her over the years on the telephone and on letters.

As they exited the plane, a Mercedes 560 SEL, an American specification, long as the limousines in America used to welcome high ranking officials during Mr. Life Goes On from foreign countries into the country from the airport to Doddan Army Barracks, was waiting idly to welcome them and take them to the Federal Palace Hotel. Efemona figured the driver was probably armed, too, with an Uzi and grenades, but neither her nor Victoria had the guts to inquire. The driver, with tribal designated facial marks on both sides of his cheeks with army uniforms and bearing white gloves on both hands, was knowledgeable in English with an accent of *TIV*.

"Good day, ladies," he said as he opened the door for them to take their seats. "My name is Cocoyamhead. I'm your designated driver throughout the duration of your stay."

Victoria was used to the men in uniform who rule, but Efemona in particular did not want to be inflicted by the virus of fear that the uniformed men had portrayed and spread throughout the Federation and in the world.

Cocoyamhead closed the door and got in front behind the wheel. He was not questioned by the women, but didn't ask questions either. You know, after years of driving for Bad Dudu and shuttling in dignitaries and VIPs from all over the world (except from America) from the airport, he knew when to engage in conversation and when to keep his mouth shut. With his tribal marks, Cocoyamhead also had large searching eyes and a large nose. Efemona wondered how a black man could have a large nose similar to a white man. In short, if not for the air conditioning in the car, Cocoyamhead was capable of consuming the little oxygen in the car alone, leaving Efemona and Victoria with none to breathe.

Efemona couldn't swallow her comment. She said, "Geez! You do have a large nose."

"That's why I'm an ordinary driver in Dudu's administration," Cocoyamhead said and became mute again.

As he taxied off the curb swiftly, Efemona and Victoria began to learn so much about Lagos and all of which means a whole lot to them. And it should be instructive to know that Victoria had never been to Ikoyi before, but Efemona had when she first met with an Arab man who almost raped her and Monica at Duba Road at Ikoyi. That was about nine years ago before my father met her at Ewu to tell her about me for the possibility of marrying her. Lagos to Victoria was a very busy city. Like many cities in the modern world, Lagos had been built on an island, which was the first defense to the British/European modern architecture. Victoria was amused, despite that it was unlike Abuja, because all her life, before she was nominated for her new post by Bad Dudu, she had only been to Benin, Ibadan, Warri, Portharcourt and main land Lagos, but Ikoyi.

Cocoyamhead drove the women and cruised the manicured flowers, rounded Tinubu Square and crossed to Ikoyi. There were plenty of armed guards, menacingly wielding guns, plain clothed security officers sniffing the air for possible signs of mutiny and sabotage. An army of outriders and motorcycle police in their best display revved their throttles and sandwiched the Mercedes 560 SEL as it swung onto the route of the Federal Palace Hotel and Casino clearing the way. The Dudu's security, obviously not wanting to be caught napping again after the greatest leader Muritala Mohammed was slain, decided to mobilize some of its awesome machinery imported from Britain, Brazil, Libya and Russia in defense of the new Matron General elect to be. It was power and post in its most formidable form, which had transisted at the Federal Palace Hotel and Casino entrance at Ikoyi, which shattered the serenity of the area. Throughout the day and night, the security men secured the ground while Victoria and Efemona went upstairs to their suites.

Above the high-rise Palace Hotel, Efemona and Victoria looked below. What they saw beside the manicured flowers along the side of the street stunned them. Hordes of men in *Agbada*-money chargers were canvassing to get foreign money sold or to buy in the black market. Efemona stared at Victoria and she said, "This is where they are. The goddamn Hausas money chargers in *Agbada* giving this country a bad name. In another hour or so, we would be chatting with *one* of them in his executive office."

*　*　*

There at the eerie heat of the busy foyer of Federal Palace and Casino, you can almost hear the grunts of the Doddan Army junta rulers tycoons with their *Agbada* on who'd made and broke the Nation as casually as they lit and crushed out their Havana Cigars. Mr. Life Goes On had built this famous Art Deco landmark in Ikoyi several years ago when Udoji award-the oil money was shared to the common man who worked. This twenty-something-story edifice, which boasts bronze-plated elevators, marble-lined corridors, passages and formal parlors, could've been created by the set designers of the Europeans.

For more than a decade, the most opulent room of this Federal Palace Hotel and Casino had remained virtually unoccupied by visiting dignitaries. As Cocoyamhead dropped Efemona and Victoria, he waited anxiously at the curb, overlooking the Bar Beach. Suite ten-forty, a suite reserved for high dignitaries once used by President Jimmy Carter, Andrew Young, Jesse Jackson, Mohammed Ali, Marion Berry, Ron Brown, Willie Brown to mention but a few was the same suite reserved for Efemona. How important I have become, Efemona thought.

It was a coincidence that from this penthouse window of the Federal Palace Hotel and Casino, The Imperial Wizard of the Ku Klux Klan, the five time hater of Blacks and minorities in South Carolina of the Year gazes out at Lagos with mournful, drooping eyes that seem to have witnessed all black people in America sadness was also in the Palace to see Bad Dudu on a private mission. For the record, the Wizard man was in Nigeria to personally apologize to Bad Dudu for his atrocities he'd exhibited against the colored people of the world for decades. And himself hope that Dudu would cease killing his own black people. That was his mission. His room was directly opposite the room reserved for Efemona. The Imperial Wizard waited in the hallway when he heard Efemona was to share the same Palace with him.

Seeing Efemona coming toward him, he bowed magnificently and kissed her foot. Efemona could see that sincerity on his face. He seemed benign and avuncular, but he has the furtive, feral charm of an old-time repentant human being.

He finally stood before Efemona and looked at her deeply in her face. "I try to be warm and ingratiating with colored people like you feel important these days. These days I travel extensively visiting all Heads of States of African countries. These days I never meet anyone I don't like anymore. These days I'm very open and honest and very caring. I've been told that you are a powerful woman, President of AWAM movement."

Efemona finally looked at the strange face before her. "And who are you, sir?"

"I'm the Imperial Wizard. You might've heard of me and my atrocities against the colored woman I shot who hails from Benin. I beg for forgiveness from you and from every other woman in your country. This is why I'm here in your country to apologize to Bad Dudu, the President of your country."

Of course the haters and leaders of the Ku Klux Klan of yesteryear were neither open nor caring nor repentant. They were die hard racists but the Imperial Wizard didn't share their philosophy anymore. For the Imperial Wizard sincerity and magnanimity, the Wizard man is as eccentric as Bad Dudu who is a billionaire. For that he hedges. He vacillates and no longer agonizes colored people in America.

Efemona looked at the very sorrowful face, patted him on his shoulder and said, "See me in America. My office hours are from eight to five. Here's my card. I'm here too, to see Bad Dudu on an urgent meeting tomorrow morning. You be good to the colored men and women of the world."

With that, Efemona, Victoria and the Imperial Wizard all parted and snuck into their respective rooms. And Efemona thought, I am now somebody!

Chapter

15

K andyman stood at the stairwell of the Federal Palace Hotel and Casino, feeling tired and exhausted after a long flight to Lagos trailing Efemona the fact that I had paid him to trail her to know what she was doing when she get to Nigeria. Kandyman was amazed at what he saw on the streets. So many beautiful women of all shapes and sizes, all lined up at the entrance to the hotel. By the way, I should tell you that Kandyman, for the purpose of this fictional story, is an American renounced journalist.

At the entrance, Kandyman saw waiters dressed in black upon white, all hovering around, ready to answer the raised tip of a finger to a whistle from customers who sat along the convinient tables at the entrance of the Palace.

As Kandyman looked up, a woman called out to him. After so many years in the business, the woman knows how to speaks pidgen and three other languages. She was from Benin. Short legged gait, a professional whore.

"I am a tourist, too," the women said, "I might be able to help you. What do you need to know?"

He raised his eyebrows and looked at her. "I was born and raised in Nigeria, but never been to this place before," Kandyman lied.

The Benin woman read his mind. He was not ready to spare a dime, she thought. Actually, she's hunting along spreading AIDS to her customers who patronize her.

Kandyman noted: To the left of the Palace Hotel are rows of sandbar beaches. Here umbrellas are pegged to the ground with chairs and tables. To the right, leading to the Dunbar Hotel, are the imitations of Jamaican huts and tents.

He walked down the aisle of the Hotel in the direction of the Jamaican huts. He would have liked to stop at the bar for a quick American beer to cool off. The cost might cost him his arms and legs. The waiters and hookers around here begging men to buy them drinks knows who is who. For him wearing a cowboy suit and cowboy hat, he's from another continent. A Yankee for that matter! They would think he has the dollar power, he thought. For one, it has already cost him more than he'd budgeted to get him to the Palace Hotel from Muritala Mohammed International Airport with a taxi. He thought: I cannot lavish what Ekiaqueta had paid me for trailing Efemona. The ride from the airport to the Palace had already cost me a thousand bucks, even though I'd told the taxi driver I was an American journalist exposing the taxi drivers of Nigeria for not using their meters. But he'd lied, too.

Though he had lied and joked, the driver was stoned-faced. Did not give a damn. The reason for that was he has to feed his family, too. The driver had looked poker-faced at the one thousand dollars shining bills Kandyman had paid him. The driver turned his head and looked behind his shoulder reacting to Kandyman's feigned face, "You must be good in exposing Clinton and Monica Lewinsky and also George Bush lying to the American public that Saddam has got weapons of mass destruction," he laughed raucously. "I think Linda Tripp was a bitch for taping Monica Lewinsky's conversations," he changed the subject and looked behind him as he drove.

"If it were in this country, Linda Tripp would be secretly murdered."

Kandyman, the renounced journalist was mute, but thinking about the thousand bucks he'd paid for a short distance.

"What is wrong in inserting a huge cigar in the carnal of a beautiful woman like Monica Lewinsky? That shows your President in America is human. That is why I will tell you that President Clinton is the greatest man in the history of great men who had lived on the surface of this earth. I'll tell you why. You see great men in history like David or Samson and Solomon for instance, were all brought down by women. And in the last several years, men like Jimmy Swaggart, Gary Hart, Jim

Baker, to name but a few were all brought down and humiliated before the public eye in America. And in this millenium, more great men had fallen on their face from grace." He looked again behind at his passenger who was listening with keen interest. "Only Bill Clinton went through these obstacles without falling from grace. All because of women."

He continued, "Common sense tells me that you must be one of those good journalists who'd exposed the President hoping that the congress would impeach him and remove him from power. I know too, that you must be one of those good journalists who wrote on Black Wednesday, or the night Mr. Gorbachev and Romania President were deposed. We'll need your assistance in this country to expose our man-Bad Dudu," he joked.

Kandyman did not wait to hear the name of the man the driver was talking about. He exited the taxi with alacrity and approached one of the waiters. He said, "Two women flew in from New York a couple of hours ago."

He gave their description to the fullest.

"Where they might be now is the question-in their suite, gaming floor, swimming pool, on the tennis courts . . . . One of them used to play for Maria Asiawo Gorretti Academy of Nursing in Benin."

The waiter nodded. In a flash, he knew who the stranger standing before him was talking about. Then he said, "I think I know who you are talking about. I saw them and I think they were the most gorgeous women this Palace has seen in ages. Why? He answered his own question. They had flesh on their cheeks. I think they must be by the beach area sunning themselves."

He was right. Efemona and Victoria were by the beach sipping on Piña Coladas. The waiter thought: If the stranger with the cowboy boots and coat and hat goes to the beach side looking sophisticated in his outfits, he certainly would look like a priest in a nudist beach. His thoughts, too, were accurate. Anyway, Kandyman looked far and beyond. He'd looked like a priest indeed. "Thank God," he said to himself, then drew in his breath.

Ebony complexioned skins, red, blue, purple, green from all over the planet, except blondes from America and England were not present.

What he'd seen were near-naked mermaids, one more beautiful than the next as far as his naked eyes could see. All bare except for small disks, the size of their nipples and a bikini bottom that consisted of a single string that slipped between their triangles. Kandyman took a deep breath again as his blood vessels began to rush to his head sending a message to his pituitary gland. He was not himself. He felt he might faint. Sodom and Gomorah hadn't committed that much sin and yet God destroyed their city. Man! Nigeria is becoming the Hollywood of Africa and God will have to apologize to the world for destroying Sodom and Gomorah, he thought. Everywhere he turned were women looking at him. Though they were salivating and laughing and blowing kisses at him for wearing cowboy attires, he was not concerned about their kisses. What was registered behind his being was, "What is the world coming down to? Efemona and Victoria were enjoying themselves naked.

He shook his head numerous times as the sun began to bake him with his suit. Then finally, he decided to turn down the beach where he'd been directed that Efemona and Victoria would be, though the waiter did not know their names.

As Kandyman strolled along the beach, his cowboy boots had accumulated enough sand. And when he stopped to shake them off his shoes, a woman from nowhere gave him a compliment of:

"You have good feet, Sir," she yelled out.

Perhaps, they might be the nicest feet she'd seen in a long time in a country where no flesh was seen on men's faces anymore as when Life Goes On had ruled.

"Thanks," Kandyman replied.

He continued to walk along with his camera and his notepad along the beach. Too many women. "Jesus!" he exclaimed.

As he looked further in the sand beach before him in the distance, he saw some men with only underwear with Uzis and assault rifles clustered on the sand. In the middle were Efemona and Victoria under a pegged down striped umbrella. He immediately recognized the gorgeous women. They were wearing white silk gowns of just about thin air with nothing underneath. Efemona recognized him as a trained American journalist. She'd seen Kandyman numerous times before at her AWAM movement rallies and in the courtrooms of Reno and Sparks, Nevada. Instantly, Efemona signalled Patricia, the Queen security woman among the women in the beach. Patricia knew what Efemona meant. The men with their rifles surrounded her and Victoria as if they would be taking turns-but the opposite. That's not the point. The thing is, they were protecting Efemona and Victoria against invasion of their privacy from Kandyman, the American journalist.

Kandyman shook his head at his own stupidity to accept trailing Efemona all for a few thousand bucks. Why has he expected to see Efemona alone when Ekiaqueta had briefed him of the life his wife wanted to live? The thought that he shouldn't have accepted the money was registered in his being. But it was too late. The women had started running towards him, bare breasts, all bouncing on his face, all surrounded him, poking him, tickling him with their painted long artificial nails. What are they up to? He loved the fun of the type, but he was on a mission or else he would not be paid his balance Ekiaqueta owes him for the news of what his wife was doing. After all, he loves investigative reporting.

"Ain't you hot?" one of the women finally asked. "We'll help you to take them off, Yankee, so you can screw as many of us as you can on the sand. How is that? Can you screw? Do you have a big dick for Efemona?"

"Won't you like to screw me on the beach?" another asked. "No! Thanks! I am on a mission," Kandyman said, as he was beginning to almost collapse from tickling.

"The mission will not be accomplished until Efemona leaves the country. Do you want a hole in your head?"

"No, please! I'm only doing my job I was hired and paid for to do."

"We suggest you leave the same way you came here if you don't want to fuck," they said, but wouldn't give him the chance. They poked and tickled him until he fell on his knees. Lord!

Jesus! Have mercy, he swallowed tonelessly. It was every man's dream to be surrounded by so many beautiful women and it was Kandyman's wishful dreams someday. But at this moment of tickling him by bare naked mermaid, it was not the type of dream he'd hoped for. He'd hoped that someday, when he becomes a millionaire after the money he would receive for the trip trailing Efemona and writing a story for the world to know who Efemona really was, he would take as many women to the Bahamas and have some fun with them as a *real man*. They were on him working with experience of King Alibaba and his forty thieves on his wallet as they stripped him naked, some licking his balls, some his neck, some his hands and some his chest and feet. The Queen of the Queens finally shook him off and sucked and sucked. "Efemona has paid us to do this," she said.

They'd exhausted him and robbed him of thousands of dollars-Efemona's laugh drowned out the roar of the sea as she watched.

"Fuck as many as you want if you have the strength, because your wife would probably divorce you when you go back home. On my words," Efemona said and laughed again and sipped on her Piña Colada.

Kandyman laid on the sand breathless.

With that all the women all walked away. They would all be rewarded by Efemona for a job well done.

....

The sun set in the West and that's what everyone knows. But in Nigeria, when some dignitaries as Efemona visit, it then set over the Federal Palace Street. But you know, the one thing that has always baffled me more than anything else is the sun setting over the Federal Palace on Ikoyi Island Street, then seeing the oranges and grapes turn to gold. As always, the traffic on this street was always congested. Although the streets were cleared before for Efemona and Victoria on their short ride from the airport to the Palace Hotel, it was filling again with rich and poor imbibing the last breath of the heat, not of the sun itself, but of terror of Bad Dudu's personal guards whipping bystanders, but also hoping to get a glimpse of Efemona, the most talked about woman in their administration of recent. They were those personal guards of course, who heard Efemona was finally in Nigeria and staying at the Palace. These guards did not stop whipping bystanders until Efemona told them to stop.

It was nearly four P.M. now, and the wind was blowing from the Atlantic Ocean. The evening breeze felt good. Efemona and Victoria strolled along the street of the Palace. This time, they hoped that Kandyman would not trail them along this famous street. Figuratively, this Ikoyi Island street was a place where King Alibaba had trained his forty thieves. To date as Efemona noted, the forty thieves had increased in numbers, graciously operating in the medieval style.

Tireless and still waiting at the curb, Cocoyamhead seeing Efemona and Victoria, thought they needed a ride outside of Federal Palace Street. But they didn't need a ride. They just wanted to have fun.

Efemona leaned on the Mercedes 560 SEL on the driver's side while Victoria leaned on the passenger's side. As Efemona carefully explained to Cocoyamhead they were not heading someplace, a gust of wind from the Atlantic Ocean caught them, plastering their thin, silky Givenchy dresses to their ass cheeks as if an impressionist painter had taken a brush to their rounded asses as confirmation of women who'd been caught in an unexpected downpour. In short, they were unaware of the picture they'd each posed to men shopping for women to lay for the night.

Since they were not going too far away from the Palace, Cocoyamhead carefully explained to them where the street began and where it ended. He had warned them that they should be careful because of the illiterate soldiers with guns terrorizing people on a daily basis, unlike himself. They chatted a few minutes with him on the curb and told him they would buzz him if they were lost. Efemona and Victoria gave him a kiss on his cheeks. Then Efemona flicked him a fifty dollar bill.

Cocoyamhead resented the bill. For one, he was adamantly against women showing off with dollars who think they are filthy rich of the dollar power knowing that him and his junta men with uniforms have the keys to the Nation's, Treasury, draining it and depositing the loot in England and Swiss Banks. He looked at the women again. He would rather sleep with them and give them millions, but how to tell them was the question. Then he just shook his head as the women walked down the street.

Efemona and Victoria, anyway, had dressed with the utmost care. They'd spend hours on their appearance, something Efemona hadn't done in weeks since she first returned from her trip until Victoria came with her good news to fetch her. The effect of their make-up was astonishingly flawless, which means that the spirit of Princess Diana had given them a hand, no doubt about that.

As they walked majestically along the street, two young females wearing sophisitcated, tight skirts with a Lebanese man walked majestically by Efemona and Victoria. The girls had a leventis shopping bag. Matter-of-factly, these two girls had just hit the jackpot with the Lebanese man who took them shopping before he lay them.

Talking about this Ikoyi Island Street where they'd shopped, I should tell you that it's a street where you see Nigerians young and old come to hang out to experience the Western tradition which led the creator to condemn Sodom and Gomorah. This particular street as Fourth Street in Reno, Fourteenth Street in Washinton D.C., or Hollywood Boulevard, Los Angeles catered to all tastes of human wants. Here one can buy illicit drugs like marijuana, cocaine, crank, harshes, heroine, opium and more which Miss Oyakilome and her cronies import for the juntas beside the crude oil profit they are hiding from their own people. Girls of all ages on this street were also available at an agreed bargain if one has the money to spend on them. On each side of this street lined prostitutes from all over the country and from elsewhere in the world. You'll see them flagging motorists, walking and licking ice cream yogurts. You'll also know them by what they wear, flimsy silky attires which the eye can penetrate to see their undergarments and pubic hairs which clothes were meant to cover.

Efemona and Victoria were surprised that more and more women in Nigeria were now coming out to shop for men, date and have orgies with whoever has the money to pay them. Thanks to my AWAM movement, Efemona said to herself. She was proud of herself and proud of the women who had come out boldly to support her movement and happy that Ikoyi Island Street has *now* become a clothing short stop where anyone could go in and select any *wrapper* they can afford to pay for. Finally, Efemona said to Victoria, "I'm impressed. My African Women Against Marriage Movement has gained recognition down here in Nigeria."

The recognintion Efemona was impressed about was that sex was now for sale for the quickies along the street behind the oleander rose flowers along the beach, in the cars and in the Palace suites. Even Reverend fathers who like it from behind parade this street in disguised clothes.

Anyway, Efemona admired the two young women as the girls admired her and Victoria. The Lebanese man smiled at Victoria and Efemona. He sure knows a good thing when he sees one, but has two women beside him already. He salivated and swallowed: "God have mercy!" he echoed to himself.

Efemona said to the Labanese man and to the girls with him, "Hello, fellows. Going licking tonight?"

They nodded and the Lebanese man said, "Are you?" "Maybe later," Efemona and Victoria chatted out and smiled.

All of them continued to stroll shoulder to shoulder. As Efemona and Victoria walked a few more strides, two beggars stood at their faces. One of them was a young woman who looked as she'd had a stroke which moved her mouth to the corner of her face. Holding her hand was a man wearing a thick goggles. When the man saw Efemona and Victoria, he took off his goggles. Efemona could see the beggar had one peculiar eye like her husband who now has a cow eye, rather than poached egg in appearance, that looked off in a different direction entirely from his other eye. He said to the gorgeous women, "Can you help us out? We are hungry. We have no money. The oil money this Nation has is only for Bad Dudu, Babagida and their in cahoots," holding the wife's hand out to Efemona.

The generous Efemona. She unzipped her purse and brought out a tight roll of crisp hundred dollar bills.

"Oh, 'scuse me," Efemona said and placed the bundle back in the purse, but brought out another bundle. This time fifty dollar bills, then pulled out one and flicked it to him. "Dollar power," Efemona said.

"Thanks, madam." They thanked Efemona and walked away happy.

* * *

Efemona and Victoria stood rooted and perplexed seeing so many women on Ikoyi Island Street where they watched the parade of starlets and whores, of gigolos, of wealthy men in Agbada, peddlers of the flesh, buyers and sellers both. As they looked and watched here and there, they saw a horticulturist work among the roses that lined the high-rise Palace Hotel as they sipped on their Piña Colada and London Gin they bought along the street. They exchanged straws and their glasses while the sun, like a huge orange dropped behind their heads as they walked. It was a perfect street to be at this time of the evening, Efemona and Victoria thought. They saw everything. All the actions, the motorists with BMW's, Mercedes Benz, Porsche, Jaguars, Rolls Royce, Lambourginis, kids with their parents, tourists, every tree and blade of grass with perfect view of unclouded vision. If the heart of the matter be told righteously, none of these materials registered on their brains. However, Efemona's eyes photographed the scenes like a Canon AE-1, perfectly focused and exposed, the shutter set correctly for the fading sun and yet the film remained blank. She was thinking too of Bad Dudu, the man she'd came to see and she thought: Was Bad Dudu so tough that no one in Nigeria can deal with him, kill the sucker!

As Efemona tried to get answers, it was not forthcoming. Then she concentrated on the horticulturist, about thirty something, slenderly built with tribal marks on his face. Though the horticulturist was handsome, he'd no flesh on his bones. Efemona figured he might be paid only *ten and ten pence*, actually a penny in Nigerian standard since Bad Dudu and Babagida ceased power and did away with Nigerian oil money. Efemona pitied him and found fascination in watching him from a distance as she walked with Victoria, the way the man had acquainted himself with the flowers, touching them lightly, muttering to them, and poking tentatively with his finger tips around their roots. Efemona whole life, merely looking at the way the man does his thing said to Victoria, "He must be an expert like my husband who like to massage the clitoris these days trying to find his way inside of me with his cow eye. His lips and tongue would be perfect inbetween your thighs," Efemona joked and tapped Victoria on her bottom. Victoria noticed that Efemona had squeezed her face when she'd mentioned 'her husband'. But she already knew why. She too lost in the mere looks of the horticulturist, asked Efemona for her camera. She focused and snapped the shutter. "Remember to develop it before I leave so you'll have yourself a copy to show men in America how men in this country now look since Bad Dudu assumed the executive hot seat."

"Are you having fun yet?" Efemona asked.

"What do you think? I'll be damn stupid if I tell you I'm not having fun with you, girlfriend," Victoria said.

Thus, Efemona became the sophisticated Queen of the most talked about Ikoyi Island Street for hookers and gigolos who are plaqued by abject poverty and are cheated of wealth, which is the reason that vendors stay open late for whatever type of business then walk the beaches and streets with no shirts on or are dressed but looks haggard. And even with their looks and the little money in their pockets they're looking for women for one night stand to sample their wares to forget their sorrows. Furthermore, amidst the heat and the curious enjoyment seekers, the homeless sit on the sidewalks and begs for help. You need not be told that a strong sense of history had mingled with the tacky Alibaba's and their forty theives. And for a minute, Efemona thought she was at Benin/ Ukpenu the home of the greatest armed robbers on earth.

Chapter

17

What a country these days! Efemona and Victoria watched the street now filled with multitudes of men and women, young and old. After about two hours of watching, Efemona said to Victoria, "I'm glad I have civilized all *these* women with my movement."

Victoria smiled and watched more women and men pass each other. I should say too, that King Alibaba and his forty thieves were among the crowd, doing what they do best to survive in the decaying country. It was the real Ikoyi at its worst and best times, the street Mr. Babagida, a good friend of mine, once told me Dele Giwa, a prominent journalist in the Nation was killed by a mail bomb over a revelation of corruption of Bad Dudu opening various accounts for Lebanese women and Thailand women. This street Babagida also told me was the place where the first lady who was taken from Bongos had an orgy with the Generals and then with Bad Dudu. And based on Babagida's own accounts, the first lady had refused to honor Bad Dudu's advances because he'd a gaunt face. However, Bad Dudu taking it personal and as a challenge for a woman he has absolute power and control over, decided to threaten her with a hole in the head, perform or both. Scared enough, she'd performed. Her vagina was too good to be true and so he forced her to marry him. This street too Babagida noted: was the street Mrs. Kudriat Abiola was murdered by Bad Dudu's son, a General in the Nigerian army. So much about this street in Nigeria, my friends!

Anyway, Efemona and Victoria continued chattering along and sipping on their drinks. As Efemona wanted to be noted among the several multitudes of people who lined the streets looking for their opposite sex for one night stand, she reached into her purse which contained various American assortment of women's paraphernalia. She dug out a bottle of Yves Saint Laurent perfume bottle out of the jumble of stuff and sprayed herself and Victoria. As they strolled, the trail of scent had assorted the gigolos and buyers and sellers sensibilities who began to salivate as they passed and at the way Efemona and Victoria walked.

Efemona stood rooted on the spot for a minute. She'd thought somebody whispered to her. She turned around, but the man walked away. Efemona and Victoria would be too damned expensive the man had thought. In reality, nature had cheated him out of everything in a country that imported crude oil to the outside world not for free but for billions of dollars. His teeth were rotten too. His shoes had all worn out. The white shirt he had on had counted years of hard labor. He couldn't afford a bar soap to clean up. But he looked at himself, no currency in his pocket except some few kobos. He shook his head and murmured to himself: why can't all women be created like Efemona and Victoria, (though he didn't actually know their names), so that the prices for laying them would be the same. He thought of his own daughter growing up. His little Iradiawa. I'll do my best to make sure she look good like Efemona and Victoria so that when he gives her away for marriage, he could get a thousand dollars or more in dowry from richer than God Bad Dudu's men who rule his country.

As Efemona and Victoria strolled along and mingled with other women, the security became tighter. The uniformed armed men on duty when they stepped down from the Mercedes 560 SEL, to watch over them has been replaced by armed guards with submachine guns rather than the ancient rifles. This time, they were also wearing khaki upon khaki designed by the Britishman, Lourd Luggard fifty years ago.

This evening was an evening Efemona remembered so well. There were plenty of men. Efemona and Victoria themselves were wearing Gucci nail high-heel leather boots high up to their knees. "Jesus!" someone among the gigolos couldn't take his eyes away from Efemona and Victoria voiced out.

Though there were plenty of AWAM members around, what they didn't know was that Efemona was their mentor. In short, most of these women had come out to get laid to have money to feed themselves and take care of their families. And the majority of these women too, were those who were married to men with ten or more wives. These women had learned to sneak out and have orgies with other men since Efemona formed her famous AWAM movement in Reno, Nevada and sent out pamphlets of her movement to all African countries, including her own country, Nigeria.

In her pamphlets she'd reached their souls stating that they don't have to wait their turn in bed with their husbands who have so many wives who don't care to make love to them anytime they needed to be laid.

It was now nine P.M. and the gigolos were still salivating, but were afraid to approach Efemona and Victoria because they looked entirely too sophisticated and because they figured that to take Efemona and Victoria to bed it would cost them a fortune. At the end, only one man whom everyone on this Ikoyi Island Street recognized and hailed as Dr. Fuck'em Good Emma, a man you can guess has rotten set of teeth, had the courage to approach them.

He had approached them for one or two reasons: Efemona and Victoria's average figures were accentuated by their perfectly flimsy silky attires. Their full bust were noticeably defined above their perfect waist. Dr. Fuck'em Good Emma then imagined he saw faint shadows where their silky sexy attires remarkably reported their proud bouncing breast would be if he was in their middle on the same bed. So he allowed himself a small smile and a cough, but told himself it was foolish fantasizing to even envision such gorgeous women in his midst. He salivated a thousand times, clenched his fingers, which long to touch their shadows. Swallowing hard, he dragged his gaze away from their chest to stare at their legs and their triangle, then stared at their faces, no blemish. "Damn! God is great creating these women flawless," he mumbled.

Finally, he told himself to make the move. It's either 'yes' or 'no'. He walked swiftly towards them, "Hello sisters. For how much?"

"Just you?"

"If you both want, I can call my friend, Ike, among the several crowd looking at both of you from a distance."

Efemona whispered to Victoria and Victoria said, "What's your name handsome man with good set of teeth," she cajoled as a matter-of-fact.

"My name is Dr. Fuck'em Good Emma."

Efemona laughed. Then she said, "You do have a fantastic name. You sure, you know how to fuck them good to have orgasm?"

Dr. Fuck'em Good Emma ignored the question. He doesn't know what orgasm is. Rather he asked, "For how much?"

"Don't worry," both women echoed.

Quickly, they hurried him to Efemona's suite. It was like magic to Dr. Fuck'em Good Emma for he'd thought they would ride with him to the slums of Ukpenu Begger Street where he lived. Rather, he was in a suite he'd not dreamed of in his life.

*　*　*

Victoria lay on the bed naked and Efemona was wearing only her negligee gown, but sat on a stool revealing her nipples and pubic hair. She got up feeling happy commanding Victoria for X- rated movie she was about to make of her with Dr. Fuck'em Good Emma. She mounted the camcorder on the tripod stand, then slowly sat down on the stool with her legs spread apart and watched Victoria perform as a Hollywood actress.

Dr. Fuck'em Good Emma took off his clothes. He'd a dick similar to a huge corn-on-the-cob. Victoria screamed looking at it baffled.

Efemona said to her, "C'mon, you can handle it," and Victoria's fear gradually melted.

Victoria hesitated for a second. "It's too big, girlfriend." "Tell you how we do it in America," Efemona said and looked at her, then brought out a giant bottle of London Gin and served her a tumbler full. She served herself and Dr. Fuck'em Good Emma too.

Victoria swallowed it and became horny. Efemona took the advantage and briefed Victoria what she wanted her to do.

Victoria held up his dick with her fingers but closed her eyes while sucking the tip of the mushroom first, then gently, very gently all the weight of the nine inch dick was in her mouth. She opened her eyes now, liking it more as she imagined. She smiled and looked at Efemona. And she thought Efemona sure knows how to enjoy in America.

Efemona pushed the button on the camcorder. It started whirring. She looked at Victoria playing the flute note. Finally, Efemona said, "Big enough. Let him in, girlfriend."

Victoria tried to shove it in herself so the huge dick would not tear her vagina. She couldn't do it herself. Dr. Fuck'em Good Emma smiled. He carefully spread her legs apart and entered her. Victoria could feel the pain, as he forced himself inside her. Once inside her, she felt better. Dr. Fuck'em Good Emma moaned out.

"Aha! The pleasing pleasure that man and woman bears. God gave me a good weapon to please the women like you who are beautiful," he said as he pumped.

Victoria, too, moaned out. "Oh, heavens. God please come down. Men and women are here forever to stay and fuck like this. You sure gave this man a good weapon to hurt women in this country who cannot afford one square meal anymore. That's why Efemona has reached out for us (them) to be prostitutes." And she *came.* And he *came.* It was the ecstasy of being able to do what they want and to do without the interference of their husbands, too, and not just the *money palava* in their country.

Victoria looked at Efemona. With sincerity on her face, she said, "Baby, I believe in AWAM movement."

Efemona became happy for the compliment. And Dr. Fuck'em Good Emma turned to Efemona and asked, "Are you ready for me?"

"Victoria will not be able to handle my camcorder to record my orgy with you. So I'll not have something of proof to show a man in America what I did for pleasure to humiliate him when I go back tomorrow, okay baby?"

With that, she got up and walked towards the bed where Dr. Fuck'em Good Emma laid on his back. She brought out a huge bundle of Naira note bills and placed -N20,000 on his exposed dick.

He smiled and said, "Forever and ever Dr. Fuck'em Good Emma believes in AWAM movement. *I will help you to promote your slogan of who is your father-in-law anyway!*"

He took the money, dressed up hurriedly and walked towards the door, feeling good about the generous gift. Efemona said to him, "If we ever meet again we will do it all over again. And remember to spend some of the money for other women who believe in my cause."

Victoria looked at Dr. Fuck'em Good Emma as he shuffled the huge currencies into his breast pockets of his ancient jacket he wore. Efemona's message to him was still fresh on his mind in the room.

Unsure whether to admit before them what he would do with the money, either to screw other women who had no jobs or fix his car, which has not ran for months, Dr. Fuck'em Good Emma simply said, "I'll surely do that."

On a hunch, Efemona asked, "How many women in this country do you think are hungry now who want well to do from America to ship them abroad?"

"Millions." he answered.

"Are you sure about that?" Efemona asked.

It was a casual reprimand that Fuck'em Good should go home and think about how the millions of men and women suffering the illness of Bad Dudu and his junta members would be saved. Anyway, Dr. Fuck'em Good Emma nodded. The only words that finally oozed out of his mouth was, "Goodbye, ladies," and he walked away, looking left and right as he, too, entered his office at the poverty room of Ekpoma University with his Ph.D. degree he shop with at Ikoyi Island Street for women who cannot afford to feed themselves, but was lucky enough for a huge gift rather than spending the few kobos he has in his pocket. Thanks to Efemona.

* * *

Efemona helped Victoria clean up the spilling of Fuck'em Good Emma's seed on her executive bed. Victoria, on the other hand, was joyful in a way, and where ever Emma's hands had touched her was good before he left. And now the silence in the room had became acrid. Victoria's hands quickly clung to Efemona's neck as though she were drowning and she was absolutely silent, silent as a child before it finally summons enough courage to scream, or before the whip lands, and the long scream begins. She doesn't know where to start to tell Efemona it was good or it was not.

That night, Sunday evening, when Dr. Fuck'em Good Emma had left, and they were dressed up, Victoria summoned up the courage and said to Efemona, "The women at Festac Town should be waiting for you."

Victoria had caught Efemona off guard. And Efemona, surprised, asked, "What women are you talking about?"

"Well, girlfriend, I arranged for a quick thirty minute stop over for you to make a speech to all the women you had reached out to through your movement at the Festac Town Convention Hall. I paid the sum of Ten thousand Naira to the town's crier to spread the news that you are in town, not only to see Bad Dudu, but to also promote your AWAM movement."

After all, Efemona would like to show off with her mother of Gucci green leather attires to the multitudes waiting. They had stayed up late talking and drinking. And Efemona had not prepared her speech. But she was smart enough to rattled them in her brain. The time had chimed Noon and quickly, Victoria radioed Cocoyamhead to get ready. "You are taking us to the Festac Town," she said.

He knew that Festac Town at that time of the day would be congested. To clear the road for Efemona and Victoria, he radioed Bad Dudu's motorcycle expert riders to clear the road. In a few minutes, they arrived and then cleared the streets.

Cocoyamhead drove down to the Convention Hall. Efemona was impressed with what she'd seen so far. The vast parking areas were filled with plenty of unmovable, smoking, rotted cars women had carried on their heads to show Efemona there were no parts in the country to fix them, far more than moving cars she'd ever seen in Reno, Nevada, except on the days she was to testify against me of how I'd assaulted her in the courts and when she had open rallies for her movement of AWAM.

Cocoyamhead parked near the cemetery where Efemona's grandmother was buried, and both women hopped out of the car and walked towards the Convention Hall. At the door, Efemona's immediate sister, Anegbo and her brother Newman were handing out pamphlets of AWAM. And in the front pew, a group of other women Efemona and Victoria didn't even know were welcoming their arrival. Quickly, Victoria hurried Efemona towards the podium. Efemona said, "So what do I owe all these women who came out to see me?"

"An ordinary speech will do, girlfriend," Victoria said.

Efemona kissed Victoria and said, "You think they would be easy to please?"

"Do the best you can. I know there are over five thousand women here already. The pews are full, and so is the security loft. I told you, women in this country are all fed up of Bad Dudu's regime. They want a change even though I am in their midst to shut me up."

It was the first time Victoria had said the truth to Efemona despite she'd been given a new post of a technical share of the pie. And Efemona registered that at the back of her mind. A revolution is needed in this country-she thought and smiled a private smile. And Victoria continued, "The people in this country, be it women, men, or children, they all want their values in the oil revenue, and they want Bad Dudu's government to consider the people they rule first before their pocketbook in Swiss Bank, British Banks, and Dubai.

And again, Efemona registered that at the back of her mind as Victoria descended and sat in the reserved seat in front. To the right of Victoria was Virginia Okonkwo, the gossiper who was wearing a white skirt and blue T-shirt. Judge Evilfall, the one and only District Master of the Family Court in Reno, Nevada, who specializes in talking to African women in Reno to divorce their husbands and take a curtain in her courtroom was there too, in the front pew. She had on a sexy Wrangler tight jeans with a cowgirl shirt and a cowgirl hat of the typical Yankee American from Reno, Nevada.

For the purpose of identification, I should tell you Evilfall was the only white woman in the crowd.

The famous Patricia, who over the years had lent her support to Efemona's cause was also there wearing a white gown with two shoulder straps and sitting on the lap of the Imperial Wizard. All these spectators had dressed with the utmost care except Efemona's mother and father. Efemona's mother had worn *Abanór (a loin cloth)* with the famous shoes she could only afford which was made from discarded tires of automobiles. Her father wore *dansiki and sokótó* with the same shoes on his feet all for the purpose of advertising and believing in their country until a savior save the country of its woes. Both sat at the back of the pew to listen to their daughter's famous speech.

Finally, Victoria stepped unto the mike and said to the audience, "Ladies," she announced with no gentlemen phrase, "Please welcome Efemona, the one and only Efemona, the new woman, with the thundering, rusty, gravelly voice, swirly hair, and the longest fingernails competing with Jim Baker's wife's nails in America."

The first movable sentence Efemona pounded to her audience was: "Be a superwoman. His Almighty never takes time to make a no woman. Every woman He creates is created to be a superwoman like me. The Almighty who created you all, gave y'all a brain faculty that's brilliant like mine," and she looked at the huge audience. "As you all learnt that I was coming here today, you all left whatever you all were doing to come down here to hear what I'd to say. It's a great determination on your part. The fact that you all are listening to me *now* is the proof of the fact that you cut from a great cloth sewn to be exhibited in the market-place for buyers to select their choice. You all are as deserving and as capable of achieving success as many other women I have inspired to be independent and be role models to others some day. As you all leave here today to go to the American Embassy and obtain a visa, America will surely recivilize you all when you get there. And when you all come back home, you all will surely be an inspiration to other women in this country, *our country.*"

Efemona bellowed further, "If you're like me, Patricia, Virginia and Evilfall, all my former mentors, sitting in the front row, every one of you would think that nothing in the world sounds more appealing than to be able to part your pudenda for different men in the comfort of your own rented apartment, set your own schedule, be your own boss, take time off whenever you feel like it. You'll feel the power of fulfillment, freedom the first to jump on stage to shake the *yansh* to show a sign that you are newly separated and single. You will feel the power of fame and fortune. You all can have all these rewards and more if you just know how to go about getting them. All you need is the solid, concrete direction from me and my mentors, that will show you all how wise it is to be independent and reap the rewards for yourselves. Now that I am here to get you all wired up about the excitement of independent life, I'll address a few of the questions you may have about my organization-AWAM movement."

The audience was not moved as she'd hoped. Then she looked up and wiped her face and drank from the bottled water beside her podium. "I know some of you are asking yourselves, how do you go about it? Well, first of all, you go out and start something with your husbands and from there on you have the power in your hands. It is the first step. After you run away, and divorce them in absentia, you quickly choose among different men on the street who most closely match your dressing style and patterns. The way they dress would tell you if they have money in the bank. It is true that culture develops some kind of art as surely as it develops language. Some primitive culture as those of my husband, Ekiaqueta, no longer interest me, because it has no real mythology or religion preaching respect for women in Nigeria or Africa in general. However, I do believe that all forms of art, our *ojeke dance*, for instance and songs still mostly relate to the women. Therefore, chant with me, my friends and be what you wannabe. Go to the discos and shake your body and *dance ojeke and the fire dance.*"

There was no applause. Efemona continued, "Too often, my friend, some women dream of an ideal lifestyle, then give up on it without really trying. Please folks, don't be a part of that. Don't delay the success, excitement and rewards that my organization called for. Make life worth living for yourselves. You must join in my movement today."

For the first time there came a big applaud from all the women. For some unbeknown reason, the news of Efemona at Festac Town got to the palmwine tappers, farmers, traders, and coffin makers who quickly carried their banners to the scene to walk around then turned their backs to Efemona. Some of them had pasted inscription of stickers, "fuck you Efemona," on their back. Soon enough, her speech was interrupted and drowned out by screaming and yelling from the women who outnumber the palmwine tappers, farmers, traders, and coffin makers.

The reason for that was that most of the men had either gone to their farms or to their coffin making shops, which gave the housewives the edge.

These men in question did not really listen to Efemona's speech. They had all watched with a bright sardonic knowingness of a smarter than smart from America-a reborn woman. Then Efemona looked into the eyes of the vindictive men and thought of how to civilize them. But they threw stones at her, intending to hurt her, and until Cocoyamhead radioed for backup of troops to calm down the disturbances, then she was able to continue. Efemona said that she was happy to note that she would be able to speak, no matter how the uncivilized men try to sabotage her. In another hour or so, I'll be appealing to Bad Dudu in his office how I feel about the uncivilized men of *our country, (my country)*.

Then the spirited Efemona declared on top of her voice, "The right of free-speech, which America believes in, is what I now believe in. Laws and cultures of our country (Nigeria) are meant to be broken because the zombies who rule are not elected by the people. And beside the question of being not elected by the people, I will tell you this is the Twenty-First Century. That things are evolving in a rapid pace. Therefore, the women of my country can do whatever pleases them. I am here to lend my support to a true democracy for everyone who believes in one vote and freedom."

Another big applaud from all the women. Efemona continued, "Myself is ending up a relationship of five years with my *ohuan* husband, which was arranged." Being a country that the majority of these women are of diverse ethnic groups and some are not knowledgeable of the meaning of ohuan she corrected herself. "I mean my goat resemblance of a husband." And then with quick reasoning, Efemona reflected how her brother Newman almost met his untimely death by the bullet because of his support to her movement. "I'd to do what I'd to do by joining with the authorities in Reno, Nevada to give Ekiaqueta, also called What Can I Say, a cow eye to allow me to exercise a new life. Judge Evilfall, also my good friend, sitting with you all here today in the front row, would preside over my divorce with What Can I Say. She is my full supporter. Evilfall is a woman who believes African women in Reno, Nevada should throw away their culture. Give her a hand of applause."

Another big applaud from all the women.

I must be frank with you that where I sat watching via satellite, my face, which was in sleep had looked so young, now was looking so old. For that a certain pain and terror passed through my nerves. There and then, I thought, insanely, as I turned my set off, remembering of Cleopatra's lament for Anthony. It was the same way I felt. But she did not know my pain where I sat watching her via satellite.

She continued, "I will listen to Evilfall because I *now* realize that Nigerian men are mean, brutal to women and under my new life, I plan to reach out to all African women in the world. I'm angry as hell about the exploitation of women in this country. Wife beating, rape and God knows that they regard you all sitting and standing before me and even me, Efemona, as a second class citizen in this country.

Another big screaming then an ovation.

Needless to tell you that my life as a man of deep silence, the son of a palmwine tapper and a farmer ended on the day Efemona was making her famous speech at Festac Convention Hall in a hazy sunny afternoon in 1995, when, at the age of forty-three, I was painfully transformed into an intellectual of a fiction writer.

Anyway, Efemona waited until the noise receded. "If I did not believe I am uniquely qualified to lead my crusade of AWAM movement, I would not be standing here today before you. I hate this soil upon which I am now standing after I have been to America and have seen how women are being treated. I know that our inexperienced, incompetent, or indecisive dictatorship junta uniform men in camouflage will not comprehend with the ground rules of America bi-laws. This is why you'll all join in my crusade to fight the repression and poverty of women in this country."

They applauded her on top of their voices.

Efemona looked around the Convention Hall and saw a number of people she knew, including her sugar daddy that once worked at the Flour Mills at Ewu, and Dr. Fuck'em Good Emma, Victoria had made a porno movie with for the eyes of Efemona alone to watch when she got back to the States. She paused and watched them sit way back in the pew before she continued.

"Three months ago, I was able to cheat my husband cold of a million dollars and has since then awarded a contract to Perini Construction Inc. of Reno, Nevada to develop about 350 acres which would harbor ninety-nine whore houses and low rent houses, including abortion clinics, theaters where women can go, sit and relax and watch American XXX movies, poolside, tennis court, chapels, amid a rustic setting of flowers and well-trimmed grass to be grown. My laborers I will employ would be uniformed men who are zombies who don't know their right hand from their left in this country who will work under the sun and the rain, day and night working for me to pay them to lay some of you to have money to take good care of yourselves. When that time comes, take the money fast from them and stick it into your bras before you part your legs for them to navigate. You also have the right to grab the money and not part your legs. If they force any of you, to perform without your consent and no money up front, write to me or call me or let Newman know. I will then fire such dubious mean spirited men and charge them for rape through international court in Hague."

"Dr. Fuck'em Good Emma did not know what Efemona meant by that. Anyway, Efemona paused then looked at her audience, then raised up her two hands close to her ears, "Back in the days when I was at Ewu Maternity and fighting with them mosquitoes, I never knew anything about rape. Now that I have been to America, it's my greatest accomplishment to let you all know that it's morally wrong that men in this country force themselves upon you even when you are tired and unable to perform. Do you all want this to continue in this country?"

The feedback was alarming. "No," they shouted.

Pointing to Evilfall where she sat in the front row, Efemona said, "Diversity is the key to tourism and Benin City and Ukpenu which is now under construction for whore houses at Ugbagwue Street would be a model street for all women who want to make it in life without their husbands. It would be a model street capitalizing on its ethnic and cultural riches for which one of the brothels would be dedicated to my greatest guest, Judge Greenfall Evilfall to take a chalet. Wouldn't that be nice that I bring in Perini Construction, an American company to fight the dust, erosion and the deluge at Ugbagwue?"

The women all shouted 'yes', but the men who stood far away watching and grinding their teeths were baffled. Evilfall reacting to the men's nay and veto, said to Efemona, "Go on with your speech, my dear. They are still primitive in this country, your country."

"Damn right, my dear," Efemona said.

After the audience stopped clapping, Efemona continued, "This my business of AWAM movement African men like Sam Okorie, Israel, Anukam and Achuko residing in Reno, Nevada all considered abomination to me is good. My mother, brothers and sisters all believe in it. I thank Judge Evilfall who suggested to me that she would grant me my divorce when I filed for it to drop my husband, which would get me a new meaning in life just as the Americans do. Now, the good news about Evilfall is that she'd promised to stay behind at Ugbagwue to share my mother's flat to lay as many black men in Benin to show an example of how it's done in America. I also owe my allegiance to Philomena Drake, who is not here today who first gave me the light on how American system supports women from all walks of life to be what they wanna be. Here I am. I'm I not chute and reborn? Don't you all like my new looks and the jewelry nestling in between my titties? It cost me thousands of dollars. All of you here today can be captain of your own faith if you move quickly. All it takes to be like me, is to run away from your husbands and put on a new knocking boots."

All the women stood ovation once more and clapped. When they sat again, Efemona was able to continue, "The number of abused women in this country increases every year. Sometimes the men kill them with blows to their head and blame it on voodoo and witchcraft. Do you all want this to keep continuing?"

"No!" they shouted.

"I can't hear you." They shouted louder for Efemona. "Women in this country continue to till the dark soil for farming and when some of them are trained for white and blue collar jobs in this country, they are under paid or their husbands squeeze their hands and take their paychecks. They are insulted on the street, in the public transportation and are denied their rights in the courts. When they wear trousers and jean pants, the traders of Akinzua Street will carry samba and beat the drums and sauce pans with spoons behind their back as they walk on the street minding their business. Do you want this to keep continuing?" If you agree that enough is enough, say before me, zombies go back to the barracks."

"Enough's enough," they screamed louder. "Zombies go to your barracks and hand over power to civilians," they chanted.

Efemona's mother, Ughulu tilted her neck to her husband and whispered to him, "Our daughter has a good message and a just cause. How about that?" She too was surprised at her daughter's oratorical speech message.

Her husband, Mr. Irabor said nothing.

Efemona was thrilled. She began, "I dedicate this year to my friend Judge Evilfall, who has agreed to share my mother's flat and lay men on a daily basis until my mother is able to pay ten years in advance for her rent. Evilfall is a dear and an angel to me."

All the women in the audience glanced in the direction of Evilfall who was at ease, happy being recognized, then yelled back at Efemona, "Register us and give us a chalet at Ugbagwue when it's completed by the great Perini Construction of America."

Efemona said to Evilfall, "Stand up for my people to know who you are."

And Evilfall stood up before the audience.

Efemona said to Evilfall, "I have introduced and sent your portraits and mug shots to the editor-in-chief of the Punch and Observer to paste them on the front page to help me advertise you on the sign boards of Benin City and Ukpenu. All the airwaves in Benin City have already aired your name, letting the men of this country know who you really are."

Evilfall had a broad smile on her face. "Thank you, Efemona. That's wonderful," she found herself saying.

"My pleasure. I guarantee you that you'll make millions from rich men of this country as you are the only white woman desperately in need to be a billionaire in America and I know you will soon become one. However my dear, you'll miss American food, especially hamburgers and cheeseburgers for some time to come and greatly miss your country, your friends and your husband, which you left behind to support my cause in my country, Nigeria, here today. You'll be homesick after sometime because there's no Deli, Burger King, no Taco Bell close to my mother's flat at Ugbagwue where you'll soon learn how to adjust to a new hostile environment in Bad Dudu Abacha's regime of the juntas, and then soon enough you will lose your self identity because of money as you intend me to do to my husband in America. Therefore, the capitalistic dollar madness in both of us will make cats and dogs of the African race to sleep with you for big bucks because you want to get rich quick like me," she smiled at Evilfall.

Evilfall, Patricia, and Virginia all boomed out laughter and stood ovation. When they finally sat, Efemona added, "I assure you Evilfall that our capitalistic madness in both of us will make you to be aggressive with the men who want you to take off your bikinis. Their hunger to navigate you will make the men of this country to bring bundles of dollars out of their retirement plan to stick them into your pudenda, that before you know it, they had wet their pants and asked you to lick them up and swallow it before they penetrate inside you."

But, you know, America in itself is a helluva place. How Efemona knew of words I don't even know their meaning since I came to America is beyond me. As I watched her make her speech via satellite, making references to pudenda twice, I summed up the courage to look up the meaning in Webster. The fact is that if I were a woman, I wouldn't let anyone take a part of my anatomy and make it so vulgar as to be unspeakable, to one word used by men purely to defile. Pudenda as I found out, is the only non- racial epithet in our general vernacular that is filthy, horrible, mean and ugly to utter except as the ultimate insult.

Pudenda, or the external genital organs of a human being and especially of a woman, is a term that derives from a verb which, believe it or not, means to be ashamed. Therefore, the power of the pudenda, and this concept that women are to be ashamed of it- seems in direct contradiction to what everyone thinks of male pudenda. You see, men can easily discuss their genitals, but not women. This is where I say my wife, Efemona is a truly reborn African woman-reformed in the American tradition. Several of the words that we use to define the male organs don't seem to make us ashamed or humiliate us. While we men may use the word to insult women, most women cringe when they hear it. Not with Efemona. All she was trying to do was make the women in her audience aware that she is now Americanized. Which she truly was.

Anyway, with that in mind, Evilfall nodded and clapped. Efemona said to her, "I estimate you'll make about $25,000 dollars a night, which will finally make you start something with your husband of twenty years marriage when you decide you had made enough money from the zombies of this country who rule my people before you go back to the States."

Evilfall stood and clapped. Efemona then finally turned to her audience who were moved to tears, cries, tears and a prolonged rumble of approval that drowned her speech. "Ancient history dictates that Nabot's Vineyard was taken away by a very jealous King who was pretty rich. The women in history must be very pretty. Don't you all think so? What I mean to tell you all is that the men will always look at you if you take good care of yourselves. This is the millenium. Men in this country still follow the example of the men in uniform who rule to beat their wives with whips, rape women, abuse their children and above all, refuse to pay us when we are nurses, teachers and then leave us or take our children from us when we speak up and then drive us away with no money in our purse to carry on with our lives. Now do you believe that these atrocities are wrong? I believe it is morally wrong. And do you believe that Ghandi's nonviolence charisma spell on the human race will solve your problems and bring you to civilization as the American women you see on television in this country, if you don't act up now? I don't think so, my friends."

Efemona looked at her audience spellbound with tears dropping from her eyes. "I want you all to make a commitment here today, now at this moment, not just to applaud me, but to support and join my effort to fight against arranged marriage that women are abused. Inequality and injustice still reign supreme in Nigeria because the men in power who rule are not well informed! If you do not believe in wearing the pants in the family, then I do not want you screaming to fool me."

Efemona turned from the podium, walked slowly away. The assembly floor erupted, the women found fascination in cheering, weeping, standing on their chairs to shout, clenching their fists and gritting their teeth. Patricia, Victoria and Virginia felt good about themselves as they all headed to their different hotels, except Evilfall who left with Efemona's mother who is to share her flat with her. And before Efemona's mother and Evilfall got to her flat, hundreds of Zombies in uniforms who were at the rally who'd guarded her with AK-47 rifles had lined up to experiment with a white woman pussy, paying big bucks they'd stolen from the Central Bank and from the Nigerian Petroleum Oil Company Trust Fund. However, some of the market women who respect their husbands in sickness and in health nayed and vetoed Efemona's conviction to leave their husband but to stay with their husbands in sickness and in health, rich or poor. At the same time, hundred who wanted out of poverty registered with AWAM movement. Some of them, after signing up, had stormed forward towards Efemona to talk to her, touch her and embrace her.

I watched via satellite how my mother-in-law clapped for her daughter, while my father-in-law looked at his wife, Ughulu and shook his head in disgust. Ughulu need not be told what my father-in-law meant when he shook his head. But she had the guts to ask her husband, for the fun of asking, while she'd frowned at him.

Efemona had hardly spent half an hour. Thus, she became a high profile visitor and a lecturer in her own country. As she descended the walkway aisle and entered the waiting car, her father said to his wife, "I'm not in favor of what our daughter, Efemona, has *now* indulged herself-spearheading a powerful movement of the African women overseas and in this country to leave their marriages.

Ughulu frowned. With vexation she said, "Efemona gave you a bundle of dollars a few weeks ago, and now you are turning your back against her? I'm divorcing you," she told her husband and left with vengeance. Before her husband got home, Ughulu had ran to Oba's Palace with every property her husband had owned in life.

All those who craned their necks through the windows of the Festac Town Convention houses around had another glimpse at the vanishing thunderous Efemona. And as the convoy of motorcycle expert riders roared out of the area, it dawned on my brothers and sisters who'd also watched Efemona from a distance, that Efemona, *Udonomoerele* (clitoris with large balls), was no longer their brother's wife alone. She has Americanized, and there was nothing they could do.

It should be informative to note that before Efemona had left Festac Town Convention Hall, she'd set up her executive office at the Mosaic Building on the twenty-fifth floor where she'd posted:

You must get out of poverty through my AWAM movement.

Never again bow down to be a lamb to the slaughter.

Through my crusade, there is a job waiting in Italy, Brazil, Thailand, England, America and Japan for any woman in this country who is tired of being penniless, repressed from tyranny of the men of this country with uniforms of brutality and insane husbands.

Advocating separation and running away are my main goals for you all to get started. Prostitution pays. Prostitution is the answer to elevate yourselves from poverty, since the oil money of this country is only in the hands of the few junta Bad Dudu Abacha's regime.

Re-education will be the benchmark of freedom and liberty for more money in your pocket through exploiting different men vying for our carnal lust. This is the millenium era, an age that will test our intelligence, our resolve and our willingness to sacrifice for ourselves without husbands.

Thus the goals of an African woman with balls had just begun. Her next move is the confrontation with the real Bad Dudu Abacha, the Caesar she'd come to see.

Chapter

18

T he evening on a Sunday, when Cocoyamhead had dropped Efemona and Victoria at the Federal Palace Hotel and Casino, after Efemona had finished regaling her audience at the Festac Convention Hall, Efemona and Victoria went to their respective suites to get ready to see Bad Dudu the next morning. As Efemona sat in the quiet of her room, she thought of Bad Dudu Abacha's regime in her being, the man she'd came to see for the impromptu job offer summit. She'd heard so much of Bad Dudu's regime and his message: Embezzle the Federal Government Treasury Fund meant for the whole people of Nigeria and then transfer it through wire fraud to the European Banks to keep it in their banks. Keep the people powerless and Dudu's regime powerful. Let Dudu and his men take care of the few from the North to import automobile tires and rice and rule for life because the Ph.Ds of Nigeria and others who co-habit the country cannot govern and take care of themselves. Trust Bad Dudu because Dudu's government knows what is good for Nigerians-a bullet in the head or detain them at *Alabon Close* to shut them up.

The time for Efemona and Victoria to see Bad Dudu was chiming closer. After Efemona had finished styling her hair, she sat down on her executive bed, but was bored. Restless, she got up and rode on the elevator to the fifth floor to pick up some famous Nigerian Newspapers at the Federal Palace Gift Shop. For sure, she'd plenty of time to read The Times, The Punch, The Sketch, and The Star Newspapers. She picked them up quickly and went to the counter to pay. To Efemona's surprise, there were several people in front of her. She joined the line, and when the man in front looked back and saw Efemona as fresh as a stranger, no bones he could count on her face, he said to her, "Is that all you have?

Come in front of me." And Efemona nodded and beamed up a good smile.

"Don't worry," Efemona said in a way of a 'being to' and remained on the line.

When Efemona finally got to the counter, the male clerk crowed out at her, *"Humm, madam, you go read all that Newspapers today?"* Though a warm, appreciative smile creased inside Efemona, male clerks in Nigeria are still very nosy. She looked into the clerk's eyes and sighed. The reason for that was that the clerk should have been quick checking her out instead of talking to her. She didn't want people to recognize her.

The clerk, too, felt a pleasurable stirring into her triangle.

Then finally, he said, "I believe people have to be nice to people. Don't you think so, madam?"

"Deaf ears." Check me out goddaminit was rather on her being. And the clerk shut his mouth, rang up the bill. "Nine forty, please."

Efemona did not even know she'd been cheated. She just wanted to get the hell out of there and she paid. In a haste, she rode the elevator back to her room. Then she opened The Punch first.

The Punch, I should tell you, was printed in Benin City, her home State. But 'The Daily Times' had carried a legacy of the British tradition since the colonial era. She did not bother to look at it or the other Newspapers. After all, she'd picked them up for the fun of it. The Daily Times, for instance, was rich and more leisurely readable and that was when Mr. Life Goes On had ruled, but not now, Efemona thought. The only problem at that time was no one knew how much of the country's oil money the parliament members surrounding Mr. Life Goes On did away with, though the paper was the voice of the elites. She tossed The Daily Times aside, became indecisive of what paper she would rather read.

The Punch, which was published in Benin where she'd schooled and knew so many people has its own flaws and setbacks. She noted instantly that it was not what it used to be when Governor Osagbovo

Ogbemudia was the Head of State in Benin. The sequence of the news and other daily events had been altered.

Actually, I had heard from my pals journalists in Nigeria who wanted a change about the front page non-news of 'The Daily Times' and other famous Newspapers. Then when I visited home, I actually took the time to look at the various Newspapers. If you had seen The Daily Times in the last decade since Bad Dudu and his groupies were in power, any Nigerian would probably notice that it isn't news that was making the front page. *Instead, it was Dog bit a man and no needles to give him an injection in the hospital,* and more so at the bottom of the paper, it was mostly about the junta members lifestyles in the formidable form from the juntas having boats and yachts in Monte Carlo, South of France and all that crap, whereas, when Life Goes On was in power, the front page of all newspapers was off-limits to news like that or to their cabinet members. I must be specific, though, because the masses nor even the well-trained investigative reporters knew not if they were hiding something in their closet. Those good old days, the front page, and all the first pages of the rest of the section, for that purpose was strictly reserved for the Newspaper first and foremost priority: The news: *like man bit a dog and the dog did not survive.*

And in the good old days, newspapers in Nigeria were not biased, they reported the news with simplicity without fear of being killed by Mr. Life Goes On until Bad Dudu ascended the throne. Anyway, there were now extraordinary interruptions to the time honored events when Efemona was in the country as a nobody. She glanced at the paper back and forth. When she was a nobody she thought: the front page had dealt mostly on Nigerian affairs, but they were now mixed with both foreign and junk news. Merely looking at the paper, Efemona saw that the first two pages were now devoted to executives and their beautiful Indians and Thai women on vacations in London and the Cayman Islands. Sports still appeared regularly where it has been, because Nigerians love soccer, boxing and lawn tennis. Advertisement, change of names were still more prominent and faithful to tradition. "Hum! Thank God," Efemona said to herself.

Going further into the paper, she noticed that marriages, births and obituaries, which used to be her favorite section, has been moved. Jeez! What's going on here? She took her time to figure it out. Goddammit! This country's zombies, when would they learn that stability is the mother of efficiency in civilized countries? Efemona cajoled and moved on.

As soon as she'd cajoled, she found it at the last page. She did not bother to look at it again. She would scan it later to see if any of her few friends had multiplied the world population or they'd died of natural causes, by armed robbers or by a hole in the head by the dictator, Bad Dudu. Efemona, therefore, gave most of her attention to the first page, which stimulated her adrenaline.

She'd read that the Nigerian economy had plummeted to an all time high into the World Global Market as a result of crude oil demand in the last few weeks, which has made top Bad Dudu Army ranking executives of Nigerian Petroleum Oil Companies to send their wives to Britain to live comfortably. Big deal! It was the same old news on the CNN and World News Tonight in the United States shortly before she departed with Victoria. She did not waste her time on the page.

Efemona scanned through the pages deeper. Then she became thirsty for London Gin and a cigarette. Damn! Victoria had introduced her to smoking again. Finally, Efemona took her paper to the canteen downstairs. There, she walked to the back and sat.

As she sat, she unfolded 'The Daily Times' on the table. Suddenly her eyes caught the caption, "EFEMONA." In such a hurry to read it, her eyes caught two headlines beside it: A TRADER SHOT BY ENRAGED WIFE; and A MAN IN A COFFIN FROM BRITAIN EN ROUTE TO NIGERIA WOKE UP. But she looked at her caption of 'Efemona,' it looked blurred. As she took the pain to stare at it for precious moments, somebody was saying something.

Efemona looked up and saw lots of people now looking at her. It looked like the place had a standard for her because only Efemona and Efemona alone could accept the definitions of why they were looking at her: that is the hideously mechanical jargon of the age still exists. Nothing has changed. She was now like a white woman in the midst of several black men and women the sun had baked in the farms. She saw some faces around her worth envy of her. Right there and then she began to believe in the vast, gray sleep she'd lost rather than coming out to the canteen to read her papers. Who knows if the security for her was still in force? She thought. Must I believe in the cures, panaceas, the howling which has afflicted this canteen where men and women come to eat and exit through the back door because they have no money to pay the owner of the *booka*? Efemona, therefore, created her standard of who she really was. The remodeled Efemona. Believe it or not, Efemona was distracted a bit. It was now up to her to find out who she really was, and it was her necessity to do that, so far as the witch doctors of the time at the Oba's Palace watching over her as she flew into the country were concerned. Therefore, there was no fear in her as if she would be poisoned and not leave the country alive. Efemona, after much thought, hunched up her head toward the somebody and said, "You talkin' to me?"

He was a man of about forty-five years old with black upon white with a note pad standing before her.

"If you wouldn't mind young man, I'm here to read my morning Newspapers. What do you want?" Efemona asked, trying to conceal her identity.

"I was wondering if you might spare me a little of your time for a few questions. We know Efemona is here in Nigeria. Do you know Efemona or have you seen Efemona?"

Efemona remembered she'd traveled in false name to see Bad Dudu, the President of all presidents in mother populous country of Africa-Nigeria. Her answer was out in a flash. "Efemona? Sure! She's the President of AWAM movement. I learnt her headquarters is in Reno, Nevada in the United States." Her tone was oratorical, no more accent of Ukpenu, menlo, as she delivered her reply with much style of the mouth and lips and jaw as First Lady Hilary Clinton, at once know-it-all and brighter than bright, former native of Ukpenu.

Efemona smiled at the man. "Efemona is now a high-priced prostitute, independent woman who knows about the law of the United States more than her husband who'd shipped her to the States. By the way, who wants to know Efemona anyway?" Efemona asked as she tried harder to conceal her identity to frustrate her interrogator.

The interrogator was not a journalist to be intimidated as such.

He said, "I do, please."

"And who the hell are you?"

"I'm Uki-Dan-be-sikun, a journalist." "A journalist?" Efemona repeated.

Uki-Dan-be-sikun looked at Efemona deeply in her face, too. And Efemona readjusted herself properly on her chair, rearranged her hair, and cupped her chin as men do. She chewed her Wrigley's Juicy Fruit Gum slowly across her mouth, then made a big bubble that sounded like a motar that has bein fired at Sandhurst Army Depot in Britain where the Generals in Nigeria got their training.

Finally, Efemona said, "You're spying on Efemona? You should know what she looks like. All journalists in Nigeria knew who Efemona was when she was a nurse at a remote village maternity at Ewu. She hardly had enough to eat. Today, as I learnt, Efemona is the talk of the Nation in this country. They said, she's teamed up with authorities in Reno, Nevada to approve a cow eye for her husband, vowed to sue him and ruin him for life, and she'd vowed to take a curtain in the famous brothels where she would service different men for big bucks and bring the dollar to her country to become a hench madam for Nigerian Bad Dudu's oil executive men who would worship her golden pussy. The most annoying thing about Efemona, sources said, is that she's also the President of AWAM movement. Her mother is from a royal family, a countess, a witch, a tyrant, and her father was a tutor, very bright and articulate. Efemona was both."

Uki-Dan-be-sikun watched Efemona finish. He could not believe that Efemona was smarter than him. What could he do?

He looked up at her. What he had wanted to say disappeared.

Finally, he retired to his former self. "You know, I was just wondering if you were the Efemona from the United States here in the country to see our Bad Dudu for the vacant post of Matron General."

"No! I might look like her."

"Okay then. Goodbye and enjoy reading your papers," he said, though he was humiliated and frustrated. The frustration he had never before received from anyone (a woman for that matter) since being a professional journalist. Efemona then smiled to herself and concentrated on her papers scanning them as fast as she could, as the time to see Bad Dudu was getting nearer. Finally, she settled on the story, "A TRADER SHOT BY AN ENRAGED WIFE," when somebody drew her attention again. She looked up. It was a waiter this time.

"What?" Efemona asked.

"I said, did you want anything to drink?" "Give me more time to decide, baby!"

Efemona had just finished reading her first story, when the waiter was saying something again. She looked up.

"What?"

"Service now or you still need more time?"

She did not want embarrassment anymore. She had not intended to be bothered. I know why the waiter is bothering me, she thought. He needs a huge tip. Anyway, Efemona said, "O.K. Give me a shot of *Ogogoro* and a bowl of escargot." She'd ordered it because its being a long time since she ate escargot.

The waiter was gone. He knew he would get a huge tip. The mere look of Efemona says it all. She's from America. Dollar power people. Though Efemona won't admit it in the open for fear of being robbed.

Efemona looked down on her paper furiously scanning the headlines. Again she saw, "EFEMONA IN NIGERIA TO SEE THE PRESIDENT, MISSION UNKNOWN." She did not bother much on reading the whole story. Victoria has already briefed her about it. Then she concentrated on, "A TRADER SHOT BY AN ENRAGED WIFE."

She read: "Mr. Esan-Aaye, 45, a prominent businessman from Ishan was shot to death early yesterday as he went home after duty by his enraged wife, Bridget Nódógbójéké Ghvamerika.

According to reliable sources, Mr. Esan-Aaye had secretly been having an affair with one Miss Theresa Obaseki who contested for the Miss Universe pageant in Los Angeles six months ago. Miss Obaseki who resided at Show him '99' street, Ukpenu, was the ex-mistress of

Babagida. Mr. Esan-Aaye, who has been madly in love, has not seen his family or made love to his wife of six years for a period of 'ninety-nine' months.

Esan Aaye had gone to see his children he'd not seen in nine months which had then triggered Mrs. Esan-Aaye's vexation to pull the trigger of his own rifle that killed him, during the sudden eruption of argument with her. He died immediately at the scene after the first shot.

Efemona sighed deeply as she finished reading it. Then she looked up and saw the waiter coming towards her. She bowed her head to the paper in pretense. And the waiter stood on her shoulder.

"What now? Plu-ease-ees-e."

"Here's your *Ogogoro* and the bowl of escargot and London Gin you ordered."

"Oh, thank you," she said and bent down to finish the story. The waiter did not go away. Rather, he looked into the paper Efemona was reading and interrupted. "They publish sad stories every day in Nigeria these days. The only good news they have published since Fela Anikulapo Kiti's death was perhaps about Efemona. The others have been mostly sad news. Two tragedies since Fela. The most baffling was, 'A man in a coffin en route from Britain to Nigeria woke up.' That's surprising! They said he woke up and would stand trial before a tribunal when Efemona leaves the country. Who is responsible for putting Umaro Diko to sleep en route to Nigeria is unknown. He'll probably get a bullet in the head. The only good story everyone is talking about is Efemona. They said Bad Dudu has nominated her for the post of Matron General."

Efemona did not utter a word. But she thought: Women have to think about so many things. Men only have to think about looking at beautiful women they cannot lay in years to come. She laughed to herself.

The waiter moved up closer to her shoulder. He had nothing to say, he has too much to say. "I hate to wait on people these days."

"Well, why do you do it? Quit it," Efemona swallowed in her being, but said nothing.

The waiter realized he must try harder to make her talk. He tried some humor. "Isn't she gorgeous," he said, looking directly into the paper Efemona was reading.

"Who is gorgeous?" Efemona asked in amazement. "I mean Mrs. Esan-Aaye, who killed her husband."

Efemona hissed. She thought the waiter was giving her the compliment. She'd wanted to stand up for him and model for him to see how gorgeous she was, too, wearing American attires. Then she remembered she was in the country with a false identity. Finally, she said to him, "Something made Mrs. Esan-Aaye to kill her husband."

The waiter did not pay attention to details. Rather, the waiter said, "I'll tell you Mr. Esan-Aaye was overdoing it. Once or twice a week was good enough for his other concubines he had here and there. But no! He's jealous that Babagida would take her and baptized her with millions of dollars. But you know, I'll say he was trifling on her, because he's got a Queen more beautiful than his own wife of six years. Nigerian women are tough these days like some American women. At Agbor the other day, a woman cut off the penis of her husband as he was sleeping, because he was too tired from screwing other women beside her. The man then bled to death on the way to the hospital with his own penis on his right hand palm. The woman figured her husband was secretly screwing other women beside her. She was just an illiterate, too, married to a University of Nevada graduate. The woman was then brought before the elders of the village, castigated first, and was dozed to death with gasoline and discarded automobile tires. The whole village witnessed the woman set ablaze and burnt to ashes."

"What?! They burnt her to ashes? That was out of line. That's why we are still backwards and barbaric in our own country. Somebody has to civilize the zombies who make our laws to degrade women, Efemona thought. She shivered, her hands on her head, looking through the window and wondering what to do. She thought of walking to Bad Dudu's office to tell him to get a life for making cruel and unusual punishment for women of her country, but she was afraid of the police and Bad Dudu's own men collecting bribes from men in Agbada coming to see their own man affixing signatures to documents before they could pass freely to see him. Anyway, Efemona concealed her identity so well. So she did what she alone could do. She became more attentive. Hearing no more words from the flippant waiter, she said, "I, myself have applied for an American visa to leave this country where women are set ablaze. In America sources said, "The woman would be a hero, through the eyes of the media. Talk shows would have her attention. Hollywood would stare her in movies and pay her millions of dollars for it. She would become an instant celebrity, signing autographs."

"I agree with you on that. But don't forget that it is only in this country that a dog can eat the bone tied on its neck. In other countries like America, the dogs cannot eat the bone tied on their necks. What do I mean by that? I mean that little things you do in America can net someone or somebody millions. You kill your dog, you make money, you burn your lips with seven-eleven coffee, you make money, you kill your husband, you make money. What else is not happening in Sodom?"

Absolutely, Efemona concurred as the waiter walked away. Then she fixed her eyes back to the paper joyously looking for the place where she'd been interrupted. She found it. But it said, "see page six."

Then she flipped through the pages, goaded with impatience. She'd overshot page six. So she backed up and found it. She read it, then looked up. The waiter was standing before her again. "Do you want any more London Gin, *Ogogoro,* escargot or you want me to serve you in your room later?"

"I will prefer you do that, please," Efemona said.

What Efemona didn't know was that the waiter, as frail and thin as he was, too, was having a crush on her. He'd never seen a gorgeous woman in years since Bad Dudu ceased power to rule his people. Efemona closed the papers and called it a day. She stood up and stepped into the elevator and told the elevator man where she was heading. She had forgotten the style of Nigerian elevator men, but now it came back to her. The man, without a word, slammed the doors of the elevator and drove the car upward. The nature of his silence conveyed his disapproval of Efemona for being rude. Efemona had said, "To the Twenty-second Floor," and that was it, though Efemona had noticed what seemed to look odd on his forehead. She stared at him and he stared at her. She'd flesh on her bones. He had none on his bones. General Bad Dudu's austerity food measure had shown on his face and so, Efemona did not recognize him. The face before her in a way has ceased. Time had done some damage on him. Before she left the country when Mr. Life Goes On was in power, she'd not seen before the drama and lines on his forehead, the deep, crooked line between the brows, the tension which now had soured the lips which nurturing food Dudu and his men eat, he cannot afford. But the man had something in mind he wanted to say: this too know women of this generation who think their shit doesn't stink and are expensive as silver and gold. He did not say. He reserved his comment until Efemona exited. But Efemona had pitied him and opened her purse and squeezed out a fifty dollar bill and handed it to him.

Efemona quietly exited the elevator and walked to her suite. She opened her door and sat on her bed, then flipped through the papers in a hurry before Victoria arrives to fetch her for the important appointment with Bad Dudu.

Having turned the paper over and over looking for a good story, she muttered to herself, "People die more in this country nowadays because of hunger and starvation anyway." She turned to the obituaries section to see if any of her relatives had died, awaiting burial, then she could attend their burial ceremonies to lavish some dollars on their coffins.

As Efemona gave death and obituary her serious attention, it was ironic, sad to her to see in bold headline, "NIGERIA MOURNS AN OIL EXECUTIVE, EMEKA NGOZIKA." Then she read about a quarter of the story. It was the Emeka she knows.

The story says: "Emeka Ngozika was on his way to Zurich for an OPEC meeting. The jet crashed shortly after take off from Muritala Mohammed Airport. There were sixty high-ranking Generals all from the South who were to attend the meeting with Ngozika in Zurich.

Sources said that Bad Dudu and Babagida had fired a huge missile at the craft to perish the Generals for their fears that when they return from the summit, they would stage a coupe to topple their administration of

Bad Dudu and Babagida. Bad and Babagida were not taking chances with the Generals from the South.

Emeka's body was found charred beyond recognition. He was the voice of the Nation to have boosted oil prices regulation with OPEC member countries to reduce Bad Dudu's pocketbook in Swiss Bank and Britain."

The one thing I realized was that Efemona was fond of Emeka Ngozika before she left the country to join the man she would hate for life. She'd the feeling that this was mainly because she recognized Emeka as her sugar daddy, from whom she would have benefited. So she mourned Emeka with all her heart, before she fell into a conscious nap.

When Efemona woke up, she found herself turning on the TV for more news of her country. Sad enough, she dropped the papers in her hand and punched the remote control. Bad Dudu was saying over and over again, "When one is surrounded by enemies, one has to be vigilant." Efemona immediately knew that the culprit had murdered her one time sugar daddy. She could not bear it.

Efemona walked towards the window. Here I am, about to rekindle a new life with Emeka after I divorce the motherfucking Ekiaqueta, the wretched man when I get back to the United States, she thought and was full of more thoughts. Then she looked through the window of her suite. The clear waters of the Atlantic Ocean was beautiful with fly boats that conveyed workers to Ikoyi and Doddan Army Barracks. And over the dock she saw the Binis and Ukpenu workers riding their bicycles home. Efemona pounded on the glass windows with her hands in a gesture of trying to jump to her death into the water. It was impossible. She walked back to her bed and sat thinking of the meeting with Bad Dudu: The meeting that would doom him for life.

*　*　*

The clock in Efemona's suite began to tick faster and faster. She knows why. Then she thought to hersoneelf: *One must not pinch a parcel that is addressed to him because one must eventually open it to find out what's inside it.* It is me and Bad Dudu. I'll teach him a lesson he will never forget. He will know that somebody is damn smarter than him. As she thought, she remembered one of St. Augustine's aphorisms, "Time." She murmured to herself: What is time? If no one asks me, I know. But if I have to explain it, I do not know. I do know Bad Dudu will fall on his face sooner. It all depends when we see each other face to face. Finally, she looked out the window down below and saw Doddan Army Barracks and their armored vehicles with soldiers sitting beside them and some standing with Uzis and modern weapons of destruction in the rain. *"Jesus! Somebody dey watch somebody for inside this rain why somebody wey no go school dey sit for executive chair! Zombie way na one way wey Fela talk na true."*

Efemona sat restless after much thought. Then she considered calling her long time friends at Ewu, Irrua, Ekpoma and especially the Aburimes who'd helped her money-wise after the delivery of our first daughter, Verita. But the phones didn't work. She clenched her fist remembering Nigeria was a very rich country and could use it's oil money to purchase more phone circuits to be launched by the Americans, Russians, Brazilians, whoever is the cheapest for the contract. And even if the phones don't work, Efemona thought, most of the people she planned to call probably might be dead.

Efemona then shook her head and said louder to herself, "Obituary in Nigeria." Still restless, she rang the waiter for a glass of Gin, her famous Gin with lime this time, the reason for that-unknown, *plus order of pounded yam with equesi soup with stockfish, escargot and cowlegs and oxtails and ponmoo which she'd missed for five good years.*

The waiter knocked. She looked through the peephole. "The talkative waiter again!" She murmured to herself. Then she opened the door.

The waiter smiled. "Here is your order, madam." He delivered and did some quick mental calculations in his head, something Nigerians are good at-mathematics in the head without ink and paper and a pen.

The waiter stood and watched Efemona open the dishes. The way the dishes looked, she could not help it. She said, "For the money I will pay for this shit, the *shit* might be very good and delicious, honey boy."

Though the honey boy took his breath away, he was dumb for words looking at the pretty face with flesh. When he recovered himself, he said finally, "Five thousand Naira, madam. But I've to tell you this madam, mind your tongue in this country! We don't eat *shit* in this country and we never will. We might be hungry, dear. By the way, do the American people eat shit in their country?" "Not that I know of," Efemona said in a way as if she's never been to America before.

"Our food in this country, especially in a Hotel like this one, is very expensive. The common man these days can't afford it," he said, then looked again at Efemona who had changed into new clothes again. The green leather monkey jacket upon black leather skirt Efemona was wearing no doubt in his heart was making a statement. It means the dollar power. He knows it. And he had so many things he'd wanted to say. He had forgotten when his eyes caught the bundle of dollars with Efemona. *He thought, well some people dey enjoy, some people dey suffer."*

Efemona pulled out two hundred dollar bills and handed it to him. "Keep the change," she said.

"Thank you, madam," he said and hurried out. He did not give a receipt. Efemona didn't care about a receipt. Quickly, she closed the door behind him, then looked down on her Gucci shoes, then her Gucci wrist watch. She'd about thirty minutes for her mother of appointments with Bad Dudu. She settled down and scraped her dishes, then drank a bottle of cold water. Victoria was by now, supposed to be on her way. Damn, why the hell hasn't she come. Has Victoria forgotten they have an appointment at eleven? Quickly, she buzzed Victoria in her suite to remind her and she said to her, "It might be a good idea if we both wear the same stuff. I have something you'll like."

"That would be wonderful. I'll be right over."

Victoria hurried to Efemona's suite. Efemona opened the door after one knock. Victoria paused, looking over her head at the blinds, which held back the morning. "I don't believe I've ever felt this way before." Finally, she said to Efemona, "Good morning."

"Good *moarning*," Efemona said with a difference. And she thought Victoria should've said, "Your welcome," but she didn't. She didn't want to embarrass Victoria this early morning, so she overlooked it.

"Did you say you have something for me to wear, too?"

Efemona handed her a gown similar to hers, but of a different color. Then Efemona put on hers and turned to Victoria, "How do I look?"

"Turn around," Victoria said.

Efemona assumed the model's pose of Naomi and Cindy Crawford, then whirled around. Victoria looked at her critically, as if she were her creation, and she watched her face for her reaction, for her comment and approval. She got it. "Very perfect. Forever, Efemona, you'll be the idol of all women in this country for wearing the most expensive Gucci stuff that fits."

Victoria looked at Efemona critically again. "Sit down a minute, girlfriend. You do have a little problem with your eyelashes. One is about fallen off. And also you need a little more red lipstick to the corners of your lips. Want me to do it for you?"

Efemona gave Victoria the brush. "Hum, hum. You look gorgeous, girlfriend."

"I try always to look entirely myself."

Efemona watched Victoria model hers, too. They looked absolutely sophisticated with their long, pencil slim vanilla and strawberry cream velvet gowns with two shoulder straps, with the simplicity of Oscar de la Renta. Efemona's long, swirly hair shone like Diana Ross, and Victoria's like Moesha's braided hair. After all, Victoria had told Efemona once before, "Bad Dudu likes attractive women." No doubt she must look good before him, being an honor of a lifetime.

They looked at themselves. Victoria lit two cigarettes and gave one to Efemona as they watched each other in the fantastic clothes and glow of their cigarettes and smiled to each other, like conspirators in their best.

Then Victoria asked, "Do you want to go a little early?" "Sure," Efemona chatted out, because it was a bad omen to see a high official of her country for the first time and not keep the time. If she was late keeping the time, as her grandmother once told her, it's a bad omen. It could result in disagreements and quarrel. And since that time her grandmother told her that, Efemona had been very conscious of the time for appointments. She would rather be there early.

Efemona smiled and pulled her elbows close to her chest. Then her small smile disappeared. She was about to call on Victoria, who'd went into the rest room when her satellite phone went off, though it was difficult to believe she would answer it. It might be Ekiaqueta, her husband calling her to find out what she was doing. The phone rang for a long time with no answer. Then another gadget caught the attention of Victoria she'd not seen before since they've been together. It was a technical gadget in air travel which was a pager Efemona stalked on her left shoulder strap on her gown. Victoria did not ask what it might be, but hurried Efemona to the elevator to downstairs.

They exited and walked side by side. Finally, Victoria said, "It was nice having Dr. Fuck'em Good Emma in my mouth and my carnal. I should thank you again for your Movement."

"My pleasure," Efemona said.

They got into the car and Cocoyamhead started driving to Doddan Army Barracks. Efemona sat beside him, his hands on the wheel staring straight ahead. Efemona and Victoria watched the streets. The traffic was heavy, but moving swiftly. Cocoyamhead swerved left, then right, jerking, slowed down, sped up and did not intend to stop until he got to his destination for the safety of the women. Then at King Side Road before he would turn on to Doddan Army Barrack, the red light that has not functioned for a decade suddenly lit up. Cocoyamhead ran it anyway because, if he stopped, he would be surrounded by violence of smoking cars and armed robbers. Neither Victoria nor Efemona said a word.

Finally, Efemona looked behind and said to Victoria, "This damn heat in Nigeria. Are you comfortable, my dear?"

"Yes. Oh yes. I am used to it here," Victoria said.

Efemona threw her right foot out the window of the passenger's side.

Victoria exclaimed, "Ooooo! What are you doing, girlfriend?" I am sorry to embarrass you. In America, the women look more sexy when they do that before their men, whom they've just met after they separate and divorce their first, second, third . . . husbands. The men drove them to the parks where the trees and the tables and chairs and the water are lit by the moon. No doubt Emeka would've salivated to see me do it before him." Cocoyamhead salivated himself. As he looked at her shiny legs, he ran into a gutter. Then, quickly, he steadied his hands on the wheel. Efemona smiled. They were silent for about five minutes when Victoria said, "Sorry about what had happened to Emeka. It's sad good able men of this country don't live long anymore. May God sanctify his grave. I know Babagida and Dudu had planned it for all the people in the aircraft to go and *quench*."

"Isn't that something? I'm mourning Emeka in Nigeria and one would be divorced, humiliated and driven into the streets of Reno."

Victoria knew Efemona was referring to Ekiaqueta and she laughed. Then they gestured at each other. But now and then their eyes or their mouths would convey something without revealing anything. Only Efemona knows what's on her mind she was planning. Good or evil!

PART III

LET ME NOW DISCUSS IN A LITTLE MORE DETAIL HOW SOOTH SAYING BY THE ROYAL DESCENDANT CAN BE VERY EFFECTIVE IN THE RUINING OF MEN.

Chapter
19

A t last Efemona and Victoria arrived at Doddan Army Barracks. Efemona saw that the building was huge and was surrounded by hordes of men wearing *shokoto and dashiki.* But the majority of the men were wearing *Agbada:* men who by trade traffic in foreign currencies. From the horse's mouth, Efemona had learned that these people were responsible for waylaying men and women foreign tourists who visited Nigeria for business. The *Agbadas* which they wore, Efemona also learned, were specially tailored at Tafawa Balewa Street in London. The designers who are paid millions, make and design the *Agbadas* with special pockets which hold bundles of different denominations of currencies in the neighborhood of five hundred thousand dollars. The Doddan Barracks in itself did not look like the White House or the Buckingham Palace. Right there and then, Efemona knew why they moved the capital to Abuja and spent billions. But this building before Efemona as she looked around was a resemblance of Sandhurst Army Canon Depot University of Britain. The only difference Efemona noted was that it was created near the Beach of Ikoyi adjacent to the towns market and the National Mosque where flies and mosquitoes wrestle with tourists.

Efemona and Victoria watched every movement in the building from afar for a long time as people dressed in *Agbada* wandered up and down the crook's building or *what they call the Dem Mayor Necromancy Healing Home where Bad Dudu and his men made the bread to rise without an oven,* a place for *Agbada* men who are not worried about the cockroaches running on the walls and how Ojukwu's scientists can help make insecticides to fight them. Efemona began to worry. But in reality it was impossible to be in the crook's building and not be in the shadows of the great crooks in power, impossible to find oneself in a place like this and not be troubled seeing men wearing those expensive *Agbadas* already described. The presence of Efemona and not just Efemona and Victoria, the place was full of tourists, with their cameras and women with heavy buttocks and thighs and their expensive *wrappers and headties*, and women from abroad mostly from Lebanon, Thailand and Philippines, which Bad Dudu sometimes has afternoon carnal lust were there to envy Efemona and Victoria for competition. But to Efemona, the place was doomed as Ukpenu, Bornu, Irrua, Ogoni and Onitsha or like all the roads in the country, as Lot's wife was trapped in salt, and doomed, cursed, in history, that those who rule her country and other African countries, like the dictators who don't know it was good to serve their people and not lead them into starvation, but then believe in foreign banks are like Lot's wife. They will all be doomed someday, Efemona thought as she watched in bafflement the atmosphere of the place.

In contrast, Sandhurst Army Canon Depot University is where they train African soldiers in Britain. Here, they have no mosquitoes and cockroaches to wrestle with the soldiers when they were firing canons during training. The place in itself is beautified with Nigerian and other African countries' money dumped in their banks, the money other African countries don't really have, which they should've spent on their starving people.

Anyway, once Efemona and Victoria were inside the building, they were fully covered. Bad Dudu wasn't taking any chances of mosquitoes beating his invitees special guests. For your information, Bad Dudu had ordered and purchased a $3 million dollar sort of a machine from Britain which was supposed to combat the mosquitoes. To his dismay, the machine, when his novice crooks had tried to put it together, it instantly developed an electrical problem. And he knew the reason: the Britishmen had tricked him again, shipping to him a used machine which has rusted. It was then that Dudu started to realize and vowed never again to do business with Britain after Efemona has come and was gone.

Therefore, the visiting of Efemona would've been a disaster if Bad Dudu had not contacted Mr. Ikemba Ojukwu to build him a resemblance of the mosquito combat machine he and his men had ordered. Ojukwu was kind enough to go to Aba where he contacted his team of engineers who quickly manufactured one for only one hundred dollars and the machine had worked perfectly.

As Efemona and Victoria walked in closer to the building that has claimed thousands of souls vying for the hot seat, there was a gathering of more tourists and soldiers in camouflage. A young man was being whipped and dragged into an army jeep and another was saying to Efemona and Victoria, "Don't let them take him. They are going to *quench* him! They are going to kill him!"

Efemona and Victoria stopped to look. One soldier grabbed the boy, but the boy held onto his sleeve as he pulled with force. There was a loud tearing noise and a seam broke open at his shoulder. The soldier twisted around to see the damage the boy had done. As a shock to him, he yelled out as he looked poker-faced at the women.

"Ori-oda! Baguomi! You tore my khaki? I'll teach you a lesson. I tell you something boy, no man born of a woman in this country gets away with tearing a soldier's khaki. I don't care who ever it is," then he swung with his AK-47. The 15 year-old boy received the nozzle of the gun to his forehead.

"God!" the boy screamed, and put his hands to his forehead to ease the pain. Another slap followed that swept his hands away from his forehead.

Quickly, Efemona hemmed herself into the circle and grabbed the boy's hand. And the boy said, "Glad you saw that! . . . how zombies, uneducated idiots terrorize us day in and day out in this country."

Efemona was mad as hell. "Listen, soldier! You can't do that to a small boy," she yelled at him.

"I only used my gun to touch him on his forehead. He's lucky I'm still in a good mood and because I don't want his blood to splash on you and your friend wearing expensive clothes. Move away and shut your mouth or you'll get the same reward yourself." The soldier, as illiterate as he was, did not know who Efemona was. But a soldier among the crowd recognized her and whispered into his buddy's ear. With that he left the boy alone and was gone. And Efemona said to the boy, "Go home and take a bath."

But the funny thing is that no running tap in the country that produces billions of barrels of crude oil daily for billions of dollars. And the boy said, "No running tap in the country except in the North where Bad Dudu hails from."

Efemon shook her head to indicate that she knew the story of the tap water when she was in the country. That was when she must travel several miles to the river to fetch water.

* * *

At the entrance to the building, there were more security men than Efemona had seen in the rain standing with their guns. Inside the passage was a soldier sitting at the desk and two others standing as alter boys over him watching every other passersby who walked in to sign on the register.

Efemona joked as she bent over to sign into the register. "Hope I'm not signing my life away in this building to the zombies."

The soldiers heard what she said. They grind their teeths but said nothing.

Then Efemona and Victoria stood for a few minutes per order of the soldier. A few seconds later, another soldier, tall with three tribal marks on each cheek came and ushered both women into an anteroom. There in the anteroom he offered them tea. They began to sip on it gently. Efemona was immediately full of more thoughts which had baffled her for decades. She knew it was the final moment to ask Bad Dudu her nagging questions when she finally saw him for the first time.

To occupy herself not to think about her thoughts, she stood up and looked at the framed pictures on the wall. The anteroom in itself was very official looking. They'd spent some of our oil money to beautify the wall, Efemona thought. There were pots of plants in four corners of the room. A Nigerian flag hung around the corner. To the right hand corner where she sat, was a highly polished Iroko table that lay idle. There were also gigantic portraits of Muritala Mohammed, Obansanjor and famous Generals who had ruled and had yet to rule. Just slightly above Bad Dudu's portrait, the man who invited her, was the portrait of the Queen of England, which almost occupied the entire damn wall.

The face Efemona was looking at was typically gaunt, mean, but fatherly. Dudu, to her, was the darkest of the dark she'd seen in a picture. He might be actually ruthless, she thought. Everything Victoria had told her about Bad Dudu had been true. But she reserved her judgement. For instance, Victoria had said to Efemona, "Bad Dudu had been attacked every now and then by demonstrating students and by journalists who are worried about our decaying economy."

Efemona was about to say something to Victoria, when another soldier walked towards them. This time he greeted and announced curtly, *"Make una follow me, ladies."*

To Efemona, that was an insult. She shook her head as she got up. Unable to take the insult, she said, "Nigerians are made more keener to speak good English to welcome men and women into an environment like this. Look at you! Zombie! Representing your Nation, speaking jargons. *'Make una follow me,'* Efemona repeated.

'Who be Una? Who are you? All you people know in this country is to carry Uzis and massacre innocent men and women. Look at you! Cant' even respect us! You don't even know if we understand *Pidgin English.* Who are you? Huh?! Answer me, sucker! You people have given this country with millions of Ph.D.s a bad image, as if all Nigerians are like you people hungry for power, but lacking education."

The soldiers knew he was wrong, but managed to grin. He'd humor as he looked at Efemona and Victoria. Quickly, he said, *"Je m'appel Yankari."*

Efemona frowned, thinking the French people are *now* Bad Dudu's guards these days. That humor just won't do. Noticing Efemona's sarcastic face, he too, became tense. He cocked his Uzi, but held his hand. So many thoughts flashed his memory. If Efemona had been alone, he would rape the daughter-of-a-bitch and then pull the trigger and dump her goddamn body in the Atlantic Ocean and then go to Bad Dudu and tell him the Efemona of a woman has changed her mind to see him or she'd gone back to the States. Anyway, he swallowed convulsively as he grinded his teeth, but walked them to Bad Dudu's executive office.

Getting to Bad Dudu's office door, he knocked once and then, stood erect in attention then quickly, raised his right hand above his furrow saying nothing and stood a few seconds. Dudu, too, raised his right hand, then looked at him and dropped his hand before him. Finally, *Je m'appel Yankari* dropped his hand and marched away. And Efemona could hear his knocking boots in the hallway. She held her laughter.

Efemona and Victoria looked at Bad Dudu who looked like a hungry medieval Neanderthal in a Moses Ten Commandment Exodus film despite all the money he may have in Nigeria and abroad. He was tall with powerful looking arms that were similar to Evander Holyfield giving him a Tarzan-like physique, but with a face of an image in the Naira note bill. The million dollar *Agbada* he wore covered up his full military uniform, which Efemona and Victoria saw with their naked eyes as he raised his arm to sip on his tea or coffee or whatever he was drinking.

While Efemona stood she imagined his gold-like brocade lace-Agbada imported from Britain, yanked off him and sold to provide bread for the hungry, or torn to pieces to clothe the naked on the streets of Ukpenu, her village, and all the art work of the Generals and ex-Generals and Prime Ministers and the Queen's portrait arts painted by the famous *Van Gogh* he'd displayed in his office sold to provide weapons for the very poor innocent souls fighting for a true democracy. Victoria was frozen in silence. It doesn't take a genius to know what was on Victoria's mind, the word Efemona could read from her expression and looks was: "You asshole motherfucking Bad Dudu with no common sense."

Bad Dudu too, stood and found himself trembling, but knew why. Who knows what questions Efemona might ask him. For the fear that he might fumble with his answers, he radioed Adam Khan to hurry up to his office, wherever he might be. He knew Adam Khan was at the Central Bank loading up briefcases full of dollars

to travel with the next morning for him. To Bad Dudu, Adam Khan can wait another hour or so. But at this moment, he needs him to come over to interpret for him if he fumbles on his answers. Finally, he looked at his guests and summed up the courage to put out his strong, firm right hand.

After the shake of the millenium, he said, "Just a minute, young ladies," and he dialed Adam Khan.

Adam Khan arrived and shook Bad Dudu's hand, but said nothing to the women. It was right there and then the women noticed for the first time that Bad Dudu carried on his shoulder a cradled Uzi with a silencer and a dart gun. On his waist was an Hausa local made balisong, the similar deadly Filipino folding knife that could be flicked open or closed with one hand, all covered up with his huge *Agbada* he wore, upon his military uniform. Above all that, he was wearing two hats and also had a .45 caliber pistol strapped in a holster around his hip. Walking back to his seat, he looked back and said, "I had to eventually banish Wole Soyinka, due to his stubbornness of not willing to condescend on my intentions to rule for life with terror."

Adam Khan smiled to that. And Bad Dudu looked at the gorgeous women and said finally, "Good morning, ladies."

"Good morning, Chief," Victoria said.

Efemona waited a few seconds and Victoria was mute. Finally, Efemona responded with a wry grin, *"Good moarning,"* with a difference.

Then she looked at Bad Dudu, who was smiling, knowing not the boomerang Efemona would unload sooner or later. And Efemona walked to him where he sat and put out her hand and said, "What a hard man I heard you are. It seemed to me you've got a bad case against pussy envy and the people of the south."

He did not know what she meant. He held her fingers a fraction longer than Victoria's during their first shake. Adam opened his mouth, but closed it only to pretend to sigh.

"Please to seat yourself and be my guest," Bad Dudu said to Efemona. And she walked towards Victoria.

Efemona and Victoria sat on the two executive chairs facing

Bad Dudu and angled themselves so as to face him more squarely. And the executive chair Bad Dudu sat was huge that his average body, even with his huge *Agbada* on, he still occupied a small portion of the enormous chair. To add salt to his injury before Efemona, he'd parked his feets on top of his huge and long desk before considering her. Not satisfied, he clasped together on top of his head his two hands, a sign of a successful emperor, a Caesar.

Efemona and Victoria looked around the office with their shining eyes of a cat. Efemona noticed a big rotating machine directed towards her. And the machine illuminated a powerful scent and a glowing flame, which to Efemona's surprise, had been attracting the flying mosquitoes, flies and cockroaches, where they met their untimely death.

As Efemona imagined what it might've been, Bad Dudu looked at her and said, "My Efemona, welcome," with a broad smile. Then he pressed on "I need you desperately in my administration to serve the men and women of this country who have fallen pray to the bullets of my soldiers, the armed robbers of this country because of poverty. To tell you the truth, most of the armed robbers of this country are from Benin and Ukpenu. Secondly Efemona, only you can help me to treat those who had fallen by the bullets to redeem their souls. You may also help render help to pregnant women during their labor. Most important Efemona, this country needs you to inspire women of this Nation to have more babies more often, the fact that lots of men of this country would eventually lose their lives fighting for my seat. By the time I called for elections, as I have always done, only to cancel it, and more men and women and children are killed, I will have no one to rule before I die."

He paused and puffed on his Havana huge cigar and looked at Efemona for her response. While a faint smile had creased his lips, a touch of defiance entered both women's eyes as they looked back at him, which seemed almost to deepen his smile as he puffed.

Efemona, too, opened her purse and reached in for a cigarette. Lighting her cigarette, she turned her face away from his piercing eyes. Victoria couldn't take his eyes away. She wanted to capture Dudu in his weirdest moments. Efemona lighted the cigarette, saying nothing, looking at him and unwilling to be the first to appeal to accept or refuse an offer she'd came to honor. They looked at each other for precious moments and non-willing to look away. As Efemona looked deeply into his eyes, she took a long savage draws on her slim cigarette and Victoria, too, lighted one for the sake of it, seeing Efemona's style, the way she held it with her long red painted fingernails.

He admired the long, shining, painted nails. And finally, he leaned forward, and suddenly, the gaze was gone. It was as if he'd assumed a different guise as he looked at them again and spoke his mind.

"Welcome, Efemona. I have chosen you among the thousands of other candidates to be among my cabinet junta members, to fill the post of Matron General for this country-*your country.*"

As he appealed to Efemona, she, too, was thinking about what pure democracy was: that form of government in which the management of public affairs remains in the hands of the people themselves, so that they make the laws, levy taxes, decide questions of war and peace, and determine all other matters of public business of such a nature as to require personal and continuous attention, as opposed to demonstration of mental proxy which is what Fela Anikulapo Kuti, the musician jazz critic coined, "demonstration of craziness" instead of democracy. Efemona also realized that in a pure democracy, civilians should rule and the army is meant to guard their Nations in times of war and therefore blamed the Britishman who set the stage in her country for the zombies to dance when they feel the need.

The more Efemona thought of this, the more anger she felt. She was expelling smoke from her nostrils when she said, "It's an honor to serve you Bad Dudu."

She did not mean it, though her words rolled off her tongue and swelled out majestically from the depth of her soul.

"You see," Efemona said, "Nigeria is the richest country in West Africa, if not Africa. Nigeria is also a text book read by the army. You know it and I know it. It explains not how to build a Nation well, but how bad to destroy its democracy, its own learned intellectuals, and its economy. And so Bad Dudu, that is why I came into the country with

Victoria, your emissary to Reno, Nevada to accept *not* your job offer, but to inform you to hand over your government to philosophers or lawyers, men of ideology with a mission who did not attend Sandhurst Army Canon Depot University of Britain, but who attended Yale, Harvard, Stanford . . . men of goodwill who has sound education. I mean not just men, but men who can be trusted with foreign leaders when they speak and exchange ideas. So, Mr. Dudu, what is the good of an invitation if it can be declined?" She smiled. "However, if you answer my questions which I have for you without fumbling, I might consider taking the job of the Matron General of this country."

Adam Khan realized that, that is why Bad Dudu had called him to come over to interpret for him with Arabic language if he should fumble. They made eye contact and Efemona was in the dark.

Dudu looked at Efemona quizzically, as if something in her tongue tone had surprised him. He stood up and walked around his desk and then paused behind the two women's chairs. Too many thoughts: I hope I answer Efemona's questions right. Clearing his throat, he squatted before Efemona's feet.

"I need you desperately. Only you, I know of, who can relieve my despair right now."

Efemona felt herself a goddess and looked away. Finally she said, "Go and sit down on your seat, Mr. Dudu."

He was willing to get a straight answer. Efemona had no straight answer yet. She stood up and took his hands and walked him to his executive seat and sat him on it. "Sit!" Her voice was soft, gentle, confident, but not too inspiring. Well, he could hold on. She rolled her hair backwards as white people do as she, too, walked back to her seat. The question she was thinking about all crowded out at once.

"By the way, what's your real name Mr. Dudu? And what's that machine beside me for? And how did you first know you would rule this rich country? And how fair are elections in this country?"

Bad Dudu stood up and walked to the direction of Adam Khan. There was nothing to say, but he had too much to answer. He suddenly felt that he was going to cry for inviting Efemona, and panic threatened to overtake him because of the questions American people had prepared for Efemona specifically for him. But he felt the questions might not be hard as such. He would give it a try. If he fumbled and Efemona declined the job offer, fine. If she accepts it, fine. So, he puffed on his Havana cigar again and looked at Efemona.

"Well, I'll start with the second question first, Efemona." "Efemona?" Bad Dudu called out, "Let me clarify to you why I prepared for your visit. You see," quoteth Bad Dudu, "In Greek mythology, the sorceress Medea, enraged at being supplanted by a rival for the affections of her husband, Jason, decided to present the new bride with a robe possessing magic properties of power. The wearer of the robe then suffered a violent death. That death-by-indirection soon finds its counterpart in what we now know as systemic insecticides which are the chemicals with extraordinary properties that are used to convert plants or animals into a sort of Medea's robe by making them actually poisonous. This is done with the purpose of killing insects and mosquitoes that may come in contact with our skin which suck human blood. As my junta cabinet members and I did not want the mosquitoes and tse-tse flies to suck my guests' blood before they leave my office, we ordered the machine beside you Efemona, from England to combat with the flies and mosquitoes. We want you to go back to America with no scars nor blemishes on your face which might worsen the acne on top of your eyelids. This we tried to prevent."

Bad Dudu puffed again on his cigar as Efemona imagined his office as one of the absolute power offices in West Africa or in Africa. She knew that to be right, and has been so for over thirty something years when Abubakar was the first to sit on the executive seat. With that in mind Bad Dudu reminisced about the good old times before he delved into how he became the all and all. And so he looked at Efemona all over again and said, "You see, Efemona, I would be damn stupid not to answer your third question beautifully in a beautiful way. I can see that Efemona in my office with me can not see herself all over as an Ukpenu woman with morals. But I can. Part of you, as I learnt, used to be horny with various sugar daddies, and part of you is now pure ebony or copper and some of you is now gold. I tell you, Efemona, that I respect that."

He looked up at her and was frozen for a moment. How to begin his answer was obscure to him. And Adam Khan murmured a few Arabic words to him, but he'd not wanted to reveal his heinous crime he committed when he was barely 14 years old. He knew Efemona, now gold plated, was not the type of a woman to forgo hearing the why. Then he cleared his throat.

"You see! My real name is Awa-nor-Kwene Mohamadu Abacha. But I prefer Major General Bad Dudu. Sometimes they call me 'the cattle mercy' because I grew up tending cattle as a little kid in Sudan. At that time, I was slim and my arms and my head were flattened like an arrow. I was called the butcherboy because there was a time when I roasted suya on the sidewalk. My friends that time all called me Yankari, because wherever I went, I amuse people as a comedian and beautiful women love me for that. I have other nicknames, as well, but I'll leave that for now while I answer your third question first.

It happened that my dad entrusted a bride for me. A beautiful woman, of course, with a legacy of fifty herds of cattle. One day I asked my wife to follow me to graze the cattles. As we were in the field, the clouds came without warning. All of a sudden there was thunder and lightning signifying rainfall was on its way. What I did, therefore, was to behead my wife and put the head in the bag to prevent the rain from falling on her newly braided hair, which I'd paid for with seven cattles to the Alahaja, who fixed her hair for her. And I'd liked the style of the braided hair so much that I couldn't have allowed the rain to fall on my newlywed's hair."

As he told the story, Efemona knew the idiot had killed his wife and didn't even know it. And she asked, "So what happened to the body after the rain stopped?"

"I left the body lying in the field with the cattles, all grazing beside her as I was saying to her, c'mon darling, get up and let's go home. She'd ignored me. So I left her behind with annoyance."

"And did you know you'd killed her then?"

"Absolutely not. Not until I got home and pulled the head out from the bag to kiss her, when my father slapped me and yelled out that I had killed her. I didn't even know what death was. It was then that I knew I was an idiot. And since that time, knowing not what mourning was, I headed out of the house to an unknown hideaway because the parents of my wife were after me and my father who'd arranged the marriage. Since the killing of my wife, death doesn't mean a damn thing to me. Away from home for several days without food, and hearing the news that Caesar had landed in Egypt and was recruiting young men in the army, it naturally took my breath away. But Egypt was far away from our country and at that time, I'd no money handy. And believe me or not, Efemona, I couldn't eat anything for days when my British teachers told us the story of Caesar in class. "What's wrong with you? Mr. Siegle, my teacher from Britain, had asked me one afternoon, being worried as his houseboy. May his soul rest in peace. "I want to wear military clothes," I had said.

"My boy! Aren't you afraid you might be killed? You should be ashamed of yourself if you are not thinking of going to a Grammar School. And you want to become a soldier when you grow up? Do you want to tell me you want to be a killer and a dictator?" I want to be like Caesar, I told him. He was annoyed with me until he died. It did not bother me a bit. I had little money stashed away for my marriage. You know at that time, it was a young man's idea, but I was still full of action and contemplation then. My blood was hot. I was lusting for carnal knowledge, but gave it up just to accomplish my objectives first. Anyway, I spent everything I had and more besides, and bought myself a toy gun and this modern military imitation clothes like this one under my *Agbada*."

He smiled and raised his right hand up, which revealed his modern military uniform. He did not know the women had already seen it. As he brought down his hand, Efemona gave a surprisingly merry laugh, which suggested that she was forecasting his downfall within her being with the worm she was given to swallow at Akinzua Palace *which in the being of the Royal breeds citizens as Efemona concerned, can tell the future of men*. Bad Dud did not know that only Victoria knew it. Adam Khan remained mute and suddenly interrupted with Arabic language. And Bad Dudu puffed on his cigar before he continued, "Then I wrote to the Queen and Lourd Luggard who told me to come to England to fulfill my ambition for they were looked upon by all Third World countries in those times. When I got to England, I threw myself at their feet. "What do you want little Caesar?" the Queen was the first to ask me. I want to wear a military uniform as Caesar does. "Allright, but why do you have to throw yourself at our feet?"

"Because I've no money to pay to achieve my goals. And you're really crazy about being a soldier, are ya?" "Yes!" "Well, we can train you at Sandhurst Army Canon Depot University for free with little strings attached." And I did not care about the strings. So I stayed in England for three years and learnt the trade of firing different weapons. My Efemona, I'll always remember Lourd Luggard. And may Allah bless his grave. They trained me and told me to keep the riches and the wealth and money of my country coming into British Banks when I became King of the Kings in Africa. Before I knew it, I soon graduated. Since then, I have become a different man. When I am feeling down, I fire the cannon and Uzis and submachine guns, which they shipped to me. Since that time, my accomplishment has been the elimination of civilian heroes of this country, through men like me. But don't get me wrong! I wouldn't say I am Caesar, but I compared myself to Caesar at a very early age, which means that I knew firsthand one thing this country's past leaders have done: the beliefs in themselves alone and therefore, I choose not to be different. I am not proud of it, but I must be frank with you that I took over to be hostile for men of this country to fear me, the same way my buddies have done.

Pardon me, Efemona! I just want to be fair and tell you the truth. Once I emulated Caesar, I fell in love with brutality. It's easy to explain why: I took chances and strived to be ruthless, different and mean like Caesar. That's the only way I could've found myself at the helm of this huge executive chair of this country. It was a challenge I readily accepted from Lourd Luggard and the Queen of England. But I know there is a lot of men out there in this country who will try to challenge my authority. The training I received was way too much for anyone to challenge me. I know that for a fact. The one thing again that the British hammered on when they gave me (us) the Northerners power was that we must honor them. In the years since they gave us the power, many of the views of my forefathers who'd ruled with iron hand law, killed, maimed, were far-sighted, that with my regime, mine is one-sided. The Britishmen believe that Nigeria truly needs a strong alternative voice. I do not want to pick on those who say we're illiterate and cannot rule, but let's face it: our country is a country at war with itself. Why it had intelligent brains like Wole Soyinka and Enahoro and Ojukwu, to mention but a few, has resources any country would envy, everything it does is suspect because of the intelligent brains from the South, and because Wole Soyinka, for instance, is the voice of the challenge to us novices in a democratic process. So a good Caesar-with a reputation for being trained as a true Caesar, can go-for-the jugular in repressing its citizens. They might say, a good leader should be clean of corruption, but in a sense, it's a democratic no-no. But it's imported. So as Caesar was a very modern man, indeed I emulated him in a way such as having mobs on his calendar, then at forty, discovering that handling a provincial army was child's play to a man accustomed to manipulating his people, then conqueror and head of state, then by force of circumstance and gaminess for destiny, a political novice, gambling not with Pompey, but with wise men of this country, the USA of Africa, the civilized men of this country made uncivilized by guns and canons and motars, then winning and ready to rule for life."

There was a dangerous quietness in Efemona's being. She was reading him as a text book as he talked. The page she was analyzing was ancient hieroglyphics when men in this country were not yet civilized, but now in this century, she realized while Nigeria was degenerating rather than moving forward as other countries with natural resources. She did not want to recollect the fact that it was in the 18th century that Britain became deeply involved in the internal affairs of Nigeria as a result of its efforts to eradicate commerce in human slavery. All she knew was that the first British Colony in her country was established in Lagos in 1861, which is now the commerce capital. And in 1900, she noted that a policy of indirect rule through the traditional rulers which had acted as agents in the Colonial Masters administration was adopted. During that time, traditional rulers, mostly from the North according to records, were not very literate and yet the Englishman gave them the elliptical power. No wonder the economy of our country has been ruined, she thought. Efemona blamed Luggard for his hindsight, though Luggard's success in Northern Nigeria at the time was as a result of indirect rule which called for governing the protectorate through the traditional rulers who themselves were not well informed in education. Her stomach became full of rocks when she recollected that under the system of indirect rule at the time, those that were made to have a technical share of the pie, were transformed into salaried district heads and so authorities, soon became responsible for peacekeeping and tax collecting within respective districts.

Aha! Efemona nodded her head, noting that what she'd thought of was a reality which was that, the Britishman tactics, rebellion, if it should exist, would be suppressed immediately by the familiar faces of the leaders and not again by the Colonial Masters themselves. Efemona then made a queer, resentful face at Bad Dudu. And watching the morning rise gradually, and still thinking of what her father had told her that most of the activities at the time were awarded the Emirs of the North through the protectorates and the local administrators were subjects to the Britishman's approval.

Damn! Efemona swallowed the bile in her gut, realizing that it was during that era that a dual system of law functioned, the notable sharia (Islamic law), though it was only in the South, where she, herself hailed from, that predominantly Christians reside, who can read and write.

Bad Dudu and Adam Khan could tell that Efemona was thinking deeply. What it was that made her make a face at Dudu as Adam Khan interpreted to him in Arabic, he couldn't tell. He puffed on his cigar and looked at Efemona deeply in the face.

"Let me tell you the machine business story, by the way. My cabinet members and I voted to purchase it. I'd negotiated a contract with Adam Khan to purchase the mosquito machine for three million pounds from Britain. For some reason, Adam Khan did what he had to do. You know how we are in this country? Adam Khan is a part of us. He knew me more than anybody else. So what he did was split the money into half, went to England and bought the machine for a fraction out of the three million pounds. He deposited some into his account and some into my account. We were all happy. And you know the British people like money. They rushed the machine to us on a First Class Delivery. But guess what, Efemona?! The machine did not function when my electricians put it together. I had to quickly invite Mr. Ikemba Ojukwu who came down to my office to try to fix it. He was unsuccessful. On his careful observation, he found out that the machine was one and the same all other Third World countries of the world had refused because it was outdated and rusted inside and we had no good engineers to make it work. Initially I had thought Mr. Ojukwu could make it work, that was why we ordered it and pocketed most of the money, hoping no one would ever know. You see, Efemona, Mr. Ojukwu is a man who believes so much in himself. He requested that I give him only one hundred Naira which is an equivalent to less than a nickel in the United States. He rushed to Aba and manufactured one in his factory, which he says cost him less than the one hundred Naira. He gladly gave us the balance of forty Naira out of the money. It is the machine on your left. You go take a look at both machines. Go on! And tell me if you notice any difference from the British made mosquito machine and that of Ikemba made at Onitsha."

Efemona, first of all, looked at Adam Khan with silent hatred. Then got up and walked to the machines and observed them carefully. Finally, she said, "How come you didn't return the other machine to Buckingham Ltd. for a full refund of the machine?"

Some kind of atavistic instinct told him where Efemona was heading. He ignored the question.

Efemona said anyway, "By the way, I don't see any difference from the imported machine and the one made by Ojukwu himself at Aba."

"I know that, Efemona. It is why I kept the machine here with that of Ojukwu to try to inform my administration members that it was time to wake up in this country. I know on the day of such meeting when I would try to put the motion on the floor, some of my junta members would hate me. But believe me, Efemona, that I am heading towards that direction, that one day I'll wipe out corruption and stamp out imported goods and approve made in Nigeria goods stamped Ibos."

Efemona and Victoria laughed mirthlessly. Efemona thought of Bad Dudu's comment: If your gut feeling is your only source of good information you're telling us now, you'd better find other of your administration not to challenge you, because you are the President, you can veto, and that's the truth. Corruption will never cease, and that's the truth and it remains to be seen. Nor have I come to listen to your crap because corruption must exist. I think you damn idiots have better topics to discuss on the day you have the nerves all of which are only maybe some figments of your exploitative, dictator innuendoes to convince me to accept the post of Matron General of this country.

Bad Dud did not know what Efemona and Victoria were each thinking. After a few seconds, he asked, "What dialects do both of you speak?" He did not wait to hear their reply. He faced Efemona. "I know you are now Americanized. Speak a little Yankee doo-doo slang I can understand, or do I still need Adam to interpret. I know you came from the real West-a little city they call Reno, in Nevada, where the judges and the Samsons and Hercules of Circus are one and the same, where the judges believe that what one judge had said can influence the others' decisions, therefore burying the truth."

They all laughed, though Efemona's laugh was a mocking type. Just in time, Judas Iscariot and Princess Akinzua walked in to save the question of the moment Efemona was thinking of answering. Judas snapped his fingers at old Adam Khan, the man whom you know by now, who after carrying his one-millionth briefcase full of millions of Nigerians crude oil money out of the country was radioed in too, to be with Bad Dudu in case he should fumble answering Efemona's question, was put out to warm the chair before Efemona and Victoria where he could drink, smoke, talk and interpret with Arabic and take it easy like the club members.

Adam Khan, of course, ignored the snapped fingers, and Judas snapped again and called out, "Hey!"

Judas winced and said, "Any good result yet from Efemona?" "The President and I were on the verge of asking Efemona to accept the job when you walked in."

Bad Dudu nodded. In truth, I'd find it less repugnant to shoot Efemona before Victoria than offer her a bribe to accept the post for which I invited her to fill.

Efemona regarded Judas Iscariot, whom as I learnt, are now good buddies, dressed in his ancient uniform of blazer and turtleneck, which to Efemona, Iscariot must've seen the outfit in a gossip clothing ad with a Corvette in the background and decided to stick with it, but changing only the colors. The only difference this time was that Iscariot had changed the turtleneck from red to blue and his blazer from white to red. In itself, the outfit would not draw much attention because he wanted to show how wretched he is and Bad Dudu can award more contracts to him to make more dubious money. At least, Iscariot had not walked in wearing a combination so iridescent sharkskin suit. So Efemona said to him, "Can I have the Omega or Rolex Seamaster?"

"I am poor. I can't afford another one."

"That's what they all say when they have all the money stacked in pillows and love seats in their houses," Efemona said and Victoria laughed.

The joke finally lapsed. Efemona said to Bad Dudu, "No, Mr. President Dudu, you don't need an interpreter."

As Bad Dudu looked again at the gorgeous women, he could feel his head aching, not from hangover at the officers' mess the day before, but from what Victoria had told him before she left for Reno, Nevada to get Efemona. She'd said, "Be careful. Efemona is full of questions like her husband who is a writer and a reporter." As Bad Dudu was in deep trance, Efemona answered his question and said, "I'm from Ukpenu, South of Benin City. Victoria, I believe is from Mberi from the Eastern part of the country, which you probably already know, but just pulling on my nerves. But tell me, Mr. Dudu! How could you and your junta members want to rule for life?"

The question baffled Princess Akinzua, and she walked from her seat, moved towards Bad Dudu, glowering, who seemed to wait for an occult go-ahead signal from Adam Khan who had it in his heart to raise his index finger to interpret for Dudu in Arabic. Because Princess Akinzua's ass was too big and covered the face of Judas and Adam Khan and slightly that of Efemona's face, she threw both arms around Bad Dudu, throwing Dudu off balance with her question. If the President answered Efemona's question right, there would be no problem. They could be awarded more contracts and more contracts in their relation's and ghost relation's name. Then the Princess grinned up into Efemona's face for the obnoxious question, and Judas was inscrutably watching, and Bad Dudu was waiting to answer the question of the century. Thus, Efemona, the African woman with balls, had just started what the American society had taught her, Dudu thought and grinded his teeth.

*   *   *

And so Efemona frustrated Bad Dudu for the first of several questions she has for him. Dudu sighed deeply, hit bottom, so to speak, because this is not the first question Bad Dudu would double fault in his answers. He stood up from his chair. He stomped again to it, missed the seat and plopped to the floor. The sheer indignity of it all only compounded the frustration he felt throughout his trying to answer the question as he'd stood before against Efemona, the relentlessly flippant mouth. He saw how hunched up her painted red lips and dark eye-brows painted with silver or gray had looked when she asked the question to cajole and humiliate him to tell him who are his forefathers anyway, who'd ruled this Nation before him. Though he had vengeance built up inside of his being, he smiled. The smile which means bombshell and damn Efemona for accepting to come see him for the vacant post. Then to tell Efemona he was the man in charge, he parked his feet on his desk, a sign of a successful emperor. Finally, he said, "I picked up the meaning of the lectures from all the British teachers who taught me and my men at Abudu Elementary School, that this country must be ruled by only men from the North. It was what first motivated me to appeal to the Queen and Lourd Luggard. I also knew my people need strong men to rule them and not eat themselves alive because life in Nigeria is war. And what do I mean by that? I mean strong men who could con and wreck the entire Nation. My definition of con men is similar to voodooism. In voodooism, as in this country, you use your opponents weakness to win. In con men's activities, namely my father's and now me, too, you use and equate their greed. The strongest make the first move, and the men you selected on your side do the rest of the job and say 'yessir, yessir, yessir!' to the strongest man on top."

Adam Khan, Judas and the Princess thought the President had fumbled with his answers. Their horns could be seen sticking out of their heads, when the President noticed the frustration on their faces.

The President did not ask why. They all sat motionless. The band that was playing in the West Wing of Doddan Army Barracks had just stopped. And Adam Khan said to all, "Why don't we all go to the West Wing and listen to the band play for Efemona and Victoria?"

Bad Dudu understood why Adam had requested him and his guests to listen to the band. He knew he'd fumbled with his answers and so he accepted to listen to the music to relax his brain for more bombshell questions from Efemona when they return back to his office.

Efemona and Victoria and all of them walked to the West Wing of the Barrack where dignitaries are welcomed to listen to *Arabic, Apala and Asonogun music.* Here, the President closed the door behind his guests. Efemona and Victoria were again in the anonymous, stage, surrounded by locked doors. Efemona found her handkerchief and wiped her forehead, thinking of the more thousand questions she would wage before the man she came to see. Bad Dudu rang for the elevator. Finally, it arrived, driven by a woman whose buttocks was heavy and eating *Gala.* They arrived at their destination and all walked out and headed to special seats reserved for Bad Dudu and his guests. They all sat and listened to *Arabic music first, then Owanbe,* and more in order of importance from the new talent Newton, who then decided on his own accord to play some jazz and R&B music for Efemona and Victoria. Newton's recent talent was outshining old talent which naturally took Bad Dudu's breath away, that seeing Newton advertised on the Daily Newspaper, he recognized the name and invited him to play for Efemona. Describing the young talent and the excerpts for Efemona from the Newspaper, then extolling the unorthodox virtues of Doddan at the West Wing where they are now and Newton playing for her to welcome her and Victoria, Efemona became joyful. She felt herself a goddess and somebody before Bad Dudu.

As they sat and watched, the *unorthodox of the crooks in Agbada, of the hungry and beggers* all filled the room, which was huge, ceilings with asbestos and Bad Dudu and his men don't even know asbestos has been banned in developed countries for causing cancer. Only Efemona knew this. She thought, what are the zombies doing with our money! She has another question to ask the President. At the far end, close to the stage, the room widened, making space for more chairs and tables. And a very wide hallway led to the restrooms. In this widened space, stood the young, talented, small band of four men and one woman.

Newton was stepping down for his break with his musicians, all. The musicians were heading down from the stage and wiping their foreheads and brows with handkerchiefs, and heading towards Efemona to shake her hand before she exited to the street door, where a soldier stood with his AK-47 guarding for intruders who would violate Efemona's privacy with Bad Dudu. Little did Efemona know that the band leader was his brother and the one and only woman in the band was also Anegbo, her famous sister, who, to refresh your memory, was the one who had *poisoned her husband- to-be with fruit from her garden and then inherited his wealth after his death.*

The heat in the room was alarming and the electric fans and air conditioners were all broken and no one in Bad Dudu's junta regime did anything to fix it. So what had happened to all the oil money this country generates for sale to the United States and to the rest of the world? Efemona pondered for another question when they go back to the President's office. The room in itself stank: Of years of dust, of regurgitated corruption, of women carnal heat and lust, of sweat, of evil atrocities to eliminate intellectuals, of banishments and of dubious talks. People stood two or three or four, all in *Agbada* and/or with their military uniforms all happier than the musicians who had been invited to play to promote their talent to Efemona. Most of the people sitting around their tables had not moved. They were all enjoying their booze. In the long hallway heading to Bad Dudu's office, the musicians stood patiently, all still wiping their faces and their brows before Efemona. In truth, they were conveying a message to Efemona, that Efemona should act on behalf of the country to tell Bad Dudu they had enough of their country's money lying idle in Britain and the Swiss Banks.

Two of the musicians stood, blandly watchful, ignoring the panhandlers who'd sneaked in, giving the soldier guarding the entrance their last *Kobo* to allow them to enter to beg the musicians for money. The policemen who walked up and down with their lips opened and their eyes closed after taking bribes from poor citizens who want to see and view Efemona from a distance, remain more blind with unnamable suspicions and fears to denounce Bad Dudu for corruption because they were into it themselves.

Efemona wished she'd not come, but was glad she'd come sitting with Bad Dudu joyfully in the room of this sweltering medieval gaunt faces, being the only stranger in her own country. Though to Efemona, it was not a new sensation, she had knowledge of this for a long time, before she'd left the country. But now she would be known after she brought down Dudu's government. The band again began to play *Sunny Ade Owanbe* music. Efemona was not too interested in folk lore music anymore, but managed to stay until the music stopped.

They all walked back to the President's office. On their way, Efemona said to Bad Dudu, "I strongly admired you for your braveness."

"And why is that, Efemona?" Dudu found himself saying. "Because your answer to my question before we went for the music leisure was shocking to me. I'll tell you the truth. I, too, have the same idea against my husband when I go back to the states."

Though Bad Dudu was relieved for a few seconds, he still was not sure if Efemona and Victoria understood him. So he turned to Efemona and said, "I can perhaps demonstrate my point with this soccer ball beside me."

Actually it was Adam Khan who'd told him what to say. "Oh! Ooh!" beamed out of Efemona. What point is he trying to convey to me now! She thought. Finally she asked anyway. "What point do you want to demonstrate, Mr. President?" Efemona asked boldly.

"That me and my junta members from the North are meant to rule in this country," Bad Dudu said with impunity.

"You go ahead and demonstrate it for us then," Efemona said, too, but having her country in her soul.

Efemona and the rest of them watched Bad Dudu stood up and pick up the soccer ball beside his desk on the floor and said, "Efemona and Victoria, please stand up and play with me."

They stood. Dudu passed the ball to Victoria and Victoria then passed it on to Efemona. Efemona dribbled and took a long shot and it hit the wall, and the ball bounced back to Dudu. Dudu, for the record, in this soccer match had scored four goals and Efemona had two assists, but fumbled to lose to 4-1 victory over the Northerners. Dudu had stunned the first goal when he tossed the ball with his head backwards and then hit the portrait of Tafawa Ballewa on the wall, which was a goal. Then Efemona passed the ball to Victoria again. Victoria tried to dribbled Bad Dudu. But Dudu was too good to be dribbled. And so, she lost the ball to Dudu, then Dudu dribbled the two women, then tossed the ball overhead of Efemona and the ball went straight and hit the picture of Shehu Shagari on the wall. To Bad Dudu and the rest of the crooks, like Adam Khan, Judas and Princess Akinzua who were watching that was a goal. And they all stood ovation and prayed a silent prayer that Dudu will not fumble again and score another goal.

When all had relaxed enough for a half-time, Victoria again passed the ball to Efemona at the mid office this time, then ran forward to dribble Dudu once, then twice, but didn't want to fumble. She halted the ball and then bent over and carried the ball with her bare hands, then ran around Dudu's desk. Adam Khan and the rest of them were amazed. They did not know what was on her mind.

"No, no, no, no, no, that's a violation of the rules," Dudu yelled out. "That's rude. Put the ball down and use your feet."

Efemona ran forward and outran Dudu for the ball, as Victoria sat the ball down. Efemona shot the ball past him, but missed her target. The ball bounced back to her. She had the ball again with her bare hands, but remembered it was a violation of the rule of the game. Then she sat the ball down and passed it on again to Victoria, but the President intercepted it and yelled out, "My aim and objective is to improve the way we play this game in this country," he explained.

Finally, Dudu struck again when he threaded the ball through the defense of Efemona and Victoria. He'd scored again on a high angled shot to the portrait of Babagida that shattered the glass of the framed portrait. He got another ovation from his crooks looting the Nigerian economy. And that made Efemona mad as hell.

Efemona passed the ball to Victoria again and Victoria passed the ball back to her. "We are yet to score even a goal," Efemona chatted out from her soul.

"Over my dead body!" Dudu said and watched Efemona dribble him, but fell, leaving Dudu with the ball. Then quickly, he took another long shot and hit the portrait of Ali Bukutu after Efemona's mistake, who then had tried to pass the ball to Victoria when she knew she'd barely made contact with Victoria. Instead of the ball flying up to the portrait of the man she'd tried successfully to aim at, the ball bobbled straight to the grateful man in *Agbada* with his proud military khaki uniform underneath and scored again from a close range on the face of another portrait of still a Northerner. That surprised Efemona. "Hum! The living and the dead go nuts in this office. It looks like you visited a burial ground to invoke the spirit to win us. I, too, will visit a burial ground to invoke my grandmother's spirit on my husband in America. So that when I go back, he would be made a complete zombie, like you Dudu."

The joke on spirits elapsed and Efemona retrieved the ball and stood looking at the portraits on the four walls. She looked directly into their faces and carried the ball with her bare hands, not caring about the noise Dudu and his crooks watching were making. Efemona fell down on her face, but picked herself up, bruised and bleeding, but limped toward the frightened Dudu, who was then aware of what Efemona was willing to do, murmuring softly as he approached to grab the ball from her to put it down.

Efemona whined, then shut her mouth to allow Victoria to retrieve the ball from her, still on the floor in pain.

"Now what, smart ass?" Dudu asked.

"Treat with Ben Gay ointment, rest and then we can play it with our bare foots again? Or a quick bullet to the brain, to relieve the pain and no more telling you to put the ball down and play it according to the rules of the game-the usual rule of the game I know of, all over the world or-?"

Adam Khan, Judas and the Princess all stood ovation for their man not fumbling. He was in control. The question scared Victoria and therefore considered treatment for Efemona as if she was in her position. Victoria knew Efemona was in serious pain and was badly hurt when she'd ran into the mosquito machine. Dudu had a soft heart. And for the sake of Allah, he considered Victoria's pleading and treated Efemona with Ben Gay.

The game resumed and Victoria applauded Efemona for her courage of not quitting. Victoria passed the ball to Efemona. And Efemona, bold enough, not caring what Dudu was saying, "Put the ball down, let's play it with our legs," it was too late. Efemona eyed the face of Obansanjo, then carefully bounced the ball on his face. "There, that's what I'm talking about."

Dudu frowned. "That's very rude of you." He looked at the joyous Efemona and said, "Lest you don't know, Romulus executed his own brother Remus for disobeying Rome's first law. And even Saddam Hussein executed his own brother for turning his back against him."

Efemona caught him in the middle of his words. "What's that supposed to mean mother-? You can execute me if you want."

Now you can tell Efemona's balls were getting larger and larger in-between her thighs.

Bad Dudu sighed deeply. He heard what Efemona had said or else they got the bullet. No one had ever challenged his words nor his authority when he was talking. Paying no attention to what Efemona said, he said, "I mean even the Pope is allowed to feel hatred, so long as it is directed against the devil."

Efemona didn't need to be told that Bad Dudu meant she was a devil for scoring the lone goal against the Northerners, who had the baton in their hands all those years, fooling the Ph.D.s and philosophers of her country. She eyed him sarcastically.

Finally, Efemona said, "My husband had told me I had the devil's horns on several occasions. Some men I have intimidated during my rally of AWAM movement in Reno, Nevada had shouted profanity at me for having the devil's horns. The President will not be the last to think that I have the devil's horns." She paused. "Mr. Dudu?" she called out. "If you believe I have the devil's horns, why don't you blow your horns and set all people you repress in this country free?"

His face became veiled, though Efemona did not care to look at his face. "The way we play the game in this country is to respect the first law of my authority: the first and foremost-Muslim brotherhood with General ranks in uniforms to rule for life. *Who talk go quench!*"

"The second law is to allow us to drain the oil reserve of this country and me and my advisers have at least ten billion dollars in foreign banks, siphoned through Lebanese businessmen and women who are *fair in complexion, like Oyinbo people,* the only people we trust most to guard us and cook for us as we rule. And if my people, whom we govern, know the truth and air their grievances through an underground movement or fliers or through newspapers without our censorship, they stay in jail for life or choose between a pound of flesh or a hole in the head, whichever one they prefer." Dudu smiled, and looked at the framed picture of a frog holding a sign of, "A clean desk is a sign of a sick mind." And Efemona caught his glance at the framed picture, which she interpreted to mean that all the documents on his desk were awaiting signature to siphon billions out of his country to foreign banks. Seeing Efemona looking at the framed picture of the frog, he diverted his gaze to look at the 'Merchant of Venice' textbook on his desk at the far right hand corner. Efemona, for the first time, saw it too, and thought perhaps he was about to take a pound of flesh from her if she was asking too many questions to humiliate him, the pound of flesh and nothing but the flesh might be taken.

She was in the midst of mobs, crooks of all time to which no General from the South eats with a golden spoon. Outside of the Doddan Barracks where she looked through the glass fronted window, she saw big lorries (cars) that had all choked on the streets, laborers from Ukpenu, from Aba, Ogoni, Bornu stood on these ghostly platforms, moving great weights of wood, water, the burden for beasts and all what not, and cursing the day Bad Dudu was born in Sudan to come to Nigeria to fool us that he was a born

Nigerian. Efemona had witnessed these hardships and lonely once before, before she left the country to America. She had seen it all, the awareness of the soldiers and policemen taking one or more Nairas from the poor motorist on roadblocks somewhere in the middle of the roads where there are no street lights. And coming to see Dudu again, Efemona felt totally estranged from Ukpenu in which she was born.

The remembrance of her loneliness at the maternity she was stationed to be paid *ten and ten pence* in a country that billions of dollars was stolen on a daily basis, erupted in her stomach. Efemona looked around in the spacious office occupied by Bad Dudu, and the loneliness she'd felt all those years before she left the country magnified and then now that she was with Dudu face to face, she wondered if more women and children growing up might be given chances to make money in an oil rich country, now with an empty treasury, Bad Dudu and his Northern crooks has emptied for their pocketbook.

She rattled in her brain why! Bad Dudu and his groupies in his administration are bold. Nothing worries them. It was the damn goddamn Sharia Courts which they believe in and fucking Lourd Luggard that started the fire in our Nation. And the Sharia is now affecting the general lives of the entire Nation. A Sharia Muslim thing that was meant by Luggard to deal with matters that were affecting the personal status of the Muslims alone. This is bullshit, Efemona thought and swallowed. She looked up at the crooked face and imagined Luggard in this present time, and the consequence of Indirect Rule he adopted, Hausa-Fulani domination to be the instrument of politics. Bullshit!

The Hausa-Fulani-a race within the Northern belt that do not believe in education, but rather in Arabic. Bullshit!

Looking at Bad Dudu again with silent hatred, it pained the fuck out of Efemona to remember that though these people couldn't read or write as herself, the Britishman saw fit, that they were the people to rule for life where she was born. Bullshit!

The remodeled Efemona! The civilized Efemona! She knew why Luggard gave them the power, because they can manipulate them to the best of their advantage, and not to the advantage of Nigeria as a Nation if they should hold fair elections in the country she was born. Bullshit!

Yes, that was the true reason Luggard almagamated North and Southern Nigeria in 1914. The almagamation has ruined us as a nation. Bullshit!

The more loneliness Efemona felt in those days when she was paid *ten and ten pence*, the more bullshit she echoed from the depth of her being. Finally, Efemona delivered in a slow cadence and with a heavy Yankee style of Reno, Nevada cowgirl accent. The message was a soul-stirring one. Considering the circumstances under which she said it and delivered it-that of genuine concern for her country, she said, "You people are dangerous for my country, Mr. Dudu."

Bad Dudu was shocked and so were Adam Khan, Judas and Princess Akinzua, all who walked out to let Dudu handle his business with Efemona the way he feels. If he chose to be insulted by a woman he invited to the country, that's his problem. As they walked out, he began to feel out of his depth. He frowned. That just won't do. With a gesture of defiance, he used his fist to hit the brick wall of his office behind his chair on which he sat.

The wall caved in. He yelled out, "You don't agree with me, that we will rule for life. I can use a relay race baton to demonstrate my point. Needless to get on our marks here or on our knees. I'll tell you right now, that I'll hand over the baton to my man."

"And who is your man?"

"Abdul Salami, my right hand man who will, perhaps, fool the Nation more than me," Dudu said with impunity.

Victoria looked at Efemona. And Efemona looked at the hole on the wall. Both women became scared, as the sound before them was like gun fire, fired from a cannon at Sandhurst Training Depot in Britain, when Dudu was there fifty years ago. The sound made them bolt out of their chairs.

Victoria finally drew herself together and sat. But Efemona, though she drew herself up against Bad Dudu's table, she, too, clutched a dainty tight fist to her breast. Finally, Efemona looked up and met Dudu's eyes. Both stared at each other, playing the same tough me or each willing to bow. Efemona wondered at the man before her. He was neither conventionally good looking nor charming. He lacked humor, mean. He has absolute power to put men behind bars for life and let them rot there. He was ruthless, so she learnt. "Geeze!" she said silently.

Bad Dudu sat motionless and frozen. But his eyes, always rigid for beautiful women from abroad, flitted to Efemona's chest. In the light of his office, he had an opportunity to observe Efemona closely for the first time *even when he was about to be disgraced and humiliated.* Efemona sighed and looked at him. Both had opposite thoughts. To Bad Dudu, Efemona wasn't too tall a woman. Her hair was long and colored gold. Her eyebrows and eyelashes were long and very dark, whether by art or by nature, he couldn't tell. He had wanted to ask Efemona: Have you transplanted your clitoris to be a dick? But he reserved the question. All he knew was anything was possible with the Americans. They must've colored the hair for her to show off to him or place a dick in her triangle. If it was, as Dudu finally concluded within himself, it was done very artistically by her salon hair dresser, or her doctors. But there was something more baffling, he thought: those funny looking spots on top of her eyelids. They must be there because of her evilness and her ability to ask questions. However, there was still something goddess-like about Efemona's face when it was in repose, and she had the most innocent eyes he had ever seen in ages-cynical, as mermaid possessed. She wore excellent clothes and she'd all the ease of manner as an American trained nurse, and yet there was something about her that was incongruous. You felt that Efemona was a mystery woman, probably because of Hollywood influence and no longer afraid to air her feelings and her views.

In contrast, Efemona had a different notion about Dudu. The main question she had always wanted to ask men of the man before her eyes, had nothing to do with the matter at hand-the invitation to accept a position under Dudu's administration. She swallowed. Dudu might know how to drag *red vines twist licorice* when he made love to women, but does that show he knows how to screw and make good love as compared to American men, who of late, made her happy screwing her for hours and then she released her passions, something unusual with African men who release before the women and then get up, leaving the woman in bed and not caring about their feelings? And if the man before her knows how to screw, will he describe it to her so she could write it in her diary and use the same method described to her by Dudu to sleep with different men of gaunt faces to humiliate a particular man in America when she returns to America? For now, she would rather confront him with the baffling questions that have puzzled her for decades. And maybe he might step down and call for an election for a true democracy for her people. Or he would meet his untimely death like the mosquitoes with the machine beside her, when she cursed him with the worm her grandmother gave her to swallow at the Oba's palace. So Efemona kept the nagging question to herself. Do gaunt faces similar to Dudu in African countries who are Presidents have more fun like the judges in Reno, Nevada who drive by Fourth and Second Street looking for black women prostitutes to navigate and make them have an orgasm even though they have no clitoris? And there Efemona and the President were each thinking opposite thoughts. It was easy for Efemona to ask more questions and move on with Dudu who seemed to have no agenda for the people he rules, but fumble with answers in mid-sentence, the moment something else popped into his head.

Dudu stood abruptly, and Efemona thought he was ready to cut a pound of flesh, but suddenly said, "Do you want me to show you around Doddan Army Barrack Depot?" which for now had ended the animosity between two powerful people: Efemona and Bad Dudu.

Chapter

20

E femona sat patiently and considered herself a philosopheress of the future of her country. Human animals, for instance, have no willpower. Bad Dudu may or may not have it. Nigeria came into her full consciousness. An inhuman animal, such as Bad Dudu, can be tempted in my own trail of thoughts. She allowed herself a small smile and wiped her lips with her tongue in a sexy American fashion. This time, she thought to herself, I will wait for the right time to tempt him. So the two women stared at the President throughout his moment of silence and thoughts. His eyes became cold and calculating. But he was calculating the impossible with Efemona. While Efemona's eyes burned into him like tongues of flaming fire, which he could not detect because he was in heat of her carnal lust, he was also no such a fool not to notice the stare of hatred for him. He could not tell, but something in his soul told him so. And just then, Efemona came up with another question for him. She asked, "Will the election you planned to hold in this country next year be fair? And I want you to tell me how fair elections in this country have been since zombies have been in charge of our executive office."

It was one of the few select issues that touched Efemona's universal nerve before she left Reno, Nevada with Victoria which she must ask the President because she knew and had been told by underground sources that personalities of great challenge to the President during election formation are place on death penalty- that of Saro Wiwa, for instance who is a renounced writer and voice of the people during elections in Nigeria, whose case made headlines when Efemona was in Nigeria.

Dudu's junta administration pronounced the death penalty, accusing him of killing his own people for his gain to ascend the nomination of running against him as the President of his country. But did Saro Wiwa actually commit the crime Dudu accused him of? Only a few people know the answer to that question. To Efemona, numerous innocent people have been executed by Bad Dudu's government, that's a fact, without question.

Anyway, Bad Dudu blamed himself for allowing Adam Khan to go after his own business. This was the time he needed him the most for Arabic interpretation of what he would say for his answer. Shall I tell Efemona the truth? He considered it a long time. Finally, the spirit of Efemona was all over him.

"I must be frank with you that during the formation of different parties in this country, *I consider myself first* and then consider the death penalty second, which is automatically in effect to those applicants who are over qualified in this country. Me, the self-described champion of the people for my party vs. the very literate personalities on death row or penalty or in exile, then we buy all the votes from North to South without challenge from anyone." Dudu paused.

"If there were protests from New York to Washington D.C. my Ambassador, I mean Mr. Gambari, was asked to secretly videotape the demonstrations and send their pictures to me where I instruct my secret police to wait their arrival at the airport and quietly silence them until the elections were over. And even when the elections were over, they were never to be seen again." He paused again.

"We stuffed ghost ballots. And what do I mean by that?"

"Geeze, you keep asking me stupid questions. How do I know? You tell me!," Efemona said.

"Sorry. I mean I'm talking about ballots arriving at polling stations at the same time in the same style envelope we printed in our head office. You know, ghost ballots when you open it and they smell *sosorobia* and *suya*." He paused.

"In our polling stations, we have no deadline." He paused.

"My system is not opened up to alternative candidates, which might spoil my candidacy for the post of President when I throw away my military uniforms: Same thing my predecessor had done. For instance, Mr. Abiola winning the elections with a landslide was never allowed to rule. He ruled in prison." He paused.

"We wring the elections. And how do we do that?" "Are you asking me? Shit, I don't know. You tell us."

"We count our goats, cattle, herons, chickens, anything we could think of that would make us win with a landslide over any party that are not really heard of that we already paid off with millions of dollars to shut them up."

Answering the questions and as it flowed from his mouth, the two women were moved. They knew all along that he was not lying. But as the women stared at him again and again, his whole body trembled under his *Agbada* and military uniform underneath. He knew again he'd fumbled for the truth. He closed his eyes, but "Why me, Efemona?" was imprinted on the back of his eyelids. He mustn't allow Efemona's spirit to burn into him to reveal secrets to her, but indeed her spirit was working the miracles. Finally, he relaxed. Her spirit might work on me, but I must not allow her to intimidate me just because she's the most qualified for the post I desperately needed someone to fill. An American trained nurse, for that matter!

As he opened his mouth, his voice was calm and reasonable. Why he does what he does was revealed. "Money," he said, "Are the chief reasons for a conqueror of the world," then he looked at Efemona and smiled. "Quote me. I know that to be true. Why do you think I do all those things I listed for you? And why do you think I seized power? I believe in Caesar, my dear!"

Dudu wondered what Efemona was thinking as he talked. Victoria's eyes also had carried Efemona back to that moment, nearly five years ago, when she was wrestling with the rats and roaches in Ewu maternity wards when she was not paid for nearly five months. Finally, Efemona smiled a thoughtful, baffled smile. Then she unloaded a word for the wise only for him to understand, that the Oval Office in D.C. might be silent for now, but sooner or later, they will quietly remove him, too, as he too, did to Mr. Abiola.

"You know, Mr. Dudu!" Efemona cried out, "One thing I cannot understand is that the Americans who believe in true democracy and who policed all the world leaders, will not help the people of this country against people like you who are dictators and oppressors."

She paused and lighted a cigarette. "You know, the Oval Office believes that the truth about assassination of foreign leaders should quietly be carried out because democracy, to the Americans, depends upon a well-informed electorate."

Efemona searched her inner soul and figured out as a philosopheress, U.S. foreign policy throughout the world. The Americans in truth, she noted, has helped plot various covert operations world-wide. So she looked at Dudu. And Dudu knew she was about to enlighten him. She said to Dudu, "You are free to count with me, if you will." She recollected before him:

- Kill Fidel Castro of Cuba.
- Kill Colonel Moammer Gadhafi of Libya.
- Kill Lumumba of Congo.
- Supply weapons to dissident in the Dominican Republic to silence Trujillo.
- Encourage South Vietnamese to plot and overthrow Diem's regime.
- Supply all the necessary intelligence and weapons that overthrew Marxist Salvador Allende from becoming President of Chile.
- Kill President Sukarno of Indonesia.
- Kill President Duvalier of Haiti.
- Go to Panama and take Noriega like a chicken to stand trial in the United States because he did not make a return to George Bush for their illegal drug transaction and informing the public that Bush was a member of the famous 'Bones and Skull' which Bush then found offensive.
- Run Idi Amin out of power.
- Bomb Saddam Hussein's empire with 120,000 air raid sorties and get Melosevic at all cost with U-2 spy planes and with modern weapons of mass destruction launching from American

Warships around the world until they lay down their arms and restore democracy to their people.

He knew Efemona was telling him the truth. He too, recollected and figured U.S. foreign policy over his head. He noted that Oval Office recalled its Ambassador from Austria because a right-wing party had won 27% of the vote in a democratic election. And the leader of the party, whom he Dudu had loyalty, Mr. Joeg Haider, who holds the same basic views as him and Patrick Buchanan, who believes the Holocaust never happened and will, of course, be given $12.3 million in election funds from the purse of the Federal Government to liquidate strong headed man like him.

- That the Americans were preventing Elian, the little Cuban boy, from returning to his father, because right-wing Cubans in Miami oppose his return because Castro is a dictator like him.
- That the Americans kept armed forces in Kuwait and Saudi Arabia to protect non-elected regimes that deny women the right to vote, drive expensive cars and hold public jobs.
- That the Americans joined with International Organizations which they spearheaded to charge Rwanda ruling government genocide.

As Dudu thought too, Efemona looked at his face, and the small mustache that he had grown over his gaunt face and lips. With his tentative smile, which Efemona denounced, she looked at him boldly in his eyes. "Why is your government so different from the governments of those men I mention in history?" Efemona said.

"I don't know, Efemona. Maybe because the American's were secretly buying my oil at a cheap price."

"Goddammit."

"By the way, am I getting on your nerves Mr. President?" "What do you expect me to say?" but he sat steadily, thinking, showing no reaction to Efemona's question. However, a line of red crept up his nerves to his neck from under his military collar. He leaned forward to her, teeth bared, menacing as a goat that fell into a pond. Finally, he said, "More names, if you can remember Efemona."

And Efemona watched him. Her spirit on him was working. Then he spat his frustration on the floor for a smart woman full of more questions for a fumbling mouth.

He was silent and she was silent, though he was breathing hard to say something. Finally, he had the guts to ask, "Are you trying to scare me or tell me that President Clinton in on his way through France or London to bomb me and my people?"

That question just won't do. Then he argued before Efemona. He gave her the facts as concrete as possible, stating that in practice, the British Administration procedures under Indirect Rule had entailed constant interaction between colonial authorities and local rulers, the system which was modified to fit the needs of each region in the country for which he was *now* the emperor. The bond that would never be broken. And that added more salt to the self-inflicted injury in the form of fumbling to explain to Efemona that, in the North, legislation took the form of a decree cosigned by the governor and the emir (King), while in Lagos *now* the commerce capital, the governors were required to seek the approval of the legislative council "to carry out its rights and duties." That was, in fact, the first iron curtain the middle-belt noticed and decided that a halt to this practice was essential. It will not be by me. Therefore, as a further indication of the iron curtain that the Britishman saw fit for my people, it has been that of higher education, which your people from the middle belt argued should (not) be used to rule in this country. Because of that, me and my junta members made a policy that gradually funded higher institutions of higher learning, such as Grammar Schools, Colleges, and Universities all in the North to help my people. We funded them with scholarships to willing students who were eager as the kids from the South to learn. His explanation to Efemona just won't do. He stood up, pulled out his pistol and put it on the table to intimidate her. And with impotent rage and fear of Clinton's reaction of what he might do to him and his administration because more men in the South were exercising their freedom at *Alabon Close Jailhouse*, he became suspicious and vicious of Bill Clinton. He looked pained, thinking Efemona might be telling him something out of the ordinary. But still, she might be right. Bill Clinton might be after him, he thought. This was not the time to show weakness. I have always been a strong man since I was born. Then he looked at Efemona and Victoria. Then he said, "My experience taught me better than before, that the Americans believe that my men who rule under me are untouchables and capable of taking risks or looking beyond their immediate obstacles and so, do not take a chance with men like us who do not value lives because we're god-like people of Prophet Mohammed."

"And why is that, Mr. Dudu?"

"Because I believe it is the reformer who is anxious for the reform and not 'my people' I rule, from which the Oval Office should expect nothing better than opposition, abhorrence and even mortal persecution of their people in my country if they should try me. Why may not my people regard as retrogression what the Americans hold dear for life as freedom itself to the Generals and the countries you have mentioned?"

He paused. The pause in itself gave Efemona a reason to think. But she was mute. He, too, knew that Bill Clinton was and still is a member of the Free Masonry, who could call his buddies all over the world and act on his stubbornness to give up his power. Then he laughed. To keep from unleashing his weakness before Efemona, he became more aggressive and more flippant than Efemona. "You know, Efemona," Dudu said, "The result of their agitation against me and my junta members would be met with repulsive defiance, because the Americans themselves need to remove the specks in their own eyes (country) before interfering with mine."

He looked at Efemona whose gaze at him might kill him if looks could kill. It didn't bother him. He became more flippant. "I understand there is evidence, and my conclusion is, that black people in America, especially in Reno, Nevada, glare at the symbol of white(s) authority, in Reno especially, from the cops and the judges who find it hard to overturn the decision of other (another) judge(s) even if he or she was wrong in passing a wrong verdict on innocents accused as Ogbebor vs. Circus Circus Hotel and Casino in Reno, Nevada. And I also understand that Ingledue and Bolshazy, both security men in them those casinos, in Reno who are on steroids as powerful as Samson and Hercules can tie black men in silver trolleys with chains and drag them along inside Circus Circus Casino while the judges and the casino owners watched and clapped for them as their testicles are dismembered from their groin as they trottle their trolleys. Above all, they were never guilty as if a black were to do that against a white man. And isn't it true that Reno, in itself, the city so called The Biggest Little City in the World was full of homeless drifters, begging by day and sleeping rough at night all because the police and sheriff's deputies apprehend underclass citizens putting them in the worst moments of their lives by lying and making up stories to charge them with? And isn't it true that they were transported and booked into Parr Jail 911 Boulevard where they employ special doctors as Dr. Protocol Andradae and Dr. Seals to surgically remove their testicles, falsified documents, then peel off the skin of their forehead to lay them as carpets to beautify their homes, their casinos and their courtrooms? Now is that justice for everyone in Reno? You answer me, Efemona! And didn't Judge Devil's Horn campaign with the slogan 'equal justice for all'? What does that tell you and the world? It means that in Reno, Nevada, there is no equal justice for the black men who hail from all over the world. Where then do you draw the line, if Judge Devil's Horn McQuaid dismisses cases of assaulted testicles and broken ear drums and broken bones of their knees?"

Efemona was stunned to know that Dudu knew more of her State she'd Naturalized. And she watched him smile. He watched her muteness with her mouth opened.

"Efemona?" he said, "I vow to fight the serpent which I know will bite me and my men to kill us. Why take chances? As the elephant is powerless over an ant that toils the soils as itself, so is the Oval Office powerless to think of striking a peaceful Nation where I rule as a leader of my country. One thing you don't know is that President Clinton is my friend and I know that he, too, is not a saint."

He was right on that, Efemona thought. The meeting that was only to last an hour was to go even longer as Mr. Isiaka walked in with the news that ten vessels had landed at Appapa Wharf to be loaded with crude oil and three billion has been paid in cash by Don't Reveal Our Secrets of Britain.

Dudu looked at him quickly, bidding him to be silent and Isiaka closed the door behind them and sat beside Victoria. The scent of Victoria as a woman Efemona has dressed up, assaulted his senses. He looked down on Victoria's shoes and smiled. His manhood began to get rigid inside him, but told himself it was not the time to start negotiation for carnal lust, with a million he was capable of lavishing for a beautiful woman. Business with Dudu first! He thought. Isiaka's mind was soon filled with the sudden image of a movie he had not seen in months. He saw two beautiful women with the President in his office as K-9, one tense, one silent, waiting for explanation of the century to fumble and flatter, where they could be read and transposed into different meaning. So it was in this office, while Efemona waited for Dudu to speak. Whatever Dudu was to say would be turned into I told you so, Victoria-that this man has Nigeria in his own pocket. But did she think Dudu gave a damn? Absolutely not.

Anyway, Efemona watched Dudu's words rain down on America as his buddy, Isiaka listened, particularly on Reno, the city she now calls home, while she relinquished those of her country- Nigeria, all for the purpose of growing a penis as the men before her she has no regards for. Then his face became blanker. Her features drawn taut, almost like a mask as she withdrew into herself again. Victoria looked at Efemona, but said nothing. She was as perplexed as Efemona. Too many thoughts were registered on their minds. How did Dudu know what he was talking about? He's just assuming. Whatever they were thinking, Isiaka didn't give a damn. He was hoping Efemona and Victoria would leave and let him discuss a quick money laundry overseas with Dudu. As Isiaka thought, Efemona thought the opposite. She told herself: The motherfucker(s) should beware. One day Clinton and his administration will get you, too. Friendship or no friendship. Noriega, the President of Panama, was a friend to George Bush, but he's now serving a life sentence in Florida.

Though he shun down Efemona's words as nothing, he immediately remembered he'd dreamed of running away from his executive chair, through a rocky mountain near Oba's Palace at Benin where he dug his feet trying to climb the walls and roofs of Oba's Palace to kill him. But his legs and arms were amputated in the Sharia court he Dudu had initiated, and so could not climb up to the Oba's room to kill him. The walls he was to climb were perhaps the oldest walls in the Kingdom of Benin, where Efemona's great, great grandparents could see far away who was coming to see them. If a pin was to move, it was already seen by the Oba way up in his Palace. How could he climb the broken glass that glittered on top of the walls, and sharp iron spears standing straight on top of the wall? And when he woke up he found himself talking to Efemona in broad daylight.

Remembering the dream and Efemona with him *now* in broad daylight, though she was with him for a purpose to help treat the lame or the destitute he wreaked havoc on in his country, he was bold enough. "Who is the strong headed Pompey in this country to challenge my junta administration? None, none, none, I said. Don't you know that making money is the chief business of all African Heads of State, except maybe one or two exceptions at the most."

Truly, Efemona searched her heart. There was no African Head of State who was not corrupt. Not even one. She smiled to that ruefully, thought she suddenly felt a wave of sick trepidation.

"You are right, Mr. President," Efemona said and flashed him a cool grin of flirtation that would doom him soon. "It's why I came with Victoria to inform you that you and your partners in Africa have wreaked havoc on the African economy, particularly our country which you rule. Tell me why you think Nigeria needs a President like you, who is not voted in as a President by the people?"

"Tell him, Efemona. *Aye-ye!* Tell him," Victoria voiced out being happy.

"Hey, Victoria! You stay out of this," Efemona warned because her grandmother's voodoo and spirit was working through her and assaulting the President.

"He could see the bloodshot eyes on Efemona's face as she began to lecture him with grievance.

"Mr. Dudu?" Efemona cried out, "You and your junta regime members should realize that no man is so dumb and stupid, not even idiots as to be incapable of joining together different words, and thereby constructing a declaration by which to make their thoughts understood. Let me tell you, Dudu, that you as a leader of this country are supposed to know: that is, if you have common sense to know by *now* that misery is supposed to be shunned in every modern society that entertains a true democracy."

"Now! Wait a minute! Are you saying I'm stupid?"

"I'm only lecturing you to tell you to learn and have common sense to govern," Efemona said.

He got up and stepped forward. "Go and sit down and listen to Efemona. She has a good message from Bill Clinton," Victoria said. And he walked towards his executive chair and sank in. Isiaka shook his head, but was of relatively no importance even though he was possessed more that the President himself. Nobody could stop her *now*.

"Mr. Dudu?" Efemona yelled at him.

He looked away because the voodoo flames from Efemona's mouth was getting a grip on him even though he didn't know that.

"Mr. Dudu? Mr. Dudu? Are you listening?" "Go on and insult me before Isiaka."

"I'll surely do that. Mr. Dudu, I said that Nigeria is already shaken by thunder and lightning born of such a collision of *'if you can't beat them, join them syndrome'*. Our entire nation is tired of this slogan. You and your junta regime should realize *now* that if all Nigerians in misery lose fast to this exaggeration, I foresee a new battle between Achilles and Hector. Don't get me wrong. I am only saying that the masses are now aware that in such an event only death can separate the innocent from the vanquished." Victoria nodded again in support which possessed Efemona more. "If you like, listen to me, because I foresee a country whereby nuclear weapons of mass destruction not yet tested by the Americans would be tried on our soil to tell you and your junta members enough is enough, to go to your Barracks, in the struggle for power. Let us not make this country another Kosovo. Enough is enough, Mr. Dudu, that time is running out for you to realize that what makes Nations great in the world are not coups and countercoups, but rather, knowing the ills of the suffering masses and solving their problems. It is what is known as essential, pure democracy,

Mr. Zombie, whatever your name is."

He sprang up again. "Did you hear that, Victoria? Efemona has just called me a zombie."

"I'll call you anything. And I will repeat it again, Zombie." "Go and sit down. She doesn't mean it. She's just telling you what she feels from the depth of her soul. Efemona watched him sink into his executive chair again, "You and your junta members should realize that the civilians have long been denied a share of the pie of this country in recent years: That us, the civilians, are now aware that in resetting a disjointed limb, one must not dislocate it in the opposite direction, but rather put it in its proper place. Therefore, Mr. Dudu, the disease we call 'us and them' is a cancer that needs to be addressed in the House of Assembly and it's now or never. And unless you and your junta members recognize its ills now, it would be highly deserving of the remark that just as men are good when approached as isolated individuals, so are they rational when they consider the affairs in the solitude of their own home. And once men are brought in crowds, they tend to lose their heads. They also can be stirred and lured into supporting policies and programs that they would reject. In that case, rational individuals will become transformed as they join a lynch mob or a revolutionary movement, which is what this country will be experiencing anytime from *now*. I want you and your junta members to realize that this country no longer has democracy, but rather has been replaced by mob rule of your regime: Mostly of the Northerners. However, Mr. Dudu, who should rule to me, be it a Northerner, Westerner, Southerner, doesn't mean anything to me because you should note that in any modern society, the rule of the wise is essential. For instance, the wise men of a country decide when, where and how a thing should be done, so that in every circumstance, one is spared the hesitation and indecision to have trust in them. Wise men of a country do not encourage corruption of *'you eat, I eat'* or *'you chop I chop'*, thereby collapsing its country's treasury to seek asylum when he feels he should retire to the country he laundered his own country's loot whereby he could ride the mule with the Queen or sit at Buckingham Palace by the fireplace with the Prime Minister, but rather bring from foreign countries to save its economy. In a Republic, just about anywhere, however organized, there are never more than forty or fifty citizens who attain a position that entitles them to command. The key issue therefore, is who has and who should have power? Well, Mr. Dudu, even in the best of democracies, where the people believe that they govern themselves, where the masses believe that it can still be suggested that power gravitates or ascends, to a small elite groups who knows how to manage the economy without borrowing billions from IMF to add to the debt of their nations, I'll be dumb therefore, not to inform you that even in a representative government lawmakers are given the chances to run for elections, because they do not only know the law, but can interpret them. Therefore, the constitution of a Nation is important just as men are able to shape them in ways of their own choosing. Good leaders and rulers who are educated are important just as men are able to shape them in ways of their own choosing. They enact the laws according to specified procedures, but the real issue is which individual and groups secure laws that promote the masses own interests. You and your juntas should not fool all the people of this country, but rather know that when the poor win, the result is pure and absolute democracy."

Efemona finally paused and smiled at Victoria. Winking her right eye she said, "Right, Victoria?"

"You betcha, girlfriend."

The Dudu of a man knew all along that he had a smarter than smart woman before him. And so, he became dumb as he shook his head a thousand times. And the number of times Dudu shook his head and gnawed his teeth, did not bother Efemona. In the first place, she wasn't counting. But who will win the battle among themselves is the question. And Efemona began to think of more questions to ask her President: Bad Dudu.

Chapter

21

One of Efemona's favorite phrases is a saying that she picked up from her father: Stupid people should not breed.

That's true. She hated stupid people *or ohuan*. She just wished they would go away and leave this world to those who have brains like her and her brothers who are all graduates out of the best Universities in Nigeria. Before Efemona decides to go off here, she explained what she meant, which is that "stupid", not the measure of IQ points or college degree, but talking about people in high office in her country who are oblivious to the rest of the world, and who, as a result, annoy the living bright philosophers and London barristers day in and day out. One example of these stupid people: idiots, whatever you may call them, who wreck their country money-wise like Marcos of the Philippines, Bad Dudu and his in cahoots in Nigeria and in general: Africa. You know all leaders who assumed power by ascending the throne killing their predecessors because they said, they were corrupt and then turn around and do the same, are all in this category. At least that's what Efemona thought.

Meanwhile, Bad Dudu has finished answering part of Efemona's political question in which he'd fumbled, but didn't even know it, or he knew it, but didn't care. But he felt dull with a sign of pain for inviting Efemona. It was chaos, he thought. He stepped towards the mosquito machine by the door to try to slow it down, because too many mosquitoes had met their untimely death and were piling into the room. He tried to open the door to alert his servants to get a coffin ready for the plenty of mosquitoes that had met their untimely death. He fumbled with the knob, but it was Oriwo, also known as Bitter Leaf, who was holding it from the outside trying to open it to see him for a quick chat before going to his own office.

"This is not the time to chat now," he said to Oriwo. "I have invited trouble upon myself and my junta regime."

Oriwo stood looking at his number one man about to fall from grace. For one, the President has never one day expressed his sadness as he has *now* before him.

"What is the matter?" he finally asked.

"Don't worry about it. I'll handle it," Dudu answered. Then he sighed deeply. He became nervous, looking at Efemona, but not because he considered himself as too barbaric, but because he could see Efemona was one of those former African women who had gone to America to be civilized, remodeled and willing to march right out over a mine entrance without looking at the warning sign by its door, then shout rape at bystanders for help against his fangs if he decided to show his insanity sooner or later. The trouble Efemona might make out of the President to collect millions in settlement through World Court would reflect his image all over the world. So he did not want to get caught up in why me idiot, had-I-known that Efemona was too smart, he wouldn't have invited her into the country.

The last question from Efemona, though he'd answered part of it, did not know if he'd fumbled it or answered Efemona critically. Realizing that, his skin was pulled across his face, which Efemona, too, noticed. She said nothing thereafter, but watched him. His lips began to draw back from his bare teeth as he stared. He almost lost his temper when he was about to say: People like Efemona think they *now* have balls after visiting the White House and chatting with Bill Clinton and talking rubbish with him to think that all Presidents are tolerant and one and the same. He quickly recollected himself and remembered the promise he made to Efemona. "I will not get mad at you, even if you asked me if I'd killed God's only son."

But he had wanted to say to hell with Efemona. Instead, he found himself answering her question, so she would accept the vacant post for which only Efemona was qualified, he thought.

Though he wants to answer her question the best he can, the why me Efemona was still registered in his being. Then he sighed again and again, looked at her and said, "Though I'd promised you I would not get mad at you, I lied, Efemona. Things might change," he laughed.

That did not bother Efemona. "Just answer my question *jare*," Efemona said.

Efemona's spirit and that of her grandmother caught him. He smiled whimsically and explained:

"It all boils down to what had happened before in this country when I was still in England learning the art of firing different cannons and motars then contemplating what to do next when I return to Nigeria. There I learnt from the Queen and Prime Minister of England that the post Colonial States have the advantage of being larger than the pre-colonial, thus more viable in the modern sense to benefit '*us*' and the British. The facts therefore, were clear to me that Nigeria would have a second advantage of a modern administrative structure as a legacy from the Colonial period if a man like me was to rule. And noting the factors which played a tremendous role in the bitterly fought Nigerian civil war of 1967- 69, I had to put on my British made camouflage army uniform to sacrifice my talent of firing the weapons under my guard. In the war, the Ibos of Eastern Nigeria gave first priority to their ethnic sense of Iboness and to the new state of Biafra. But Nigerians outside of Biafra, whom my mentor Mr. Gowon was the figure head, had to think twice whether it was worth a considerable sacrifice to maintain Nigeria as one, rather than seeing it break up into a number of ethnically divided States. With that, I'd to influence Mr. Gowon that I knew how to fire different weapons and should not give up hope, when the facts were clear to me that the Iboman self identity as Ibos was stronger than their National loyalty to Nigeria. I tell you right now that what the Ibos wanted to do was to drive the Hausas to their cattle field, which I vehemently had denounced as an insult. There is no doubt in my mind that the Ibos wanted to enjoy the oil money themselves. This is why my junta regime and I decided that we will empty the oil reserves and steal the money and dump it anywhere we want in the world. As the most populous country of Africa, Nigeria had possibilities and other developments that could have hardly been achieved if it were allowed to break up. These were my reasons for deciding that I will wear a military uniform like Caesar until I die. I refused to go back to the cattle farms where they think I belong in Sudan. As long as I live, the Iboman will never be trusted again in this country. I remain the Caesar of my country, my dear. Come closer to me and give me a kiss. Come on my dear!"

Oriwo laughed and gave a thumbs-up to Bad Dudu. Efemona and Victoria did not see it as funny. The thing is, Efemona had reminded him of history which he'd forgotten. "It was your buddy's slogan that says 'to keep Nigeria one, is a task that must be done.'

"Who is your buddy, my dear?"

"Gowon," Efemona answered, then she added, "Why haven't you formed a new slogan now after the war that would say, 'to keep Nigeria divided by Zamfara Sharia law is a task that must be carried out.' But you know, Mr. Dudu, I think it would be better for the Northerners and Southerners to go their separate ways."

The spirit of Efemona was getting into his blood. "I say, come closer and give me a kiss, my dear!" he said and looked at Efemona and smiled a sardonic smile.

Efemona smiled a demonic smile too, and whined on her seat. With her eyes shining as those of a cat, she said, "I'll give you a kiss if you agree with me that the editor of The Heartbreak Newspaper was right when he wrote, "On Aburi we stand."

Bad Dudu shivered, then coughed. His eyes became red when he remembered the famous speech made by Mr. Ikemba Ojukwu at Aburi. This goddamn stupid Efemona, he thought. But Efemona was not stupid as he thought. He stood up and was rooted on the spot, looking at Efemona as she, too, stood up and jutted her elbows out, her hands on her hips in a fashion of what can you do, asshole. I'm an American. She looked at him sarcastically, "I understand that when the Financial Times Correspondent based in Lagos wrote about Bad Dudu to account for the $12.5 billion in oil sales during the Gulf War, you bundled the correspondent out of Nigeria within 24 hours. Ending up in Britain, he was cajoled and humiliated. That aside, you have the audacity to make an application to World Bank to borrow $15 billion under five seconds which would bring up our economy where it was in the seventies. I am glad the World Bank or IMF, whatever they call them, did not honor your application for the loan. I know you would've slaughtered most Southerners for the money, then add the loot to your growing account in Swiss Bank. Give you a kiss, you said, Mr. Dudu? I will give you a kiss if you promise me you will take me to the Astoria Prince Hotel in Britain where you and your Generals spend $10,000 dollars a night of our oil money alone to fool around with mistresses from Lebanon, Brazil, Thailand and the Philippines."

Bitter Leaf and Bad Dudu were getting more irritated as they stared at Efemona, the way she was posed, her hands still on her hips. Then Dudu furtively glanced at the closed door and the mosquito machine. Registered on his *mugoo* dumb brain were the Lebanese women, not much prettier than Nigerian women eating shit these days with no money to take care of themselves and to feed their children. His thoughts were plenty and did not want to show it. He knows a famous Nigerian journalist had perhaps trailed him to the famous Astoria Prince Hotel room XJ, which was unlocked when he was making love to two Filipino women at the same time on one bed. He'd remembered how he yelled out to him to get lost and respect his privacy when he was butt naked. Suddenly, his eyes swung up to Efemona, imagining her psychological profile and background. Finally, he said, "No offense taken, Efemona."

"Tell you the truth, Dudu, I don't care if offense was taken. I know that when the journalist caught you red handed you went totally apeshit! Huh? Kiss you, you mean? I'll kiss you if Katangora, the famous journalist, is left alone with his editors to write about the truth in this country."

His head began to ache. He looked at Efemona's face, she's even more demon possessed than he thought. He shook and nodded his head several times, noting that Efemona was trying to germinate a penis in broad daylight. If she accepts the post of Matron General for which I invited her to fill, I will make sure afterwards she remains in line with everyone else in the country I have absolute control over. My Allah! Efemona thinks her shit doesn't stink anymore because she'd been to America to be Americanized. I'll teach her a lesson if she doesn't know that no matter how smart and beautiful or how wide or small the vagina of a woman might be a man rich or poor, with a big or small penis, still had to *fuck'am*. He was about building up the courage to eliminate those negative thoughts from his heart when Efemona added more salt to his injury.

"Accept your post of Matron General for this country and give you a kiss as well, you mean? I'll honor the post and kiss you if you agree that it is an insult to the Ph.D.s holders of this country with no jobs, while Bad Dudu with no education sits in *this* enormous chair of *this* office with air conditioning, signing signatures to release crates of banned items into the country to your Generals who are Hausas who already have billions in Swiss Banks, making the people of this country from the South to suffer and eat shit on the sidewalk of Ikoyi. To crown it all, I understand that you personally had bought the famous EKO LAI MERIDIAN HOTEL in your name with $10.5 million dollars of our oil money fooling all the people with Ph.D.s of this country who could manage our economy better than you."

As Efemona talked, she looked out the window and saw her village at Ukpenu was completely in the dark. Nigerian Electric Power Authority (NEPA) had perhaps failed again because of lack of transformers imported from Mexico and Brazil all lying waste in the high seas with no money to claim them. A country with oil revenue sales of up to $50 billion dollars a year. She looked at Dudu again. Then she said, "My village is also a part of Nigeria, isn't it?"

He did not know why she asked. "Yes we are one, my dear," he answered.

"Well, my village has no light and only you and your Generals have billions in Swiss Banks, the oil money meant for every one of us in this country. And do you think I am happy with the fact that when I call my father and mother in America to reach them, I am told all the trunck lines are busy for a country with billions of oil sale revenue that can fetch Nigeria enough circuit for the country so the telephones can work effectively and only you have billions in Swiss Banks and the money has no inherent use to the people of Nigeria except to the Swiss government. You think about it, Mr. Dudu. One of your Generals in your Administration can afford to pay the American government to launch as many satellites with only $2 billion dollars or less for the phones in this country to function better. Isn't it a shame on you and your Generals who have fooled the people of this country buying homes in Britain, yachts on the Cayman Islands worth millions, Lamborghinis and Rolls Royces' for various mistresses overseas?!"

Oriwo was not himself. Dudu himself nodded his frustration, but with thanks to Efemona, and with not enough strength to answer. Within a few moments, he succumbed to her words. His eyes began to blink abnormally. And almost immediately, he was breathing heavily, having found truth in Efemona's grievance. He looked at her quizzically with some thoughts he feels she might have knowledge about or might pretend she has no knowledge about. Finally, he played with the idea of telling Efemona a joke. "You've been running your mouth all this time. And if you run it more than you have I assure you that I will ask Oriwo to straddle your legs and put pepper in your vagina while I sit back and watch your reaction." Not again, Efemona thought.

Efemona knew nothing more humiliating and disgraceful than that when she was growing up and disobeying her mother leaving the house without giving her mother notice and sleeping around with various men. Mad enough one day, as her mother couldn't take it any more, she opened her vagina and poured granulated pepper into her vagina. Realizing that she couldn't go out for several months as a result of the hot chili in her vagina, she mellowed down a bit. Dudu noticed her mellowness and capitalized on it.

"Are you listening to me, Efemona? "Yes, I'm listening, Mr. Dudu."

"Give me the respect and call me Mr. President, though that's not my point now. I guess you would like to know the characteristics and profile of a notorious woman like Efemona before me, born in township of Benin, but raised at Ukpenu and how different they are from Aba, Owerri, Enugu, Port Harcourt, Irrua, Ewu, Kano, Sokoto, Jos, Bornu and other African countries. The signs of a typical notorious woman whom her husband had shipped to America who wanted to be independent to come to Nigeria to be a hench madam to run for

Presidential election of this country to live the life of the Americans or the Romans is all registered in my brain, Efemona."

She did not wait for the President to finish.

"What are they? Tell me Mr. Dudu. Oh! Excuse me. Tell me, Mr. President."

"First, the notorious woman takes the man's children and runs away to another big city like New Jersey where the man cannot find her and their children. While in New Jersey or another city, she takes a curtain in a red light district, where she then continues to service different men. When her husband will hire a private investigator to locate her whereabouts, and her husband visits her to beg her to come back home so they can raise their children together in the traditional African way, she refuses the offer, basing her 'no response' on reflections of how her mother was married to different men and because the American society has recivilized her. When she looked at the very sorrowful face of her husband, she will call on her first son of the man: like Ehimare, get me a bottle of Heineken from the fridge while she sat on the man's couch, the system then entrusted to her, then stretched and crossed her legs on the center table. She does that to humiliate her husband perhaps and to tell him she has grown a penis in-between her legs and because the man's privilege has been taken away by the system and therefore the man can't do shit in her own rented apartment. If, for instance, Ehimare was not quick enough to get her the bottle of Heineken from the fridge, she will yell out louder and call on Ehimare's name, which was the same way the boy's father used to call his son to get him a bottle of beer from the fridge when he returned from work. And when the boy finally abandoned his toys and got her the drink, she gives him a hard knock on his forehead, while the boy feels excruciating pain and cries, the man sits and watches his son cry out in anguish and pain, but dare not say a word, afraid that the notorious woman would call the cops or the sheriffs on him to cuff him and send his ass to jail. But if the husband did not react to the humiliation, she will get up and reach for her remote control on the center table and punch the button to click the music of humiliation for the man, from a stereo system rack she bought with the child support payment the man was paying supposedly meant to feed his children. And when the music clicked, she will listen to fire traditional music CDs recorded at Oba's Royal Palace which her mother had bought and shipped to her on how to humiliate the man who was kind enough to marry her and take her away from the culture of poverty I personally inflicted on my people of this country."

He paused. "And is that all?"

"I'm not finished, goddammit," Dudu yelled back. "Go ahead.

I'm still listening," Efemona yelled back.

"Oriwo gave a thumbs up for Dudu again. He knew he was doing good. He wouldn't let the daughter-of-a-bitch get away scott free. "You know, a notorious woman like you, Efemona is one who jumps on stage when Femi Kuti, the son of Fela Anikulapo Kuti, is performing in Reno's Wingfield Park. While all the married African women who are dedicated to their husbands all sit and watch Femi. The notorious woman like Efemona will go on stage and dance and shake her butt to humiliate her husband she'd divorced who might be in the audience watching. But in reality, a notorious woman like you, Efemona is not actually humiliating her husband. She's actually advertising herself for the rich and famous of Reno, Nevada to notice her, leaving her three children to wonder what kind of mother they have. A notorious woman like you, Efemona, will call the cops to arrest her husband a thousand times for little or nothing to gain fame and independence. A notorious woman like you, Efemona flirt with the judges of Reno, and with her ex- husband's friends so that they will be on her side to ask the husband to pay child support to her to become a hench madam and use the money to enrich her pocketbook and those of her parents and immediate brothers and sisters while neglecting those on her husband's side. A notorious woman like you, Efemona, are those who boldly tell their husband 'who is your father anyway', after they tied their husband's penis to a bed frame after they'd made love to her despite that the husband's father arranged the marriage for his son to know the notorious woman like you. He sighed finally. He'd much to say about a notorious woman like Efemona. *Avanlagbe. Okuntarlagbe Efemona.*"

Efemona didn't quite remember what those words meant. But she knew they were curses. Dudu explained to her anyway, "I say thunder and bullets with stones will reign upon you in my office if you keep running your mouth against me and my junta members."

You know, I can only tell you here that Bad Dudu broke into my thoughts where I sat, sipping on my red wine and watching them through American high tech of Radio Shack bringing technology into living rooms. The thing is, I, too, had an experience with an African woman born and raised in Benin in Nigeria with the notorious profiles of what Bad Dudu had described Efemona to be. My experience was with a woman I will call Miss BI. After we divorced and the American justice system made her rich and me poorer, she became free as the air. Fully independent, she'd access to collect child support, alimony, welfare, food stamps, to name but a few. Though the system gave her everything I'd sweat for before I married her, it did not pain me as much as when I visited her, when she told me to sit on the floor. However, it pained the fuck out of me that on another occasion, I'd visited her to beg her to let me see my children, when I met Mr. Georgia making a violent love on my couch. The humiliating part was that Mr. Georgia was once my friend. To humiliate me even further, after they were done, Miss BI asked me to clean off the mess they had made on the couch. With shame and the love I'd for my three children who were locked up in the room upstairs, I quickly cleaned it up and sprayed perfume in the living room which made the place stink, but better than the foul odor that emanated from their private parts, which I'd endured but could've made my children sick. When I was done cleaning, I begged her to bring the children along with her to the John Ascuaga's Nugget Hotel and Casino. A place I realized I shouldn't have suggested because on my arrival, Miss BI and Mr. Georgia were already waiting for me with my children.

Here, Miss BI got offended that I'd purposely sprayed the room to tell her that Mr. Georgia stunk. And Mr. Georgia, without hearing my explanation, took a notorious woman's words over mine and had a dagger to the ready to slash my throat. Thank God Chukwuma Achuko, a man I will describe as a Reno, Nevada playboy and has many women friends, good looking and some charm of a true Iboman gentleman and all of the macho posturing of a good ol' pal welcome home. Honest or principled are the good words most women use to describe him. Anyway, he was by me to tell me not to do what I'd intended. Otherwise, I would say Mr. Georgia still today is the luckiest man that had lived to fuck my ex-woman on any couch, drink my booze, and upon that, had the nerve to pull a dagger on me at the John Ascuaga's Nugget and Casino while my children watched where they sat helplessly like children with no father. I tell you the truth, a crime of the worst century would've been committed by me. Mr. Achuko led me out of that thought of vengeance.

On another occasion and for the love of my children, I'd gone to visit Miss BI again after the last humiliation I'd entertained. She welcomed me in, quite allright. But still, I already knew that I was not to sit on my couch that I'd bought with my hard earned money before I married her. To avoid her calling the cops as she'd done in the past, I sat on the floor. A few minutes later, she got up from her seat and went to her bar and fixed herself a glass of home made Bloody Mary and purposefully left it on the dinner table. I watched her walk back and took her seat without the drink, then stretched her legs on top of the center table.

Actually, I knew what she was about. All she was up to was to show that she is the head of the household and by no means I dare not say something to her, but warm my butt on the floor. I must admit that I was tasty for a beer too, but dare not ask. How could I ask a woman who is the head of her household to give me a drink when she stretched her legs on the center table and fully relaxed, with no worries whatsoever, only to think of enjoyment in America, in a country I brought this notorious Miss BI? Well, I swallowed the little pride I had left.

Finally, staring at me on the floor, she yelled at my son, Ozie, and I thought she was about to tell him to get me a bottle of beer. With alacrity, Ozie yanked off from my arms on the floor.

She said to him, "Get me the glass of Bloody Mary on the dining table."

Ozie fetched her the drink. Sipping on it, I said, "You know what, Miss BI? I think it's morally wrong for an African woman to come to America to live the life of the Americans. And you know my father who arranged my marriage with you thinks you will respect our tradition until death do us part."

She looked at me and laughed. That famous saying of Efemona, the Efemona I also knew through a good friend whom I was told became notorious in this Biggest Little City in the World, also pulped out from her mouth. And that was, "Who is your father, anyway?"

With that, my flaming red eye instinct told her something to say to me, "You must leave now or I'll call the cops."

Thus, the profile of a notorious description of African woman by Bad Dudu who want out of marriage also suit the psychological profile of Miss BI as I whinned my Radio Shack toy device and watched Efemona and Dudu far away in another Continent.

Anyway, so much of African woman from Nigeria who wants to be independent. Efemona knew the President was telling the truth too. Saying nothing, expressionless, she watched him unfurled the arm of his Agbada he wore over his military uniform.

Efemona whispered to Victoria. "Do you think Dudu is right about his description of a notorious woman?"

"For the record, no, girlfriend. But you must keep him engaged in talking so we know how sick he really is for knowing who is notorious and who isn't."

Efemona nodded. Oriwo has nothing to say. But for the record, he thumb-ups for his man again. And standing still over Victoria's shoulder, and looking at Bad Dudu, Efemona saw that his cheeks were flushed from his good times get together with his acquaintances the previous night possibly, she thought. She began to observe him. Maybe too much Remimartins shots was the reason he came up with the signs of a typical notorious woman like me. Maybe not, she might be mistaken. But looking at his eyes, she was all along sure that he is a man who likes to enjoy and drink too much and socialize, because the mere look at his eyes says it all. His eyes were larger as those of John the Baptist eating locust in the garden, which is because of his shiny remnants of his uninterrupted sleep with his buddies which had contributed to his gaunt face look to remember the notorious woman profiles. His mere looks says it all that he'd never, Efemona had presumed, looked more handsome, more masculine, sexier to his mistresses all over the world. Why they liked him was money. Nothing else. Finally, Efemona, as smart as ever, asked, "Mr. President, why can't men from Benin, or any other part of the riverian areas of the South where the bread and butter of this country is, rule this country with their Ph.D.s they obtained from Yale, Oxford, Harvard and Stanford?"

His eyes quickly riveted on her lips, which he parted with the intention to argue or give her a straight answer. But the straight answer he'd hoped to give or to argue about died unspoken. He looked at Efemona again. Nonplussed, he splayed his hand to his chest where he sat in a gesture of true Caesar. Why him was again imprinted on his mind. His jaw Victoria and Bitter Leaf could see turned to iron. And Efemona noticed too that his crooked teeth similar to those of a dog watching his masters meat hanging by the fireplace and then salivating, he clinched and unclenched his fists.

That just won't do. His cervical vertebra Efemona probably guessed must've shrunk an inch. Though Dudu recovered his nerves and self, from the stupid question she threw before him, he looked mean. Seething with an impotent rage, he uttered, "Efemona, you better control your mouth. I've warned you before with style. Bare in mind I will not warn you again. Next time you pose any hard question to me, I'll ring the bell to alert the fathers of wickedness guarding me, who will not only answer your smart questions, but who will pull out each hair of your pudenda or cunt or whatever the Americans call vagina, one by one." And his hand mistakenly hit the bell, which he hadn't mean to.

And three figures, all six-footers, were standing before Efemona and Victoria. Men who perhaps are Israelis who pity no one, challenging the President, who were on the register for monthly payment services rendered or not. He too, was surprised to see the three men standing in the room.

"Did the bell go off?"

"Yes, my lord," Esemuede was the first to respond. He barely could pronounce their name tags when Bad Dudu said, "It was by accident."

They stood guard anyway as Bad Dudu excused himself to the restroom. "I'll be back ladies."

* * *

The phone began to ring in Dudu's office and no one dare pick it up to say 'hello', except by Efemona who thinks Dudu is not God as he might think, which baffled the three Israeli guards. They could not restrain Efemona, because Dudu hadn't told them anything was amiss.

"Hello!" the line went dead.

"The motherfucker hung up," Efemona cursed and walked back to her seat.

The President came in with a fresh washed face. To the Israeli guards, Efemona had become persona non grata in Dudu's office. Efemona didn't know this. Dudu sat down and overlooked the Israeli standing guard over everyone, then looked at Efemona, "Maybe I should tell you a joke, Efemona."

"Go right ahead," Efemona said.

"I want you to picture behind your brain, that it was a woman talking to God."

He swiveled his chair around.

"Why do you think God made a man so handsome and strong and sexy?"

"Allah says so you'll like him."

"Well, Allah! Why did you make man so handsome and dominating?"

"Allah says so you'll like him."

"Well then, Allah, why did you make man so stupid?" "Allah says so he'll like you, Efemona."

The joke did not move Efemona. So he thought: What kind of a woman is Efemona? At least every now and then when he tells the joke to other women how stupid he really was for being the fly that buzzes around different women hole *yanshes* to love them, they laugh to it.

"How abnormal!" he sighed. Then a very faint, wry thought crossed his face. And finally, he swiveled his enormous chair around, and Efemona looked at his novice stupid political mask of a Rogue or Scoundrel as both looked out the window of the enormous plate- glass window which offered a magnificent panoramic view of Alabon Close at Kirikiri holding cell with the broad silver sweep of the Julius Berger Canal he told Nigerians he dug with a billion dollars far away. Efemona knew the Rogue did not finance the goddamn canal with a billion dollars. He might have spent half of what he claimed while the rest had ended up with Adam Khan to travel with and find a bank in Tahiti to dump the loot. In the distance, Efemona and Dudu Abacha saw the Federal Palace and EkO LAI MERIDIAN and the National Mosque he recently financed with another billion dollars for his Muslim brothers to like him. He was a Muslim. The women before him were Catholic.

"Hum, that Mosque looks magnificent. Where is the Catholic Church Cathedral for the Catholics to worship? If I am not mistaken, that Mosque was built with the Nation's oil revenue money? Isn't it, Bad Dudu?"

He did not reason to know where Efemona was heading. Only the Israelis, Oriwo and Victoria all knew what Efemona meant. Or he knew, but didn't quickly remembered when he had affixed his first signature to a document to swing a $10 billion of Federal money to Britain's Barclays Bank and another $5 billion to Swiss Bank after he'd seized power and built the National Mosque to fool the Nation. And that was when he was imitating Caesar to do and undo, and a hole in the head with whoever challenges him. And since no one was bold enough to challenge him, he then conducted a merciless campaign against elections for a true democracy and party formation in general. A hole in the head against a civilian President heighten his pride, and then he boasted and dare any strong headed Pompey to challenge him to reduce his self-esteem. Beyond guns and motars lay his ultimate goal. Rule; fool the people, give the relay-race baton to his next man in line to rule when he had drained enough oil money. Turning around with impotent anger he responded to Efemona's comment about Aburi and the neglect of the Catholic Cathedral building opposite the National Mosque, the Catholic faith worshipers contributed money to build themselves, but ran out of money to complete it. *"Aburi-kor-Aburi-ni.* Ojukwu can speak all the English and Oxford English in the Dictionary at Aburi, me and my partners who rule hold on tight to the Presidency of this Nation with AK- 47 rifles, sniper rifles, V-40 percussion grenades, Mauser automatics, Uzis submachine guns, C-4s and gelinite the Britishman gave us to defend ourselves if Ogboru tried to take the post from us with force. Education or no education. You hear me, Efemona? I want you to open your eyes and ears wide open. By the way, what can you do if I built thousands of mosques with Federal oil money. Nothing, Efemona! I want you to know that." "What?" Victoria drew her eyes from Efemona and turned to face Bad Dudu. Then she said, "But, with sound education you can stand with world leaders and express yourself on the podium as Wole Soyinka, the Nobel Prize winner."

"The Hausa crooks rulers of this country don't attend summits with world leaders and will never will" Dudu said.

Efemona gave Victoria a high five and said, "Good point you made." Then she looked at the gaunt-faced Dudu, "Why is education not important?" she asked.

"I don't think I can explain that any longer because I already told you that men with Uzis and Khaki uniform camouflage on, don't go to summits to represent their country and spark from their mouth mechanical and carpenter jargons to be laughed at."

"And you are happy at that?," Efemona asked.

Efemona became wilder. She began to lecture him with grievance. She said, "Let me tell you something you'll remember from this moment on. You see, hard-nosed non elected official like you Dudu may find my lectures naïve, but it is the truth. Face the reality that the Ibos of this country are a perfect genius of a race not only in this country, but in Africa. I want you to realize that political and economic issues are setting this country backwards from development because of you and your junta regime and cronies.

As a flirt, she smiled and walked up to him and held his hands. She squeezed it hard as a man would have done. Looking at him squarely, deeply in the eye, she went on, "I suggest that the Federal Government recognized and trust the Ibos, award them contracts for research in the field of science, so that by the year 2050, most other Third World Countries could rely on Nigeria for supplies of immediate needs rather than Nigeria importing bicycles from Korea and toothpicks from Hong Kong. I will also tell you that your junta regime for which you are the king of the kings in Africa, should recognize the Ibos and call back to the country all the scientists who left the country after the Biafra-Nigeria civil war to develop the *Ogunigbe bombs* and other viable products needed in Third World Countries. I know this is not an easy task for you at this moment of your money laundry to drain our country bone dry, but I want you to put it in consideration though I also know that demographic currents is undeniable in this respect, but if you try to remove the 'US' and 'THEM' syndrome Nigeria could become the giant of Africa and eventually a world power like India. I will tell you that though this demographic current is undeniable perhaps that you Bad Dudu and Babagida are the main problem that Nigeria has. For instance, Mr. Dudu, the great oil boom during Udoji era, in this country has long been replaced by dwindling economy. My friend here, Victoria, sitting here with me in your office know too, that Nigeria businesses, accustomed to foreign investments for the last decade has long shrunk and replaced by foreign investments pulling out with worker shortages. Since you ceased power by a hole in the head, immigration has shrinked compared to when Nigeria had a Civilian Government who has common sense and education to rule and govern.

These demographic changes since you assumed power to me all point to one clear conclusion, which is that if businesses want qualified employees from foreign countries, the junta members and Dudu as their figure head should be advised by people like me (Efemona) who is now well informed. What foreign investments find attractive are what generates loyalty to both the investors and the country itself. The environment should be conducive to both parties. And these days, the environment in Nigeria with the outside world is no longer conducive except to Bad Dudu Abacha, Babagida and your cronies in all the Nigerian banks siphoning money abroad."

The passions she'd unleashed lecturing him stunned him. He looked into her eyes. "Is what you are saying to me right?"

"Yes." Then Efemona dropped her eyes. "Every Ph.D. holder in this country are watching their steps against you. Why don't you let them rule and see a difference in people's lives in this country? I'll tell you Mr. Dudu, that in most countries, those factors I have listed are important, and are best for Nigerians too. For instance, America and Mexico, Japan and America. Canada and Brazil and so on and so forth. In these regards, a high sense of participation in decision making process does not matter where one hails from in this country, being you a Hausa, Ibo, Yoruba, Benin, or Efik as long as they are well informed with ideologies. These grouping Bad Dudu, are what make up for an effective democratically elected government. Not realizing these illnesses you have rotted Nigerians into, Nigeria will remain an Isola Bella: that wash-tiny basin where Napoleon made his first morning toilet. How smart a woman can be, Dudu thought and became dumb.

Everything Efemona had said went through his right ear as he tried to listen and then passed through or had been retained at his left ear. As his left ear could not retain more lectures, he made believe that he was craving for a Havana cigar. Then he strike a match, and the Havana cigar he had on the tray had burned out leaving the precariously huge ash on the tray. He hissed and blew out the match. Looking at Efemona, he said, "All Presidents in the world are not the same. I will tell you the difference between Bad Dudu Abacha's Authoritarian Government and the government of Bill Clinton's Administration whom women of your type can lecture."

"Are you listening to me, Efemona?"

"Yes, I'm listening. Your Israeli guards are listening too. Go ahead, tell me."

"The difference is that when I send those who challenge my authority to prison, I asked my special men I imported from Israel to poison them. Whereas in America while they incarcerate the less privileged who cram their jails and prisons, they employ psychiatrist doctors to evaluate them to make believe they are sick and therefore keep them for life. I mean they label them to be a threat to the community and thereby keeping them behind bars for life. Don't you know why they do that? It is because the judges and their cops or Jail Industries use them to acquire millions and millions of dollars. Doing that, the judges who are corrupt as me and my cronies and their congressmen . . . can afford to purchase a whole section of heaven from God which I am prepared to outbid them for anyway. Isn't it true that the judges of Reno makes bizarre decisions because the casino owners or the gurus already paid them millions when it involves their security men crunching testicles of men like Mr. Ogbebor in Reno, Nevada and they all made their decisions to favor their white cronies because the testicles of Mr. Ogbebor fetch them billions in their pocketbooks? So what is the difference in what I do in this country and what they do in Reno and in America in general?"

As he talked, he stared down at Victoria's face for a while then looking up and meeting Efemona's gaze. This time, he couldn't hold his vexation burning inside of him. He said, "Who the hell are you, Efemona to think that all Presidents are one and the same, to come to my office on my invitation to lecture me? I invited you into this country to give you a position under my Administration. So! Bad weed or marijuana we have in this country is not enough to get you high? I can visualize that you've joined the Americans in Reno, Nevada snorting cocaine, smoking crack, crank, heroine and shooting needles through your female genitals. If not, who are you to tell me what I'm doing in this country is morally wrong and zombie-like? Allahdammit!"

"Do you want us to bound her?" Esemuede, the Israel guard asked, seeing his man tense.

"I'll take care of Efemona myself. Y'all can leave."

They left Dudu alone in the office to handle his business.

Victoria was relieved.

Aha! Efemona thought. It is difficult to teach a pig from Sudan who came to Nigeria to fool the people to sing. What I say does not only annoy the pig, it wastes the teacher its own time. To crown it all, Victoria and Efemona saw his face flushed and his brown walnut eyes bigger than those of John the Baptist eating locust out of hunger, glowed like a tiger's eyes in the dark. It did not bother Efemona. She too was prepared for the worst. No matter what!

Victoria bent her head to the floor. Efemona could not tell why. And the tension between Efemona and Dudu in his spacious office grew deeper. Both began to murmur something, no other can hear and reply to. To Victoria it was like one of those moments of misunderstanding among thieves where there is a palpable shift in leadership or compromise when sharing their loots. Victoria senses this and turned the sword in the President's wound to make him bleed more. Then she whispered to Efemona, "Don't give up."

"Hum, me give up?"

The Dudu of a man did not give up either.

"You have been shooting needles in your clitoris to get high before coming into my office, huh? Americana?!"

Efemona looked at him perplexed. She sat like a woman in a trance. How did he know? Maybe his instincts or because he saw my eyes red. She told herself, No. The Dudu of a man is hallucinating. No he is mad enough. Anything is possible with the man when he's annoyed. He doesn't forgive like me. Realizing this, she showed a sign of coming to bow. No. If I bow before the idiot, who am I then? A Royal nonentity? Hell No! She sneezed once, then another followed. She blew her nose with Victoria's handkerchief in a bewildered fashion. "You have an Uzi tied around your waist. You might as well just use it with the silencer now," though a pair of familiar horizontal lines appeared between her forehead.

"If you leave this office alive, you will know that my name is not Bad Dudu Abacha. Over my dead body. Over my dead body," he yelled out with annoyance.

The tide began to change. At last Efemona felt an atmosphere, as when the lights in a room go out during thunder and lightening in Benin and Ukpenu and the house with its four walls and closed doors becomes suddenly quiet and dangerous to the naked eyes to see. The two women became terrified. Their faces snap to alert, fearing Dudu might pull the .45 Browning automatic pistol. If he does, nobody would know what happened to them. Her husband in Reno, Nevada would not give a damn.

Victoria worsened her thoughts. "Girlfriend, you be quiet. You must be out of your mind. You are not talking to President Bill Clinton in the Oval Office. And let me tell you something, you don't argue with a man with a loaded weapon. I don't want to die in this manner. I want to die of natural causes," she yelled. "Do you understand me? Do you hear me?"

The boomerang had struck. Efemona found fire shot from her nerves. Too many thoughts. Was it a plan for Victoria to lure her into the country like a lamb to the slaughter house? And her blood would be used to paint the walls of the President's office? She found herself gritting her teeth. To her, it was an invitation to her mugging. Her nostrils began to quiver though the President did not notice. Her fingernails grew an inch, when Bad Dudu stared at her again and again and his eyes glowed as flames.

He could not hold himself. "Victoria?" "Yes, Mr. President?"

"Tell Efemona how I punish those who defy me, challenge me and ask stupid questions to make the President not be himself."

"Oh. Okay. But human rights activists and Amnesty International might be after your ass, my dear."

"Go ahead, tell her. I don't care."

Well Victoria has his permission. Victoria hesitated. "Tell me, my dear," Efemona pleaded in a soft, but harsh voice.

"Well, I let you decide for yourself after I tell you the heinous crimes of the President. If you still want to run your mouth, that's all up to you."

"You are holding us up. Go ahead, tell me. I don't give a fuck," Efemona, the Amercicana said.

"Well, there are four rooms in this spacious office of the President. In one of the rooms is a holding cell for a man or a woman to be punished. And the rest of the rooms are punishment rooms. The man was allowed to choose for himself which of the rooms he wanted. The man opened the first room, and before him was a bucket of ice cold water. He immediately knew what it was meant for. So he declined to be punished in the room. Next, he opened the second room, and there was a bowl of shaving cream inside it. He was not such a fool not to know what the room and the shaving cream was there for. So he declined the room. Next, he opened the last room which had a chair and was full of cow and horse dung. At least he would sit down, forget his troubles and relax, he thought. So he chose the room and sat on the chair feeling happy. "You know what happened afterwards?"

"No, tell me," Efemona said.

"Ten minutes later the President torturers opened the door and said to him, "Okay, my friend. Your break is over. Time to bend your head over the cow shit and start eating.""

"Thank you, my dear, for telling your friend what I'm capable of," Dudu said.

The worm her grandmother gave her to swallow before she drowned in Nigeria potholes moved in her stomach. To Efemona, it was telling her don't let the President see her fear. And right then, her only goal since Victoria has joined the President was to be calm or even tougher. She made herself straighter on her seat. It was a question of pride: A remodeled African Ukpenu woman who Americanized and Naturalized mustn't beg and show weakness. The Americans were there to rescue them in times of trouble. To say the least, American judges from Reno, Nevada who are biased when it boils down to black versus black thing or black versus white thing, who only see the wrong black people commit against white and not white against Ogbebor, a black, the man whose testicle now hung at Circus Circus Hotel and Casino, were behind her. At least Efemona therefore mustn't show a sign of weakness. She decided that a little bit of comedy might work the miracle, if not, she would try seduction.

Finally, Efemona said, "Upon your words or whatever evil you are planning. Well, upon my words too." She walked towards Bad Dudu who was now standing baffled, contemplating. "Don't you know how to entertain a joke, *Mr. Aporaka face?*" Efemona said and grabbed his balls. But you know, I still think you are a dunce and a motherfucker. Give me a kiss" and the kiss she'd long denied him was about to begin.

Dudu laughed. The worm seduction has caught him. He found himself kissing and licking her red lips. She peeled the two shoulder straps off her shoulders. Her breasts hung unrestrained before his eyes. They were the type he loved. Victoria opened her mouth. What she wanted to say, died within her soul. Her new sex appeal caught Dudu, she thought, and winked her right eye at him.

Well, Dudu thought: Efemona started it. He walked to where he'd his music boom box. At least it was music while he worked and signed signatures to embezzle government funds out of his country. But this time it was music of romance with Efemona. He switched on the FM stereo system. By coincidence, Fela Anikulapo Kuti was singing his famous *"E speak Oyinbo pass Englishman."*

Though he didn't like Fela and never will, because Fela had ridiculed him a lot through his music, he reserved his animosity at this crucial moment just to dance with Efemona. So he took her to the spacious floor and moved his footsteps to the rhythm of the song. He found himself humming a different version of the lyrics to suit the moment to humiliate her. He sang along with Fela. I regret Fela's music is the one and only song playing in my favorite station at this crucial moment. My mentors who'd ruled this country didn't like him. They even killed his mother and burnt down Fela's home all to shut him up and dance to our whims and caprices. He was too strong headed. Anyway, I have no choice now. I know you and your Southerners love his music and the nonsense against us he preached. "I'll sing along with Fela this time, just for you."

The jazzy saxophone beat has just finished and Fela was now singing the opening verse of his lyrics. Dudu sang in a rough, untrained, novice coaxed voice of *apétési or gworo and Ubiaroko grass*:

> *"Efemona speak American slang*
> *Pass American people,*
> *I say Efemona speak American*
> *Motherfucking slang pass American*
> *Ghetto men."*

After they danced and he thought he'd humiliated Efemona in his own way, he took her by her elbow and walked her over to her seat and stood for a moment over her head. Then he walked back to his seat. Then he sat very still and looked straight into Efemona's eyes. "I understand you are the only one and only woman from Nigeria who knows how to dance Ójeké for the judges and the entire city of Reno, Nevada population?"

"And what's wrong with that?" Efemona asked sharply. "For your information, I only dance it to humiliate men who think women are of low class in the world, men who are as stupid as yourself, spraying money on foreign women carnals and men with dubious characters like you and Ekiaqueta, my husband."

The one thing the President noted was that with Efemona, she's always to the ready to reply to his words, with no fear. Mad enough, he raised his eye brows, *"Gbejayléghé, atilogun, be-ojéké mamen onokana,* Miss never afraid."

Within now and the next few minutes I will dance all the named dance you just mentioned. But first let me satisfy your appetite for my carnal lust," and she walked up to him and rubbed her titties on his face and mouth and withdrew them slightly from his face. There his anger quickly transformed into boobs lust. His eyes moved up to her obliging nipples as dark as wood ebony, disobediently erect before him.

As he looked at the boobs before his mouth, an Ibo phrase of *papa bomboy anwulugo* popularly used by Onitsha women to insult Irrua men was registered on his mind. The meaning which was not too far away from what Efemona was up to: The father of my three children is dead, but inwardly happy about the inheritance, she would acquire. And what did he leave behind for her? Man! He left nothing except an old car, an old bicycle and a little hut. Efemona therefore was a profile of what he envisioned in his heart. She was capable of poisoning her husband to acquire his wealth just like *me* laundry Government funds overseas all for myself and my family.

As he thought of this imprinted heinous phrase on his mind, Efemona caught one of her titties by her right hand and pushed it into his mouth. "This is how to entertain a joke." Seducing him, she slowly lowered her gown down, way down below her thighs. He was surprised at what he was looking at. "Man!" Bad Dudu thought, Nigerian women from abroad these days are good looking as Lebanese women, though his heart was pounding, and his lungs labored. Perspiration poured forth from his forehead to his face, as blood rushed to concentrate in his manhood. He moaned involuntarily when Efemona finally revealed the huge triangular womanhood avenue which was sufficiently covered around her mound with bushy dark hairs. With happiness, he yelled out, "Elijah the prophet is great." He salivated again. Astonished, he said, "Efemona, if somebody walks in and sees us . . ."

"So what? They will have me too if they are real men," she said. "But don't worry though, Victoria is guarding the door and besides, what do you care when you are the King, the Caesar with military uniform in power. The absolute man in power. Who on earth therefore, will have the power to challenge strong headed Pompey like you?"

As his eyes became normal and transfixed into Efemona's covered dark bushy mound, and the repellent nipples, perhaps now better looking than copper type, he then remembered a secret he'd hidden for years: £8 million pounds to sleep with a blond British woman secretly arranged by a Lebanese pimp in Britain was imprinted on his mind which he now had started to regret about. Finally Efemona said, "Mr. Dudu, I came in two modes to honor your invitation. First, to appeal to you about my people suffering. Secondly, to humiliate my husband, Ekiaqueta in America. That is why I want to fuck you." Bending over, she picked up her panties on the floor she'd slipped down before him and slipped it into his Agbada pocket and smiled.

"Sit down, baby. I'll teach you how Congressmen and women does it in D.C." Bad Dudu stood baffled and perplexed. Then Efemona pulled one arm of his excess Agbada over his head to rest on his other arm while it left him with only his military uniforms. Finally, she gave him a light push on his chest with her palm and he fell on his oversize executive seat. He thought then smiled, what a precociously seductive woman of Lolita caliber of the famous Vladimir Nabokov's novel. As he thought, his dick hurt in his khaki pant. He moaned something in Arabic which Efemona didn't quite understood. She bent over and pulled down his khaki pant to his knees. His manhood was huge. As they say, a man's huge size is the same as his middle finger.

"Can you handle it?" Dudu asked.

"Ain't no stupid dick rich enough is too big for me, baby." She opened her legs. The more Efemona was teasing him, opening up her legs and then closing them, the more he salivates like a dog in the butcher's shop watching the masters meat and licking its own balls. Finally, she sat on the rigid dick and with her two hands to his cheeks, she brought his lips to hers and kissed him. He returned the kiss and never intended to stop kissing her. Every now and then he clasped his head between her feminine boobs and thrust his mouth to one of them when he fumbled with his kissing.

"I love it," she moaned softly. "Suck the titties, baby. Suck it harder."

He took a breast in each hand and squeezed harder while he sucked until his jaw ached. He grabbed her hips and thrust her down, then up, then down, then up, then down. Slowly, faster, slowly, faster-. While he found himself moaning Arabic joy of ecstasy words she didn't even understand, she too was enjoying it more than him.

As she began to secrete and ooze out the charm and secretion of the Royal curses in her blood to caught him, she opened one of his buttons on his military khaki shirt and sank her long resemblance of Flo Jo nails into his chest. He grunted with a mix of pleasure and pain not knowing Efemona has taken his blood in her fingers to wash it into the jar of blood for doomed men the Royals of Akinzua Palace keep for record purposes to hurt men of his type. On that pleasure note, the phone rang without interest to pick it up. Could have been any of the leaders in other African countries as tough as himself. Dudu was carried away, and almost laughed when Efemona was singing Fela Anikulapo song of:

Zombie-o-zombie
Zombie-o-zombie

For him. He'd to quickly cram one of her breasts into his mouth to suppress his laughter, and Efemona cursed him, *"I know you go die on top of toto."* Oh! Pardon me. Efemona meant to say, Dudu will die on top of pussy.

The phone rang for a long time before Etinlinhadoya, his secretary picked it up and answered, "Please call back. I think the President is having a meeting."

"Yeah right," Efemona murmured. "He's fucking his brains out on the hot seat with me while Abiola's spirit haunts him and Babagida for denying him the seat as the President elect of this country."

He began to enjoy the fuck more than Efemona. Efemona asked, "Let's say you were to fall sick or have a stroke after fucking me would you treat yourself in this country?"

"No, my dear," his reply chatted out. "Why not?"

"Because, the hospitals in this country are not well equipped, no medicine. Why do I have to treat myself in this country when doctors in this country are not qualified as British and American doctors." To Efemona it shows how stupid he really was when he was the brain behind why people die often in Nigerian hospitals. He did not know why Efemona asked him. He knew he'd wealth outside of his own country and when he falls sick he would travel to abroad to get his first class American or European treatment which to Efemona, the people he afflicted with the virus of poverty can not afford one square meal a day. On that answer and note, the curse of Efemona's pussy or vagina of any other woman was upon him.

"I'll tell you right now, Mr. Dudu, that my pussy and *one other* India apple damshells is what you will enjoy in your life as a dictator of this country before you die. The fool did not read any meaning to the soothsaying of Efemona. He was enjoying the thrusting of his huge dick into Efemona who closed her arms tightly around his head then raised her clasped hands towards heavens and began softly to whisper and pray to God and the gods of Ukpenu and Benin and Ogoni-not only for an erotic chant in his ears after her pussy, but praying also that God would please-touch- Dudu's soul for him to call for election for the people of her country before He calls him on the judgement day after eating the one and only India damshell I have predicted. She continued to twist her butt making him to like it even more than her. As she was punishing him with her pagan instincts and therefore unable to come she whispered soft words revealed by angels of the Lord to him: "You see, Dudu, Nigeria has well educated men. They who can make policies better than Sandhurst Army Cannon Depot University trained soldiers. Ain't you ashamed that you and your predecessor who'd ruled this country has ruined the life of the founding fathers of this country? The very literate men of this country who fought for the Independence of this country from Britain, you and your men drove them into exile? Ain't you sad that Tony Enahoro is regretting ever fighting for Independence for us. That Zik died a pauper? Awolowo was only given a humiliated burial? Ain't you ashamed that he didn't rule this country to inform the Britishmen that not all men in Nigeria are one and illiterate to devalue and ruin our economy to launder money in all the Banks in Britain to re-build their fallen Empire? That Sandhurst trained soldiers like you can only ruin this Nation? And they will wrench it out of disillusion and cynicism? I doubt that you Bad Dudu Abacha and your man Babagida have that capabilities and philosophical ideology which Zikiwe, Enahoro, Awolowo, Gani, Tae Solarin, Chinua Achebe, Dr. Usman Yuguda, Cyprain Ikwensi, Wole Soyinka, Dr. Hassan Adamu all have. Even you too know that they are men with American ideologies with sound education. To me, the doctrine of personalism that you and your men borrowed from Britain no longer is appealing to the people of this Nation. I tell you right now that it is *now* yam and cassava subtlety. It does not make sense at all any more. And if you were a grassroots politician who'd a talent and a personal magnetism to sway my people, I advise you to sell them to Wole Soyinka, or Achebe, because these people are well informed and the people of this country know their record and respect them in literature. But you and Babagida and your mentors and junta regime doesn't have that knowledge and charm among leaders of the world except in Britain. Y'all are savages, brute dictators which make Nations to be anarchy. Please arrange for an election and let the people of this country vote in their man. Is that too much to ask? Huh?!"

He moaned the pleasure of release when Efemona gripped him tighter on his head and moaned her last words of: "Please Bad Dudu."

He'd sucked her titties like a hungry baby and she doubted if he was even listening as he was enjoying the fuck. "Talk to me," she moaned too. But he wouldn't talk, at least for a few seconds for the joy of precious release. His climax wasn't as vocal but was just as tempestuous. For forty-five seconds afterwards his mouth was fixed to her breast, and her head was resting on his shoulder. "Talk to me, Dudu!"

He was short of words. Then she got up pissed and pushed his mouth away from her breast. *"Geez-esuz! Come chop na come die?* No manners at all? Want to bite my breast off because you like it too much?!"

"Are you alright?" Victoria asked and was by her side to the rescue.

"Yes am alright. Dudu just want to suck them until I have no milk to feed my four month old baby."

They laughed. "Why would you want to do that, Mr. President?"

"I figured no other woman in this country who are hungry enough have enough milk in their breasts to feed me when Efemona was gone," he joked.

Efemona and Dudu looked at each other. Finally they sat up. Their torsos gleamed with perspiration. He looked at her again and told himself she's too gorgeous a woman. "What a tigress you are, Efemona? I doubt any one of my several Lebanese women, except maybe Thailand women compared with you. British blondes are not good. For now only him know the story of the British blondes as he smiled to himself and saw the mess of puddle on his thighs and on his executive chair. Allah have mercy for Efemona for seducing me and he bowed his head thinking.

Chapter

22

T he heathy Israeli guards, Esemueda, Poisonous and Hemlock, who left Dudu alone to handle his business the best way he saw fit, all drove out onto Doddan Army Barrack recreation Officer's Mess for healthy Generals alone, where they eat free food of: stockfish and pepper soup, thinking who Efemona might be as they chew and swallow their stockfish and cow legs. The more than 80,000 acres of Federal Government property had computed to something like about 120 square feet of mostly habituated Government Offices of the Hausas nepotism arena. There are, however, few Yorubas, suya sellers and cattle rearers inside the offices themselves, with millions of pounds, yens, dollars and more of foreign currencies in their Agbada pockets and don't even know how much they load up of Federal funds in their huge Agbadas.

Esemuede, Poisonous and Hemlock guard these other Generals when the President doesn't need their services.

As I said, the place stank of Hausa nepotism, which I think is the reason why Ph.D. holders don't have jobs and aren't able to feed their families. But still, that doesn't mean they have started eating shit in the country. They would rather rack their brains, steal with weapons and kill or come up with '419' activities.

Anyway, on the apropos of Poisonous and Hemlock's silence in the General Officer's Club, Esemuede said to them, "I think Efemona might be a powerful woman who came with a mission to reduce Bad Dudu and Dudu doesn't even know it."

"I hope he radios us soon to hang the daughter-of-a-bitch for another $2 million bucks," Poisonous said.

"Yeah, right. And that would add to our existing $10 million dollars in Israeli Banks to fight the Palestinians," Hemlock said.

On that note, Esemuede ordered three more shots of Cognac.

And Esemuede was about to ask another question, when Hemlock choked as he gulped his shot of the Cognac when

Babangida, also known as the Political Leper, walked in.

Lest you don't know, the military in Nigeria is perhaps the foremost Nigerian bastion of Hausa nepotism, which is fixed and clearly defined in respect to order, responsibilities, duties, and in case the top guns needed guidance, there's a manual for the Israeli paid soldiers of fortune who snoop around intellectuals tables of the Yorubas and Bendelites to know what they were planning against Bad Dudu and Babagida.

Once or twice, these three Israelis had related to Bad Dudu about some men from Benin who were planning a coup to depose him. And Bad Dudu acted on their information and then told them to poison them one by one. After they were all poisoned and died, Bad Dudu quietly paid them with a loaded suitcase containing a billion dollars and life became more exciting for them being in Nigeria and rubbing shoulders with the Generals who don't value lives of the poor.

Babangida quietly sat near the juke box and slotted in some Kobos to play his selected favorite of Mina music, the traditional music he grew up with, then walked back to the counter and declared enough booze for all in the Officers Mess Club. As a slow smooth duper of Government Funds, he doesn't talk much, neither does his wife. He'd declared the booze to shut everyone in the General's Club up. He ate his stockfish and British, French and American imported salad and wiped his mouth, then walked away. He does that every day, when he was not signing signatures to release ships in the high seas loaded with Nigerian crude oil.

As he was gone, Hemlock said, "But you know, I think Babangida is one of the smartest few in Dudu's regime, that has committed the gravest misdeeds against Nigerians and is even unrepentant-like Dudu we all are working for. Unlike other Generals, Babagida has close to $500 billion in Swiss Banks and that's not including what he has in British Banks."

"Do you know why he's able to get away with so many atrocities and the loot, it was because Nigerians are not so much civilized as the Palestinians in the Middle East against us in Israel," Poisonous corrected.

"If a Nigerian can come up with $5 billion today for me, I'll get the motherfucker the same way he masterminded the killing of Emeka Ngozika and all the Southern Generals going for OPEC meeting in Zurich. For the killing of those Generals that he had promised to pay me $4 billion but never did. He thinks he's the smartest General duper Nigerians have produced. Shit! He can only run, but cannot hide as history is beckoning on him for his role in the socio-political and suffering of the masses, the atrocities he committed against literate men fed up of his signatures on the papers when Dudu had cold or *iba* that retired him for three months. Fawehinmi also wants the idiot arrested for his crimes of looting the Central Bank of Nigeria," Hemlock grieved.

Esemuede listened, but no words to express his bitterness against Babangida. But in reality, all three men are one and the same. Finally, they finished their drinks and headed back to their special office well equipped like the gym where they torture civilians for Bad Dudu Abacha.

* * *

Meanwhile, Efemona and Bad Dudu had finished making the love of the millenium. And as she sat up first, she said the last word of 'please' again with a wry, proud, grown-up exasperation, as a flirt submitting to the powers imposed by a superior higher than her. She did not look at Dudu's face again at least for several minutes, but was busy looking at his thighs and the seed that might have been another Dudu Jr. in her womb that flowed out of her as she thrust herself up and down his huge dick or penis, whatever Africans now call it as the Americans. Then she took some Kleenex from her purse and stuck them into herself and pulled her dress up. Dudu's military uniform became hopelessly wrinkled because of the starch, which had absorbed most of the sweat for the pagan punishment Efemona made him suffer before

378

he could come, to flood her womanhood. The sweat, though, which might be noticeable, would not be noticeable when he slipped on his Agbada again in the proper fashion. Even when she Kleenexed him, his lap was still uncomfortably sticky, which is no problem because his Agbada would cover it, and no one would notice. When she was finally done cleaning him up, she said to him, "Mr. Dudu, I know you like to fuck. Victoria would be sixty-nining with you on your desk if you adjust your manners. But you know, I have never witnessed a man throughout my love making and experimenting with various huge dicks, biting a woman's breasts as hard as you did to me. By the way, are you a cannibal, a dog, or a sadist? But please don't bite those of Victoria. She doesn't like pain." Little did Efemona know that the man she was talking to had slumped into his executive seat and dozed off into a deep slumber. And Efemona began to wonder: Maybe the fumes from her vagina put him to sleep or that Dudu must've had enough tea and *gworo* and *suya* with rum and plenty of Lebanese young women he fooled around with and navigated with the power of Viagra the previous night, before her, that made him so tired.

Efemona looked at Victoria and said, "What do you think?" "I think we better give him a few minutes to recuperate," Victoria said.

"Well then, I think we should step out to the General's Club and have something to eat. I'm starving after the fuck of humiliating Ekiaqueta down here at the Doddan Barracks, my dear." Victoria laughed.

And on Efemona's suggestion, Victoria picked up Dudu's ball point on his desk and left him a note on his steno pad which read: *Bad Dudu, Efemona and I will be back shortly. We went to the General's Club for lunch. Efemona might've more questions for you when we return. Enjoy your nap.*

* * *

They went in to lunch in the glass-fronted General's Club only for Generals and American VIPs. The Americans on special invitation to see Bad Dudu have code names and badges to identify them. Efemona and Victoria had it because they'd traveled from Reno enroute to Lagos in false name as I said before. This glass-fronted General's Club has recently been built by Bad Dudu for his wife to make dubious money and it was similar to the Crystal Cathedral in Los Angeles. Efemona placed Victoria on her left.

The waiter, a tall Sudanese man who worked for the First Lady with white gloves on both of his hands seated them at an elegant table, with candles and silverware. It was the same table ex-President Jimmy Carter and his daughter Amy and Andrew Young had dined with President Shagari two decades ago. The food here compared favorably with the best of Reno restaurants as the Harrah's Roof Garden and other restaurants in the area Efemona had dined in Reno before she'd traveled with Victoria to see Bad Dudu on his invitation. This General's Club cuisine was no different. Efemona ordered *Ngwoogwoo, stockfish, pepper soup* for the fun of it, while Victoria could not decide what to eat. For one, she had never before eaten in such a good restaurant displaying American cuisine before her. By the time she finally placed her order, Efemona was half way into her *Ngwoogwoo*. Victoria ordered french fries, hamburger, egg rolls, whole boiled pig foot, whole smoked salmon and whole chicken. How could she finish all the food she'd ordered, Efemona thought.

"I know you cannot finish all the food you have ordered," Efemona voiced out.

"Opportunity comes only but once in your lifetime. I'll stuff my purse and parcel the rest to my people in the village who have not tasted chicken for the past three years because it's too damn expensive these days, through Dudu's men who have price ceilings on suya, goat, rams, herons and cattle meat imported from Australia.

Efemona had not meant to ask that kind of stupid question when she knew everyone in her country except the Generals themselves, eat well and spend our money on British and American cuisine in the General's members only Club.

With that thought, they began to enjoy themselves. The place was cool except for the dragon flies fighting with the women on their hands to their mouths. "Dammit," Efemona said. "With all the crude oil revenue nature blessed this country with to benefit every hard working farmer of this country."

"Damn right, my dear. The zombies believe in Britain, Swiss Dubai and the Cayman Banks rather than fighting poverty, the deluge and the dragon flies of this country," Victoria said.

As Victoria was fully relaxed and eating the American cuisine she had never before tasted if not for Efemona, Efemona excused herself and headed into the men's restroom. She closed the door behind her and meditated for a few seconds. After meditation, she turned herself into a dragon fly and flew back into the President's office. Here she flew around his head *seven times* avoiding the mosquito machine itself not to be the victim of death first before Dudu on what she planned to do. After flying around Dudu's head *seven times*, she transformed herself again to a human being and did an oddly relevant traditional Royals ritual to cast her famous Royals spell on the President.

Looking at him, she said out loud, "I tell you how to be a statesman, the people you rule will love and respect you and you too will respect their feelings. And when you die, the whole Nation will mourn you and feel sadness. I promise you no one in this country will mourn your death that I, Efemona forecast to you today."

He was still deep into his nap and never knew Efemona had came to cast the Spell of the Royals on him.

Noticing that the President would never woke up until she told him so. She then walked to the wine and his liquor cabinet and opened what she believed Dudu drinks regularly while signing signatures to release tires in the high seas imported by civilian businessmen, but ceased by his Generals in the high seas to punish the businessmen to be poor. Then she opened the half consumed bottles of Cognac, Jack Daniels and added some voodoo herbs into it. When she was done, she transformed herself again into the dragonfly and flew back into the men's room to become what she was before. Turning into Efemona again, she walked out and joined Victoria at the table still enjoying herself with American hamburgers and fries.

Then Efemona allowed Victoria to swallow the food she had in her mouth before she asked, "Do ordinary people come in here often to dine?"

"No. Who go give monkey banana?"

That pissed Efemona off even more. "I'll tell you a little secret, Victoria, that when we get back to the President's office, I will have to record my conversation with him. This is a special day for me. You might not know this. But it is the truth."

Victoria laughed. "What's so fucking funny about that?" "Just thinking about the Nobel Prize you'll receive in the near future," Victoria said.

"I hope so," Efemona said.

Victoria drank a bottled water of Aquafina, which she'd never before dreamt of drinking. And after drinking half of the bottle, she replaced the cap and tightened it and placed it along with her unconsumed whole chicken and whole boiled pig foot in her purse. Though the Generals in the Club were wondering what she was doing, they were dumbfounded. The women were gorgeously dressed, they might be the mistresses of other Generals from abroad, they thought.

The women headed out majestically and walked towards the President's office. A few steps out of the General's Club, Victoria said, "The Army Captains and Generals from the North are really the ones who enjoy most in this country and it sounds to me they know that Nigerians are afraid to challenge them."

"That's another reason I came with you to challenge the President and not the mere vacant post he wants me to fill. When I was growing up my teachers used to say, the Hausas are very honest. But in truth, they are slow poison. Do you want to tell me we have a true democracy in this country? I tell you that we don't have equal amenities for all, but some people get more of it than others." These are some of my grievances and I want to pose it before him when we get to his office. And you sit and watch what I came into the country to do," Efemona said. "Good luck, girl friend," Victoria said.

*　*　*

It was now a typically hot Lagos-Ikoyi afternoon, with a soft breeze from the Atlantic that carries the resinous tyrmine of riches of gold and silver and bundles of currencies through the seas to their Agbada as the rich Generals walked the long hallways of corrupt and nepotism building where *bread was made to rise without oven*, as I said before. And Efemona and Victoria walked in casually without interference from the nosy guard whom Efemona had insulted before.

The truth about that is if I were in his shoes, I wouldn't want to be insulted with a saltery mouth and Yankee slangs of the Americans.

Anyway, they walked in without *"Hey madams, where una dey go?"* and Bad Dudu was still in deep slumber with his neck tilted to the left of his executive chair, his custom hat on his head had fell on the floor. Efemona smiled and walked a few calculated steps in his direction where he sat, snoring heavily with an unusual guttural gurgling vibration. And even with his unusual guttural sound, it did not stop tse-tse flies from buzzing around his nose until two retreated to the top of his military hat. The two stubborn tse-tse flies had avoided the direction of the mosquito machine because they were in the likeness of Efemona's namesake from the Royal Palace to help put the President into a state of dreaming to tell him that he would enjoy his last days on earth.

Due to the temperature of the room, a rancid vapor had emanated from his nostrils which was due to his guttural snoring Efemona had lured him into with her paganistic instincts voodoo. She smiled when she looked at his condition she led him into and then picked up the hat on the floor and placed it on top of his military hat and immediately the President jerked up like a puppet manipulated by a robot, but fell back to his nap.

"Hum! Look at your nose dripping cattah," Victoria said and added, "And you are ruling. Some leaders of great other countries might come in here to see our President in this condition to think that all Nigerians are like you, zombie, for a country with clean and decent people with common sense." With his unusual guttural snoring, the only big anopheles mosquito in the room that has not met its untimely death buzz around his nose and the breeze from his nose send him around the mosquito machine and was captured. Meanwhile, Bad Dudu was having bad dreams. He'd dreamt that he'd jumped down from a moving vehicle, and had ran along a lonely road crying for help as the car sped away without him. As he tried to run after his car, his

$2 million native hat specially made for him by his father-in-law in Sudan flew off of his head in a terrible harmattan wind. As he tried to run after it, a woman was standing by him waving and saying nothing.

"Is he dreaming or what? Come on wake up, we are back," Efemona yelled at him and pinched his nose with her pagan voodoo toothpick in her hand. And he jerked up again. "These damn mosquitoes in this country," he found himself saying and opened his eyes not knowing Efemona had pinched him and wanted him to die.

"Look at you! You have a big booger in your nose, Mr. President." "Please give me the Kleenex on top of the liquor cabinet, my dear, if you will."

With annoyance, Victoria walked to the liquor cabinet and squeezed out a hand full and handed it to him. "Here! Wipe your nose," she yelled at him—as a sign to tell him that people like him shouldn't rule the Nation. But he did not get it.

"By the way, did I fall asleep on my gorgeous visitors?"

"Yes. You embarrassed us and the Nation at large, Mr. Dudu," Efemona said.

"Sorry about that," he said and looked at Efemona.

Only Allah and Prophet Mohammed knew why he apologized. Then he fumbled into his ashtray and extracted the half Havana cigar, which had formed a precariously huge ash and stuck it between his lips. He had not really meant to screw the daughter-of-a-bitch. But she did seduction number one on him. He knew the bitch had more questions for him more than fumbled response. So he reached for his lighter on the table and lit his cigar. He puffed and puffed for the craving of the flavor hardly pausing for breath, holding it with his right hand to his lips. Finally, he sat it down on the tray where it belonged.

Efemona looked at him too, fully alert. "Are you ready to answer more questions?"

"Just go right ahead and ask me any questions."

"Okay, Mr. President. All the weapons you mentioned, I mean snipers, rifles, motars, cannons, Uzis and fighter planes and jets, why are they stationed in Kaduna and not decentralized in Nigeria?"

He looked at the ceiling above him and sighed as usual. "Because all my junta members believe they should be there. The British government who makes most of our decisions for us because we pump in Nigerian money into their banks and so had warned us not to decentralize the arms now in Kaduna, because if we do, we are fucked and our powers would diminish and they will never support us again if men from the Southern part of this country should occupy the executive office where I now sat. It is the reason why I believe that the British empire existed for the colonization of the world and purposely for this country for which I now rule." "Goddammit! You got to be out of your mind, Mr. Dudu.

How dare you say that? Mr. Dudu, I have a different notion about the British Empire. But don't get mad more than you've been if I tell you the truth about the British people."

"Go ahead, tell me about British people, which my military junta and I know more than you before you were even born."

"Well, Mr. Dudu, I personally believe that the British Empire existed for the ruining of the world at large, especially for my country, Nigeria. They are inhuman people. I don't mean the ordinary citizens of Britain. I mean their Government and their philosophy about our country, when they colonized us. Look what they left behind in my country: Corruption, nepotism and giving the not-so-bright people like you power to rule."

As Efemona talked, she wondered if the hungry could be armed with the proceeds of his gold Rolex watch if sold in Christie Auction, to replace him and his kangaroo courts and the junta for karma and retribution of those he'd killed.

Victoria swallowed the bile in her throat. "And you said 'us'.

Who is 'us'?" she interrupted the President.

Deep in thought, Dudu said, "Never mind."

"What do you mean never mind? I didn't come all the way from Reno, NV to be told never mind. Jesus! I wish Christ would come down now to tell you how I feel right now, sucker," Efemona said.

Victoria managed a weak smile and slapped her friend on the back for a sign of support.

He thought Victoria slapped Efemona on her back for a good reason, then he said, "Both of you can ridicule me as much as you can. Smile and wink at each other as much as you can. By the way, what do you know about Christ? You weren't born when I wore my first imitation of Caesar's uniform and bought my first imitation of toy gun waylaying innocent people on the street for *Naira and Kobo* before I went to Britain, got trained and graduated at Sandhurst. If you want to know more about Jesus Christ, you ask me, my dear. I will tell you HE was a revolutionary just like me, but with a different message. His message was to the poor, preaching equal social and economic justice to the masses. Mine is to repress, rule, kill and make the masses suffer. The men Christ chose for his disciples can tell you that if they were still alive today. I mean his twelve disciples or comrades or working men or proletarians or whatever you may call them. The women he loved were whores like you, Efemona. That's why Christ and I are different. I like women who are not whores and are married who submit to their husbands. So what do you know about Jesus and his father God? You were still in your mother's womb when I fired my first Uzi that killed Ironsi and put my brother on the throne. Efemona, you know nothing, my dear," he mocked.

I must tell you that where I sat in my living room watching, I was stunned at what the President had said. I shook my head in disgust, noting that he was blaspheming against the creator of heaven and the earth. Efemona and Victoria were stunned, too.

"Now he's blaspheming against his creator," Efemona looked at Victoria and said with exclamation. Then she looked at Dudu and bolted out from her chair. "You called me a whore? Yes! I might be a whore, but don't forget that if a woman sleeps alone, it is the fault of the man. Men. I will tell you, Dudu, that all men, including yourself will render their account on the day of judgement, especially if the widowed, the divorced and the separated like me, soon to be, invite a man to sleep with her and he declines. You will be surprised that God will forgive all sins, but never will forgive the man who turned down the woman who want to be laid. God has a reason for that and that is, if the man sleeps with the widowed, the divorced or the separated, HE forgives the man's sins, and HE is then pleased with the man, just as Archangel Gabriel. If God had, for instance, followed these men who turned down invitations on widows, the divorced, or the separated, and had never gone to see Mary, Christ would never have been born and given a life. You might think that is logic, but it is not, Mr. Dudu, just to let you know, fool."

I shook my head where I sat. How Efemona, my wife, knew that was astonishing to me. The President, too, began to reason to see things the way Efemona was seeing things. But as a Caesar in the image of Caesar on the hot seat in his Nation with absolute power, he did not want to admit it. He let Efemona finish her story. At this time, I could not wait to hear Efemona's immediate continuance of her argument before him. But on my return from the bathroom, Efemona was saying, "I'll tell you the path which God follows, Mr. President. HE follows the one leading to Mary's. Mary, you know, was a widow and I, too will follow Mary's path in Reno, Nevada."

He nodded his head. Deep in thought, he looked at the two women before him. They were gorgeous. He could send for their husbands and have them hanged and would then take them away from their men who allows Efemona and Victoria to sleep alone. Finally, he said, "That's why some tyrant leaders, Dudu not alone, in African countries kill men who have beautiful women and let them sleep alone, going to their farms and coming home to tell the women 'not tonight', because they are too tired. Me! I'm never tired because I sign signatures all day."

I was surprised to see him pause, but got up abruptly and shake his head left and right. Then he said, "Efemona, let's not talk about God now because I believe you don't know that much about God. You might know a little. Just a little. Do you know how God made man? And the first words this animal, man, said to God? Me and my junta advisors know and we were there listening to *them.*"

My little boy, Oziengbe, had woke up and came to sit on my lap, a sign to tell me he was hungry. So I got up and carried him on my shoulder, then took my gadget toy of Radio Shack technology which allows us these days to see our loved ones far away, to the kitchen and sat it on the dinette table. As I was humming a thought on my mind that Efemona had met her counterpart who is ruthless and good in argument, unlike me, who is dumb and unable to express myself except on the paper, I saw Efemona got up and said to Dudu, "Please tell me and Victoria what the words man created by God first spoke to God. Even if you answer me to convince me, I'll still tell you that you are blaspheming against your creator though, Efemona said, baffled. Her grandmother, once the Princess of voodoo practice in Benin never told her what the first words were. Anyway, as I was preparing Oziengbe some quick snacks, I saw Dudu said, "Creator my ass. This earth is the heaven and the hell. If you have killed men and seized their wealth to enjoy yourself with it, you are in heaven. It is like me killing, raping, draining the country of billions, every day, five days a week."

Oziengbe looked at the picture in the gadget and said to me, "That looks like my mama, daddy. Does that man with the big nose and the hat on want to strike mama, or what?"

"No," I said, "Efemona is arguing with him because she claimed she knows more than him, the man who has lived on this earth before her."

"Oh, is that what it is?"

"I believe so," and he was quiet.

I gave him his sandwich of bread with chicken baloney. As he sat down to eat, I sat and watched from afar. Anyway, Bad Dudu was now saying, "You see, God had woke up one early morning and has no one to speak to. With the powers of the universe acting on HIM alone, HE molded a calf similar to those of your grandmother at Akenzua Palace, from the earth resembling HIMSELF. But the calf did not talk to HIM. Then he put on his eye glasses and cut HIMSELF a cane from the bushes within and whipped the calf. Then it jumped up standing erect. At least HE was surprised, too. So he left him there for a little while. On the seventh day after resting enough, God came back to look at him. HE was surprised to see that the sun had baked him to black, which was what he least had wanted to see. HE'd expected to see someone fair in complexion like HIM. So furious, when HE saw the color, HE said, 'Go, go, go, just go away and suffer, but multiply the earth. Eat yourselves alive if you can. That's why our forefathers sold their sons and daughters. And that is what we are doing. I have no creator. My father and my mother are my creators."

"Don't be blasphemous," Efemona said after listening to him again argue blindly.

"You know," Victoria said, "He has every reason to blaspheme against his creator. Money is power."

"Do you mean to tell me this gaunt face, leader of First World will reject to shake his hands in a summit of leaders of the world, has money?" Efemona asked in whisper.

Victoria said nothing, brought out a few Kobos from her purse and shook them in her palms before her and him. The sound was of silver similar to American quarters, nickels and dimes. *"Oh! Ncho- cho man?"* Efemona asked.

"That's right," Victoria said and nodded.

Efemona looked at the President and smiled. Finally she gave a thumbs-up for him. Turning to Efemona, Victoria said, "Him and his men are the people draining our oil money. They have billions in Britain and Swiss Banks."

Efemona herself loves money. It does not matter how she gets it. Hearing that the President has *Ncho-cho*, she too, was thinking fast on how to con him of millions if she could. He might be a fool in various carnals of women, but he'd learned to be careful with Efemona, the smarter than smart of all mother of smart women of Africa.

The office of the President was so quiet after Victoria reflected to Efemona how rich he was. Efemona stood and walked a few steps to him and stopped, looking at him and adjusting to the quietness and the nuances of Bad Dudu, the way her grandmother had taught her to look at evil, mean spirited men, poor or rich.

Finally Efemona said to Victoria turning her head away from the face of Dudu, "For some time now, I have been having awful dreams about my country that children these days in my country now carry chairs and desks on their heads to school." Victoria winked her left eye to Efemona signifying to Efemona it was not the right time to ask him why! So she walked back to her seat and sat. The President had relighted his huge Havana cigar again and did not hear what Efemona had said to Victoria. Anyway, the pagan voodoo worm Efemona's grandmother gave her to swallow before she died moved in her diaphragm which was the one that alerted her to come across men with lots of money. Why the worm had failed to instruct her if I was rich before she got involved with me was still a mystery to her. Then she looked up at Dudu again. She had always wanted to meet famous men with lots of money. But not the blood money of the Federal Government Dudu and his in cahoots crooks are embezzling night and day out of her country. She pressed her lower abdomen with her index finger and the worm moved up where she can recall what the voodoo worm wants her to do to Dudu. So as Victoria looked at her again, and she, Efemona looked up at the President in the fashion of having lots of the blood money of the masses stocked up in various banks in the world, it was as if the crack of a leather whip was introduced into her skin. Efemona smiled an evil smile at him. Carefully choosing her words from Cleopatra, Efemona said to Dudu, "I'll love you to death. I'll love you with other Kings who are rich with round strong arms, such as those you have. And when I am tired of loving you, I'll whip you to death or sue you to acquire more wealth, but you Dudu, shall always be my zombie hero: my nice, kind, wise, good old soldier among African kings of the kings." She laughed. He too, laughed. He did not know what she was up to. The spirit of her grandmother had caught him again.

He looked at Efemona and her shining demonic eyes. "But you have insulted me by saying I'm old. What you don't know is that I have a bounty of grey hairs, but bounty of wealth."

"I already know that. It is the money God blessed Nigerian soil with to nurture every citizen of this country," Efemona replied sharply.

He still wasn't paying attention to what Efemona was gearing at, which shows how stupid he really was. He said, "I believe you have been the most notorious and dangerous among women I have invited into the country from abroad to assume a vacant post, but suddenly found myself answering unanswerable questions.

One thing you don't know is that my junta members and I all have old and young sweeties too, even younger than you think you are."

"That is not the point, Dudu Zombie Dudu," Efemona said and hunched her evil eyes up at him.

"Do you think I'm happy that your children and grandchildren all go to school in Britain enjoying the National oil wealth you looted out of this country and the poor children of this country, including my brothers and sisters, now carry chairs and desks on their heads to school every morning-chairs and desks their parents and my parents borrowed money in the bank to buy so they can be educated? No! I'm not happy about that! I want you to know that."

Where I sat in my living room in Reno, Nevada I watched Babangida sneeze seven times and almost choked to death for the blood Government masses embezzled funds he has in Swiss, Britain, Cayman, France and Germany that made Nigerian children to carry chairs and desks on their heads to school. Still, Dudu did not get it which touched my nerves the more, because I had equally sent money to my brothers and sisters to buy their own chairs and desks so they don't drop out of elementary school and be laughed at in the near future by Babangida and Dudu's children who are now enjoying the wealth of the Nation, their fathers stole from the Nigerian government. Come to think about it, and where it hurts me so bad, was that the chairs and desks had cost me about a million Naira. How many parents in Nigeria can afford that kind of money? Absolutely only the zombies who had ruled our Nation and drained the National Treasury bone dry possibly could. The fact though, was that it was not the cost of the chairs and desks that touched my nerves, but rather the fact that I'd to wash dishes and pots in American kitchens and restaurants so my brothers and sisters can be in school in a country that imports crude oil to foreign countries just as Saudi Arabia, Kuwait, Iraq and Iran. In most of these oil producing countries College students in these countries drive at least a Volkswagens car to school.

It also touched my nerves that my friend from Aba, Mr. Okafor, a family man of five, a complete gentleman had to lose five fingers at an American fast food restaurants washing giant pots to be able to send money to his brothers and sisters to buy chairs and desks so they can go to school and have a chair to sit on and a desk to spread their notebooks.

I must tell you that it did not only touch my nerves, but also reminded me of how I had washed dishes at St. Mary's Hospital for seven years and a packer at Loyal Extrusions for another five years. And the funny thing about my working for so long at St. Mary's Hospital had been that Adriene Josephs of the Food Service Department had pretended to like me. A lady whom I will describe as a class 'A' type personality, hard working, goal oriented, driven to demanding the best for her employees who were white to get benefits, but refusing to settle for raises when it involves black men from Nigeria. I knew that to be because I had common sense to observe and because actions speak louder than words.

Anyway, she was an intelligent woman who quickly grasps the overall significance rather than searching for details. I will also tell you that she had a natural ability-an intuitive sense-that enables her to perceive what food the chefs should prepare quickly in the kitchen at peak period and so on and so forth. As a matter-of-fact, Adriene was the first American to ask me if it was true that Africans still live on top of trees as Apes and Monkeys. The question, which I found offensive, when she was reviewing my application for a kitchen helper. With all the years I busted my ass working for a minimum wage with no benefits and receiving insults from everyone in the kitchen for being so dark coming to America to wash dishes, heavy duty pots and scrubbing the kitchen floors, I still was not given a raise or even a thank you for the excellent job I was doing. The fact was, I was the only black man who had worked at St. Mary's kitchen for five years at the time. With my intention to quit, Adriene finally assured me that within a couple of months, I would receive a promotion and a raise. The reason for the speculation as I soon found out was ACLU got into their business for not promoting a black man. As a result of that Adriene secretly informed me that I will soon be promoted to the level of a Head pot washer if I can beat the record of cleaning two heavy duty dirty giant pots within fifteen seconds. What a humiliation, I thought. I took the humiliation and insult for all the Nigerians in America and especially in Reno, Nevada to remind Bad Dudu and Babangida's junta regime that Nigerians abroad are not supposed to receive insolence from anyone in the world if not their stupidity and greediness to drain Nigeria bone dry of its resources and not creating jobs for College graduates and University graduates. And above all, killing students who came home to Nigeria to challenge their junta regime.

Anyway, because of ACLU threats, to act on my behalf for promotion and a raise, St. Mary's Hospital was finally willing to promote me with strings attached-which was, I must show that I can beat the record set by another minority-a Mexican a decade ago before I was hired who later retired and died in his sleep from complications from chemicals he'd used to clean the pots. The funny part of the whole thing about the promise of my promotion was not assured me through commitment in writing. Six months passed by. My raise and promotion eventually faded away despite that I'd practiced hard to beat the record of five seconds set by Jose Jesus, a Mexican. The news that a Nigerian had set a new record of washing giant pots in the kitchen restaurants across America was carried by AP wire services, which was grounds that I might be fired before I even get the promotion and a raise.

My instincts told me I might be fired so I called my friend, Babangida at Ikoyi and asked his opinion on what to do because I was about to be humiliated and degraded. His advice to me was encouraging. "Ain't you a Nigerian?! Come on, steal their meat or whatever you lay your hands on." I could tell that he was mad as hell that I was not as sharp in thinking as he was with Bad Dudu. He hung the phone up on me. With that in mind, I built up an animosity against St. Mary's Food Service Department for discrimination, that on my lunch break when everyone was out of the kitchen, I would go into their cold room housing the goodies such as the prime ribs, steaks, lobsters, chicken breasts and shrimp with a trash bag then load it up. After the load up, I will sneak out of the cold room and walk a few calculated steps out of the kitchen and dump it in the back of my car and rush it all home after work.

For quite some time Adriene didn't seem to have any knowledge of who was what! Who would believe that it was Babangida who gave me the idea? Anyway, I became greedy. I overloaded the damn trash bag one day with just about everything I laid my hands on to ship it to my folks in Nigeria who were starving to death when it busted in the middle of everyone waiting in the time clock area to clock in. Everyone in line looked at me as if I were a rock in the middle of Lake Victoria.

If the heart of the matter be told truthfully, I shouldn't have listened to Babangida. Because of that, it was the first embarrassed look I got since my arrival to the United States. "Wow-ooo! He's getting away with it. The African from Nigeria is damn too smart. Check that out," a Filipino nurse on the line had grumbled.

"He's smarter than us. Why didn't we think of that all these years we have been busting our asses?" a Mexican said. "Haven't we been scrubbing the floors here on minimum wage?" Quickly, I hauled them back into the damn trash bag, not caring what they were saying and walked out to my car. Somehow the news got around. My fellow employees thought I was sick or something for doing that. Getting no promotion or a raise, what would you do if you were in my shoes? Well, I did not regret doing it. That afternoon, I walked straight to Adriene and said to her, "Ain't no one smarter than a Nigerian. Let's call it even," and that got her mad. I walked out on her anyway.

It also touched my nerves when I remembered the insolence of a high magnitude I received being a Nigerian working for Loyal Extrusions, a plant where hours worked by a Nigerian and Mexicans were ducked by payroll clerks, notably by Holy Shit and Gerald Fuck Da Nigga on a regular basis. Holy Shit, for instance, was slightly younger than Honey Fleming, Tanya, Holly Jackson and Miss Janice Beck. Some of these women gossip all day in the plant facility about one particular Nigerian who claimed he's a writer, but working overtime. It did not move the Nigerian, *which of course was me.* Honey Fleming, the proud lesbian, was the brain behind why I was being repressed because she claimed she couldn't understand my accent the way I talked which made my boss to move me way behind the machines so we don't see each other as regularly as before when she was walking by. Anyway, among these mean women which nature had punished to be on their monthly period (PMS) every day of the week and 365 days of the year, at Loyal Extrusions, Janice and Holly Jackson were the only two who were extremely respectful and cultured. Holy Shit, for instance, was the smartest among them. She has a dubious character of ducking employee hours. By the time I knew this I was short of words to express my bitterness before her in her office for ducking my hours on every pay period. The thing was,

I was so preoccupied with the writing of this book that Holy Shit was able to cheat and duck my hours on pay days. By the time I found out, I had ended up on the street of Reno, homeless, while Holy Shit had bought herself a brand new 4x4 Tracker truck, which gave me the concern to investigate why I ended up on the sidewalk of Reno. But before I realized this, all the women I mentioned above knew what was going on, mocking me as they passed by me on the floor at Loyal Extrusions facility. And on the whole, Honey Fleming, for instance, was always getting on my nerves, purposefully looking for me to mock me with those Japanese panda bear eyes. Honey was thirty- five (or was she forty?) mean pussy and brat. Mean lil' daughter- of-a-bitch who kept Loyal Extrusions a gossip place. My outstanding memory working in this plant rests on the time that I had to walk into her office one afternoon when I couldn't take her insults and bullshit any more, that I'd to pee on the asshole's head where she sat gossiping about me. But anyhow, Honey was not autistic or anything, just that she was mean and evil. Maybe she'd experienced a bad birth delivery which rendered her assless too, and mean.

For the record, Tanya, who was sitting next to her buddy gossiping about me became surprised and had to jump up to avoid my shitting on her own head, too. This particular bitch, I will tell you, has a flabby titties and proud of it. A mean and racial women like her, I make her eat my shit before she pay me to make love to her. What really annoys me about Tanya is that she thinks she's the all and all at Loyal Extrusions. Despite the fact that her eyes were always on the opposite when she walked past my area where I work all day sweating, I had the courage to say 'Hi' to her one afternoon, only to ignore me and looked at me as an ape or something. This happened not one time, but thrice. I figured this was my time to tell Tanya my pen has taken over to inform her that she's a stinking, ugly, bitch, motherfucking stupid fool and idiot. I hope the next time we see each other again Tanya will have learned manners and respect for her elders.

With all these negatives at Loyal Extrusions of humiliation against me and Holy Shit ducking my hours and cutting herself huge checks from not only me, but from the Mexicans whom the personnel communicate with daily with sign languages, I had to call my man, Babangida at Ikoyi on the telephone to relate my bitterness. What he did tell me on the phone made some sense to me. He told me, "Tame the Holy Shit for Christ sake to tell her no one all over the world can cheat a Nigerian and get away scot free, but that only Nigerians are blessed to be crooks, it doesn't matter where they are in the world."

Babangida became mad as hell as I told him what Nigerians go through every day overseas with racial bitches. Hanging up the phone on me, I could not sleep that night, only to think of a way to tame Holy Shit to dance to my whims and caprices as a true Nigerian.

Anyway, it all happened by Nigerian voodoo that Holy had to become my sex slave. The thing was, I had just got off work and was awaiting the City's Bus at the bus stop when Holy saw me standing in the rain. She pulled over her 4x4 Tracker white truck and asked me to hop in beside her on the passenger's side and soon enough her glazed blue eyes began to flirt with me.

Driving with happiness, I flirt back with Holy Shit. Her flirtatious glances became full fledged hot looks that I couldn't resist. I noticed she was attracted to me and I was attracted to her. Serendipity was on the move, for Christ sake. Why Holy stopped for me after ducking my hours and buying herself a new car from the hours she ducked other employees I think was not only because of my Nigerian voodoo that'd caught her but rather was not going to be the frustrated woman her mother was who did not experiment with a Nigerian dick before she died. And number two, Holy was determined to find out if Nigerian dudes had bigger ding dongs than white American dudes. Anyway, she drove me to one of the downtown casino hotels where she quickly paid for two nights just for me and her. I confess here that Holy Shit was a good virgin I'd never come across in a long time. Though she was mean at work with me, my Nigerian voodoo spirit had caught her to get naked for me to feel her body and sodomized her the way she wanted it. I started getting really worried about four thirty-five in the morning when I found out her glazed blue eyes were still glazed and her mean look was still registered on her face as it was when we started screwing from the start. Her virginal was also intact, too, not because

I hadn't made a tripple of penetration at it, but because my penis had been stunned into giving up by the cement hardness of her vaginal lips. As I investigated the reason why the pussy was like as it was under the bedside lamp, I looked at what seemed to be a normal pussy. Anyway, I woke her up because it was time for us to go to work. On our way, I corrupted her mind, a way of taming her to become mine and whenever I was busy working on the manuscripts, she should swap my time card for me, being at work or not. She had no objection with it. Which shows how powerful my dick had satisfied her. She even apologized to me on how she was the brain behind the ducking of employees' hours. And she'd the impetus to ask me, "By the way, weren't you surprised that most Mexicans grumble about their pay checks every pay day? And weren't you complaining about it too until you got fed up of coming into my office to pay you what I'd ducked from you?"

I sighed and nodded my head. But I said to her after she had finished, "Would you from now on do me a favor now that we are good friends?"

"What favor do you want me to do for you?" she asked with remorseful tongue sticking out to kiss my lips.

"Well, I want you to clock me in and out at work, five days a week."

"That's no problem."

Thus I tamed the bitch until I finished writing this chapter. And even when I'd finished writing this chapter, I purposefully would not show up at work while I was in the money, getting paid without showing up at work. Three months later, Holy Shit signed her home title and her 4x4 Tracker truck over to me. I still was not satisfied, so I began to pimp her to the homeless men on the street who'd almost forgotten the pleasure derived from carnal navigation of women, both ugly or beautiful. When she finally contracted the AIDS virus, I let her die like a chicken. I was not remorseful because Nigerians believe in the adage, *"Do me I do you. And God no go vex."* With the news of what had happened to Holy Shit, everyone at Loyal Extrusions realized that Nigerians are tough people, and that no one should underestimate a Nigerian to tame an American woman with hamburgers and cheese to get even. Nigerians are good at that, folks!

The mere thought that I remembered these thoughts as Efemona cautioned Dudu about school children carrying chairs and desks on their heads to school while the juntas and Dudu all have billions in foreign banks, I did not only give a thumbs-up for Efemona, I soloquized almost jumping to my feet before I realized I was watching my wife via satellite in Nigeria.

Anyway, back with Efemona, the African woman with balls, Victoria looked up at the face of the President looking sour, thinking of the children going hungry to their schools in the morning with their chairs and desks on top of their heads. To relieve the President's mind from these children who find themselves born into poor homes, Victoria said to him, "Ain't that a shame I haven't even formally introduced Efemona to you since we walked into your office and Efemona and I have said things we shouldn't have said? So much of your vexation, Mr. Dudu. *Make una introduce unaselves.* Oh excuse me, Mr. President. Efemona is here. It is my pleasure to introduce her to you."

With that note, happiness could be seen on Dudu's face. Efemona will not ask any more questions to upset his stomach, he thought. He stood up and walked up to Efemona, put out his strong firm right hand. And he said, "Good day Efemona. I am pleased to have you here in my office."

Efemona ignored his hand. But she said, *"As Salam aleykum,"* she ridiculed. "I'm pleased too, Mr. President." *"Wa aleyka Salam,"* growled the President.

The thing is, this sudden rememberance of Efemona greeting the President in the muslin fashion is an everyday infernal muslim greetings which had been adopted even by unbelievers to get the day going without trouble in a country inhabited with Christians and muslims. For that reason, Efemona's natural courtesty got the better of him. Then he walked to his seat and sat. Looking at Efemona, he said, "As I said before, your name was drawn up for the post of Matron General for this country to oversee the running of the hospitals of this country and its General Healthcare problem this Nation has faced over the years. You are the most qualified and the most experienced person for the job. I'm offering you the vacant position with high pay scale with housing allowance and most important, you can date any of my junta members, *since you no longer qualify as suger daughter, but mommy daddy.* How many children did you say you have now, three?" he joked.

"Yes, three," Efemona laughed in return.

"Then you now qulaify as Ikebe! Ikebe! sugar father! Mommy! daddy old! old Ikebe! daddy daddy-young sugar in my junta regime," he joked again. Finally he walked two steps away from his chair with a bright, forced encouraging *thiefman* smile. Then he added, "Coffee, tea, *UnLondon Gin, madam?"* with a wry grin like the sketch of a fatherly servant about to serve an obedient child. What Efemona had long waited for to happen because she, too, was thirsty.

As the President was half way to the wine and hard liquor cabinet, Efemona said, *"Undouble Gordon London Gin."*

"Ah! Bien sûr madam."

He brought Efemona and Victoria their gin double shots and *double, double, double* shots of Cognac for himself.

And they all touched glasses.

"A la vôtre, m'sieu," they said.

Efemona didn't quite remember how to say I'm still married but will soon divorce the son-of-a-bitch when she returns to the States. Anyway, she said instead, *"Merci, pour le Undouble London Gin, m'sieu!"*

Then he smiled with a magnificent slight bow and said, *"De rien, madam."*

They all drank in silence for a few seconds. Efemona watched as Dudu sipped on his gin. She couldn't hold herself and she said,

"My God, the President does have a big Adam's apple I have never seen in ages."

Victoria looked up, "Sure he does."

They were all mute for another few seconds. The President downed his *double, double, double* on a second sip, then he looked at Efemon directly in her eyes and finally he said, "Men with unique characteristics like the Adam's apple of mine were created to command and rule. It is in history, my dear. Take a look at those great men in history who had ruled all over the world before me. They all had unique features about them which made them great leaders: Richard Nixon, big ears and big nose. Henry Kissinger, big ears and deep accent. Brezhnev, the former Soviet Union great leader, big eye brows. Muritala Mohammed, your late former head-of-state, big eyes as the moon. Mr. O-"

"Okay! Okay! Okay! Okay! Mr. President, Okay!" Efemona was repeating for him to stop. Finally, he stopped.

"I didn't know you were that enlightened," Victoria said to the President and looked at Efemona.

The President didn't want Efemona to attack him with education so he said quickly, "Efemona, you look very healthy and pretty. Victoria, too. Efemona, you have become very beautiful, more than my wife now. I'll invite you someday after today, for you to help me teach my wife the secret of your make-up. She would love you to death, Efemona if-, rather than she go to Europe to spend one million dollars to do her nails. I believe you fixed your long nails you display before me by yourself."

"By the way, the women of this country could be healthy and pretty if they could afford three square meals a day."

He was busy lighting his huge Havana cigar and did not hear Efemona. The compliment, on the other hand, did not stop Efemona. She knew all along why the President has too much power. Money was the key to his ruthlessness and why he would rule for life.

He walked to the wine and liquor cabinet again and served himself, then his guests. The spacious office became silent with an austerity of the ascetic. The walls shone on their eyes. The carpet which has recently been imported from Britain was beautiful. Apart from the few photos that Dudu had damaged their glasses when he dribbled the women tossing the soccer ball over his head to score several goals to one, there still remained thousands of portraits of the living and the dead on the wall. No one but the Almighty alone could tell how happy Dudu was when Efemona began to apply more lipstick to her lips, then shadow boxing in front of the huge mirrors of the portraits of Queen Elizabeth before her. At least Efemona has run out of questions for him, he thought. He was relieved. Right there in his thoughts, he'd an overwhelming purpose that gave meaning to his thoughts and thinking. He began to eye Efemona from the corners of his eyes as Efemona began to brush her hair. The way he looked portrayed him as wry, amused eyes, at least for his guests consumption. His natural cynicism he kept veiled as far as Efemona could see.

As she was done with her make-up, she looked at Dudu. Then she said, "I honestly don't know how you function on this hot seat without a law degree. Even some Nigerian professors who attended Yale, Harvard and Stanford have trouble wondering Why! Why! Why! As the laws of our Constitution you have made now pile up faster than what Lourd Luggard, Margarette Thatcher, John Major and Blair had intended."

He found it difficult to respond. Rather he said, "I measure up to all those great leaders with unique characteristics I mentioned, my dear."

"I'm not your dear. But anyway, that brought me back to ask you what you meant by *Ikebe, Ikebe, sugar father, mommy daddy, old, old, Ikebe sugar,* Mr. President."

"It means you can sleep around with any of my junta members who rule this Nation with me, married or single after work at the General's Officers Mess Club, because we have billions and we have the power to lay women VIPs we invited into the country. And for you to be happy with *real men*, I'll give you an office at Abuja, close to my office inside the Black House. How is that? You are my first pick for the job, Efemona."

"Would there be enough *London Gordon Gin undouble, undouble?* That's my favorite, Mr. Dudu. It does not only make me flippant with my husband in America, it also makes me more horny," Efemona joked, too.

"I'll have it plentiful for you when at work or after work, Efemona. *Undouble gin* shouldn't be a problem. But mind you, mind you that I am about to make some changes, just because you are in the country, to be sure, but aside from a handful of my rich and powerful old Generals in the Nigerian Army, there has never been beautiful women dining with us in the General's Officers Mess Club. Most often, I go there to dine when Generals are there, the place is fairly partisan in regard to who is on the line for the relay race baton. I mean, for instance, Bad Dudu and Ogboru were not as likely to be at the corner table as my junta members who support me and know who was on the line to rule. Just for you

Efemona, I'll instruct all Generals to undermine your flippant tongue when you are dining with them and can't stand our Arabic slang."

Finally, he dropped the glass of drink containing Jack Daniels shots on the table and some of the colored liquid splashed on Efemona and Victoria. It was on Victoria's left breast. He'd done it on purpose, because Victoria, according to Efemona, was supposed to be sixty-nining with him on his huge desk. They had forgotten, but not him. And he said, looking at the replent nipple from the two shoulder straps of her velvety gown, "Can I lick it?"

Victoria looked at Efemona in a manner of look-what-this- idiot-has-done, soiling our expensive dresses and not at all remorseful. Efemona, never short of words, said, "That's what I'm talking about. Dudu and his junta members have no manners," shaking her head. Then she took off her sunglasses from her face and balanced it back on her head as white people do.

Efemona had went with Victoria to Nigeria or more precisely, been conned to Nigeria to accept a post that would net her millions of dollars through Bad Dudu's regime. Was that enough to insult her every now and then? Efemona thought as the President said, "It was about time you took the glasses off your eyes." With that sarcastic remark, Efemona glared at him as if she might slap the fuck out of him to cast the demon out of him, but then she remembered the President was rich and he could go to any length with her and to worsen the situation, she'd screwed him on the hot seat and he might publish it in the papers that her pussy was not gold but as the Golden Gate Bridge.

The President, too, could tell that both women were annoyed. Finally, he said, "I'm sorry, my dear-s, It's just that I was hungry for Victoria carnal, and to suck her titties." For the insult of no manners Efemona thought the President had he said to Efemona, "You are in my office to accept a position. Please to warm your seat and be seated and listen to me. I'll appreciate it if you don't use foul language to curse me out." Then he stood up from his oversized chair. And Efemona stared down at him. "Not in this office for which no one voted you in. You must be out of your senses," Efemona said, seething with rage. Then she attacked again. Victoria became mute, but looked on at the African woman with balls, talking to the President any way she feels. Her mouth working more than normal after swallowing her shot of *London gin undouble.* "You know what, Mr. President? I think you are a cunt sucker," Efemona said, bristling as Victoria stifled her impulse to choke with laughter, but bowed her head. "You answer me, motherfucker. Why didn't you receive me and Victoria at Abuja, the new capital? Do you mean to tell me if the Queen and Prime Minister of Britain were to visit you and your junta members tomorrow, you would welcome them in this slum? Where would you receive them? Tell me, what do you call insult…?! I tell you motherfucker, cunt sucker, that you insulted us."

Actually, where I sat watching my Efemona, I began to feel out of depth. How had my father not done his homework before tying me up with a woman of Efemona's personality, not respecting men?! What would've meant a reversal of the situation with Efemona was saved by the bell on the door of the President's office. The door opened, and a young female runner walked in and walked the length of the spacious office, over the Britishlike made carpet, and detoured around the Great Seal of Nigerian emblem, then back towards Dudu's desk, which sat in front of the Julius Berger Canal in the distance. The young female runner handed him a letter and he did not even look at it or the girl. The young girl walked out the same way she'd walked in. But Efemona noticed that the girl did not march on the Great Seal so she stood up and walked on it to piss the sucker off more, more than he'd been. He got offended, but did not know why Efemona had done that.

Anyway, it was ironic that Dudu had never traveled to England, United States or to the European countries, since he, too, toppled the man with two hats on he claimed was corrupt. So he knew not what motherfucker, cunt sucker and bitch meant. And so the President laughed. Hah!-ha-ha-ha-ha-ha-a-a-a-.

Victoria knew that in her mind sooner or later, the President will find out himself and might decide to be ruthless. To avoid that, she said to Efemona, "For my sake, please give him a little respect."

"You stay out of this and be quiet," Efemona warned Victoria. Facing the President, she yelled, "When shall the zombies give up arms and let the very smart people like me rule my damn country, cunt sucker?"

He laughed even louder. "Hah-ha-ha-ha-ha-a-a-a-a-a-h. He read a different meaning to Efemona's abuses which showed how naïve the world at large had alienated people like him from the world. "Enough is enough of my jutna members robbing the poor people of this country with power of weapons the Britishman gave us. They are mis-using the arms to kill poor women going to their local market to sell *ugborele.* I am going to deploy my junta's honest men on the street at night to stop the armed robbers that it will no longer be tolerated killing innocent people going to market. Above all, when that has materialized, I will stamp out corruption," Dudu said.

Victoria, who was held spellbound with the President's message of wiping out corruption, wiped some tears from her eyes. And Efemona looked at the President. She said to him, "How would you wipe out corruption when yourself believes in Britain, foreign banks and award thousands of ghost contracts year after year, swinging the kickbacks from such contracts to Europe, cunt sucker, motherfucking asshole?"

"Here I go," Dudu voice out with amazement. Efemona is something, he thought. Then using Shakespeare's words out ot the 'Merchant of Venice' he had on his desk, he exclaimed, "A Daniel come to judgement in my office."

He was now aware that Efemona has been cursing him. At least his common sense had told him that. To Dudu, Efemona is very rude to remind him of foreign banks and ghost contracts he awards every year. He lost his temper and fired back with annoyance. He is fluent to speak 45 out of more than 450 dialects of his country. He yelled out, *"Oui."* But *oui* was French. He had for one minute forgotten Efemona's dialect. As pissed as he was, he sat up and moved closer to her. Pointing his index finger at her, some kind of actavistic instincts reminded him of her dialect. He could not help himself. He delivered curses upon curses on her not only in her language, but in other different ethnic dialects. To hell with Efemona. If she wants to accept my vacant post fine or you can go back where you came from. This country doesn't need people like you challenging the MAN. *"Enay-wolo-ne-mame. Ne- Bini-be-Esam moe ghekwo-Nó-Oghvaragbon-ekwo-Ragbon-opia. Agbonmerele.* You got the balls?! Not afraid, huh?! Your balls are bigger than mine, huh?! *Awa Ukin. Dog Ukin. Gbo-ojeke nosi Royals nu dógbe ghva Amerika mame onokana.*"

For a minute Victoria thought the President was going to pick up his pistol on his desk and blow Efemona's brains out. But he paused. "Calm down, Mr. President," Victoria begged.

"I'll appreciate it if you don't tell me to calm down. Why don't you tell Efemona to stop reminding me where I hide the Nation's money in the world. It is not her business to inform me." He became more tense. "This nowadays women, like Efemona, a devil who never would've dreamt of going to America if not for blind men like Ekiaqueta or What Can I Say or whatever his name meant, who saw you as cute, when their husband takes them to America they sell their masters to the white man, spread their legs for different men to humiliate them, prove too know, jail them, then take a curtain in the red light districts neighborhoods populated by drunks, prostitutes like you, Efemona, who went to America to sleep with homosexuals then experimented with lesbianism before fucking American wide horses and donkeys all for the love of money, sucking different pricks as big as watermelons, as saxophones and trumpets, forgetting that Africans, men or women have morals and culture and these are abominations of the white man per se, will come to my office to insult me!"

"If you and your junta members were not siphoning the Nation's money out of the country, and had created jobs, I'll not form the most powerful organization on earth. My organization of African Women Against Marriage movement helps women of this country to obtain visas to held overseas to sell their carnals in Italy, Spain, Britain, in fact anywhere in the world when Nigerians outside of Nigeria should be respected with dignity. Because of you, the women of this country, outside of Nigeria have lost their self identity and dignity and culture. The men of this country are no exception. Some have turned homosexuals abroad to be able to send their parents dollars and pounds to feed themselves. Because of you and your junta regime, who instilled poverty on the people of this country, fellow human beings have now resorted to cannibalizing on their fellows with flesh, grilling their feet, their hearts and saving some for later, pending when you relinquish the hot seat for which no one voted you in. Motherfucker!"

The mere mention of men cannibalizing on human flesh reminded Dudu of Mr. Orji. Though he didn't show remorse for the culture of poverty he and his junta regime inflicted on the people of Nigeria, and men and women selling their butts for dollars and pounds, he was bent on silencing Efemona for telling him the truth. He looked at Efemona with animosity and hatred. "Now tell me, smart woman, which one of the abominations have you, yourself specialized in just because you want to get rich quick just like me and my junta members to come to Nigeria for men of this country to worship you as a hench Maddam? *Gbakana woman! Tu pah Norma woman?!* Huh?! Over my dead body. I tell you that any more ugly remarks against me and my junta members would be met with sad news to your parents and that is, if they know you are in town. But if they don't know that you are in town, you will vanish overnight or right now! Oval Office or Reno without Efemona. Now is that clear, smart woman?"

He waited for her 'yes' or 'no'. There was none.

"Efemona?" Dudu called. "I invited you to either honor my vacant post or refuse it. I did not invite you to challenge me or to lecture me. At this moment, I have no reason to pressure you for the post. It is too late. Let me refresh your memory with some names to see if you still remember them. The names of course are men of this country who tried to tell me they were too smart to uncover my atrocities and embezzlement. He started to name names:

"Minere Amakeri. Do you know him?" "No."

"Thompson Irabor-not your own father. Do you know him?" "No."

"Dele Giwa. Do you know him?" "No." "Nosa Igiebor. Do you know him?" "No." "And Saro Wiwa. Do you know him?" "No."

Efemona remembered a few of them, but had lied. Dudu has every reason to boast to remind Efemona he is still the Caesar. "Well," he said as he looked at Efemona, "I'll make sure you shit in your gown in the middle of your Village market at Ukpenu. I have the power to do to you what my junta mentors and recent members and I had done to the men whom you don't know."

"Victoria?" Efemona called out. "Do you remember or know who those people Dudu had mentioned are?"

"Yes! They were all great journalists Nigeria had, had and produced. Minere Amakeri," Victoria explained, "Was a reporter in Port Harcourt, River State, for the Nigerian Observer based in Benin City, the Edo state. He had covered a press conference of the Nigerian Union of Teachers, River State Branch, on July 27, 1973. The Union demanded better conditions for the teachers in the state and gave an ultimatum to stage an industrial action if their demands were not considered. The Union's demand and ultimatum were then published by the Nigerian Observer on July 30, 1973. Commander Alfred Diete-Spiff, the then Governor, got him arrested by secret men in uniform and then took him to the Governor's office where the Governor personally bullied and tortured him, his hair shaved from his head and private parts and was also given 24 lashes of the cane on his bare butt and back before he was locked up in a toilet for 27 hours. And it was the handiwork of Dudu who gave the orders to the then Governor."

Dudu nodded his head as Victoria told what she knew in detail. "Tell Efemona who the others were, my dear. Don't be afraid. Go on, tell her. Alladammit! I want Efemona to know that *man dey pas man* in some ugly ways."

The ever inquisitve Efemona, never afraid, wanted to know. Then she said, "Tell me, Victoria. You think I am afraid? Hell no! Fuck Dudu!"

"The rest of the stories of these men will make you shit in your underwear, my friend."

"I don't care. Tell me," Efemona insisted.

"Well, Mr. Thompson and Mr. Irabor were both victims of Decree No. 4 of 1984 which was an obnoxious gag law directly aimed at silencing the press in Nigeria under the junta regime. The other two journalists, Tunde Thompson and Ndika Irabor of the Guardian were jailed for two years each for knowing too much. And Mr. Dele Giwa at the time was the Chief Editor of News Watch magazine. He was killed by a parcel bomb he received in his home which was rumored was sent to him by the President himself."

Dudu nodded and looked into Efemona's eyes for her reaction. He got none. Anyway, he gave a thumbs-up to Victoria. Victoria added, "Mr. Nosa Ijiebor was editor-in-chief of Tell Magazine. He too, suffered various forms of punishment from our *man,* the dictator, for calling for a true democratic civilian rule for Nigerians. And Saro Wiwa, Dudu determined was writing stuff that was detrimental to his regime and then constantly hammering on support and open rally for Mr. Abiola."

As Victoria recalled these ugly events one by one, Efemona shivered but tried not to show it. Dudu looked at Efemona and nodded at her with a whisk of his left eye, which was a sign of "Me and my juntas are the brain behind the several journalists we have shut up who can never write any more stuff detrimental to our regime. The voodoo and the worm her grandmother gave her to swallow which made her to be bold moved again in her stomach. And she knew that the President can no do shit. So with all might in her being, she said, "You can't do shit. *Udaleuison.*"

"That must be alien's language, Efemona. If you are so bold, why don't you say it in English, Yoruba, Ibo or Hausa?" the President said and looked at Victoria.

"What did Efemona mean by that?"

"I'm not an interpreter," Victoria said, but smiled and looked at Efemona and then to Dudu.

"You don't want to know," Victoria found herself saying to Dudu.

The worm moved again in Efemona's stomach. With that, she stood up. Looking at Dudu with absolute hatred, she voiced out, "Why are you asking Victoria? You should ask me. I said, you can't do shit, asshole."

Chapter
23

D udu can't shake off the feeling that he had invited Efemona to the country for his own ruin. Try as he might, he could not anticipate the subject which the young female errand runner with a letter to him had summoned him to discuss immediately with Israeli guards and Adam Khan. Not that the letter to him would be a summon for him to discuss, per se, an authoritarian leader doesn't discuss anything with the men whom he registered on payroll whether they have jobs to do or not. An authoritarian leader did the talking with his men who carry his briefcases full of foreign currencies for him overseas and they assimiliate with responses of 'Yes, sir' or 'No, sir' at the appropriate times. As the errand young woman left, Efemona began to eye Dudu and certain with herself that she'd not broken the rules by informing him to change his ways of corruption, nepotism and money laundering outside of his country. Which left some open alternatives that either Bad Dudu was actually going to yank off all the hairs in her private parts or ordered to submit to Esemuede and his fellow torturers who have no mercy for anyone once they were paid and told to carry out the order. Efemona then closed her eyes and bit her lips in protest, but without Dudu's knowing.

As Efemona thought, the President was thinking her opposite. He remembered how pleased Buckingham Palace in England regarded his bravery and his satisfactory marks as a brute and one of the most brutal leaders among leaders of the world, and yet Efemona is still alive talking shit and challenging him. How he'd earned satisfactory marks by virtue of his hard work and dedication to duty when he was attending Sandhurst Army Cannon Depot where he learned the trade of firing artileries. In firing motars, for instance, he was first in his class with credits of three hundred out of possible three hundred and twenty. In mathematics, physics, chemistry, English and French, he was nowhere, though, close to the Southern Generals in the same class with him who'd maintained straight A's. But on the roll of general merit, he stood out number one among five hundred students for nepotism, crook ways, killing and signatures on papers for recruiting cronies around the world. Which brought me to the point of my political thinking! Does that signify that Nigerian army officers who actually trained in England shouldn't be able to think as the Americans? Let's face the reality! Academy of Sandhurst or West Point in America are one and the same. These two world known Academies are established for the possiblity that officers who graduated and trained there should be able to build roads, harbors and bridges in their countries. In America, for instance, officers who trained at West Point Academy are proud of themselves in that they prove the value of their training on how to build solid harbors, roads and bridges, whereas Nigerian trained officers who came back after training at Sandhurst cannot build roads, design harbors and bridges. When they do decide to build roads and bridges and harbors, they give the contract to Strabarg, Julius Berger and Buckingham Palace Oni and Sons whereby the said companies give them half of what the contract was, then deposit the loot for them in foreign banks. For those of you who don't know, and for those children growing up in Nigeria, pardon my expression, that is how to be a true Nigerian when you occupy any Government office. But you know, the Academy of Sandhurst was supposed to be a reputation for Civil Engineering just as West Point, that was supposed to redeem that modern sentiment of engineering. In real sense, Sandhurst Academy doesn't teach the Nigerian officers engineering. What they teach them there is crook ways, how to topple and assassinate, and how easy it is to open foreign accounts in Britain after graduation.

The thing is, from any good training academy in Europe, Britain and America combined, the soldiers there are trained well. Efemona and I know that from eight until eleven P.M., the cadets were in training classrooms. In the first Nigerian classrooms the zombies-are taught Fundamentals of Brutalism, crook ways, how to topple and how to open accounts at Barclay's in England, while their counterparts in England or America tackled mathematics, physics, which included calculus, analytical geometry and conic sections, drawing and designing which included landscaping and topography and chemistry and philosophy. The later was all composed of instruction in mechanics, electricity, astronomy, light, heat and magnetism, with texts which included *Newton's Principles and Gregory's Treatise on Mechanics*. At about eleven and Noon, the cadets were allowed to return to their quarters to study. This is the time, the Nigerian cadets training with other cadets of Europe, England and America are given a special handout to read on how to be proper crooks on the paper manipulations of swindling Government funds to pay for thier training. For the credit for that, they were given one hour every day and different handouts to look into when they were exercising their free hour. After that comes the dinner hour which was at one, and at two came formation followed by studies and recitation in foreign language until four. The textbooks, none of which were written by African authors, were *Gil Blas* and Voltaire's *Histoire* de Charles XII. From four until sunset it was military exercises. Two hours every other afternoon were devoted to *artillery* practices. And again, the academy specialized the Nigerians on this more than engineering and learning in their classrooms. Then at sunset, dress parade and roll call were followed by dinner. And on every table where the Nigerian cadets were seated on the dinner tables, were placed human skulls, which is to remind them that killing was permissable toppling another leader of their country. After dinner and each robbing the heads of the skulls with their boths hands, they were dismissed to retire to their quarters to wrestle more on self thinking on how they will siphon billions of their nation's money to England and other foreign countries. During this period of their thinking, their quarters were not inspected which is to allow them to think critically on how they would pay the British trainers for educating them.

Realizing all this, Efemona looked at Dudu now standing and his back to the wall thinking always the why on his mind for inviting her.

Victoria stared at the thiefman, Dudu, momentarily nonplussed when he faced them again. Efemona and Victoria now noticed that Dudu had added another inch to his height, was now half an inch taller than he was, more gaunt face with gray black hair still covered by his military hat and his custom hat and was in a constant state of angry disarray, and brown eyes so dark that they looked too brown at times, beneath his bushy brows which met above the bridge of his huge nose, which gave him a more animal-like predatory look.

Then he heard a knock on the door. Without a word to the women before him, Dudu went to the door and opened it. Esemuede, Poisonous and Hemlock were waiting just outside. They stepped into the room and watched Efemona and Victoria, like a triple of trained guard dogs waiting for their master to give them a go ahead that would loosen them on Efemona for challenging their man.

"Yes! What are you all here for again? I have told you all, I can handle Efemona myself," Dudu voiced out furious.

The three spun on their heels and walked briskly away, their heads down, thinking what kind of charm Efemona had used to charm him.

After too much thought about Efemona and thinking of how to avoid her nonchalant attitude of too much question asking, he said, "You know, I'm afraid I have an important meeting to attend to in a few minutes. I would like to answer most of your questions if you still have any, but I'm sorry I have to go now," and he looked directly into Efemona's eyes, and then to Victoria. "Would you young women wait for me or we call it a day of Efemona in the country?"

"Will they castigate us at the meeting if we go with you?!" Efemona asked with her diabolical squeezed face. Then she hissed. The President did not pay attention to her squeezed face nor heard her hiss. He got up before the two women and was unable to answer the question. Efemona got up, too, and reached out to Victoria's right hand. "Come on, get up. What is he? Let's go with him."

And he thought, well, the Oval Office knew Efemona is in the country. They must've told her not to give him any moment of an inch from him. No matter what he said to Efemona to avoid her going with him, she would defy his words. So he let his vexation unwind. "Oh! Well, you follow me," he found himself saying finally.

Actually, he'd no meeting to attend. He'd just wanted to take a break and stroll the length of the long hallway and have some fresh air then get himself together for more tormenting questions from Efemona. Anyway, they all walked out with the President and walked the long hallway with him. As they walked, Victoria thought it was the right time to tell him what a true democracy was. She did not know how to begin. After much dabbling in her being, the issue of whether the Nigerian government should just do away with the army because they have and are still destroying our economy flashed her memory. She looked up at Efemona and said, "Of all the Greek nation-states, only the Spartans maintained a standing army and in truth they are the people who invented democracy."

That touched him. And he looked at Victoria critically as if to say I am an authority on the subject. But he said anyway, "Which doesn't mean the people of Athens couldn't fight when they were called upon to do so by their governor. The same thing applies to my own people whom I govern with authoritarian hand. Though in actuality, where I hail from in the North, might be a state of mostly cattle reaners who are chosen by the British during their Protectorate era of Nigeria, and then later became crooks of all time with the weapons of bullets and pen on the ink on paper defrauding the nation's wealth, we are averse to taking up arms in our own defense to maintain the superiority of the leadership of this country."

To show more authority on the subject for which Efemona and I are novice, he said looking at Efemona and Victoria, "Do you know who the Persians are who invaded their soil?"

He answered his own question. "The Spartan Army and the Athenian Navy."

I'll tell you that my thoughts again were broken into when this subject came up where I sat watching Efemona via satellite in my living room in Reno, Nevada. I soloquized again and bolted off my couch when Victoria said to Dudu, "I'll tell you, Mr. Dudu, that a standing illiterate army who cannot build roads, schools, harbors and bridges and a democracy are incompatible. A tyrant like Dudu, for instance, is using the army to subjugate his own people."

"That's exactly why the Englishman gave us the power for the masses to fear us. Our system of government will remain and will always be conduceive to tyranny if any strong headed Pompey try me and my juntas ruling now, and those who are yet to receive the baton from me when I drained enough of the Nation's oil money. I'd to use the military mostly my junta supporters to knock some sense into those who challenge and defy my authority like Abiola, Wole Soyinka and a whole lot of literate men of this country. So far I eliminated all of them except Wole Soyinka and Enahoro, both who survived my fangs because they're damned too smart scholars who the world recognized and had protected them through exile to be able to evade me."

"And that means in actuality Nigeria has no true democracy because of people like you as a leader," Efemona said.

Dudu looked down on Efemona's Gucci shoes as they began to walk back to his office unable to reflect on what he'd said over and over. So he said, "You know, Efemona, I'll let Victoria answer that question for me."

Victoria smiled. "Democracy," she said, "Became part of the Englishman's language in the early16ᵗʰ century, according to history and it was borrowed from the Union of two Greek roots: One, it refers to direct government by enfranchised citizens. Then in the seventeenth century, the term democracy had acquired bad humor in England during the time of Cromwell and the Great Glorious Revolution, which the conservatives later termed the Government of the Common People or what they coined the 'rabble', the worst conceivable form of government in those days is what I think you have now have adopted again in this country."

"My God!" Dudu cracked up. "Right now I must admit to my know it all women that I am now bored with the subject of political matters and issues. Why don't we discuss something else," he retorted.

"What is wrong in telling you that you and your junta regime have damaged this country's democracy which this country had enjoyed during Zikiwe and Enahoro?" Efemona interrupted.

He squeezed his face with no response, but endured it just because it was Efemona and the American people are behind her, gave her the power to challenge him, because in America, women have the power.

Victoria who could not hold her thoughts despite his facial expression said, "It used to be that in a true democracy, like our Republic as I perceive it, was supposed to embrace: One, that the people are the source of all political power. Two, that through representatives which are chosen by the masses, laws are made. And three, that all representatives must submit themselves and their actions to a public scrutiny by the people they are to govern. And that's what elections are all about in a democratic government which you claim Nigeria has but which I say we don't have," Victoria argued on his face with sincerity.

With that, she reached for her glass containing her shots of London Gin she'd left behind to walk with the President in the hallway. Then she stood and raised it in the Dudu's face. Efemona too, rose to her feet, then slowly, by force of circumstance, Dudu rose to his feet to avoid more rebuk. Finally, they all touched glasses and sat, and Efemona said, "To the Americans, and their intrepid foes in Oval Office who will free the people of Nigeria from the iron law of a dictator tyrant Bad Dudu."

"Amen."

He'd been fooled to join the chorus, because Efemona's spirit was getting into his veins. So he did not know when he said, "Amen instead of "Allah" along with the women.

"As I recall, Napoleon Boneparte was elected Emperor by the French people. But today who's to say a thing like that would ever happen in this country since Zikiwe and Enahoro, and all other Nationalists this country respected during the struggle for our independence? We all know what happened after the independence ceremony. Elections were held and were fair. It is not so today!" Victoria made sure Dudu got the message. Efemona gave her a high five.

Come to think of these political issues of good government, Victoria brought up as a reflection for the President to sit down and think about it did not mean a thing to him. The reason for that was because Dudu and Babangida were the scourge of the crude oil of the Delta areas, notably, Ogoni, Eleme, Burutu, Portharcourt and-which is why rumor has it that Dudu and Babangida had over five hundred cutthroats at their backyards. Their headquarters sources said were located somewhere in the Dem Mayor Room, the room where they made the bread to rise without oven, a barracoon of thieves in Agbada and murderers, complete with women they lavish millions in their carnals.

* * *

Efemona downed her *undouble* shots of London Gin. After downing it, she stood up and walked to the window and looked far and beyond the rice farms at Agbede and the Julius Berger canal Dudu claimed he dug with billions of dollars. Though the canal was beautiful and the vast acres of the rice farms beside it was huge, not enough to feed the Nation, the money Dudu claimed he paid the contractors for both projects was not worth it. But the beauty did not fail to impress her. On both sides, the canal was hemmed in by several fly boats with an occasional opening where the rich and famous Bad Dudu junta members stalled their boats, standing on their boats fishing. As Efemona viewed, a dense fog clung the canal like cotton, dissipating slowly as the sun began to rise before her. She could not help it and finally she said to Dudu. "But you know, I can't help but tell you I love the dense of fog in the distance away."

"It's even more beautiful at dusk when the canal is tasty for blood and that's when it turns blood red, then gold in the middle distance, and finally indigo blue as you'll observes further."

For a minute Efemona reasoned that he might pull the trigger and kill her and dump her body into the canal. She let that die in her being. And in the distance, she saw a huge man in the resemblance of Babangida, the one the masses nicknamed the 'politcal leper' who is proved to be worth his weight in gold bullion bullying a man who'd won an election with a landslide. It might've been Mr. Abiola or a farmer she'd known at Ukpenu. She wasn't quite sure. Anyway, the man's boat was not of the standard of Babangida himself stood upon. Babangida was yelling and cursing at the man, to get lost with his boat to wherever he'd came from to fish in the canal. The man resisted. With his resistance, Babangida got offended. And with his military uniform of brutality Dudu had honored him with a day before, he jumped on the man's boat, and capsized the boat and the man drowned. Babangida swimmed ashore with his life vest and looked at the man and his boat drowning, "I told you no one from the South survives our fangs. The Doddan Barrack executive chair is restricted to only men from the North."

* * *

Efemona shook her head in disgust. It could've been her father. No one except her has seen the tragedy. It is how to be a Hausa wearing khaki in Nigeria, she thought. With her diabolical mind of her own, she turned and walked back to her seat.

"You won't believe what I saw in the distance, Victoria," she said to Victoria.

"What is it?"

"A man just drowned. And I think it was the man who had won the election."

Victoria was lost and did not ask further questions.

Then Efemona began to retrace the village beside the canal and the rice farms in her heart. The village were shanties, a disheveled alien home in ramshackle order. There were no good tard roads or good streets nor rhyme or reason for anyone to live there. The reason some people live there was because of poverty Dudu and Babangida inflicted on the people of Nigeria. As for the denizens of this jungle cruel village and disolate godforsaken place, Efemona vowed to fight Dudu with any diabolical might. The truth to that was that since she'd left the country to join her husband, the thought that when she returned to Nigeria, the village where most of the crude oil is tapped would've been transformed into a beautiful city like Reno, Nevada, and she could call the village 'The Biggest Little Village In The World.' But things hadn't changed. On top of that eye sorely foul place, there were dirty, naked children with no clothes on in this modern era, a village where children should have the best. With that, Efemona bite her lips: Babangida and Dudu and their junta in cahoots will pay a grave price for their actions against the people that live in those shanties, Efemona thought.

Finally, Efemona raised her head up to look at Bad Dudu and at the same time Babangida was registered in her being. Reflecting on the way these two Generals had treated those who spoke out against their regime, there was such a naked malice in her face, that Dudu himself could see. So he asked, "Efemona?! What's the matter?" He turned his attention on her and muttered something too that Efemona was certainly sure was not complimenting her, but a ridicule of a smart woman, *"Enaywolo-ne-Bini be-Esan moeghekwo, nó-Oghvaragbon Ekwo-Ragbon Opia. Agbonmerele-nokwo."*

Victoria, looking at Dudu's ridicule savage lips, whispered to Efemona. And both got their second good look at the man who is the terror to the people of Nigeria, ditching out orders at the Doddan Army Barracks. Dudu, as they looked, had a muscular build and stood nearly six feet tall. His hair was darkened with just for men still wearing his famous two hats. He had side whiskers framed which framed his gaunt face. To them he would not be considered handsome as a leader of any country, but he has money of his nation stashed away in foreign countries. His nose was crooked like that of a lion in a cage zoo waiting to devour. His brown eyes of a sadist monster looking were set too far apart from his gaunt face which formed a miserable line, then meeting at the bridge of his huge nose. To crown it all, he has that animal grace to his movement which is why he was able to score four goals to one over the Southerners. Among those qualities they have seen, the aura of brutality was registered on his face. Both women figured Dudu had to be a very wicked man and a violent individual but who mostly didn't carry out his executions, but by paid killers from Israel. That's why the people with Ph.D.s of Nigeria feared him. With that look and that note of malice and animosity, Efemona said to Dudu, "Mr. Dudu, take down your pants. I want to fuck you again. Your dick was huge for my carnal and I loved it. It sure did fill up my wide and used gate."

He loved different *yanshes.* How can he refuse? Different *yanshes and holes* of different women and that was one of the resons he ceased power to take advantage of the women of other past leaders he'd killed.

Efemona's hole which he'd navigated before in Efemona's way, was free. He was paying no *dime, nickel* and *Kobo* for it. But if it were *yanshes* of Lebanese, Thai women, he could pay millions for it. He opened his mouth to say something, but Efemona was already all over him. He became mesmerized again in Efemona carnal lust whose titties were already in his mouth. The spirit of Efemona was working on him. He smiled. Efemona was striking and a good seductress. She was not too tall. Her flawless skin was ebony and possibly blessed with a good father and a good mother. Whichever of them was good or bad to make Efemona be what she was, was none of his business. He rubbed his fingers gently over her hair which were long and swirly as Diana Ross', curly, shining black as those of a 'being to' to America, loose which fell to her shoulders. Her painted red lips as Marilyn Monroe's took his breath away, talkless of her *yansh* which Clinton might like to insert his famous Havana, before drowning into it. And her mamalian glands are those that put men into slumber. With all these qualities of a woman already all over him, her yansh, lips and mamalian glands are mine as of now. Looking at her nose that was somehow caved in as Ukpenulike, and lips that were full and beautifully sculptured as Marilyn Monroe, which were slightly parted before him and working, teasing him to reveal a glimmer of white pagan set of teeth he began to salivate for her carnal. To crown it all, she wore a velvet backless gown with two shoulder straps easy enough to slip up and enter her. Allah have mercy! Efemona was simply the most beautiful woman *now* he'd ever seen next to his Lebanese mistresses. "Okay! Let's not waste time. Sit on it, babe," he finally said, as her carnal medicine lust had caught him.

And Efemona sat on the rigid huge dick and slowly, the huge dick was inside her. As Efemona pumped up and down, she forgot that she was the one in control to ask questions. And Dudu capitalized on her quietness of her rolling the buttocks on his dick and asked her questions she'd never thought anyone would ask her.

The President asked, "Efemona? By the way, how did you meet Ekiaqueta who took you to America to now become internationally acclaimed as an American woman?"

"Actually it was by accident. Had Ekiaqueta's father opened his eyes wide open."

"Allah day!" Efemona said. "You know since families in Nigerina cannot afford three square meals a day, mothers who cared for their young daughters ripe for marriage began to shop for men for them. I mean rich men from abroad. Sometimes we do our homework ourselves. Some women come to my grandmother for potions to catch rich men from America. But for me, I did it with Royal voodoo. So, when the men then laugh with the young women, me Efemona included, they are caught with the potion. That is how I caught Ekiaqueta, my husband. After we caught him with the potion we take them as sheep to the slaughter in our arms why we watch them behave like goats, *ohuan* or cattle to our fathers and mothers who without hesitation had known what had happened. Without *Much Ado About Nothing,* our parents introduce themselves to the goats, *ohuan* or cattle in the name of men. Our parents then ask 'us' if we take a liking to the man we have caught with our potion, before they tell them to provide for us. Whether they like it or not, they must keep the young women like me in a nice home, buy us nice clothes, shoes and expensive jewelry and *Nukarlary* and on top of that they must train us in an expensive institution of higher learning. And say, for instance, the man already has a wife who is perhaps a dunce, we can ask the man to let her go before we move into his house and later at the end when our voodoo has really worked its miracles, we loot their homes and run away and find other men in the same manner. That's why some men these days say there are notorious women out there who will do anything to get men, because the austerity measure in this country is way too high due to Bad Dudu draining the Nation's treasury."

Efemona was to ask him a question, too. But this time he was in control as Efemona pumped harder enjoying the size and fitness of his huge dick into her.

"What do your friends know you by?" a question of retaliation. She pumped down his huge dick and her mouth twitched in a wry moan of pleasure. "My friends I hang out with in America call me the Egyptian Jezebel, a consequence of my reputed fondness for Gordon

Gin spirit which renders my mouth to vibrate and more flippant more than Ekiaqueta, the man I married."

Though she was moaning soft words of pleasure, she was still not able to *come*. And Dudu was liking it even more. With his stamina, he carried her up and leaned her against the long desk and Efemona brought her ass close to him, her hands holding the edge of the desk as the President entered her, assaulting her carnal with his huge weapon. He noticed she was not feeling a thing, though she was liking it more than him, then he asked, "What do you say your grandmother does for a living?"

"She was the Princess of voodoo at Oba's Palace in Benin."

He did not know what Efemona meant by Voodoo because a typical Hausa man only believes in Sandhurst Army Cannon Depot training, where they learn the art of artilery fire, and when they graduate, they come back to Nigeria to cease power in the Dem Mayor office where they make the dough to rise without oven and where arguments were settled and insults directed to them by those who challenge them were repaid at the point of bullet to the brain. "Explain to me," he found himself saying as he forced himself again and again inside her.

"Okay! I say my grandmother was a Voodoo Princess who cast spells on people like you for their wickedness. The spell she cast can bring good luck or bad luck to people. She can also use it to bring harm upon bad people. She uses *elephant tusk, Ezzykjworo, dry cameleon, tortoise shell* and other gadgets I can't recall."

He felt a sudden chill in his dick and brain as he entered her deeper.

"Voodoo?" he pronounced. The medicine in her vagina was beginning to work its way to his pituitary gland and veins.

"Yes," Efemona thrusted her ass backwards to him. "You mean to tell me you've never heard of *Udeleukin Okannoyaukin of Benin Royal family?* Even decent and moral men of good characters, churchgoers come to Benin to see my grandmother for advice and voodoo."

"I have never heard of Okannoyaukin."

He thrust himself in and out as she too began to roll her buttocks left and right as if dancing Owanbe. "She is a Voodoo Princess, and she has great power to bring you down before I leave the country. People might say she's evil but I say she's a goddess. Her name is heard far and wide in the nation and overseas because her Voodoo pracitce is a religion. She originated it in Oba's Palace- the Royal family of Benin where the Americans in Reno, Nevada now know I am a Royal born. In Benin, the god Voodoo is an all- powerful being. Everything that happens is its doing. Most often, it too can be malicious as you, Dudu. The symbol of Voodoo is the snake. One who practices Voodoo is able to communicate directly with this god. My grandmother is the Queen. Only, in Voodoo practices of Okan-noyaukin in Oba's Palace in Benin where my grandmother is the Princess can one ask for a curse for people like you, Dudu and Babangida for ruining my Nation. At this moment of your thrusting your huge self into me, your name has been registered through my vagina in her grave, *that you go die on top of toto.*

"To curse me or to bless me?" he asked.

She moaned. He did not hear what she answered. But she was saying: "Oh! No one has more powerful magic than my grandmother, despite what you may have heard about her. My grandmother's powers are only used against the bad to bring bad people to their knees. For instance, the armed robber who shot and killed my husband's mother would never have been caught if not for my grandmother who cast her spell to make the man come forward to confess and then he was burnt to ashes before the King at his Palace. Same thing will apply to you, because you are a thief, a rogue and scoundrel who inflicted hardship on the people of this country."

As he thrust himself for the last time for release, the billions he had stolen from the Government flashed into his brain. Then he released, and then he suddenly felt some powers had gone out of him like Jesus Christ. Was it the power of release? Efemona knew it wasn't. It was the spirit of her grandmother who'd drowned in the potholes of Ukpenu street at Benin that caught him. And sooner or later Efemona predicted, one would know who the real Princess of Voodoo prophet was.

PART IV

Chapter

24

T he meeting that was to take half an hour with the President was taking forever. I was getting drunk, frequently getting up and using the bathroom. As I came out of the bathroom for the sixth time, I tippietoed into the children's room. They had all dozed to the edge of their beds, their coverlets tossed away from their bodies. So I rearranged them all and covered them up with their coverlets. Then I walked back into the living room and switched on my gadget again. The President had stood still, his index finger almost touching Efemona's nose, saying, *"Eki- rail-etoua onokana. I say I go shave your hair from your head and yank out all your pubic hairs from your toto onokana one by one."*

As I began to wonder what Efemona must've said to provoke the President again there came a knock on the door. I walked briskly to the door, though it was not the right moment for me to abandon my gadget watching. I opened the door. It was Miss Uluebeka, for the record, is my children's nanny. With her standing before me, I knew the time had chimed the hour for my children to get ready for school. Wow! It must've been more than six hours, I have been watching Efemona with the President, I thought.

Miss Uluebeka hurried up and got the kids ready, then quickly she prepared a good meal for us. She'd provided us with a good meal of oatmeal, bacon, scrambled eggs, muffins and grape fruit. A widow by standard, her husband was a good man who later became a victim of frequent Reno police harrassment on the sidewalk of Reno being that he had once been arrested before on charges of verbal abuse of his wife. Since that time, he was stopped and frisked on the sidewalk on numerous occasions by RPD, who then added more ingredients of made up false accusations, before charging him for whatever crime that came out of their mouth first when he was stopped.

As the children's nanny had taken the children to school, I switched on my gadget again, and I saw the President more tense than he'd been. I almost thought for a minute that he was about to strike my wife and get it all over with. But instead, he stood still like Tarzan over Efemona's shoulder saying, "Don't they harrass innocent men and women of low income in Reno, Nevada? You must not be from America then! My juntas and I watch all day and night how innocent men and women are cornered on the streets and alleys of Reno and then are arrested for jaywalking, resisting arrest, and in most cases are beaten, their limbs broken, while judges like Hickman and McQuaid stood guard and watch making sure the victims stay in jail for 60 days or more to make blood money on their heads. Myself and my junta members are aware that the Mafia owners of the casinos in Reno, Nevada are part of the problem who pay the judges millions, and buy them yachts and homes in the Carribean to insinuate them to deny motions filed in their courtrooms."

Efemona just stared at him as he began to ridicule the City that gave her a new meaning to her feminine life then making her a citizen of Reno, Nevada. To add insult to his foolery, Efemona said to Victoria, *"Wetin be toto self?"*

"Oh! Now she doesn't know what *toto* is! *Tell 'am'.*" *"The President, means sey e-go remove your hair by the roots from your vagina."* Efemona hissed on him.

"You can hiss. But I no sey, the judges for Reno and their police be like us wey dey rule for Nigeria. I no sey dem they make blood money for there, and dem dey arrest innocent people and break their limbs before dem charge them for jaywalking and blah-blah-blah . . ." he became tense again.

"Calm down please, Mr. President." Victoria appealed. "Calm down, please! At least for my sake!"

He paused and looked at Victoria. But then I found some element of truth from what Dudu was saying. Though I did not know what Efemona had said to him that provoked him to that extent to make such references to Reno, because I'd walked to the kitchen to get a glass of water, I couldn't have been more sorrowful to remember how my good friend, Kandison, a man with three children, a Master's Degree holder who maintains a steady job, pays his taxes, could be stopped in front of his home for jaywalking and resisting an arrest. The fact is black people in Reno, Nevada are the victims of their laws made by the judges and the mafias of their casinos. I witnessed it a thousand times. My first terrible experience was at Circus Circus Hotel and Casino, at the heart of downtown Reno, Nevada. It was a beautiful summer day and Kandison had just finished making love to his mistress on the Casino Tower, Twenty-Third Floor who came to visit him from Los Angeles, California, when I ran into him by the casino elevator on the west side. We chatted and exchanged a few pleasantries. Within a few minutes of my stalking away with my buddy, Achuko, there were people out on the floor, near the elevator, all of them running in the direction of where Kandison had sat on the chair by the slot machine where I'd met him. All the men and women in the vicinity were all whites. Among them were security dogs yapping at heels, some of the security men whom Judge Hickman and Judge McQuaid nicknamed Samson, Goliath and Hercules were all there with their mace and whips and knives and revolvers and electric guns. As I looked back, I saw that it was a babble of excitement that has risen from this gathering of humanity.

"Good Lord!" Chuckuma Achuko exclaimed seeing the gathering where we had both greeted our bosom friend. "Come on, let's go back and see what the hell is going on there," he'd said to me. So I trailed behind Achuko in the same direction, him wearing an expression of a grim resolve. Down beneath where Kandison was sitting by the slot machine, the huge crowd had multiplied so that Achuko and I had to shouldered our way through the crowd. Another few feet from the elevator we heard the angry voices of Samson, Goliath and Hercules. So we stopped. What we'd seen was heinous on its face.

Samson, Goliath and Hercules were holding and wrestling down Kandison, a very thin man of 120 pounds. Samson was gripping Kandison's left arm, Goliath his right and Hercules had arm locked around to his neck in a tight grip that his eyes were rolling, which was the excitement of the crowd and the gamblers. If Achuko and I had not known Kandison, we would've assumed that Kandison their prisoner had snatched a purse. What was really funny about the whole thing was Kandison wasn't fat. He was just skinny-chested, neck of an ostrich, his arms thin, his legs, though can move were ostrich too. Now you know that even the breeze can move my man Kandison.

Anyway, with his status, he likes to dress neatly with suits, the best Italian made and shoes to match. At all times, it looks like what he normally wears were bestowed upon him by the Lord. His hair was shaven like Michael Jordan, though his was like that of a coconut. The outstanding visible quality was his nose which God had bestowed upon his face perfectly that when he put on sun shades, it was as if they have been surgically grafted on the bridge of his nose. But the nose Achuko and I were looking at when we first met him was not the same nose we'd saw him with earlier. It seems to me that his nose *now* huge, had been broken several times not only by Samson, Goliath and Hercules, but by RPD too, who he told us has been after him since he published his first title of the novel: 'The Court Circus Mess/Underclass and Injustice', a somewhat fictional true story of the system of law and justice in Reno, Nevada repressing the less privileged.

Based on an eye witness accounts from the crowd, Kandison was just sitting near the slot machine, and waiting for the ex- mistresses of Judge Hickman, of Ingledue, and Bolshazy with whom Kandison was now having an affair for them to come down from the tower to join him on the casino floor. For some reason, Samson, Goliath and Hercules knew Felicity Da Wild Horse was Judge Hickman's mistress, and Cat and Irene where Ingledue and Bolshazy and for that reason had to deal with Kandison for being bold enough in Reno, not only to humiliate a judge on a wheelchair but also the security men of Circus Circus Hotel & Casino. But to the onlookers, the story was different. Kandison was just being taken advantage of because he was black and poor. Achuko and I had no doubt about that, that it was the truth.

As we looked at Kandison, standing rigidly, his leg unable to compromise his wishes to stand upright, and yet the RPD were there with their chains on his arms and legs, it made Achuko and I to wonder where the blood money the city of Reno was making from poor slim men and women, they had taken advantage of on the sidewalk and on the Casino Gaming Floor, was spent even when the judges like Hickman of the City's Municipal Court and Judge McQuaid of the Federal Court knew their officers and security men of their Casinos were lying against innocent accused.

Well, I can understand why Kandison's sultry mouth was working, a man who hardly can talk and express himself when talking, but except on the paper with a pen. When Achuko and I looked at him, he doesn't look like a man that does drugs or alcohol for his voice to protest the injustice against him in the casino where thousands and multitudes of whites were gambling, and only him sitting with no money in his pocket except the pocket money Felicity Da Wild Horse and the rest of the women had given him for screwing them night and day, what these men can no longer do except to eat the pussy. But God on this day blessed Kandison for his voice to be heard. It was stentorically clear for the Americans all over the 52 states to hear his plight.

He was saying, "I haven't done anything wrong. I am just waiting for my mistresses to come down from the tower. Please don't hurt me and please don't put those chains on my arms, legs and neck. I am not a criminal. I am invited for the blackjack tournament tomorrow morning. I have paid my entry fees."

"Shut up! You're a con artist," a judge I recognized as Hickman yelled at him on his wheelchair.

"Beg your pardon?! I'll appreciate it if you recount your words against me, your Honor," Kandison yelled back despite the terrible slap on his face by Goliath to shut him up.

Hickman did not buy that. "I'll say it again that you are a thief, a con artist. Is that too much to admit?"

"All my life since I came to Reno in 1979, I have had no problems with anyone until I got married to Omoya from Nigeria. I am not going to talk about that because that's another story of its own. Anyway, I am a man of extreme intelligence, with three lovable children, and with a Master's Degree in Political Science to remove me from that concept of a con artist, your Honor. The reason I am bound in chains before you as a criminal is because I'm black and because I have been arrested once before. I assure you that's why I'm being picked on, on the sidewalk and in the Casinos where you're now watching me with your scornful rabbit eyes."

Achuko and I knew that was the truth and nothing but the truth. As we watched, a spectator among the crowd also a black man who told us he was from California, who said he'd just been released from Parr Jail Boulevard after a week, with his backpack, tapped on my shoulders. I was wondering where I had seen him before, when he said, "Tell the man in chains to bail out after they book him into Parr Boulevard. Otherwise, the officers who are hungry to make blood money commission and be hailed as top cops, of Reno will continually add more charges against him each day-what they call 'Addbooking'. Before he knows it, a bail that was set at $20,000 dollars would amount to $100,000 dollars."

Achuko and I already knew that to be true. So we nodded our heads. As Kandison pleaded for his dear life, Samson also known as Ingledue, the brute, shook his head and glowered at him and placed his right foot on his chest as Kandison fell.

"I better go get a knife to operate on his testicles before the cops ship him to Parr Boulevard," Hercules, also known as Bolshazy, said to his superior.

As Samson re-cuffed him tighter on his wrists, he yelled at Hercules, "Brand him on his forehead."

"Yes, sir," Hercules said. "I will do whatever you say, boss." "Where is all the 'silver you have silver mined' in Circus Circus Hotel and Casino for the past 22 years?" Hercules yelled at Kandison on the floor who was now bleeding from his nostrils.

"I don't have any."

"You liar," Hercules yelled again with his fists clenched on his face after branding and UPCing him on his forehead with an '86ed' hot iron.

And Kandison in the wake of all that just lay helpless. Who was to speak out for him against false allegations which he was charged? No one in Reno, because in the RPD, they are all white. In the casinos of

Reno, Nevada, the security men who arrest blacks, spot black people the moment they walk into the casinos, then branding them on their forehead with an 'X' or '86', are all white. In Reno Municipal Court, the judges are all whites. In the Federal Court, the judges are all white. And at ninth Circuit Court, the judges are all whites. In their Supreme Court, the judges are all whites. Denying appeals and motions and throwing out cases of brutality of black men by RPD and of Samson, Goliath and Hercules of Reno Casinos is nothing new just because they are all making dubious blood money from the Mafia owners of the Casinos. "Remove one of his testicles and break his left knee. After that give him a blow on his left ear to render him deaf," Goliath instructed.

A man among the crowd, a good Samaritan I presumed, finally rebuked that idea, stating to them it was against Nature and God to castrate a living human being if it was not his willingness to donate his body parts for scientific research and more so, it looks that Kandison is not a rapist, murderer and child molester to receive such a cruel and unusual punishment while he was minding his business before he was spotted and then was wrestled to the ground. Achuko and I nodded at the words of the man we didn't even know. And as he looked at us in return, he said, "But you know, it is not a laughing matter. Someone's got to speak the truth to save a man's life who has lived in this community for 22 years with no grave crimes until his wife Omoya, whom he shipped into Reno, Nevada from the culture of poverty in their country called the cops on him for verbal abuse. Since that time, the cops of The Biggest Little City have kept their eyes on him on the sidewalk." "You don't know what you are talking about," Goliath yelled at the good Samaritan. "We have seen Kandison on numerous occasions in this casino 'silver mining'. And now he's bold enough not of screwing our mistresses but screwing the mistress of Judge Hickman on our property. We'll appreciate it if you'll let us handle our business, sir. Or we'll bound you, too along with him. Whichever you prefer, pardner."

"Why are you defending him?" Ingledue asked the good Samaritan who looked just like him. A tall, huge, mean man weighing at least 265 pounds, bearing the features of a brute, as a substantial obstacle. His tallness and hugeness kept onlookers three steps backwards as he stood now with his hands planted on his hips, his chin jutting out belligerently, and his eyes flashing defiance and animosity against the man he cuffed. What can I do to the good Samaritan, he was thinking. Even God doesn't challenge Ingledue when he'd cuffed anyone who is helpless or underclass. With that notion, he said to the man, "You better watch your tongue, or you'll regret the day you were given life."

The man did not care. He was huge, too. His hair shaved off as Ingledue. As huge as Bolshazy and Hercules too. In reality, could toss the three captors around as though they were chicken. So Hercules and Bolshazy did not want to provoke him as Ingledue did.

"Well, I am defending the man you guys cuffed because this is a free country. What can you do? I'll repeat it before the President of this Country and before the Mafia y'all are working for, that you cannot castrate a man for a concurted story of silver mining without a fair trial. The reason he came to this country I guess is to have a good education and a good life, the amenities he doesn't have in his country because of Bad Dudu and his junta's regime. With the jury of the peers in this country, we have to show a good example to other Third World countries in the world that we are the most civilized people on the face of the planet earth."

Ingledue was mute. Achuko and I knew as much that, that was in fact true. So we shook our heads in support. Hickman after watching and after much thought knew that a reputation of castrating innocents accused of 'silver mining' despite no proof and they might have a huge dick to sodomize his mistress, finally realized that the business of castration was not good for Reno. Temporarily, he told Samson, Goliath and Hercules to stop. The reason for that was he wanted the crowd to disperse.

"If you castrate him I'll die with you," Achuko, who couldn't take it any more among us in the crowd said out loud. Everyone fell silent as Achuko stepped forward with his huge biceps, barrell-chested, and with his shining beefy forehead and shaved head and his neck bigger than Ingledue's. The whole crowd looked at him as the crowd looked at Pilate for Crucification of Christ. But still, Samson, Goliath and Hercules did not wash their hands.

"It is better to arrest him than to castrate him in the public for what he did not do," Achuko told them.

Hickman winched his eyes to the captors as a sign that they should hold on. On that note, the crowd began to disperse and Achuko stalked away to where I was standing in the distance. As I began to congratulate him, I saw that they stripped Kandison naked. And with con artist style, Hickman dropped a ballisong knife, the Filipino folding knife type, then dropped it beside Kandison. Samson and Hercules both laughed. Samson quickly took the knife on the floor and cut Kandison open from his scrotum, then took out one of his testicles with bravado, then hung it on the roof of Circus Circus Hotel & Casino reminding the poor of Reno, Nevada what they can do! Absolutely nothing! And on top of that, Goliath and Hercules stomped on his chest, kicked his back, his face, groin, buttocks and feet with their huge fists and legs bigger than those of elephants. As Achuko and I rushed back to the scene, Kandison's month was already ruined, not from Samson, Goliath and Hercules alone, but from RPD who also joined the hungry savages, thirsty for Kandison's blood. But on careful observation, these hungry savages in their superiority of State given uniform of brutality who parade only on blacks neighborhood on 24 hours basis, who had no intention of bearing children of their own except that their own life is bent on making blood money and commission, what they know best to boost the jail population, are never-the-less better than Kandison in any way, because they are filthy, ugly homosexuals and human devourers as vultures, sadist and hungry fools motherfuckers. Yes motherfuckers! My pen had taken over!

We stood and looked at Kandison's ugly condition. It was too late for Achuko to act. All we could do was shake our heads and walk away.

As we walked a short distance away from the scene, I asked Achuko, "Do you think Kandison will get a fair trial despite he's the one all white skinheads RPD and Samson, Goliath and Hercules has assaulted in the presence of the multitudes?"

Before Achuko could respond, a man walking behind us said with distructed sincerity, "You know damn well this is Reno, Nevada where fair trials are bane of constitution-denied."

That summed up the thoughts the President envisioned in me. But still, I had no way to get hold of Dudu to tell him that what he'd seen in movies or on the sidewalk of Reno streets and their casinos were true and that I'd witnessed it first hand. The thing is, the telephones in Nigeria don't work. Otherwise I would have called him to tell him that what he'd seen on Reno sidewalks was in fact true. Anyway the President was still mad as hell at Efemona. "No, no, no, no, no, no! Women like Efemona, they visit the country and sleep with famous men and politicians like Fela Anikulapo Kuti and give them AIDS," he said rebuking Victoria's pleading to calm down.

"Don't even try to bring Fela into this because when he was alive you and your junta cronies did not like him."

"Never will I tolerate nonsense from too know women who visited America and came on my invitation to insult me and my junta regime in my office. *I still think I'll yank all the roots of your hair from your toto.*"

He stood still, his index finger in his mouth biting it hard. What can he do to Efemona, he was thinking. Caesars of the world don't bow down even to a Queen. Even the Queen or a queen too can not pee into a bottle. It is me and you. Keep on running your mouth against me, he thought.

"Calm down please, Mr. President," Victoria voiced out again.

I will yank off all your hairs from your vagina by the root. The words re-echoed and reverberated in Efemona's brain. So looking into his eyes, as her blood ran cold in her veins, she did not doubt that Dudu meant precisely what he had said he would do, because he's a brute. It was like when her mother warned her not to defy her curfew and she did. The next thing that happened after that was chili pepper grounded then inserted into her vagina. She did not respond.

Dudu, on the other hand, knew Efemona probably would never give up. Facing Victoria, he said, "Allright, Victoria. I thought it's nice to inform Efemona where she now belongs. She's no longer a Nigerian. She has inherited a Western lifestyle, a life similar to Sodom and Gomorrah of San Francisco where they practice lesbianism and homosexuality. He looked at Efemona again, *"Udelelagbe . . . Avan nonsi-nenelagbe. Okuntar nonsi yor grandmother lagbe. Idegunlagbe for coming to ruin me.,"* the curses he'd remembered of Efemona's own dialect all followed out from his mouth.

Efemona tried to speak. The President overpowered her words. "Yes or no? Answer me. Anyway, I know what's best to do to you. I will silence you and bribe President Clinton with 100 million barrels of my Nation's sweet crude oil. *The oil wey you people dey cry for e go soon finish. Emi-ohanabelagbe-onokana. Ena-agbon, be Ena-Elimi kifieneghofia. Ugborele Ukin.* Devil, I say you are! You hear me?! I guess your father trained you but your mother didn't train you to have good etiquette on how to be a proper Nigerian wife to respect your elders not even your husband whom I believe you probably have tormented because the American laws allows that and because he's poor."

"Calm down please, Mr. President," Victoria appealed again. "Victoria?" Dudu called out. "I can't help. Tell me what I have done wrong! Was it a crime that I asked you to go to Reno, Nevada to get Efemona to fill the post of Matron General for which hunger claimed had Mrs. Obaze?"

And she said, "I don't know Mr. President."

"I'd wanted to remove her from the culture of poverty. I guess I made the biggest mistake of my life. Which now leaves me to ask your friend what she has in-between her thighs. Efemona?" he yelled out at her as he frowned, "Tell me, what do you have in- between your thighs? Men's genitals or a clitoris? I'll seriously doubt it if you merely tell me you are a woman. So what do you have in- between your legs? Allah dammit?!" He sighed. If he had not screwed the daughter-of-a-bitch, he would've thought she has a dick. But still Efemona must've fooled him, making him to believe she has a hole like a woman. Anything was possible with the goddamned Americans who are competing with God and Allah. They must've affixed a dick in place of her female genitals.

Which leaves me with the same thought as I sat patiently watching them in my living room. As I watched Dudu from afar, I saw that his face became more gaunt, hardened enough as to congeal. Efemona turned and saw his flaming eyes. She began to recite a Voodoo spell of the Royals in the pit of her stomach. Then finally, she attacked.

"Didn't your forefathers sold their sons and daughters to the white man for exchange of mirrors and whiskey all for the love of money?! Why is what I do to my husband a concern here to you, Mr. Dudu? You think seriously about calling for elections in this country. If I torment my husband in America that's my problem, not yours."

He bite his lips. "Victoria?" Dudu called upon again. "You said to me to calm down. I tell you Efemona got the balls."

For those of you who don't know that American citizens all over the world got the nerves, they can do and undo, I agree here to confirm that truth. An American, for instance, has the freedom of expression. He can challenge the President of his country and call him names. He can burn the flag of his country in protest of what he deemed is wrong. They can wave their hands in a high profile executive meetings in a kind of parody of a hipster and walk out over arguments. For several years, it had been their fancy as Americans that they belonged in any society uptown in the world, precisely because the foot of history as Americans contested their right to be anywhere in the world. Efemona and I knew this because when she'd joined me, it was the first thing I'd gisted her. Therefore, the game of who is who was heating up in her heart. She did not bother to know if his eyes were flaming any more.

Her adrenaline was flowing, and she'd trouble keeping her malice within her being. Though she was quiet, only Almighty knew what Efemona was thinking of as an American, but still a Nigerian in blood. Suddenly it dawned on Efemona as an American citizen, not to let Dudu intimidate her. And besides, she was in control. The Voodoo spell and worm her grandmother gave her to swallow gives her signs of what she would do to suit the moment. Why should I even be scared of him at all, a zombie for that matter, *ohuan*, sheep, gaunt face, asshole, she thought. Finally, she raised her eyebrows, "Mr. President, I don't fear you. Oval Office protects human rights all over the world for what men and women believes in," she said and sprang to her feet. She's vexed. She was short of words to express her anger. She walked two steps to exit the door and Victoria grabbed her Gucci purse made of gold and silver, the two most precious and expensive metals of the earth, which I had suffered to buy for her.

"Efemona, please don't leave me here," Victoria pleaded. "You are here on a special mission with the President."

She knew Victoria, as the eye of a needle. She gave her the respect and she sat. The President forced a smile. "Look, Efemona," he said in a manner of a father and daughter relationship. "I invited you into the country to accept or refuse an offer from me. I'm now contemplating-" he paused. "Just because of you, I've decided to hand over power to civilians not because you have prayed to God when we mated twice on my executive seat, but because of World opinion against my junta regime who rule this Nation of very literate people made illiterate for decades with guns on their temple when they voice out their concern about their country they love so dearly and blessed in nature with mineral resources," he paused and sighed.

In his sighness, and judging from the way he's paused which was different from his usual way of pausing, Efemona knew she'd scored yet another one on him, with her diabolical Voodoo might of her grandmother. With that advantage over him, she said with boldness, "Just because you are wearing a million dollar native Agbada over your military uniform doesn't give you the right and liberty to insult me. I am an American. I want you to remember that from this moment on. You can shoot me if you want."

With that flippant vibration from her mouth, I was scared, where I'd sat noting that I'll have no *hole* to release the fruit of another child if she was shot. And true, no other woman would like me with my cow eye. If the President got mad enough and pulled the trigger and killed my wife, no woman will love me with a cow eye. Man! I began to shiver where I sat waiting for Efemona to retract her words. I began to think. Let it not become a class struggle between an American citizen and a dictator of his country. You know dictators of their countries don't give a fuck. That was my concern. Thank God, he'd fogotten he had a weapon on the table, or most probably he wanted Efemona to insult him more than she'd been before he decided to act in a brutal manner. I was glad that rather than a bullet in her temple, he fired back with words of humiliation. "*Wahoo.* America has bred one," he said. "*Gbejeleghe be atilogun be Ojéké mame Onokana. Aponiyeke.* Hotter than

July now, huh? Americana! Moonwalk like Michael Jackson for me to see. *Enagwolo-nay yar-Amerika.*"

Victoria could not contain herself. She bursted out laughing at the President who *now* has turned comedian. And Efemona looked at Victoria too, very amazed. *"What is the Zancho-idiot* motherfucker talking about?"

He listened for Victoria to explain though he didn't know what motherfucker meant. He thought he heard the word *zancho* and *i-d-i-o-t*. But he didn't ask. He knew that *zancho* was a Spanish word meaning screw around with all the beautiful women from India, Thailand and Lebanon who are divorced, separated, now living in Nigeria. And if they were not married, visit them when their husbands were sweating it out in their farms and taking advantage of their wives because they are poor women who desperately needed the devil or God, whoever heard their prayers first, to redeem them from poverty. Victoria finally looked at Efemona and explained.

"Dudu said if it pleases you, you are free to dance all the named dances of the Royals at Akinzua Palace for him to see even including Michael Jackson's famous dance—the moonwalk dance."

"That's not a problem. In a few minutes, I will, honey." Efemona and Victoria laughed uproariously as they both looked at him now dejected.

At a time, I felt sorry for the President whom I now perceived to have had enough. Unfortunately, he doesn't know that somebody had pity for him, which was me. Apparently, what Efemona was doing to him was enough to say, I had had enough, I no longer need your services. Part of the problem was Mr. Bawuh himself who'd chosen Efemona among several candidates who qualified for the post. Dudu smiled to himself. A General was at the brink of his downfall. Yeah! He could not believe his world. But actually, I admired his courage to take all the insults for a man of a high caliber can only take so much. Even as he sat still, thinking, Efemona had the nerves to say to him, "If you want me to Moonwalk for you to see, you'll be surprised I'll do it better than Michael Jackson."

He did not protest that. Though he frowned, revealing his eyes, now ball-like, like those of a frog, he knew Efemona wasn't lying about that. His right index finger was again in his mouth. Biting it hard, he began to think deeply. How can an ordinary nurse who was taken away from the village, a High School dropout, come to my office to ridicule and reduce me and my junta regime.?! There's no doubt in my mind Efemona probably has a big clitoris bigger than my balls, my tongue or *she doesn't have any*. I know I'm not educated as she thinks she now does going to America to learn all that bullshit of mechanical jargons of slang learning from the ghettos. He couldn't think any more. "Efemona," he said, "I will, with my executive powers, ban all women of this country, young or old, High School graduates or dropouts, Grammar School girls who attended Maria Asiawo Gorritti Academy of Nursing School from going abroad," America emphasized.

In a country where both men and young women finding a way to leave the country to venture to other parts of the world and Efemona is the architect of the powerful movement, only God knew how Efemona must've felt. Victoria noticed it too as Efemona squirmed on her seat. In truth, Dudu got her. He too, saw her reaction. Efemona thought without saying a word to provoke the moment. My AWAM movement would be doomed. Her ultimate goal when she finished reducing the President was to held back to America to devote her new life to AWAM, which she had already publicized in America and sent pamphlets to Italy, Benin, Cotonu, Cameroon, Belgium, London, Brazil, Spain, Argentina, Peru, El Salvador and to Dudu's home towm, Bornu near Ogoni. With those thoughts, she came to her senses after the worm her grandmother gave her to swallow moved in her diaphragm. The worm had told her you don't want to make a mistake now. You are fully in control. Don't you remember you have filed for your brothers and sisters to come to America, and you have advocated the need for young women of this country to leave their husbands and held abroad? She sighed, the next thing she remembered was that she had filed secretly for divorce in America and after the divorce was granted her, she would sue her husband, which her husband was unaware of. She began to think quickly. I've got good things going! I already asked Patricia, my friend, to rent me an apartment secretly where I will service men of all colors for the money, without the knowledge of my husband. I now reach out to other women of all colors to follow my example and I am at their side at all times at Senator Washington office to testify for the women that the divorce papers the men marrying us brought from Nigeria are fake. I now preside and regale over large audiences for a purpose in Reno, Nevada. Soon to live my life the way the Romans do. I will then be on top of the world wearing green leather attires and jackets as a symbol and statement of the dollar power. If Dudu should ban all the women I have already reached out to held abroad, then my mission in life is defeated and Ekiaqueta, my husband would be happy. Then she looked down at the carpet and shook her head.

Victoria said to her, "Girlfriend, don't get yourself stresed out over what you think you cannot finish." Which I think was good advice from a good friend to my wife. As I glanced at my wife to see how she reacted to Victoria's statement, I saw her smiling a diabolical smile. But I had forgotten what she told me that kind of smile was. But anyway, I should point out that Efemona, my wife, is a feminist. The women's movement of AWAM she formed is for every woman who deemed it necessary to better their lives without no man's involvement in their lives. The thing is, women of Efemona's type who followed her lead soon owned properties, entered into contracts, had decent educations with the money they made from selling their carnals in red light districts and from divorce granted them that burned their husbands to their heels. And on top of the divorce and alimony which netted them millions, Efemona advocated for them to grow penises, which meant that all women are eligible for equal pay with men.

Anyway, Efemona said to the President, as she pushed out her tongue. "Don't you know how to entertain a joke? She walked up to him as she had always done when the worm inside her told her what to do. Then she kissed him on his lips.

He smiled and licked his lips, then put out his firm black dog fingers. Efemona took it with pride, smiled and murmured to herself, "I am somebody. You are a zombie President," though she suppressed her anger and replaced it with a clear, smooth type of mockery laughter. In the distance, I could tell she let a minute pass.

Finally, she said, "Now, tell me, Mr. President, why are you putting two hats on and wearing Agbada over your military uniforms and knocking on black boots?" a question no one has dared ask him before.

It was an easy question for him, he thought, so the 'why me' was not imprinted on his brain. And so he laughed aloud. "Only if it makes you happy and stop insulting me in my office, Efemona," he said and smiled too, as he tried to be friendly and forget the past insults and ridicule.

I saw Victoria look at Efemona for a quick glance, then sipped on her *undouble, double undouble London Gin.* All along, she had wished that Efemona would ask him that question. She smiled and stood up abruptly, then gave Efemona a high five, what she too, has learned from the new remodeled Efemona as an American. She said, "I have waited all along for you to ask him that question rather than beating around the bush. I think the people of this country might want to know why actually the President is wearing two hats and wearing (cattle) black boots and Agbada worth over five million dollars over his military uniforms when the Nation at large men and women (except your elite Clubs of the Generals) of this country and some people in the villages don't even know the color of Naira, our legal tender for debts."

Come to think about it, Victoria was right because I have been to some remote villages at Bornu, near Ogoni where Bad Dudu hails from. The cattle farmers don't even know Nigeria has Naira and Kobo for legal tender. In Bornu, near Ogoni, the people still trade by barter. Sometimes, they use cowries and the Sea Shells as legal tender which makes me wonder what Bad Dudu will give for his answer. Anyway, as a true Caesar and conqueror and as the man with the Nation's money all stashed away in foreign banks, he answered with an authoritarian tone.

He explained, "An Agbada as big and expensive like mine before my gorgeous women is supposed to send a message to *all* African countries leaders not to compete with the juntas of my country. You see, Efemona, you probably already know this, that in Africa *we,* the rich and famous, especially the leaders, have a way we exhibit our fame and riches to our guests understanding, if *we* have attained milions and billions in

Britain, Switzerland, the Cayman Islands or elsewhere *our* cronies help *us* deposit the money outside our country in foreign banks. Britain and Swiss Banks are the authoritarian leaders first and foremost priority than the people he rules who are wrought in poverty. When an authoritarian leader attains the billions he usually wears two hats or three or more hats depending on who the VIP coming from abroad to see (him) really is. Each time an authoritarian leader stood up abruptly and took off his hats before his guests and puts it on over and over again, it represents how much in billions he has attained in Britain. I am sure you will want me to demostrate it for both of you?"

I looked away for a second, then reached over to my television and pressed the on button as I watched my gadget. Ted Kopple was saying, "An earthquake had struck Southern California." I sympathized with the people while I imagined myself at the helm of the destruction the earthquake had done to the victims' homes. Getting bored with that news, I was again tempted to look at my gadget to see what the President was prepared to do. Anyway, before I looked up, both women said, "Demonstrate it for us, Mr. President."

I guess he now knew Efemona is materialistic and could entice her with his reaches to shut her up from asking him arrogant questions. Quickly, I saw him stood up, then yanked off the military hat first and placed it on top of his executive table. Then he took off his custom hat. Finally, he looked at the women. "When I say ready, you say go."

"Ready?"

"Go," they echoed.

He felt he has now a moral obligation to tell them how an authoritarian leader without thorough education can be foolish. As he stood, I noticed from my gadget, that he has a Colonel's and General's eagle tag on his Agbada's left breast huge pocket as he scanned the women's facial expressions of their pronouncement, "Go," sincerity. I watched him for a full minute, noting that the women were quiet and waiting for him to demonstrate it. Could he have been lying to them or was he pulling their strings to make Efemona relaxed and not ask any more questions? I thought so myself. No sooner I'd thought so, that I saw the sincerity on his face, motivated by patriotism and a sense of a thief about spelling out corruption to the women rather than telephoning the Queen of England when he was due on the calendar of his wall of the Dem Mayors office, to visit England to ride the mule with the Prime Minister and the Queen and then deposit a billion pounds into Barclay's Bank of Buckingham Avenue. Anyway, I could see the women were getting worried when I saw Bad Dudu finally flipped the hat up and then caught it with his nose like a clown and the hat stood on his huge nose firmly. The women laughed. Then he grabbed the hat after a few seconds from his nose and said, "Keep counting," he voiced out, as he started to put the hat on again over and over on his head. He'd caught them unaware. Anyway, Victoria and Efemona realized that and started counting: *"One-two-three-four-five -six-seven-eight-nine-ten-eleven-twelve- billion,"* they pronounced billion because he'd stopped putting on the hat over and over. They figured he has twelve billion pounds in Britain. However, they had missed the count when Dudu sneezed. Efemona had wanted him to start all over again. Victoria disagreed, believing that she had counted eleven instead of twelve which Efemona had chanted. Rather than asking him to start all over again they settled their little discrepancy at eleven billion.

Come to think about it, while Efemona had missed the count Efemona of all people, I reasoned that when the President had sneezed, she must've said, "Oh! Bless you," as anyone would in America. And I was right on that when I'd watched the replay on my gadget. She'd said, "Bless you, Mr. President." But I tell you that Nigerians who'd never traveled to America are alien to the bless you stuff. So the President didn' know what Efemona meant. There was no response from the President. He looked up at Efemona and smiled.

"I said bless you," Efemona repeated, then cease the time to explain to him. "In America" Efemona said, "When one next to you sneezes, you say to them 'bless you'. Most of the time, the person blessed responds with a 'thank you' note, while the blesser replys back with 'your welcome'." The President nodded. After a few seconds of the lecture, the remodeled Americana Efemona, the President said, "Oh, well, I thank you."

"Oh! Your welcome, Mr. President," Efemona said as a ridicule. Efemona turned to Victoria, "What was the count?"

"I thought we settled that at eleven billion?" "Oh! I forgot," Efemona said.

Seeing his guests in disagreement, Dudu said, "What is the disagreement about?" Victoria could not help it, but said the truth. "Efemona think that, twelve billion pounds is just but a chicken change the masses heard you have across the globe."

Dudu almost went bizarre, but held himself as a man. Finally, he said, "Why are you impatient? I haven't said I was done," he assured Efemona.

"Oh! I'm sorry, Mr. President."

He accepted her apology. Then he began with the Agbada. Dudu explained, "The number of times an authoritarian leader unfolds and refolds the big wide sleeves of his Agbada up, backwards up to his shoulders, it represents millions. The right sleeves of my Agbada represent Swiss Bank and the left sleeve represent Cayman Island Mercantile Bank. Each fold backwards represents one million. You get it?!"

They nodded. Finally, he said, "Ready?" "Go," they said.

They watched him fold the right sleeve up first. Efemona and Victoria counted: *"One-two-three-four-five-six-seven-eight-nine-ten- eleve n-twelve-thirteen-fourteen-fifteen-sixteen-million Swiss Bank,"* Victoria pronounced before Efemona. Efemona had missed the count, because Dudu had coughed and had to ask him, "Need some water, juice, *Cognac undouble?*" as in America when one was choking.

"No thanks," Dudu found himself saying.

"The President is learning very fast," Efemona said to Victoria and added, "So what's the count?"

"Sixteen," Victoria said. Was I hallucinating? I thought I counted seventeen, Efemona thought. She didn't want to embarrass Victoria. So she agreed with Victoria.

Dudu smiled and gave them a thumbs up. Looking at them he said, *"Linda! Linda! Linda!"* words he has always known to mean beautiful.

He was a bit carried away. Though I myself had enjoyed speaking different languages and willing to learn more, I figured it was not the right time to take me aback to my Secondary School days. And I know Efemona was thinking the same thing. Looking instead like an adolescent who'd lots of things to say on her mind she figured it was not the time to bring up a subject of linguistics either. To cut the President short of his intentions, she said with a word of seven letters, *"Gracias,"* a Spanish word I believe to mean 'good'.

Victoria knew she was in the middle of two good ping pong players. With some deep seated atavistic instinct, words her father frequently used to hail her when she did well at school Mid-Term Examinations, flashed her memory. *"Merci, Merci, Merci."* He'd never thought that his office would be turned into, to speaking different languages. He looked up at the women, "Where was I?" he asked.

"Your next is the left Agbada sleeve, Mr. President," Victoria said.

I saw Dudu on my gadget coughed. And I thought he was about to cough out all the billions he did away with out of his country to wrought Nigerians in poverty. My wish thinking did not happen. Instead of coughing out the billions, I saw huge smoke coming out of his mouth. My God! The smoke was from his Havana cigar. Anyway, Efemona said, "We are waiting, Mr. President."

The spirit of Efemona caught him again. "Oh well, I'm ready," he said.

"We are ready too," they echoed.

He started to fold the left sleeve up his arm. The women counted: *"One-two-three-four-five-six-seven-eight-nine-ten-eleven- twelve-thirteen-fourteen-fifiteen-sixteen-seventeen-eighteen-nineteen-twenty-million Swedish National Bank,"* Efemona pronounce before Victoria. And Victoria thought she'd counted nineteen. Actually, I'd counted twenty along with the President. I guess that Victoria had missed the count because Dudu had blinked his left eyeball. And Efemona didn't want to argue. So they settled the count at nineteen million.

But by my imagination, I was thinking wow, the President has all that money and his face looks as gaunt as a farmer?! And I guess Efemona was imagining the same thought. As the President finished spelling out his loot over the years, he sat down and looked out the window of the West wing beside the mosquito machine. There were businessmen in huge Agbada and some of them wearing suits of Italian made. With all these men on que up to see him, he'd hoped to discharge Efemona and Victoria and then call it a day. Efemona he thought was bad for his business. But the spirit of Efemona had caught him. He did not know how to tell her. As he thanked the women they focused more on his gaunt face. At the same time, Efemona looked up and saw with surprise, a copy of the 'Merchant of Venice' on his table. She called out to Victoria. "Did you see what I saw on the President's table?"

Victoria was not paying attention. She was focused on his gaunt face and thinking so many thoughts. Though she was lost for Efemona's question, Efemona reminded her what she'd seen on his table. "The President has a copy of 'The Merchant of Venice'," Efemona answered her own question.

"No wonder Dudu doesn't forgive those who try to topple his Administration of the juntas," Victoria said.

That irritated Efemona as she looked at his face again becoming more gaunt. "Tell me," Efemona said, "How many pounds of flesh have you taken from men and women of this country, since you assumed this post of Presidency for which no one voted you? Be truthful with me. And if you are truthful with me I can then decide if I'll honor the post of Matron General for this country." "To tell you the truth, I don't keep track, my dear. I hope that answered your question, my dear."

"You coward! Sandhurst trained men are not supposed to be cowards."

He looked up at the pictures of Heads of State in Africa on the wall of his office. I could see him shake his head in a no, no, fashion. Then he looked at Efemona, "You really think you know everything, Efemona? But I tell you, you don't know anything. Look at you name calling the real Caesar of African Heads of State a coward. But I tell you that Khadafi of Libya and myself were trained together at Sandhurst. Yes, Sandhurst," he resonated.

In the distance, I watched Dudu's mouth drop. I figured the 'why me' he'd always thought of Efemona for knowing too much was again registered at the back of his mind. Anyway, he looked at Efemona sternly as Victoria tilter her neck close to Efemona for a whisper conversation. Efemona is a thoroughly American rebreed. He had no choice than to tell her the truth, how brave he was at Sandhurst. He said, "Margarette Thatcher and Queen Elizabeth taught Khadafi and I in class and since then I knew not to forgive. Pound of flesh is pound of flesh taken if anyone try me and my Junta members who are loyal to me. I'll repeat in your face that I'm not a coward."

I noticed that both women sensed a sincerity on his face about that. But Efemona said, "Khadafi doesn't take pound of flesh from his own people. He only take from the Yankees and from the Europeans," Efemona reminded him. Victoria nodded in support.

The 'why me' again was imprinted on his eyelids as he looked at Efemona. Then he looked at Victoria, sort of surprised, then stood up and walked towards her seat. "Yes . . . Efemona."

I almost cracked up, but didn't. Though he was Efemona's superior, and Efemona didn't care to give him the respect that he deserved, he was old enough for Efemona to be her grand, grand, grand daughter. So he put his hand on her shoulder. He said to Efemona, "Efemona, you will be a very good Matron General of this country, at this point in time, I don't think it's going to happen, because you'll get caught up in the power struggle between my Juntas who didn't want you in my administration in the first place anyway. Even if you decided to take the post, my loyal Junta members, will continue to move you up and down the board. *Somewhere in the back of your mind you know that's how to be a true Nigerian.* It wasn't going to happen to you. My aim was to protect you until you retire by yourself. Here, with me in the Dem Mayors office, where the bread rise without oven you could have got on with your life and your career and . . ."

Unfortunately, Efemona was not interested. She shook off his huge black dog fingers away from her shoulder, and gave him a nasty look.

The President seemed confused. But was not irritated, but something was clicking in his brain. He looked at his watch. Then he shook his head and walked back to his seat and sat.

As he turned his back and walked to his seat, Victoria made some light chatter with Efemona for her bravery and not giving up, and it was the time Efemona was in deep thought of jubilation in her heart. Far away across the Ocean only me knew her thoughts. She was thinking: I Efemona was chosed among thousands of women lower on the gold scale standard of different ethnic groups of Nigerian women by Mr. Ojie, to cherish, honor and be a proper housewife to his son who is now a tough talking daughter-of-a- bitch, is now sitting before the most talked about President of Presidents in the world, challenging him and ridiculing him. Efemona, who was chosen on a promise to bear as many children as I could and then serve my husband, Ekiaqueta when I join him in America now stare wonderfully at the table in front of a zombie President.

Efemona then carefully excused herself and stood up. Facing the direction of the entrance, she brought out some Kleenex from her purse and wiped out tears from the corners of her eyes. Then she sneezed to fool the President. She then walked back to her seat and sat. She could hold on no longer to the question in her heart, so she said to Victoria, "Why is it that all African Heads of State's faces appeared gaunt even with all the millions and billions they have in their country and in overseas? In America, for instance, millionaires such as Bill Cosby, Andrew Young, Osie Davis and others all appears to have flesh on their cheeks, but African Presidents?"

"I guess because they invest in their countries and eat good food," Victoria said and looked at Efemona, and then looked at the President's face again. Efemona was right, she thought. Finally, she said, "You should know why, girlfriend. It is because they only eat *Apu* and *Eba* on a daily basis which they swallow with *equesi* or *ogbono soup* with plenty of *stockfish* in the soup."

Come to think about that for a second, I realized that Victoria was right, because *stockfish* to me which rich Dudu and some Nigerians import from Norway, is not fresh fish and for the most part one is unable to chew it, even with plenty of hours of boiling it soft for consumption the ingredients and the flavor of it all is then eroded out.

Victoria said, "*Stockfish* to me is not rich enough to make one healthy. Maybe I should retract that. Even the common man cannot afford *stockfish* these days. Only the rich people like Dudu can afford it. He eats it twenty-four hours of the day, compared to Bill Cosby and the rest of the people you mentioned who changes their diet on a regular basis. However, you should join me to congratulate our President and his Junta members at Doddan Army Barracks, the fact that our young women, including me, these days have sugar daddies we look up to who take good care of us at their General Officers Mess Club where we dine with them. Here they order for us shrimp, cow legs, pepper soup, which gives them an erection. Basically in their Mess, they take advantage of us when they have fed us to satisfaction. And what do I mean by that? I mean that five or more erect penises then penetrate one vagina. As they line up over one vagina after feeding us, the whole place then turns into *junkalization* of different words as they shout and spit on the floor and yelled out, *Iwoyouoriri-Agwu-Anal e-Kedu-Kilode-Bawoni-Bakwomi-Bodiaye-Emabinu* and other rubbish vibration from their mouth. When these words start vibrating from their mouths, we know that they have chalets already rented to lure (us) women to, to rape us."

I watched Victoria pause and look at the face of the President. To my amazement, I saw that the President nodded too. The reason I think he nodded was probably because he remembered Eko Lai Meridian Hotel a few blocks away from Doddan Barracks where he navigates every night when he was off work signing signatures to embezzle Government funds to Swiss Banks.

Anyway Victoria said to Efemona, "My dear, you are a registered nurse now, a dietician et all. Please recommend what food your Presidents in Africa, including our own President Dudu, should eat."

Efemona sipped on her *undouble, double, undouble.* She cleared her throat, then looked at the face of the President. "Mr. President, I recommend that you should eat imported hamburgers with cheese and fries every weekday on your lunch breaks. Occasionally import Kentucky Fried Chicken or build one Kentucky restaurant and Taco Bell in Lagos. Above all, eat plenty of salads and vegetables. *Eba, fufu* and *garri* with plenty of stockfish in the equesi soup with *bitter leaf* and *okazi leaves* just won't do."

He laughed. "Hah-ha-ha-ha-aaaaa. Linda-Gracias-Merci," the President incorporated out as part of the lectures from Efemona. "I'll surely visit the hamburger restaurants more often," he assured Efemona. And Efemona thought: One foolish President among African countries.

* * *

The next several minutes passed uneventfully, despite the stockfish, hamburgers and Kentucky Fried Chicken lectures. There was no knock on the President's door and the phones had ceased to ring all day because Efemona was talking nonsense with him. Victoria went on for a minute, "Speaking in generalities," she finally hit the nail on the head, beginning with a high profile member of Dudu's regime who choked on eating too much stockfish on a daily basis and raping young women just because these women cannot afford to buy bar soaps and nail polish to paint their fingernails. Victoria was saying, "I found the atrocities of Izekor and his dictatorial behavior at the General's Officers Mess Club to be unwarranted with young women of fourteen and fifteen years old. But don't take my word for it. I do know that there are several people out there who have seen him take advantage of these poor girls in Eko Lai Meridian Hotel, penetrating their vaginas and the women screaming for help. Most of what I have seen myself which I presume you Dudu already knows something about, will not shock you but bring no credit on the young women either who have spoken out through AWAM movement of Efemona. These young women I tell you are being taken advantage of, because of your corruption, bribery, election voting denial, and moreso, sexual misconduct at Doddan Army Barracks."

Despite the fact that everything Victoria had said and has more to say, were to be true, and likewise for his consumption, Dudu had the sense that he was attending the Seventeenth Century witch trial in England when he was attending Sandhurst Army Cannon Depot University, where witnesses after witness got up and told stories about one of their neighbors. The only thing different was the defendant was missing. Dudu was not missing. He was prepared to listen to whatever criticism Victoria was making.

Anyway, Dudu and his guests all settled back to their drinks. Efemona glanced around the walls, as if taking attendance of the remaining photos on his huge office wall. Victoria caught Dudu's eyes looking away. Finally, Efemona's eyes jammed that of Dudu. Victoria looked back at Dudu again, sort of guessing they were all at an impasse until she figured out at the bottom of her heart that Bad Dudu was one of the richest man in Africa and by no means will listen to Izekor taking advantage of young women of fourteen and fifteen when he has the money to buy them lipstick and nailpolish. But still, Victoria tried to recall some of his dubious activities of life as imparted to her by some of the great journalists before they were shot for expressing their 'Freedom of Expression' on the paper. For that reason, she turned again to Bad Dudu and she said, "Mr. Dudu, would you mind taking me on a cruise on your next visit to the Cayman Islands and spend some of those millions and billions you have all over the globe on me, since there are no more bold journalists to expose people like Izekor on your Authoritarian dubious regime."

"Not until after we sixty-nine on my desk as Efemona promised you will with me," he smiled, but retracted that statement, then said, "I can take you and Efemona and two more young women with us if Efemona accepts the post for which I invited her to fill for me."

"Mr. Dudu?"

"Yes, my Efemona."

"Well, I mean to inform you that I'll only be available after my divorce with my husband in America," she said and shrugged. Then she turned to Victoria, "If Dudu doesn't take you along and the women he'd mapped out on his mind, I can take you with me and go to the Bahamas and enjoy ourselves."

He knows Efemona can compete with him with the dollar power when she divorces her husband. Because in America, when the women divorce their husbands, they amass all the wealth and sweat the man has suffered all his life for. He just shook his head and laughed.

Efemona found fascination watching him. The worm in her stomach moved. So, she thought the time was perfect to tell him that it was a nation of illiterates that men with khaki uniforms rule their people. A President, she noted, had to be elected by the people to assume the post of the *Presidency*. That in itself was absolute democracy-government of the people by the people. Looking at him with animosity as she has always been when there was no joke telling, she explained, "I thought a President of any country, including ours was supposed to be wearing double breasted suits rather than two hats and Agbada upon black boots?"

Victoria picked up the meaning fast. She did not want Dudu to fumble with his answer. Victoria said, "This is Nigeria, my dear. You are not in America, Britain, nor Italy. And don't you know in this country it is coup, coup, coup and counter coup de tat?"

I was surprised that the President did not thank Victoria for answering that question for him. Still facing her, he said, "Tell Efemona that she is in Nigeria and that some people make their money by farming the land, some by trade, but me. The thing is, I can make Efemona a billionaire, but she thinks she has more dollars than me. I will appreciate it if you tell Efemona that the British pounds and schillings are stronger than the dollar in international monetary standard. The one thing though, I will not fail to let you both know is that for the love of money, I love power. Who is the leader in Africa, for instance, who wouldn't like to phone the Queen, John Major, Tony Blair, Margarette Thatcher on a daily basis? By the way, y'all need more *undouble, London Gin undouble ladies?*"

I thought by now Efemona had had enough. Anyway, she nodded with Victoria. And the President got up and walked to the wine and liquor cabinet. He served himself Cognac and served his guests *double, double, undouble, undouble of London Gin,* that Efemona loves dearly.

"Thanks," they said. "Y'all welcome," he said.

They all began to enjoy their drinks because no swarm of flies or mosquitoes had inhabited the room. The mosquito machine was still working. Efemona could tell why, the fact that all the insects in the room were deflected by the fan of the machine and by no means were not struggling the liquor from her on her lips. As she gulped her *undouble,* she looked at the President who was now getting intoxicated and she knew her medicine was getting into her nerves. The President had not bothered to shut his mouth. He continued, "African countries need strong men like Idi Amen, Fidel Castro, Khadafi, Ikemba Ojukwu, Anikulapo Kuti and me to bring the people of this country to civilization. There is nothing wrong by what my mentors and I do. What do I mean by that? I mean liquidating the treasury of our Central Bank. It is pretty legitimate and that is because no one is bold enough to challenge 'us'."

I saw him turn his face and look at the gorgeous women as they too, angled themselves looking at him squarely in his face. "Victoria?" he called upon, "You should've enlightened Efemona before coming with her to see me. But anyway, I think Efemona is just too Americanized to understand that my junta men are saving my people from themselves. If I didn't seize power by coup, my people would be eating each other up alive. I'm glad it is only Clifford Orji who is cannibalizing on his fellow human beings and other men have not joined in the chorus."

"Are you happy about that? You should know it is because of you and your Juntas ruining our Nation that made men to cannibalize on their fellows. You damned motherfucker."

He was getting assaulted by Cognac Efemona had poisoned and his eyes were beginning to roll left and right. Not waiting for Efemona to ask more questions, he continued, "Didn't you hear of the news in the United States the terror Anini caused in Benin City and Ukpenu, your home State, Efemona? Just to give you an example. It was me that put up a million dollars ransom on his head to get him dead or alive. I also put up another million for Umaro Diko to be shipped back to Nigeria in a crate for embezzling billions of dollars of Nigerian Government funds for which my signatures were missing. And the reason I put up the million dollars for Anini to be caught dead or alive was because he was killing my Junta members and policemen on roadblocks who were taking one Naira bribes from motorists and market women. You know I paid the man who arrested Anini in cash."

Efemona hissed. "Hum-hum! How much is that compared to what you stole away from Nigeria Treasury to European countries?" she said.

That rang a bell in his brain. He looked dejected. "What you fail to understand," he managed to continue, "Is that Anini could've wiped out the whole people of your village at Ukpenu if I didn't put up the ransom."

That sent a chilling effect on Efemona and Victoria too. "I apologize," Efemona said, "I just haven't been current on domestic affairs on the news of Nigeria lately because of my AWAM movement in America."

The worn inside her had told her to apoligize. And the President accpeted her apology and vowed that he would abolish high ranking officials of his regime, including himself from going to England to ride the mule with the Queen and Prime Minister. With that thought, an idea leaped into Efemona. The worm had moved in her stomach. Then as nonchalantly as she could, she reached her sunglasses from her head and put it on again. Then she looked at Dudu. Her mouth began to vibrate, "Now I understand why there is coup, coup and counter coup in our country. How could you wipe out corruption in this country when only you have all those millions and billions in different banks in the Universe? If you are serious, Mr. Dudu, you need to make arrangements to bring all the money back to our country."

"A second Daniel come to judgement! There we go again. Just when I thought we were beginning to understand one another, you are-"

"We can never understand each other until you give up this executive chair for which you don't fit in and for which millions of men and women have lost their lives . . . and for which millions of Nigerians from North to South, East to West who are literate, qualified, Mr. President."

I was surprised that on that note, he looked at the women with an unpleasant face with matching expressions and waved his hand in dismissal of Efemona's wishes. Then he put his drink down and stared at Efemona. For some reason, what he was thinking was not going to happen. Efemona would not accept bribes to shut her fucking mouth despite that Ukpenu is rotted in unmitigated poverty, and that, if he was to bribe her with one million dollars, here in Nigeria, the money would have the same effect as a billion dollars in Reno, Nevada where the poor are arrested on the sidewalk to boost Jail Industry. The money would then swell on Efemona's head in Reno if she accepts it and at the same time, she would be a focus of the judges and cops and the Mafia if they don't like her to take the money away from her through arrest for jaywalking on the sidewalk when the judges set her bail for a million dollars. That thought of bribery died within him. Bribing her, she would have more questions for him anyway, he thought. Anyway, he shook his head again and again. Then finally he answered Efemona.

"We do have a problem there. And by the way, I think that Efemona is smarter than a true Nigerian now, more than the President, too. Amerikana," he mocked and laughed. Then supressing his own laughter for which Efemona and Victoria did not participate, he said, "I must be very frank and honest with you, Efemona . . . and you Victoria, that if I know the way to bring back all the money I have in foreign banks, overseas, I'll do it, overnight. Besides, the Lebanese businessmen that I do business with don't tell me how much I have acquired because, he too, has his own cut whenever he make huge deposit for me overseas."

From every indication, Efemona knew Dudu was finally getting

dozed with the spell in the Cognac she'd poisoned. She knew also that sooner or later he would reveal all his misdeeds to her before he die. So she stared at his mouth for the moment of truth and let him continue with no interruptions.

"You see," Dudu said, "The fact is that the white man too, is a cunning creature. I've personally called and written a series of memos to all the Bank Managers of the Universe where I have accounts. But do you know that they bluntly have refused to give me back all the millions and billions in one withdrawal?"

"No, Mr. President. I didn't know that."

"Oh, yes they refused to give me my money back in one huge withdrawl. I am upset and regretting ever making those huge transactions of laundering Government funds away from my country through Lebanese crooks. I'm sad that even with all the millions and billions of dollars and pounds and German marks I have in *Obodoyinbo,* I mean foreign countries, the white man still doesn't recognize who I am. For instance, I was in Germany and France a few months ago to withdraw and balance my account I have in their countries. Do you know that I underwent a series of questioning before I could withdraw just only one million dollars out of ten billion dollars I have in both countries? Their humiliating question is enough for me to stop depositing money in their banks. I plan to send a memo to other African leaders that the white man doesn't regard us even if we can afford to buy the Heaven and the Earth from the creator."

"Like what kind of humiliating questions, Mr. Dudu?" Victoria finally interrupted as if she wasn't listening.

He did not waste time to respond. "I mean like, do you have an ID, sir? Your social security, sir, your instate ID sir? Give me a break! They don't even care to know if I'm the President of Zimbaqwue, the President of Namibia, Cairo, Sudan, Kenya, Togo, Ivory Coast, Ghana or even the President of Nigeria, the most populous country in Africa. Oh! I'll take back just one country in Africa which is Egypt that I mentioned. Being that the people are fair in complexion, the white man respects them like white people. And anyway, back on what I was saying, more humiliating yet, even with all my billions in their banks, I stay on the line too before I'm served. And do you know what is most insulting to the African Leaders of the World including me, all the white women on the line in the banks seeing us too dark as charcoal, would grab their purses to their chest even in broad daylight as if we would grab it from them and start running. Today, that tells me that an African can be the Head of State of his country, and actor in the United States, an Ambassador in Europe, but still their white women still humiliate us in that fashions which has finally got to my nerves and not even to mention waiting for the elevators with them. And in most cases they don't even want to share the elevator with us!

My penis shrank when the President related his bitterness, despite that the spell and poison Efemona cast into the Cognac the President was drinking was having an effect on him. With that ugly remark about the white man and their women against Africans and African American nationals who are in Reno, Nevada, the President broke into my thoughts again to remind me of my experience with the typical rednecks and their ways of putting down black people in an establishment, or work environment and in their Courts and in their University classrooms.

Truly, I had experienced discrimination in the highest degree in most institutions that I have worked. For instance, I have worked in almost all the casinos in Reno without a raise which made me to find an asylum with Loyal Extrusion Inc., a place I will describe as a sinister sepulchral environment because black people have no future there. At least that's what I was told. It was there I finally met two distinguished gentlemen with Godly minds. Gordy Case and Jamie Sorensen will both remain in my mind as good men without racial bias. Though these two men may have believed Edgar Wallace, that killing is permissible if it is war, but horrible if it is murder, Gordy Case and Jamie respected me for who I was. Though their mere looks will instill that notion that they are perhaps racist, because they tell jokes that stink, I clearly don't see them as racists. Unlike their counterparts who are Professors in the Universities, and some other establishments I had worked where I was reduced as a nonentity and looked down upon, where they ordered me around, make me perform odd jobs they will not offer a white man, but still I resisted the urge to quit any of my jobs until I was fired.

Anyway, Gordy and Jamie were one of those people whose telephone voice matched their looks. But in reality, these two gentlemen will in fact, from my observation at Loyal Extrusions defend and rescue a black man dying by the sword in a battle field. Having said that, I will also balance my phrases that under no circumstances shall man judge another human being from the way they look, not share the elevator with them and also grabbing their purses close to their chest . . . . The truth is, I have been judged too, in the courtrooms of Reno, lied against by Samsons, Goliath and Hercules (security men) at Circus Circus Hotel and Casino and the judge found me guilty on arraignment. Before my arraignment I couldn't help but approach Gordy Case for an advance. Not only did he approve my advance withdrawal, he went into his pocket to make up the difference to pay off the fine for me. How can a poor man like me repay these two gentlemen? Well I am still hoping to write a bestseller of criticism so I can take them to Athens, the most romantic City in the world to introduce them to some rolling buttocks of Athens women, with my money. I mean women who would have straight blonde hair that tumble over their shoulders, and American women with characteristics coquettish twist of their head, whom I'll tame to carry the message across America that black people don't snatch purses in broad daylight. I mean women whose blouse are unbuttoned and the whiteness of their breasts contrasted sharply with their deep Mediterranean tans. Women who had roofs of their own bathed in the soft blue glow of the moon that fell into their rooms through their French doors leading to their balconies where the romantic pleasures will first start with the women. So much of Gordy, Jamie and me in Athens with beautiful women when I'd made it. I rest my case on that.

*　*　*

Another hour chimed by as the President held the two women spellbound, though Efemona knew it was her spell that caught him with the Cognac. Both remembered their last words to each other which rang in their ears. Efemona's muscles of her back after a long time of sitting and listening to him contracted and straightened up, but twirling to face Dudu the con artist. And Dudu's mind as well as Efemona could tell, had taken off in directions that he wouldn't have allowed if he'd been in full control of his thought process. His thought process at this time was strictly Efemona's handiwork. She knew it. What his mind was telling him to reveal to Efemona and Victoria now was that Dem Mayor office where he sat and embezzled Government funds would eventually become his last battlefield since Efemona had come to ruin him asking him all kinds of nonsense questions and not bowing down to him as everyone in the country does. He had talked and talked and talked.

Efemona believed her President. She was very relaxed and she loved to see that Nigeria completely wipe out the disease of corruption and nepotism in a vast ethnic Nation of diverse dialects. So she nodded along with everything Bad Dudu was saying, though she was the brain behind the truth of what he was actually saying. Finally, Victoria said, "Just don't embezzle Nigerian funds meant for the people of Nigeria again. Don't you know African countries, including ours, need the little money nature blessed them with? The poor of this Country would be happier if they too, have a technical share of the pie? My parents can't even feed themselves in a country that produces billions of barrels of crude oil like Saudi Arabia and most OPEC countries."

She stood up and walked towards him, and she continued, "You tell me, you alone have those millions and billions of Nigerian funds in foreign countries. When another power hungry member of your relay race Junta seize power and you happen to fall a victim to the bullet the money is forever lost in those countries."

"You are right, my dear," Dudu said.

He watched Victoria wiped some tears from her eyes with her left hand. He knew Victoria meant her words of sincerity saying, "Nigeria is a very rich country, blessed with natural resources. Even stupid people are supposed to be rich and able to care for their families. Most people believe this, why can't I too, be rich? In Nigeria, everyone is supposed to have enough."

He looked at both women. And he imagined himself lying with both of them and him in the middle in one of the resorts in Cayman Islands-fumbling with their titties and waking up to a good peaceful morning. After a deep silence, Dudu said, "You see, little did I know that the white man is a trickish being. It's an insult to Bad Dudu, the President of this country, and particularly to my guests facing me now. This *THING* has been bothering me for two decades now, that if I relate how the Queen and Prime Minister of England conned my Lebanese pimp that acted on my behalf, Efemona might blow the whistle."

Efemona knew she was about to score yet another one on him with her spell in his Cognac. What is it that the President kept as a secret for two decades that he wanted to reveal to them? Efemona and Victoria found themselves thinking and guessing in their hearts. Finally, Efemona asked, "Do you want us to guess?"

"If una fit guess am, I go dash una $5 million dollars." He reached over the pockets of his Agbada and brought out huge bundles of currencies in the neighborhood of $5 million dollars and dropped them on his desk.

"Wowooo! Some people dey enjoy for this country-o," Victoria said with amazement seeing currencies she'd never seen before all her life and

more surprised that an Agbada worn by Hausas, could hold as much as five million dollars. They began to guess. Who would like to miss an opportunity to make $5 million dollars in a second without actually working and sweating for it? No one I know of. As Efemona wants to be an overnight millionaire, she said to Victoria, "Girlfriend, let's keep guessing," and Efemona alone guessed more than forty reasons within ten seconds, ranging from, "I think you quarreled with your wife last night, you didn't have *some* last night, you lost your temper and sliced off the clitoris of your wife for not giving you *some*, you lost big money on the stock market, you lost your cattle boot worth $10 million and on and on and on."

"No," he said and laughed too.

Only Victoria was so close. She'd guessed, "You planned with your son Mohammed to murder Kudirat, the wife of Abiola, the Presidential elect. After that you have $20 million dollars oil deal to be auctioned off to the British."

"No. But you were so close," he said and laughed again. "So close. That's just but a fraction of my . . ." he paused.

After more guessing, none of them came nearer his secret. Then Efemona said, "You tell us, Mr. Dudu. I know you've been an asshole. I promise I will not blow the whistle."

"O.K." he said. Massaging his pounding temples, he took off his military green beret hat with his right hand. Then he swung it a couple of times and said, "Please promise me you'll not blow the whistle. Not that I don't trust you and Victoria, but I do have my reasons. If any of you do, a pound of flesh or a hole in the head will befall both of you. I'll not care who among you. Is that clear?"

The women were mute. And with that threat, Victoria looked at Efemona, thinking that it would be impossible for Efemona to keep the secret longer than the President had done for two decades. She doubted that Efemona could knowing that Efemona is the prime candidate to get the hole in the head because herself is good in keeping secrets. How Efemona could keep the secret is the question. As Efemona began to say, "I'll . . ." Victoria sprang to her feet. She closed her eyes and found herself saying, "No, no, no, please no, Efemona please, please, Efemona . . ." he might pull the triggers.

"You be quiet, Victoria. This is supposed to be a free country- though not quite. Your money buys you anything you want in the market if you can afford it. Who does the President think he is- Adolf Hitler? Big deal. Just because he's wearing a military uniform? I bet he'd never get any nearer to the war front line and he calls himself a General and a President. General my ass," Efemona hissed, "General speaking jargons on the Executive seat, giving the people of this country with Ph.D.s a bad name, screwing and raping young women on the sidewalk because of his khaki uniforms," she hissed again, clenching and unclenching her fists.

The President opened his mouth but was unable to say something. And Efemona's fear about him had long melted away. She was not the type again, to be intimidated. After all, she'd screwed him on his Executive seat twice which gave her the edge coupled with her spell on him through the poison in his Cognac. So Efemona went on anyway, "Chant with me girlfriend," she said, "That Efemona will not blow the whistle."

Victoria was relieved.

They chanted together. "Efemona and I will not blow the whistle."

* * *

Bad Dudu became confident. Efemona peeped into her purse. Her tape recorder was still working. "Go ahead. I'll not blow the whistle," she repeated.

Dudu cleared his throat. He'd not really meant to do what he now wanted to do. Efemona's spell was working. "You know," Dudu said, "The Queen and the Prime Minister of England once arranged for me through my Lebanese pimp to ride the mule with a blond and after that lay her at the Buckingham Palace, which was a good idea to me because I'd never before slept with a white woman or traveled to Britain. All my business transactions before this time, has been done through the internet super highway high tech and I thought I needed a change to travel to England and fulfill my dreams of blond carnal lust. It pained the fuck out of me that I had paid $10 million pounds under the table to the pimp to deliver it to the Queen and Prime Minister of England who'd signed the fucking bout with the blond for two nights."

"$10 million pounds to lay (with) an English woman for two nights?" Victoria repeated.

"Jesus fucking Christ," Efemona bellowed.

"Here we go again! I have already told you people who that criminal Christ was. I don't want to hear about him and his father-God!"

"That's not the question now, Mr. Dudu. Please continue. We are listening," Efemona pleaded.

"By the way, how did you send the money?" Victoria asked. "I sent the money through the Lebanese pimp who knows about wire fraud more than I do. First, he'd routed the money through an account in Zurich one Friday morning. Then later that same day he came back to my office and sent a fax (message) to the Queen and Prime Minister that the money was on its way. Five hours later, the Queen and Prime Minister buzzed me in my office that they wanted the money re-routed to Barclay's Bank in Britain instead of Zurich. And I authorized my Lebanese crook pimp to do what he'd to do in the computers."

"You authorized that huge transaction just to navigate a blond," Efemona repeated, then crossed her legs contentedly letting her eyes rest on him, wondering as she lighted her cigarette and inhaled deeply. When she'd gotten the nicotine flavor, Efemona turned to him, "What was the name of the blond you were to lay with, if I may ask, Mr. President?"

"Vanna Major," he lied. Efemona and Victoria knew he gave the wrong name.

"And did you ever navigate her after you paid that much money for a blond whore carnal?"

He looked at her, pained, and answered slowly in a manner of I'm very sorry for what all the leaders of this country, mostly from the North have done, siphoning the Nation's money to overseas and using the money to lay whores all over the world while Nigerian women can not afford to buy nail polish and . . . .

"No, my dear. Her carnal navigation never happened. The special room inside the Buckingham Palace they told my pimp I should meet the blond naked never existed."

"Never existed?" both women, mad as hell, echoed on cue as if instincts told them to at the same time. But Efemona was more touched.

I saw her lose her temper and sprang to her feet then pointed her index finger to his face. And I guess the reason for that was probably because of the poverty level in her country and yet Dudu has $10 million pounds to pay over for a blond pussy, whereas it was because of poverty in her country that made her to form her AWAM movement, the movement she founded which secretly sends young women abroad to sell their carnals to be able to feed themselves and their families. The pain in her stomach after remembering AWAM movement, she lashed out at Dudu, "I learnt the poor man in this country doesn't eat eggs any more because it's too damn expensive and the eggs to even spend the money on, if they do have the money, to buy it. And you motherfucker know that the pressing problem that divided this country remained unsolved and my people still go to bed hungry every night and you sent $10 million pounds to England just to navigate a blond pussy."

She had tears in her eyes. Wiping them slowly away with her left hand she continued, "Look at India! Nigeria is richer than India. India went World Nuclear Power on March 15, 1998, and you are fucking a bitch for $10 million pounds motherfucker."

Dudu caught Efemona's index finger pointed at his nose. That in itself did not stop Efemona. "You cunt sucker! I'd to come see you to give beggars standing at the Federal Palace Hotel, and at the Airport and at the National Mosque and at the Doddan Army Barracks where you sit comfortably signing signatures, worrying not what you'll eat for breakfast, lunch and dinner, money to feed themselves. Do you know how that makes me feel? Let go of me!" she shouted through the depth of her voice.

Stone-faced but near tears too, Bad Dudu faced Efemona and Victoria in the spacious quiet Executive Office and said, "One day, I hope that both of you, including the people whom I rule will find it in their hearts to forgive the past leaders before forgiving me."

From my living room, I saw him sighed heavily. Seeing him sigh, Efemona said, "Well, Victoria and I will forgive you. But I doubt if my grandmother who drowned in the potholes of Ukpenu will forgive you, neither do I think the people of this country you rotted in poverty would. You can appeal to the people of this country by yourself when I leave for the States."

The bomb inside Efemona as the President sighed relieving his pain, I would say can possibly exterminate the judges of Reno who'd found me guilty for what I did not do. But still, when I looked at my wife, Efemona, from afar in my Radio Shack gadget, I saw that her face was like that of an innocent baby still in the womb but as dangerous as a rattle snake with vengeance for the people of her country still eating *garri* night and day.

"Go on and tell us what kind of pussy the blond was to have. Was it gold or silver that no black woman in Nigeria or in Africa might have?" Efemona asked.

"And what made you do it?" Victoria asked, immediately following Efemona's question.

He looked away, then reached for his Havana cigar and lighted it. When it glowed, he puffed on it. His voice, when he finally spoke was mellow, but sorrowful. The Cognac spell was still working. "My pimp told me that if I was stingy paying over the money secretly through him to the Queen and Prime Minister who would arranged the fucking bout with the blond, another African Head of State was willing to pay $20 million pounds for the *toto*. And where was the African Head of State from? From Ethiopia. I thought then how can an Ethiopian Head of State compete with an OPEC country when he should use the money to fight the drought in his country? Only Allah knew how angry I was. I then immediately summoned other African Heads of State and some members of my Military Juntas for an impromptu summit. The meeting which took place in a comfortable rain- proofed cabin in the Ajegule area, 80 miles away from Doddan Army Barracks, made me feel good about myself to reduce the goddamn Ethiopian Head of State for even trying to outbid my price. Anyway, all the African Heads of State except Ethiopian, Moi refused to honor the meeting. All others had arrived secretly at irregular intervals and were all members of the OAU. They came to support me to rebuke Arapi Moi for trying to top my bid. When the last man came I then shut the secret cabin door. My Israeli guards, Esemuede, Poisonous and Hemlock took positions against intruders from Fela Anikulapo Kuti who was against me and other leaders who'd ruled before me draining our oil money and from Abiola's men who wanted to rule this country with all cost. As we quietly sat around a tall, long rectangular table, I served *suya* and tea to everyone present. And for your information, these buddies of mine as African Heads of State had met before under tense clandestine upheaval urging Ian Smith and Botha of South Africa to step down. I trusted my buddies as they trusted me. You see! Efemona! I shouldn't be telling both of you this because the first bullet is reserved for people like you, Efemona who knows too much, gossip a lot and who might blow the whistle to Journalists of this country who hate my guts."

"But you can't stop now. Just round up quickly, Mr. President," Efemona said with spell charm from her mouth.

Victoria concurred with a nod and a smile. The President I saw from a distance in my living room looked sad. With the fake sadness look on his face, he continued, "I, the Authoritarian Leader, was the chairman of the occasion. The urgency of the meeting I said to all my buddies present was that I desperately needed to send $20 million pounds to Britain through my Lebanese pimp, to the Queen and Prime Minister of Britain to arrange a suite/cocoon with a blond in Buckingham. My grievance, I told my buddies, was that Arapi Moi was about to sabotage my bid by toppling my bid to lay the blond first. I also told my *follow-follow* Authoritarian Leaders of Africa who attended my impromptu meeting to rebuke Moi that Nigeria will remain and will always be the leader to civilize other African countries."

"How can you civilize other African countries when we have millions of graduates with no jobs in Nigeria, roaming the streets and some had turned armed robbers?" Victoria interrupted.

"Girlfriend please, let the President finish," Efemona cautioned. "I'm sorry, girlfriend. I wasn't thinking," Victoria said. "Please continue,

Mr. President." Victoria said to him to get him wired up with Efemona's charm.

I saw his lips trembled and he asked, "Where was I?"

He did not wait to hear where he'd stopped. He reminded himself. "I informed my buddies that the bargain with the blond had already been struck with the Queen and Prime Minister of England and the blond has agreed to sleep with me for two nights and for the urgency of her carnal lust, I planned to travel within the next couple of days to meet her at Room Vanna 107. After we all had our dinner, I decide that the time was ripe to call for a vote. I rose. Standing tough like Tarzan and speaking Pidgin English, I said to my Lebanese pimp seated on my right hand: $10 million pounds to sleep with a blond without Moi topping my bid with $10 million pounds higher than my bid to screw the British blond for the first time in my life: I took the attendance myself. Read my lips and see how we'd voted young ladies:

"Katanga from Bornu." "Yes."

"Ahijou, Cameroon." "No."

"Babagida, Mina." "Yes."

"Ogbemudia, Benin" "No."

"Awo, Ibadan."

"Oh, excuse me. I forgot he's late. I voted for him, 'No'." "Mohammed Muritala Sokoto. He's late, but I voted yes for him. Barclay's Bank of England has voted to use his millions he left behind to renovate the Bank and the remaining millions used to feed the homeless sleeping rough at the Buckingham Palace entrance."

"Ojukwu, Portharcourt."

"Fuck' em motherfuckers. They teamed up with Nigerian soldiers during the Biafra-Nigerian civil war."

"Yes or no, please." "No."

"Mr. Bruce Langfield, Scotland Yard, Britain." "100%. Keep the money coming fools."

"Is that a yes or no, please?"

"Yes."

"Mobutu, Kenya. Is he here?"

"He's late," his son said. "I voted yes for my father," Moboya said.

"Mr. Walker, America."

"Our blondes need big African and American ding dongs, man. They love their dicks. You are welcomed if the British blond changes her mind. Our blondes will screw dogs, cows and horses for the money, man. Efemona, the famous African woman, who left Ukpenu to join her husband in America, residing in Reno, Nevada knows that already. Walker assured me."

"I take that for yes. I told him."

I watched Efemona laugh from a distance so far away, but so close with Radio Shack gadget in my living room. The reason for her raucous laughter was unclear to me.

"Idi Amin, Uganda."

"Fuck the sons and daughters-of-a-bitches." "Yes or no, please. I said to him."

"I say fuck the Queens and the Americans," Idi Amin said. "I'll take that for a No," I shook my head to make Amin know that he was not welcomed to the meeting, because he was mean to the British people, especially to the Queen and her entourage who visited him at the basement of his Palace bowing down to him in the specially built Palace to humiliate the Queen of all people."

"The noise was getting too much in the cabin. All of us were getting high on Cognac and *Ubiaroko grass: what the Americans call weed.* That's when I slammed the gavel. Ooooorder I yelled out from the depth of my soul. Everyone please be seated and let's get the meeting over with and move ahead with other issues facing us in Nigeria and in Africa."

"Fela Anikulapo Kuti, Abeokuta."

"Oh! 'cuse me. He's deceased now. I forgot. But his son was at the meeting. He voted No for him. For the first time, Femi said, he was carrying on everything his father believes in. I didn't quesion him because my counterparts already silenced their family. I mean to zero."

"Sani Abacha, Sudan."

"He fell *yakatani* and never woke. I voted for him yes. Nigeria is sad because he left no will and he has billions in Britain and Swiss Banks. It's already liquidated by the Queen and Prime Minister of Britain. The money they said would be used to renovate Buckingham Palace."

"Lumummba Jr., Zaire." "No."

"Shagari, Jos."

"He's asleep. I voted for him yes. His money is feeding the jailbirds in Britain, Scotland Yard."

"Moi."

"My counterparts and OAU members rebuked him in absentia for all the homes he built in Boston, Miami with his Country's Government funds he embezzled and . . . and for his bold courage to compete with me."

"Zagamu, Kaduna." "Yes."

"Abiola, Ondo."

"I must rule," I heard him say. He was really pissed when I told him he couldn't rule. The Clinton's administration must remember that I won the election and yet ruling in prison. Is that democracy in the sense of the American ideology? He was asking. What do you call democracy in Nigeria? So I remembered Ivan Ikoku whom we just gave a face on the Naira note bill. And also Mr. Awolowo who had the Socialist idea and the British told us not to allow him to rule and then died a paupa! For that reason ladies and gentlemen I frowned, ordered him hemlock tea to shut him up. To me it was democracy at its best. His daughter voted No for him via satellite from Houston, Texas. No living will. Britain is still debating over his millions of pounds and dollars in British Banks. I know in my heart the millions would eventually be used to buy new clothes for Prince Williams and his brother."

"Colonel Moammer Khadhafi, Libya."

"I believe in International Brotherhood of Freedom Fighters.

Armed them with bombs, grenades, maime them abroad or hold them for ransom. The Yankees are not fit to live."

"Yes or no, please."

"I say fuck the Yankees and the Britishman. They killed my daughter during their raid on my palace for being strong headed at their policies in the Third World."

"I take that for a No." "Jerry Rawlings, Ghana."

"No. It's time African Heads of State wake up to Nuclear Arms Race as India has done. And let me make this clear to everyone.

If this resolution is passed with or without my vote, the white man will come back and use the money to purchase all the uranium in Africa and then test their new weapons in our backyards to kill us and our children. In reality it did make some sense, but I did not buy it."

"I, the chairman, voted yes. The resolution was passed. And please promise me these names will not be publicly revealed."

"We absolutely promise," Efemona and Victoria echoed. "The white man you and I know are cunning creatures," Dudu said again and again.

"You must have a strong reason for that more than you have told us," Victoria said.

He bent his head. Raising up his head, he said, "They played on my intelligence at the Buckingham Palace. I never thought I'll be a looney at my age." He was silent for a minute as Efemona looked at him to fall from grace. Looking at Efemona, too, he made some quick remarkable pleasantries to fool the women, because Efemona was asking him what happened to the more than $100 billion dollars crude oil sale during the Gulf War for which he wouldn't have explained. But Efemona was not the type to be fooled. She let it slide for a moment.

He was still saying, "You and Victoria certainly belong to the Hollywood, Miami and Joe Conforte's women of Mustang Ranch beauty pageant molds of Reno, Nevada. I Dudu, had visited the Mustang Ranch when Conforte had problems with the Federal Government for tax invasion or whatever they call it. I was to help bail out Conforte with $7 million dollars, not only buying his stock, but also to navigate several of his beauty queens at the Ranch. I was humiliated by the women. They said my Agbada dress was too big and by the time I pulled it over my head before I screw, they would lose two or three customers waiting in line to screw them."

I think I remember that particular day that Dudu visited the Mustang Ranch. Holy Shit, the girl that I had in there at the Ranch to make money for me had actually called me to the Ranch that a figure with a gaunt face wearing what he called Agbada what the Nevadans had never seen before was at the Ranch and his accent was difficult to understand. I was at the dinner table when she'd called, so I donned on my Levi's 501 Jeans and a T-shirt and headed there to show an example to him of what he should've worn. As I got there, the place was absolutely jammed packed at the bar. There were perhaps more than 100 people who were milling about in the twinkles of light that bounced off the eternal disco hall. What made Dudu different to be singled out in the crowd was that all the men there were dressed in Yankee style Western semi-casual mode while the women, men were trying to lay with their money were dressed in whore-like, incredibly short mini skirts that feature furlongs of prime time thigh, topped by ultra-tight tank tops and nasty blouses with necklines that plunge to the dark depth of the male libido and the male's wallet. As I paid six dollars for one tiny four ounce beer, the buzzer sounded, and all the women quickly move to the center of the huge spacious lobby. It was line up time for the new men that were coming in. As I said before, I was there at the suggestion of Holy Shit, a blond who was bent on making fast money for me. For her, the Ranch was a place blondes go to, to make fast money with their carnals. With the certainty of the IRS take over of the Ranch, which she'd seen on the news, she informed and begged me if she could go to the Ranch to make fast money for me. In all my years of residing in Reno, I had never walked through those infamous gates if not for Holy who wanted to make money for me. Anyway, I tapped Dudu on the shoulder.

"Where are you from?" I asked.

"Nigeria," he said, then added, "I thought I come to Reno, Nevada to enjoy myself with blondes and let the people of Reno know that African leaders can think more with their *little heads* (penis) rather than with their big heads. I am surprised that the girls and their managers here at the Ranch don't know who I am in Nigeria. The girls turned me down saying my Agbada was too big and blah-blah-blah. What they don't know was that I had $5 million dollars stuffed in my Agbada pockets to lavish."

With his pompousness to lavish Nigerian funds, which vexed me the most, I left him there to be ridiculed more by the women. Holy Shit knew I was mad as hell, but didn't know why. But as I got home and turned on the TV, an anchor man I can't recall was casting the news saying: An African Head of State wearing a huge Agbada, presumably from Nigeria was turned down by whores at the Ranch. What the women didn't know was that he'd close to $7 million dollars to lavish for the women. He vowed never to come to Reno Mustange Ranch again to be insulted. So much about the Ranch episode with Bad Dudu.

Dudu was still talking to Efemona and Victoria, "What the blondes at the Ranch and their manager didn't know was that I had $7 million dollars in bundles stuffed inside my Agbada pocket to lay all the women which never happened because of my Agbada that was too big. It was the reason I'd yeilded to the Queen and Prime Minister's suggestion through the pimp to meet the British blond at the Buckingham Palace for two nights romantic affair."

Efemona and Victoria sat still and watched Dudu rain down more secrets. It was essential that they think clearly now. Efemona had to deal with Dudu and then salvage the acceptance of being Matron General for which she was invited to fill. Finally, Efemona made a motion to Victoria. She said, "Thanks for the compliments anyway. I still can't imagine the life of my people haunted by people like you, Dudu and your Juntas who share a collective history of self-consciousness that is genetically inclined. This in fact has made the entire population of this Country to think madness of you and your Juntas. Give my people the chance to choose their real man through election process. Military rule to me is anarchy. By the way, I think it might be a good idea to abolish the Army anyway in Nigeria. It is my suggestion to you, Mr. President."

"I would love to. But as I said before, my people would be eating themselves alive."

"What do you mean eating themselves alives? The truth is, you're the one eating up my people substance alive," Efemona said knowing that it was an excuse not to hand over power to civilians.

Chapter

25

The President pulled himself together after he explained his thwarted high hope to navigate the carnal of a British blond.

After puffing on his Havana cigar and gulping down another *triple undouble* shots of Cognac, he took a deep breath, and Efemona saw by his body movement which showed, that he looked at her funny. All said and done, Dudu still had the pistol on the desk, and there wasn't much keeping him from pulling the trigger. Except, Efemona thought, Dudu might have other plans for Efemona, something he'd been thinking about for the last few minutes when he finished relating his truth about $10 million dollars to screw a blond from England. And at the same time, thinking of the $100 billion dollar crude oil sale which was unaccounted for during the Gulf War. For now, Dudu hadn't known the pistol was still on the desk to kill her, so there was no reason to remind him. But still, Efemona couldn't resist the opportunity to fuck with his mind and perhaps draw him into answering more questions. Efemona reasoned, with her Voodoo spell flame in her mouth that only she knew she has within her; maybe this is the right time to tell him her own problems. Then Efemona went on to tell Dudu everything about her early life at Ukpenu, how she'd corresponded with Ekiaqueta, her husband, in America thinking that Ekiaqueta was a multimillionaire, before she joined him in Reno, Nevada after a brief introduction and he's treating her like a slave, and how she would wish that the women in Nigeria she'd introduced into her AWAM movement were given preferential treatment just like in America. Through her Crocodile tears, another of her trickish Voodoo spells on him, she'd watched the President closely to see if she'd touched his elephant heart for sympathy.

However, the sympathy she'd longed to see from him was not registered on his face. That gave Efemona another concern to increase the Voodoo flame of more flippant vibration from her mouth. Still, there was no pity, no expression at all that she could see. Her situation suddenly became unbearable when the President suddenly spun his chair around to face the window of his office, but staring at nothing in particular, leaving Efemona and Victoria to stare at his back. As he remained in that position for a while with his thumb in his mouth, thinking, Efemona thought: I will know who is who. My grandmother's Voodoo worm in me or Sandhurst motars and cannons for terrorizing the people of this country.

That moment after her thoughts, the worm moved in her stomach. The spell caught the President and suddenly he turned his chair around. Then he said, "Efemona?! I'm sorry to hear what you are going through with your husband in Reno, Nevada. I'll also look into the problems of women in this country for the need to employ more women in the work force, particularly in my Junta Administration. But I tell you, Efemona, that I'll be dumb and stupid to inform you that our culture, tradition and ways of life would be altered because of you. However, I will see to that, too, in one hundred years to come. I will tell you why."

"Why, Mr. President?" Efemona asked with a loud voice, as if a dog had bitten into her flesh.

"I've researched my heart to know that in politics of this country, there has never been a woman bold enough or educated enough as you think you now are to shatter the political glass ceiling of Doddan Army Barracks. And more so, to defy the sexism of the African Continent: women in politics. What do I mean by that? I mean women who will go where no women in African hemisphere has gone before and in Africa as a whole-perhaps to the 'Black House' at Abuja, or to the hot seat of mine. It will never happen. Such women, no matter how educated, may have an office next to mine, but will *never, never* rule in this country. By the way, why did you bring up that issue?"

"Because I feel that women need a strong voice in the political issues of this country," Efemona answered with her Voodoo spell again. "I know, Mr. President, that I, Efemona, qualify for this hot seat you now sit before me. For your information, I also found myself asking that same question-that paragon of sexism you brought up. I am in a better position to let you know, Mr. Dudu, that in America, men running for public offices during elections can quarrel, fight and even viciously attack each other. But, they are much more willing to let the past go by, to adopt a political spectrum of no permanent friends and no permanent enemies. For instance, in the state of Nevada where I attained my Citizenship, Harry Reid lost one of the closest races U.S. Senate seat in history to Paul Laxalt in 1974. How about Al Gore and George W. Bush? That aside, Harry Reid is now working with Paul Laxalt in the same office. How about that?! Even George Bush Senior had no problem taking Bill Clinton on a tour of the White House. He shook his hand and they hugged. I tell you, Mr. President, that is what civility is and that's what politics is supposed to be. Men in American politics and most developed countries can pummel each other, but they don't hold animosity, because they know that in politics they can't afford to do that. They don't hang their opponents after the election is over. They hand over to whoever wins. And whoever wins doesn't rule in prison. The loser backs the winner up during swear-in and crises.

In contrast, it is not so in Nigeria, where I was born, where you now seated yourself as God or the Authoritarian Leader even though no one voted you into office to rule. Coupled with that, you have the nerve to hang farmers and market women who voice out their concern against your Junta Administration. Those who are not killed are driven into exile. How about that, Mr. President? Mr. Dudududu?"

He could not stand Efemona again lecturing him. With all that, he knew Efemona was talking sense into him, but still, he said, "Efemona, I swear that isn't true. I swear that isn't true." Then he turned again to face the window as he spun the chair around, apparently not sure if Efemona would accept the post of Matron General he had invited her to fill and all of a sudden, she's to be watched as an impediment to his progress in dwindling the Nation's Economy. Then she too, called on his name.

"I don't want to hear it," he said as he turned around his chair. "Efemona?! I don't care what you say to convince me. In the first place, I don't think you know what you are talking about. Even if I cannot read, I have men in my Administration who read and interpret for me. The other day, my secretary read the TIME magazine, which featured Nevada's women in politics who are vicious against others and each other. For instance, Idigun, my secretary, interpreted to me that women in the Nevada political spectrum are much worse than men are when dealing with antagonism. He gave me a series of evidence to believe, to back his allegations up. He gave me an example of a powerful woman in Nevada: Senate Minority Leader, Titus vs. other women on the County Commission. He even cited Jan Jones vs. Commissioner Yvonne Atkinson Gates. Sexism in politics . . . can only exist in America, because America gave women the chance. By the way, you know what I am talking about."

"No I don't. Tell us!"

"I mean in America, where Oval Office gave 'Equal Rights' to women to talk shit and challenge men during elections, or Women vs. Women, quote and unquote, women like to constantly contrast themselves: like who has the longest fingernails and who wears the most expensive material of Gucci and so on and so forth. Is that what you want to introduce and bring to this country where I rule as the Caesar of this Nation? You've got to be kidding me, Efemona! Warm yourself that seat you are seated. Overall, do you know what politics boils down to? It boils down to making dubious money. Kill or be killed to assume being a county commissioner, a judge, a governor or . . . . Why do you think in American politics men or women running for politics spend millions to be heard by the people who they try to sway their hearts and to vote for them? And when they win, don't they forget their promises they made to the people? I mean the people they represent in their Counties-to go fuck themselves? And what they promise they would do they never, never accomplish? It is because money is the chief reason for a conqueror of the World, of a State, of a Country-whatever you may call it. Now! Did you know that Jon Corzine spent $2 million dollars a week on TV ads to win New Jersey's democratic Senate nomination? And at least another $200,000 to investigate his republican opponent-Floria? I bet you don't! I don't even want to enlighten you on Presidential elections in America, how much they spend and all that stuff. All I am trying to make you aware of is there is no difference from Military rule and elected officials by the people. We all have the same motive and that motive is money and fame to lay and entice beautiful women in the world. One has a choice among women in the world who are married to poor men, but beautiful. We can humiliate their husbands and take their wives. Give me a break, Efemona! I will repeat it that you don't know nothing."

She became mute. She knew where the President was heading. She dare not admit to herself, otherwise her mission for all women in Nigeria and Africa in general would be thwarted. Efemona then looked down as if she wasn't listening. Finally her head went up in slow motion as the Voodoo worm moved in her stomach. And the President, too, looked at Efemona with new interest of her carnal lust. So he set aside sexism in politics and returned to Efemona's former concerns of the why's she was invited to see him. Looking at her, he said, "I strongly suggest though that you keep all the grievance you may have about yourself at least for the time being. I trust Victoria that she would keep our conversation in this room. I mean everything we discussed here in my office today, mine and your problems. I have my reasons for that which you already know."

Efemona and Victoria were lost for a minute. Efemona, trying to remember, exchanged her left leg for the other. The President smiled and looked at her. "You see," he added, "I must confess to you that there are those in my Junta regime who would like to wipe out corruption and those who believe in foreign Banks than in Nigerian Banks. I am one of those people. Ojukwu can grumble. Where is he now? I silenced him. Me and my men in power all from the North and muslims will continue to embezzle Nigerian crude oil money sales until we exhaust every penny Nigeria generates from its revenue.

He'd contradicted himself on that based on his remorse of sending $10 million pounds to Britain through a pimp to navigate a blond in

Britain. I think the reason for that was that he was getting assaulted by Cognac spell, Efemona thought.

Efemona was in deep thought. Dudu must vacate the post of the executive seat for which no one voted him.

* * *

Efemona wondered if Dudu was right. And she realized that he would never know that his end was near and there would never be any way for him to know. She felt that Dudu has not only treated the people of Nigeria with disrespect, he disregarded their well-being as well for having all those millions and billions for himself in foreign Banks and yet, killing and maiming his people to shut them up. She realized that children born in Nigeria will not have good heroes to emulate if Dudu will survive another year in office. Dudu and Efemona made eye contact and held it a fraction before Efemona turned away her face as a dismissal of his regime within a few more hours when the Voodoo spell in her mouth would drive him to insanity before he follow one of his female concubines home where he would die like a chicken on top of her carnal. She sighed deeply. Hum hum! This gaunt face is able to play on the minds of my people in this country? Her mind raced down to the poverty of the people in her country again as if an iron whip had been introduced into her bare back.

Though Efemona was not very impressed about how Dudu responded to her concern about the women of Nigeria, she vowed in her heart that her brother, Newman would help her to carry on her movement of AWAM in Nigeria when she was gone back to America. Suddenly, Dudu spun his chair around in an usual style. He did not know what Efemona was thinking. But he said, after facing the women again, "Let me say this once and for all, that is, any revelation of the secret information which has been discussed in my office remain with the three of us and outside of this office is grounds for a bullet in the head. Revealing my secret that would make my Junta members to hate me is grounds for treason against the President and both of you could be hanged or shot by firing squad of my no mercy Generals in my

Administration, American citizen or not. I tell you that firing squad is also typical of my regime to those who rebel against my Authoritarian leadership. Efemona and Victoria are no exception. In a few minutes I will take you both to see Siro Wiwa where he's waiting for my approval to be silenced with a bullet to his temple. Bare in mind that I don't accept pleading for leniency from other World leaders. My words of death against a rebel of my words is death."

I watched from afar. My penis shrunk again, as my Efemona looked poker-faced, unmoved. And I knew what my Efemona was thinking: Jesus! What a man so ill-hearted! But in her heart, her laugh remained, and she still seemed, in a kind of loggerhead but of joyless helplessness if the Voodoo spell in her didn't silence Dudu on top of his mistress. In that case, he would commit more atrocities against the people who voice out their concern for the country they love so well in which they were born. As she thought, the worm in her diaphragm moved, which told her to blink her left eyelash. And she blinked it. The President blinked his right one. And what that meant was that they were both thinking the opposite. Somebody must die and be humiliated like a chicken in the world was Efemona's thought. And the President thought of more signatures and approval on papers to make more money was at the back of his mind.

As the spell caught him more than ever, he looked at Efemona and said, "I would be glad if you submit your resumé today to assume the post of Matron General of this country without challenge."

Stupid, foolish idiot who doesn't know that I came with Victoria to bring his Authoritarian Regime down, Efemona murmured to Victoria.

*　*　*

I took my eyes away from my Radio shack gadget toy bringing high tech technology into homes, for a minute and opened the door to let the kids in after their long day at school. As they undressed and put on their street clothes and were on the lunch table, food which were prepared by their nanny, a good meal of beef stew and clam chowder and potato salad which I also ate before they arrived, I told them their mama has not yet returned. I sat with them while they ate and we chatted which was my routine every day after they'd returned from school to ask and tease them what they did at school.

On this particular day, which was now on a Tuesday afternoon in Reno, Nevada, I asked my children, not particularly directing the question to any one of them, "So what's new? What did you guys do at school today? Good subjects? Good instructors? . . . and blah, blah, blah," just to talk anyway. My daughter Verita, who had turned eleven, was the first to respond. "An interesting subject today for me in social studies taught by Miss Benny. She said that there is no distinctly Native American criminal class except Congress, and that Mark Twain was the first to observe that."

I began to think, why would my eleven-year-old daughter pick that phrase up amidst everything her teacher had said in her class. But in reality I praised my daughter who is destined to be an actress and if that fails will try to become a writer, lawyer or a Political Scientist. And my daughter asked, "Daddy, do you believe in class struggle?"

My God! An eleven-year-old girl could ask me an intelligent question like that! The first thing that came to my being was her mother and the President of Nigeria, Efemona wants to bring down his Government. There in my heart, too, I remembered the Socialist Doctrine, which is somewhat vague on the subject of criminals like Dudu himself. And I believe that Miss Benny, reflecting on Mark Twain before a class of sixth graders, gets most of her thoughts and opinions from nineteenth-century radicals who believed that the Oppressive Capitalist system created crime and criminals themselves. Anyway, Ehimare and his immediate junior, Oz, did not seem to be interested in discussing anything with me on what they did at school except that they were busy swallowing their meal.

They all finished eating and I requested if they would go for a quick visit to the Judas Iscariot home. They all shouted yes. So I did not take a vote or veto this day. We all headed out and strolled to Judas' home about three blocks away from my place. As we strolled, I put my arm around Verita and she put her arm around mine. She said, "We don't seem to talk much anymore, Daddy."

"Because you are at school and Daddy tries to stay indoors most of the time because of my eyes," I replied, making no reference to the cow eye on my face.

"You can always call me on your breaks at school on my cell phone."

"I can?"

"Yes you can."

After a few seconds she said, "There's been a lot of things going on around you and mommy."

"Yes, but nothing to be concerned about because you are too young to know."

After another few seconds, she said, "I know things are not alright between you and mom."

I saw that coming again and replied without hesitation, "The relationship between a husband and wife is no one else's business, my Veri-Veri, not even to their children. I want you to remember that as you mature in life and when you marry."

"I'm not sure that's true. My brothers and I have a direct interest in your happiness and well-being. We love you both as you love us." Unfortunately, I didn't want to tell her that her mother has Americanized and is living the life of the Romans. But I did say though, "I want you to honor and cherish your husband until death do both of you part," and I added, "the only way I will advise you to divorce your husband is if he's a rapist, a thief, a con- artist, drug user and abuser, or a killer. Other than that, money is not everything, it doesn't even buy happiness. It might buy material stuff, but eventually those material things would decay. And remember that Daddy loves you and your two brothers despite that I am poor. However, your mom's and your daddy's happiness and well-being are not necessarily tied to our marriage."

"That's what I'm talking about. I know you guys are having some problems."

"Yes, but not with each other. I already told you about the life your mother wants to live. Subject closed. Okay!"

We reached the doorstep of Judas Iscariot and stood facing each other. Verita said, "When is mommy coming back from Nigeria?"

"After she accomplishes her mission," I replied.

I knocked on the door while I was in deep thought. And yet my deep thought increased when no one answered the door. And Verita asked, "Daddy, what's wrong?"

I could not help but replied, "I suppose happiness and separation or divorce are incompatible. All are natural biological things. And maybe one day, my staying in doors to write this book after work because of my new look will not mean a thing to your mother. Efemona and I will not have a good adult relationship with you and your brothers anymore."

"Do you really mean that?"

"Of course. I always have the belief that animals in the wilds of Kenya or Yankari in Nigeria who leave their nests someday will certainly find their parents again and recognize them."

Having said that to make my daughter happy, I knew it was not going to happen with me and her mother anymore. Our relationship had been tarnished. Anyway, I knocked again and again, and no one answered the door. So we headed back to the house. In a few minutes after our arrival to the house and watching the Discovery Channel of how animals eat or be eaten, for a while, they all dozed off on the couch. Quietly, I switched on my gadget toy again, which was for my eyes only, the debacle between two great personalities I never want to come across if I believe in life after death. Dudu and Efemona.

Anyway, I saw Dudu excuse himself and headed into an adjoining room, which might-I believe was a restroom. And Victoria looked at Efemona and said, "He will not think of violence against us if he releases most of the liquor in his system." With that, the worm in Efemona's stomach moved. The pistol and the huge $5 million dollars in bundles was still lying still on his desk. Efemona smiled. If anyone was smart in the world, Efemona was the one. She took the pistol and stuck it in her purse. Then she loaded the bundles too, as much as her purse could load. Then she grabbed the purse of Victoria and loaded the remaining bundles into it and both sat still, waiting for him. I was surprised Dudu came out of the restroom and noticed nothing. Efemona's Voodoo spirit in his cognac began to work in him like a pig. To accomplish her objective, Efemona brought up a discussion. She said to Dudu, "Setting aside what my husband is doing to me in America, today is my saddest day in life."

"Why is that, Efemona?" Dudu asked in amazement.

"After reading the Daily Times yesterday and seeing you announce the Nation's mourning of Mr. Emeka Ngozika. Ngozika was my good friend when I was still in Nigeria. And over the years, I kept in contact with him over the phone, since my husband has a habit of violating my rights. Besides, Mr. President, I've planned to divorce him when I get back to the States."

Actually, I know Efemona more than anyone else. What she was doing as the worm in her stomach moved was reminding Dudu of his atrocities when he ordered the plane carrying Emeka and other high-profile military Generals from the South downed by bazooka to perish all the men on board so that they can not topple his Government.

Anyway, Efemona added, "Divorcing my husband in America, I could make a fortune. It is the American way. I have three children by him, which is a prerequisite to qualify me for dissolution of community properties. I'm interested to work for you, but not at this time. It was surely an honor, Mr. Dudu to remember me and the good job I've done for my country while I was here six years ago. I'll only tell you, Mr. President, that if you want me in your Administration, you're gonna hafta give me some time for at least another year or so to think about it. I would have accepted the offer of Matron General, but my leave of absence expires in the year 2025. Right now, my only objective in mind is to face my husband in the Court of Law in America. He has little money in the bank that I want the court to take a look into. It's not much, but the judges of Reno, Nevada would take it from him and give it to me. I love America. Don't get me wrong. That doesn't mean I don't love my motherland."

What a trickish woman, I thought. Though Dudu bowed his head in disappointment, he was in a way happy, that Efemona has a dubious mind to acquire wealth from her husband, which was the same thing he was doing in his country: embezzling Government funds. The only thing different from the intentions of Efemona, he thought, was: Government vs. Individual wealth accumulation.

Finally, he said to Efemona, "Well, this new post death had claimed Maddam Obaze would've elevated you Efemona. You would've made a new name for yourself when you make speeches all over the world. In short, you had a hundred percent chance to meet First Ladies of the world. What could've been more appealing than that? Besides, you would be making all kinds of money like (us) me.

"Tell the President you are already making speeches all over the world," Victoria, more bold at heart, now that Efemona had a weapon with her, pointed out.

Efemona looked at the President. "I'm already making speeches around the world, but that is not the point. My calendar is already booked with appointments for this year. I'll call you, Mr. President. Trust me."

"I'll hold the post for you for one year. How is that, Efemona?"
"Bee-oootiful."

Victoria looked at the face of the President, "Keep your fingers crossed. A year from now is at our palms. You heard her. I believe Efemona will call you if the telephones in Nigeria are not always busy when people from America calls. I mean to say if the phones goes through" and she laughed.

That mere mention of 'if the telephone goes through' made Efemona's clitoris to shrink. He shrugged instead. "All right," he said, but praying in his heart that Efemona won't bring up the issue of the phones again that don't work in the country for discussion which might bring up the subject of draining the Nigerian Treasury again for which he knows he's responsible.

Efemona and Victoria managed a smile seeing his reaction. "I appreciate your concern and generosity to hold the post of Matron General for one year for me. But remember, Mr. President, this world is unstable. If you don't hear from me, give someone else a chance to make money from the oil revenue of this country."

He felt dejected. He knew as much there was no need to pressure Efemona for the post. He stood up and put out his hand. Efemona took it. Then to Victoria. And Victoria took it too. Then walking back to his executive seat, he sighed deeply. He felt a kind of defeat. He was thinking: Shall I put a bullet to their skulls now that I've revealed my secrets to them and Efemona would be gone to the States feeling happy, refusing his offer? He could not withstand the humiliation. The women had walked up to the door to leave in pretense when he said, "Ladies, have a seat. We have more to talk about."

What is it the President wants to talk about other than he lost his pistol and $5 million dollars he slapped on the desk out of his Agbada to swell his ego's?! Victoria was thinking and blaming Efemona in her heart. Now he would kill them without looking back. But he'd lost it. His mind was someplace else, not the pistol, not the money, but the secret. Anyway, the women sat. Quickly, he walked to the wine and liquor cabinet and served himself a glass full of cognac and gulped it down. The spirit of Efemona from her grandmother caught him more than ever in the cognac. After gulping it, he served himself another glass full then served the women their taste. They did not refuse it. They accepted it and they all drank silently. Finally, the President said to Efemona, "The reason I call both of you back is because I forgot to inform you that when you make a lot of dollars from your divorce in America, you should remember to ship some to your country. And remember that my junta and I are here to help redeposit it in Britain for a higher interest rate," he mocked and ridiculed.

Victoria thought as much that he wanted to start something. As she thought, Efemona looked at the face of the scoundrel Dudu, but just didn't care. She wanted to say something. But he over- powered Efemona. He said, "Remember young lady, that any revelation of what we discussed here today must remain with the three of us and outside of the three of us is a pound of flesh or a hole in the head, just to remind you both."

Victoria's blood shivered, almost to the point of wetting herself. Efemona relieved her from it when she said with humor, "Hope those mosquito machines remain in your office for life to serve other dignitaries and not seen in Upper Volta for a profit of one thousand Naira in your damn ass," she ridiculed too, knowing that the moment she leaves the country, Dudu would organize with his Lebanese crooks to sell it and deposit the proceeds for him in Britain-Nigerian style.

And that's how to be a true Nigerian. Though he looked pained that Efemona remembered him of what he also had in mind about the mosquito machine the moment Efemona leaves the country, he just didn't know what to think of Efemona, the one and only Efemona, the remodeled African woman. He bit his lips. Then he remembered Doddan Army Barracks full of contradictions. He allowed himself a small laugh. Too many thoughts: like Doddan, where his signature alone is needed to embezzle Government funds through various cronies was apparent. Efemona should know that the truth and purpose for that is to deny any other ethnic group from sitting on the hot seat. And if the heart of the matter be righteously told, it is that so many heads had been lost-of those who feel that Dudu was not fit to rule and he should hold elections. Here I am with Efemona humiliating me! Efemona should know that in irony, of course, that only Dudu and his junta members can hand over the baton, cloaked themselves in the air conditioned Executive Office to give orders to our body guards as if it were sanctifying grace could enjoy, the gleaming door to his adjoining office is the Kiri-Kiri Annex (Jail). Efemona should know that no man as strong as Pompey in History, however strong-hearted, had ever come out of the room without giving a full account of how he'd planned a coup to overthrow the President. Efemona should know that here, the men and women even mention their friends' names who are innocent as virgins just to satisfy his interrogators he imported from Israel but trained in Siberia. Looking at Efemona after downing his fourth glass of cognac, he stood up and walked to Efemona as he was boiling, then pointed his index finger in her face as he has always done. But this time, he was more tense. Victoria knew nothing could stop him now. She and Efemona were about to die. She was relieved again when the President merely said to Efemona with vexation, "I've the power to sell the mosquito machine to any African Head of State who requests it for little or nothing."

His behavior became irrational. The President walked and opened the Kiri-Kiri Annex door opposite him in the spacious office and said to the women, "I know both of you are not afraid."

The door they all now stared, at the request of Bad Dudu, has a sign on it. "VERY PRIVATE." "Come in here and see for yourselves," he said to the women and laughed, then swayed and almost fell *Yakatani* on his butt.

Efemona and Victoria didn't need to be told what the room was used for. They already knew by imagination. There were the usual familiar faces of Esemuede, Poisonous and Hemlock all standing guard with their submachine guns standing erect as soon as the President opened the door. Perhaps, they thought, they had a job to do. But Dudu waved them aside. "They are still my visitors," he said quickly, knowing that they would grab the women immediately and strap them to the electric chair or gurney in the room used for torturing men and women who challenge Dudu's regime.

As he waved them aside, he said to the women, particularly not looking at them, but the room in itself. "I replace my former guards with Esemuede, Poisonous and Hemlock a couple of weeks ago. The former were getting too lenient and sympathetic to men and women who challenge my Authoritarian regime."

The three new men, Esemuede, Poisonous and Hemlock, Efemona and Victoria of course already knew, but never knew they were all doctors, too. "These three doctors standing before both of you are good in what they do," he told them.

All looked like bullies. Inconsequential-looking mean and also dressed in Khaki upon Khaki with doctors' white aprons. They had needles and .357 Magnums in their holsters. The place in itself looked like an operating room or the gym, well-equipped like a health club where the President works out or takes his naps during his lunch breaks. It was not the case. It was a room Efemona and Victoria noticed to be for testing every part of the human anatomy: like for stretching and shrinking. The machines, they noted, were one of a kind. Over the machines and gurneys are high-powered fluorescent light bulbs that glared their hot white rays at young men of 40 years and above. At least Efemona and Victoria thought, this is one of the power rooms of murder in Doddan Army Barracks, they knew men talked about, and might had existed for over forty years since it first opened and some brute like Dudu from the North was also ruling at the time.

Anyway, Efemona reached into her purse and took out her slim cigarrette pack, took out one and lighted it, despite the sign on the wall that said 'No Smoking'. The three Israeli torturers or doctors on duty looked at Efemona and said nothing. The President began to walk them around each machine and gurney all which had a man tied to it. He said out loud to the men waiting for their punishment of death, "Hey listen! When I come to your gurney, I want you to introduce yourself to the two women with me."

The first man, strapped to what looked like an electric chair, introduced himself as Saro Wiwa. As he saw the young gorgeous women, he said, "Sisters, please help me out of the torturous hands of Dudu the brute."

"Ah! They are not here to help any one of you out. As a matter of fact, one of them might be joining you in here if she continues to run her mouth and ridicule me and my Junta regime. For now, I brought them in here to know how I get my information and who want to topple my regime."

His legs were belted around the arms of the electric chair. His hands against the headrest. Needles sticked all over his body as if being treated with the modern medicine of acupuncture. But it was strictly the opposite. He was naked, too. Wires attached to his private parts. And Poisonous stood over him as Dudu gave his orders. First he said to Poisonous, "Tell the women what this room is used for."

Efemona and Victoria listened as Poisonous related to them everything, while Dudu stood and nodded and looked on. Efemona and Victoria had only one thought: The Doddan Army Barracks is a barbaric, uncomfortable place heavily guarded as an artillery post, because the President and his juntas couldn't allow Clinton to come to Nigeria through France or London to arrest him for human rights abuse and violations.

For a while, the President, Efemona and Victoria all stood looking at each other. Efemona covered her eyes and imagined she was Wiwa, whose naked handsome body was bathed in a pool of sweat, his weary face washed in tears. Seeing with her eyes how the President paid Israeli men a fortune to torture his people, Efemona was glad to decline his offer of the vacant post of Matron General, a post that also might require her to perform autopsies and lie about how they had died.

They watched Wiwa scream and beg, gasping as the President watched him confess a number of men who tried to topple him or writing to uncover his misdeeds or for him to relinquish the hot seat. As Wiwa begged for mercy, Dudu knew his arrogance of power still belonged to him, and must not be questioned. And there was Poisonous, the technician doctor with plenty of needles injecting Wiwa and saying, "I'm about to inject one more solution in your veins that would send your blood rushing to your head until you felt that your skull would burst open, only then could you name more names, if you have any. It is better to let me know now before I start."

What was funny to Efemona was that Poisonous also consoled him. "Don't worry, it is not lethal. I have many more solutions to test. I was taught in Siberia a few weeks ago after Dudu shipped my partners and I from Israel, following a failed coup. It was to be tested on men like you. Then he looked at Wiwa. "I am now eager to test you. Are you ready to confess?"

Wiwa shook his head, looked at Efemona and Victoria knowing full well he was doomed and the gorgeous women cannot help him. "Listen to me very carefully. If you happen to recall the names of all the Journalists writing bad stuff about Bad Dudu, your President, or the names of those involved in the last aborted coup, then perhaps I can sympathize with you and talk to the President to spare you alone among the other two here," he said and gave him a shock on his penis, a very courageous torturer, Efemona noted.

He'd not wanted to hear what Wiwa was confessing. Rather, Wiwa coughed out more grievance from the depth of his soul. He confessed: "Due east of the tip of Porthancourt, Warri and other areas, where the dung of the masses of my people fertilizes the soil to generate more crude oil, the roads are bad, the waters are bad and polluted. This is water that was supposed to breed wealth of fish, but not anymore. The livelihood of many locals here had lies in the fishing industry and trade once before and much of it supplying the daily needs of the local restaurants and street (bookas) resturants. And even at this moment when my people-our people- cannot fish the waters, the returns from the sale of crude oil from this part of the country supposed to benefit the people living in the densely populated areas."

He knew nothing would stop Bad Dudu, the man with authoritarian arrogance of power to stop his torture and execution. The torturer, Poisonous gave him another shock to make him shut up. Wiwa did not. He confessed more of his sins before Efemona and Victoria. "Many refineries in this part of the country, lure the Americans, the French, the British and the Canadians for more crude oil profits. And where are the profits for my people living in these areas? Portharcourt, Eleme, Warri and most refineries in these areas have no good roads, talkless of Ogoni where the environment has been degraded and its inhabitants still live in tharched huts and slums and in the dark."

His speeches became faint when Poisonous gave him the last shock. Efemona and Victoria looked away. While Victoria had wet herself, Efemona tried to fight back the waves of nausea that threatened her merely looking at Wiwa. With the Voodoo worm in her, that moved, she reacted to Dudu's barbaric method of employing technicians to silence great men in her country. Then Efemona walked towards Wiwa with vexation to try to pull off the needles. Poisonous grabbed her hand, "You think you got the balls?" he said and looked at Bad Dudu.

With that, the President said to the women, "It's time we go back to my office," though he'd not meant it to be so soon. But he had had enough of Efemona always trying to hurt his intentions. His downing a series of shots of *undouble cognac* was also playing a part on him as a demonic Nebuchadnezzar, the king of ancient Babylon. They had barely sat when Efemona walked to the liquor cabinet and served him. And she thought as he took the drink from her: I will make you a *wino* and *alcoholic* before you die a miserable death on top of *toto*. He gulped it and started to laugh, though he controlled his anomie, hearing a knock on the door.

"Come in," Dudu yelled out.

Abdulsalam swept in and faced Dudu. With happiness, he said to Dudu, paying no attention to Efemona and Victoria. "The job is done. Umaro Diko arrived in a coffin heavily drugged and he is now talking. Our hired killers are in my office waiting to be paid for his kidnapping."

Though his speech was barely heard, Abdulsalam understood him. *"Okay. Tell them sey I go soon finish with my visitors."*

He tried to hide his slurred speech, which was of low voice full of confidence and of contempt he'd not had in about a month. As Abdulsalam hurried out, Dudu said to Efemona, "I want you to work for me-like it or not-starting from now on."

Where I sat in my living room, my penis shrank again. If only Efemona would just say okay, I accept the offer. Man! I was surprised to hear, "Not when you are killing innocent students, babies and their mothers when they carry banners on the streets of Nigeria to protest against your junta Administration. I already told you I will not accept your post of Matron General. By the way, don't you know Wiwa is a citizen for truth against your Authoritarian regime? If you let him live, I can work for you. I'll tell you, though, that you can't force me to start working for you now." And her voice was harsh. "Dudu," Efemona called upon, "I have always been very curious to have this privilege to meet with you to ask you why?!, why?!, why?!" she said and suddenly became aggressive. "First of all, I don't have a mind, Mr. Dudu . . ."

I thought where I sat watching my Efemona from afar: Why wouldn't she have the mind when she has the President's weapon and $5 million in her purse if Dudu remembers and decided to act stupid with his Uzi? But I guess Efemona knew that Dudu had forgotten he even had it on the desk. For that, I know Efemona trusted herself then coupled with the Voodoo spell charm against the President. To crown it all, she can fire any kind of weapon, a legacy of American tradition to teach women to shoot to kill their husbands, a rapist attacker, or a molester. Her eyes were constantly moving and watching his movement. She watched the President gnawed his teeth. "By the way," the President asked, "How much do you make, now, in America from the job you do? I'll topple it!" he said and stood up staggering.

"Sit down, Mr. President," Victoria, who was no longer afraid, said. She knew Efemona had a motive for recording all their conversations. If nothing else, Bill Clinton and all the judges of Reno, Nevada were backing Efemona up. She knew it. And that was the truth.

The President shrugged. His face became more gaunt. Efemona knew she had defeated him, a man who obviously has enjoyed life, respected by Kings among Kings of Africa. Efemona walked up to him. His head was down in deep thought. Then she said, "Talk to me, Mr. President. Tell us all the atrocities you have committed in this country with your junta members, then I can decide if I would assume my newly assigned duties of the Matron General for this country today. Nothing but the truth. Otherwise . . ." Efemona threatened while her eyes caught him, their lips smiled and her eyelashes blinked.

The President could almost see her eyelashes blinking faster and faster, another of Efemona's spells on him.

"Well I was the man who pronounced the death sentence on some men from Benin to be executed when George Bush Sr. was after me and my junta militia for smuggling tons and tons of cocaine into his country. The six men got a hole in the head. You want to know where those missing students who went to America to study are, who tried to expose me and my junta members through investigative journalism . . . ?"

"Don't you want to know, Victoria," Efemona looked at Victoria and asked.

"What do you think?"

Listening to Efemona, she wanted to remind her that she was no longer afraid of Dudu and were now both in cahoots at bringing down the Authoritarian leader, and were inside the cage together with the gorilla, and the thrills and chills were going to be more than vicarious when they were finished with him.

At Efemona's suggestion, the subject quickly turned to fooling him. Then they watched him staggered to a huge cupboard near the mosquito machine and opened it. "What's he doing?" Victoria asked.

"Let's go see what he's got going in there," Efemona said.

Inside the cupboard, as he opened it before them, there were several heads like Stalin's Soviet Republic where brains were embalmed.

"These over here," Dudu pointed out, "Are those who tried to topple me and my men out of office, and those over there are the students from New York University and U.C. Berkley whom my Ambassador to the United Nations, Mr. Gambari secretly videotaped demonstrating about my Authoritarian regime outside of the Nigerian Embassy in New York to make Bill Clinton be after me for human rights abuses. And those over there are Nigerian students in Nigerian Universities who know too much, writing nonsense about my regime and Babangida, and those over there are the market women who carry placards against me and my juntas, and those little heads were the children in their mother's and father's elbows when my secret policemen invaded their homes and the kids wailed. Any problem with that? Huh?!" he said and broke out with a raucous laughter and slapped the cupboard.

That touched Victoria and she shook her head before him. She could not contain herself. She exclaimed, "Jesus! Does it not ever cross your heart that children of today are men of tomorrow? The difference between them and adults is that you took their lives when they were still helpless creatures."

"You are right. But who will challenge me is the question, my dear," he said and laughed. Then he slammed the cupboard and walked back to his seat and sank in. As he got up and walked towards Efemona and Victoria, he thought of the idea of silencing them, then looked back.

Efemona watched him sink into his seat again and asked, "More *undouble*, Mr. President?" She waited for no response. She went ahead and filled up his glass with cognac and handed it to him. Downing it at once, he talked and talked about women who know more than their masters, smarter than himself, who have gone to America to be Americanized, the truth flooding out from his mouth, how he would want all the smart women like Efemona sent to Alabon close where they would be hanged, the way he'd seized power, and how many heads in the history of Nigeria he'd taken and their body parts sold to the Merchants in Venice for them to make bar soaps, and how he would be the first to buy it to wash his face.

With that, Efemona had had it. She took out the pistol from her purse. "Don't do anything stupid or I'll blow your motherfucking brains out. Get up slowly, sucker, and drop the Uzi on your shoulder to the floor. Nice and slow to avoid bloodshed in here, motherfucker," she yelled at Dudu.

Wowooo! I might die now at the hand of a woman I'd invited he reasoned.

He obeyed. "Victoria get over there and pick up the Uzi that has taken a lot of souls and throw it out the window as far as you can."

She did as she was commanded.

For the first time, Dudu knew he had lost his power. So he looked at Efemona, "You came on my invitation to ruin me? How long will your power last?"

"What power?" Efemona asked and pointed the pistol in his face.

"The power the Yankees gave you to come on my invitation to ruin me."

"Shut up, motherfucker! The Yankees also gave me the power to record our conversations. And the first thing I will do when I get back to the States is play it before the CIA, to tell them how wicked you are. You asshole!"

He sighed. From afar, I could see that Dudu had lost his strength. Efemona could kill him. I just stood helpless. But I commend Dudu for his boldness. Even with the pistol pointed at him, he was still bold as a military man. "You can only shoot your chicken husband in America. Besides, everything I may have said and told you are not true"

"Shut up. The heads in the cupboard are evidence, Mr. Dudu," Efemona said.

To the President, everything seemed stunted and misshapen. The only color of a really dark man beyond dark on his face suggested too much *undouble, undouble* of *cognac*. And his office, like the Oval Office in America or Buckingham Palace in England would now be frozen as Lot's wife in History was trapped on salt, and doomed, therefore, as its history that overwhelming, omnipresent gift of God through Efemona could not be questioned, to be the property of the grey, unquestioning mediocre. He wished he hadn't told the whore his secrets for Efemona to reveal to the Oval Office and their CIA for covert actions against him. He sighed deeply, feeling sorry for Efemona's husband who probably had told her about his plans and objectives, and how he would take advantage of the white man in America who came to Africa to trick the African people and then took them hostage as slaves. And Efemona would reveal his secrets and even testify before the Senate Committee how dubious her husband is and her husband, who thought he was smart enough, would be jailed because of a whore like Efemona.

Efemona, who didn't care what the President was thinking, said to Victoria, "Let's get the hell out of here from this brute."

And they bolted out of the room and slammed the door behind them. He staggered to the door and opened it. Efemona looked back. "I'll see what I can do to bring down your government," she yelled at Dudu.

With his blurred speech, he raised his head up and yelled out to Efemona, "I'll send you someplace where the wicked cease from troubling and toppling a Leader like me."

"Whatever you meant by that, I'll send you there first. Trust me on that, asshole!" Efemona yelled back.

I shook my head where I sat. 'What a woman!' were the last ten words that were registered in my being.

The President walked in and stood rooted in the middle of his spacious office. Pride had deserted him. Grief, bitterness and pain clawed its way from the bottom of his stomach to his firm Tarzan-like hands. But still, to his credit, Dudu didn't interfere by asking Idigunlagbe, his secretary, questions to offer him comfort. He looked around him. The lights were shining on his face, so he reached on to the switch on the wall and turned them off for concealment of darkness to lend some comfort to his mood. Then he walked to his Executive Chair and sat. As a man with a lion's heart, he didn't need to cry. And for several minutes, he kept his face buried on his desk and suffered the aftershock of the violent catharsis of Efemona's voice commanding him. The tremors came in waves, significant, but not that sufficient to produce another tidal wave of emotion he'd suffered with women of whore categories.

Eventually he raised his head up, expecting to see Efemona and Victoria standing before him, both gloating at him. He was alone, but noticed that a dim light from the cupboard shot out its rays to the spacious room. Barely standing on his feet, he rubbed and wiped his right hand palm across his face. He was leaning toward revenge against his rage and anger. But the women were out of his reach. Soon enough, he realized he was in total darkness and again turned on the light. The light again casted its rays onto his face to remind him to pick up a steaming cup of poisoned coffee Efemona had made for him when they'd left the Dem Mayor punishment room. He sipped on it once, then saw another fourth bottle of half empty Cognac liquor bottle uncapped. Immediately, he smelled its pungent bouquet and grabbed it, then gulped it down his throat.

As Efemona and Victoria walked majestically out of the site of Doddan Army Barrack, Efemona thought about the possibility of another terror like Idi Amin of Uganda, if the spell she casted on Dudu through the Cognac did not work its miracle for him to hold down one of his several mistresses the CIA had lined up for him to navigate their carnal with special Viagra made in the Senate floor of the CIA in Washington D.C., there would be more heads taken by Bad Dudu. Then she gritted her teeth as she walked and thought more thoughts. It would've been a thing of joy if Dudu the savage was having animosity against *only* the white man who came to Africa to destroy the Cultured Religion of the African race by planting their Churches all over African soil after successfully persuading their forefathers to stop worshipping *Idols,* the *only* form of communication with their superior Being they'd known then. It would have been better if Dudu had sent his men to boomerang those savages in Reno, Nevada, notably, the Samsons and Hercules of Circus Circus Hotel and Casino, who break the limbs of black people in their casinos. It would even be honored by other African countries if he'd sent people to reprimand some judges in Reno, Nevada who were biased against Ogbebor then finding him guilty always for what he did not do after being stopped and harrassed on numerous occasions on the sidewalk of Reno streets, rather than killing his own people and worse yet, doing away with Nigerian crude oil money and depositing it's loot in foreign Banks, the money the white man will eventually use to make amarments to kill all African people in Africa.

Meanwhile, Dudu stood again and walked around his table. His present mood would not compromise with what's on his mind. He looked at his desk and did an oddly irreverant riff on the edge of the table. His eyes were about closed and his dark head on his long, dark neck that was supposed to be covered by the collar of his military uniform seemed to become elongated as a tortoise peeping out from its shell for a praying mantis to feed on. Something really abnormal appeared on his face which had not been there before, since he toppled his enemies, a kind of passionate, triumphant rage and agony. Then his Tarzan-like free moving body was utterly still, as though he was confessing to the Pope for his forgiveness of all his sins, being held in readiness for a communion more total than flesh could bear.

Finally, he realized he could not hold himself any longer. So he buzzed Abdulsalam. As he dialed his number, his hands were shaking.

"Get over here now!" Dudu finally managed to say.

'Salam was in his office within a few seconds. And he was surprised to see his man in such condition, looking at Dudu, whose eyes now seemed as those of John the Baptist eating locust in the wilderness as a result of hunger. Somehow 'Salam knew something was terribly wrong with Dudu. In the condition Dudu was in, he knew that he was the runner-up for his Executive seat. Dudu looked at 'Salam and assimilated him. "I will be gone," he said, "But for how long I do not know."

'Salam looked at him in the eye with shock and Dudu raised his hands and lay them on his shoulder and kissed him on both cheeks, then took his arm and walked him to the hot seat. He stood for a minute and looked at the enormous seat, then sat 'Salam on it.

"Remember world opinion is on our ass. Our junta regime Generals cannot visit America and other famous World leaders-because of our human right violations and-. But still, I have my reasons to believe that Bawuh had sold me to Clinton's Administration, by picking Efemona out of thousands of names that were qualified for the post of Matron General. I have no doubt in my mind that Bill Clinton's Administration has something to do with my being in this shape, to look like a drone and stupid to have carnal knowledge of Efemona, who then used her powers of Oval Office to dance on my stupidity."

"Tell me exactly what's amiss?!" 'Salam said.

With blurred speech, he narrated a little to him. After about half an hour, Dudu walked him upstairs where the names and register of men of high esteem and caliber he had killed in the neighborhood of one thousand were kept. In there, Dudu had a pot of strong coffee on a small burner. 'Salam helped himself and made himself a cup from it. Then Dudu said, "Please to take attendance of these books in here. They are classified books on human atrocities and embezzlement of Government funds out of this country. 'Salam began to scan the shelves. Gently, he removed one of the books and wiped the red dust off of it and then looked at it and handed it to Dudu. Dudu took the book and replaced it where it had been. Then he picked one by himself. This time it was Islamic Koran Jihad study for Muslims of the North who are mostly Generals in line for the relay race baton to rule. Here, 'Salam knew he was the next in line to rule without being told.

After the tour upstairs, Dudu found it difficult to climb the stairs down. But he managed. The insult of Efemona humiliating him brewed back from the bottom of his stomach to his head. He could not withstand it. He said to 'Salam, "Sit and wait for me in here. I'll be back."

He took one of the keys to the cars of the Executive privilege and headed to the door. And I was wondering why Abdulsalam did not take the keys from him. I can tell you the reason for that. That was because Nigeria has no definition for alcoholics. Alcoholics can drive on Nigerian roads and kill individuals walking home to their farms and local markets. And the truth about that is: Alcoholism has not been defined by the Federal Government.

Anyway, Dudu turned around and said to 'Salam, "Oh! One more thing I forgot to tell you. Handover as soon as you can."

"Do you have any particular individual in mind I should hand over to?" 'Salam asked.

He looked at him in the eyes. The words slugged out. "To Obansanjo."

"Any special reason for that?"

"I believe he is a good kid. He belongs to 'us' rather than 'them'. Don't forget to tell him Uganda's Airspace is now open for business now that Idi Amin is out of office and he could carry a billion dollars across their airspace with Nigerian Airforce One and he would not be questioned."

'Salam nodded. Dudu fished out a letter from his Agbada pocket and handed it to him and immediately headed toward the door. He'd written and warned that he had been ruined by a woman named Efemona whom Bawuh had recommended to fill the post of Matron General.

Dudu admitted his mistakes: "My dear comrades," he wrote,: "I want you all to watch out for a woman named Efemona. She would be a powerful woman to bring this Country to Civilization or perhaps sell us again into slavery to the white man. In that case, the power of the Hausas would cease to exist in Nigeria. Efemona would enslave us and use us as paper towels to wipe her shit from her ass. And I believe I said a lot I shouldn't have said. Just a few minutes ago I heard it over the radio, the atrocities I have committed with my Junta members. She'd vowed that Babangida and I would vomit all the Government funds we embezzled over the years, since being leaders of this Nation. The worst of all, a pompous Journalist from the West has published it in the Obiagele Newspaper, due to be released sometime this evening. The media, all who hate my guts, would be nosing around for the heads in the cupboard for evidence. Our enemies would love to see the heads. Don't let them see it. Efemona's ambition is to sell us. Whoever is not sold would be shipped to Reno, Nevada where their skins would be surgically removed to lay as carpets for Judge McQuaid, who was not there on the casino floor to make his decision that, "Ogbebor has not admitted or denied" silver mining on the Gaming floor of Circus Circus machines. Don't forget to send a fax message to Judge McQuaid, and all the other judges who find Ogbebor guilty for what he did not do that they will all fall on their faces and go naked by the power of Efemona's grandmother's Voodoo that has caught me too. Help me tell all the judges too, that they should kiss the place where the sun don't shine because they were all biased against Ogbebor in Reno, Nevada. My fellow comrades, be advised. Never, never get drunk with beautiful women. They are evil and they can bring men down to their knees with too much socialization. Above all, never, never, never leave documents exposed. Always destroy evidence as I wish you would do with this letter you are now reading. Carry my message across. Bye and good luck, comrades."

* * *

Abdulsalam sat on his new executive seat and finished reading the letter. After reading it, he ran outside to confront Bad Dudu that he had nothing to worry about. It was too late. The damage had been done. Dudu had sneaked into one of the several cars for Executive privilege and drove up Carter Bridge Expressway and headed home for his wife to see him for the last time. Though he'd driven himself home safely, his vision when he was driving was blurred and he realized his nerves were not compromising with the steering wheel. He pulled over to the curb and rested a few minutes, then zoomed off again, realizing he might be seen and be kidnapped by those who don't like him and punish him the same way he'd punished men and women of Nigeria.

He managed to get home. Quickly, he told his wife what was wrong with him. The spell in the Cognac had caught him and was working in his veins. He said to his wife with blurred speech, "You know darling, some men like women with the spirit of adventure. That's how we met, isn't it? Since our discovering ourselves, it added spiciness and suspense to our lives. James Bond didn't fuck shrinking violets, did he?"

"No," she answered him with sadness, noting that she was getting wrinkles over her face and Dudu was probably screwing young women behind her back, though she didn't really care as long as he didn't bring them home. Besides, she has access to his Bank accounts all over the world, likewise to suitcases in the neighborhood of thirty-two all loaded with foreign currencies. Why would she be worried?

"I know you want to fuck by reminding me when we were youths. My dear, you have my permission to screw young women," his wife said. Actually, Efemona's spell was working all the way around, even to the extent of the CIA's involvement in his life.

"You mean I cannot navigate your carnal for the last time?" "I'm on my PMS monthly shit," his wife said.

The spell in the Cognac was pushing him to say what he didn't mean to say to his wife. Feeling blue and restless, he picked up the

phone, the only phone in the entire Country that was functioning Day, Noon and Night to ring when dialed to be received by his mistresses. And likewise was that of his driver. So he dialed his driver. "C'mon over and drive me to see Lara, my mistress from Thailand."

His driver, who was also a General having an orgy with two women, part of the life of the Generals from the North who'd dwindled the economy of Nigeria, said to Dudu on the other end, "I'll be right over. Give me a few minutes to release my passion of joy into my mistress' carnals I flew into the country from Brazil yesterday."

After releasing, he dressed up hurriedly and headed out and promised his mistresses he wouldn't be long.

Though Dudu was burning with carnal heat navigation, he knew his driver had always been punctual and never been late to drive him up to see Lara, his one of several mistresses. In the presence of his wife, he called Lara. Lara had also been on the President's payroll, whether he screwed her or not, on a monthly basis. "Hey, I'll be right over," he found himself saying. And he added, "I have something I want to experiment with you tonight, my dear Lara."

The driver honked. He kissed his wife for the last time and said, "Get me two Havanas on the shelf."

She walked over and took two of the Havana cigars and stuck them into his Agbada. Then he headed out and took his seat in the Rolls Royce and his driver drove slowly over to Lara, a driveway off Mbadiwe Street where he'd built a $3 million dollar home for her- a secluded area still a jungle where he usually went to relax with her without the fear of anyone tailing him. Recently he had not deposited cash into Lara's account. Maybe he had forgotten and that was why he had called to tell her he was coming right over to fuck and pay her what he owed her in back payment for the past three months. Did he forget or was Dudu taking advantage of her for being young and beautiful?! But Lara was from Thailand and so he regarded her as a blond or a white woman.

His driver drove slowly through the narrow part of Mbadiwe flood covered potholed street and finally came to a stop behind an iroko tree. Then Dudu looked here and there in anticipation that no one was watching him. Under the tree was cool and shady, but beyond the branches the moon shun through. He lit one of his Havana cigars and balanced it in the left side corner of his lips, smiled to himself and nodded. He puffed and exhaled. Finally, he said to his driver, "After a while you can come into the house and sit and wait in the study. Meanwhile, watch and make sure no one is in the jungle to see me walk into the house."

"You know damn well I love my job, Mr. President," his driver said.

As he was walking into the house staggering, he remembered what Efemona had put him through. For a woman to disarm him was a shame. And that was his pain and not the heads in the cupboard. Why should I worry about that when I am God-like and unmoved by strong-headed Pompeys like Abiola, Dele Giwa, Ojukwu, Fela Anikulapo Kuti, Gana Fawehinmi and Wole Soyinka? He shook his head and thought as he walked and swayed into the house without knocking: How can a man of my caliber suffer from a diarrhea of words and a constipation of ideas when I was with Efemona and Victoria in my office? To worsen his condition, Stagger Lee announced on his LateNight News: "The President was disarmed in his office early today by Efemona, a Naturalized Citizen of the United States whose acquaintance was Victoria. The whereabouts of Victoria after Efemona left for the United States is unknown. Sources said that Efemona might have taken her into the American Embassy for protection."

Two hungry farmers who were in the jungle saw a Rolls Royce pull over beside an iroko tree in front of the house they've never seen before since being hunters in the area. They viewed with their binoculars. They saw he was Bad Dudu and what the hell was he doing there at this time of night? They grumbled in their hearts. Dudu walked into the house and walked straight into his den, carpeted, and finished in pine paneling, American style. Lara followed him into the den, which she had refurnished in Thailand style, with a huge king sized bed and five pillows. She turned on the lights. Her new dozen mounted animal heads stared down at him from the walls, glassy-eyed, with the trace of a smile around their mouths, as if they too, were pretty happy to have been killed by Bad Dudu. It was the spirit and spell of Efemona that got the Oval Office wired up that they too, have had enough of Dudu's atrocities against mankind in Nigeria to buy Lara over through covert means to oust him. So the taxidermist, CIA or Efemona's spell had a sick sense of humor. Still, Bad Dudu knew nothing. Didn't know as much his end was at the tip of Lara's fingers and her hole. He swayed behind her and put his hands on her shoulder, then looked down at her behind. Finally, he said, "So what's cookin', good lookin'?"

She could tell that he'd had enough of Gworo and Cola-nuts and smelling enough booze to put her to sleep, before even fucking her. But she replied to him, "I couldn't sleep and I thought you know you are owing me three months back payment of fucking me."

"Well, thought it was nice I came over to inform you the deposit into your bank account would be made first thing in the morning. And what's for dinner?"

"Me," and she got naked before him. Her thick pubic hairs and copper-like clitoris caught his eyes, and he too, started stripping off his Agbada and his military uniform one after the other quickly. She stood in the middle of the room, naked, while Dudu circled around her. Out of the corner of her eye, she saw his huge dick was up.

Dudu looked at her, "Go for it, darling."

She took a deep breath, closed her eyes, and with one finger she lowered his erect penis to her lips. When it was over, though not really over until he navigated real hole, Dudu said, "Swallow it."

She swallowed it and Dudu commanded her, "Now is the time for bed show."

She did not hesitate. She went to the huge bed and laid on her back. And the President made a joke. "When I was young, I used to swim in Niagara Falls, but now I go to Viagra falls. Do you have Viagra for me?"

She stood up and walked to her closet and brought out a full bottle of Viagra the CIA had given her to put him to sleep and never to wake up again. She opened it and handed him two for his weight. He swallowed it.

Lara went back to the bed and lay on her back and Dudu stared at her pubic hair, then regarded her medium breasts and nipples staring at him. She had a good body, good muscle tone and good skin if one overlooked a few mosquito bites since she came to Ikoyi on the invitation of Bad Dudu through Lebanese pimps. Her long hair falling over her face had been dyed as a blond, but her hair over her mode was still very dark. Lara stirred and turned on her stomach. Bad Dudu, the carnal navigatorer, looked at her rounded rump and felt himself harder and harder.

He lay next to her on the bed and put his hand between her legs, his fingers entering her. That was not enough. He incited a huge Havana cigar into her and sniffed it, then put it on the bed head board, waiting for it to dry before lighting it up. After that, he reached for her clitoris and massaged it.

She squirmed a little, clearly not enjoying going from a sound sleep to having a man's fingers in her no matter how much he was paying her on ghost register account on a monthly basis.

"What's the matter with you, Lara? You are not responding the way you normally do when I'm here fucking you."

"Because I feel humiliated. My culture in Thailand does not allow cigars inside women."

Dudu wiped the huge cigar on the sheets and consoled her. She was upset. "Here, you are not hard enough." She handed him another two pills of Viagra, and he swallowed them.

He became more irrational and blood concentrated in his manhood more than it should have been. His head began to swell, but could still think. He stood up, layed beside her again. And she knew it was time for him to go where the wicked must go and they would not be missed. Bad Dudu too, was thinking in his own way as he became helpless and the room began to revolve around him. So he thought, Well, even if the masses wouldn't miss me, my Junta members of a small elite who rule and have the baton ready in their right hand with all the power and money would miss him. That's what matters. There would be no tears from the pew or from market women, from farmers and students and children as when Mao of China and other great leaders of other countries died and their people cried and wished they lived forever. No!

The flame on him was out as his eyes stared wondrously on her mode, lifeless.

* * *

The two farmers who kept vigil with their hunters' head lamp watched from a distance as Lara and Dudu's driver became irrational themselves, calling on Dudu to 'please wake up' to free them from his peer's bullet who would take over when he was buried. But in actuality, Lara knew what had happened. The driver had no knowledge. With fear, he headed out and and drove to Doddan Army Barrack and informed Abdulsalam.

Lara dressed up hurriedly and headed up to the roof of her building where her Cessina T-70 Bad Dudu had purchased for her was laying idle. She loaded her Cessina with the few items she could carry to Thailand where the CIA Chief was waiting for her to pay her off at the Ritz Hotel in Downtown Thailand off American Embassy Road.

In the air flying to Thailand, she'd several thoughts: I should've yanked off his Agbada, Rolex watch and his hat worth another $15 million dollars coupled with what the CIA was owing me. Meanwhile, panic gripped the men in uniforms at Doddan Army Barrack when Dudu's driver related the sad news of his untimely death like Abiola he too had hired the Israeli's to poison with rycine.

The two farmers who watched from a distance with their binoculars and saw what'd happened to Bad Dudu, saw his mouth opened and his eyes wide opened. Why would the driver drive away alone without Bad Dudu? And why would the woman they saw continued to load up the plane on her roof, carrying just about anything? With that thought, they walked majestically to the house.

Dudu was there alone on the bed. His eyes were wide open and flies resting on his lips and penis and nose. The two farmers helped themselves to his Rolex watch and his custom hat and his Agbada worth $15 million dollars. Before they left the house, one of the farmers zipped down his eyelids and slammed the door. "God is great," they said and smiled.

*   *   *

On her way home to America, Efemona had listened to her walkman tape recorder play the conversations she had with Bad Dudu and smiled. The President with his boastful voice was clear. From, "Come here and see for yourself," to the abuses and insults of: "What do you have inbetween your legs?!" Then he laughed uproarously. Efemona asking, "More undouble Cognac, Mr. President?"

His voice, hard. Insult upon insult to her in particular, unaware that Efemona had a toy recorder. She listened to how he put down President Bill Clinton and dare him to send his men and his guards would fight to the last man. She saw the brute sprang to his feet with slurred speech, but well composed of his revelations to her. "If you don't mind your tongue, I'll take a pound of flesh from both of you and have the Merchants from Venice come in and make a bid on your skulls for display in their museums. And she remembered how Victoria had reacted to the £10 million pounds to navigate a white woman in England. Above all, he was boastful, "You come here to tell me you know too much now huh, Americana?" The way he concluded his boast: There is, of course, nothing they can do. "Who is the strong-headed Pompey to try me and my Generals? We are more powerful than God. We are the Kings of the Kings," and dribbling the soccer ball behind his back, he seemed like a god. "The coffin that came with you into the country was my handiwork," he'd said and boasted.

Efemona had enough. She turned off the recorder. Efemona felt herself again. She knew she'd ruined him and he must be brought down by those families who'd missed their loved ones and unaccounted for, for decades. She saw the heads in the cupboard and that was proof of his heinous crime. As she read in the newspapers enroute to Reno, Nevada, that Dudu slept on top of *toto* and never woke up, she realized how powerful her Voodoo worm her grandmother gave her to swallow had been effective. Then an enroute on KLM flight from Holland to San Francisco the TV on board was on. "PRESIDENT BAD DUDU OF NIGERIA IS DEAD," appeared in bold headline of 'Obeageli Newspaper', Abdulsalam was casting his news from it. He also had said, "It would be two to three days before the coroner can conclude what caused the President's death. It was apparent that he was with Efemona. But the identity of the woman Efemona was with is unknown. Anyone who knew the identity of the other woman with Efemona should report to 'Salam within forty-eight hours for a huge reward. My administration is working night and day with the Prime Minister of Britain to request

President Bill Clinton to extradite Efemona to face charges of driving Bad Dudu nut to answer questions she has knowledge about and of stolen Federal Government weapon."

The TV shut off itself after the news of the hour. "Bullshit," Efemona said and added, *"Uwe-be-Eghonose daleisun."*

A man behind Efemona said, "That sounds like an alien language."

"Whatever. I'm just happy he passed out on top of pussy and the money he stole would not be buried with him," Efemona said.